THE NEIL GAIMAN READER

ALSO BY NEIL GAIMAN

Novels
The Ocean at the End of the Lane
Graveyard Book
Anansi Boys
Coraline
American Gods
Stardust
Neverwhere
Good Omens (with Terry Pratchett)

Collections
Trigger Warning
Fragile Things
Smoke and Mirrors

Illustrated Stories
The Truth Is a Cave in the Black Mountains (illustrated by Eddie Campbell)
The Sleeper and the Spindle (illustrated by Chris Riddell)

For Younger Readers
Fortunately, the Milk (illustrated by Skottie Young)
Hansel and Gretel (illustrated by Lorenzo Mattotti)
Instructions (illustrated by Charles Vess)
Odd and the Frost Giants (illustrated by Brett Helquist)
Crazy Hair (illustrated by Dave McKean)
Blueberry Girl (illustrated by Charles Vess)
The Dangerous Alphabet (illustrated by Gris Grimly)
M Is for Magic (illustrated by Teddy Kristiansen)

Nonfiction
Art Matters (illustrated by Chris Riddell)
Make Good Art
The View from the Cheap Seats

THE NEIL GAIMAN READER

Selected Fiction

NEIL GAIMAN

wm
WILLIAM MORROW *An Imprint of* HarperCollins*Publishers*

HarperCollins books may be purchased for educational, business, or
sales promotional use. For information, please email the Special Markets
Department at SPsales@harpercollins.com.

FIRST EDITION

Frontispiece photograph by Majdanski/Shutterstock, Inc.

Library of Congress Cataloging-in-Publication Data has been applied for.

ISBN 978-0-06-303185-2

20 21 22 23 24   LSC   10 9 8 7 6 5 4 3 2 1

CONTENTS

FOREWORD

Thanks to Neil Gaiman, spiders now stop me dead in my tracks. This is a truly weird turn of events, worthy of one of his novels, that now, instead of trying to shoo them away or smash them, I stand frozen, and wonder if this eight-legged brother is about to tell me something that it's been trying to share since before the slave ships. Something that I'm only now ready to hear. I would explain more, but that would turn this into a foreword for just one novel, *Anansi Boys,* when this collection is so much more.

Besides, what brought me here was not spiders, but Tori Amos. This already sounds like the line of a '90s song, and the line I'm writing about is from 1992, and is actually hers: *If you need me, me and Neil'll be hanging out with the Dream King.* The lyric clearly means something to Amos and to Gaiman, but it meant something else to a young obsessive of them both. By that time, I had been reading Neil's work for years. But that one line made me think Amos had done something else. She went into his work and found herself. I remember hearing that song and thinking, "So I'm not the only one who believes in Neil's world more than my own."

I still think I live in Gaiman's world more than my own. For us maladjusted misfits, an escape to his worlds was all that enabled us to endure ours. I would say that Gaiman creates the kind of work that begets obsessions, but that seems too easy. All great art has its devotees, but Gaiman, particularly for other writers and oddballs, regardless of genre or art form, gives us permission to never let go of the world of wonder that we're all told at some time to leave behind. Of course, the best writers know this is a scam—there is no fantasy world standing opposite the real world, because it's all real. Not allegory, or fable, but real.

Which might explain why I devoured *American Gods* when it came out in 2001, a year that badly needed an escape into fantasy. Except that escape was not what it gave me. The novel proposed something way more radical: the idea that the forgotten gods were still around, adjusting quite badly to their twilight, and just because we no longer believed in them didn't mean that they had stopped messing with us. And it wasn't just the continued machinations of gods, but the continued importance of myths. After all, a myth was a religion once, and a reality before that, and myths still tell us more about ourselves than religion ever could. Neil Gaiman is a mythmaker, but also a dream restorer. It never even occurred to me that I needed a character to be rescued from simply being relegated to folklore, until he took the stuff of childhood rhymes, half-forgotten, and gave them living, breathing, combative souls. Then he threw them into a present that they weren't always ready for, and certainly wasn't ready for them.

This collection abounds in fantastic beasts, normal people with weird powers, weird people with normal struggles, worlds above this one, worlds below, and the real world, which is not a real as you might think. Some stories travel through strange realms in three pages. Some don't end so much as stop, and some don't begin so much as pause and wait for you to catch up. Some stories take up an entire city, others a bedroom. Some have the stuff of childhood, with very adult consequences, while others show what happens when grown-up people lose what it means to be a child. And then there are some stories that let you off with a warning, while others leave you so arrested that peeling yourself away from them will take days.

There's more. Toni Morrison once wrote that Tolstoy could never have known that he was writing for a black girl in Lorraine, Ohio. Neil could never have known that he was writing for a confused Jamaican kid who, without even knowing it, was still staggering from centuries of erasure of his own gods and monsters. Sure, myths were religions once, but they are at the core of a people's and a nation's identity. So, when I saw Anansi, on the other side of erasure, responding to being rubbed out and forgotten, I found myself wondering who the hell was this man from the UK who had just restored our story. I understood what being taken away from our myths meant for me, but I had never considered what it meant for the myth.

If Gaiman's comics and graphic novels turned me into one kind of fan, his fiction turned me into another. I envy the person who, by picking up this collection, will be reading Neil for the first time. But on the other hand, people who know all of the Beatles' songs still pick up compilations, and they do so for a reason. This is an introduction by way of throwing you in the deep end, touching on nearly everything that has sealed Gaiman's reputation as one of our masters of fantasy. And yet even for the person who's read quite a bit of his work, there is still much to discover, even in the old stuff. Like I said, there are people who own every album but still buy the greatest hits, and it's not because of nostalgia.

It's that by putting these stories beside each other, a curious new narrative emerges: that of the writer. The excerpt from *Neverwhere* is brilliant enough on its own but sandwiched between "Don't Ask Jack" and "The Daughter of Owls," all three pieces take on a new dimension. Put together, it's the *theme* that becomes the story. The secret lives of children, the world of terror and wonder that we leave them to when we turn off the light and close the door. What happens when the door stays closed. What happens when one world moves on and the other does not. It doesn't escape the reader that "Neverwhere" sounds similar to "Neverland," another place where a cost is paid when children never grow up. But it does something to you, entering one world still feeling the effects (and bringing the subtext) of the one you have just left behind, taking the fears and wonders of one story to another. Or even better, seeing, as you move through the collection, what keeps Gaiman awake at night.

Other odd things happen in this volume. The way we read certain characters in "I, Cthulhu" shades how we react to their names cropping up several stories later. Those characters never really appear in the second story, but it doesn't even matter. They have left such a stamp on our imagination that we barely realize that the dread that comes to the latter story is one *we* bring to it. The subtext of foreboding, the sense that anything could happen is coming from us. This is what great collections do: recontextualize stories, even the ones you've read before, and give you brand new ways to read them. Together, they also reveal aspects of story you might not have been aware of when they were apart. Side-splitting humour, for instance. Humour and horror have always been inseparable bedfellows: horror making humour funnier; humour making horror more horrifying. The opening punch of the story "We Can Get Them For You Wholesale" is hilarious not just because of how dark and ridiculous it gets, but because it is punctuated by that most British of qualities, cheapness. Just how far are you willing to go, if there's a bargain to be had? Spoiler: The end of the world.

Maybe a better comparison for this collection is the Beatles' "White Album": massive in size and scope, with individually brilliant pieces presented together because the only context they need is how good they are. In this volume is funny stuff. Scary stuff. Fantasy stuff. Mystery stuff. Ghost stuff. Kid stuff. Stuff you have read, and much that you haven't.

Stories that reinforce all that you know about Neil Gaiman's work and stories that will confound what you know. It's tempting to say that the great thing about this or any storyteller is that he never grew up, but that's not quite it. In fact, when I was a younger, one of the thrills of Gaiman's work was how it left me feeling so *adult* for reading them.

Meaning of course that if you've read Neil's work for as long as I have, then you recognize the rather wicked irony that it took worlds of make believe to make you feel grown up. These characters may have powers, see visions, come from imaginary homelands or do weird, wonderful, sometimes horrible things. But they also come loaded with internal troubles, are riddled with personal conflicts, and sometimes live and die (and come back to life) based on the complicated choices they make. And here I used to think that it was the fairies that were simplistic and the people who were complex.

There's something so very Christian, or rather Protestant, about the idea of dismissing the imagination as a sign of growing up, and as a diligent student of dead social realist writers, I believed it. But realism is speculation too. And if you were a black nerd like me, a white family from an impossibly clean suburb experiencing nothing more than the drama of crushing ennui as they tear their lives apart just by talking about it was as fantastical as Superman.

Being no fan of H. P. Lovecraft I've of course saved him for the end. You can't talk about a modern fantasist without bring Mr. Mountains of Madness into the room, which is funny given how much he would have hated being in any space with so many others not like him. But when I read Neil Gaiman, I don't see Lovecraft at all, not even in "I, Cthulhu." The ghost I see hovering is Borges. Like Jorge Luis, Neil is not writing speculative fiction. He is so given over to these worlds that he has gone beyond speculating about them to living in them. Like Borges, he writes about things as if they have already happened, describes worlds as if we are already living in them, and shares stories as if they are solid truths that he's just passing along. I don't think I really believe that in reading great fiction I find myself, so much as I find where I want to be. Because Neil's stories leave you feeling that his is the world we've always lived in, and it's the "real" world that is the stuff of make-believe.

Marlon James

PREFACE

The worst conversations, for me, are normally with taxi drivers.

They say, "So what do you do, then?" and I say, "I write things."

"What kind of things?"

"Um. All sorts," I say, and I sound unconvincing. I can hear it in my voice.

"Yeah? What sort of stuff is all sorts, then? Fiction, nonfiction, books, TV?"

"Yes. That sort of thing."

"So, what sort of thing do you write? Fantasy? Mysteries? Science fiction? Literary fiction? Children's books? Poetry? Reviews? Funny? Scary? What?"

"All of that, really."

Then the drivers sometimes shoot me a look in the mirror and decide I am taking the mickey, and are quiet, and sometimes they keep going. The next question is always, "Anything I've heard of?"

So, then I list the titles of books I've written, and all but one of the taxi drivers who have asked the question have nodded, and said they've never actually heard of the books, or me, but they will be sure to look them up. Sometimes they ask how to spell my name. (The one taxi driver who pulled over to the side of the road, then got out of the car and then hugged me and had me sign something for his wife was an anomaly, but one that I really liked.)

And I feel awkward for not being somebody who writes one thing—mysteries, say, or ghost stories. Someone who is easy to explain in taxis.

This is a book for all those taxi drivers. But it's not just for them. It is a book for anybody who, having asked me what I do, and then having asked me what I write, wants to know what book of mine they should read.

Because the answer for me is always, "What kind of things do you like?" And then I try and point them at the thing I've written that is closest to what they want to read.

In this book you will find short stories, novelettes and novellas, and even some extracts from novels. (You won't find any comics or criticism, nor will you find essays, screenplays or poetry.)

The stories, short and long, are in here because I'm proud of them, and you can dip into them and dip out again. They cover all kinds of genres and subjects, and mostly what they have in common is that I wrote them. The other thing they have in common is they were chosen by readers on the Internet, when we asked people to vote for the stories they liked best. This meant that I didn't have to try and choose favorites. I let the votes for individual stories be our guide to what went in here, and I didn't put my thumb on the scales to add or lose any stories, except for one. It's a fable called "Monkey and the Lady," and I slipped it into this book because it hasn't been collected anywhere and has only ever appeared in the book it was written for, Dave McKean's 2017 anthology *The Weight of Words*. It's a story I love, very much, although I could not tell you why.

The extracts from novels were harder to choose, and in these I let myself be guided by my beloved editor, Jennifer Brehl. In my head nothing from a novel stands alone, and thus you cannot take extracts from books out of context—except I remember finding a paperback, as a boy, that must have belonged to my father, called *A Book of Wit and Humour*, edited by Michael Barsley, which mostly consisted of extracts from novels. I still have it. I fell in love with selected passages that then sent me to seek out books I delight in and take pleasure in rereading to this day, like Stella Gibbons's glorious novel of dark and dreadful Sussex farmhouse doings, *Cold Comfort Farm*, or Caryl Brahms and S. J. Simon's magical Shakespearian comedy *No Bed for Bacon*. So perhaps someone reading this will decide, on the basis of the pages presented here, that *American Gods* or *Stardust* (to take two very different novels that both happen to have me as an author) might be their cup of tea, and worth investigating further. I'd like that.

The stories in this book are printed in order of publication, not in order of how much people loved them, earliest stories first. You can see me trying to find out who I am as a writer, trying on other people's hats and glasses and wondering if they suit me, before, eventually, discovering who I had been all along. I encourage you to browse. To start where it suits you, to read whatever tale you feel like reading at that moment.

I love being a writer.

I love being a writer because I'm allowed to do whatever I want, when I write. There aren't any rules. There aren't even any guardrails. I can write funny things and sad things, big stories and small. I can write to make you happy or write to chill your blood. I am certain that I would have been a more commercially successful author if I'd just written a book, that was in most ways like the last book, once a year, but it wouldn't have been half as much fun.

I'll be sixty soon. I've been writing professionally since I was twenty-two. I hope very much that I have another twenty, perhaps even thirty years of writing left in me; there are so many stories I still want to tell, after all, and it's starting to feel like, if I just keep going, I may one day have an answer for anyone, even a taxi driver, who wants to know what kind of a writer I am.

I may even find out myself.

If you have been on the road with me all these years, reading these stories and novels as they appeared, thank you. I appreciate it and you. If this is our first encounter, then I hope you find something in these pages that amuses you, distracts you, makes you wonder or makes you think—or that simply makes you want to read on.

Thank you for coming, my reader.

Enjoy yourself.

Neil Gaiman
May 2020
Isle of Skye

WE CAN GET THEM FOR YOU WHOLESALE

1984

P ETER PINTER HAD never heard of Aristippus of the Cyrenaics, a lesser-known follower of Socrates who maintained that the avoidance of trouble was the highest attainable good; however, he had lived his uneventful life according to this precept. In all respects except one (an inability to pass up a bargain, and which of us is entirely free from that?), he was a very moderate man. He did not go to extremes. His speech was proper and reserved; he rarely overate; he drank enough to be sociable and no more; he was far from rich and in no wise poor. He liked people and people liked him. Bearing all that in mind, would you expect to find him in a lowlife pub on the seamier side of London's East End, taking out what is colloquially known as a "contract" on someone he hardly knew? You would not. You would not even expect to find him in the pub.

And until a certain Friday afternoon, you would have been right. But the love of a woman can do strange things to a man, even one so colorless as Peter Pinter, and the discovery that Miss Gwendolyn Thorpe, twenty-three years of age, of 9, Oaktree Terrace, Purley, was messing about (as the vulgar would put it) with a smooth young gentleman from the accounting department—*after*, mark you, she had consented to wear an engagement ring, composed of real ruby chips, nine-carat gold, and something that might well have been a diamond (£37.50) that it had taken Peter almost an entire lunch hour to choose—can do very strange things to a man indeed.

After he made this shocking discovery, Peter spent a sleepless Friday night, tossing and turning with visions of Gwendolyn and Archie Gibbons (the Don Juan of the Clamages accounting department) dancing and swimming before his eyes—performing acts that even Peter, if he were pressed, would have to admit were most improbable. But the bile of jealousy had risen up within him, and by the morning Peter had resolved that his rival should be done away with.

Saturday morning was spent wondering how one contacted an assassin, for, to the best of Peter's knowledge, none were employed by Clamages (the department store that employed all three of the members of our eternal triangle and, incidentally, furnished the ring), and he was wary of asking anyone outright for fear of attracting attention to himself.

Thus it was that Saturday afternoon found him hunting through the Yellow Pages.

ASSASSINS, he found, was not between ASPHALT CONTRACTORS and ASSESSORS (QUANTITY); KILLERS was not between KENNELS and KINDERGARTENS; MURDERERS was not between MOWERS and MUSEUMS. PEST CONTROL looked promising; however closer investigation of the pest control advertisements showed them to be almost solely concerned with "rats, mice, fleas, cockroaches, rabbits, moles, and rats" (to quote from one that Peter felt was rather hard on rats) and not really what he had in mind. Even so, being of a careful nature, he dutifully inspected the entries in that category, and at the bottom of the second page, in small print, he found a firm that looked promising.

'Complete discreet disposal of irksome and unwanted mammals, etc.' went the entry, 'Ketch, Hare, Burke and Ketch. The Old Firm.' It went on to give no address, but only a telephone number.

Peter dialed the number, surprising himself by so doing. His heart pounded in his chest, and he tried to look nonchalant. The telephone rang once, twice, three times. Peter was just starting to hope that it would not be answered and he could forget the whole thing when there was a click and a brisk young female voice said, "Ketch Hare Burke Ketch. Can I help you?"

Carefully not giving his name, Peter said, "Er, how big—I mean, what size mammals do you go up to? To, uh, dispose of?"

"Well, that would all depend on what size sir requires."

He plucked up all his courage. "A person?"

Her voice remained brisk and unruffled. "Of course, sir. Do you have a pen and paper handy? Good. Be at the Dirty Donkey pub, off Little Courtney Street, E3, tonight at eight o'clock. Carry a rolled-up copy of the *Financial Times*—that's the pink one, sir—and our operative will approach you there." Then she put down the phone.

Peter was elated. It had been far easier than he had imagined. He went down to the newsagent's and bought a copy of the *Financial Times,* found Little Courtney Street in his *A–Z of London,* and spent the rest of the afternoon watching football on the television and imagining the smooth young gentleman from accounting's funeral.

IT TOOK PETER a while to find the pub. Eventually he spotted the pub sign, which showed a donkey and was indeed remarkably dirty.

The Dirty Donkey was a small and more or less filthy pub, poorly lit, in which knots of unshaven people wearing dusty donkey jackets stood around eyeing each other suspiciously, eating crisps and drinking pints of Guinness, a drink that Peter had never cared for. Peter held his *Financial Times* under one arm as conspicuously as he could, but no one approached him, so he bought a half of shandy and retreated to a corner table. Unable to think of anything else to do while waiting, he tried to read the paper, but, lost and confused by a maze of grain futures and a rubber company that was selling something or other short (quite what the short somethings were he could not tell), he gave it up and stared at the door.

He had waited almost ten minutes when a small busy man hustled in, looked quickly around him, then came straight over to Peter's table and sat down.

He stuck out his hand. "Kemble. Burton Kemble of Ketch Hare Burke Ketch. I hear you have a job for us."

He didn't look like a killer. Peter said so.

"Oh, lor' bless us, no. I'm not actually part of our workforce, sir. I'm in sales."

Peter nodded. That certainly made sense. "Can we—er—talk freely here?"

"Sure. Nobody's interested. Now then, how many people would you like disposed of?"

"Only one. His name's Archibald Gibbons and he works in Clamages accounting department. His address is . . ."

Kemble interrupted. "We can go into all that later, sir, if you don't mind. Let's just quickly go over the financial side. First of all, the contract will cost you five hundred pounds . . ."

Peter nodded. He could afford that and in fact had expected to have to pay a little more.

". . .although there's always the special offer," Kemble concluded smoothly.

Peter's eyes shone. As I mentioned earlier, he loved a bargain and often bought things he had no imaginable use for in sales or on special offers. Apart from this one failing (one that so many of us share), he was a most moderate young man. "Special offer?"

"Two for the price of one, sir."

Mmm. Peter thought about it. That worked out at only £250 each, which couldn't be bad no matter how you looked at it. There was only one snag. "I'm afraid I don't *have* anyone else I want killed."

Kemble looked disappointed. "That's a pity, sir. For two we could probably have even knocked the price down to, well, say four hundred and fifty pounds for the both of them."

"Really?"

"Well, it gives our operatives something to do, sir. If you must know"—and here he dropped his voice—"there really isn't enough work in this particular line to keep them occupied. Not like the old days. Isn't there just *one* other person you'd like to see dead?" Peter pondered. He hated to pass up a bargain, but couldn't for the life of him think of anyone else. He liked people. Still, a bargain was a bargain . . .

"Look," said Peter. "Could I think about it and see you here tomorrow night?"

The salesman looked pleased. "Of course, sir," he said. "I'm sure you'll be able to think of someone."

The answer—the obvious answer—came to Peter as he was drifting off to sleep that night. He sat straight up in bed, fumbled the bedside light on, and wrote a name down on the back of an envelope, in
case he forgot it. To tell the truth, he didn't think that he could forget
it, for it was painfully obvious, but you can never tell with these late-
night thoughts.

The name that he had written down on the back of the envelope
was this: *Gwendolyn Thorpe*.

He turned the light off, rolled over, and was soon asleep, dreaming peaceful and remarkably unmurderous dreams.

KEMBLE WAS WAITING for him when he arrived in the Dirty Donkey
on Sunday night. Peter bought a drink and sat down beside him.

"I'm taking you up on the special offer," he said by way of greeting.

Kemble nodded vigorously. "A very wise decision, if you don't
mind me saying so, sir."

Peter Pinter smiled modestly, in the manner of one who read the
Financial Times and made wise business decisions. "That will be four
hundred and fifty pounds, I believe?"

"Did I say four hundred and fifty pounds, sir? Good gracious me,
I do apologize. I beg your pardon, I was thinking of our bulk rate.
It would be four hundred and seventy-five pounds for two people."

Disappointment mingled with cupidity on Peter's bland and
youthful face. That was an extra £25. However, something that
Kemble had said caught his attention.

"Bulk rate?"

"Of course, but I doubt that sir would be interested in that."

"No, no, I am. Tell me about it."

"Very well, sir. Bulk rate, four hundred and fifty pounds, would
be for a large job. Ten people."

Peter wondered if he had heard correctly. "Ten people? But that's
only forty-five pounds each."

"Yes, sir. It's the large order that makes it profitable."

"I see," said Peter, and "Hmm," said Peter, and "Could you be here
the same time tomorrow night?"

"Of course, sir."

Upon arriving home, Peter got out a scrap of paper and a pen. He wrote the numbers one to ten down one side and then filled it in as follows:

1. . . . *Archie G.*

2. . . . *Gwennie.*

3. . . .

and so forth.

Having filled in the first two, he sat sucking his pen, hunting for wrongs done to him and people the world would be better off without.

He smoked a cigarette. He strolled around the room.

Aha! There was a physics teacher at a school he had attended who had delighted in making his life a misery. What was the man's name again? And for that matter, was he still alive? Peter wasn't sure, but he wrote *The Physics Teacher, Abbot Street Secondary School* next to the number three. The next came more easily—his department head had refused to raise his salary a couple of months back; that the raise had eventually come was immaterial. *Mr. Hunterson* was number four.

When he was five, a boy named Simon Ellis had poured paint on his head while another boy named James somebody-or-other had held him down and a girl named Sharon Hartsharpe had laughed. They were numbers five through seven, respectively.

Who else?

There was the man on television with the annoying snicker who read the news. He went on the list. And what about the woman in the flat next door with the little yappy dog that shat in the hall? He put her and the dog down on nine. Ten was the hardest. He scratched his head and went into the kitchen for a cup of coffee, then dashed back and wrote *My Great-Uncle Mervyn* down in the tenth place. The old man was rumored to be quite affluent, and there was a possibility (albeit rather slim) that he could leave Peter some money.

With the satisfaction of an evening's work well done, he went off to bed.

Monday at Clamages was routine; Peter was a senior sales assistant in the books department, a job that actually entailed very little. He clutched his list tightly in his hand, deep in his pocket, rejoicing in the feeling of power that it gave him. He spent a most enjoyable lunch hour in the canteen with young Gwendolyn (who did not know that he had seen her and Archie enter the stockroom together) and even smiled at the smooth young man from the accounting department when he passed him in the corridor.

He proudly displayed his list to Kemble that evening.

The little salesman's face fell.

"I'm afraid this isn't ten people, Mr. Pinter," he explained. "You've counted the woman in the next-door flat *and* her dog as one person. That brings it to eleven, which would be an extra"—his pocket calculator was rapidly deployed—"an extra seventy pounds. How about if we forget the dog?"

Peter shook his head. "The dog's as bad as the woman. Or worse."

"Then I'm afraid we have a slight problem. Unless . . ."

"What?"

"Unless you'd like to take advantage of our wholesale rate. But of course sir wouldn't be . . ."

There are words that do things to people; words that make people's faces flush with joy, excitement, or passion. *Environmental* can be one; *occult* is another. *Wholesale* was Peter's. He leaned back in his chair. "Tell me about it," he said with the practiced assurance of an experienced shopper.

"Well, sir," said Kemble, allowing himself a little chuckle, "we can, uh, *get* them for you wholesale, seventeen pounds fifty each, for every quarry after the first fifty, or a tenner each for every one over two hundred."

"I suppose you'd go down to a fiver if I wanted a thousand people knocked off?"

"Oh no, sir," Kemble looked shocked. "If you're talking those sorts of figures, we can do them for a quid each."

"One *pound?*"

"That's right, sir. There's not a big profit margin on it, but the high turnover and productivity more than justifies it."

Kemble got up. "Same time tomorrow, sir?"

Peter nodded.

One thousand pounds. One thousand people. Peter Pinter didn't even *know* a thousand people. Even so . . . there were the Houses of Parliament. He didn't like politicians; they squabbled and argued and carried on so.

And for that matter . . .

An idea, shocking in its audacity. Bold. Daring. Still, the idea was there and it wouldn't go away. A distant cousin of his had married the younger brother of an earl or a baron or something . . .

On the way home from work that afternoon, he stopped off at a little shop that he had passed a thousand times without entering. It had a large sign in the window—guaranteeing to trace your lineage for you and even draw up a coat of arms if you happened to have mislaid your own—and an impressive heraldic map.

They were very helpful and phoned him up just after seven to give him their news.

If approximately fourteen million, seventy-two thousand, eight hundred and eleven people died, he, Peter Pinter, would be *King of England.*

He didn't have fourteen million, seventy-two thousand, eight hundred and eleven pounds: but he suspected that when you were talking in those figures, Mr. Kemble would have one of his special discounts.

MR. KEMBLE DID.

He didn't even raise an eyebrow.

"Actually," he explained, "it works out quite cheaply; you see, we wouldn't have to do them all individually. Small-scale nuclear weapons, some judicious bombing, gassing, plague, dropping radios in swimming pools, and then mopping up the stragglers. Say four thousand pounds."

"Four thou—? That's incredible!"

The salesman looked pleased with himself. "Our operatives will be glad of the work, sir." He grinned. "We pride ourselves on servicing our wholesale customers."

The wind blew cold as Peter left the pub, setting the old sign swinging. It didn't look much like a dirty donkey, thought Peter. More like a pale horse.

Peter was drifting off to sleep that night, mentally rehearsing his coronation speech, when a thought drifted into his head and hung around. It would not go away. Could he—could he *possibly* be passing up an even larger saving than he already had? Could he be missing out on a bargain?

Peter climbed out of bed and walked over to the phone. It was almost 3 A.M., but even so . . .

His Yellow Pages lay open where he had left it the previous Saturday, and he dialed the number.

The phone seemed to ring forever. There was a click and a bored voice said, "Burke Hare Ketch. Can I help you?"

"I hope I'm not phoning too late . . ." he began.

"Of course not, sir."

"I was wondering if I could speak to Mr. Kemble."

"Can you hold? I'll see if he's available."

Peter waited for a couple of minutes, listening to the ghostly crackles and whispers that always echo down empty phone lines.

"Are you there, caller?"

"Yes, I'm here."

"Putting you through." There was a buzz, then "Kemble speaking."

"Ah, Mr. Kemble. Hello. Sorry if I got you out of bed or anything. This is, um, Peter Pinter."

"Yes, Mr. Pinter?"

"Well, I'm sorry it's so late, only I was wondering . . . How much would it cost to kill everybody? Everybody in the world?"

"Everybody? All the people?"

"Yes. How much? I mean, for an order like that, you'd have to have some kind of a big discount. How much would it be? For everyone?"

"Nothing at all, Mr. Pinter."

"You mean you wouldn't do it?"

"I mean we'd do it for nothing, Mr. Pinter. We only have to be asked, you see. We always have to be asked."

Peter was puzzled. "But—when would you start?"

"Start? Right away. Now. We've been ready for a long time. But we had to be asked, Mr. Pinter. Good night. It *has* been a *pleasure* doing business with you."

The line went dead.

Peter felt strange. Everything seemed very distant. He wanted to sit down. What on earth had the man meant? "We always have to be asked." It was definitely strange. Nobody does anything for nothing in this world; he had a good mind to phone Kemble back and call the whole thing off. Perhaps he had overreacted, perhaps there was a perfectly innocent reason why Archie and Gwendolyn had entered the stockroom together. He would talk to her; that's what he'd do. He'd talk to Gwennie first thing tomorrow morning . . .

That was when the noises started.

Odd cries from across the street. A catfight? Foxes probably. He hoped someone would throw a shoe at them. Then, from the corridor outside his flat, he heard a muffled clumping, as if someone were dragging something very heavy along the floor. It stopped. Someone knocked on his door, twice, very softly.

Outside his window the cries were getting louder. Peter sat in his chair, knowing that somehow, somewhere, he had missed something. Something important. The knocking redoubled. He was thankful that he always locked and chained his door at night.

They'd been ready for a long time, but they had to be asked . .

WHEN THE THING came through the door, Peter started screaming, but he really didn't scream for very long.

"I, CTHULHU"

1986

I.

CTHULHU, THEY CALL ME. Great Cthulhu. Nobody can pronounce it right.

Are you writing this down? Every word? Good. Where shall I start—mm? Very well, then. The beginning. Write this down, Whateley.

I was spawned uncounted aeons ago, in the dark mists of Khhaa'yngnaiih (no, of course I don't know how to spell it. Write it as it sounds), of nameless nightmare parents, under a gibbous moon. It wasn't the moon of this planet, of course, it was a real moon. On some nights it filled over half the sky and as it rose you could watch the crimson blood drip and trickle down its bloated face, staining it red, until at its height it bathed the swamps and towers in a gory dead red light.

Those were the days.

Or rather the nights, on the whole. Our place had a sun of sorts, but it was old, even back then. I remember that on the night it finally exploded we all slithered down to the beach to watch. But I get ahead of myself.

I never knew my parents.

My father was consumed by my mother as soon as he had fertilized her and she, in her turn, was eaten by myself at my birth. That is my first memory, as it happens. Squirming my way out of my mother, the gamy taste of her still in my tentacles.

Don't look so shocked, Whateley. I find you humans just as revolting.

Which reminds me, did they remember to feed the shoggoth? I thought I heard it gibbering.

I spent my first few thousand years in those swamps. I did not like this, of course, for I was the color of a young trout and about four of your feet long. I spent most of my time creeping up on things and eating them and in my turn avoiding being crept up on and eaten.

So passed my youth.

And then one day—I believe it was a Tuesday—I discovered that there was more to life than food. (Sex? Of course not. I will not reach that stage until after my next estivation; your piddly little planet will long be cold by then). It was that Tuesday that my Uncle Hastur slithered down to my part of the swamp with his jaws fused.

It meant that he did not intend to dine that visit, and that we could talk.

Now, that is a stupid question, even for you, Whateley. I don't use either of my mouths in communicating with you, do I? Very well then. One more question like that and I'll find someone else to relate my memoirs to. And you will be feeding the shoggoth.

We are going out, said Hastur to me. Would you like to accompany us?

We? I asked him. Who's we?

Myself, he said, Azathoth, Yog-Sothoth, Nyarlathotep, Tsathoggua, Iä! Shub-Niggurath, young Yuggoth and a few others. You know, he said, the boys. (I am freely translating for you here, Whateley, you understand. Most of them were a-, bi-, or trisexual, and old Iä! Shub Niggurath has at least a thousand young, or so it says. That branch of the family was always given to exaggeration.) We are going out, he concluded, and we were wondering if you fancied some fun.

I did not answer him at once. To tell the truth I wasn't all that fond of my cousins, and due to some particularly eldritch distortion of the planes I've always had a great deal of trouble seeing them clearly. They tend to get fuzzy around the edges, and some of them—Sabaoth is a case in point—have a great many edges.

But I was young, I craved excitement. "There has to be more to life than this!" I would cry, as the delightfully fetid charnel smells of the swamp miasmatized around me, and overhead the ngau-ngau and zitadors whooped and skrarked. I said yes, as you have probably guessed, and I oozed after Hastur until we reached the meeting place.

As I remember we spent the next moon discussing where we were going. Azathoth had his hearts set on distant Shaggai, and Nyarlathotep had a thing about the Unspeakable Place (I can't for the life of me think why. The last time I was there everything was shut). It was all the same to me, Whateley. Anywhere wet and somehow, subtly *wrong* and I feel at home. But Yog-Sothoth had the last word, as he always does, and we came to this plane.

You've met Yog-Sothoth, have you not, my little two-legged beastie? I thought as much.

He opened the way for us to come here.

To be honest, I didn't think much of it. Still don't. If I'd known the trouble we were going to have I doubt I'd have bothered. But I was younger then.

As I remember our first stop was dim Carcosa. Scared the shit out of me, that place. These days I can look at your kind without a shudder, but all those people, without a scale or pseudopod between them, gave me the quivers.

The King in Yellow was the first I ever got on with.

The tatterdemalion king. You don't know of him? Necronomicon page seven hundred and four (of the complete edition) hints at his existence, and I think that idiot Prinn mentions him in De Vermis Mysteriis. And then there's Chambers, of course.

Lovely fellow, once I got used to him.

He was the one who first gave me the idea.

What the unspeakable hells is there to do in this dreary dimension? I asked him.

He laughed. When I first came here, he said, a mere color out of space, I asked myself the same question. Then I discovered the fun one can get in conquering these odd worlds, subjugating the inhabitants, getting them to fear and worship you. It's a real laugh.

Of course, the Old Ones don't like it.

The old ones? I asked.

No, he said, Old Ones. It's capitalized. Funny chaps. Like huge starfish-headed barrels, with filmy great wings that they fly through space with.

Fly through space? Fly? I was shocked. I didn't think anybody flew these days. Why bother when one can sluggle, eh? I could see why they called them the old ones. Pardon, Old Ones.

What do these Old Ones do? I asked the King.

(I'll tell you all about sluggling later, Whateley. Pointless, though. You lack wnaisngh'ang. Although perhaps badminton equipment would do almost as well.) (Where was I? Oh yes.)

What do these Old Ones do, I asked the King.

Nothing much, he explained. They just don't like anybody else doing it.

I undulated, writhing my tentacles as if to say "I have met such beings in my time," but fear the message was lost on the King.

Do you know of any places ripe for conquering? I asked him.

He waved a hand vaguely in the direction of a small and dreary patch of stars. There's one over there that you might like, he told me. It's called Earth. Bit off the beaten track, but lots of room to move.

Silly bugger.

That's all for now, Whateley.

Tell someone to feed the shoggoth on your way out.

II.

IS IT TIME ALREADY, Whateley?

Don't be silly. I know that I sent for you. My memory is as good as it ever was. Ph'nglui mglw'nafh Cthulhu R'lyeh wgah'nagl fthagn.

You know what that means, don't you?

In his house at R'lyeh dead Cthulhu waits dreaming.

A justified exaggeration, that; I haven't been feeling too well recently.

It was a joke, one-head, a joke. Are you writing all this down? Good. Keep writing. I know where we got up to yesterday.

R'lyeh.

Earth.

That's an example of the way that languages change, the meanings of words. Fuzziness. I can't stand it. Once on a time R'lyeh was the Earth, or at least the part of it that I ran, the wet bits at the start. Now it's just my little house here, latitude 47" 9' south, longitude 126" 43' west.

Or the Old Ones. They call us the Old Ones now. Or the Great Old Ones, as if there were no difference between us and the barrel boys.

Fuzziness.

So I came to Earth, and in those days it was a lot wetter than it is today. A wonderful place it was, the seas as rich as soup and I got on wonderfully with the people. Dagon and the boys (I use the word literally this time). We all lived in the water in those far-off times, and before you could say *Cthulhu fthagn* I had them building and slaving and cooking. And being cooked, of course.

Which reminds me, there was something I meant to tell you. A true story.

There was a ship, a-sailing on the seas. On a Pacific cruise. And on this ship was a magician, a conjurer, whose function was to entertain the passengers. And there was this parrot on the ship.

Every time the magician did a trick the parrot would ruin it. How? He'd tell them how it was done, that's how. "He put it up his sleeve," the parrot would squawk. Or "he's stacked the deck" or "it's got a false bottom."

The magician didn't like it.

Finally the time came for him to do his biggest trick.

He announced it.

He rolled up his sleeves.

He waved his arms.

At that moment the ship bucked and smashed over to one side.

Sunken R'lyeh had risen beneath them. Hordes of my servants, loathsome fish-men, swarmed over the sides, seized the passengers and crew and dragged them beneath the waves. R'lyeh sank below the waters once more, awaiting that time when dread Cthulhu shall rise and reign once more.

Alone, above the foul waters, the magician—overlooked by my little batrachian boobies, for which they paid heavily—floated, clinging to a spar, all alone. And then, far above him he noticed a small green shape. It came lower, finally perching on a lump of nearby driftwood, and he saw it was the parrot.

The parrot cocked its head to one side and squinted up at the magician. "Alright," it says, "I give up. How did you do it?"

Of course it's a true story, Whateley.

Would black Cthulhu, who slimed out of the dark stars when your most eldritch nightmares were suckling at their mothers' pseudo-mammaria, who waits for the time that the stars come right to come forth from his tomb-palace, revive the faithful and resume his rule, who waits to teach anew the high and luscious pleasures of death and revelry, would he lie to you?

Sure I would.

Shut up Whateley, I'm talking. I don't care where you heard it before.

We had fun in those days. Carnage and destruction, sacrifice and damnation, ichor and slime and ooze, and foul and nameless games. Food and fun. It was one long party, and everybody loved it except those who found themselves impaled on wooden stakes between a chunk of cheese and pineapple.

Oh, there were giants on the earth in those days.

It couldn't last forever.

Down from the skies they came, with filmy wings and rules and regulations and routines and Dho-Hna knows how many forms to be filled out in quintuplicate. Banal little bureaucruds, the lot of them. You could see it just looking at them: Five-pointed heads—every one you looked at had five points, arms whatever, on their heads (which I might add were always in the same place). None of them had the imagination to grow three arms or six, or one hundred and two. Five, every time.

No offense meant.

We didn't get on.

They didn't like my party.

They rapped on the walls (metaphorically). We paid no attention. Then they got mean.

Argued. Bitched. Fought.

Okay, we said, you want the sea, you can have the sea. Lock, stock, and starfish-headed barrel. We moved onto the land—it was pretty swampy back then—and we built Gargantuan monolithic structures that dwarfed the mountains.

You know what killed off the dinosaurs, Whateley? We did. In one barbecue.

But those pointy-headed killjoys couldn't leave well enough alone. They tried to move the planet nearer the sun—or was it further away? I never actually asked them. Next thing I knew we were under the sea again.

You had to laugh.

The city of the Old Ones got it in the neck. They hated the dry and the cold, as did their creatures. All of a sudden they were in the Antarctic, dry as a bone and cold as the lost plains of thrice-accursed Leng.

Here endeth the lesson for today, Whateley.

And will you please get somebody to feed that blasted shoggoth?

III.

(Professors Armitage and Wilmarth are both convinced that not less than three pages are missing from the manuscript at this point, citing the text and length. I concur.)

The stars changed, Whateley.

Imagine your body cut away from your head, leaving you a lump of flesh on a chill marble slab, blinking and choking. That was what it was like. The party was over.

It killed us.

So we wait here below. Dreadful, eh?

Not at all. I don't give a nameless dread. I can wait.

I sit here, dead and dreaming, watching the ant-empires of man rise and fall, tower and crumble.

One day—perhaps it will come tomorrow, perhaps in more to-morrows than your feeble mind can encompass—the stars will be rightly conjoined in the heavens, and the time of destruction shall be upon us: I shall rise from the deep and I shall have dominion over the world once more.

Riot and revel, blood-food and foulness, eternal twilight and nightmare and the screams of the dead and the not-dead and the chant of the faithful.

And after?

I shall leave this plane, when this world is a cold cinder orbiting a lightless sun. I shall return to my own place, where the blood drips nightly down the face of a moon that bulges like the eye of a drowned sailor, and I shall estivate.

Then I shall mate, and in the end I shall feel a stirring within me, and I shall feel my little one eating its way out into the light.

Um.

Are you writing this all down, Whateley? Good.

Well, that's all. The end. Narrative concluded.

Guess what we're going to do now? That's right.

We're going to feed the shoggoth.

NICHOLAS WAS . . .

1989

OLDER THAN SIN, and his beard could grow no whiter. He wanted to die.

The dwarfish natives of the Arctic caverns did not speak his language, but conversed in their own, twittering tongue, conducted incomprehensible rituals, when they were not actually working in the factories.

Once every year they forced him, sobbing and protesting, into Endless Night. During the journey he would stand near every child in the world, leave one of the dwarves' invisible gifts by its bedside. The children slept, frozen into time.

He envied Prometheus and Loki, Sisyphus and Judas. His punishment was harsher.

Ho.

Ho.

Ho.

BABYCAKES

1990

A FEW YEARS BACK all the animals went away.

We woke up one morning, and they just weren't there anymore.

They didn't even leave us a note, or say good-bye. We never figured out quite where they'd gone.

We missed them.

Some of us thought that the world had ended, but it hadn't. There
just weren't any more animals. No cats or rabbits, no dogs or whales,
no fish in the seas, no birds in the skies.

We were all alone.

We didn't know what to do.

We wandered around lost, for a time, and then someone pointed
out that just because we didn't have animals anymore, that was no
reason to change our lives. No reason to change our diets or to cease
testing products that might cause us harm.

After all, there were still babies.

Babies can't talk. They can hardly move. A baby is not a rational,
thinking creature.

We made babies.

And we used them.

Some of them we ate. Baby flesh is tender and succulent.

We flayed their skin and decorated ourselves in it. Baby leather is soft and comfortable.

Some of them we tested.

We taped open their eyes, dripped detergents and shampoos in, a drop at a time.

We scarred them and scalded them. We burnt them. We clamped them and planted electrodes into their brains. We grafted, and we froze, and we irradiated.

The babies breathed our smoke, and the babies' veins flowed with our medicines and drugs, until they stopped breathing or until their blood ceased to flow.

It was hard, of course, but it was necessary. No one could deny that.

With the animals gone, what else could we do?

Some people complained, of course. But then, they always do. And everything went back to normal.

Only . . .

Yesterday, all the babies were gone.

We don't know where they went. We didn't even see them go. We don't know what we're going to do without them.

But we'll think of something. Humans are smart. It's what makes us superior to the animals and the babies.

We'll figure something out.

CHIVALRY

1992

M RS. WHITAKER FOUND the Holy Grail; it was under a fur coat.
Every Thursday afternoon Mrs. Whitaker walked down to
the post office to collect her pension, even though her legs were no
longer what they were, and on the way back home she would stop in
at the Oxfam Shop and buy herself a little something.

The Oxfam Shop sold old clothes, knickknacks, oddments, bits
and bobs, and large quantities of old paperbacks, all of them dona-
tions: secondhand flotsam, often the house clearances of the dead.
All the profits went to charity.

The shop was staffed by volunteers. The volunteer on duty this afternoon was Marie, seventeen, slightly overweight, and dressed in a
baggy mauve jumper that looked like she had bought it from the shop.

Marie sat by the till with a copy of *Modern Woman* magazine, filling out a "Reveal Your Hidden Personality" questionnaire. Every
now and then, she'd flip to the back of the magazine and check the
relative points assigned to an A), B), or C) answer before making up
her mind how she'd respond to the question.

Mrs. Whitaker puttered around the shop.

They still hadn't sold the stuffed cobra, she noted. It had been
there for six months now, gathering dust, glass eyes gazing balefully
at the clothes racks and the cabinet filled with chipped porcelain and
chewed toys.

Mrs. Whitaker patted its head as she went past.

She picked out a couple of Mills & Boon novels from a bookshelf—
Her Thundering Soul and *Her Turbulent Heart,* a shilling each—and
gave careful consideration to the empty bottle of Mateus Rosé with
a decorative lampshade on it before deciding she really didn't have
anywhere to put it.

She moved a rather threadbare fur coat, which smelled badly of
mothballs. Underneath it was a walking stick and a water-stained
copy of *Romance and Legend of Chivalry* by A. R. Hope Moncrieff,
priced at five pence. Next to the book, on its side, was the Holy Grail.
It had a little round paper sticker on the base, and written on it, in felt
pen, was the price: 30p.

Mrs. Whitaker picked up the dusty silver goblet and appraised it
through her thick spectacles.

"This is nice," she called to Marie. Marie shrugged.

"It'd look nice on the mantelpiece." Marie shrugged again.

Mrs. Whitaker gave fifty pence to Marie, who gave her ten pence
change and a brown paper bag to put the books and the Holy Grail
in. Then she went next door to the butcher's and bought herself a
nice piece of liver. Then she went home.

The inside of the goblet was thickly coated with a brownish-red
dust. Mrs. Whitaker washed it out with great care, then left it to soak
for an hour in warm water with a dash of vinegar added. Then she
polished it with metal polish until it gleamed, and she put it on the
mantelpiece in her parlor, where it sat between a small soulful china
basset hound and a photograph of her late husband, Henry, on the
beach at Frinton in 1953.

She had been right: It did look nice.

For dinner that evening she had the liver fried in breadcrumbs
with onions. It was very nice.

The next morning was Friday; on alternate Fridays Mrs. Whitaker
and Mrs. Greenberg would visit each other. Today it was Mrs. Greenberg's turn to visit Mrs. Whitaker. They sat in the parlor and ate
macaroons and drank tea. Mrs. Whitaker took one sugar in her tea,
but Mrs. Greenberg took sweetener, which she always carried in her
handbag in a small plastic container.

"That's nice," said Mrs. Greenberg, pointing to the Grail. "What is it?"

"It's the Holy Grail," said Mrs. Whitaker. "It's the cup that Jesus drunk out of at the Last Supper. Later, at the Crucifixion, it caught His precious blood when the centurion's spear pierced His side."

Mrs. Greenberg sniffed. She was small and Jewish and didn't hold with unsanitary things. "I wouldn't know about that," she said, "but it's very nice. Our Myron got one just like that when he won the swimming tournament, only it's got his name on the side."

"Is he still with that nice girl? The hairdresser?"

"Bernice? Oh yes. They're thinking of getting engaged," said Mrs. Greenberg.

"That's nice," said Mrs. Whitaker. She took another macaroon. Mrs. Greenberg baked her own macaroons and brought them over every alternate Friday: small sweet light brown biscuits with almonds on top.

They talked about Myron and Bernice, and Mrs. Whitaker's nephew Ronald (she had had no children), and about their friend Mrs. Perkins who was in hospital with her hip, poor dear.

At midday Mrs. Greenberg went home, and Mrs. Whitaker made herself cheese on toast for lunch, and after lunch Mrs. Whitaker took her pills; the white and the red and two little orange ones.

The doorbell rang.

Mrs. Whitaker answered the door. It was a young man with shoulder-length hair so fair it was almost white, wearing gleaming silver armor, with a white surcoat.

"Hello," he said.

"Hello," said Mrs. Whitaker.

"I'm on a quest," he said.

"That's nice," said Mrs. Whitaker, noncommittally.

"Can I come in?" he asked.

Mrs. Whitaker shook her head. "I'm sorry, I don't think so," she said.

"I'm on a quest for the Holy Grail," the young man said. "Is it here?"

"Have you got any identification?" Mrs. Whitaker asked. She

knew that it was unwise to let unidentified strangers into your home when you were elderly and living on your own. Handbags get emptied, and worse than that.

The young man went back down the garden path. His horse, a huge gray charger, big as a shire-horse, its head high and its eyes intelligent, was tethered to Mrs. Whitaker's garden gate. The knight fumbled in the saddlebag and returned with a scroll.

It was signed by Arthur, King of All Britons, and charged all persons of whatever rank or station to know that here was Galaad, Knight of the Table Round, and that he was on a Right High and Noble Quest. There was a drawing of the young man below that. It wasn't a bad likeness.

Mrs. Whitaker nodded. She had been expecting a little card with a photograph on it, but this was far more impressive.

"I suppose you had better come in," she said.

They went into her kitchen. She made Galaad a cup of tea, then she took him into the parlor.

Galaad saw the Grail on her mantelpiece, and dropped to one knee. He put down the teacup carefully on the russet carpet. A shaft of light came through the net curtains and painted his awed face with golden sunlight and turned his hair into a silver halo.

"It is truly the Sangrail," he said, very quietly. He blinked his pale blue eyes three times, very fast, as if he were blinking back tears.

He lowered his head as if in silent prayer.

Galaad stood up again and turned to Mrs. Whitaker. "Gracious lady, keeper of the Holy of Holies, let me now depart this place with the Blessed Chalice, that my journeyings may be ended and my geas fulfilled."

"Sorry?" said Mrs. Whitaker.

Galaad walked over to her and took her old hands in his. "My quest is over," he told her. "The Sangrail is finally within my reach."

Mrs. Whitaker pursed her lips. "Can you pick your teacup and saucer up, please?" she said.

Galaad picked up his teacup apologetically.

"No. I don't think so," said Mrs. Whitaker. "I rather like it there. It's just right, between the dog and the photograph of my Henry."

"Is it gold you need? Is that it? Lady, I can bring you gold . . ."

"No," said Mrs. Whitaker. "I don't want any gold thank *you*. I'm simply not interested."

She ushered Galaad to the front door. "Nice to meet you," she said.

His horse was leaning its head over her garden fence, nibbling her gladioli. Several of the neighborhood children were standing on the pavement, watching it.

Galaad took some sugar lumps from the saddlebag and showed the braver of the children how to feed the horse, their hands held flat. The children giggled. One of the older girls stroked the horse's nose.

Galaad swung himself up onto the horse in one fluid movement. Then the horse and the knight trotted off down Hawthorne Crescent.

Mrs. Whitaker watched them until they were out of sight, then sighed and went back inside.

The weekend was quiet.

On Saturday Mrs. Whitaker took the bus into Maresfield to visit her nephew Ronald, his wife Euphonia, and their daughters, Clarissa and Dillian. She took them a currant cake she had baked herself.

On Sunday morning Mrs. Whitaker went to church. Her local church was St. James the Less, which was a little more "Don't think of this as a church, think of it as a place where like-minded friends hang out and are joyful" than Mrs. Whitaker felt entirely comfortable with, but she liked the vicar, the Reverend Bartholomew, when he wasn't actually playing the guitar.

After the service, she thought about mentioning to him that she had the Holy Grail in her front parlor, but decided against it. On Monday morning Mrs. Whitaker was working in the back garden. She had a small herb garden she was extremely proud of: dill, vervain, mint, rosemary, thyme, and a wild expanse of parsley. She was down on her knees, wearing thick green gardening gloves, weeding, and picking out slugs and putting them in a plastic bag. Mrs. Whitaker was very tenderhearted when it came to slugs.

She would take them down to the back of her garden, which bordered on the railway line, and throw them over the fence.

She cut some parsley for the salad. There was a cough behind her. Galaad stood there, tall and beautiful, his armor glinting in the morning sun. In his arms he held a long package, wrapped in oiled leather.

"I'm back," he said.

"Hello," said Mrs. Whitaker. She stood up, rather slowly, and took off her gardening gloves. "Well," she said, "now you're here, you might as well make yourself useful."

She gave him the plastic bag full of slugs and told him to tip the slugs out over the back of the fence.

He did.

Then they went into the kitchen. "Tea? Or lemonade?" she asked.

"Whatever you're having," Galaad said.

Mrs. Whitaker took a jug of her homemade lemonade from the fridge and sent Galaad outside to pick a sprig of mint. She selected two tall glasses. She washed the mint carefully and put a few leaves in each glass, then poured the lemonade.

"Is your horse outside?" she asked.

"Oh yes. His name is Grizzel."

"And you've come a long way, I suppose."

"A very long way."

"I see," said Mrs. Whitaker. She took a blue plastic basin from under the sink and half-filled it with water. Galaad took it out to Grizzel. He waited while the horse drank and brought the empty basin back to Mrs. Whitaker.

"Now," she said, "I suppose you're still after the Grail."

"Aye, still do I seek the Sangrail," he said. He picked up the leather package from the floor, put it down on her tablecloth and unwrapped it. "For it, I offer you this."

It was a sword, its blade almost four feet long. There were words and symbols traced elegantly along the length of the blade. The hilt was worked in silver and gold, and a large jewel was set in the pommel.

"It's very nice," said Mrs. Whitaker, doubtfully.

"This," said Galaad, "is the sword Balmung, forged by Wayland Smith in the dawn times. Its twin is Flamberge. Who wears it is un-conquerable in war, and invincible in battle. Who wears it is incapable of a cowardly act or an ignoble one. Set in its pommel is the sardonynx Bircone, which protects its possessor from poison slipped into wine or ale, and from the treachery of friends."

Mrs. Whitaker peered at the sword. "It must be very sharp," she said, after a while.

"It can slice a falling hair in twain. Nay, it could slice a sunbeam," said Galaad proudly.

"Well, then, maybe you ought to put it away," said Mrs. Whitaker.

"Don't you want it?" Galaad seemed disappointed.

"No, thank you," said Mrs. Whitaker. It occurred to her that her late husband, Henry, would have quite liked it. He would have hung it on the wall in his study next to the stuffed carp he had caught in Scotland, and pointed it out to visitors.

Galaad rewrapped the oiled leather around the sword Balmung and tied it up with white cord.

He sat there, disconsolate.

Mrs. Whitaker made him some cream cheese and cucumber sandwiches for the journey back and wrapped them in greaseproof paper. She gave him an apple for Grizzel. He seemed very pleased with both gifts.

She waved them both good-bye.

That afternoon she took the bus down to the hospital to see Mrs. Perkins, who was still in with her hip, poor love. Mrs. Whitaker took her some homemade fruitcake, although she had left out the walnuts from the recipe, because Mrs. Perkins's teeth weren't what they used to be.

She watched a little television that evening, and had an early night.

On Tuesday the postman called. Mrs. Whitaker was up in the boxroom at the top of the house, doing a spot of tidying, and, taking each step slowly and carefully, she didn't make it downstairs in time. The postman had left her a message which said that he'd tried to deliver a packet, but no one was home.

Mrs. Whitaker sighed.

She put the message into her handbag and went down to the post office.

The package was from her niece Shirelle in Sydney, Australia. It contained photographs of her husband, Wallace, and her two daughters, Dixie and Violet, and a conch shell packed in cotton wool.

Mrs. Whitaker had a number of ornamental shells in her bedroom. Her favorite had a view of the Bahamas done on it in enamel. It had been a gift from her sister, Ethel, who had died in 1983.

She put the shell and the photographs in her shopping bag. Then, seeing that she was in the area, she stopped in at the Oxfam Shop on her way home.

"Hullo, Mrs. W.," said Marie.

Mrs. Whitaker stared at her. Marie was wearing lipstick (possibly not the best shade for her, nor particularly expertly applied, but, thought Mrs. Whitaker, that would come with time) and a rather smart skirt. It was a great improvement.

"Oh. Hello, dear," said Mrs. Whitaker.

"There was a man in here last week, asking about that thing you bought. The little metal cup thing. I told him where to find you. You don't mind, do you?"

"No, dear," said Mrs. Whitaker. "He found me."

"He was really dreamy. Really, really dreamy," sighed Marie wistfully. "I could of gone for him.

"And he had a big white horse and all," Marie concluded. She was standing up straighter as well, Mrs. Whitaker noted approvingly.

On the bookshelf Mrs. Whitaker found a new Mills & Boon novel—*Her Majestic Passion*—although she hadn't yet finished the two she had bought on her last visit.

She picked up the copy of *Romance and Legend of Chivalry* and opened it. It smelled musty. EX LIBRIS FISHER was neatly handwritten at the top of the first page in red ink.

She put it down where she had found it.

When she got home, Galaad was waiting for her. He was giving the neighborhood children rides on Grizzel's back, up and down the street.

"I'm glad you're here," she said. "I've got some cases that need moving."

She showed him up to the boxroom in the top of the house. He moved all the old suitcases for her, so she could get to the cupboard at the back.

It was very dusty up there.

She kept him up there most of the afternoon, moving things around while she dusted.

Galaad had a cut on his cheek, and he held one arm a little stiffly.

They talked a little while she dusted and tidied. Mrs. Whitaker told him about her late husband, Henry; and how the life insurance had paid the house off; and how she had all these things, but no one really to leave them to, no one but Ronald really and his wife only liked modern things. She told him how she had met Henry during the war, when he was in the ARP and she hadn't closed the kitchen blackout curtains all the way; and about the sixpenny dances they went to in the town; and how they'd gone to London when the war had ended, and she'd had her first drink of wine.

Galaad told Mrs. Whitaker about his mother Elaine, who was flighty and no better than she should have been and something of a witch to boot; and his grandfather, King Pelles, who was well-meaning although at best a little vague; and of his youth in the Castle of Bliant on the Joyous Isle; and his father, whom he knew as "Le Chevalier Mal Fet," who was more or less completely mad, and was in reality Lancelot du Lac, greatest of knights, in disguise and bereft of his wits; and of Galaad's days as a young squire in Camelot.

At five o'clock Mrs. Whitaker surveyed the boxroom and decided that it met with her approval; then she opened the window so the room could air, and they went downstairs to the kitchen, where she put on the kettle.

Galaad sat down at the kitchen table.

He opened the leather purse at his waist and took out a round white stone. It was about the size of a cricket ball.

"My lady," he said, "This is for you, an you give me the Sangrail."

Mrs. Whitaker picked up the stone, which was heavier than it looked, and held it up to the light. It was milkily translucent, and deep inside it flecks of silver glittered and glinted in the late-afternoon sunlight. It was warm to the touch.

Then, as she held it, a strange feeling crept over her: Deep inside she felt stillness and a sort of peace. *Serenity*, that was the word for it; she felt serene.

Reluctantly she put the stone back on the table. "It's very nice," she said.

"That is the Philosopher's Stone, which our forefather Noah hung in the Ark to give light when there was no light; it can transform base metals into gold; and it has certain other properties," Galaad told her proudly. "And that isn't all. There's more. Here." From the leather bag he took an egg and handed it to her. It was the size of a goose egg and was a shiny black color, mottled with scarlet and white. When Mrs. Whitaker touched it, the hairs on the back of her neck prickled. Her immediate impression was one of incredible heat and freedom. She heard the crackling of distant fires, and for a fraction of a second she seemed to feel herself far above the world, swooping and diving on wings of flame.

She put the egg down on the table, next to the Philosopher's Stone.

"That is the Egg of the Phoenix," said Galaad. "From far Araby it comes. One day it will hatch out into the Phoenix Bird itself; and when its time comes, the bird will build a nest of flame, lay its egg, and die, to be reborn in flame in a later age of the world."

"I thought that was what it was," said Mrs. Whitaker.

"And, last of all, lady," said Galaad, "I have brought you this." He drew it from his pouch, and gave it to her. It was an apple, apparently carved from a single ruby, on an amber stem.

A little nervously, she picked it up. It was soft to the touch—deceptively so: Her fingers bruised it, and ruby-colored juice from the apple ran down Mrs. Whitaker's hand.

The kitchen filled—almost imperceptibly, magically—with the smell of summer fruit, of raspberries and peaches and strawberries and red currants. As if from a great way away she heard distant voices raised in song and far music on the air.

"It is one of the apples of the Hesperides," said Galaad, quietly. "One bite from it will heal any illness or wound, no matter how deep; a second bite restores youth and beauty; and a third bite is said to grant eternal life."

Mrs. Whitaker licked the sticky juice from her hand. It tasted like fine wine.

There was a moment, then, when it all came back to her—how it was to be young: to have a firm, slim body that would do whatever she wanted it to do; to run down a country lane for the simple unladylike joy of running; to have men smile at her just because she was herself and happy about it.

Mrs. Whitaker looked at Sir Galaad, most comely of all knights, sitting fair and noble in her small kitchen.

She caught her breath.

"And that's all I have brought for you," said Galaad. "They weren't easy to get, either."

Mrs. Whitaker put the ruby fruit down on her kitchen table. She looked at the Philosopher's Stone, and the Egg of the Phoenix, and the Apple of Life.

Then she walked into her parlor and looked at the mantelpiece: at the little china basset hound, and the Holy Grail, and the photograph of her late husband Henry, shirtless, smiling and eating an ice cream in black and white, almost forty years away.

She went back into the kitchen. The kettle had begun to whistle. She poured a little steaming water into the teapot, swirled it around, and poured it out. Then she added two spoonfuls of tea and one for the pot and poured in the rest of the water. All this she did in silence.

She turned to Galaad then, and she looked at him.

"Put that apple away," she told Galaad, firmly. "You shouldn't offer things like that to old ladies. It isn't proper."

She paused, then. "But I'll take the other two," she continued, after a moment's thought. "They'll look nice on the mantelpiece. And two for one's fair, or I don't know what is."

Galaad beamed. He put the ruby apple into his leather pouch. Then he went down on one knee, and kissed Mrs. Whitaker's hand.

"Stop that," said Mrs. Whitaker. She poured them both cups of tea, after getting out the very best china, which was only for special occasions.

They sat in silence, drinking their tea.

When they had finished their tea they went into the parlor. Galaad crossed himself, and picked up the Grail.

Mrs. Whitaker arranged the Egg and the Stone where the Grail had been. The Egg kept tipping on one side, and she propped it up against the little china dog.

"They do look very nice," said Mrs. Whitaker.

"Yes," agreed Galaad. "They look very nice."

"Can I give you anything to eat before you go back?" she asked.

He shook his head.

"Some fruitcake," she said. "You may not think you want any now, but you'll be glad of it in a few hours' time. And you should probably use the facilities. Now, give me that, and I'll wrap it up for you."

She directed him to the small toilet at the end of the hall, and went into the kitchen, holding the Grail. She had some old Christmas wrapping paper in the pantry, and she wrapped the Grail in it, and tied the package with twine. Then she cut a large slice of fruitcake and put it in a brown paper bag, along with a banana and a slice of processed cheese in silver foil.

Galaad came back from the toilet. She gave him the paper bag, and the Holy Grail. Then she went up on tiptoes and kissed him on the cheek.

"You're a nice boy," she said. "You take care of yourself."

He hugged her, and she shooed him out of the kitchen, and out of the back door, and she shut the door behind him. She poured herself another cup of tea, and cried quietly into a Kleenex, while the sound of hoofbeats echoed down Hawthorne Crescent.

On Wednesday Mrs. Whitaker stayed in all day.

On Thursday she went down to the post office to collect her pension. Then she stopped in at the Oxfam Shop.

The woman on the till was new to her. "Where's Marie?" asked Mrs. Whitaker.

The woman on the till, who had blue-rinsed gray hair and blue spectacles that went up into diamante points, shook her head and shrugged her shoulders. "She went off with a young man," she said. "On a horse. Tch. I ask you. I'm meant to be down in the Heathfield shop this afternoon. I had to get my Johnny to run me up here, while we find someone else."

"Oh," said Mrs. Whitaker. "Well, it's nice that she's found herself a young man."

"Nice for her, maybe," said the lady on the till, "But some of us were meant to be in Heathfield this afternoon."

On a shelf near the back of the shop Mrs. Whitaker found a tarnished old silver container with a long spout. It had been priced at sixty pence, according to the little paper label stuck to the side. It looked a little like a flattened, elongated teapot.

She picked out a Mills & Boon novel she hadn't read before. It was called *Her Singular Love*. She took the book and the silver container up to the woman on the till.

"Sixty-five pee, dear," said the woman, picking up the silver object, staring at it. "Funny old thing, isn't it? Came in this morning." It had writing carved along the side in blocky old Chinese characters and an elegant arching handle. "Some kind of oil can, I suppose."

"No, it's not an oil can," said Mrs. Whitaker, who knew exactly what it was. "It's a lamp."

There was a small metal finger ring, unornamented, tied to the handle of the lamp with brown twine.

"Actually," said Mrs. Whitaker, "on second thoughts, I think I'll just have the book."

She paid her five pence for the novel, and put the lamp back where she had found it, in the back of the shop. After all, Mrs. Whitaker reflected, as she walked home, it wasn't as if she had anywhere to put it.

MURDER MYSTERIES

1992

The Fourth Angel says:

> Of this order I am made one,
> From Mankind to guard this place
> That through their Guilt they have foregone
> For they have forfeited His Grace;
> Therefore all this must they shun
> Or else my Sword they shall embrace
> And myself will be their Foe
> To flame them in the Face.

—CHESTER MYSTERY CYCLE,
The Creation and Adam and Eve, 1461

THIS IS TRUE.

Ten years ago, give or take a year, I found myself on an enforced stopover in Los Angeles, a long way from home. It was December, and the California weather was warm and pleasant.

England, however, was in the grip of fogs and snowstorms, and no planes were landing there. Each day I'd phone the airport, and each day I'd be told to wait another day.

This had gone on for almost a week.

I was barely out of my teens. Looking around today at the parts of my life left over from those days, I feel uncomfortable, as if I've received a gift, unasked, from another person: a house, a wife, children, a vocation. Nothing to do with me, I could say, innocently. If it's true that every seven years each cell in your body dies and is replaced, then I have truly inherited my life from a dead man; and the misdeeds of those times have been forgiven, and are buried with his bones.

I was in Los Angeles. Yes.

On the sixth day I received a message from an old sort-of-girlfriend from Seattle: she was in L.A., too, and she had heard I was around on the friends-of-friends network. Would I come over?

I left a message on her machine. Sure.

That evening: a small, blonde woman approached me as I came out of the place I was staying. It was already dark.

She stared at me, as if she were trying to match me to a description, and then, hesitantly, she said my name.

"That's me. Are you Tink's friend?"

"Yeah. Car's out back. C'mon. She's really looking forward to seeing you."

The woman's car was one of the huge old boatlike jobs you only ever seem to see in California. It smelled of cracked and flaking leather upholstery. We drove out from wherever we were to wherever we were going.

Los Angeles was at that time a complete mystery to me; and I cannot say I understand it much better now. I understand London, and New York, and Paris: you can walk around them, get a sense of what's where in just a morning of wandering, maybe catch the subway. But Los Angeles is about cars. Back then I didn't drive at all; even today I will not drive in America. Memories of L.A. for me are linked by rides in other people's cars, with no sense there of the shape of the city, of the relationships between the people and the place. The regularity of the roads, the repetition of structure and form, mean that when I try to remember it as an entity, all I have is the boundless profusion of tiny lights I saw from the hill of Griffith Park one night, on my first trip to the city. It was one of the most beautiful things I had ever seen, from that distance.

"See that building?" said my blonde driver, Tink's friend. It was a redbrick Art Deco house, charming and quite ugly.

"Yes."

"Built in the 1930s," she said, with respect and pride.

I said something polite, trying to comprehend a city inside which fifty years could be considered a long time.

"Tink's real excited. When she heard you were in town. She was so excited."

"I'm looking forward to seeing her again."

Tink's real name was Tinkerbell Richmond. No lie.

She was staying with friends in a small apartment clump, somewhere an hour's drive from downtown L.A.

What you need to know about Tink: she was ten years older than me, in her early thirties; she had glossy black hair and red, puzzled lips, and very white skin, like Snow White in the fairy stories; the first time I met her I thought she was the most beautiful woman in the world.

Tink had been married for a while at some point in her life and had a five-year-old daughter called Susan. I had never met Susan— when Tink had been in England, Susan had been staying on in Seattle, with her father.

People named Tinkerbell name their daughters Susan.

Memory is the great deceiver. Perhaps there are some individuals whose memories act like tape recordings, daily records of their lives complete in every detail, but I am not one of them. My memory is a patchwork of occurrences, of discontinuous events roughly sewn together: The parts I remember, I remember precisely, whilst other sections seem to have vanished completely.

I do not remember arriving at Tink's house, nor where her flatmate went.

What I remember next is sitting in Tink's lounge with the lights low, the two of us next to each other, on her sofa.

We made small talk. It had been perhaps a year since we had seen

one another. But a twenty-one-year-old boy has little to say to a
thirty-two-year-old woman, and soon, having nothing in common,
I pulled her to me.

She snuggled close with a kind of sigh, and presented her lips to
be kissed. In the half-light her lips were black. We kissed for a little
on the couch, and I stroked her breasts through her blouse and then
she said:

"We can't fuck. I'm on my period."

"Fine."

"I can give you a blowjob, if you'd like."

I nodded assent, and she unzipped my jeans, and lowered her head
to my lap.

After I had come, she got up and ran into the kitchen. I heard her
spitting into the sink, and the sound of running water: I remember
wondering why she did it, if she hated the taste that much. Then she
returned and we sat next to each other on the couch.

"Susan's upstairs, asleep," said Tink. "She's all I live for. Would
you like to see her?"

"I don't mind."

We went upstairs. Tink led me into a darkened bedroom. There
were child-scrawl pictures all over the walls—wax-crayoned drawings of winged fairies and little palaces—and a small fair-haired girl
was asleep in the bed.

"She's very beautiful," said Tink, and kissed me. Her lips were still
slightly sticky. "She takes after her father."

We went downstairs. We had nothing else to say, nothing else to
do. Tink turned on the main light. For the first time, I noticed tiny
crow's feet at the corners of her eyes, incongruous on her perfect
Barbie doll face.

"I love you," she said.

"Thank you."

"Would you like a ride back?"

"If you don't mind leaving Susan alone . . . ?"

She shrugged, and I pulled her to me for the last time. At night Los
Angles is all lights. And shadows.

A blank, here, in my mind. I simply don't remember what happened next. She must have driven me back to the place where I was staying—how else would I have gotten there? I do not even remember kissing her good-bye. Perhaps I simply waited on the sidewalk and watched her drive away.

Perhaps.

I do know, however, that once I reached the place I was staying, I just stood there, unable to go inside, to wash, and then to sleep, unwilling to do anything else.

I was not hungry. I did not want alcohol. I did not want to read or talk. I was scared of walking too far, in case I became lost, bedeviled by the repeating motifs of Los Angeles, spun around and sucked in so I could never find my way home again. Central Los Angeles sometimes seems to me to be nothing more than a pattern, like a set of repeating blocks: a gas station, a few homes, a mini-mall (doughnuts, photo developers, Laundromats, fast foods), and repeat until hypnotized; and the tiny changes in the mini-malls and the houses only serve to reinforce the structure.

I thought of Tink's lips. Then I fumbled in a pocket of my jacket and pulled out a packet of cigarettes.

I lit one, inhaled, blew blue smoke into the warm night air.

There was a stunted palm tree growing outside the place I was staying, and I resolved to walk for a way, keeping the tree in sight, to smoke my cigarette, perhaps even to think; but I felt too drained to think. I felt very sexless, and very alone.

A block or so down the road there was a bench, and when I reached it I sat down. I threw the stub of the cigarette onto the pavement, hard, and watched it shower orange sparks.

Someone said, "I'll buy a cigarette off you, pal. Here."

A hand in front of my face, holding a quarter. I looked up.

He did not look old, although I would not have been prepared to say how old he was. Late thirties, perhaps. Mid-forties. He wore a long, shabby coat, colorless under the yellow streetlamps, and his eyes were dark.

"Here. A quarter. That's a good price."

I shook my head, pulled out the packet of Marlboros, offered him one. "Keep your money. It's free. Have it."

He took the cigarette. I passed him a book of matches (it advertised a telephone sex line; I remember that), and he lit the cigarette. He offered me the matches back, and I shook my head. "Keep them. I always wind up accumulating books of matches in America."

"Uh-huh." He sat next to me and smoked his cigarette. When he had smoked it halfway down, he tapped the lighted end off on the concrete, stubbed out the glow, and placed the butt of the cigarette behind his ear.

"I don't smoke much," he said. "Seems a pity to waste it, though."

A car careened down the road, veering from one side to the other. There were four young men in the car; the two in the front were both pulling at the wheel and laughing. The windows were wound down, and I could hear their laughter, and the two in the backseat (*"Gaary, you asshole! What the fuck are you onnn, mannnn?"*), and the pulsing beat of a rock song. Not a song I recognized. The car looped around a corner, out of sight.

Soon the sounds were gone, too.

"I owe you," said the man on the bench.

"Sorry?"

"I owe you something. For the cigarette. And the matches. You wouldn't take the money. I owe you."

I shrugged, embarrassed. "Really, it's just a cigarette. I figure, if I give people cigarettes, then if ever I'm out, maybe people will give me cigarettes." I laughed, to show I didn't really mean it, although I did. "Don't worry about it."

"Mm. You want to hear a story? True story? Stories always used to be good payment. These days . . ."—he shrugged—". . . not so much."

I sat back on the bench, and the night was warm, and I looked at my watch: it was almost one in the morning. In England a freezing new day would already have begun: a workday would be starting for those who could beat the snow and get into work; another handful of old people, and those without homes, would have died, in the night, from the cold.

"Sure," I said to the man. "Sure. Tell me a story."

He coughed, grinned white teeth—a flash in the darkness—and he began.

"First thing I remember was the Word. And the Word was God. Sometimes, when I get *really* down, I remember the sound of the Word in my head, shaping me, forming me, giving me life.

"The Word gave me a body, gave me eyes. And I opened my eyes, and I saw the light of the Silver City.

"I was in a room—a silver room—and there wasn't anything in it except me. In front of me was a window that went from floor to ceiling, open to the sky, and through the window I could see the spires of the City, and at the edge of the City, the Dark.

"I don't know how long I waited there. I wasn't impatient or anything, though. I remember that. It was like I was waiting until I was called; and I knew that sometime I would be called. And if I had to wait until the end of everything and never be called, why, that was fine, too. But I'd be called, I was certain of that. And then I'd know my name and my function.

"Through the window I could see silver spires, and in many of the other spires were windows; and in the windows I could see others like me. That was how I knew what I looked like.

"You wouldn't think it of me, seeing me now, but I was beautiful. I've come down in the world a way since then.

"I was taller then, and I had wings.

"They were huge and powerful wings, with feathers the color of mother-of-pearl. They came out from just between my shoulder blades. They were so good. My wings.

"Sometimes I'd see others like me, the ones who'd left their rooms, who were already fulfilling their duties. I'd watch them soar through the sky from spire to spire, performing errands I could barely imagine.

"The sky above the City was a wonderful thing. It was always light, although lit by no sun—lit, perhaps, by the City itself; but the quality of light was forever changing. Now pewter-colored light, then brass, then a gentle gold, or a soft and quiet amethyst . . ."

The man stopped talking. He looked at me, his head on one side. There was a glitter in his eyes that scared me. "You know what amethyst is? A kind of purple stone?"

I nodded.

My crotch felt uncomfortable.

It occurred to me then that the man might not be mad; I found this far more disquieting than the alternative.

The man began talking once more. "I don't know how long it was that I waited in my room. But time didn't mean anything. Not back then. We had all the time in the world.

"The next thing that happened to me, was when the Angel Lucifer came to my cell. He was taller than me, and his wings were imposing, his plumage perfect. He had skin the color of sea mist, and curly silver hair, and these wonderful gray eyes . . .

"I say *he*, but you should understand that none of us had any sex, to speak of." He gestured toward his lap. "Smooth and empty. Nothing there. You know."

"Lucifer shone. I mean it—he glowed from inside. All angels do. They're lit up from within, and in my cell the Angel Lucifer burned like a lightning storm.

"He looked at me. And he named me.

" 'You are Raguel,' he said. 'The Vengeance of the Lord.'

"I bowed my head, because I knew it was true. That was my name. That was my function.

" 'There has been a . . . a wrong thing,' he said. 'The first of its kind. You are needed.'

"He turned and pushed himself into space, and I followed him, flew behind him across the Silver City to the outskirts, where the City stops and the Darkness begins; and it was there, under a vast silver spire, that we descended to the street, and I saw the dead angel.

"The body lay, crumpled and broken, on the silver sidewalk. Its wings were crushed underneath it and a few loose feathers had already blown into the silver gutter.

"The body was almost dark. Now and again a light would flash inside it, an occasional flicker of cold fire in the chest, or in the eyes, or in the sexless groin, as the last of the glow of life left it forever.

"Blood pooled in rubies on its chest and stained its white wing feathers crimson. It was very beautiful, even in death.

"It would have broken your heart.

"Lucifer spoke to me then. 'You must find who was responsible

for this, and how; and take the Vengeance of the Name on whosoever caused this thing to happen.'

"He really didn't have to say anything. I knew that already. The
hunt, and the retribution: it was what I was created for, in the Beginning; it was what I *was*.

" 'I have work to attend to,' said the Angel Lucifer.

"He flapped his wings once, hard, and rose upward; the gust of
wind sent the dead angel's loose feathers blowing across the street.

"I leaned down to examine the body. All luminescence had by
now left it. It was a dark thing, a parody of an angel. It had a perfect,
sexless face, framed by silver hair. One of the eyelids was open, revealing a placid gray eye; the other was closed. There were no nipples on the chest and only smoothness between the legs.

"I lifted the body up.

"The back of the angel was a mess. The wings were broken and
twisted, the back of the head staved in; there was a floppiness to the
corpse that made me think its spine had been broken as well. The
back of the angel was all blood.

"The only blood on its front was in the chest area. I probed it with
my forefinger, and it entered the body without difficulty.

"*He fell*, I thought. *And he was dead before he fell.*

"And I looked up at the windows that ranked the street. I stared
across the Silver City. *You did this*, I thought. *I will find you, whoever
you are. And I will take the Lord's vengeance upon you.*"

The man took the cigarette stub from behind his ear, lit it with a
match. Briefly I smelled the ashtray smell of a dead cigarette, acrid
and harsh; then he pulled down to the unburnt tobacco, exhaled blue
smoke into the night air.

"The angel who had first discovered the body was called Phanuel.

"I spoke to him in the Hall of Being. That was the spire beside
which the dead angel lay. In the Hall hung the . . . the blueprints,
maybe, for what was going to be . . . all this." He gestured with the
hand that held the stubby cigarette, pointing to the night sky and the
parked cars and the world. "You know. The universe."

"Phanuel was the senior designer; working under him were a
multitude of angels laboring on the details of the Creation. I watched

him from the floor of the Hall. He hung in the air below the Plan, and angels flew down to him, waiting politely in turn as they asked him questions, checked things with him, invited comment on their work. Eventually he left them and descended to the floor.

" 'You are Raguel,' he said. His voice was high and fussy. 'What need have you of me?'

" 'You found the body?'

" 'Poor Carasel? Indeed I did. I was leaving the Hall—there are a number of concepts we are currently constructing, and I wished to ponder one of them, *Regret* by name. I was planning to get a little distance from the City—to fly above it, I mean, not to go into the Dark outside, I wouldn't do that, although there has been some loose talk amongst . . . but, yes. I was going to rise and contemplate.

" 'I left the Hall, and . . . ' he broke off. He was small, for an angel. His light was muted, but his eyes were vivid and bright. I mean really bright. 'Poor Carasel. How could he *do* that to himself? How?'

" 'You think his destruction was self-inflicted?'

"He seemed puzzled—surprised that there could be any other explanation. 'But of course. Carasel was working under me, developing a number of concepts that shall be intrinsic to the universe when its Name shall be Spoken. His group did a remarkable job on some of the real basics—*Dimension* was one, and *Sleep* another. There were others.

" 'Wonderful work. Some of his suggestions regarding the use of individual viewpoints to define dimensions were truly ingenious.

" 'Anyway. He had begun work on a new project. It's one of the really major ones—the ones that I would usually handle, or possibly even Zephkiel.' He glanced upward. 'But Carasel had done such sterling work. And his last project was *so* remarkable. Something apparently quite trivial that he and Saraquael elevated into . . .' he shrugged. 'But that is unimportant. It was *this* project that forced him into nonbeing. But none of us could ever have foreseen . . .'

" 'What was his current project?'

"Phanuel stared at me. 'I'm not sure I ought to tell you. All the new concepts are considered sensitive until we get them into the final form in which they will be Spoken.'

"I felt myself transforming. I am not sure how I can explain it to you, but suddenly I wasn't me—I was something larger. I was trans-figured: I was my function.

"Phanuel was unable to meet my gaze.

" 'I am Raguel, who is the Vengeance of the Lord,' I told him. 'I serve the Name directly. It is my mission to discover the nature of this deed, and to take the Name's vengeance on those responsible. My questions are to be answered.'

"The little angel trembled, and he spoke fast.

" 'Carasel and his partner were researching *Death*. Cessation of life. An end to physical, animated existence. They were putting it all together. But Carasel always went too far into his work—we had a terrible time with him when he was designing *Agitation*. That was when he was working on *Emotions* . . .'

" 'You think Carasel died to—to research the phenomenon?'

" 'Or because it intrigued him. Or because he followed his re-search just too far. Yes.' Phanuel flexed his fingers, stared at me with those brightly shining eyes. 'I trust that you will repeat none of this to any unauthorized persons, Raguel.'

" 'What did you do when you found the body?'

" 'I came out of the Hall, as I said, and there was Carasel on the sidewalk, staring up. I asked him what he was doing, and he did not reply. Then I noticed the inner fluid, and that Carasel seemed unable, rather than unwilling, to talk to me.

" 'I was scared. I did not know what to do.

" 'The Angel Lucifer came up behind me. He asked me if there was some kind of problem. I told him. I showed him the body. And then . . . then his Aspect came upon him, and he communed with the Name. He burned so bright.

" 'Then he said he had to fetch the one whose function embraced events like this, and he left—to seek you, I imagine.

" 'As Carasel's death was now being dealt with, and his fate was no real concern of mine, I returned to work, having gained a new—and, I suspect, quite valuable—perspective on the mechanics of *Regret*.

" 'I am considering taking *Death* away from the Carasel and Sara-quael partnership. I may reassign it to Zephkiel, my senior partner, if he is willing to take it on. He excels on contemplative projects.'

"By now there was a line of angels waiting to talk to Phanuel. I felt I had almost all I was going to get from him.

" 'Who did Carasel work with? Who would have been the last to see him alive?'

" 'You could talk to Saraquael, I suppose—he was his partner, after all. Now, if you'll excuse me . . .'

"He returned to his swarm of aides: advising, correcting, suggesting, forbidding."

The man paused.

The street was quiet now; I remember the low whisper of his voice, the buzz of a cricket somewhere. A small animal—a cat perhaps, or something more exotic, a raccoon, or even a jackal—darted from shadow to shadow among the parked cars on the opposite side of the street.

"Saraquael was in the highest of the mezzanine galleries that ringed the Hall of Being. As I said, the universe was in the middle of the Hall, and it glinted and sparkled and shone. Went up quite a way, too . . ."

"The universe you mention, it was, what, a diagram?" I asked, interrupting for the first time.

"Not really. Kind of. Sorta. It was a blueprint; but it was full-sized, and it hung in the Hall, and all these angels went around and fiddled with it all the time. Doing stuff with *Gravity* and *Music* and *Klar* and whatever. It wasn't really the universe, not yet. It would be, when it was finished, and it was time for it to be properly Named."

"But . . ." I grasped for words to express my confusion. The man interrupted me.

"Don't worry about it. Think of it as a model if that makes it easier for you. Or a map. Or a—what's the word? Prototype. Yeah. A Model-T Ford universe." He grinned. "You got to understand, a lot of the stuff I'm telling you, I'm translating already; putting it in a form you can understand. Otherwise I couldn't tell the story at all. You want to hear it?"

"Yes." I didn't care if it was true or not; it was a story I needed to hear all the way through to the end.

"Good. So shut up and listen.

"So I met Saraquael in the topmost gallery. There was no one else about—just him, and some papers, and some small, glowing models.

" 'I've come about Carasel,' I told him.

"He looked at me. 'Carasel isn't here at this time,' he said. 'I expect him to return shortly.'

"I shook my head.

" 'Carasel won't be coming back. He's stopped existing as a spiritual entity,' I said.

"His light paled, and his eyes opened very wide. 'He's dead?'

" 'That's what I said. Do you have any ideas about how it happened?'

" 'I . . . this is so sudden. I mean, he'd been talking about . . . but I had no idea that he would . . .'

" 'Take it slowly.' "

"Saraquael nodded.

"He stood up and walked to the window. There was no view of the Silver City from his window—just a reflected glow from the City and the sky behind us, hanging in the air, and beyond that, the Dark. The wind from the Dark gently caressed Saraquael's hair as he spoke. I stared at his back.

" 'Carasel is . . . no, was. That's right, isn't it? *Was.* He was always so involved. And so creative. But it was never enough for him. He always wanted to understand everything—to experience what he was working on. He was never content to just create it—to understand it intellectually. He wanted *all* of it.

" 'That wasn't a problem before, when we were working on properties of matter. But when we began to design some of the Named emotions . . . he got too involved with his work.

" 'And our latest project was *Death*. It's one of the hard ones—one of the big ones, too, I suspect. Possibly it may even become the attribute that's going to define the Creation for the Created: If not for *Death*, they'd be content to simply exist, but with *Death*, well, their lives will have meaning—a boundary beyond which the living cannot cross . . .'

" 'So you think he killed himself?'

" 'I know he did,' said Saraquael. I walked to the window and

looked out. Far below, a *long* way, I could see a tiny white dot. That
was Carasel's body. I'd have to arrange for someone to take care of
it. I wondered what we would do with it; but there would be someone who would know, whose function was the removal of unwanted
things. It was not my function. I knew that.

" 'How?'

"He shrugged. 'I know. Recently he'd begun asking questions—
questions about *Death*. How we could know whether or not it was
right to make this thing, to set the rules, if we were not going to
experience it ourselves. He kept talking about it.'

" 'Didn't you wonder about this?'

"Saraquael turned, for the first time, to look at me. 'No. That *is*
our function—to discuss, to improvise, to aid the Creation and the
Created. We sort it out now, so that when it all Begins, it'll run like
clockwork. Right now we're working on *Death*. So obviously that's
what we look at. The physical aspect; the emotional aspect; the phil-
osophical aspect . . .

" 'And the *patterns*. Carasel had the notion that what we do here
in the Hall of Being creates patterns. That there are structures and
shapes appropriate to beings and events that, once begun, must continue until they reach their end. For us, perhaps, as well as for them.
Conceivably he felt this was one of his patterns.'

" 'Did you know Carasel well?'

" 'As well as any of us know each other. We saw each other here;
we worked side by side. At certain times I would retire to my cell
across the City. Sometimes he would do the same.'

" 'Tell me about Phanuel.'

"His mouth crooked into a smile. 'He's officious. Doesn't do
much—farms everything out and takes all the credit.' He lowered
his voice, although there was no other soul in the gallery. 'To hear
him talk, you'd think that *Love* was all his own work. But to his
credit, he does make sure the work gets done. Zephkiel's the real
thinker of the two senior designers, but he doesn't come here. He
stays back in his cell in the City and contemplates; resolves problems
from a distance. If you need to speak to Zephkiel, you go to Phanuel,
and Phanuel relays your questions to Zephkiel . . .'

"I cut him short. 'How about Lucifer? Tell me about him.'

" 'Lucifer? The Captain of the Host? He doesn't work here . . . He has visited the Hall a couple of times, though—inspecting the Creation. They say he reports directly to the Name. I have never spoken to him.'

" 'Did he know Carasel?'

" 'I doubt it. As I said, he has only been here twice. I have seen him on other occasions, though. Through here." He flicked a wingtip, indicating the world outside the window. "In flight."

" 'Where to?'

"Saraquael seemed to be about to say something, then he changed his mind. 'I don't know.'

"I looked out of the window at the Darkness outside the Silver City. 'I may want to talk with you some more, later,' I told Saraquael.

" 'Very good.' " I turned to go.

" 'Sir? Do you know if they will be assigning me another partner? For *Death?*'

" 'No,' I told him. 'I'm afraid I don't.'

"In the center of the Silver City was a park—a place of recreation and rest. I found the Angel Lucifer there, beside a river. He was just standing, watching the water flow.

" 'Lucifer?'

"He inclined his head. 'Raguel. Are you making progress?'

" 'I don't know. Maybe. I need to ask you a few questions. Do you mind?'

" 'Not at all.'

" 'How did you come upon the body?'

" 'I didn't. Not exactly. I saw Phanuel standing in the street. He looked distressed. I inquired whether there was something wrong, and he showed me the dead angel. And I fetched you.'

" 'I see.'

"He leaned down, let one hand enter the cold water of the river. The water splashed and rolled around it. 'Is that all?'

" 'Not quite. What were you doing in that part of the city?'

" 'I don't see what business that is of yours.'

" 'It is my business, Lucifer. What were you doing there?'

" 'I was . . . walking. I do that sometimes. Just walk and think.
And try to understand.' He shrugged.

" 'You walk on the edge of the City?'

"A beat, then 'Yes.'

" 'That's all I want to know. For now.'

" 'Who else have you talked to?'

" 'Carasel's boss and his partner. They both feel that he killed
himself—ended his own life.'

" 'Who else are you going to talk to?'

"I looked up. The spires of the City of the Angels towered above
us. 'Maybe everyone.'

" 'All of them?'

" 'If I need to. It's my function. I cannot rest until I understand
what happened, and until the Vengeance of the Name has been taken
on whosoever was responsible. But I'll tell you something I *do* know.'

" 'What would that be?' Drops of water fell like diamonds from
the Angel Lucifer's perfect fingers.

" 'Carasel did not kill himself.'

" 'How do you know that?'

" 'I am Vengeance. If Carasel had died by his own hand,' I explained to the Captain of the Heavenly Host, 'there would have been
no call for me. Would there?'

"He did not reply.

"I flew upward into the light of the eternal morning.

"You got another cigarette on you?"

I fumbled out the red and white packet, handed him a cigarette.

"Obliged.

"Zephkiel's cell was larger than mine.

"It wasn't a place for waiting. It was a place to live, and work, and
be. It was lined with books, and scrolls, and papers, and there were
images and representations on the walls: pictures. I'd never seen a
picture before.

"In the center of the room was a large chair, and Zephkiel sat
there, his eyes closed, his head back.

"As I approached him, he opened his eyes.

"They burned no brighter than the eyes of any of the other angels I had seen, but somehow they seemed to have seen more. It was something about the way he looked. I'm not sure I can explain it. And he had no wings.

" 'Welcome, Raguel,' he said. He sounded tired.

" 'You are Zephkiel?' I don't know why I asked him that. I mean, I knew who people were. It's part of my function, I guess. Recognition. I know who *you* are.

" 'Indeed. You are staring, Raguel. I have no wings, it is true, but then my function does not call for me to leave this cell. I remain here, and I ponder. Phanuel reports back to me, brings me the new things, for my opinion. He brings me the problems, and I think about them, and occasionally I make myself useful by making some small suggestions. That is my function. As yours is vengeance.'

" 'Yes.'

" 'You are here about the death of the Angel Carasel?'

" 'Yes.'

" 'I did not kill him.'

"When he said it, I knew it was true.

" 'Do you know who did?'

" 'That is *your* function, is it not? To discover who killed the poor thing and to take the Vengeance of the Name upon him.'

" 'Yes.'

"He nodded.

" 'What do you want to know?'

"I paused, reflecting on what I had heard that day. 'Do you know what Lucifer was doing in that part of the City before the body was found?'

"The old angel stared at me. 'I can hazard a guess.'

" 'Yes?'

" 'He was walking in the Dark.'

"I nodded. I had a shape in my mind now. Something I could almost grasp. I asked the last question:

" 'What can you tell me about *Love*?'

"And he told me. And I thought I had it all.

"I returned to the place where Carasel's body had been. The remains had been removed, the blood had been cleaned away, the stray feathers collected and disposed of. There was nothing on the silver sidewalk to indicate it had ever been there. But I knew where it had been.

"I ascended on my wings, flew upward until I neared the top of the spire of the Hall of Being. There was a window there, and I entered.

"Saraquael was working there, putting a wingless mannikin into a small box. On one side of the box was a representation of a small brown creature with eight legs. On the other was a representation of a white blossom.

" 'Saraquael?'

" 'Hm? Oh, it's you. Hello. Look at this. If you were to die and to be, let us say, put into the earth in a box, which would you want laid on top of you—a spider, here, or a lily, here?'

" 'The lily, I suppose.'

" 'Yes, that's what I think, too. But *why?* I wish . . .' He raised a hand to his chin, stared down at the two models, put first one on top of the box, then the other, experimentally. 'There's so much to do, Raguel. So much to get right. And we only get one chance at it, you know. There'll just be one universe—we can't keep trying until we get it right. I wish I understood why all this was so important to Him . . .'

" 'Do you know where Zephkiel's cell is?' I asked him.

" 'Yes. I mean, I've never been there. But I know where it is.'

" 'Good. Go there. He'll be expecting you. I will meet you there.'

"He shook his head. 'I have work to do. I can't just . . .'

"I felt my function come upon me. I looked down at him, and I said, 'You will be there. Go now.'

"He said nothing. He backed away from me toward the window, staring at me; then he turned and flapped his wings, and I was alone.

"I walked to the central well of the Hall and let myself fall, tumbling down through the model of the universe: it glittered around me, unfamiliar colors and shapes seething and writhing without meaning.

"As I approached the bottom, I beat my wings, slowing my descent, and stepped lightly onto the silver floor. Phanuel stood between two angels who were both trying to claim his attention.

" 'I don't care how aesthetically pleasing it would be,' he was explaining to one of them. 'We simply cannot put it in the center. Background radiation would prevent any possible life-forms from even getting a foothold; and anyway, it's too unstable.'

"He turned to the other. 'Okay, let's see it. Hmm. So that's *Green*, is it? It's not exactly how I'd imagined it, but. Mm. Leave it with me. I'll get back to you.' He took a paper from the angel, folded it over decisively.

"He turned to me. His manner was brusque, and dismissive. 'Yes?'

" 'I need to talk to you.'

" 'Mm? Well, make it quick. I have much to do. If this is about Carasel's death, I have told you all I know.'

" 'It is about Carasel's death. But I will not speak to you now. Not here. Go to Zephkiel's cell: he is expecting you. I will meet you there.'

"He seemed about to say something, but he only nodded, walked toward the door.

"I turned to go when something occurred to me. I stopped the angel who had the *Green*. 'Tell me something.'

" 'If I can, sir.'

" 'That thing.' I pointed to the universe. 'What's it going to be *for*?'

" 'For? Why, it is the universe.'

" 'I know what it's called. But what purpose will it serve?'

"He frowned. 'It is part of the plan. The Name wishes it; He requires *such and such*, to *these* dimensions and having *such and such* properties and ingredients. It is our function to bring it into existence, according to His wishes. I am sure *He* knows its function, but He has not revealed it to me.' His tone was one of gentle rebuke.

"I nodded, and left that place.

"High above the City a phalanx of angels wheeled and circled and dove. Each held a flaming sword that trailed a streak of burning brightness behind it, dazzling the eye. They moved in unison through the salmon pink sky. They were very beautiful. It was—you know on summer evenings when you get whole flocks of birds performing their dances in the sky? Weaving and circling and clustering and breaking apart again, so just as you think you understand the pattern, you realize you don't, and you never will? It was like that, only better.

"Above me was the sky. Below me, the shining City. My home. And outside the City, the Dark.

"Lucifer hovered a little below the Host, watching their maneuvers.

" 'Lucifer?'

" 'Yes, Raguel? Have you discovered your malefactor?'

" 'I think so. Will you accompany me to Zephkiel's cell? There are others waiting for us there, and I will explain everything.'

"He paused. Then, 'Certainly.'

"He raised his perfect face to the angels, now performing a slow revolution in the sky, each moving through the air keeping perfect pace with the next, none of them ever touching. 'Azazel!'

"An angel broke from the circle; the others adjusted almost imperceptibly to his disappearance, filling the space, so you could no longer see where he had been.

" 'I have to leave. You are in command, Azazel. Keep them drilling. They still have much to perfect.'

" 'Yes, sir.'

"Azazel hovered where Lucifer had been, staring up at the flock of angels, and Lucifer and I descended toward the City.

" 'He's my second-in-command,' said Lucifer. 'Bright. Enthusiastic. Azazel would follow you anywhere.'

" 'What are you training them for?'

" 'War.'

" 'With whom?'

" 'How do you mean?'

" 'Who are they going to fight? Who else *is* there?'

"He looked at me; his eyes were clear, and honest. 'I do not know. But He has Named us to be His army. So we will be perfect. For Him. The Name is infallible and all-just and all-wise, Raguel. It cannot be otherwise, no matter what—' He broke off and looked away.

" 'You were going to say?'

" 'It is of no importance.'

" 'Ah.'

"We did not talk for the rest of the descent to Zephkiel's cell."

I looked at my watch; it was almost three. A chill breeze had begun to blow down the L.A. street, and I shivered. The man noticed, and he paused in his story. "You okay?" he asked.

"I'm fine. Please carry on. I'm fascinated."

He nodded.

"They were waiting for us in Zephkiel's cell: Phanuel, Saraquael, and Zephkiel. Zephkiel was sitting in his chair. Lucifer took up a position beside the window.

"I walked to center of the room, and I began.

" 'I thank you all for coming here. You know who I am; you know my function. I am the Vengeance of the Name, the arm of the Lord. I am Raguel.

"The Angel Carasel is dead. It was given to me to find out why he died, who killed him. This I have done. Now, the Angel Carasel was a designer in the Hall of Being. He was very good, or so I am told . . .

" 'Lucifer. Tell me what you were doing before you came upon Phanuel, and the body.'

" 'I have told you already. I was walking.'

" 'Where were you walking?'

" 'I do not see what business that is of yours.'

" '*Tell me.*'

"He paused. He was taller than any of us, tall, and proud. 'Very well. I was walking in the Dark. I have been walking in the Darkness for some time now. It helps me to gain a perspective on the City—being outside it. I see how fair it is, how perfect. There is nothing more enchanting than our home. Nothing more complete. Nowhere else that anyone would want to be.'

" 'And what do you do in the Dark, Lucifer?'

"He stared at me. 'I walk. And . . . There are voices in the Dark. I listen to the voices. They promise me things, ask me questions, whisper and plead. And I ignore them. I steel myself and I gaze at the City. It is the only way I have of testing myself—putting myself to any kind of trial. I am the Captain of the Host; I am the first among the Angels, and I must prove myself.'

"I nodded. 'Why did you not tell me this before?'

"He looked down. 'Because I am the only angel who walks in the Dark. Because I do not want others to walk in the Dark: I am strong enough to challenge the voices, to test myself. Others are not so strong. Others might stumble, or fall.'

" 'Thank you, Lucifer. That is all, for now.' I turned to the next angel. 'Phanuel. How long have you been taking credit for Carasel's work?'

"His mouth opened, but no sound came out.

" 'Well?'

" 'I . . . I would not take credit for another's work.'

" 'But you did take credit for *Love*?'

"He blinked. 'Yes. I did.'

" 'Would you care to explain to us all what *Love* is?' I asked.

"He glanced around uncomfortably. 'It's a feeling of deep affection and attraction for another being, often combined with passion or desire—a need to be with another.' He spoke dryly, didactically, as if he were reciting a mathematical formula. 'The feeling that we have for the Name, for our Creator—that is *Love* . . . amongst other things. *Love* will be an impulse that will inspire and ruin in equal measure. We are . . .' He paused, then began once more. 'We are very proud of it.'

"He was mouthing the words. He no longer seemed to hold any hope that we would believe them.

" 'Who did the majority of the work on *Love*? No, don't answer. Let me ask the others first. Zephkiel? When Phanuel passed the details on *Love* to you for approval, who did he tell you was responsible for it?'

"The wingless angel smiled gently. 'He told me it was his project.'

" 'Thank you, sir. Now, Saraquael: whose was *Love*?'

" 'Mine. Mine and Carasel's. Perhaps more his than mine, but we worked on it together.'

" 'You knew that Phanuel was claiming the credit for it?'

" '. . . Yes.'

" 'And you permitted this?'

" 'He . . . he promised us that he would give us a good project of our own to follow. He promised that if we said nothing we would be given more big projects—and he was true to his word. He gave us *Death*.'

"I turned back to Phanuel. 'Well?'

" 'It is true that I claimed that *Love* was mine.'

" 'But it was Carasel's. And Saraquael's.'

" 'Yes.'

" 'Their last project—before *Death*?'

" 'Yes.'

" 'That is all.'

"I walked over to the window, looked at the silver spires, looked at the Dark. And I began to speak.

" 'Carasel was a remarkable designer. If he had one failing, it was that he threw himself too deeply into his work.' I turned back to them. The Angel Saraquael was shivering, and lights were flickering beneath his skin. 'Saraquael? Who did Carasel love? Who was his lover?'

"He stared at the floor. Then he stared up, proudly, aggressively. And he smiled.

" 'I was.'

" 'Do you want to tell me about it?'

" 'No.' A shrug. 'But I suppose I must. Very well, then.

" 'We worked together. And when we began to work on *Love* . . . we became lovers. It was his idea. We would go back to his cell whenever we could snatch the time. There we touched each other, held each other, whispered endearments and protestations of eternal devotion. His welfare mattered more to me than my own. I existed for him. When I was alone, I would repeat his name to myself and think of nothing but him.

" 'When I was with him . . .' he paused. He looked down. 'Nothing else mattered.'

"I walked to where Saraquael stood, lifted his chin with my hand, stared into his gray eyes. 'Then why did you kill him?'

" 'Because he would no longer love me. When we started to work on *Death*, he . . . he lost interest. He was no longer mine. He belonged to *Death*. And if I could not have him, then his new lover was welcome to him. I could not bear his presence—I could not endure to have him near me and to know that he felt nothing for me. That was what hurt the most. I thought . . . I hoped . . . that if he was gone, then I would no longer care for him—that the pain would stop.

" 'So I killed him. I stabbed him, and I threw his body from our window in the Hall of Being. But the pain has *not* stopped.' It was almost a wail.

"Saraquael reached up, removed my hand from his chin. 'Now what?'

"I felt my aspect begin to come upon me; felt my function possess me. I was no longer an individual—I was the Vengeance of the Lord.

"I moved close to Saraquael and embraced him. I pressed my lips to his, forced my tongue into his mouth. We kissed. He closed his eyes.

"I felt it well up within me then: a burning, a brightness. From the corner of my eye, I could see Lucifer and Phanuel averting their faces from my light; I could feel Zephkiel's stare. And my light became brighter and brighter until it erupted—from my eyes, from my chest, from my fingers, from my lips: a white searing fire.

"The white flames consumed Saraquael slowly, and he clung to me as he burned.

"Soon there was nothing left of him. Nothing at all.

"I felt the flame leave me. I returned to myself once more.

"Phanuel was sobbing. Lucifer was pale. Zephkiel sat in his chair, quietly watching me.

"I turned to Phanuel and Lucifer. 'You have seen the Vengeance of the Lord,' I told them. 'Let it act as a warning to you both.'

"Phanuel nodded. 'It has. Oh, it has. I . . . I will be on my way, sir. I will return to my appointed post. If that is all right with you?'

" 'Go.'

"He stumbled to the window and plunged into the light, his wings beating furiously.

"Lucifer walked over to the place on the silver floor where Saraquael had once stood. He knelt, stared desperately at the floor as if he were trying to find some remnant of the angel I had destroyed, a fragment of ash, or bone, or charred feather, but there was nothing to find. Then he looked up at me.

" 'That was not right,' he said. 'That was not just.' He was crying; wet tears ran down his face. Perhaps Saraquael was the first to love, but Lucifer was the first to shed tears. I will never forget that.

"I stared at him impassively. 'It was justice. He killed another. He was killed in his turn. You called me to my function, and I performed it.'

" 'But . . . he *loved*. He should have been forgiven. He should have been helped. He should not have been destroyed like that. That was *wrong*.'

" 'It was His will.'

"Lucifer stood. 'Then perhaps His will is unjust. Perhaps the voices in the Darkness speak truly, after all. How *can* this be right?'

" 'It is right. It is His will. I merely performed my function.'

"He wiped away the tears with the back of his hand. 'No,' he said, flatly. He shook his head, slowly, from side to side. Then he said, 'I must think on this. I will go now.'

"He walked to the window, stepped into the sky, and he was gone.

"Zephkiel and I were alone in his cell. I went over to his chair. He nodded at me. 'You have performed your function well, Raguel. Shouldn't you return to your cell to wait until you are next needed?' "

The man on the bench turned toward me: his eyes sought mine. Until now it had seemed—for most of his narrative—that he was scarcely aware of me; he had stared ahead of himself, whispered his tale in little better than a monotone. Now it felt as if he had discovered me and that he spoke to me alone, rather than to the air, or the City of Los Angeles. And he said:

"I knew that he was right. But I *couldn't* have left then—not even if I had wanted to. My aspect had not entirely left me; my function was not completely fulfilled. And then it fell into place; I saw the whole picture. And like Lucifer, I knelt. I touched my forehead to the silver floor. 'No, Lord,' I said. 'Not yet.'

"Zephkiel rose from his chair. 'Get up. It is not fitting for one angel to act in this way to another. It is not right. Get up!'

"I shook my head. 'Father, You are no angel,' I whispered.

"Zephkiel said nothing. For a moment, my heart misgave within me. I was afraid. 'Father, I was charged to discover who was responsible for Carasel's death. And I do know.'

" 'You have taken your Vengeance, Raguel.'

" '*Your* Vengeance, Lord.'

"And then He sighed and sat down once more. 'Ah, little Raguel. The problem with creating things is that they perform so much better than one had ever planned. Shall I ask how you recognized me?'

" 'I . . . I am not certain, Lord. You have no wings. You wait at the center of the City, supervising the Creation directly. When I destroyed Saraquael, You did not look away. You know too many things. You . . .' I paused and thought. 'No, I do not know how I know. As You say, You have created me well. But I only understood who You were, and the meaning of the drama we had enacted here for You, when I saw Lucifer leave.'

" 'What did you understand, child?'

" 'Who killed Carasel. Or, at least, who was pulling the strings. For example, who arranged for Carasel and Saraquael to work together on *Love,* knowing Carasel's tendency to involve himself too deeply in his work?'

"He was speaking to me gently, almost teasingly, as an adult would pretend to make conversation with a tiny child. 'Why should anyone have "pulled the strings," Raguel?'

" 'Because nothing occurs without reason; and all the reasons are Yours. You set Saraquael up: yes, he killed Carasel. But he killed Carasel so that *I* could destroy *him*.'

" 'And were you wrong to destroy him?'

"I looked into His old, old eyes. 'It was my function. But I do not think it was just. I think perhaps it was needed that I destroy Saraquael, in order to demonstrate to Lucifer the Injustice of the Lord.'

"He smiled, then. 'And whatever reason would I have for doing that?'

" 'I . . . I do not know. I do not understand—no more than I understand why You created the Dark or the voices in the Darkness. But You did. You caused all this to occur.'

"He nodded. 'Yes. I did. Lucifer must brood on the unfairness of Saraquael's destruction. And that—amongst other things—will precipitate him into certain actions. Poor sweet Lucifer. His way will be the hardest of all my children; for there is a part he must play in the drama that is to come, and it is a grand role.'

"I remained kneeling in front of the Creator of All Things.

" 'What will you do now, Raguel?' He asked me.

" 'I must return to my cell. My function is now fulfilled. I have taken Vengeance, and I have revealed the perpetrator. That is enough. But—Lord?'

" 'Yes, child.'

" 'I feel dirty. I feel tarnished. I feel befouled. Perhaps it is true that all that happens is in accordance with Your will, and thus it is good. But sometimes You leave blood on Your instruments.'

"He nodded, as if He agreed with me. 'If you wish, Raguel, you may forget all this. All that has happened this day.' And then He said, 'However, you will not be able to speak of this to any other angel, whether you choose to remember it or not.'

" 'I will remember it.'

" 'It is your choice. But sometimes you will find it is easier by far not to remember. Forgetfulness can sometimes bring freedom, of a sort. Now, if you do not mind,' he reached down, took a file from a stack on the floor, opened it, 'there is work I should be getting on with.'

"I stood up and walked to the window. I hoped He would call me back, explain every detail of His plan to me, somehow make it all better. But He said nothing, and I left His Presence without ever looking back."

The man was silent, then. And he remained silent—I couldn't even hear him breathing—for so long that I began to get nervous, thinking that perhaps he had fallen asleep or died.

Then he stood up.

"There you go, pal. That's your story. Do you think it was worth a couple of cigarettes and a book of matches?" He asked the question as if it was important to him, without irony.

"Yes," I told him. "Yes. It was. But what happened next? How did you . . . I mean, if . . ." I trailed off.

It was dark on the street now, at the edge of daybreak. One by one the streetlamps had begun to flicker out, and he was silhouetted against the glow of the dawn sky. He thrust his hands into his pockets. "What happened? I left home, and I lost my way, and these days home's a long way back. Sometimes you do things you regret, but there's nothing you can do about them. Times change. Doors close behind you. You move on. You know?

"Eventually I wound up here. They used to say no one's ever originally from L.A. True as Hell in my case."

And then, before I could understand what he was doing, he leaned down and kissed me, gently, on the cheek. His stubble was rough and prickly, but his breath was surprisingly sweet. He whispered into my ear: "I never fell. I don't care what they say. I'm still doing my job, as I see it."

My cheek burned where his lips had touched it. He straightened up. "But I still want to go home."

The man walked away down the darkened street, and I sat on the bench and watched him go. I felt like he had taken something from me, although I could no longer remember what. And I felt like something had been left in its place—absolution, perhaps, or innocence, although of what, or from what, I could no longer say.

An image from somewhere: a scribbled drawing of two angels in flight above a perfect city; and over the image a child's perfect hand print, which stains the white paper blood-red. It came into my head unbidden, and I no longer know what it meant.

I stood up.

It was too dark to see the face of my watch, but I knew I would get no sleep that day. I walked back to the place I was staying, to the house by the stunted palm tree, to wash myself and to wait. I thought about angels and about Tink; and I wondered whether love and death went hand in hand.

The next day the planes to England were flying again.

I felt strange—lack of sleep had forced me into that miserable state in which everything seems flat and of equal importance; when nothing matters, and in which reality seems scraped thin and threadbare. The taxi journey to the airport was a nightmare. I was hot, and tired, and testy. I wore a T-shirt in the L.A. heat; my coat was packed at the bottom of my luggage, where it had been for the entire stay.

The airplane was crowded, but I didn't care.

The stewardess walked down the aisle with a rack of newspapers: the *Herald Tribune, USA Today,* and the *L.A.Times.* I took a copy of the *Times,* but the words left my head as my eyes scanned over them. Nothing that I read remained with me. No, I lie. Somewhere in the back of the paper was a report of a triple murder: two women and a small child. No names were given, and I do not know why the report should have registered as it did.

Soon I fell asleep. I dreamed about fucking Tink, while blood ran sluggishly from her closed eyes and lips. The blood was cold and viscous and clammy, and I awoke chilled by the plane's air-conditioning, with an unpleasant taste in my mouth. My tongue and lips were dry. I looked out of the scratched oval window, stared down at the clouds, and it occurred to me then (not for the first time) that the clouds were in actuality another land, where everyone knew just what they were looking for and how to get back where they started from.

Staring down at the clouds is one of the things I have always liked best about flying. That, and the proximity one feels to one's death.

I wrapped myself in the thin aircraft blanket and slept some more, but if further dreams came then they made no impression upon me.

A blizzard blew up shortly after the plane landed in England, knocking out the airport's power supply. I was alone in an airport elevator at the time, and it went dark and jammed between floors. A dim emergency light flickered on. I pressed the crimson alarm button until the batteries ran down and it ceased to sound; then I shivered in my L.A. T-shirt in the corner of my little silver room. I watched my breath steam in the air, and I hugged myself for warmth.

There wasn't anything in there except me; but even so, I felt safe and secure. Soon someone would come and force open the doors. Eventually somebody would let me out; and I knew that I would soon be home.

TROLL BRIDGE

1993

THEY PULLED UP most of the railway tracks in the early sixties, when I was three or four. They slashed the train services to ribbons. This meant that there was nowhere to go but London, and the little town where I lived became the end of the line.

My earliest reliable memory: eighteen months old, my mother away in hospital having my sister, and my grandmother walking with me down to a bridge, and lifting me up to watch the train below, panting and steaming like a black iron dragon.

Over the next few years they lost the last of the steam trains, and with them went the network of railways that joined village to village, town to town.

I didn't know that the trains were going. By the time I was seven they were a thing of the past.

We lived in an old house on the outskirts of the town. The fields opposite were empty and fallow. I used to climb the fence and lie in the shade of a small bulrush patch, and read; or if I were feeling more adventurous I'd explore the grounds of the empty manor beyond the fields. It had a weed-clogged ornamental pond, with a low wooden bridge over it. I never saw any groundsmen or caretakers in my forays through the gardens and woods, and I never attempted to enter the manor. That would have been courting disaster, and besides, it was a matter of faith for me that all empty old houses were haunted.

It is not that I was credulous, simply that I believed in all things dark and dangerous. It was part of my young creed that the night was full of ghosts and witches, hungry and flapping and dressed completely in black.

The converse held reassuringly true: daylight was safe. Daylight was always safe.

A ritual: on the last day of the summer school term, walking home from school, I would remove my shoes and socks and, carrying them in my hands, walk down the stony flinty lane on pink and tender feet. During the summer holiday I would put shoes on only under duress. I would revel in my freedom from footwear until the school term began once more in September.

When I was seven I discovered the path through the wood. It was summer, hot and bright, and I wandered a long way from home that day.

I was exploring. I went past the manor, its windows boarded up and blind, across the grounds, and through some unfamiliar woods. I scrambled down a steep bank, and I found myself on a shady path that was new to me and overgrown with trees; the light that penetrated the leaves was stained green and gold, and I thought I was in fairyland.

A little stream trickled down the side of the path, teeming with tiny, transparent shrimps. I picked them up and watched them jerk and spin on my fingertips. Then I put them back.

I wandered down the path. It was perfectly straight, and overgrown with short grass. From time to time I would find these really terrific rocks: bubbly, melted things, brown and purple and black. If you held them up to the light you could see every color of the rainbow. I was convinced that they had to be extremely valuable, and stuffed my pockets with them.

I walked and walked down the quiet golden-green corridor, and saw nobody.

I wasn't hungry or thirsty. I just wondered where the path was going. It traveled in a straight line, and was perfectly flat. The path never changed, but the countryside around it did. At first I was walking along the bottom of a ravine, grassy banks climbing steeply on each side of me. Later, the path was above everything, and as I walked I could look down at the treetops below me, and the roofs of occasional distant houses. My path was always flat and straight, and I walked along it through valleys and plateaus, valleys and plateaus. And eventually, in one of the valleys, I came to the bridge.

It was built of clean red brick, a huge curving arch over the path. At the side of the bridge were stone steps cut into the embankment, and, at the top of the steps, a little wooden gate.

I was surprised to see any token of the existence of humanity on my path, which I was by now convinced was a natural formation, like a volcano. And, with a sense more of curiosity than anything else (I had, after all, walked hundreds of miles, or so I was convinced, and might be *anywhere*), I climbed the stone steps, and went through the gate.

I was nowhere.

The top of the bridge was paved with mud. On each side of it was a meadow. The meadow on my side was a wheat field; the other field was just grass. There were the caked imprints of huge tractor wheels in the dried mud. I walked across the bridge to be sure: no trip-trap, my bare feet were soundless.

Nothing for miles; just fields and wheat and trees.

I picked an ear of wheat, and pulled out the sweet grains, peeling them between my fingers, chewing them meditatively.

I realized then that I was getting hungry, and went back down the stairs to the abandoned railway track. It was time to go home. I was not lost; all I needed to do was follow my path home once more.

There was a troll waiting for me, under the bridge.

"I'm a troll," he said. Then he paused, and added, more or less as an afterthought, "Fol rol de ol rol."

He was huge: his head brushed the top of the brick arch. He was more or less translucent: I could see the bricks and trees behind him, dimmed but not lost. He was all my nightmares given flesh. He had huge strong teeth, and rending claws, and strong, hairy hands. His hair was long, like one of my sister's little plastic gonks, and his eyes bulged. He was naked, and his penis hung from the bush of gonk hair between his legs.

"I heard you, Jack," he whispered in a voice like the wind. "I heard you trip-trapping over my bridge. And now I'm going to eat your life."

I was only seven, but it was daylight, and I do not remember being scared. It is good for children to find themselves facing the elements of a fairy tale—they are well equipped to deal with these.

"Don't eat me," I said to the troll. I was wearing a stripy brown T-shirt, and brown corduroy trousers. My hair also was brown, and I was missing a front tooth. I was learning to whistle between my teeth, but wasn't there yet.

"I'm going to eat your life, Jack," said the troll.

I stared the troll in the face. "My big sister is going to be coming down the path soon," I lied, "and she's far tastier than me. Eat her instead."

The troll sniffed the air, and smiled. "You're all alone," he said. "There's nothing else on the path. Nothing at all." Then he leaned down, and ran his fingers over me: it felt like butterflies were brushing my face—like the touch of a blind person. Then he snuffled his fingers, and shook his huge head. "You don't have a big sister. You've only a younger sister, and she's at her friend's today."

"Can you tell all that from smell?" I asked, amazed.

"Trolls can smell the rainbows, trolls can smell the stars," it whispered sadly. "Trolls can smell the dreams you dreamed before you were ever born. Come close to me and I'll eat your life."

"I've got precious stones in my pocket," I told the troll. "Take them, not me. Look." I showed him the lava jewel rocks I had found earlier.

"Clinker," said the troll. "The discarded refuse of steam trains. Of no value to me."

He opened his mouth wide. Sharp teeth. Breath that smelled of leaf mold and the underneaths of things. "Eat. Now."

He became more and more solid to me, more and more real; and the world outside became flatter, began to fade.

"Wait." I dug my feet into the damp earth beneath the bridge, wiggled my toes, held on tightly to the real world. I stared into his big eyes. "You don't want to eat my life. Not yet. I—I'm only seven. I haven't *lived* at all yet. There are books I haven't read yet. I've never been on an airplane. I can't whistle yet—not really. Why don't you let me go? When I'm older and bigger and more of a meal I'll come back to you."

The troll stared at me with eyes like headlamps. Then it nodded.

"When you come back, then," it said. And it smiled.

I turned around and walked back down the silent straight path where the railway lines had once been.

After a while I began to run.

I pounded down the track in the green light, puffing and blowing, until I felt a stabbing ache beneath my ribcage, the pain of stitch; and, clutching my side, I stumbled home.

THE FIELDS STARTED to go, as I grew older. One by one, row by row, houses sprang up with roads named after wildflowers and respectable authors. Our home—an aging, tattered Victorian house—was sold, and torn down; new houses covered the garden.

They built houses everywhere.

I once got lost in the new housing estate that covered two meadows I had once known every inch of. I didn't mind too much that the fields were going, though. The old manor house was bought by a multinational, and the grounds became more houses.

It was eight years before I returned to the old railway line, and when I did, I was not alone.

I was fifteen; I'd changed schools twice in that time. Her name was Louise, and she was my first love.

I loved her gray eyes, and her fine light brown hair, and her gawky way of walking (like a fawn just learning to walk, which sounds really dumb, for which I apologize): I saw her chewing gum, when I was thirteen, and I fell for her like a suicide from a bridge.

The main trouble with being in love with Louise was that we were best friends, and we were both going out with other people.

I'd never told her I loved her, or even that I fancied her. We were buddies.

I'd been at her house that evening: we sat in her room and played *Rattus Norvegicus,* the first Stranglers LP. It was the beginning of punk, and everything seemed so exciting: the possibilities, in music as in everything else, were endless. Eventually it was time for me to go home, and she decided to accompany me. We held hands, innocently, just pals, and we strolled the ten-minute walk to my house.

The moon was bright, and the world was visible and colorless, and the night was warm.

We got to my house. Saw the lights inside, and stood in the driveway, and talked about the band I was starting. We didn't go in.

Then it was decided that I'd walk *her* home. So we walked back to her house.

She told me about the battles she was having with her younger sister, who was stealing her makeup and perfume. Louise suspected that her sister was having sex with boys. Louise was a virgin. We both were.

We stood in the road outside her house, under the sodium-yellow streetlight, and we stared at each other's black lips and pale yellow faces.

We grinned at each other.

Then we just walked, picking quiet roads and empty paths. In one of the new housing estates, a path led us into the woodland, and we followed it.

The path was straight and dark, but the lights of distant houses shone like stars on the ground, and the moon gave us enough light to see. Once we were scared, when something snuffled and snorted in front of us. We pressed close, saw it was a badger, laughed and hugged and kept on walking.

We talked quiet nonsense about what we dreamed and wanted and thought.

And all the time I wanted to kiss her and feel her breasts, and maybe put my hand between her legs.

Finally I saw my chance. There was an old brick bridge over the path, and we stopped beneath it. I pressed up against her. Her mouth opened against mine.

Then she went cold and stiff, and stopped moving.

"Hello," said the troll.

I let go of Louise. It was dark beneath the bridge, but the shape of the troll filled the darkness.

"I froze her," said the troll, "so we can talk. Now: I'm going to eat your life."

My heart pounded, and I could feel myself trembling. "No."

"You said you'd come back to me. And you have. Did you learn to whistle?"

"Yes."

"That's good. I never could whistle." It sniffed, and nodded. "I am pleased. You have grown in life and experience. More to eat. More for me."

I grabbed Louise, a taut zombie, and pushed her forward. "Don't take me. I don't want to die. Take *her*. I bet she's much tastier than me. And she's two months older than I am. Why don't you take her?"

The troll was silent.

It sniffed Louise from toe to head, snuffling at her feet and crotch and breasts and hair.

Then it looked at me.

"She's an innocent," it said. "You're not. I don't want her. I want you."

I walked to the opening of the bridge and stared up at the stars in the night.

"But there's so much I've never done," I said, partly to myself. "I mean, I've never. Well, I've never had sex. And I've never been to America. I haven't . . ." I paused. "I haven't *done* anything. Not yet."

The troll said nothing.

"I could come back to you. When I'm older." The troll said nothing.

"I *will* come back. Honest I will."

"Come back to me?" said Louise. "Why? Where are you going?"

I turned around. The troll had gone, and the girl I had thought I loved was standing in the shadows beneath the bridge.

"We're going home," I told her. "Come on."

We walked back and never said anything.

She went out with the drummer in the punk band I started, and, much later, married someone else. We met once, on a train, after she was married, and she asked me if I remembered that night.

I said I did.

"I really liked you, that night, Jack," she told me. "I thought you were going to kiss me. I thought you were going to ask me out. I would have said yes. If you had."

"But I didn't."

"No," she said. "You didn't." Her hair was cut very short. It didn't suit her.

I never saw her again. The trim woman with the taut smile was not the girl I had loved, and talking to her made me feel uncomfortable.

I MOVED TO London, and then, some years later, I moved back again, but the town I returned to was not the town I remembered: there were no fields, no farms, no little flint lanes; and I moved away as soon as I could, to a tiny village ten miles down the road.

I moved with my family—I was married by now, with a toddler—into an old house that had once, many years before, been a railway station. The tracks had been dug up, and the old couple who lived opposite us used it to grow vegetables.

I was getting older. One day I found a gray hair; on another, I heard a recording of myself talking, and I realized I sounded just like my father.

I was working in London, doing A&R for one of the major record companies. I was commuting into London by train most days, coming back some evenings.

I had to keep a small flat in London; it's hard to commute when the bands you're checking out don't even stagger onto the stage until midnight. It also meant that it was fairly easy to get laid, if I wanted to, which I did.

I thought that Eleanora—that was my wife's name; I should have mentioned that before, I suppose—didn't know about the other women; but I got back from a two-week jaunt to New York one winter's day, and when I arrived at the house it was empty and cold.

She had left a letter, not a note. Fifteen pages, neatly typed, and every word of it was true. Including the PS, which read: *You really don't love me. And you never did.*

I put on a heavy coat, and I left the house and just walked, stunned and slightly numb.

There was no snow on the ground, but there was a hard frost, and the leaves crunched under my feet as I walked. The trees were skeletal black against the harsh gray winter sky.

I walked down the side of the road. Cars passed me, traveling to and from London. Once I tripped on a branch, half-hidden in a heap of brown leaves, ripping my trousers, cutting my leg.

I reached the next village. There was a river at right angles to the road, and a path I'd never seen before beside it, and I walked down the path, and stared at the partly frozen river. It gurgled and plashed and sang.

The path led off through fields; it was straight and grassy.

I found a rock, half-buried, on one side of the path. I picked it up, brushed off the mud. It was a melted lump of purplish stuff, with a strange rainbow sheen to it. I put it into the pocket of my coat and held it in my hand as I walked, its presence warm and reassuring.

The river meandered away across the fields, and I walked on in silence.

I had walked for an hour before I saw houses—new and small and square—on the embankment above me.

And then I saw the bridge, and I knew where I was: I was on the old railway path, and I'd been coming down it from the other direction.

There were graffiti painted on the side of the bridge: FUCK and BARRY LOVES SUSAN and the omnipresent NF of the National Front. I stood beneath the bridge in the red brick arch, stood among the ice cream wrappers, and the crisp packets and the single, sad, used condom, and watched my breath steam in the cold afternoon air.

The blood had dried into my trousers.

Cars passed over the bridge above me; I could hear a radio playing loudly in one of them.

"Hello?" I said, quietly, feeling embarrassed, feeling foolish. "Hello?"

There was no answer. The wind rustled the crisp packets and the leaves.

"I came back. I said I would. And I did. Hello?"

Silence.

I began to cry then, stupidly, silently, sobbing under the bridge.

A hand touched my face, and I looked up.

"I didn't think you'd come back," said the troll.

He was my height now, but otherwise unchanged. His long gonk hair was unkempt and had leaves in it, and his eyes were wide and lonely.

I shrugged, then wiped my face with the sleeve of my coat. "I came back."

Three kids passed above us on the bridge, shouting and running.

"I'm a troll," whispered the troll, in a small, scared voice. "Fol rol de ol rol."

He was trembling.

I held out my hand and took his huge clawed paw in mine. I smiled at him. "It's okay," I told him. "Honestly. It's okay."

The troll nodded.

He pushed me to the ground, onto the leaves and the wrappers and the condom, and lowered himself on top of me. Then he raised his head, and opened his mouth, and ate my life with his strong sharp teeth.

WHEN HE WAS finished, the troll stood up and brushed himself down. He put his hand into the pocket of his coat and pulled out a bubbly, burnt lump of clinker rock.

He held it out to me.

"This is yours," said the troll.

I looked at him: wearing my life comfortably, easily, as if he'd been wearing it for years. I took the clinker from his hand, and sniffed it. I could smell the train from which it had fallen, so long ago. I gripped it tightly in my hairy hand.

"Thank you," I said.

"Good luck," said the troll.

"Yeah. Well. You too."

The troll grinned with my face.

It turned its back on me and began to walk back the way I had come, toward the village, back to the empty house I had left that morning; and it whistled as it walked.

I've been here ever since. Hiding. Waiting. Part of the bridge.

I watch from the shadows as the people pass: walking their dogs, or talking, or doing the things that people do. Sometimes people pause beneath my bridge, to stand, or piss, or make love. And I watch them, but say nothing; and they never see me.

Fol rol de ol rol.

I'm just going to stay here, in the darkness under the arch. I can hear you all out there, trip-trapping, trip-trapping over my bridge.

Oh yes, I can hear you.

But I'm not coming out.

SNOW, GLASS, APPLES

1994

I DO NOT KNOW what manner of thing she is. None of us do. She killed her mother in the birthing, but that's never enough to account for it.

They call me wise, but I am far from wise, for all that I foresaw fragments of it, frozen moments caught in pools of water or in the cold glass of my mirror. If I were wise I would not have tried to change what I saw. If I were wise I would have killed myself before ever I encountered her, before ever I caught him.

Wise, and a witch, or so they said, and I'd seen his face in my dreams and in reflections for all my life: sixteen years of dreaming of him before he reined his horse by the bridge that morning and asked my name. He helped me onto his high horse and we rode together to my little cottage, my face buried in the gold of his hair. He asked for the best of what I had; a king's right, it was.

His beard was red-bronze in the morning light, and I knew him, not as a king, for I knew nothing of kings then, but as my love. He took all he wanted from me, the right of kings, but he returned to me on the following day and on the night after that: his beard so red, his hair so gold, his eyes the blue of a summer sky, his skin tanned the gentle brown of ripe wheat.

His daughter was only a child: no more than five years of age when I came to the palace. A portrait of her dead mother hung in the princess's tower room: a tall woman, hair the color of dark wood, eyes nut-brown. She was of a different blood to her pale daughter.

The girl would not eat with us.

I do not know where in the palace she ate.

I had my own chambers. My husband the king, he had his own rooms also. When he wanted me he would send for me, and I would go to him, and pleasure him, and take my pleasure with him.

One night, several months after I was brought to the palace, she came to my rooms. She was six. I was embroidering by lamplight, squinting my eyes against the lamp's smoke and fitful illumination. When I looked up, she was there.

"Princess?"

She said nothing. Her eyes were black as coal, black as her hair; her lips were redder than blood. She looked up at me and smiled. Her teeth seemed sharp, even then, in the lamplight.

"What are you doing away from your room?"

"I'm hungry," she said, like any child.

It was winter, when fresh food is a dream of warmth and sunlight; but I had strings of whole apples, cored and dried, hanging from the beams of my chamber, and I pulled an apple down for her.

"Here."

Autumn is the time of drying, of preserving, a time of picking apples, of rendering the goose fat. Winter is the time of hunger, of snow, and of death; and it is the time of the midwinter feast, when we rub the goose fat into the skin of a whole pig, stuffed with that autumn's apples; then we roast it or spit it, and we prepare to feast upon the crackling.

She took the dried apple from me and began to chew it with her sharp yellow teeth.

"Is it good?"

She nodded. I had always been scared of the little princess, but at that moment I warmed to her and, with my fingers, gently, I stroked her cheek. She looked at me and smiled—she smiled but rarely— then she sank her teeth into the base of my thumb, the Mound of Venus, and she drew blood.

I began to shriek, from pain and from surprise, but she looked at me and I fell silent.

The little princess fastened her mouth to my hand and licked and sucked and drank. When she was finished, she left my chamber. Beneath my gaze the cut that she had made began to close, to scab, and to heal. The next day it was an old scar: I might have cut my hand with a pocketknife in my childhood.

I had been frozen by her, owned and dominated. That scared me, more than the blood she had fed on. After that night I locked my chamber door at dusk, barring it with an oaken pole, and I had the smith forge iron bars, which he placed across my windows.

My husband, my love, my king, sent for me less and less, and when I came to him he was dizzy, listless, confused. He could no longer make love as a man makes love, and he would not permit me to pleasure him with my mouth: the one time I tried, he started violently, and began to weep. I pulled my mouth away and held him tightly until the sobbing had stopped, and he slept, like a child.

I ran my fingers across his skin as he slept. It was covered in a multitude of ancient scars. But I could recall no scars from the days of our courtship, save one, on his side, where a boar had gored him when he was a youth.

Soon he was a shadow of the man I had met and loved by the bridge. His bones showed, blue and white, beneath his skin. I was with him at the last: his hands were cold as stone, his eyes milky blue, his hair and beard faded and lusterless and limp. He died unshriven, his skin nipped and pocked from head to toe with tiny, old scars.

He weighed near to nothing. The ground was frozen hard, and we could dig no grave for him, so we made a cairn of rocks and stones above his body, as a memorial only, for there was little enough of him left to protect from the hunger of the beasts and the birds.

So I was queen.

And I was foolish, and young—eighteen summers had come and gone since first I saw daylight—and I did not do what I would do, now.

If it were today, I would have her heart cut out, true. But then I would have her head and arms and legs cut off. I would have them disembowel her. And then I would watch in the town square as the hangman heated the fire to white-heat with bellows, watch unblinking as he consigned each part of her to the fire. I would have archers around the square, who would shoot any bird or animal that came close to the flames, any raven or dog or hawk or rat. And I would not close my eyes until the princess was ash, and a gentle wind could scatter her like snow.

I did not do this thing, and we pay for our mistakes.

They say I was fooled; that it was not her heart. That it was the heart of an animal—a stag, perhaps, or a boar. They say that, and they are wrong.

And some say (but it is *her* lie, not mine) that I was given the heart, and that I ate it. Lies and half-truths fall like snow, covering the things that I remember, the things I saw. A landscape, unrecognizable after a snowfall; that is what she has made of my life.

There were scars on my love, her father's thighs, and on his ballock-pouch, and on his male member, when he died.

I did not go with them. They took her in the day, while she slept, and was at her weakest. They took her to the heart of the forest, and there they opened her blouse, and they cut out her heart, and they left her dead, in a gully, for the forest to swallow. The forest is a dark place, the border to many kingdoms; no one would be foolish enough to claim jurisdiction over it. Outlaws live in the forest. Robbers live in the forest, and so do wolves. You can ride through the forest for a dozen days and never see a soul; but there are eyes upon you the entire time.

They brought me her heart. I know it was hers—no sow's heart or doe's would have continued to beat and pulse after it had been cut out, as that one did.

I took it to my chamber.

I did not eat it: I hung it from the beams above my bed, placed it on a length of twine that I strung with rowan berries, orange-red as a robin's breast, and with bulbs of garlic.

Outside the snow fell, covering the footprints of my huntsmen, covering her tiny body in the forest where it lay.

I had the smith remove the iron bars from my windows, and I would spend some time in my room each afternoon through the short winter days, gazing out over the forest, until darkness fell.

There were, as I have already stated, people in the forest. They would come out, some of them, for the Spring Fair: a greedy, feral, dangerous people; some were stunted—dwarfs and hunchbacks; others had the huge teeth and vacant gazes of idiots; some had fingers like flippers or crab claws. They would creep out of the forest each year for the Spring Fair, held when the snows had melted.

As a young lass I had worked at the fair, and they had scared me then, the forest folk. I told fortunes for the fairgoers, scrying in a pool of still water; and later, when I was older, in a disk of polished glass, its back all silvered—a gift from a merchant whose straying horse I had seen in a pool of ink.

The stallholders at the fair were afraid of the forest folk; they would nail their wares to the bare boards of their stalls—slabs of gingerbread or leather belts were nailed with great iron nails to the wood. If their wares were not nailed, they said, the forest folk would take them and run away, chewing on the stolen gingerbread, flailing about them with the belts.

The forest folk had money, though: a coin here, another there, sometimes stained green by time or the earth, the face on the coin unknown to even the oldest of us. Also they had things to trade, and thus the fair continued, serving the outcasts and the dwarfs, serving the robbers (if they were circumspect) who preyed on the rare travelers from lands beyond the forest, or on gypsies, or on the deer. (This was robbery in the eyes of the law. The deer were the queen's.)

The years passed by slowly, and my people claimed that I ruled them with wisdom. The heart still hung above my bed, pulsing gently in the night. If there were any who mourned the child, I saw no evidence: she was a thing of terror, back then, and they believed themselves well rid of her.

Spring Fair followed Spring Fair: five of them, each sadder, poorer, shoddier than the one before. Fewer of the forest folk came out of the forest to buy. Those who did seemed subdued and listless. The stallholders stopped nailing their wares to the boards of their stalls. And by the fifth year but a handful of folk came from the forest—a fearful huddle of little hairy men, and no one else.

The Lord of the Fair, and his page, came to me when the fair was done. I had known him slightly, before I was queen.

"I do not come to you as my queen," he said.

I said nothing. I listened.

"I come to you because you are wise," he continued. "When you were a child you found a strayed foal by staring into a pool of ink; when you were a maiden you found a lost infant who had wandered far from her mother, by staring into that mirror of yours. You know secrets and you can seek out things hidden. My queen," he asked, "what is taking the forest folk? Next year there will be no Spring Fair. The travelers from other kingdoms have grown scarce and few, the folk of the forest are almost gone. Another year like the last, and we shall all starve."

I commanded my maidservant to bring me my looking glass. It was a simple thing, a silver-backed glass disk, which I kept wrapped in a doeskin, in a chest, in my chamber.

They brought it to me then, and I gazed into it:

She was twelve and she was no longer a little child. Her skin was still pale, her eyes and hair coal-black, her lips blood-red. She wore the clothes she had worn when she left the castle for the last time—the blouse, the skirt—although they were much let-out, much mended. Over them she wore a leather cloak, and instead of boots she had leather bags, tied with thongs, over her tiny feet.

She was standing in the forest, beside a tree.

As I watched, in the eye of my mind, I saw her edge and step and flitter and pad from tree to tree, like an animal: a bat or a wolf. She was following someone.

He was a monk. He wore sackcloth, and his feet were bare and scabbed and hard. His beard and tonsure were of a length, over-grown, unshaven.

She watched him from behind the trees. Eventually he paused for the night and began to make a fire, laying twigs down, breaking up a robin's nest as kindling. He had a tinderbox in his robe, and he knocked the flint against the steel until the sparks caught the tinder and the fire flamed. There had been two eggs in the nest he had found, and these he ate raw. They cannot have been much of a meal for so big a man.

He sat there in the firelight, and she came out from her hiding place. She crouched down on the other side of the fire, and stared at him. He grinned, as if it were a long time since he had seen another human, and beckoned her over to him.

She stood up and walked around the fire, and waited, an arm's length away. He pulled in his robe until he found a coin—a tiny copper penny—and tossed it to her. She caught it, and nodded, and went to him. He pulled at the rope around his waist, and his robe swung open. His body was as hairy as a bear's. She pushed him back onto the moss. One hand crept, spiderlike, through the tangle of hair, until it closed on his manhood; the other hand traced a circle on his left nipple. He closed his eyes and fumbled one huge hand under her skirt. She lowered her mouth to the nipple she had been teasing, her smooth skin white on the furry brown body of him.

She sank her teeth deep into his breast. His eyes opened, then they closed again, and she drank.

She straddled him, and she fed. As she did so, a thin blackish liquid began to dribble from between her legs . . .

"Do you know what is keeping the travelers from our town? What is happening to the forest people?" asked the Lord of the Fair.

I covered the mirror in doeskin, and told him that I would personally take it upon myself to make the forest safe once more.

I had to, although she terrified me. I was the queen.

A foolish woman would have gone then into the forest and tried to capture the creature; but I had been foolish once and had no wish to be so a second time.

I spent time with old books. I spent time with the gypsy women (who passed through our country across the mountains to the south, rather than cross the forest to the north and the west).

I prepared myself and obtained those things I would need, and when the first snows began to fall, I was ready.

Naked, I was, and alone in the highest tower of the palace, a place open to the sky. The winds chilled my body; goose pimples crept across my arms and thighs and breasts. I carried a silver basin, and a basket in which I had placed a silver knife, a silver pin, some tongs, a gray robe, and three green apples.

I put them on and stood there, unclothed, on the tower, humble before the night sky and the wind. Had any man seen me standing there, I would have had his eyes; but there was no one to spy. Clouds scudded across the sky, hiding and uncovering the waning moon.

I took the silver knife and slashed my left arm—once, twice, three times. The blood dripped into the basin, scarlet seeming black in the moonlight.

I added the powder from the vial that hung around my neck. It was a brown dust, made of dried herbs and the skin of a particular toad, and from certain other things. It thickened the blood, while preventing it from clotting.

I took the three apples, one by one, and pricked their skins gently with my silver pin. Then I placed the apples in the silver bowl and let them sit there while the first tiny flakes of snow of the year fell slowly onto my skin, and onto the apples, and onto the blood.

When dawn began to brighten the sky I covered myself with the gray cloak, and took the red apples from the silver bowl, one by one, lifting each into my basket with silver tongs, taking care not to touch it. There was nothing left of my blood or of the brown powder in the silver bowl, nothing save a black residue, like a verdigris, on the inside.

I buried the bowl in the earth. Then I cast a glamour on the apples (as once, years before, by a bridge, I had cast a glamour on myself), that they were, beyond any doubt, the most wonderful apples in the world, and the crimson blush of their skins was the warm color of fresh blood.

I pulled the hood of my cloak low over my face, and I took ribbons and pretty hair ornaments with me, placed them above the apples in the reed basket, and I walked alone into the forest until I came to her dwelling: a high sandstone cliff, laced with deep caves going back a way into the rock wall.

There were trees and boulders around the cliff face, and I walked quietly and gently from tree to tree without disturbing a twig or a fallen leaf. Eventually I found my place to hide, and I waited, and I watched.

After some hours, a clutch of dwarfs crawled out of the hole in the cave front—ugly, misshapen, hairy little men, the old inhabitants of this country. You saw them seldom now.

They vanished into the wood, and none of them espied me, though one of them stopped to piss against the rock I hid behind.

I waited. No more came out.

I went to the cave entrance and hallooed into it, in a cracked old voice.

The scar on my Mound of Venus throbbed and pulsed as she came toward me, out of the darkness, naked and alone.

She was thirteen years of age, my stepdaughter, and nothing marred the perfect whiteness of her skin, save for the livid scar on her left breast, where her heart had been cut from her long since.

The insides of her thighs were stained with wet black filth.

She peered at me, hidden, as I was, in my cloak. She looked at me hungrily. "Ribbons, goodwife," I croaked. "Pretty ribbons for your hair . . ."

She smiled and beckoned to me. A tug; the scar on my hand was pulling me toward her. I did what I had planned to do, but I did it more readily than I had planned: I dropped my basket and screeched like the bloodless old peddler woman I was pretending to be, and I ran.

My gray cloak was the color of the forest, and I was fast; she did not catch me.

I made my way back to the palace.

I did not see it. Let us imagine, though, the girl returning, frustrated and hungry, to her cave, and finding my fallen basket on the ground.

What did she do?

I like to think she played first with the ribbons, twined them into her raven hair, looped them around her pale neck or her tiny waist.

And then, curious, she moved the cloth to see what else was in the basket, and she saw the red, red apples.

They smelled like fresh apples, of course; and they also smelled of blood. And she was hungry. I imagine her picking up an apple, pressing it against her cheek, feeling the cold smoothness of it against her skin.

And she opened her mouth and bit deep into it . . .

By the time I reached my chambers, the heart that hung from the roof beam, with the apples and hams and the dried sausages, had ceased to beat. It hung there, quietly, without motion or life, and I felt safe once more.

That winter the snows were high and deep, and were late melting. We were all hungry come the spring.

The Spring Fair was slightly improved that year. The forest folk were few, but they were there, and there were travelers from the lands beyond the forest.

I saw the little hairy men of the forest cave buying and bargaining for pieces of glass, and lumps of crystal and of quartz rock. They paid for the glass with silver coins—the spoils of my stepdaughter's depredations, I had no doubt. When it got about what they were buying, townsfolk rushed back to their homes and came back with their lucky crystals, and, in a few cases, with whole sheets of glass.

I thought briefly about having the little men killed, but I did not. As long as the heart hung, silent and immobile and cold, from the beam of my chamber, I was safe, and so were the folk of the forest, and, thus, eventually, the folk of the town.

My twenty-fifth year came, and my stepdaughter had eaten the poisoned fruit two winters back, when the prince came to my palace. He was tall, very tall, with cold green eyes and the swarthy skin of those from beyond the mountains.

He rode with a small retinue: large enough to defend him, small enough that another monarch—myself, for instance—would not view him as a potential threat.

I was practical: I thought of the alliance of our lands, thought of the kingdom running from the forests all the way south to the sea; I thought of my golden-haired bearded love, dead these eight years; and, in the night, I went to the prince's room.

I am no innocent, although my late husband, who was once my king, was truly my first lover, no matter what they say.

At first the prince seemed excited. He bade me remove my shift, and made me stand in front of the opened window, far from the fire, until my skin was chilled stone-cold. Then he asked me to lie upon my back, with my hands folded across my breasts, my eyes wide open—but staring only at the beams above. He told me not to move, and to breathe as little as possible. He implored me to say nothing. He spread my legs apart.

It was then that he entered me.

As he began to thrust inside me, I felt my hips raise, felt myself begin to match him, grind for grind, push for push. I moaned. I could not help myself.

His manhood slid out of me. I reached out and touched it, a tiny, slippery thing.

"Please," he said softly. "You must neither move nor speak. Just lie there on the stones, so cold and so fair."

I tried, but he had lost whatever force it was that had made him virile; and, some short while later, I left the prince's room, his curses and tears still resounding in my ears.

He left early the next morning, with all his men, and they rode off into the forest.

I imagine his loins, now, as he rode, a knot of frustration at the base of his manhood. I imagine his pale lips pressed so tightly together. Then I imagine his little troupe riding through the forest, finally coming upon the glass-and-crystal cairn of my stepdaughter. So pale. So cold. Naked beneath the glass, and little more than a girl, and dead.

In my fancy, I can almost feel the sudden hardness of his manhood inside his britches, envision the lust that took him then, the prayers he muttered beneath his breath in thanks for his good fortune. I imagine him negotiating with the little hairy men—offering them gold and spices for the lovely corpse under the crystal mound.

Did they take his gold willingly? Or did they look up to see his men on their horses, with their sharp swords and their spears, and realize they had no alternative?

I do not know. I was not there; I was not scrying. I can only imagine . . .

Hands, pulling off the lumps of glass and quartz from her cold body. Hands, gently caressing her cold cheek, moving her cold arm, rejoicing to find the corpse still fresh and pliable.

Did he take her there, in front of them all? Or did he have her carried to a secluded nook before he mounted her?

I cannot say.

Did he shake the apple from her throat? Or did her eyes slowly open as he pounded into her cold body; did her mouth open, those red lips part, those sharp yellow teeth close on his swarthy neck, as the blood, which is the life, trickled down her throat, washing down and away the lump of apple, my own, my poison?

I imagine; I do not know.

This I do know: I was woken in the night by her heart pulsing and beating once more. Salt blood dripped onto my face from above. I sat up. My hand burned and pounded as if I had hit the base of my thumb with a rock.

There was a hammering on the door. I felt afraid, but I am a queen, and I would not show fear. I opened the door.

First his men walked into my chamber and stood around me, with their sharp swords, and their long spears.

Then he came in; and he spat in my face.

Finally, she walked into my chamber, as she had when I was first a queen and she was a child of six. She had not changed. Not really.

She pulled down the twine on which her heart was hanging. She pulled off the rowan berries, one by one; pulled off the garlic bulb— now a dried thing, after all these years; then she took up her own, her pumping heart—a small thing, no larger than that of a nanny goat or a she-bear—as it brimmed and pumped its blood into her hand.

Her fingernails must have been as sharp as glass: she opened her breast with them, running them over the purple scar. Her chest gaped, suddenly, open and bloodless. She licked her heart, once, as the blood ran over her hands, and she pushed the heart deep into her breast.

I saw her do it. I saw her close the flesh of her breast once more. I saw the purple scar begin to fade.

Her prince looked briefly concerned, but he put his arm around her nonetheless, and they stood, side by side, and they waited.

And she stayed cold, and the bloom of death remained on her lips, and his lust was not diminished in any way.

They told me they would marry, and the kingdoms would indeed be joined. They told me that I would be with them on their wedding day.

It is starting to get hot in here.

They have told the people bad things about me; a little truth to add savor to the dish, but mixed with many lies.

I was bound and kept in a tiny stone cell beneath the palace, and I remained there through the autumn. Today they fetched me out of the cell; they stripped the rags from me, and washed the filth from me, and then they shaved my head and my loins, and they rubbed my skin with goose-grease.

The snow was falling as they carried me—two men at each hand, two men at each leg—utterly exposed, and spread-eagled and cold, through the midwinter crowds, and brought me to this kiln.

My stepdaughter stood there with her prince. She watched me, in my indignity, but she said nothing.

As they thrust me inside, jeering and chaffing as they did so, I saw one snowflake land upon her white cheek, and remain there without melting.

They closed the kiln door behind me. It is getting hotter in here, and outside they are singing and cheering and banging on the sides of the kiln.

She was not laughing, or jeering, or talking. She did not sneer at me or turn away. She looked at me, though; and for a moment I saw myself reflected in her eyes.

I will not scream. I will not give them that satisfaction. They will have my body, but my soul and my story are my own, and will die with me.

The goose-grease begins to melt and glisten upon my skin. I shall make no sound at all. I shall think no more on this.

I shall think instead of the snowflake on her cheek.

I think of her hair as black as coal, her lips, redder than blood, her skin, snow-white.

ONLY THE END OF THE
WORLD AGAIN

1994

I T WAS A bad day: I woke up naked in the bed with a cramp in my
stomach, feeling more or less like hell. Something about the quality of the light, stretched and metallic, like the color of a migraine,
told me it was afternoon.

The room was freezing—literally: there was a thin crust of ice
on the inside of the windows. The sheets on the bed around me
were ripped and clawed, and there was animal hair in the bed. It
itched.

I was thinking about staying in bed for the next week—I'm always
tired after a change—but a wave of nausea forced me to disentangle
myself from the bedding and to stumble, hurriedly, into the apartment's tiny bathroom.

The cramps hit me again as I got to the bathroom door. I held
on to the door frame and I started to sweat. Maybe it was a fever; I
hoped I wasn't coming down with something.

The cramping was sharp in my guts. My head felt swimmy. I
crumpled to the floor, and, before I could manage to raise my head
enough to find the toilet bowl, I began to spew.

I vomited a foul-smelling thin yellow liquid; in it was a dog's
paw—my guess was a Doberman's, but I'm not really a dog person; a
tomato peel; some diced carrots and sweet corn; some lumps of half-

chewed meat, raw; and some fingers. They were fairly small pale fingers, obviously a child's.

"Shit."

The cramps eased up, and the nausea subsided. I lay on the floor with stinking drool coming out of my mouth and nose, with the tears you cry when you're being sick drying on my cheeks.

When I felt a little better, I picked up the paw and the fingers from the pool of spew and threw them into the toilet bowl, flushed them away.

I turned on the tap, rinsed out my mouth with the briny Innsmouth water, and spat it into the sink. I mopped up the rest of the sick as best I could with washcloth and toilet paper. Then I turned on the shower and stood in the bathtub like a zombie as the hot water sluiced over me.

I soaped myself down, body and hair. The meager lather turned gray; I must have been filthy. My hair was matted with something that felt like dried blood, and I worked at it with the bar of soap until it was gone. Then I stood under the shower until the water turned icy.

There was a note under the door from my landlady. It said that I owed her for two weeks' rent. It said that all the answers were in the Book of Revelation. It said that I made a lot of noise coming home in the early hours of this morning, and she'd thank me to be quieter in future. It said that when the Elder Gods rose up from the ocean, all the scum of the Earth, all the nonbelievers, all the human garbage and the wastrels and deadbeats would be swept away, and the world would be cleansed by ice and deep water. It said that she felt she ought to remind me that she had assigned me a shelf in the refrigerator when I arrived and she'd thank me if in the future I'd keep to it.

I crumpled the note, dropped it on the floor, where it lay alongside the Big Mac cartons and the empty pizza cartons and the long-dead dried slices of pizza.

It was time to go to work.

I'd been in Innsmouth for two weeks, and I disliked it. It smelled fishy. It was a claustrophobic little town: marshland to the east, cliffs to the west, and, in the center, a harbor that held a few rotting fishing boats and was not even scenic at sunset. The yuppies had come to Innsmouth in the eighties anyway, bought their picturesque fisherman's cottages overlooking the harbor. The yuppies had been gone for some years now, and the cottages by the bay were crumbling, abandoned.

The inhabitants of Innsmouth lived here and there in and around the town and in the trailer parks that ringed it, filled with dank mobile homes that were never going anywhere.

I got dressed, pulled on my boots, put on my coat, and left my room. My landlady was nowhere to be seen. She was a short pop-eyed woman who spoke little, although she left extensive notes for me pinned to doors and placed where I might see them; she kept the house filled with the smell of boiling seafood: huge pots were always simmering on the kitchen stove, filled with things with too many legs and other things with no legs at all.

There were other rooms in the house, but no one else rented them. No one in their right mind would come to Innsmouth in winter.

Outside the house it didn't smell much better. It was colder, though, and my breath steamed in the sea air. The snow on the streets was crusty and filthy; the clouds promised more snow.

A cold salty wind came up off the bay. The gulls were screaming miserably. I felt shitty. My office would be freezing, too. On the corner of Marsh Street and Leng Avenue was a bar, The Opener, a squat building with small dark windows that I'd passed two dozen times in the last couple of weeks. I hadn't been in before, but I really needed a drink, and besides, it might be warmer in there. I pushed open the door.

The bar was indeed warm. I stamped the snow off my boots and went inside. It was almost empty and smelled of old ashtrays and stale beer. A couple of elderly men were playing chess by the bar. The barman was reading a battered old gilt-and-green-leather edition of the poetical works of Alfred, Lord Tennyson.

"Hey. How about a Jack Daniel's, straight up?"

"Sure thing. You're new in town," he told me, putting his book facedown on the bar, pouring the drink into a glass.

"Does it show?"

He smiled, passed me the Jack Daniel's. The glass was filthy, with a greasy thumbprint on the side, and I shrugged and knocked back the drink anyway. I could barely taste it.

"Hair of the dog?" he said. "In a manner of speaking."

"There is a belief," said the barman, whose fox-red hair was tightly greased back, "that the *lykanthropoi* can be returned to their natural forms by thanking them, while they're in wolf form, or by calling them by their given names."

"Yeah? Well, thanks."

He poured another shot for me, unasked. He looked a little like Peter Lorre, but then, most of the folk in Innsmouth look a little like Peter Lorre, including my landlady.

I sank the Jack Daniel's, this time felt it burning down into my stomach, the way it should.

"It's what they say. I never said I believed it."

"What *do* you believe?"

"Burn the girdle."

"Pardon?"

"The *lykanthropoi* have girdles of human skin, given to them at their first transformation by their masters in Hell. Burn the girdle."

One of the old chess players turned to me then, his eyes huge and blind and protruding. "If you drink rainwater out of a wargwolf's pawprint, that'll make a wolf of you, when the moon is full," he said. "The only cure is to hunt down the wolf that made the print in the first place and cut off its head with a knife forged of virgin silver."

"Virgin, huh?" I smiled.

His chess partner, bald and wrinkled, shook his head and croaked a single sad sound. Then he moved his queen and croaked again.

There are people like him all over Innsmouth.

I paid for the drinks and left a dollar tip on the bar. The barman was reading his book once more and ignored it.

Outside the bar big wet kissy flakes of snow had begun to fall, settling in my hair and eyelashes. I hate snow. I hate New England. I hate Innsmouth: it's no place to be alone, but if there's a good place to be alone, I've not found it yet. Still, business has kept me on the move for more moons than I like to think about. Business, and other things.

I walked a couple of blocks down Marsh Street—like most of Innsmouth, an unattractive mixture of eighteenth-century American Gothic houses, late-nineteenth-century stunted brownstones, and late-twentieth prefab gray-brick boxes—until I got to a boarded-up fried chicken joint, and I went up the stone steps next to the store and unlocked the rusting metal security door.

There was a liquor store across the street; a palmist was operating on the second floor.

Someone had scrawled graffiti in black marker on the metal: JUST DIE, it said. Like it was easy.

The stairs were bare wood; the plaster was stained and peeling. My one-room office was at the top of the stairs.

I don't stay anywhere long enough to bother with my name in gilt on glass. It was handwritten in block letters on a piece of ripped cardboard that I'd thumbtacked to the door.

LAWRENCE TALBOT

ADJUSTOR

I unlocked the door to my office and went in.

I inspected my office, while adjectives like *seedy* and *rancid* and *squalid* wandered through my head, then gave up, outclassed. It was fairly unprepossessing—a desk, an office chair, an empty filing cabinet; a window, which gave you a terrific view of the liquor store and the empty palmist's. The smell of old cooking grease permeated from the store below. I wondered how long the fried chicken joint had been boarded up; I imagined a multitude of black cockroaches swarming over every surface in the darkness beneath me.

"That's the shape of the world that you're thinking of there," said a deep dark voice, deep enough that I felt it in the pit of my stomach.

There was an old armchair in one corner of the office. The remains of a pattern showed through the patina of age and grease the years had given it. It was the color of dust.

The fat man sitting in the armchair, his eyes still tightly closed, continued: "We look about in puzzlement at our world, with a sense of unease and disquiet. We think of ourselves as scholars in arcane liturgies, single men trapped in worlds beyond our devising. The truth is far simpler: there are things in the darkness beneath us that wish us harm."

His head was lolled back on the armchair, and the tip of his tongue poked out of the corner of his mouth.

"You read my mind?"

The man in the armchair took a slow deep breath that rattled in the back of his throat. He really was immensely fat, with stubby fingers like discolored sausages. He wore a thick old coat, once black, now an indeterminate gray. The snow on his boots had not entirely melted.

"Perhaps. The end of the world is a strange concept. The world is always ending, and the end is always being averted, by love or foolishness or just plain old dumb luck.

"Ah well. It's too late now: The Elder Gods have chosen their vessels. When the moon rises . . ."

A thin trickle of drool came from one corner of his mouth, oozed down in a thread of silver to his collar. Something scuttled from his collar into the shadows of his coat.

"Yeah? What happens when the moon rises?"

The man in the armchair stirred, opened two little eyes, red and swollen, and blinked them in waking.

"I dreamed I had many mouths," he said, his new voice oddly small and breathy for such a huge man. "I dreamed every mouth was opening and closing independently. Some mouths were talking, some whispering, some eating, some waiting in silence."

He looked around, wiped the spittle from the corner of his mouth, sat back in the chair, blinking puzzledly. "Who are you?"

"I'm the guy who rents this office," I told him.

He belched suddenly, loudly. "I'm sorry," he said in his breathy voice, and lifted himself heavily from the armchair. He was shorter than I was, when he was standing. He looked me up and down blearily. "Silver bullets," he pronounced after a short pause. "Old-fashioned remedy."

"Yeah," I told him. "That's so obvious—must be why I didn't think of it. Gee, I could just kick myself. I really could."

"You're making fun of an old man," he told me.

"Not really. I'm sorry. Now, out of here. Some of us have work to do."

He shambled out. I sat down in the swivel chair at the desk by the window and discovered, after some minutes, through trial and error, that if I swiveled the chair to the left, it fell off its base.

So I sat still and waited for the dusty black telephone on my desk to ring while the light slowly leaked away from the winter sky.

Ring.

A man's voice: *Had I thought about aluminum siding?* I put down the phone.

There was no heating in the office. I wondered how long the fat man had been asleep in the armchair.

Twenty minutes later the phone rang again. A crying woman implored me to help her find her five-year-old daughter, missing since last night, stolen from her bed. The family dog had vanished, too.

I don't do missing children, I told her. *I'm sorry: too many bad memories.* I put down the telephone, feeling sick again.

It was getting dark now, and, for the first time since I had been in Innsmouth, the neon sign across the street flicked on. It told me that MADAME EZEKIEL performed TAROT READINGS AND PALMISTRY.

Red neon stained the falling snow the color of new blood.

Armageddon is averted by small actions. That's the way it was. That's the way it always has to be.

The phone rang a third time. I recognized the voice; it was the aluminum siding man again. "You know," he said chattily, "transformation from man to animal and back being, by definition, impossible, we need to look for other solutions. Depersonalization, obviously, and likewise some form of projection. Brain damage? Perhaps. Pseudoneurotic schizophrenia? Laughably so. Some cases have been treated with intravenous thioridazine hydrochloride."

"Successfully?"

He chuckled. "That's what I like. A man with a sense of humor. I'm sure we can do business."

"I told you already. I don't need aluminum siding."

"Our business is more remarkable than that and of far greater importance. You're new in town, Mr. Talbot. It would be a pity if we found ourselves at, shall we say, loggerheads?"

"You can say whatever you like, pal. In my book you're just another adjustment, waiting to be made."

"We're ending the world, Mr. Talbot. The Deep Ones will rise out of their ocean graves and eat the moon like a ripe plum."

"Then I won't ever have to worry about full moons anymore, will I?"

"Don't try to cross us," he began, but I growled at him, and he fell silent.

Outside my window the snow was still falling.

Across Marsh Street, in the window directly opposite mine, the most beautiful woman I had ever seen stood in the ruby glare of her neon sign, and she stared at me.

She beckoned with one finger.

I put down the phone on the aluminum siding man for the second time that afternoon, and went downstairs, and crossed the street at something close to a run; but I looked both ways before I crossed.

She was dressed in silks. The room was lit only by candles and stank of incense and patchouli oil.

She smiled at me as I walked in, beckoned me over to her seat by the window. She was playing a card game with a tarot deck, some version of solitaire. As I reached her, one elegant hand swept up the cards, wrapped them in a silk scarf, placed them gently in a wooden box.

The scents of the room made my head pound. I hadn't eaten anything today, I realized; perhaps that was what was making me lightheaded. I sat down across the table from her, in the candlelight.

She extended her hand and took my hand in hers.

She stared at my palm, touched it, softly, with her forefinger.

"Hair?" She was puzzled.

"Yeah, well. I'm on my own a lot." I grinned. I had hoped it was a friendly grin, but she raised an eyebrow at me anyway.

"When I look at you," said Madame Ezekiel, "this is what I see. I see the eye of a man. Also I see the eye of a wolf. In the eye of a man I see honesty, decency, innocence. I see an upright man who walks on the square. And in the eye of a wolf I see a groaning and a growling, night howls and cries, I see a monster running with blood-flecked spittle in the darkness of the borders of the town."

"How can you see a growl or a cry?"

She smiled. "It is not hard," she said. Her accent was not American. It was Russian, or Maltese, or Egyptian perhaps. "In the eye of the mind we see many things."

Madame Ezekiel closed her green eyes. She had remarkably long eyelashes; her skin was pale, and her black hair was never still—it drifted gently around her head, in the silks, as if it were floating on distant tides.

"There is a traditional way," she told me. "A way to wash off a bad shape. You stand in running water, in clear spring water, while eating white rose petals."

"And then?"

"The shape of darkness will be washed from you."

"It will return," I told her, "with the next full of the moon."

"So," said Madame Ezekiel, "once the shape is washed from you, you open your veins in the running water. It will sting mightily, of course. But the river will carry the blood away."

She was dressed in silks, in scarves and cloths of a hundred different colors, each bright and vivid, even in the muted light of the candles.

Her eyes opened.

"Now," she said, "the tarot." She unwrapped her deck from the black silk scarf that held it, passed me the cards to shuffle. I fanned them, riffed and bridged them.

"Slower, slower," she said. "Let them get to know you. Let them love you, like . . . like a woman would love you."

I held them tightly, then passed them back to her.

She turned over the first card. It was called *The Warwolf.* It showed darkness and amber eyes, a smile in white and red.

Her green eyes showed confusion. They were the green of emeralds. "This is not a card from my deck," she said and turned over the next card. "What did you do to my cards?"

"Nothing, ma'am. I just held them. That's all."

The card she had turned over was *The Deep One.* It showed something green and faintly octopoid. The thing's mouths—if they were indeed mouths and not tentacles—began to writhe on the card as I watched.

She covered it with another card, and then another, and another. The rest of the cards were blank pasteboard.

"Did you do that?" She sounded on the verge of tears.

"No."

"Go now," she said.

"But—"

"*Go.*" She looked down, as if trying to convince herself I no longer existed.

I stood up, in the room that smelled of incense and candlewax, and looked out of her window, across the street. A light flashed briefly in my office window. Two men with flashlights were walking around. They opened the empty filing cabinet, peered around, then took up their positions, one in the armchair, the other behind the door, waiting for me to return. I smiled to my-self. It was cold and inhospitable in my office, and with any luck they would wait there for hours until they finally decided I wasn't coming back.

So I left Madame Ezekiel turning over her cards, one by one, staring at them as if that would make the pictures return; and I went downstairs and walked back down Marsh Street until I reached the bar.

The place was empty now; the barman was smoking a cigarette, which he stubbed out as I came in.

"Where are the chess fiends?"

"It's a big night for them tonight. They'll be down at the bay. Let's see. You're a Jack Daniel's? Right?"

"Sounds good."

He poured it for me. I recognized the thumbprint from the last time I had the glass. I picked up the volume of Tennyson poems from the bar top.

"Good book?"

The fox-haired barman took his book from me, opened it, and read:

"Below the thunders of the upper deep;
Far, far beneath in the abysmal sea,
His ancient dreamless, uninvaded sleep
The Kraken sleepeth . . ."

I'd finished my drink. "So? What's your point?"

He walked around the bar, took me over to the window. "See? Out there?"

He pointed toward the west of the town, toward the cliffs. As I stared a bonfire was kindled on the cliff tops; it flared and began to burn with a copper-green flame.

"They're going to wake the Deep Ones," said the barman. "The stars and the planets and the moon are all in the right places. It's time. The dry lands will sink, and the seas shall rise . . ."

" 'For the world shall be cleansed with ice and floods, and I'll thank you to keep to your own shelf in the refrigerator,' " I said.

"Sorry?"

"Nothing. What's the quickest way to get up to those cliffs?"

"Back up Marsh Street. Hang a left at the Church of Dagon till you reach Manuxet Way, then just keep on going." He pulled a coat off the back of the door and put it on. "C'mon. I'll walk you up there. I'd hate to miss any of the fun."

"You sure?"

"No one in town's going to be drinking tonight." We stepped out, and he locked the door to the bar behind us.

It was chilly in the street, and fallen snow blew about the ground like white mists. From street level, I could no longer tell if Madame Ezekiel was in her den above her neon sign or if my guests were still waiting for me in my office.

We put our heads down against the wind, and we walked.

Over the noise of the wind I heard the barman talking to himself:

"Winnow with giant arms the slumbering green," he was saying.

"There hath he lain for ages and will lie

Battening upon huge seaworms in his sleep,

Until the latter fire shall heat the deep;

Then once by men and angels to be seen,

In roaring he shall rise . . ."

He stopped there, and we walked on together in silence with blown snow stinging our faces.

And on the surface die, I thought, but said nothing out loud.

Twenty minutes' walking and we were out of Innsmouth. Manuxet Way stopped when we left the town, and it became a narrow dirt path, partly covered with snow and ice, and we slipped and slid our way up it in the darkness.

The moon was not yet up, but the stars had already begun to come out. There were so many of them. They were sprinkled like diamond dust and crushed sapphires across the night sky. You can see so many stars from the seashore, more than you could ever see back in the city.

At the top of the cliff, behind the bonfire, two people were waiting—one huge and fat, one much smaller. The barman left my side and walked over to stand beside them, facing me.

"Behold," he said, "the sacrificial wolf." There was now an oddly familiar quality to his voice.

I didn't say anything. The fire was burning with green flames, and it lit the three of them from below: classic spook lighting.

"Do you know why I brought you up here?" asked the barman, and I knew then why his voice was familiar: it was the voice of the man who had attempted to sell me aluminum siding.

"To stop the world ending?"

He laughed at me then.

The second figure was the fat man I had found asleep in my office chair. "Well, if you're going to get eschatalogical about it . . ." he murmured in a voice deep enough to rattle walls. His eyes were closed. He was fast asleep.

The third figure was shrouded in dark silks and smelled of patchouli oil. It held a knife. It said nothing.

"This night," said the barman, "the moon is the moon of the Deep Ones. This night are the stars configured in the shapes and patterns of the dark old times. This night, if we call them, they will come. If our sacrifice is worthy. If our cries are heard."

The moon rose, huge and amber and heavy, on the other side of the bay, and a chorus of low croaking rose with it from the ocean far beneath us.

Moonlight on snow and ice is not daylight, but it will do. And my eyes were getting sharper with the moon: in the cold waters men like frogs were surfacing and submerging in a slow water dance. Men like frogs, and women, too: it seemed to me that I could see my landlady down there, writhing and croaking in the bay with the rest of them.

It was too soon for another change; I was still exhausted from the night before; but I felt strange under that amber moon.

"Poor wolf-man," came a whisper from the silks. "All his dreams have come to this: a lonely death upon a distant cliff."

I will dream if I want to, I said, *and my death is my own affair.* But I was unsure if I had said it out loud.

Senses heighten in the moon's light; I heard the roar of the ocean still, but now, overlaid on top of it, I could hear each wave rise and crash; I heard the splash of the frog people; I heard the drowned whispers of the dead in the bay; I heard the creak of green wrecks far beneath the ocean.

Smell improves, too. The aluminum siding man was human, while the fat man had other blood in him.

And the figure in the silks . . .

I had smelled her perfume when I wore man-shape. Now I could smell something else, less heady, beneath it. A smell of decay, of putrefying meat and rotten flesh.

The silks fluttered. She was moving toward me. She held the knife.

"Madame Ezekiel?" My voice was roughening and coarsening. Soon I would lose it all. I didn't understand what was happening, but the moon was rising higher and higher, losing its amber color and filling my mind with its pale light.

"Madame Ezekiel?"

"You deserve to die," she said, her voice cold and low. "If only for what you did to my cards. They were old."

"I don't die," I told her. " 'Even a man who is pure in heart, and says his prayers by night.' Remember?"

"It's bullshit," she said. "You know what the oldest way to end the curse of the werewolf is?"

"No."

The bonfire burned brighter now; burned with the green of the world beneath the sea, the green of algae and of slowly drifting weed; burned with the color of emeralds.

"You simply wait till they're in human shape, a whole month away from another change; then you take the sacrificial knife and you kill them. That's all."

I turned to run, but the barman was behind me, pulling my arms, twisting my wrists up into the small of my back. The knife glinted pale silver in the moonlight. Madame Ezekiel smiled.

She sliced across my throat.

Blood began to gush and then to flow. And then it slowed and stopped . . .

—*The pounding in the front of my head, the pressure in the back. All a roiling change a how-wow-row-now change a red wall coming toward me from the night*
—*I tasted stars dissolved in brine, fizzy and distant and salt*
—*my fingers prickled with pins and my skin was lashed with tongues of flame my eyes were topaz I could taste the night*

My breath steamed and billowed in the icy air.

I growled involuntarily, low in my throat. My forepaws were touching the snow.

I pulled back, tensed, and sprang at her.

There was a sense of corruption that hung in the air, like a mist, surrounding me. High in my leap, I seemed to pause, and something burst like a soap bubble . . .

I was deep, deep in the darkness under the sea, standing on all fours on a slimy rock floor at the entrance of some kind of citadel built of enormous rough-hewn stones. The stones gave off a pale glow-in-the-dark light; a ghostly luminescence, like the hands of a watch.

A cloud of black blood trickled from my neck.

She was standing in the doorway in front of me. She was now six, maybe seven feet high. There was flesh on her skeletal bones, pitted and gnawed, but the silks were weeds, drifting in the cold water, down there in the dreamless deeps. They hid her face like a slow green veil.

There were limpets growing on the upper surfaces of her arms and on the flesh that hung from her ribcage.

I felt like I was being crushed. I couldn't think anymore.

She moved toward me. The weed that surrounded her head shifted. She had a face like the stuff you don't want to eat in a sushi counter, all suckers and spines and drifting anemone fronds; and somewhere in all that I knew she was smiling.

I pushed with my hind legs. We met there, in the deep, and we struggled. It was so cold, so dark. I closed my jaws on her face and felt something rend and tear.

It was almost a kiss, down there in the abysmal deep . . .

I LANDED SOFTLY on the snow, a silk scarf locked between my jaws. The other scarves were fluttering to the ground. Madame Ezekiel was nowhere to be seen.

The silver knife lay on the ground in the snow. I waited on all fours in the moonlight, soaking wet. I shook myself, spraying the brine about. I heard it hiss and spit when it hit the fire.

I was dizzy and weak. I pulled the air deep into my lungs. Down, far below, in the bay, I could see the frog people hanging on the surface of the sea like dead things; for a handful of seconds, they drifted back and forth on the tide, then they twisted and leapt, and each by each they *plop-plopped* down into the bay and vanished beneath the sea.

There was a scream. It was the fox-haired bartender, the pop-eyed aluminum siding salesman, and he was staring at the night sky, at the clouds that were drifting in, covering the stars, and he was screaming. There was rage and there was frustration in that cry, and it scared me.

He picked up the knife from the ground, wiped the snow from the handle with his fingers, wiped the blood from the blade with his coat. Then he looked across at me. He was crying. "You bastard," he said. "What did you do to her?"

I would have told him I didn't do anything to her, that she was still on guard far beneath the ocean, but I couldn't talk anymore, only growl and whine and howl.

He was crying. He stank of insanity and of disappointment. He raised the knife and ran at me, and I moved to one side.

Some people just can't adjust even to tiny changes. The barman stumbled past me, off the cliff, into nothing.

In the moonlight blood is black, not red, and the marks he left on the cliff side as he fell and bounced and fell were smudges of black and dark gray. Then, finally, he lay still on the icy rocks at the base of the cliff until an arm reached out from the sea and dragged him, with a slowness that was almost painful to watch, under the dark water.

A hand scratched the back of my head. It felt good.

"What was she? Just an avatar of the Deep Ones, sir. An eidolon, a manifestation, if you will, sent up to us from the uttermost deeps to bring about the end of the world."

I bristled.

"No, it's over—for now. You disrupted her, sir. And the ritual is most specific. Three of us must stand together and call the sacred names while innocent blood pools and pulses at our feet."

I looked up at the fat man and whined a query. He patted me on the back of the neck sleepily.

"Of course she doesn't love you, boy. She hardly even exists on this plane in any material sense."

The snow began to fall once more. The bonfire was going out.

"Your change tonight, incidentally, I would opine, is a direct result of the selfsame celestial configurations and lunar forces that made tonight such a perfect night to bring back my old friends from Underneath . . ."

He continued talking in his deep voice, and perhaps he was telling me important things. I'll never know, for the appetite was growing inside me, and his words had lost all but the shadow of any meaning; I had no further interest in the sea or the cliff-top or the fat man.

There were deer running in the woods beyond the meadow: I could smell them on the winter's night's air.

And I was, above all things, hungry.

I WAS NAKED when I came to myself again, early the next morning, a half-eaten deer next to me in the snow. A fly crawled across its eye, and its tongue lolled out of its dead mouth, making it look comical and pathetic, like an animal in a newspaper cartoon.

The snow was stained a fluorescent crimson where the deer's belly had been torn out.

My face and chest were sticky and red with the stuff. My throat was scabbed and scarred, and it stung; by the next full moon, it would be whole once more.

The sun was a long way away, small and yellow, but the sky was blue and cloudless, and there was no breeze. I could hear the roar of the sea some distance away.

I was cold and naked and bloody and alone. *Ah well*, I thought, *it happens to all of us in the beginning. I just get it once a month.*

I was painfully exhausted, but I would hold out until I found a deserted barn or a cave; and then I was going to sleep for a couple of weeks.

A hawk flew low over the snow toward me with something dangling from its talons. It hovered above me for a heartbeat, then dropped a small gray squid in the snow at my feet and flew upward. The flaccid thing lay there, still and silent and tentacled in the bloody snow.

I took it as an omen, but whether good or bad I couldn't say and I didn't really care anymore; I turned my back to the sea, and on the shadowy town of Innsmouth, and began to make my way toward the city.

DON'T ASK JACK

1995

NOBODY KNEW WHERE the toy had come from, which great-grandparent or distant aunt had owned it before it was given to the nursery.

It was a box, carved and painted in gold and red. It was undoubtedly attractive and, or so the grown-ups maintained, quite valuable—perhaps even an antique. The latch, unfortunately, was rusted shut, and the key had been lost, so the Jack could not be released from his box. Still, it was a remarkable box, heavy and carved and gilt.

The children did not play with it. It sat at the bottom of the old wooden toy box, which was the same size and age as a pirate's treasure chest, or so the children thought. The Jack-in-the-Box was buried beneath dolls and trains, clowns and paper stars and old conjuring tricks, and crippled marionettes with their strings irrevocably tangled, with dressing-up clothes (here the tatters of a long-ago wedding dress, there a black silk hat, crusted with age and time) and costume jewelry, broken hoops and tops and hobbyhorses. Under them all was Jack's box.

The children did not play with it. They whispered among themselves, alone in the attic nursery. On gray days when the wind howled about the house and rain rattled the slates and pattered down the eaves, they told each other stories about Jack, although they had never seen him. One claimed that Jack was an evil wizard, placed in the box as punishment for crimes too awful to describe; another (I am certain that it must have been one of the girls) maintained that Jack's box was Pandora's Box and he had been placed in the box as guardian to prevent the bad things inside it from coming out once more. They would not even touch the box, if they could help it, although when, as happened from time to time, an adult would comment on the absence of that sweet old Jack-in-the-Box, and retrieve it from the chest, and place it in a position of honor on the mantelpiece, then the children would pluck up their courage and, later, hide it away once more in the darkness.

The children did not play with the Jack-in-the-Box. And when they grew up and left the great house, the attic nursery was closed up and almost forgotten.

Almost, but not entirely. For each of the children, separately, remembered walking alone in the moon's blue light, on his or her own bare feet, up to the nursery. It was almost like sleepwalking, feet soundless on the wood of the stairs, on the threadbare nursery carpet. Remembered opening the treasure chest, pawing through the dolls and the clothes and pulling out the box.

And then the child would touch the catch, and the lid would open, slow as a sunset, and the music would begin to play, and Jack came out. Not with a pop and a bounce: he was no spring-heeled Jack. But deliberately, intently, he would rise from the box and motion to the child to come closer, closer, and smile.

And there in the moonlight, he told them each things they could never quite remember, things they were never able entirely to forget.

The oldest boy died in the Great War. The youngest, after their parents died, inherited the house, although it was taken from him when he was found in the cellar one night with cloths and paraffin and matches, trying to burn the great house to the ground. They took him to the madhouse, and perhaps he is there still.

The other children, who had once been girls and now were women, declined, each and every one, to return to the house in which they had grown up; and the windows of the house were boarded up, and the doors were all locked with huge iron keys, and the sisters visited it as often as they visited their eldest brother's grave, or the sad thing that had once been their younger brother, which is to say, never.

Years have passed, and the girls are old women, and owls and bats have made their homes in the old attic nursery, rats build their nests among the forgotten toys. The creatures gaze uncuriously at the faded prints on the wall, and stain the remnants of the carpet with their droppings.

And deep within the box within the box, Jack waits and smiles, holding his secrets. He is waiting for the children. He can wait forever.

EXCERPT FROM *NEVERWHERE*

1996

RICHARD WAITED AGAINST the wall, next to Door. She said very little; she chewed her fingernails, ran her hands through her reddish hair until it was sticking up in all directions, then tried to push it back down again. She was certainly unlike anyone he had ever known. When she noticed him looking at her she shrugged and shimmied down further into her layers of clothes, deeper into her leather jacket. Her face looked out at the world from inside the jacket. The expression on her face made Richard think of a beautiful homeless child he had seen, the previous winter, behind Covent Garden: he had not been certain whether it was a girl or a boy. Its mother was begging, pleading with the passersby for coins to feed the child, and the infant that she carried in her arms. But the child stared out at the world, and said nothing, although it must have been cold and hungry. It just stared.

Hunter stood by Door, looking back and forth down the platform. The Marquis had told them where to wait, and had slipped away. From somewhere, Richard heard a baby begin to cry. The Marquis slipped out of an exit-only door, and walked toward them. He was chewing on a piece of candy.

"Having fun?" asked Richard. A train was coming toward them, its approach heralded by a gust of warm wind.

"Just taking care of business," said the Marquis. He consulted the piece of paper, and his watch. He pointed to a place on the platform. "This should be the Earl's Court train. Stand behind me here, you three." Then, as the Underground train—a rather boring-looking, normal train, Richard was disappointed to observe—rumbled and rattled its way into the station, the Marquis leaned across Richard, and said to Door, "My lady? There is something that perhaps I should have mentioned earlier."

She turned her odd-colored eyes on him. "Yes?"

"Well," he said, "the Earl might not be *entirely* pleased to see me."

The train slowed down and stopped. The carriage that had pulled up in front of Richard was quite empty: its lights were turned off; it was bleak and empty and dark. From time to time Richard had noticed carriages like this one, locked and shadowy, on Tube trains, and had wondered what purpose they served. The other doors on the train hissed open, and passengers got on and got off. The doors of the darkened carriage remained closed. The Marquis drummed on the door with his fist, an intricate rhythmic rap. Nothing happened. Richard was just wondering if the train would now pull out without them on it, when the door of the dark carriage was pushed open from the inside. It opened about six inches, and an elderly, bespectacled face peered out at them.

"Who knocks?" he said.

Through the opening, Richard could see flames burning, and people, and smoke inside the car. Through the glass in the doors, however, he still saw a dark and empty carriage. "The Lady Door," said the Marquis, smoothly, "and her companions."

The door slid open all the way, and they were in Earl's Court.

❊✖❊

There was straw scattered on the floor, over a layer of rushes. There was an open log fire, sputtering and blazing in a large fireplace. There were a few chickens, strutting and pecking on the floor. There were seats with hand-embroidered cushions on them, and there were tapestries covering the windows and the doors.

Richard stumbled forward as the train lurched out of the station.

He reached out, grabbed hold of the nearest person, and regained his balance. The nearest person happened to be a short, gray, elderly man-at-arms, who would have looked, Richard decided, exactly like a recently retired government employee, were it not for the tin hat, the surcoat, the rather clumsily knitted chain mail, and the spear; instead he looked like a recently retired government employee who had, somewhat against his will, been dragooned into his local amateur dramatic society, where he had been forced to play a man-at-arms.

The little gray man blinked shortsightedly at Richard, as Richard grabbed him, and then he said, lugubriously, "Sorry about that."

"My fault," said Richard.

"I know," said the man.

An enormous Irish wolfhound padded down the aisle, and stopped beside a lute player, who sat on the floor picking at a gladsome melody in a desultory fashion. The wolfhound glared at Richard, snorted with disdain, then lay down and went to sleep. At the far end of the carriage an elderly falconer, with a hooded falcon on his wrist, was exchanging pleasantries with a small knot of damozels of a certain age. Some passengers obviously stared at the four travelers; others, just as obviously, ignored them. It was, Richard realized, as if someone had taken a small medieval court and put it, as best they could, in one carriage of an Underground train.

A herald raised his bugle to his lips and played a tuneless blast, as an immense, elderly man, in a huge fur-lined dressing gown and carpet slippers, staggered through the connecting door to the next compartment, his arm resting on the shoulder of a jester in shabby motley. The old man was larger than life in every way: he wore an eye patch over his left eye, which had the effect of making him look slightly helpless and unbalanced, like a one-eyed hawk. There were fragments of food in his red-gray beard, and what appeared to be pajama pants were visible at the bottom of his shabby fur gown.

That, thought Richard, correctly, *must be the Earl.*

The Earl's jester, an elderly man with a pinched, humorless mouth and a painted face, looked like he had fled from a life as an all-round entertainer near the bottom of the bill in the Victorian music halls a hundred years before. He led the Earl to a throne-like carved wooden seat, in which, a trifle unsteadily, the Earl sat down. The wolfhound got up, padded down the length of the carriage, and settled itself at the Earl's slippered feet.

Earl's Court, thought Richard. *Of course.* And then he began to wonder whether there was a Baron in Barons Court tube station, or a Raven in Ravenscourt, or . . .

The little old man-at-arms coughed asthmatically, and said, "Right then, you lot. State your business." Door stepped forward. She held her head up high, suddenly seeming taller and more at ease than Richard had previously seen her, and she said, "We seek an audience with His Grace the Earl."

The Earl called down the carriage. "What did the little girl say, Halvard?" he asked. Richard wondered if he were deaf.

Halvard, the elderly man-at-arms, shuffled around, and cupped his hand to his mouth. "They seek an audience, Your Grace," he shouted, over the rattle of the train.

The Earl pushed aside his thick fur cap and scratched his head, meditatively. He was balding underneath his cap. "They do? An audience? How splendid. Who are they, Halvard?"

Halvard turned back to them. "He wants to know who you all are. Keep it short, though. Don't go on."

"I am the Lady Door," announced Door. "The Lord Portico was my father."

The Earl brightened at this, leaned forward, peered through the smoke with his one good eye. "Did she say she was Portico's oldest girl?" he asked the jester.

"Yus, Your Grace."

The Earl beckoned to Door. "Come here," he said. "Come-come-come. Let me look at you." She walked down the swaying carriage, grabbing the thick rope straps that hung from the ceiling as she went, to keep her balance. When she stood before the Earl's wooden chair she curtseyed. He scratched at his beard, and stared at her. "We were all quite devastated to hear of your father's unfortunate—" said the Earl, and then he interrupted himself, and said, "Well, all your family, it was a . . ." And he trailed off, and said, "You know I had warmest regards for him, did a bit of business together . . . Good old

Portico . . . full of ideas . . ." He stopped. Then he tapped the jester on the shoulder, and whispered, in a querulous boom, loud enough that it could be heard easily over the noise of the train, "Go and make jokes at them, Tooley. Earn your keep."

The Earl's fool staggered up the aisle with an arthritic mop and a rheumatic mow. He stopped in front of Richard. "And who might you be?" he asked.

"Me?" said Richard. "Um. Me? My name? It's Richard. Richard Mayhew."

"*Me?*" squeaked the Fool, in an elderly, rather theatrical imitation of Richard's Scottish accent. "*Me?* Um. *Me?* La, nuncle. 'Tis not a man, but a mooncalf." The courtiers sniggered, dustily.

"And I," de Carabas told the jester, with a blinding smile, "call myself the Marquis de Carabas." The Fool blinked.

"De Carabas the thief?" asked the jester. "De Carabas the body snatcher? De Carabas the traitor?" He turned to the courtiers around them. "But this cannot be de Carabas. For why? Because de Carabas has long since been banished from the Earl's presence. Perhaps it is instead a strange new species of *stoat*, who grew particularly large." The courtiers tittered uneasily, and a low buzz of troubled conversation began. The Earl said nothing, but his lips were pressed together tightly, and he had begun to tremble.

"I am called Hunter," said Hunter to the jester.

The courtiers were silent then. The jester opened his mouth, as if he were going to say something, and then he looked at her, and he closed his mouth again. A hint of a smile played at the corner of Hunter's perfect lips. "Go on," she said. "Say something funny."

The jester stared at the trailing toes of his shoes. Then he muttered, "My hound hath no nose."

The Earl, who had been staring at the Marquis de Carabas like a slow-burning fuse, pop-eyed, white-lipped, unable to believe the evidence of his senses, now exploded to his feet, a gray-bearded volcano, an elderly berserker. His head brushed the roof of the carriage. He pointed at the Marquis, and shouted, spittle flying, "I will not stand for it, I will not. Make him come forward."

Halvard waggled a gloomy spear at the Marquis, who sauntered to the front of the train, until he stood, beside Door, in front of the Earl's throne. The wolfhound growled in the back of its throat.

"You," said the Earl, stabbing the air with a huge, knotted finger. "I know you, de Carabas. I haven't forgotten. I may be old, but I haven't forgotten."

The Marquis bowed. "Might I remind Your Grace," he said, urbanely, "that we had a deal? I negotiated the peace treaty between your people and the Raven's Court. And in return you agreed to provide a little favor." *So there is a raven's court,* thought Richard. He wondered what it was like.

"A little favor?" said the Earl. He turned a deep beetroot color. "Is that what you call it? I lost a dozen men to your foolishness in the retreat from White City. I lost an eye."

"And if you don't mind my saying so, Your Grace," said the Marquis, graciously, "that is a very fetching patch. It sets off your face perfectly."

"I swore . . . ," fulminated the Earl, beard bristling, "I swore . . . that if you ever set foot in my domain I would . . ." He trailed off. Shook his head, confused, and forgetful. Then he continued. "It'll come back to me. I do not forget."

"He might not be entirely pleased to see you?" whispered Door to de Carabas.

"Well, he's not," he muttered back.

Door stepped forward once more. "Your Grace," she said, loudly, clearly, "de Carabas is here with me as my guest and my companion. For the fellowship there has ever been between your family and mine, for the friendship between my father and—"

"He abused my hospitality," boomed the Earl. "I swore that . . . if he ever again entered my domain I would have him gutted and dried . . . like, like something that's been . . . um . . . gutted, first, and then . . . um . . . dried . . ."

"Perchance—a kipper, my lord?" suggested the jester.

The Earl shrugged. "It is of no matter. Guards, seize him." And they did. While neither of the guards would ever see sixty again, each of them was holding a crossbow, pointed at the Marquis, and their hands did not tremble, neither with age nor fear. Richard looked at Hunter. She seemed untroubled by this, watching it almost with amusement, like someone watching a piece of drama played out for their benefit.

Door folded her arms, and stood taller, putting her head back, raising her pointed chin. She looked less like a ragged street pixie; more like someone used to getting her own way. The opal eyes flashed. "Your Grace, the Marquis is with me as my companion, on my quest. Our families have been friends for a long time now—"

"Yes. They have," interrupted the Earl, helpfully. "Hundreds of years. Hundreds and hundreds. Knew your grandfather, too. Funny old fellow. Bit vague," he confided.

"But I am forced to say that I will take an act of violence against my companion as an act of aggression against myself and my house." The girl stared up at the old man. He towered over her. They stood for some moments, frozen. He tugged on his red and gray beard, agitatedly, then he thrust out his lower lip like a small child. "I will not have him here," he said.

The Marquis took out the golden pocket watch he had found in Portico's study. He examined it, carelessly. Then he turned to Door, and said, as if none of the events around them had occurred, "My lady, I will obviously be of more use to you off this train than on. And I have other avenues to explore."

"No," she said. "If you go, we all go."

"I don't think so," said the Marquis. "Hunter will look after you as long as you stay in London Below. I'll meet you at the next market. Don't do anything too stupid in the meantime." The train was coming into a station.

Door fixed the Earl with her look: there was something more ancient and powerful in those huge opal-colored eyes in their pale heart-shaped face than her young years would have seemed to allow. Richard noticed that the room fell quiet whenever she spoke. "Will you let him go in peace, Your Grace?" she asked.

The Earl ran his hands over his face, rubbed his good eye and his eye patch, then looked back at her. "Just make him go," said the Earl. He looked at the Marquis. "Next time"—he ran a thick old finger across his Adam's apple—"kipper."

The Marquis bowed low. "I'll see myself out," he said to the guards, and stepped toward the open door. Halvard raised his crossbow, pointed it toward the Marquis' back. Hunter reached out her hand, and pushed the end of the crossbow back down toward the floor. The Marquis stepped onto the platform, turned and waved an ironic good-bye flourish at them. The door hissed closed behind him.

The Earl sat down on his huge chair at the end of the carriage. He said nothing. The train rattled and lurched through the dark tunnel. "Where are my manners?" muttered the Earl to himself. He looked at them with one staring eye. Then he said it again, in a desperate boom that Richard could feel in his stomach, like a bass drum beat. *"Where are my manners?"* He motioned one of the elderly men-at-arms to him. "They will be hungry after their journey, Dagvard. Thirsty too, I shouldn't wonder."

"Yes, Your Grace."

"Stop the train!" called the Earl. The doors hissed open and Dagvard scuttled off onto a platform. Richard watched the people on the platform. No one came into their carriage. No one seemed to notice that anything was at all odd, or in any way unusual.

Dagvard walked over to a vending machine on the side of the platform. He took off his helmet. Then he rapped, with one mailed glove, on the side of the machine. "Orders from the Earl," he said. "Choc'lits." A ratcheting whirr came from deep in the guts of the machine, and it began to spit out dozens of Cadbury Fruit and Nut chocolate bars, one after another. Dagvard held his metal helmet below the opening to catch them. The doors began to close. Halvard put the handle of his pike between the doors, and they opened again, and began bumping open and shut on the pike handle. *"Please stand clear of the doors,"* said a loudspeaker voice. *"The train cannot leave until the doors are all closed."*

The Earl was staring at Door lopsidedly, with his one good eye. "So. What brings you here to me?" he asked.

She licked her lips. "Well, indirectly, Your Grace, my father's death."

He nodded, slowly. "Yes. You seek vengeance. Quite right too." He coughed, then recited, in a basso profundo, *"Brave the battling blade, flashes the furious fire, steel sword sheathed in hated heart, crimsons the . . . the . . . something. Yes."*

"Vengeance?" Door thought for a moment. "Yes. That was what my father said. But I just want to understand what happened, and to protect myself. My family had no enemies." Dagvard staggered back onto the train then, his helmet filled with chocolate bars and cans of Coke; the doors were permitted to close, and the train moved off once more.

RICHARD WAS HANDED a bar of vending-machine-sized Cadbury Fruit and Nut chocolate, and a large silver goblet, ornamented around the rim with what appeared to Richard to be sapphires. The goblet was filled with Coca-Cola. The jester, whose name appeared to be Tooley, cleared his throat, loudly. "I would like to propose a toast to our guests," he said. "A child, a bravo, a fool. May they each get what they deserve."

"Which one am I?" whispered Richard to Hunter.

"The fool, of course," she said.

"In the old days," said Halvard dismally, after sipping his Coke, "we had wine. I prefer wine. It's not as sticky."

"Do all the machines just give you things like that?" asked Richard.

"Oh yes," said the old man. "They listen to the Earl, y'see. He rules the Underground. The bit with the trains. He's lord of the Central, the Circle, the Jubilee, the Victorious, the Bakerloo—well, all of them except the Underside Line."

"What's the Underside Line?" asked Richard.

Halvard shook his head, and pursed his lips. Hunter brushed Richard's shoulder with her fingers. "Remember what I told you about the shepherds of Shepherd's Bush?"

"You said I didn't want to meet them, and there were some things I was probably better off not knowing."

"Good," she said. "So now you can add the Underside Line to the list of things you're better off not knowing."

Door came back down the carriage toward them. She was smiling. "The Earl's agreed to help us," she said. "Come on. He's meeting us in the library." Richard was almost proud of the way he didn't say "What library?" or point out that you couldn't put a library on a train. Instead he followed Door toward the Earl's empty throne, and round the back of it, and through the connecting door behind it, and into the library. It was a huge stone room, with a high wooden ceiling. Each wall was covered with shelves. Each shelf was laden with objects: there were books, yes. But the shelves were filled with a host of other things: tennis rackets, hockey sticks, umbrellas, a spade, a notebook computer, a wooden leg, several mugs, dozens of shoes, pairs of binoculars, a small log, six glove puppets, a lava lamp, various CDs, records (LPs, 45s and 78s), cassette tapes and eight-tracks, dice, toy cars, assorted pairs of dentures, watches, flashlights, four garden gnomes of assorted sizes (two fishing, one of them mooning, the last smoking a cigar), piles of newspapers, magazines, grimoires, three-legged stools, a box of cigars, a plastic nodding-head Alsatian, socks . . . The room was a tiny empire of lost property.

"This is his real domain," muttered Hunter. "Things lost. Things forgotten."

There were windows, set in the stone wall. Through them, Richard could see the rattling darkness and the passing lights of the Underground tunnels. The Earl was sitting on the floor with his legs splayed, patting the wolfhound and scratching it underneath the chin. The jester stood beside him, looking embarrassed. The Earl clambered to his feet when he saw them. His forehead creased. "Ah. There you are. Now, there was a reason I asked you here, it'll come to me . . ." He tugged at his red-gray beard, a tiny gesture from such a huge man.

"The Angel Islington, Your Grace," said Door, politely.

"Oh yes. Your father had a lot of ideas, you know. Asked me about them. I don't trust change. I sent him to Islington." He stopped. Blinked his one eye. "Did I tell you this already?"

"Yes, Your Grace. And how can *we* get to Islington?"

He nodded as if she had said something profound. "Only once by the quick way. After that you have to go the long way down. Dangerous."

Door said, patiently, "And the quick way is?"

"No, no. Need to be an opener to use it. Only good for Portico's family." He rested a huge hand on her shoulder. Then his hand slid up to her cheek. "Better off staying here with me. Keep an old man warm at night, eh?" He leered at her, and touched her tangle of hair with his old fingers. Hunter took a step toward Door. Door gestured with her hand: *No. Not yet.*

Door looked up at the Earl, and said, "Your Grace, I *am* Portico's oldest daughter. How do I get to the Angel Islington?" Richard found himself amazed that Door was able to keep her temper in the face of the Earl's obviously losing battle with temporal drift.

The Earl winked his single eye in a solemn blink: an old hawk, his head tipped on one side. Then he took his hand from her hair. "So you are. So you are. Portico's daughter. How is your dear father? Keeping well, I hope. Fine man. Good man."

"How do we get to the Angel Islington?" said Door, but there was a tremble in her voice.

"Hmm? Use the Angelus, of course."

Richard found himself imagining the Earl sixty, eighty, five hundred years ago: a mighty warrior, a cunning strategist, a great lover of women, a fine friend, a terrifying foe. There was still the wreckage of that man in there somewhere. That was what made him so terrible, and so sad. The Earl fumbled on the shelves, moving pens and pipes and peashooters, little gargoyles and dead leaves. Then, like an aged cat stumbling on a mouse, he seized a small, rolled-up scroll, and handed it to the girl. "Here y'go, lassie," said the Earl. "All in here. And I suppose we'd better drop you off where you need to go."

"You'll drop us off?" asked Richard. "In a train?"

The Earl looked around for the source of the sound, focused on Richard, and smiled enormously. "Oh, think nothing of it," he boomed. "Anything for Portico's daughter." Door clutched the scroll tightly, triumphantly.

Richard could feel the train beginning to slow, and he, and Door, and Hunter were led out of the stone room, and back into the carriage. Richard peered out at the platform, as they slowed down.

"Excuse me. What station is this?" he asked. The train had stopped, facing one of the station signs: BRITISH MUSEUM, it said. Somehow, this was an oddity too many. He could accept the Mind the Gap Thing, and the Earl's Court, and even the strange library. But damn it, like all Londoners, he knew his Tube map, and this was going too far. "There isn't a British Museum station," said Richard, firmly.

"There isn't?" boomed the Earl. "Then, mm, then you must be very careful as you get off the train." And he guffawed, delightedly, and tapped his jester on the shoulder. "Hear that, Tooley? I am as funny as you are."

The jester smiled as bleak a smile as ever was seen. "My sides are splitting, my ribs are cracking, and my mirth is positively uncontainable, Your Grace," he said.

The doors hissed open. Door smiled up at the Earl. "Thank you," she said.

"Off, off," said the vast old man, shooing Door and Richard and Hunter out of the warm, smoky carriage onto the empty platform. And then the doors closed, and the train moved away, and Richard found himself staring at a sign which, no matter how many times he blinked—nor even if he looked away from it and looked back suddenly to take it by surprise—still obstinately persisted in saying:

BRITISH MUSEUM

THE DAUGHTER OF OWLS

1996

From *The Remaines of Gentilisme & Judaisme* by John Aubrey, R.S.S. (1686–87), (pp 262–263)

I HAD THIS STORY from my friend Edmund Wyld Esq. who had it from Mr Farringdon, who said it was old in his time. In the Town of Dymton a newly-born girl was left one night on the steps of the Church, where the Sexton found her there the next morning, and she had hold of a curious thing, *viz.:*—yᵉ pellet of an Owle, which when crumbled showed the usual composition of an Hoot-owles's pellet, thus: skin and teeth and small bones.

The old wyves of the Town sayed as follows: that the girl was the daughter of Owls, and that she should be burnt to death, for she was not borne of woeman. Notwithstanding, wiser Heads and Greybeards prevayled, and the babe was taken to the Convent (for this was shortly after the Papish times, and the Convent had been left empty, for the Townefolke thought it was a place of Dyvills and such, and Hoot-owles and Screach-owles and many bats did make theyr homes in the tower) and there she was left, and one of the wyves of the Towne each day went to the Convent and fed the babe &c.

It was prognostickated that yᵉ babe would dye, wᶜʰ she did not doe: instead she grew year onn and about until she was a mayd of xiiii summers. She was the prittiest thing you ever did see, a fine young lass, who spent her dais and nights behind high stone walls with no-one never to see, but a Towne wyfe who came every morn. One market daie the good-wife talked too loudly of the girl's pritty-ness, & also that she could not speak, for she had never learned the manner of it.

The men of Dymton, the grey-beards and the young men, spoke to-gether, saying: if wee were to visit her, who would know? (Mean-ing by *visit*, that they did intend to ravish her.)

It was putt about thus: that ye menfolk would go a-hunting all in a company, when the Moon would be fulle: wch it beeing, they crep't one by one from theyr houses and mett outside the Convent, & the Reeve of Dymton unlocked the gate & one by one they went in. They found her hiding in the cellar, being startled by ye noyse.

The Maid was more pritty even than they had heard: her hair was red wch was uncommon, & she wore but a white shift, & when she saw them she was much afrayd for she had never seen no Men be-fore, save only the woemen who brought her vittles: & she stared at them with huge eyes & she uttered small cries, as if she were implor-ing them nott to hurte her.

The Townefolk merely laughed for they meant mischiefe & were wicked cruel men: & they came at her in the moon's light.

Then the girl began a-screaching & a-wayling, but that did not stay them from theyr purpos. & the grate window went dark & the light of the moon was blockt: & there was the sound of mighty wings; but the men did not see it as they were intent on theyr ravishment.

The folk of Dymton in theyr beds that night dreamed of hoots & screaches and howells: & of grate birds: & they dreamed that they were become littel mice & ratts.

On the morrow, when the sun was high, the goodwives of the Town went through Dymton a-hunting High & Low for theyr Hus-bands & theyr Sonnes; w^ch, coming to the Convent, they fownd, on the Cellar stones, ye pellets of owles: & in the pellets they discovered hair & buckles & coins, & small bones: & also a quantity of straw upon the floor.

And the men of Dymton was none of them seen agane. However, for some years therafter, some said they saw yᵉ Maid in high Places, like the highest Oke trees & steeples &c; this being always in the dusk, and at night, & no-one could rightly sware, if it were her or no.

(She was a white figure:—but Mʳ E. Wyld could not remember him rightly whether folk said that she wore cloathes or was naked.)

The truth of it I know not, but it is a merrye tale & one wᶜʰ I write down here.

THE GOLDFISH POOL
AND OTHER STORIES

1996

I T WAS RAINING when I arrived in L.A., and I felt myself surrounded by a hundred old movies.

There was a limo driver in a black uniform waiting for me at the airport, holding a white sheet of cardboard with my name misspelled neatly upon it.

"I'm taking you straight to your hotel, sir," said the driver. He seemed vaguely disappointed that I didn't have any real luggage for him to carry, just a battered overnight bag stuffed with T-shirts, underwear, and socks.

"Is it far?"

He shook his head. "Maybe twenty-five, thirty minutes. You ever been to L.A. before?"

"No."

"Well, what I always say, L.A. is a thirty-minute town. Wherever you want to go, it's thirty minutes away. No more."

He hauled my bag into the boot of the car, which he called the trunk, and opened the door for me to climb into the back.

"So where you from?" he asked, as we headed out of the airport into the slick wet neon-spattered streets.

"England."

"England, eh?"

"Yes. Have you ever been there?"

"Nosir. I've seen movies. You an actor?"

"I'm a writer."

He lost interest. Occasionally he would swear at other drivers, under his breath.

He swerved suddenly, changing lanes. We passed a four-car pileup in the lane we had been in.

"You get a little rain in this city, all of a sudden everybody forgets how to drive," he told me. I burrowed further into the cushions in the back. "You get rain in England, I hear." It was a statement, not a question.

"A little."

"More than a little. Rains every day in England." He laughed. "And thick fog. Real thick, thick fog."

"Not really."

"Whaddaya mean, no?" he asked, puzzled, defensive. "I've seen movies."

We sat in silence then, driving through the Hollywood rain; but after a while he said: "Ask them for the room Belushi died in."

"Pardon?"

"Belushi. John Belushi. It was your hotel he died in. Drugs. You heard about that?"

"Oh. Yes."

"They made a movie about his death. Some fat guy, didn't look nothing like him. But nobody tells the real truth about his death. Y'see, he wasn't alone. There were two other guys with him. Studios didn't want any shit. But you're a limo driver, you hear things."

"Really?"

"Robin Williams and Robert De Niro. They were there with him. All of them going doo-doo on the happy dust."

The hotel building was a white mock-gothic chateau. I said goodbye to the chauffeur and checked in; I did not ask about the room in which Belushi had died.

I walked out to my chalet through the rain, my overnight bag in my hand, clutching the set of keys that would, the desk clerk told me, get me through the various doors and gates. The air smelled of wet dust and, curiously enough, cough mixture. It was dusk, almost dark.

Water splashed everywhere. It ran in rills and rivulets across the courtyard. It ran into a small fishpond that jutted out from the side of a wall in the courtyard.

I walked up the stairs into a dank little room. It seemed a poor kind of a place for a star to die.

The bed seemed slightly damp, and the rain drummed a maddening beat on the air-conditioning system.

I watched a little television—the rerun wasteland: *Cheers* segued imperceptibly into *Taxi,* which flickered into black and white and became *I Love Lucy*—then stumbled into sleep.

I dreamed of drummers intermittently drumming, only thirty minutes away.

The phone woke me. "Hey-hey-hey-hey. You made it okay then?"

"Who is this?"

"It's Jacob at the studio. Are we still on for breakfast, hey-hey?"

"Breakfast . . . ? "

"No problem. I'll pick you up at your hotel in thirty minutes. Reservations are already made. No problems. You got my messages?"

"I . . ."

"Faxed 'em through last night. See you."

The rain had stopped. The sunshine was warm and bright: proper Hollywood light. I walked up to the main building, walking on a carpet of crushed eucalyptus leaves—the cough medicine smell from the night before.

They handed me an envelope with a fax in it—my schedule for the next few days, with messages of encouragement and faxed handwritten doodles in the margin, saying things like *"This is Gonna be a Blockbuster!"* and *"Is this Going to be a Great Movie or What!"* The fax was signed by Jacob Klein, obviously the voice on the phone. I had never before had any dealings with a Jacob Klein.

A small red sports car drew up outside the hotel. The driver got out and waved at me. I walked over. He had a trim, pepper-and-salt beard, a smile that was almost bankable, and a gold chain around his neck. He showed me a copy of *Sons of Man.*

He was Jacob. We shook hands.

"Is David around? David Gambol?"

David Gambol was the man I'd spoken to earlier on the phone when arranging the trip. He wasn't the producer. I wasn't certain quite what he was. He described himself as "attached to the project."

"David's not with the studio anymore. I'm kind of running the project now, and I want you to know I'm really psyched. Hey-hey."

"That's good?"

We got in the car. "Where's the meeting?" I asked.

He shook his head. "It's not a meeting," he said. "It's a breakfast." I looked puzzled. He took pity on me. "A kind of premeeting meeting," he explained.

We drove from the hotel to a mall somewhere half an hour away while Jacob told me how much he enjoyed my book and how delighted he was that he'd become attached to the project. He said it was his idea to have me put up in the hotel—"Give you the kind of Hollywood experience you'd never get at the Four Seasons or Ma Maison, right?"—and asked me if I was staying in the chalet in which John Belushi had died. I told him I didn't know, but that I rather doubted it.

"You know who he was with, when he died? They covered it up, the studios."

"No. Who?"

"Meryl and Dustin."

"This is Meryl Streep and Dustin Hoffman we're talking about?"

"Sure."

"How do you know this?"

"People talk. It's Hollywood. You know?"

I nodded as if I did know, but I didn't.

PEOPLE TALK ABOUT books that write themselves, and it's a lie. Books don't write themselves. It takes thought and research and backache and notes and more time and more work than you'd believe.

Except for *Sons of Man*, and that one pretty much wrote itself.

The irritating question they ask us—us being writers—is:

"Where do you get your ideas?"

And the answer is: Confluence. Things come together. The right ingredients and suddenly: *Abracadabra!*

It began with a documentary on Charles Manson I was watching more or less by accident (it was on a videotape a friend lent me after a couple of things I *did* want to watch): there was footage of Manson, back when he was first arrested, when people thought he was innocent and that it was the government picking on the hippies. And up on the screen was Manson—a charismatic, good-looking, messianic orator. Someone you'd crawl barefoot into Hell for. Someone you could kill for.

The trial started; and, a few weeks into it, the orator was gone, replaced by a shambling, apelike gibberer, with a cross carved into its forehead. Whatever the genius was was no longer there. It was gone. But it had been there.

The documentary continued: a hard-eyed ex-con who had been in prison with Manson, explaining, "Charlie Manson? Listen, Charlie was a joke. He was a nothing. We laughed at him. You know? He was a nothing!"

And I nodded. There was a time before Manson was the charisma king, then. I thought of a benediction, something given, that was taken away.

I watched the rest of the documentary obsessively. Then, over a black-and-white still, the narrator said something. I rewound, and he said it again.

I had an idea. I had a book that wrote itself.

The thing the narrator had said was this: that the infant children Manson had fathered on the women of The Family were sent to a variety of children's homes for adoption, with court-given surnames that were certainly not Manson.

And I thought of a dozen twenty-five-year-old Mansons. Thought of the charisma-thing descending on all of them at the same time. Twelve young Mansons, in their glory, gradually being pulled toward L.A. from all over the world. And a Manson daughter trying desperately to stop them from coming together and, as the back cover blurb told us, "realizing their terrifying destiny."

I wrote *Sons of Man* at white heat: it was finished in a month, and

I sent it to my agent, who was surprised by it ("Well, it's not like your other stuff, dear," she said helpfully), and she sold it after an auction—my first—for more money than I had thought possible. (My other books, three collections of elegant, allusive and elusive ghost stories, had scarcely paid for the computer on which they were written.)

And then it was bought—prepublication—by Hollywood, again after an auction. There were three or four studios interested: I went with the studio who wanted me to write the script. I knew it would never happen, knew they'd never come through. But then the faxes began to spew out of my machine, late at night—most of them enthusiastically signed by one Dave Gambol; one morning I signed five copies of a contract thick as a brick; a few weeks later my agent reported the first check had cleared and tickets to Hollywood had arrived, for "preliminary talks." It seemed like a dream.

The tickets were business class. It was the moment I saw the tickets were business class that I knew the dream was real.

I went to Hollywood in the bubble bit at the top of the jumbo jet, nibbling smoked salmon and holding a hot-off-the-presses hardback of *Sons of Man*.

SO. BREAKFAST.

They told me how much they loved the book. I didn't quite catch anybody's name. The men had beards or baseball caps or both; the women were astoundingly attractive, in a sanitary sort of way.

Jacob ordered our breakfast, and paid for it. He explained that the meeting coming up was a formality.

"It's your book we love," he said. "Why would we have bought your book if we didn't want to make it? Why would we have hired *you* to write it if we didn't want the specialness you'd bring to the project. The *you-ness*."

I nodded, very seriously, as if literary me-ness was something I had spent many hours pondering.

"An idea like this. A book like this. You're pretty unique."

"One of the uniquest," said a woman named Dina or Tina or possibly Deanna.

I raised an eyebrow. "So what am I meant to do at the meeting?"

"Be receptive," said Jacob. "Be positive."

THE DRIVE TO the studio took about half an hour in Jacob's little red car. We drove up to the security gate, where Jacob had an argument with the guard. I gathered that he was new at the studio and had not yet been issued a permanent studio pass.

Nor, it appeared, once we got inside, did he have a permanent parking place. I still do not understand the ramifications of this: from what he said, parking places had as much to do with status at the studio as gifts from the emperor determined one's status in the court of ancient China.

We drove through the streets of an oddly flat New York and parked in front of a huge old bank.

Ten minutes' walk, and I was in a conference room, with Jacob and all the people from breakfast, waiting for someone to come in. In the flurry I'd rather missed who the someone was and what he or she did. I took out my copy of my book and put it in front of me, a talisman of sorts.

Someone came in. He was tall, with a pointy nose and a pointy chin, and his hair was too long—he looked like he'd kidnapped someone much younger and stolen their hair. He was an Australian, which surprised me.

He sat down.

He looked at me.

"Shoot," he said.

I looked at the people from the breakfast, but none of them were looking at me—I couldn't catch anyone's eye. So I began to talk: about the book, about the plot, about the end, the showdown in the L.A. nightclub, where the good Manson girl blows the rest of them up. Or thinks she does. About my idea for having one actor play all the Manson boys.

"Do you believe this stuff?" It was the first question from the Someone.

That one was easy. It was one I'd already answered for at least two dozen British journalists.

"Do I believe that a supernatural power possessed Charles Manson for a while and is even now possessing his many children? No. Do I believe that something strange was happening? I suppose I must do. Perhaps it was simply that, for a brief while, his madness was in step with the madness of the world outside. I don't know."

"Mm. This Manson kid. He could be Keanu Reeves?"

God, no, I thought. Jacob caught my eye and nodded desperately. "I don't see why not," I said. It was all imagination anyway. None of it was real.

"We're cutting a deal with his people," said the Someone, nodding thoughtfully.

They sent me off to do a treatment for them to approve. And by *them,* I understood they meant the Australian Someone, although I was not entirely sure.

Before I left, someone gave me $700 and made me sign for it: two weeks' per diem.

I SPENT TWO days doing the treatment. I kept trying to forget the book, and structure the story as a film. The work went well. I sat in the little room and typed on a notebook computer the studio had sent down for me, and printed out pages on the bubble-jet printer the studio sent down with it. I ate in my room.

Each afternoon I would go for a short walk down Sunset Boulevard. I would walk as far as the "almost all-nite" bookstore, where I would buy a newspaper. Then I would sit outside in the hotel courtyard for half an hour, reading a newspaper. And then, having had my ration of sun and air, I would go back into the dark, and turn my book back into something else.

There was a very old black man, a hotel employee, who would walk across the courtyard each day with almost painful slowness and water the plants and inspect the fish. He'd grin at me as he went past, and I'd nod at him.

On the third day I got up and walked over to him as he stood by the fish pool, picking out bits of rubbish by hand: a couple of coins and a cigarette packet.

"Hello," I said.

"Suh," said the old man.

I thought about asking him not to call me sir, but I couldn't think of a way to put it that might not cause offense. "Nice fish."

He nodded and grinned. "Ornamental carp. Brought here all the way from China."

We watched them swim around the little pool.

"I wonder if they get bored."

He shook his head. "My grandson, he's an ichthyologist, you know what that is?"

"Studies fishes."

"Uh-huh. He says they only got a memory that's like thirty seconds long. So they swim around the pool, it's always a surprise to them, going 'I never been here before.' They meet another fish they known for a hundred years, they say, 'Who are you, stranger?' "

"Will you ask your grandson something for me?" The old man nodded. "I read once that carp don't have set life spans. They don't age like we do. They die if they're killed by people or predators or disease, but they don't just get old and die. Theoretically they could live forever."

He nodded. "I'll ask him. It sure sounds good. These three—now, this one, I call him Ghost, he's only four, five years old. But the other two, they came here from China back when I was first here."

"And when was that?"

"That would have been, in the Year of Our Lord Nineteen Hundred and Twenty-four. How old do I look to you?"

I couldn't tell. He might have been carved from old wood. Over fifty and younger than Methuselah. I told him so.

"I was born in 1906. God's truth."

"Were you born here, in L.A.?"

He shook his head. "When I was born, Los Angeles wasn't nothin' but an orange grove, a long way from New York." He sprinkled fish food on the surface of the water. The three fish bobbed up, pale-white silvered ghost carp, staring at us, or seeming to, the O's of their mouths continually opening and closing, as if they were talking to us in some silent, secret language of their own.

I pointed to the one he had indicated. "So he's Ghost, yes?"

"He's Ghost. That's right. That one under the lily—you can see his tail, there, see?—he's called Buster, after Buster Keaton. Keaton was staying here when we got the older two. And this one's our Princess."

Princess was the most recognizable of the white carp. She was a pale cream color, with a blotch of vivid crimson along her back, setting her apart from the other two.

"She's lovely."

"She surely is. She surely is all of that."

He took a deep breath then and began to cough, a wheezing cough that shook his thin frame. I was able then, for the first time, to see him as a man of ninety.

"Are you all right?"

He nodded. "Fine, fine, fine. Old bones," he said. "Old bones."

We shook hands, and I returned to my treatment and the gloom.

I PRINTED OUT the completed treatment, faxed it off to Jacob at the studio.

The next day he came over to the chalet. He looked upset.

"Everything okay? Is there a problem with the treatment?"

"Just shit going down. We made this movie with . . ." and he named a well-known actress who had been in a few successful films a couple of years before. "Can't lose, huh? Only she is not as young as she was, and she insists on doing her own nude scenes, and that's not a body anybody wants to see, believe me.

"So the plot is, there's this photographer who is persuading women to take their clothes off for him. Then he *shtups* them. Only no one believes he's doing it. So the chief of police—played by Ms. Lemme Show the World My Naked Butt—realizes that the only way she can arrest him is if she pretends to be one of the women. So she sleeps with him. Now, there's a twist . . ."

"She falls in love with him?"

"Oh. Yeah. And then she realizes that women will always be imprisoned by male images of women, and to prove her love for him, when the police come to arrest the two of them she sets fire to all the photographs and dies in the fire. Her clothes burn off first. How does that sound to you?"

"Dumb."

"That was what we thought when we saw it. So we fired the director and recut it and did an extra day's shoot. Now she's wearing a wire when they make out. And when she starts to fall in love with him, she finds out that he killed her brother. She has a dream in which her clothes burn off, then she goes out with the SWAT team to try to bring him in. But he gets shot by her little sister, who he's also been *shtupping*."

"Is it any better?"

He shakes his head. "It's junk. If she'd let us use a stand-in for the nude sequences, maybe we'd be in better shape."

"What did you think of the treatment?"

"What?"

"My treatment? The one I sent you?"

"Sure. That treatment. We loved it. We all loved it. It was great. Really terrific. We're all really excited."

"So what's next?"

"Well, as soon as everyone's had a chance to look it over, we'll get together and talk about it."

He patted me on the back and went away, leaving me with nothing to do in Hollywood.

I decided to write a short story. There was an idea I'd had in England before I'd left. Something about a small theater at the end of a pier. Stage magic as the rain came down. An audience who couldn't tell the difference between magic and illusion, and to whom it would make no difference if every illusion was real.

THAT AFTERNOON, ON my walk, I bought a couple of books on Stage Magic and Victorian Illusions in the "almost all-nite" bookshop. A story, or the seed of it anyway, was there in my head, and I wanted to explore it. I sat on the bench in the courtyard and browsed through the books. There was, I decided, a specific atmosphere that I was after.

I was reading about the Pockets Men, who had pockets filled with every small object you could imagine and would produce whatever you asked on request. No illusion—just remarkable feats of organization and memory. A shadow fell across the page. I looked up.

"Hullo again," I said to the old black man.

"Suh," he said.

"Please don't call me that. It makes me feel like I ought to be wearing a suit or something." I told him my name.

He told me his: "Pious Dundas."

"Pious?" I wasn't sure that I'd heard him correctly. He nodded proudly.

"Sometimes I am, and sometimes I ain't. It's what my mamma called me, and it's a good name."

"Yes."

"So what are you doing here, suh?"

"I'm not sure. I'm meant to be writing a film, I think. Or at least, I'm waiting for them to tell me to start writing a film."

He scratched his nose. "All the film people stayed here, if I started to tell you them all now, I could talk till a week next Wednesday and I wouldn't have told you the half of them."

"Who were your favorites?"

"Harry Langdon. He was a gentleman. George Sanders. He was English, like you. He'd say, 'Ah, Pious. You must pray for my soul.' And I'd say, 'Your soul's your own affair, Mister Sanders,' but I prayed for him just the same. And June Lincoln."

"June Lincoln?"

His eyes sparkled, and he smiled. "She was the queen of the silver screen. She was finer than any of them: Mary Pickford or Lillian Gish or Theda Bara or Louise Brooks. . . . She was the finest. She had 'it.' You know what 'it' was?"

"Sex appeal."

"More than that. She was everything you ever dreamed of. You'd see a June Lincoln picture, you wanted to . . ." he broke off, waved one hand in small circles, as if he were trying to catch the missing words. "I don't know. Go down on one knee, maybe, like a knight in shinin' armor to the queen. June Lincoln, she was the best of them. I told my grandson about her, he tried to find something for the VCR, but no go. Nothing out there anymore. She only lives in the heads of old men like me." He tapped his forehead.

"She must have been quite something."

He nodded.

"What happened to her?"

"She hung herself. Some folks said it was because she wouldn't have been able to cut the mustard in the talkies, but that ain't true: she had a voice you'd remember if you heard it just once. Smooth and dark, her voice was, like an Irish coffee. Some say she got her heart broken by a man, or by a woman, or that it was gambling, or gangsters, or booze. Who knows? They were wild days."

"I take it that you must have heard her talk."

He grinned. "She said, 'Boy, can you find what they did with my wrap?' and when I come back with it, then she said, 'You're a fine one, boy.' And the man who was with her, he said, 'June, don't tease the help' and she smiled at me and gave me five dollars and said 'He don't mind, do you, boy?' and I just shook my head. Then she made the thing with her lips, you know?"

"A *moue*?"

"Something like that. I felt it here." He tapped his chest. "Those lips. They could take a man apart."

He bit his lower lip for a moment, and focused on forever. I wondered where he was, and when. Then he looked at me once more.

"You want to see her lips?"

"How do you mean?"

"You come over here. Follow me."

"What are we . . . ? " I had visions of a lip print in cement, like the handprints outside Grauman's Chinese Theatre.

He shook his head, and raised an old finger to his mouth. *Silence.*

I closed the books. We walked across the courtyard. When he reached the little fish-pool, he stopped.

"Look at the Princess," he told me.

"The one with the red splotch, yes?"

He nodded. The fish reminded me of a Chinese dragon: wise and pale. A ghost fish, white as old bone, save for the blotch of scarlet on its back—an inch-long double-bow shape. It hung in the pool, drifting, thinking.

"That's it," he said. "On her back. See?"

"I don't quite follow you."

He paused and stared at the fish.

"Would you like to sit down?" I found myself very conscious of Mr. Dundas's age.

"They don't pay me to sit down," he said, very seriously. Then he said, as if he were explaining something to a small child, "It was like there were gods in those days. Today, it's all television: small heroes. Little people in the boxes. I see some of them here. Little people.

"The stars of the old times: They was giants, painted in silver light, big as houses . . . and when you met them, they were *still* huge. People believed in them.

"They'd have parties here. You worked here, you saw what went on. There was liquor, and weed, and goings-on you'd hardly credit. There was this one party . . . the film was called *Hearts of the Desert*. You ever heard of it?"

I shook my head.

"One of the biggest movies of 1926, up there with *What Price Glory* with Victor McLaglen and Dolores del Río and *Ella Cinders* starring Colleen Moore. You heard of them?" I shook my head again.

"You ever heard of Warner Baxter? Belle Bennett?"

"Who were they?"

"Big, big stars in 1926." He paused for a moment. *"Hearts of the Desert.* They had the party for it here, in the hotel, when it wrapped. There was wine and beer and whiskey and gin—this was Prohibition days, but the studios kind of owned the police force, so they looked the other way; and there was food, and a deal of foolishness; Ronald Colman was there and Douglas Fairbanks—the father, not the son—and all the cast and the crew; and a jazz band played over there where those chalets are now.

"And June Lincoln was the toast of Hollywood that night. She was the Arab princess in the film. Those days, Arabs meant passion and lust. These days . . . well, things change.

"I don't know what started it all. I heard it was a dare or a bet; maybe she was just drunk. I thought she was drunk. Anyhow, she got up, and the band was playing soft and slow. And she walked over here, where I'm standing right now, and she plunged her hands right into this pool. She was laughing, and laughing, and laughing . . .

"Miss Lincoln picked up the fish—reached in and took it, both hands she took it in—and she picked it up from the water, and then she held it in front of her face.

"Now, I was worried, because they'd just brought these fish in from China and they cost two hundred dollars apiece. That was before I was looking after the fish, of course. Wasn't me that'd lose it from my wages. But still, two hundred dollars was a whole lot of money in those days.

"Then she smiled at all of us, and she leaned down and she kissed it, slow like, on its back. It didn't wriggle or nothin', it just lay in her hand, and she kissed it with her lips like red coral, and the people at the party laughed and cheered.

"She put the fish back in the pool, and for a moment it was as if it didn't want to leave her—it stayed by her, nuzzling her fingers. And then the first of the fireworks went off, and it swum away.

"Her lipstick was red as red as red, and she left the shape of her lips on the fish's back. —There. Do you see?"

Princess, the white carp with the coral red mark on her back, flicked a fin and continued on her eternal series of thirty-second journeys around the pool. The red mark did look like a lip print.

He sprinkled a handful of fish food on the water, and the three fish bobbed and gulped to the surface.

I walked back in to my chalet, carrying my books on old illusions. The phone was ringing: it was someone from the studio. They wanted to talk about the treatment. A car would be there for me in thirty minutes.

"Will Jacob be there?"

But the line was already dead.

THE MEETING WAS with the Australian Someone and his assistant, a bespectacled man in a suit. His was the first suit I'd seen so far, and his spectacles were a vivid blue. He seemed nervous.

"Where are you staying?" asked the Someone. I told him.

"Isn't that where Belushi . . . ? "

"So I've been told."

He nodded. "He wasn't alone, when he died."

"No?"

He rubbed one finger along the side of his pointy nose. "There were a couple of other people at the party. They were both directors, both as big as you could get at that point. You don't need names. I found out about it when I was making the last Indiana Jones film."

An uneasy silence. We were at a huge round table, just the three of us, and we each had a copy of the treatment I had written in front of us. Finally I said:

"What did you think of it?"

They both nodded, more or less in unison.

And then they tried, as hard as they could, to tell me they hated it while never saying anything that might conceivably upset me. It was a very odd conversation.

"We have a problem with the third act," they'd say, implying vaguely that the fault lay neither with me nor with the treatment, nor even with the third act, but with them.

They wanted the people to be more sympathetic. They wanted sharp lights and shadows, not shades of gray. They wanted the heroine to be a hero. And I nodded and took notes.

At the end of the meeting I shook hands with the Someone, and the assistant in the blue-rimmed spectacles took me off through the corridor maze to find the outside world and my car and my driver.

As we walked, I asked if the studio had a picture anywhere of June Lincoln.

"Who?" His name, it turned out, was Greg. He pulled out a small notebook and wrote something down in it with a pencil.

"She was a silent screen star. Famous in 1926."

"Was she with the studio?"

"I have no idea," I admitted. "But she was famous. Even more famous than Marie Prevost."

"Who?"

" 'A winner who became a doggie's dinner.' One of the biggest stars of the silent screen. Died in poverty when the talkies came in and was eaten by her dachshund. Nick Lowe wrote a song about her."

"Who?"

" '*I knew the bride when she used to rock and roll.*' Anyway, June Lincoln. Can someone find me a photo?"

He wrote something more down on his pad. Stared at it for a moment. Then wrote down something else. Then he nodded.

We had reached the daylight, and my car was waiting.

"By the way," he said, "you should know that he's full of shit."

"I'm sorry?"

"Full of shit. It wasn't Spielberg and Lucas who were with Belushi. It was Bette Midler and Linda Ronstadt. It was a coke orgy. Everybody knows that. He's full of shit. And he was just a junior studio accountant for chrissakes on the Indiana Jones movie. Like it was his movie. Asshole."

We shook hands. I got in the car and went back to the hotel.

THE TIME DIFFERENCE caught up with me that night, and I woke, utterly and irrevocably, at 4 A.M.

I got up, peed, then I pulled on a pair of jeans (I sleep in a T-shirt) and walked outside.

I wanted to see the stars, but the lights of the city were too bright, the air too dirty. The sky was a dirty, starless yellow, and I thought of all the constellations I could see from the English countryside, and I felt, for the first time, deeply, stupidly homesick.

I missed the stars.

I WANTED TO work on the short story or to get on with the film script. Instead, I worked on a second draft of the treatment.

I took the number of Junior Mansons down to five from twelve and made it clearer from the start that one of them, who was now male, wasn't a bad guy and the other four most definitely were.

They sent over a copy of a film magazine. It had the smell of old pulp paper about it, and was stamped in purple with the studio name and with the word ARCHIVES underneath. The cover showed John Barrymore, on a boat.

The article inside was about June Lincoln's death. I found it hard to read and harder still to understand: it hinted at the forbidden vices that led to her death, that much I could tell, but it was as if it were

hinting in a cipher to which modern readers lacked any key. Or perhaps, on reflection, the writer of her obituary knew nothing and was
hinting into the void.

More interesting—at any rate, more comprehensible—were the
photos. A full-page, black-edged photo of a woman with huge eyes
and a gentle smile, smoking a cigarette (the smoke was airbrushed
in, to my way of thinking very clumsily: had people ever been taken
in by such clumsy fakes?); another photo of her in a staged clinch
with Douglas Fairbanks; a small photograph of her standing on the
running board of a car, holding a couple of tiny dogs.

She was, from the photographs, not a contemporary beauty. She
lacked the transcendence of a Louise Brooks, the sex appeal of a Mar-
ilyn Monroe, the sluttish elegance of a Rita Hayworth. She was a
twenties starlet as dull as any other twenties starlet. I saw no mystery
in her huge eyes, her bobbed hair. She had perfectly made-up cupid's
bow lips. I had no idea what she would have looked like if she had
been alive and around today.

Still, she was real; she had lived. She had been worshipped and
adored by the people in the movie palaces. She had kissed the fish,
and walked in the grounds of my hotel seventy years before: no time
in England, but an eternity in Hollywood.

I WENT IN to talk about the treatment. None of the people I had
spoken to before were there. Instead, I was shown in to see a very
young man in a small office, who never smiled and who told me how
much he loved the treatment and how pleased he was that the studio
owned the property.

He said he thought the character of Charles Manson was particularly cool, and that maybe—"once he was fully dimensionalized"—
Manson could be the next Hannibal Lecter.

"But. Um. Manson. He's real. He's in prison now. His people killed
Sharon Tate."

"Sharon Tate?"

"She was an actress. A film star. She was pregnant and they killed
her. She was married to Polanski."

"*Roman* Polanski?"

"The director. Yes."

He frowned. "But we're putting together a deal with Polanski."

"That's good. He's a good director."

"Does he know about this?"

"About what? The book? Our film? Sharon Tate's death?"

He shook his head: none of the above. "It's a three-picture deal. Julia Roberts is semiattached to it. You say Polanski doesn't know about this treatment?"

"No, what I said was—"

He checked his watch.

"Where are you staying?" he asked. "Are we putting you up somewhere good?"

"Yes, thank you," I said. "I'm a couple of chalets away from the room in which Belushi died."

I expected another confidential couple of stars: to be told that John Belushi had kicked the bucket in company with Julie Andrews and Miss Piggy the Muppet. I was wrong.

"Belushi's dead?" he said, his young brow furrowing. "Belushi's not dead. We're doing a picture with Belushi."

"This was the brother," I told him. "The brother died, years ago."

He shrugged. "Sounds like a shithole," he said. "Next time you come out, tell them you want to stay in the Bel Air. You want us to move you out there now?"

"No, thank you," I said. "I'm used to it where I am."

"What about the treatment?" I asked.

"Leave it with us."

I FOUND MYSELF becoming fascinated by two old theatrical illusions I found in my books: "The Artist's Dream" and "The Enchanted Casement." They were metaphors for something, of that I was certain; but the story that ought to have accompanied them was not yet there. I'd write first sentences that did not make it to first paragraphs, first paragraphs that never made it to first pages. I'd write them on the computer, then exit without saving anything.

I sat outside in the courtyard and stared at the two white carp and the one scarlet and white carp. They looked, I decided, like Escher drawings of fish, which surprised me, as it had never occurred to me there was anything even slightly realistic in Escher's drawings.

Pious Dundas was polishing the leaves of the plants. He had a bottle of polisher and a cloth.

"Hi, Pious."

"Suh."

"Lovely day."

He nodded, and coughed, and banged his chest with his fist, and nodded some more.

I left the fish, sat down on the bench.

"Why haven't they made you retire?" I asked. "Shouldn't you have retired fifteen years ago?"

He continued polishing. "Hell no, I'm a landmark. They can *say* that all the stars in the sky stayed here, but *I* tell folks what Cary Grant had for breakfast."

"Do you remember?"

"Heck no. But *they* don't know that." He coughed again. "What you writing?"

"Well, last week I wrote a treatment for this film. And then I wrote another treatment. And now I'm waiting for . . . something."

"So what *are* you writing?"

"A story that won't come right. It's about a Victorian magic trick called 'The Artist's Dream.' An artist comes onto the stage, carrying a big canvas, which he puts on an easel. It's got a painting of a woman on it. And he looks at the painting and despairs of ever being a real painter. Then he sits down and goes to sleep, and the painting comes to life, steps down from the frame and tells him not to give up. To keep fighting. He'll be a great painter one day. She climbs back into the frame. The lights dim. Then he wakes up, and it's a painting again . . ."

". . . AND THE other illusion," I told the woman from the studio, who had made the mistake of feigning interest at the beginning of the meeting, "was called 'The Enchanted Casement.' A window hangs in the air and faces appear in it, but there's no one around. I think I can get a strange sort of parallel between the enchanted casement and probably television: seems like a natural candidate, after all."

"I like *Seinfeld*," she said. "You watch that show? It's about nothing. I mean, they have whole episodes about nothing. And I liked Garry Shandling before he did the new show and got mean."

"The illusions," I continued, "like all great illusions, make us question the nature of reality. But they also frame—pun, I suppose, intentionalish—the issue of what entertainment would turn into. Films before they had films, telly before there was ever TV."

She frowned. "Is this a movie?"

"I hope not. It's a short story, if I can get it to work."

"So let's talk about the movie." She flicked through a pile of notes. She was in her mid-twenties and looked both attractive and sterile. I wondered if she was one of the women who had been at the breakfast on my first day, a Deanna or a Tina.

She looked puzzled at something and read: *"I Knew the Bride When She Used to Rock and Roll?"*

"He wrote that down? That's not this film."

She nodded. "Now, I have to say that some of your treatment is kind of . . . *contentious*. The Manson thing . . . well, we're not sure it's going to fly. Could we take him out?"

"But that's the whole point of the thing. I mean, the book is called *Sons of Man;* it's about Manson's children. If you take him out, you don't have very much, do you? I mean, this is the book you bought." I held it up for her to see: my talisman. "Throwing out Manson is like, I don't know, it's like ordering a pizza and then complaining when it arrives because it's flat, round, and covered in tomato sauce and cheese."

She gave no indication of having heard anything I had said. She asked, "What do you think about *When We Were Badd* as a title? Two *d*'s in Badd."

"I don't know. For this?"

"We don't want people to think that it's religious. *Sons of Man.* It sounds like it might be kind of anti-Christian."

"Well, I do kind of imply that the power that possesses the Manson children is in some way a kind of demonic power."

"You do?"

"In the book."

She managed a pitying look, of the kind that only people who know that books are, at best, properties on which films can be loosely based, can bestow on the rest of us.

"Well, I don't think the studio would see that as appropriate," she said.

"Do you know who June Lincoln was?" I asked her.

She shook her head.

"David Gambol? Jacob Klein?"

She shook her head once more, a little impatiently. Then she gave me a typed list of things she felt needed fixing, which amounted to pretty much everything. The list was TO: me and a number of other people, whose names I didn't recognize, and it was FROM: Donna Leary.

I said Thank you, Donna, and went back to the hotel.

I WAS GLOOMY for a day. And then I thought of a way to redo the treatment that would, I thought, deal with all of Donna's list of complaints.

Another day's thinking, a few days' writing, and I faxed the third treatment off to the studio.

Pious Dundas brought his scrapbook over for me to look at, once he felt certain that I was genuinely interested in June Lincoln— named, I discovered, after the month and the president, born Ruth Baumgarten in 1903. It was a leatherbound old scrapbook, the size and weight of a family Bible.

She was twenty-four when she died.

"I wish you could've seen her," said Pious Dundas. "I wish some of her films had survived. She was so big. She was the greatest star of all of them."

"Was she a good actress?"

He shook his head decisively. "Nope."

"Was she a great beauty? If she was, I just don't see it."

He shook his head again. "The camera liked her, that's for sure. But that wasn't it. Back row of the chorus had a dozen girls prettier'n her."

"Then what was it?"

"She was a star." He shrugged. "That's what it means to be a star."

I turned the pages: cuttings, reviewing films I'd never heard of— films for which the only negatives and prints had long ago been lost, mislaid, or destroyed by the fire department, nitrate negatives being a notorious fire hazard; other cuttings from film magazines: June Lincoln at play, June Lincoln at rest, June Lincoln on the set of *The Pawnbroker's Shirt,* June Lincoln wearing a huge fur coat—which somehow dated the photograph more than the strange bobbed hair or the ubiquitous cigarettes.

"Did you love her?"

He shook his head. "Not like you would love a woman . . ." he said.

There was a pause. He reached down and turned the pages. "And my wife would have killed me if she'd heard me say this . . ."

Another pause.

"But yeah. Skinny dead white woman. I suppose I loved her." He closed the book.

"But she's not dead to you, is she?"

He shook his head. Then he went away. But he left me the book to look at.

The secret of the illusion of "The Artist's Dream" was this: It was done by carrying the girl in, holding tight on to the back of the canvas. The canvas was supported by hidden wires, so, while the artist casually, easily, carried in the canvas and placed it on the easel, he was also carrying in the girl. The painting of the girl on the easel was arranged like a roller blind, and it rolled up or down.

"The Enchanted Casement," on the other hand, was, literally, done with mirrors: an angled mirror which reflected the faces of people standing out of sight in the wings.

Even today many magicians use mirrors in their acts to make you think you are seeing something you are not.

It was easy, when you knew how it was done.

"BEFORE WE START," he said, "I should tell you I don't read treatments. I tend to feel it inhibits my creativity. Don't worry, I had a secretary do a précis, so I'm up to speed."

He had a beard and long hair and looked a little like Jesus, although I doubted that Jesus had such perfect teeth. He was, it appeared, the most important person I'd spoken to so far. His name was John Ray, and even I had heard of him, although I was not entirely sure what he did: his name tended to appear at the beginning of films, next to words like EXECUTIVE PRODUCER. The voice from the studio that had set up the meeting told me that they, the studio, were most excited about the fact that he had "attached himself to the project."

"Doesn't the précis inhibit your creativity, too?"

He grinned. "Now, we all think you've done an amazing job. Quite stunning. There are just a few things that we have a problem with."

"Such as?"

"Well, the Manson thing. And the idea about these kids growing up. So we've been tossing around a few scenarios in the office: try this for size. There's a guy called, say, Jack Badd—two *d*'s, that was Donna's idea—"

Donna bowed her head modestly.

"They put him away for satanic abuse, fried him in the chair, and as he dies he swears he'll come back and destroy them all."

"Now, it's today, and we see these young boys getting hooked on a video arcade game called *Be Badd*. His face on it. And as they play the game he like, starts to possess them. Maybe there could be something strange about his face, a Jason or Freddy thing." He stopped, as if he were seeking approval.

So I said, "So who's making these video games?"

He pointed a finger at me and said, "You're the writer, sweetheart. You want us to do all your work for you?"

I didn't say anything. I didn't know what to say.

Think movies, I thought. *They understand movies.* I said, "But surely, what you're proposing is like doing *The Boys from Brazil* without Hitler."

He looked puzzled.

"It was a film by Ira Levin," I said. No flicker of recognition in his eyes. "*Rosemary's Baby.*" He continued to look blank. "*Sliver.*"

He nodded; somewhere a penny had dropped. "Point taken," he said. "You write the Sharon Stone part, we'll move heaven and earth to get her for you. I have an in to her people."

So I went out.

THAT NIGHT IT was cold, and it shouldn't have been cold in L.A., and the air smelled more of cough drops than ever.

An old girlfriend lived in the L.A. area and I resolved to get hold of her. I phoned the number I had for her and began a quest that took most of the rest of the evening. People gave me numbers, and I rang them, and other people gave me numbers, and I rang them, too.

Eventually I phoned a number, and I recognized her voice.

"Do you know where I am?" she said.

"No," I said. "I was given this number."

"This is a hospital room," she said. "My mother's. She had a brain hemorrhage."

"I'm sorry. Is she all right?"

"No."

"I'm sorry."

There was an awkward silence.

"How are you?" she asked.

"Pretty bad," I said.

I told her everything that had happened to me so far. I told her how I felt.

"Why is it like this?" I asked her.

"Because they're scared."

"Why are they scared? What are they scared of?"

"Because you're only as good as the last hits you can attach your name to."

"Huh?"

"If you say yes to something, the studio may make a film, and it will cost twenty or thirty million dollars, and if it's a failure, you will have your name attached to it and will lose status. If you say no, you don't risk losing status."

"Really?"

"Kind of."

"How do you know so much about all this? You're a musician, you're not in films."

She laughed wearily: "I live out here. Everybody who lives out here knows this stuff. Have you tried asking people about their screenplays?"

"No."

"Try it sometime. Ask anyone. The guy in the gas station. Any-one. They've all got them." Then someone said something to her, and she said something back, and she said, "Look, I've got to go," and she put down the phone.

I couldn't find the heater, if the room had a heater, and I was freezing in my little chalet room, like the one Belushi died in, same uninspired framed print on the wall, I had no doubt, same chilly dampness in the air.

I ran a hot bath to warm myself up, but I was even chillier when I got out.

WHITE GOLDFISH SLIDING to and fro in the water, dodging and dart-ing through the lily pads. One of the goldfish had a crimson mark on its back that might, conceivably, have been perfectly lip-shaped: the miraculous stigmata of an almost-forgotten goddess. The gray early-morning sky was reflected in the pool.

I stared at it gloomily. "You okay?"

I turned. Pious Dundas was standing next to me.

"You're up early."

"I slept badly. Too cold."

"You should have called the front desk. They'd've sent you down a heater and extra blankets."

"It never occurred to me."

His breathing sounded awkward, labored.

"You okay?"

"Heck no. I'm old. You get to my age, boy, you won't be okay ei-ther. But I'll be here when you've gone. How's work going?"

"I don't know. I've stopped working on the treatment, and I'm stuck on 'The Artist's Dream'—this story I'm doing about Victorian stage magic. It's set in an English seaside resort in the rain. With the magician performing magic on the stage, which somehow changes the audience. It touches their hearts."

He nodded, slowly. " 'The Artist's Dream' . . ." he said. "So. You see yourself as the artist or the magician?"

"I don't know," I said. "I don't think I'm either of them."

I turned to go and then something occurred to me.

"Mister Dundas," I said. "Have you got a screenplay? One you wrote?"

He shook his head.

"You *never* wrote a screenplay?"

"Not me," he said.

"Promise?"

He grinned. "I promise," he said.

I went back to my room. I thumbed through my UK hardback of *Sons of Man* and wondered that anything so clumsily written had even been published, wondered why Hollywood had bought it in the first place, why they didn't want it, now that they had bought it.

I tried to write "The Artist's Dream" some more, and failed miserably. The characters were frozen. They seemed unable to breathe, or move, or talk.

I went into the toilet, pissed a vivid yellow stream against the porcelain. A cockroach ran across the silver of the mirror.

I went back into the sitting room, opened a new document, and wrote:

I'm thinking about England in the rain,
a strange theatre on the pier: a trail
of fear and magic, memory and pain.

The fear should be of going bleak insane,
the magic should be like a fairy tale.
I'm thinking about England in the rain.

The loneliness is harder to explain—
an empty place inside me where I fail,
of fear and magic, memory and pain.

I think of a magician and a skein
of truth disguised as lies. You wear a veil.
I'm thinking about England in the rain . . .

The shapes repeat like some bizarre refrain
and here's a sword, a hand, and there's a grail
of fear and magic, memory and pain.

The wizard waves his wand and we turn pale,
tells us sad truths, but all to no avail.
I'm thinking about England, in the rain
of fear and magic, memory and pain.

I didn't know if it was any good or not, but that didn't matter. I had written something new and fresh I hadn't written before, and it felt wonderful.

I ordered breakfast from room service and requested a heater and a couple of extra blankets.

THE NEXT DAY I wrote a six-page treatment for a film called *When We Were Badd,* in which Jack Badd, a serial killer with a huge cross carved into his forehead, was killed in the electric chair and came back in a video game and took over four young men. The fifth young man defeated Badd by burning the original electric chair, which was now on display, I decided, in the wax museum where the fifth young man's girlfriend worked during the day. By night she was an exotic dancer.

The hotel desk faxed it off to the studio, and I went to bed.

I went to sleep, hoping that the studio would formally reject it and that I could go home.

IN THE THEATER of my dreams, a man with a beard and a baseball cap carried on a movie screen, and then he walked offstage. The silver screen hung in the air, unsupported.

A flickery silent film began to play upon it: a woman who came out and stared down at me. It was June Lincoln who flickered on the screen, and it was June Lincoln who walked down from the screen and sat on the edge of my bed.

"Are you going to tell me not to give up?" I asked her.

On some level I knew it was a dream. I remember, dimly, understanding why this woman was a star, remember regretting that none of her films had survived.

She was indeed beautiful in my dream, despite the livid mark which went all the way around her neck.

"Why on earth would I do that?" she asked. In my dream she smelled of gin and old celluloid, although I do not remember the last dream I had where anyone smelled of anything. She smiled, a perfect black-and-white smile. "I got out, didn't I?"

Then she stood up and walked around the room.

"I can't believe this hotel is still standing," she said. "I used to fuck here." Her voice was filled with crackles and hisses. She came back to the bed and stared at me, as a cat stares at a hole.

"Do you worship me?" she asked.

I shook my head. She walked over to me and took my flesh hand in her silver one.

"Nobody remembers anything anymore," she said. "It's a thirty-minute town."

There was something I had to ask her. "Where are the stars?" I asked. "I keep looking up in the sky, but they aren't there."

She pointed at the floor of the chalet. "You've been looking in the wrong places," she said. I had never before noticed that the floor of the chalet was a sidewalk and each paving stone contained a star and a name—names I didn't know: Clara Kimball Young, Linda Arvidson, Vivian Martin, Norma Talmadge, Olive Thomas, Mary Miles Minter, Seena Owen . . .

June Lincoln pointed at the chalet window. "And out there." The window was open, and through it I could see the whole of Hollywood spread out below me—the view from the hills: an infinite spread of twinkling multicolored lights.

"Now, aren't those better than stars?" she asked.

And they were. I realized I could see constellations in the streetlamps and the cars.

I nodded.

Her lips brushed mine.

"Don't forget me," she whispered, but she whispered it sadly, as if she knew that I would.

I woke up with the telephone shrilling. I answered it, growled a mumble into the handpiece.

"This is Gerry Quoint, from the studio. We need you for a lunch meeting."

Mumble something mumble.

"We'll send a car," he said. "The restaurant's about half an hour away."

THE RESTAURANT WAS airy and spacious and green, and they were waiting for me there.

By this point I would have been surprised if I *had* recognized any-one. John Ray, I was told over hors d'oeuvres, had "split over contract disagreements," and Donna had gone with him, "obviously."

Both of the men had beards; one had bad skin. The woman was thin and seemed pleasant.

They asked where I was staying, and, when I told them, one of the beards told us (first making us all agree that this would go no fur-ther) that a politician named Gary Hart and one of the Eagles were both doing drugs with Belushi when he died.

After that they told me that they were looking forward to the story.

I asked the question. "Is this for *Sons of Man* or *When We Were Badd?* Because," I told them, "I have a problem with the latter."

They looked puzzled.

It was, they told me, for *I Knew the Bride When She Used to Rock and Roll.* Which was, they told me, both High Concept and Feel Good. It was also, they added, Very Now, which was important in a town in which an hour ago was Ancient History.

They told me that they thought it would be a good thing if our hero could rescue the young lady from her loveless marriage, and if they could rock and roll together at the end.

I pointed out that they needed to buy the film rights from Nick Lowe, who wrote the song, and then that, no, I didn't know who his agent was.

They grinned and assured me that that wouldn't be a problem.

They suggested I turn over the project in my mind before I started on the treatment, and each of them mentioned a couple of young stars to bear in mind when I was putting together the story. And I shook hands with all of them and told them that I certainly would.

I mentioned that I thought that I could work on it best back in England.

And they said that that would be fine.

SOME DAYS BEFORE, I'd asked Pious Dundas whether anyone was with Belushi in the chalet, on the night that he died.

If anyone would know, I figured, he would.

"He died alone," said Pious Dundas, old as Methuselah, unblinking. "It don't matter a rat's ass whether there was anyone with him or not. He died alone."

IT FELT STRANGE to be leaving the hotel.

I went up to the front desk.

"I'll be checking out later this afternoon."

"Very good, sir."

"Would it be possible for you to . . . the, uh, the groundkeeper. Mister Dundas. An elderly gentleman. I don't know. I haven't seen him around for a couple of days. I wanted to say good-bye."

"To one of the groundsmen?"

"Yes."

She stared at me, puzzled. She was very beautiful, and her lipstick was the color of a blackberry bruise. I wondered whether she was waiting to be discovered.

She picked up the phone and spoke into it, quietly.

Then, "I'm sorry, sir. Mister Dundas hasn't been in for the last few days."

"Could you give me his phone number?"

"I'm sorry, sir. That's not our policy." She stared at me as she said it, letting me know that she *really* was *so* sorry . . .

"How's your screenplay?" I asked her.

"How did you know?" she asked.

"Well—"

"It's on Joel Silver's desk," she said. "My friend Arnie, he's my writing partner, and he's a courier. He dropped it off with Joel Silver's office, like it came from a regular agent or somewhere."

"Best of luck," I told her.

"Thanks," she said, and smiled with her blackberry lips.

INFORMATION HAD TWO Dundas, P's listed, which I thought was both unlikely and said something about America, or at least Los Angeles.

The first turned out to be a Ms. Persephone Dundas.

At the second number, when I asked for Pious Dundas, a man's voice said, "Who is this?"

I told him my name, that I was staying in the hotel, and that I had something belonging to Mr. Dundas.

"Mister. My grandfa's dead. He died last night."

Shock makes clichés happen for real: I felt the blood drain from my face; I caught my breath.

"I'm sorry. I liked him."

"Yeah."

"It must have been pretty sudden."

"He was old. He got a cough." Someone asked him who he was talking to, and he said nobody, then he said, "Thanks for calling."

I felt stunned.

"Look, I have his scrapbook. He left it with me."

"That old film stuff?"

"Yes."

A pause.

"Keep it. That stuff's no good to anybody. Listen, mister, I gotta run."

A click, and the line went silent.

I went to pack the scrapbook in my bag and was startled, when a tear splashed on the faded leather cover, to discover that I was crying.

I STOPPED BY the pool for the last time, to say good-bye to Pious Dundas, and to Hollywood.

Three ghost-white carp drifted, fins flicking minutely, through the eternal present of the pool.

I remembered their names: Buster, Ghost, and Princess; but there was no longer any way that anyone could have told them apart.

The car was waiting for me, by the hotel lobby. It was a thirty-minute drive to the airport, and already I was starting to forget.

THE PRICE

1997

TRAMPS AND VAGABONDS have marks they make on gateposts and trees and doors, letting others of their kind know a little about the people who live at the houses and farms they pass on their travels. I think cats must leave similar signs; how else to explain the cats who turn up at our door through the year, hungry and flea-ridden and abandoned?

We take them in. We get rid of the fleas and the ticks, feed them, and take them to the vet. We pay for them to get their shots, and, indignity upon indignity, we have them neutered or spayed.

And they stay with us: for a few months, or for a year, or forever.

Most of them arrive in summer. We live in the country, just the right distance out of town for the city dwellers to abandon their cats near us.

We never seem to have more than eight cats, rarely have less than three. The cat population of my house is currently as follows: Hermione and Pod, tabby and black respectively, the mad sisters who live in my attic office and do not mingle; Snowflake, the blue-eyed long-haired white cat, who lived wild in the woods for years before she gave up her wild ways for soft sofas and beds; and, last but largest, Furball, Snowflake's cushionlike calico long-haired daughter, orange and black and white, whom I discovered as a tiny kitten in our garage one day, strangled and almost dead, her head poked through an old badminton net, and who surprised us all by not dying but instead growing up to be the best-natured cat I have ever encountered.

And then there is the black cat. Who has no other name than the Black Cat and who turned up almost a month ago. We did not realize he was going to be living here at first: he looked too well-fed to be a stray, too old and jaunty to have been abandoned. He looked like a small panther, and he moved like a patch of night.

One day, in the summer, he was lurking about our ramshackle porch: eight or nine years old, at a guess, male, greenish-yellow of eye, very friendly, quite unperturbable. I assumed he belonged to a neighboring farmer or household.

I went away for a few weeks, to finish writing a book, and when I came home he was still on our porch, living in an old cat bed one of the children had found for him. He was, however, almost unrecognizable. Patches of fur had gone, and there were deep scratches on his gray skin. The tip of one ear was chewed away. There was a gash beneath one eye, a slice gone from one lip. He looked tired and thin.

We took the Black Cat to the vet, where we got him some antibiotics, which we fed him each night, along with soft cat food.

We wondered who he was fighting. Snowflake, our beautiful white near-feral queen? Raccoons? A rat-tailed, fanged possum?

Each night the scratches would be worse—one night his side would be chewed up; the next it would be his underbelly, raked with claw marks and bloody to the touch.

When it got to that point, I took him down to the basement to recover beside the furnace and the piles of boxes. He was surprisingly heavy, the Black Cat, and I picked him up and carried him down there, with a cat basket, and a litter box, and some food and water. I closed the door behind me. I had to wash the blood from my hands when I left the basement.

He stayed down there for four days. At first he seemed too weak to feed himself: a cut beneath one eye had rendered him almost one-eyed, and he limped and lolled weakly, thick yellow pus oozing from the cut in his lip.

I went down there every morning and every night, and I fed him and gave him antibiotics, which I mixed with his canned food, and I dabbed at the worst of the cuts, and spoke to him. He had diarrhea, and, although I changed his litter daily, the basement stank evilly.

The four days that the Black Cat lived in the basement were a bad four days in my house: the baby slipped in the bath and banged her head and might have drowned; I learned that a project I had set my heart on—adapting Hope Mirrlees's novel *Lud-in-the-Mist* for the BBC—was no longer going to happen, and I realized that I did not have the energy to begin again from scratch, pitching it to other networks or to other media; my daughter left for summer camp and immediately began to send home a plethora of heart-tearing letters and cards, five or six each day, imploring us to bring her home; my son had some kind of fight with his best friend, to the point that they were no longer on speaking terms; and, returning home one night, my wife hit a deer that ran out in front of the car. The deer was killed, the car was left undriveable, and my wife sustained a small cut over one eye.

By the fourth day, the cat was prowling the basement, walking haltingly but impatiently between the stacks of books and comics, the boxes of mail and cassettes, of pictures and of gifts and of stuff. He mewed at me to let him out and, reluctantly, I did so.

He went back onto the porch and slept there for the rest of the day.

The next morning there were deep new gashes in his flanks, and clumps of black cat hair—his—covered the wooden boards of the porch.

Letters arrived that day from my daughter, telling us that camp was going better and she thought she could survive a few days; my son and his friend sorted out their problem, although what the argument was about—trading cards, computer games, *Star Wars*, or A Girl—I would never learn. The BBC executive who had vetoed *Lud-in-the-Mist* was discovered to have been taking bribes (well, "questionable loans") from an independent production company and was sent home on permanent leave: his successor, I was delighted to learn when she faxed me, was the woman who had initially proposed the project to me before leaving the BBC.

I thought about returning the Black Cat to the basement, but decided against it. Instead, I resolved to try and discover what kind of animal was coming to our house each night and from there to formulate a plan of action—to trap it, perhaps.

For birthdays and at Christmas, my family gives me gadgets and gizmos, pricy toys which excite my fancy but, ultimately, rarely leave their boxes. There is a food dehydrator and an electric carving knife, a breadmaking machine, and, last year's present, a pair of see-in-the-dark binoculars. On Christmas Day I had put the batteries into the binoculars and had walked about the basement in the dark, too impatient even to wait until nightfall, stalking a flock of imaginary starlings. (You were warned not to turn it on in the light: that would have damaged the binoculars and quite possibly your eyes as well.) Afterward I had put the device back into its box, and it sat there still, in my office, beside the box of computer cables and forgotten bits and pieces.

Perhaps, I thought, if the creature, dog or cat or raccoon or what-have-you, were to see me sitting on the porch, it would not come, so I took a chair into the box-and-coatroom, little larger than a closet, which overlooks the porch, and, when everyone in the house was asleep, I went out onto the porch and bade the Black Cat goodnight.

That cat, my wife had said, when he first arrived, *is a person.* And there was something very personlike in his huge leonine face: his broad black nose, his greenish-yellow eyes, his fanged but amiable mouth (still leaking amber pus from the right lower lip).

I stroked his head, and scratched him beneath the chin, and wished him well. Then I went inside and turned off the light on the porch.

I sat on my chair in the darkness inside the house with the see-in-the-dark binoculars on my lap. I had switched the binoculars on, and a trickle of greenish light came from the eyepieces.

Time passed, in the darkness.

I experimented with looking at the darkness with the binoculars, learning to focus, to see the world in shades of green. I found myself horrified by the number of swarming insects I could see in the night air: it was as if the night world were some kind of nightmarish soup, swimming with life. Then I lowered the binoculars from my eyes and stared out at the rich blacks and blues of the night, empty and peaceful and calm.

Time passed. I struggled to keep awake, found myself profoundly missing cigarettes and coffee, my two lost addictions. Either of them would have kept my eyes open. But before I had tumbled too far into the world of sleep and dreams, a yowl from the garden jerked me fully awake. I fumbled the binoculars to my eyes and was disappointed to see that it was merely Snowflake, the white cat, streaking across the front garden like a patch of greenish-white light. She vanished into the woodland to the left of the house and was gone.

I was about to settle myself back down when it occurred to me to wonder what exactly had startled Snowflake so, and I began scanning the middle distance with the binoculars, looking for a huge raccoon, a dog, or a vicious possum. And there was indeed something coming down the driveway toward the house. I could see it through the binoculars, clear as day.

It was the Devil.

I had never seen the Devil before, and, although I had written about him in the past, if pressed would have confessed that I had no belief in him, other than as an imaginary figure, tragic and Miltonian. The figure coming up the driveway was not Milton's Lucifer. It was the Devil.

My heart began to pound in my chest, to pound so hard that it hurt. I hoped it could not see me, that, in a dark house, behind window glass, I was hidden.

The figure flickered and changed as it walked up the drive. One moment it was dark, bull-like, minotaurish, the next it was slim and female, and the next it was a cat itself, a scarred, huge gray-green wildcat, its face contorted with hate.

There are steps that lead up to my porch, four white wooden steps in need of a coat of paint (I knew they were white, although they were, like everything else, green through my binoculars). At the bottom of the steps, the Devil stopped and called out something that I could not understand, three, perhaps four words in a whining, howling language that must have been old and forgotten when Babylon was young; and, although I did not understand the words, I felt the hairs raise on the back of my head as it called.

And then I heard, muffled through the glass but still audible, a low growl, a challenge, and—slowly, unsteadily—a black figure walked down the steps of the house, away from me, toward the Devil. These days the Black Cat no longer moved like a panther, instead he stumbled and rocked, like a sailor only recently returned to land.

The Devil was a woman, now. She said something soothing and gentle to the cat, in a tongue that sounded like French, and reached out a hand to him. He sank his teeth into her arm, and her lip curled, and she spat at him.

The woman glanced up at me then, and if I had doubted that she was the Devil before, I was certain of it now: the woman's eyes flashed red fire at me, but you can see no red through the night-vision binoculars, only shades of a green. And the Devil saw me through the window. It saw me. I am in no doubt about that at all.

The Devil twisted and writhed, and now it was some kind of jackal, a flat-faced, huge-headed, bull-necked creature, halfway between a hyena and a dingo. There were maggots squirming in its mangy fur, and it began to walk up the steps.

The Black Cat leapt upon it, and in seconds they became a rolling, writhing thing, moving faster than my eyes could follow.

All this in silence.

And then a low roar—down the country road at the bottom of our drive, in the distance, lumbered a late-night truck, its blazing headlights burning bright as green suns through the binoculars. I lowered them from my eyes and saw only darkness, and the gentle yellow of headlights, and then the red of rear lights as it vanished off again into the nowhere at all.

When I raised the binoculars once more, there was nothing to be seen. Only the Black Cat on the steps, staring up into the air. I trained the binoculars up and saw something flying away—a vulture, perhaps, or an eagle—and then it flew beyond the trees and was gone.

I went out onto the porch, and picked up the Black Cat, and stroked him, and said kind, soothing things to him. He mewled piteously when I first approached him, but, after a while, he went to sleep on my lap, and I put him into his basket, and went upstairs to my bed, to sleep myself. There was dried blood on my T-shirt and jeans, the following morning.

That was a week ago.

The thing that comes to my house does not come every night. But it comes most nights: we know it by the wounds on the cat, and the pain I can see in those leonine eyes. He has lost the use of his front left paw, and his right eye has closed for good.

I wonder what we did to deserve the Black Cat. I wonder who sent him. And, selfish and scared, I wonder how much more he has to give.

SHOGGOTH'S OLD PECULIAR

1998

ENJAMIN LASSITER WAS coming to the unavoidable conclusion
that the woman who had written *A Walking Tour of the British
Coastline*, the book he was carrying in his backpack, had never been
on a walking tour of any kind, and would probably not recognize the
British coastline if it were to dance through her bedroom at the head
of a marching band, singing "I'm the British Coastline" in a loud and
cheerful voice while accompanying itself on the kazoo.

He had been following her advice for five days now and had little
to show for it, except blisters and a backache. *All British seaside resorts
contain a number of bed-and-breakfast establishments, who will be only too
delighted to put you up in the "off-season."* was one such piece of advice.
Ben had crossed it out and written in the margin beside it: *All British
seaside resorts contain a handful of bed-and-breakfast establishments, the
owners of which take off to Spain or Provence or somewhere on the last day
of September, locking the doors behind them as they go.*

He had added a number of other marginal notes, too. Such as *Do
not repeat not under any circumstances order fried eggs again in any roadside cafe* and *What is it with the fish-and-chips thing?* and *No they are not.*
That last was written beside a paragraph which claimed that, if there
was one thing that the inhabitants of scenic villages on the British
coastline were pleased to see, it was a young American tourist on a
walking tour.

For five hellish days, Ben had walked from village to village, had drunk sweet tea and instant coffee in cafeterias and cafes and stared out at gray rocky vistas and at the slate-colored sea, shivered under his two thick sweaters, got wet, and failed to see any of the sights that were promised.

Sitting in the bus shelter in which he had unrolled his sleeping bag one night, he had begun to translate key descriptive words: *charming* he decided, meant *nondescript; scenic* meant *ugly but with a nice view if the rain ever lets up; delightful* probably meant *We've never been here and don't know anyone who has.* He had also come to the conclusion that the more exotic the name of the village, the duller the village.

Thus it was that Ben Lassiter came, on the fifth day, somewhere north of Bootle, to the village of Innsmouth, which was rated neither *charming, scenic,* nor *delightful* in his guidebook. There were no descriptions of the rusting pier, nor the mounds of rotting lobster pots upon the pebbly beach.

On the seafront were three bed-and-breakfasts next to each other: Sea View, Mon Repose, and Shub Niggurath, each with a neon VACANCIES sign turned off in the window of the front parlor, each with a CLOSED FOR THE SEASON notice thumbtacked to the front door.

There were no cafes open on the seafront. The lone fish-and-chip shop had a CLOSED sign up. Ben waited outside for it to open as the gray afternoon light faded into dusk. Finally a small, slightly frog-faced woman came down the road, and she unlocked the door of the shop. Ben asked her when they would be open for business, and she looked at him, puzzled, and said, "It's Monday, dear. We're never open on Monday." Then she went into the fish-and-chip shop and locked the door behind her, leaving Ben cold and hungry on her doorstep.

Ben had been raised in a dry town in northern Texas: the only water was in backyard swimming pools, and the only way to travel was in an air-conditioned pickup truck. So the idea of walking, by the sea, in a country where they spoke English of a sort, had appealed to him. Ben's hometown was double dry: it prided itself on having banned alcohol thirty years before the rest of America leapt onto the Prohibition bandwagon, and on never having got off again; thus all Ben knew of pubs was that they were sinful places, like bars, only with cuter names. The author of *A Walking Tour of the British Coastline* had, however, suggested that pubs were good places to go to find local color and local information, that one should always "stand one's round," and that some of them sold food.

The Innsmouth pub was called the Book of Dead Names and the sign over the door informed Ben that the proprietor was one A. *Al-Hazred*, licensed to sell wines and spirits. Ben wondered if this meant that they would serve Indian food, which he had eaten on his arrival in Bootle and rather enjoyed. He paused at the signs directing him to the Public Bar or the Saloon Bar, wondering if British Public Bars were private like their Public Schools, and eventually, because it sounded more like something you would find in a Western, going into the Saloon Bar.

The Saloon Bar was almost empty. It smelled like last week's spilled beer and the day-before-yesterday's cigarette smoke. Behind the bar was a plump woman with bottle-blonde hair. Sitting in one corner were a couple of gentlemen wearing long gray raincoats and scarves. They were playing dominoes and sipping dark brown foam-topped beerish drinks from dimpled glass tankards.

Ben walked over to the bar. "Do you sell food here?"

The barmaid scratched the side of her nose for a moment, then admitted, grudgingly, that she could probably do him a ploughman's.

Ben had no idea what this meant and found himself, for the hundredth time, wishing that *A Walking Tour of the British Coastline* had an American-English phrase book in the back. "Is that food?" he asked.

She nodded.

"Okay. I'll have one of those."

"And to drink?"

"Coke, please."

"We haven't got any Coke."

"Pepsi, then."

"No Pepsi."

"Well, what do you have? Sprite? 7UP? Gatorade?"

She looked blanker than previously. Then she said, "I think there's a bottle or two of cherryade in the back."

"That'll be fine."

"It'll be five pounds and twenty pence, and I'll bring you over your ploughman's when it's ready."

Ben decided as he sat at a small and slightly sticky wooden table, drinking something fizzy that both looked and tasted a bright chemical red, that a ploughman's was probably a steak of some kind. He reached this conclusion, colored, he knew, by wishful thinking, from imagining rustic, possibly even bucolic, ploughmen leading their plump oxen through fresh-ploughed fields at sunset and because he could, by then, with equanimity and only a little help from others, have eaten an entire ox.

"Here you go. Ploughman's," said the barmaid, putting a plate down in front of him.

That a ploughman's turned out to be a rectangular slab of sharp-tasting cheese, a lettuce leaf, an undersized tomato with a thumbprint in it, a mound of something wet and brown that tasted like sour jam, and a small, hard, stale roll, came as a sad disappointment to Ben, who had already decided that the British treated food as some kind of punishment. He chewed the cheese and the lettuce leaf, and cursed every ploughman in England for choosing to dine upon such swill.

The gentlemen in gray raincoats, who had been sitting in the corner, finished their game of dominoes, picked up their drinks, and came and sat beside Ben. "What you drinkin'?" one of them asked, curiously.

"It's called cherryade," he told them. "It tastes like something from a chemical factory."

"Interesting you should say that," said the shorter of the two. "Interesting you should say that. Because I had a friend worked in a chemical factory and he *never drank cherryade*." He paused dramatically and then took a sip of his brown drink. Ben waited for him to go on, but that appeared to be that; the conversation had stopped.

In an effort to appear polite, Ben asked, in his turn, "So, what are *you* guys drinking?"

The taller of the two strangers, who had been looking lugubrious, brightened up. "Why, that's exceedingly kind of you. Pint of Shoggoth's Old Peculiar for me, please."

"And for me, too," said his friend. "I could murder a Shoggoth's. 'Ere, I bet that would make a good advertising slogan. 'I could murder a Shoggoth's.' I should write to them and suggest it. I bet they'd be very glad of me suggestin' it."

Ben went over to the barmaid, planning to ask her for two pints of Shoggoth's Old Peculiar and a glass of water for himself, only to find she had already poured three pints of the dark beer. *Well,* he thought, *might as well be hung for a sheep as a lamb,* and he was certain it couldn't be worse than the cherryade. He took a sip. The beer had the kind of flavor which, he suspected, advertisers would describe as *full-bodied,* although if pressed they would have to admit that the body in question had been that of a goat.

He paid the barmaid and maneuvered his way back to his new friends.

"So. What you doin' in Innsmouth?" asked the taller of the two. "I suppose you're one of our American cousins, come to see the most famous of English villages."

"They named the one in America after this one, you know," said the smaller one.

"Is there an Innsmouth in the States?" asked Ben.

"I should say so," said the smaller man. "He wrote about it all the time. Him whose name we don't mention."

"I'm sorry?" said Ben.

The little man looked over his shoulder, then he hissed, very loudly, "H. P. Lovecraft!"

"I told you not to mention that name," said his friend, and he took a sip of the dark brown beer. "H. P. Lovecraft. H. P. bloody Lovecraft. H. bloody P. bloody Love bloody craft." He stopped to take a breath. "What did *he* know. Eh? I mean, what did he bloody know?"

Ben sipped his beer. The name was vaguely familiar; he remembered it from rummaging through the pile of old-style vinyl LPs in the back of his father's garage. "Weren't they a rock group?"

"Wasn't talkin' about any rock group. I mean the writer."

Ben shrugged. "I've never heard of him," he admitted. "I really mostly only read Westerns. And technical manuals."

The little man nudged his neighbor. "Here. Wilf. You hear that? He's never heard of him."

"Well. There's no harm in that. *I* used to read that Zane Grey," said the taller.

"Yes. Well. That's nothing to be proud of. This bloke—what did you say your name was?"

"Ben. Ben Lassiter. And you are . . . ? "

The little man smiled; he looked awfully like a frog, thought Ben. "I'm Seth," he said. "And my friend here is called Wilf."

"Charmed," said Wilf.

"Hi," said Ben.

"Frankly," said the little man, "I agree with you."

"You do?" said Ben, perplexed.

The little man nodded. "Yer. H. P. Lovecraft. I don't know what the fuss is about. He couldn't bloody write." He slurped his stout, then licked the foam from his lips with a long and flexible tongue. "I mean, for starters, you look at them words he used. *Eldritch*. You know what *eldritch* means?"

Ben shook his head. He seemed to be discussing literature with two strangers in an English pub while drinking beer. He wondered for a moment if he had become someone else, while he wasn't looking. The beer tasted less bad, the farther down the glass he went, and was beginning to erase the lingering aftertaste of the cherryade.

"*Eldritch*. Means weird. Peculiar. Bloody odd. That's what it means. I looked it up. In a dictionary. And *gibbous*?"

Ben shook his head again.

"*Gibbous* means the moon was nearly full. And what about that one he was always calling us, eh? Thing. Wossname. Starts with a *b*. Tip of me tongue . . ."

"Bastards?" suggested Wilf.

"Nah. Thing. You know. *Batrachian*. That's it. Means looked like frogs."

"Hang on," said Wilf. "I thought they was, like, a kind of camel."

Seth shook his head vigorously. "S'definitely frogs. Not camels. Frogs."

Wilf slurped his Shoggoth's. Ben sipped his, carefully, without pleasure.

"So?" said Ben.

"They've got two humps," interjected Wilf, the tall one.

"Frogs?" asked Ben.

"Nah. Batrachians. Whereas your average dromederary camel, he's only got one. It's for the long journey through the desert. That's what they eat."

"Frogs?" asked Ben.

"Camel humps." Wilf fixed Ben with one bulging yellow eye. "You listen to me, matey-me-lad. After you've been out in some trackless desert for three or four weeks, a plate of roasted camel hump starts looking particularly tasty."

Seth looked scornful. "You've never eaten a camel hump."

"I might have done," said Wilf.

"Yes, but you haven't. You've never even been in a desert."

"Well, let's say, just supposing I'd been on a pilgrimage to the Tomb of Nyarlathotep . . ."

"The black king of the ancients who shall come in the night from the east and you shall not know him, you mean?"

"Of course that's who I mean."

"Just checking."

"Stupid question, if you ask me."

"You could of meant someone else with the same name."

"Well, it's not exactly a common name, is it? Nyarlathotep. There's not exactly going to be two of them, are there? 'Hullo, my name's Nyarlathotep, what a coincidence meeting you here, funny them bein' two of us,' I don't exactly think so. Anyway, so I'm trudging through them trackless wastes, thinking to myself, I could murder a camel hump . . ."

"But you haven't, have you? You've never been out of Innsmouth harbor."

"Well . . . No."

"There." Seth looked at Ben triumphantly. Then he leaned over and whispered into Ben's ear, "He gets like this when he gets a few drinks into him, I'm afraid."

"I heard that," said Wilf.

"Good," said Seth. "Anyway. H. P. Lovecraft. He'd write one of his bloody sentences. Ahem. 'The gibbous moon hung low over the eldritch and batrachian inhabitants of squamous Dulwich.' What does he mean, eh? *What does he mean?* I'll tell you what he bloody means. What he bloody means is that the moon was nearly full, and everybody what lived in Dulwich was bloody peculiar frogs. That's what he means."

"What about the other thing you said?" asked Wilf.

"What?"

"*Squamous.* Wossat mean, then?"

Seth shrugged. "Haven't a clue," he admitted. "But he used it an awful lot."

There was another pause.

"I'm a student," said Ben. "Gonna be a metallurgist." Somehow he had managed to finish the whole of his first pint of Shoggoth's Old Peculiar, which was, he realized, pleasantly shocked, his first alcoholic beverage. "What do you guys do?"

"We," said Wilf, "are acolytes."

"Of Great Cthulhu," said Seth proudly.

"Yeah?" said Ben. "And what exactly does that involve?"

"My shout," said Wilf. "Hang on." Wilf went over to the barmaid and came back with three more pints. "Well," he said, "what it involves is, technically speaking, not a lot right now. The acolytin' is not really what you might call laborious employment in the middle of its busy season. That is, of course, because of his bein' asleep. Well, not exactly *asleep.* More like, if you want to put a finer point on it, *dead.*"

" 'In his house at Sunken R'lyeh dead Cthulhu lies dreaming,' " interjected Seth. "Or, as the poet has it, 'That is not dead what can eternal lie—' "

" 'But in Strange Aeons—' " chanted Wilf. "—and by *Strange* he means *bloody peculiar*—"

"Exactly. We are not talking your normal Aeons here at all."

" 'But in Strange Aeons even Death can die.' "

Ben was mildly surprised to find that he seemed to be drinking another full-bodied pint of Shoggoth's Old Peculiar. Somehow the taste of rank goat was less offensive on the second pint. He was also delighted to notice that he was no longer hungry, that his blistered feet had stopped hurting, and that his companions were charming, intelligent men whose names he was having difficulty in keeping apart. He did not have enough experience with alcohol to know that this was one of the symptoms of being on your second pint of Shoggoth's Old Peculiar.

"So right now," said Seth, or possibly Wilf, "the business is a bit light. Mostly consisting of waiting."

"And praying," said Wilf, if he wasn't Seth.

"And praying. But pretty soon now, that's all going to change."

"Yeah?" asked Ben. "How's that?"

"Well," confided the taller one. "Any day now, Great Cthulhu (currently impermanently deceased), who is our boss, will wake up in his undersea living-sort-of quarters."

"And then," said the shorter one, "he will stretch and yawn and get dressed—"

"Probably go to the toilet, I wouldn't be at all surprised."

"Maybe read the papers."

"—And having done all that, he will come out of the ocean depths and consume the world utterly."

Ben found this unspeakably funny. "Like a ploughman's," he said.

"Exactly. Exactly. Well put, the young American gentleman. Great Cthulhu will gobble the world up like a ploughman's lunch, leaving but only the lump of Branston pickle on the side of the plate."

"That's the brown stuff?" asked Ben. They assured him that it was, and he went up to the bar and brought them back another three pints of Shoggoth's Old Peculiar.

He could not remember much of the conversation that followed. He remembered finishing his pint, and his new friends inviting him on a walking tour of the village, pointing out the various sights to him. "That's where we rent our videos, and that big building next door is the Nameless Temple of Unspeakable Gods and on Saturday mornings there's a jumble sale in the crypt . . ."

He explained to them his theory of the walking tour book and told them, emotionally, that Innsmouth was both *scenic* and *charming*. He told them that they were the best friends he had ever had and that Innsmouth was *delightful*.

The moon was nearly full, and in the pale moonlight both of his new friends did look remarkably like huge frogs. Or possibly camels.

The three of them walked to the end of the rusted pier, and Seth and/or Wilf pointed out to Ben the ruins of Sunken R'lyeh in the bay, visible in the moonlight, beneath the sea, and Ben was overcome by what he kept explaining was a sudden and unforeseen attack of seasickness and was violently and unendingly sick over the metal railings into the black sea below . . .

After that it all got a bit odd.

BEN LASSITER AWOKE on the cold hillside with his head pounding and a bad taste in his mouth. His head was resting on his backpack. There was rocky moorland on each side of him, and no sign of a road, and no sign of any village, scenic, charming, delightful, or even picturesque.

He stumbled and limped almost a mile to the nearest road and walked along it until he reached a petrol station.

They told him that there was no village anywhere locally named Innsmouth. No village with a pub called the Book of Dead Names. He told them about two men, named Wilf and Seth, and a friend of theirs, called Strange Ian, who was fast asleep somewhere, if he wasn't dead, under the sea. They told him that they didn't think much of American hippies who wandered about the countryside taking drugs, and that he'd probably feel better after a nice cup of tea and a tuna and cucumber sandwich, but that if he was dead set on wandering the country taking drugs, young Ernie who worked the afternoon shift would be all too happy to sell him a nice little bag of homegrown cannabis, if he could come back after lunch.

Ben pulled out his *A Walking Tour of the British Coastline* book and tried to find Innsmouth in it to prove to them that he had not dreamed it, but he was unable to locate the page it had been on—if ever it had been there at all. Most of one page, however, had been ripped out, roughly, about halfway through the book.

And then Ben telephoned a taxi, which took him to Bootle railway station, where he caught a train, which took him to Manchester, where he got on an airplane, which took him to Chicago, where he changed planes and flew to Dallas, where he got another plane going north, and he rented a car and went home.

He found the knowledge that he was over 600 miles away from the ocean very comforting; although, later in life, he moved to Nebraska to increase the distance from the sea: there were things he had seen, or thought he had seen, beneath the old pier that night that he would never be able to get out of his head. There were things that lurked beneath gray raincoats that man was not meant to know. *Squamous.* He did not need to look it up. He knew. They were *squamous.*

A couple of weeks after his return home Ben posted his annotated copy of *A Walking Tour of the British Coastline* to the author, care of her publisher, with an extensive letter containing a number of helpful suggestions for future editions. He also asked the author if she would send him a copy of the page that had been ripped from his guidebook, to set his mind at rest; but he was secretly relieved, as the days turned into months, and the months turned into years and then into decades, that she never replied.

THE WEDDING PRESENT

1998

AFTER ALL THE joys and the headaches of the wedding, after the madness and the magic of it all (not to mention the embarrassment of Belinda's father's after-dinner speech, complete with family slide show), after the honeymoon was literally (although not yet metaphorically) over and before their new suntans had a chance to fade in the English autumn, Belinda and Gordon got down to the business of unwrapping the wedding presents and writing their thank-you letters—thank-yous enough for every towel and every toaster, for the juicer and the breadmaker, for the cutlery and the crockery and the teas made and the curtains.

"Right," said Gordon. "That's the large objects thank-you'd. What've we got left?"

"Things in envelopes," said Belinda. "Checks, I hope."

There were several checks, a number of gift tokens, and even a £10 book token from Gordon's Aunt Marie, who was poor as a church mouse, Gordon told Belinda, but a dear, and who had sent him a book token every birthday as long as he could remember. And then, at the very bottom of the pile, there was a large brown businesslike envelope.

"What is it?" asked Belinda.

Gordon opened the flap and pulled out a sheet of paper the color of two-day-old cream, ragged at top and bottom, with typing on one side. The words had been typed with a manual typewriter, something Gordon had not seen in some years. He read the page slowly.

"What is it?" asked Belinda. "Who's it from?"

"I don't know," said Gordon. "Someone who still owns a typewriter. It's not signed."

"Is it a letter?"

"Not exactly," he said, and he scratched the side of his nose and read it again.

"Well," she said in an exasperated voice (but she was not really exasperated; she was happy. She would wake in the morning and check to see if she were still as happy as she had been when she went to sleep the night before, or when Gordon had woken her in the night by brushing up against her, or when she had woken him. And she was). "Well, what is it?"

"It appears to be a description of our wedding," he said. "It's very nicely written. Here," and he passed it to her.

She looked it over.

It was a crisp day in early October when Gordon Robert Johnson and Belinda Karen Abingdon swore that they would love each other, would support and honor each other as long as they both should live. The bride was radiant and lovely, the groom was nervous, but obviously proud and just as obviously pleased.

That was how it began. It went on to describe the service and the reception clearly, simply, and amusingly.

"How sweet," she said. "What does it say on the envelope?"

" 'Gordon and Belinda's Wedding,' " he read.

"No name? Nothing to indicate who sent it?"

"Uh-uh."

"Well, it's very sweet, and it's very thoughtful," she said. "Whoever it's from."

She looked inside the envelope to see if there was something else inside that they had overlooked, a note from whichever one of her friends (or his, or theirs) had written it, but there wasn't, so, vaguely relieved that there was one less thank you note to write, she placed the cream sheet of paper back in its envelope, which she placed in a box file, along with a copy of the wedding banquet menu, and the invitations, and the contact sheets for the wedding photographs, and one white rose from the bridal bouquet.

Gordon was an architect, and Belinda was a vet. For each of them what they did was a vocation, not a job. They were in their early twenties. Neither of them had been married before, nor even seriously involved with anyone. They met when Gordon brought his thirteen-year-old golden retriever, Goldie, gray-muzzled and half-paralyzed, to Belinda's surgery to be put down. He had had the dog since he was a boy and insisted on being with her at the end. Belinda held his hand as he cried, and then, suddenly and unprofessionally, she hugged him, tightly, as if she could squeeze away the pain and the loss and the grief. One of them asked the other if they could meet that evening in the local pub for a drink, and afterward neither of them was sure which of them had proposed it.

The most important thing to know about the first two years of their marriage was this: they were pretty happy. From time to time they would squabble, and every once in a while they would have a blazing row about nothing very much that would end in tearful reconciliations, and they would make love and kiss away the other's tears and whisper heartfelt apologies into each other's ears. At the end of the second year, six months after she came off the pill, Brenda found herself pregnant.

Gordon bought her a bracelet studded with tiny rubies, and he turned the spare bedroom into a nursery, hanging the wallpaper himself. The wallpaper was covered with nursery rhyme characters, with Little Bo Peep, and Humpty Dumpty, and the Dish Running Away with the Spoon, over and over and over again.

Belinda came home from the hospital, with little Melanie in her carry-cot, and Belinda's mother came to stay with them for a week, sleeping on the sofa in the lounge.

It was on the third day that Belinda pulled out the box file to show her wedding souvenirs to her mother and to reminisce. Already their wedding seemed like such a long time ago. They smiled at the dried brown thing that had once been a white rose, and clucked over the menu and the invitation. At the bottom of the box was a large brown envelope.

" 'Gordon and Belinda's Marriage,' " read Belinda's mother.

"It's a description of our wedding," said Belinda. "It's very sweet. It even has a bit in it about Daddy's slide show."

Belinda opened the envelope and pulled out the sheet of cream paper. She read what was typed upon the paper, and made a face. Then she put it away without saying anything.

"Can't I see it, dear?" asked her mother.

"I think it's Gordon playing a joke," said Belinda. "Not in good taste, either."

Belinda was sitting up in bed that night, breastfeeding Melanie, when she said to Gordon, who was staring at his wife and new daughter with a foolish smile upon his face, "Darling, why did you write those things?"

"What things?"

"In the letter. That wedding thing. You know."

"I don't know."

"It wasn't funny."

He sighed. "What are you talking about?"

Belinda pointed to the box file, which she had brought upstairs and placed upon her dressing table. Gordon opened it and took out the envelope. "Did it always say that on the envelope?" he asked. "I thought it said something about our wedding." Then he took out and read the single sheet of ragged-edged paper, and his forehead creased. "I didn't write this." He turned the paper over, staring at the blank side as if expecting to see something else written there.

"You didn't write it?" she asked. "Really you didn't?" Gordon shook his head. Belinda wiped a dribble of milk from the baby's chin. "I believe you," she said. "I thought you wrote it, but you didn't."

"No."

"Let me see that again," she said. He passed the paper to her. "This is so weird. I mean, it's not funny, and it's not even true." Typed upon the paper was a brief description of the previous two years for Gordon and Belinda. It had not been a good two years, according to the typed sheet. Six months after they were married, Belinda had been bitten in the cheek by a Pekingese, so badly that the cheek needed to be stitched back together. It had left a nasty scar. Worse than that, nerves had been damaged, and she had begun to drink, perhaps to numb the pain. She suspected that Gordon was revolted by her face, while the new baby, it said, was a desperate attempt to glue the couple together.

"Why would they say this?" she asked.

"They?"

"Whoever wrote this horrid thing." She ran a finger across her cheek: it was unblemished and unmarked. She was a very beautiful young woman, although she looked tired and fragile now.

"How do you know it's a 'they'?"

"I don't know," she said, transferring the baby to her left breast. "It seems a sort of 'they'-ish thing to do. To write that and to swap it for the old one and to wait until one of us read it. . . . Come on, little Melanie, there you go, that's such a fine girl . . ."

"Shall I throw it away?"

"Yes. No. I don't know. I think . . ." She stroked the baby's forehead. "Hold on to it," she said. "We might need it for evidence. I wonder if it was something Al organized." Al was Gordon's youngest brother.

Gordon put the paper back into the envelope, and he put the envelope back into the box file, which was pushed under the bed and, more or less, forgotten.

Neither of them got much sleep for the next few months, what with the nightly feeds and the continual crying, for Melanie was a colicky baby. The box file stayed under the bed. And then Gordon was offered a job in Preston, several hundred miles north, and since Belinda was on leave from her job and had no immediate plans to go back to work, she found the idea rather attractive. So they moved.

They found a terraced house on a cobbled street, high and old and deep. Belinda filled in from time to time at a local vet's, seeing small animals and housepets. When Melanie was eighteen months old, Belinda gave birth to a son, whom they called Kevin after Gordon's late grandfather.

Gordon was made a full partner in the firm of architects. When Kevin began to go to kindergarten, Belinda went back to work.

The box file was never lost. It was in one of the spare rooms at the top of the house, beneath a teetering pile of copies of *The Architects' Journal* and *The Architectural Review*. Belinda thought about the box file, and what it contained, from time to time, and, one night when Gordon was in Scotland overnight consulting on the remodeling of an ancestral home, she did more than think.

Both of the children were asleep. Belinda went up the stairs into the undecorated part of the house. She moved the magazines and opened the box, which (where it had not been covered by magazines) was thick with two years of undisturbed dust. The envelope still said "Gordon and Belinda's Marriage" on it, and Belinda honestly did not know if it had ever said anything else.

She took out the paper from the envelope, and she read it. And then she put it away, and sat there, at the top of the house, feeling shaken and sick.

According to the neatly typed message, Kevin, her second child, had not been born; the baby had been miscarried at five months. Since then Belinda had been suffering from frequent attacks of bleak, black depression. Gordon was home rarely, it said, because he was conducting a rather miserable affair with the senior partner in his company, a striking but nervous woman ten years his senior. Belinda was drinking more, and affecting high collars and scarves to hide the spiderweb scar upon her cheek. She and Gordon spoke little, except to argue the small and petty arguments of those who fear the big arguments, knowing that the only things that were left to be said were too huge to be said without destroying both their lives.

Belinda said nothing about the latest version of "Gordon and Belinda's Marriage" to Gordon. However, he read it himself, or something quite like it, several months later, when Belinda's mother fell ill, and Belinda went south for a week to help look after her.

On the sheet of paper that Gordon took out of the envelope was a portrait of a marriage similar to the one that Belinda had read, although, at present, his affair with his boss had ended badly, and his job was now in peril.

Gordon rather liked his boss, but could not imagine himself ever becoming romantically involved with her. He was enjoying his job, although he wanted something that would challenge him more than it did.

Belinda's mother improved, and Belinda came home again within the week. Her husband and children were relieved and delighted to see her.

It was Christmas Eve before Gordon spoke to Belinda about the envelope.

"You've looked at it too, haven't you?" They had crept into the children's bedrooms earlier that evening and filled the hanging Christmas stockings. Gordon had felt euphoric as he had walked through the house, as he stood beside his children's beds, but it was a euphoria tinged with a profound sorrow: the knowledge that such moments of complete happiness could not last; that one could not stop Time.

Belinda knew what he was talking about. "Yes," she said, "I've read it."

"What do you think?"

"Well," she said. "I don't think it's a joke anymore. Not even a sick joke."

"Mm," he said. "Then what is it?"

They sat in the living room at the front of the house with the lights dimmed, and the log burning on the bed of coals cast flickering orange and yellow light about the room.

"I think it really is a wedding present," she told him. "It's the marriage that we aren't having. The bad things are happening there, on the page, not here, in our lives. Instead of living it, we are reading it, knowing it could have gone that way and also that it never did."

"You're saying it's magic, then?" He would not have said it aloud, but it was Christmas Eve, and the lights were down.

"I don't believe in magic," she said, flatly. "It's a wedding present. And I think we should make sure it's kept safe."

On Boxing Day she moved the envelope from the box file to her jewelry drawer, which she kept locked, where it lay flat beneath her necklaces and rings, her bracelets and her brooches.

Spring became summer. Winter became spring.

Gordon was exhausted. By day he worked for clients, designing, and liaising with builders and contractors; by night he would sit up late, working for himself, designing museums and galleries and public buildings for competitions. Sometimes his designs received honorable mentions, and were reproduced in architectural journals.

Belinda was doing more large animal work, which she enjoyed, visiting farmers and inspecting and treating horses, sheep, and cows. Sometimes she would bring the children with her on her rounds.

Her mobile phone rang when she was in a paddock trying to examine a pregnant goat who had, it turned out, no desire to be caught, let alone examined. She retired from the battle, leaving the goat glaring at her from across the field, and thumbed the phone open. "Yes?"

"Guess what?"

"Hello, darling. Um. You've won the lottery?"

"Nope. Close, though. My design for the British Heritage Museum has made the short list. I'm up against some pretty stiff contenders, though. But I'm on the short list."

"That's wonderful!"

"I've spoken to Mrs. Fulbright and she's going to have Sonja baby-sit for us tonight. We're celebrating."

"Terrific. Love you," she said. "Now got to get back to the goat."

They drank too much champagne over a fine celebratory meal. That night in their bedroom as Belinda removed her earrings, she said, "Shall we see what the wedding present says?"

He looked at her gravely from the bed. He was only wearing his socks. "No, I don't think so. It's a special night. Why spoil it?" She placed her earrings in her jewelry drawer, and locked it.

Then she removed her stockings. "I suppose you're right. I can imagine what it says, anyway. I'm drunk and depressed and you're a miserable loser. And meanwhile we're . . . well, actually I *am* a bit tiddly, but that's not what I mean. It just sits there at the bottom of the drawer, like the portrait in the attic in *The Picture of Dorian Gray*."

" 'And it was only by his rings that they knew him.' Yes. I remember. We read it in school."

"That's really what I'm scared of," she said, pulling on a cotton nightdress. "That the thing on that paper is the real portrait of our marriage at present, and what we've got now is just a pretty picture. That it's real, and we're not. I mean"—she was speaking intently now, with the gravity of the slightly drunk—"don't you ever think that it's too good to be true?"

He nodded. "Sometimes. Tonight, certainly."

She shivered. "Maybe really I *am* a drunk with a dog bite on my cheek, and you fuck anything that moves and Kevin was never born and—and all that other horrible stuff."

He stood up, walked over to her, put his arms around her. "But it isn't true," he pointed out. "This is real. You're real. I'm real. That wedding thing is just a story. It's just words." And he kissed her, and held her tightly, and little more was said that night. It was a long six months before Gordon's design for the British Heritage Museum was announced as the winning design, although it was derided in *The Times* as being too "aggressively modern," in various architectural journals as being too old-fashioned, and it was described by one of the judges, in an interview in the *Sunday Telegraph,* as "a bit of a compromise candidate—everybody's second choice."

They moved to London, letting their house in Preston to an artist and his family, for Belinda would not let Gordon sell it. Gordon worked intensively, happily, on the museum project. Kevin was six and Melanie was eight. Melanie found London intimidating, but Kevin loved it. Both of the children were initially distressed to have lost their friends and their school. Belinda found a part-time job at a small animal clinic in Camden, working three afternoons a week. She missed her cows.

Days in London became months and then years, and, despite occasional budgetary setbacks, Gordon was increasingly excited. The day approached when the first ground would be broken for the museum.

One night Belinda woke in the small hours, and she stared at her sleeping husband in the sodium-yellow illumination of the streetlamp outside their bedroom window. His hairline was receding, and the hair at back was thinning. Belinda wondered what it would be like when she was actually married to a bald man. She decided it would be much the same as it always had been. Mostly happy. Mostly good.

She wondered what was happening to the *them* in the envelope. She could feel its presence, dry and brooding, in the corner of their bedroom, safely locked away from all harm. She felt, suddenly, sorry for the Belinda and Gordon trapped in the envelope on their piece of paper, hating each other and everything else.

Gordon began to snore. She kissed him, gently, on the cheek, and said, "Shhh." He stirred, and was quiet, but did not wake. She snuggled against him and soon fell back into sleep herself.

After lunch the following day, while in conversation with an importer of Tuscan marble, Gordon looked very surprised and reached a hand up to his chest. He said, "I'm frightfully sorry about this," and then his knees gave way, and he fell to the floor. They called an ambulance, but Gordon was dead when it arrived. He was thirty-six years old.

At the inquest the coroner announced that the autopsy showed Gordon's heart to have been congenitally weak. It could have gone at any time.

For the first three days after his death, Belinda felt nothing, a profound and awful nothing. She comforted the children, she spoke to her friends and to Gordon's friends, to her family and to Gordon's family, accepting their condolences gracefully and gently, as one accepts unasked-for gifts. She would listen to people cry for Gordon, which she still had not done. She would say all the right things, and she would feel nothing at all.

Melanie, who was eleven, seemed to be taking it well. Kevin abandoned his books and computer games, and sat in his bedroom, staring out of the window, not wanting to talk.

The day after the funeral her parents went back to the countryside, taking both the children with them. Belinda refused to go. There was, she said, too much to do.

On the fourth day after the funeral she was making the double bed that she and Gordon had shared when she began to cry, and the sobs ripped through her in huge ugly spasms of grief, and tears fell from her face onto the bedspread and clear snot streamed from her nose, and she sat down on the floor suddenly, like a marionette whose strings had been cut, and she cried for the best part of an hour, for she knew that she would never see him again.

She wiped her face. Then she unlocked her jewelry drawer and took out the envelope and opened it. She pulled out the cream-colored sheet of paper and ran her eyes over the neatly typed words. The Belinda on the paper had crashed their car while drunk and was about to lose her driving license. She and Gordon had not spoken for days. He had lost his job almost eighteen months earlier and now spent most of his days sitting around their house in Salford. Belinda's job brought in what money they had. Melanie was out of control: Belinda, cleaning Melanie's bedroom, had found a cache of five- and ten-pound notes. Melanie had offered no explanation for how an eleven-year-old girl had come by the money, had just retreated into her room and glared at them, tight-lipped, when quizzed. Neither Gordon nor Belinda had investigated further, scared of what they might have discovered. The house in Salford was dingy and damp, such that the plaster was coming away from the ceiling in huge crumbling chunks, and all three of them had developed nasty bronchial coughs.

Belinda felt sorry for them.

She put the paper back in the envelope. She wondered what it would be like to hate Gordon, to have him hate her. She wondered what it would be like not to have Kevin in her life, not to see his drawings of airplanes or hear his magnificently tuneless renditions of popular songs. She wondered where Melanie—the other Melanie, not *her* Melanie but the there-but-for-the-grace-of-God Melanie—could have got that money and was relieved that her own Melanie seemed to have few interests beyond ballet and Enid Blyton books.

She missed Gordon so much it felt like something sharp being hammered into her chest, a spike, perhaps, or an icicle, made of cold and loneliness and the knowledge that she would never see him again in this world.

Then she took the envelope downstairs to the lounge, where the coal fire was burning in the grate, because Gordon had loved open fires. He said that a fire gave a room life. She disliked coal fires, but she had lit it this evening out of routine and out of habit, and because not lighting it would have meant admitting to herself, on some absolute level, that he was never coming home.

Belinda stared into the fire for some time, thinking about what she had in her life, and what she had given up; and whether it would be worse to love someone who was no longer there, or not to love someone who was.

And then, at the end, almost casually, she tossed the envelope onto the coals, and she watched it curl and blacken and catch, watched the yellow flames dancing amidst the blue.

Soon the wedding present was nothing but black flakes of ash which danced on the updrafts and were carried away, like a child's letter to Santa Claus, up the chimney and off into the night.

Belinda sat back in her chair, and closed her eyes, and waited for the scar to blossom on her cheek.

WHEN WE WENT TO SEE THE END OF THE WORLD BY DAWNIE MORNINGSIDE, AGE 11¼

1998

W HAT I DID on the founders day holiday was, my dad said we were going to have a picnic, and, my mum said where and I said I wanted to go to Ponydale and ride the ponies, but my dad said we were going to the end of the world and my mum said oh god and my dad said now, Tanya, its time the child got to see what was what and my mum said no, no, she just meant that shed thought that Johnsons Peculiar Garden of Lights was nice this time of year.

My mum loves Johnsons Peculiar Garden of Lights, which is in Lux, between 12th street and the river, and I like it too, especially when they give you potato sticks and you feed them to the little white chipmunks who come all the way up to the picnic table.

This is the word for the white chipmunks. Albino.

Dolorita Hunsickle says that the chipmunks tell your fortune if you catch them but I never did. She says a chipmunk told her she would grow up to be a famous ballerina and that she would die of consumption unloved in a boardinghouse in Prague.

So my dad made potato salad. Here is the recipe.

My dads potato salad is made with tiny new potatoes, which he boils, then while their warm he pours his secret mix over them which is mayonnaise and sour cream and little onion things called chives which he sotays in bacon fat, and crunchy bacon bits. When it gets cool its the best potato salad in the world, and better than the potato salad we get at school which tastes like white sick.

We stopped at the shop and got fruit and Coca-Cola and potato sticks, and they went into the box and it went into the back of the car and we went into the car and mum and dad and my baby sister, We Are On Our Way!

Where our house is, it is morning, when we leave, and we got onto the motorway and we went over the bridge over twilight, and soon it got dark. I love driving through the dark.

I sit in the back of the car and I got all scrunched singing songs that go lah lah lah in the back of my head so my dad has to go, Dawnie darling stop making that noise, but still I go lah lah lah.

Lah lah lah.

The motorway was closed for repairs so we followed signs and this is what they said: DIVERSION.

Mummy made dad lock his door, while we were driving, and she made me to lock my door too.

It got more darker as we went.

This is what I saw while we drived through the center of the city, out of the window. I saw a beardy man who ran out when we stopped at the lights and ran a smeary cloth all over our windows.

He winked at me through the window, in the back of the car, with his old eyes.

Then he wasnt there anymore, and mummy and daddy had an arguement about who he was, and whether he was good luck or bad luck. But not a bad arguement.

Their were more signs that said DIVERSION, and they were yellow.

I saw a street where the prettiest men Id ever seen blew us kisses and sung songs, and a street where I saw a woman holding the side of her face under a blue light but her face was bleeding and wet, and a street where there were only cats who stared at us.

My sister went loo loo, which means look and she said kitty.

The baby is called Melicent, but I call her Daisydaisy. Its my secret name for her. Its from a song called Daisydaisy, which goes, Daisydaisy give me your answer do Im half crazy over the love of you it wont be a stylish marriage I cant afford a carriage but youll look sweet upon the seat of a bicycle made for two.

Then we were out of the city, into the hills.

Then there were houses that were like palaces on each side of the road, set far back.

My dad was born in one of those houses, and he and mummy had the arguement about money where he says what he threw away to be with her and she says oh, so your bringing that up again are you?

I looked at the houses. I asked my Daddy which one Grandmother lived in. He said he didnt know, which he was lying. I dont know why grownups fib so much, like when they say Ill tell you later or well see when they mean no or I wont tell you at all even when your older.

In one house there were people dancing in the garden. Then the road began to wind around, and daddy was driving us through the countryside through the dark.

Look! said my mother. A white deer ran across the road with people chasing it. My dad said they were a nuisance and they were a pest and like rats with antlers, and the worst bit of hitting a deer is when it comes through the glass into the car and he said he had a friend who was kicked to death by a deer who came through the glass with sharp hooves.

And mummy said oh god like we really needed to know that, and daddy said well it happened Tanya, and mummy said honestly your incorigible.

I wanted to ask who the people chasing the deer was, but I started to sing instead going lah lah lah lah lah lah.

My dad said stop that. My mum said for gods sake let the girl express herself, and Dad said I bet you like chewing tinfoil too and my mummy said so whats that supposed to mean and Daddy said nothing and I said arent we there yet?

On the side of the road there were bonfires, and sometimes piles of bones.

We stopped on one side of a hill. The end of the world was on the other side of the hill, said my dad.

I wondered what it looked like. We parked the car in the car park. We got out. Mummy carried Daisy. Daddy carried the picnic basket. We walked over the hill, in the light of the candles they set by the path. A unicorn came up to me on the way. It was white as snow, and it nuzzled me with its mouth.

I asked daddy if I could give it an apple and he said it probably has fleas, and Mummy said it didnt. and all the time its tail went swish swish swish.

I offered it my apple it looked at me with big silver eyes and then it snorted like this, hrrrmph, and ran away over the hill.

Baby Daisy said loo loo.

This is what it looks like at the end of the world, which is the best place in the world.

There is a hole in the ground, which looks like a very wide big hole and pretty people holding sticks and simatars that burn come up out of it. They have long golden hair. They look like princesses, only fierce. Some of them have wings and some of them dusnt.

And theres a big hole in the sky too and things are coming down from it, like the cat-heady man, and the snakes made out of stuff that looks like glitter-jel like I putted on my hair at Hallowmorn, and I saw something that looked like a big old buzzie fly, coming down from the sky. There were very many of them. As many as stars.

They dont move. They just hang there, not doing anything. I asked Daddy why they weren't moving and he said they were moving just very very slowly but I dont think so.

We set up at a picnic table.

Daddy said the best thing about the end of the world was no wasps and no moskitos. And mummy said there werent alot of wasps in Johnsons Peculiar Garden of Lights either. I said there werent alot of wasps or moskitos at Ponydale and there were ponies too we could ride on and my Dad said hed brought us here to enjoy ourselves.

I said I wanted to go over to see if I could see the unicorn again and mummy and daddy said dont go too far.

At the next table to us were people with masks on. I went off with Daisydaisy to see them.

They sang Happy Birthday to you to a big fat lady with no clothes on, and a big funny hat. She had lots of bosoms all the way down to her tummy. I waited to see her blow out the candles on her cake, but there wasnt a cake.

Arent you going to make a wish? I said.

She said she couldnt make any more wishes. She was too old. I told her that at my last birthday when I blew out my candles all in one go I had thought about my wish for a long time, and I was going to wish that mummy and Daddy wouldn't argue any more in the night. But in the end I wished for a shetland pony but it never come.

The lady gave me a cuddle and said I was so cute that she could just eat me all up, bones and hair and everything. She smelled like sweet dried milk.

Then Daisydaisy started to cry with all her might and mane, and the lady putted me down.

I shouted and called for the unicorn, but I didnt see him. Sometimes I thought I could hear a trumpet, and sometimes I thought it was just the noise in my ears.

Then we came back to the table. Whats after the end of the world I said to my dad. Nothing he said. Nothing at all. Thats why its called the end.

Then Daisy was sick over Daddys shoes, and we cleaned it up.

I sat by the table. We ate potato salad, which I gave you the recipe for all ready, you should make it its really good, and we drank orange juice and potato sticks and squishy egg and cress sandwiches. We drank our Coca-cola.

Then Mummy said something to Daddy I didnt hear and he just hit her in the face with a big hit with his hand, and mummy started to cry.

Daddy told me to take Daisy and walk about while they talked.

I took Daisy and I said come on Daisydaisy, come on old daisybell because she was crying too, but Im too old to cry.

I couldnt hear what they were saying. I looked up at the cat face man and I tried to see if he was moving very very slowly, and I heard the trumpet at the end of the world in my head going dah dah dah.

We sat by a rock and I sang songs to Daisy lah lah lah lah lah to the sound of the trumpet in my head dah dah dah.

Lah lah lah lah lah lah lah lah.

Lah lah lah.

Then mummy and daddy came over to me and they said we were going home. But that everything was really all right. Mummys eye was all purple. She looked funny, like a lady on the television.

Daisy said owie. I told her yes, it was an owie. We got back in the car.

On the way home, nobody said anything. The baby slept.

There was a dead animal by the side of the road somebody had hit with a car. Daddy said it was a white deer. I thought it was the unicorn, but mummy told me that you cant kill unicorns but I think she was lying like grownups do again.

When we got to Twilight I said, if you told someone your wish, did that mean it wouldnt come true?

What wish, said Daddy?

Your birthday wish. When you blow out the candles.

He said, Wishes dont come true whether you tell them or not. Wishes, he said. He said you cant trust wishes.

I asked Mummy, and she said, whatever your father says, she said in her cold voice, which is the one she uses when she tells me off with my whole name.

Then I slept too.

And then we were home, and it was morning, and I dont want to see the end of the world again. And before I got out of the car, while mummy was carrying in Daisydaisy to the house, I closed my eyes so I couldn't see anything at all, and I wished and I wished and I wished and I wished. I wished wed gone to Ponydale. I wished wed never gone anywhere at all. I wished I was somebody else.

And I wished.

THE FACTS IN THE CASE OF THE DEPARTURE OF MISS FINCH

1998

To BEGIN AT the end: I arranged the thin slice of pickled ginger, pink and translucent, on top of the pale yellowtail flesh, and dipped the whole arrangement—ginger, fish, and vinegared rice—into the soy sauce, flesh-side down; then I devoured it in a couple of bites.

"I think we ought to go to the police," I said.

"And tell them what, exactly?" asked Jane.

"Well, we could file a missing persons report, or something. I don't know."

"And where did you last see the young lady?" asked Jonathan, in his most policemanlike tones. "Ah, I see. Did you know that wasting police time is normally considered an offense, sir?"

"But the whole circus . . ."

"These are transient persons, sir, of legal age. They come and go. If you have their names, I suppose I can take a report . . ."

I gloomily ate a salmon skin roll. "Well, then," I said, "why don't we go to the papers?"

"Brilliant idea," said Jonathan, in the sort of tone of voice which indicates that the person talking doesn't think it's a brilliant idea at all.

"Jonathan's right," said Jane. "They won't listen to us."

"Why wouldn't they believe us? We're reliable. Honest citizens. All that."

"You're a fantasy writer," she said. "You make up stuff like this for a living. No one's going to believe you."

"But you two saw it all as well. You'd back me up."

"Jonathan's got a new series on cult horror movies coming out in the autumn. They'll say he's just trying to get cheap publicity for the show. And I've got another book coming out. Same thing."

"So you're saying that we can't tell anyone?" I sipped my green tea.

"No," Jane said, reasonably, "we can tell anyone we want. It's making them believe us that's problematic. Or, if you ask me, impossible."

The pickled ginger was sharp on my tongue. "You may be right," I said. "And Miss Finch is probably much happier wherever she is right now than she would be here."

"But her name isn't Miss Finch," said Jane, "it's——" and she said our former companion's real name.

"I know. But it's what I thought when I first saw her," I explained. "Like in one of those movies. You know. When they take off their glasses and put down their hair. 'Why, Miss Finch. You're beautiful.' "

"She certainly was that," said Jonathan, "in the end, anyway." And he shivered at the memory.

There. So now you know: that's how it all ended, and how the three of us left it, several years ago. All that remains is the beginning, and the details.

For the record, I don't expect you to believe any of this. Not really. I'm a liar by trade, after all; albeit, I like to think, an honest liar. If I belonged to a gentlemen's club I'd recount it over a glass or two of port late in the evening as the fire burned low, but I am a member of no such club, and I'll write it better than ever I'd tell it. So here you will learn of Miss Finch (whose name, as you already know, was not Finch, nor anything like it, since I'm changing names here to disguise the guilty) and how it came about that she was unable to join us for sushi. Believe it or not, just as you wish. I am not even certain that I believe it anymore. It all seems such a long way away.

I could find a dozen beginnings. Perhaps it might be best to begin in a hotel room, in London, a few years ago. It was 11:00 A.M. The phone began to ring, which surprised me. I hurried over to answer it.

"Hello?" It was too early in the morning for anyone in America to be phoning me, and there was no one in England who was meant to know that I was even in the country.

"Hi," said a familiar voice, adopting an American accent of monumentally unconvincing proportions. "This is Hiram P. Muzzledexter of Colossal Pictures. We're working on a film that's a remake of *Raiders of the Lost Ark* but instead of Nazis it has women with enormous knockers in it. We've heard that you were astonishingly well supplied in the trouser department and might be willing to take on the part of our male lead, Minnesota Jones . . ."

"Jonathan?" I said. "How on earth did you find me here?"

"You knew it was me," he said, aggrieved, his voice losing all trace of the improbable accent and returning to his native London.

"Well, it sounded like you," I pointed out. "Anyway, you didn't answer my question. No one's meant to know that I was here."

"I have my ways," he said, not very mysteriously. "Listen, if Jane and I were to offer to feed you sushi—something I recall you eating in quantities that put me in mind of feeding time at London Zoo's Walrus House—and if we offered to take you to the theater before we fed you, what would you say?"

"Not sure. I'd say 'Yes' I suppose. Or 'What's the catch?' I might say that."

"Not exactly a catch," said Jonathan. "I wouldn't exactly call it a *catch*. Not a real catch. Not really."

"You're lying, aren't you?"

Somebody said something near the phone, and then Jonathan said, "Hang on, Jane wants a word." Jane is Jonathan's wife.

"How are you?" she said.

"Fine, thanks."

"Look," she said, "you'd be doing us a tremendous favor—not that we wouldn't love to see you, because we would, but you see, there's someone . . ."

"She's your friend," said Jonathan, in the background.

"She's *not* my friend. I hardly know her," she said, away from the phone, and then, to me, "Um, look, there's someone we're sort of lumbered with. She's not in the country for very long, and I wound up agreeing to entertain her and look after her tomorrow night. She's pretty frightful, actually. And Jonathan heard that you were in town from someone at your film company, and we thought you might be perfect to make it all less awful, so please say yes."

So I said yes.

In retrospect, I think the whole thing might have been the fault of the late Ian Fleming, creator of James Bond. I had read an article the previous month, in which Ian Fleming had advised any would-be writer who had a book to get done that wasn't getting written to go to a hotel to write it. I had, not a novel, but a film script that wasn't getting written; so I bought a plane ticket to London, promised the film company that they'd have a finished script in three weeks' time, and took a room in an eccentric hotel in Little Venice.

I told no one in England that I was there. Had people known, my days and nights would have been spent seeing them, not staring at a computer screen and, sometimes, writing.

Truth to tell, I was bored half out of my mind and ready to welcome any interruption.

Early the next evening I arrived at Jonathan and Jane's house, which was more or less in Hampstead. There was a small green sports car parked outside. Up the stairs, and I knocked at the door. Jonathan answered it; he wore an impressive suit. His light brown hair was longer than I remembered it from the last time I had seen him, in life or on television.

"Hello," said Jonathan. "The show we were going to take you to has been canceled. But we can go to something else, if that's okay with you."

I was about to point out that I didn't know what we were originally going to see, so a change of plans would make no difference to me, but Jonathan was already leading me into the living room, establishing that I wanted fizzy water to drink, assuring me that we'd still be eating sushi and that Jane would be coming downstairs as soon as she had put the children to bed.

They had just redecorated the living room, in a style Jonathan described as Moorish brothel. "It didn't set out to be a Moorish brothel," he explained. "Or any kind of a brothel really. It was just where we ended up. The brothel look."

"Has he told you all about Miss Finch?" asked Jane. Her hair had been red the last time I had seen her. Now it was dark brown; and she curved like a Raymond Chandler simile.

"Who?"

"We were talking about Ditko's inking style," apologized Jonathan. "And the Neal Adams issues of *Jerry Lewis*."

"But she'll be here any moment. And he has to know about her before she gets here."

Jane is, by profession, a journalist, but had become a bestselling author almost by accident. She had written a companion volume to accompany a television series about two paranormal investigators, which had risen to the top of the bestseller lists and stayed there.

Jonathan had originally become famous hosting an evening talk show, and had since parlayed his gonzo charm into a variety of fields. He's the same person whether the camera is on or off, which is not always true of television folk.

"It's a kind of family obligation," Jane explained. "Well, not exactly *family.*"

"She's Jane's friend," said her husband, cheerfully.

"She is *not* my friend. But I couldn't exactly say no to them, could I? And she's only in the country for a couple of days."

And who Jane could not say no to, and what the obligation was, I never was to learn, for at the moment the doorbell rang, and I found myself being introduced to Miss Finch. Which, as I have mentioned, was not her name.

She wore a black leather cap, and a black leather coat, and had black, black hair, pulled tightly back into a small bun, done up with a pottery tie. She wore makeup, expertly applied to give an impression of severity that a professional dominatrix might have envied. Her lips were tight together, and she glared at the world through a pair of definite black-rimmed spectacles—they punctuated her face much too definitely to ever be mere glasses.

"So," she said, as if she were pronouncing a death sentence, "we're going to the theater, then."

"Well, yes and no," said Jonathan. "I mean, yes, we are still going out, but we're not going to be able to see *The Romans in Britain*."

"Good," said Miss Finch. "In poor taste anyway. Why anyone would have thought that nonsense would make a musical I do not know."

"So we're going to a circus," said Jane, reassuringly. "And then we're going to eat sushi."

Miss Finch's lips tightened. "I do not approve of circuses," she said.

"There aren't any animals in this circus," said Jane.

"Good," said Miss Finch, and she sniffed. I was beginning to understand why Jane and Jonathan had wanted me along.

The rain was pattering down as we left the house, and the street was dark. We squeezed ourselves into the sports car and headed out into London. Miss Finch and I were in the backseat of the car, pressed uncomfortably close together.

Jane told Miss Finch that I was a writer, and told me that Miss Finch was a biologist.

"Biogeologist actually," Miss Finch corrected her. "Were you serious about eating sushi, Jonathan?"

"Er, yes. Why? Don't you like sushi?"

"Oh, I'll eat *my* food cooked," she said, and began to list for us all the various flukes, worms, and parasites that lurk in the flesh of fish and which are only killed by cooking. She told us of their life cycles while the rain pelted down, slicking nighttime London into garish neon colors. Jane shot me a sympathetic glance from the passenger seat, then she and Jonathan went back to scrutinizing a handwritten set of directions to wherever we were going. We crossed the Thames at London Bridge while Miss Finch lectured us about blindness, madness, and liver failure; and she was just elaborating on the symptoms of elephantiasis as proudly as if she had invented them herself when we pulled up in a small back street in the neighborhood of Southwark Cathedral.

"So where's the circus?" I asked.

"Somewhere around here," said Jonathan. "They contacted us

about being on the Christmas special. I tried to pay for tonight's show, but they insisted on comping us in."

"I'm sure it will be fun," said Jane, hopefully. Miss Finch sniffed.

A fat, bald man, dressed as a monk, ran down the pavement toward us. "There you are!" he said. "I've been keeping an eye out for you. You're late. It'll be starting in a moment." He turned around and scampered back the way he had come, and we followed him. The rain splashed on his bald head and ran down his face, turning his Fester Addams makeup into streaks of white and brown. He pushed open a door in the side of a wall.

"In here."

We went in. There were about fifty people in there already, dripping and steaming, while a tall woman in bad vampire makeup holding a flashlight walked around checking tickets, tearing off stubs, selling tickets to anyone who didn't have one. A small, stocky woman immediately in front of us shook the rain from her umbrella and glowered about her fiercely. "This'd better be gud," she told the young man with her—her son, I suppose. She paid for tickets for both of them.

The vampire woman reached us, recognized Jonathan and said, "Is this your party? Four people? Yes? You're on the guest list," which provoked another suspicious stare from the stocky woman.

A recording of a clock ticking began to play. A clock struck twelve (it was barely eight by my watch), and the wooden double doors at the far end of the room creaked open. "Enter . . . of your own free will!" boomed a voice, and it laughed maniacally. We walked through the door into darkness.

It smelled of wet bricks and of decay. I knew then where we were: there are networks of old cellars that run beneath some of the overground train tracks—vast, empty, linked rooms of various sizes and shapes. Some of them are used for storage by wine merchants and used-car sellers; some are squatted in, until the lack of light and facilities drives the squatters back into the daylight; most of them stand empty, waiting for the inevitable arrival of the wrecking ball and the open air and the time when all their secrets and mysteries will be no more.

A train rattled by above us.

We shuffled forward, led by Uncle Fester and the vampire woman, into a sort of a holding pen where we stood and waited.

"I hope we're going to be able to sit down after this," said Miss Finch.

When we were all settled the flashlights went out, and the spotlights went on.

The people came out. Some of them rode motorbikes and dune buggies. They ran and they laughed and they swung and they cackled. Whoever had dressed them had been reading too many comics, I thought, or watched *Mad Max* too many times. There were punks and nuns and vampires and monsters and strippers and the living dead.

They danced and capered around us while the ringmaster—identifiable by his top hat—sang Alice Cooper's song "Welcome to My Nightmare," and sang it very badly.

"I know Alice Cooper," I muttered to myself, misquoting something half-remembered, "and you, sir, are no Alice Cooper."

"It's pretty naff," agreed Jonathan.

Jane shushed us. As the last notes faded away the ringmaster was left alone in the spotlight. He walked around our enclosure while he talked.

"Welcome, welcome, one and all, to the Theater of Night's Dreaming," he said.

"Fan of yours," whispered Jonathan.

"I think it's a *Rocky Horror Show* line," I whispered back.

"Tonight you will all be witnesses to monsters undreamed-of, freaks and creatures of the night, to displays of ability to make you shriek with fear—and laugh with joy. We shall travel," he told us, "from room to room—and in each of these subterranean caverns another nightmare, another delight, another display of wonder awaits you! Please—for your own safety—I must reiterate this!—do not leave the spectating area marked out for you in each room—on pain of doom, bodily injury, and the loss of your immortal soul! Also, I must stress that the use of flash photography or of any recording devices is utterly forbidden."

And with that, several young women holding pencil flashlights led us into the next room.

"No seats then," said Miss Finch, unimpressed.

The First Room

In the first room a smiling blonde woman wearing a spangled bikini, with needle tracks down her arms, was chained by a hunchback and Uncle Fester to a large wheel.

The wheel spun slowly around, and a fat man in a red cardinal's costume threw knives at the woman, outlining her body. Then the hunchback blindfolded the cardinal, who threw the last three knives straight and true to outline the woman's head. He removed his blindfold. The woman was untied and lifted down from the wheel. They took a bow. We clapped.

Then the cardinal took a trick knife from his belt and pretended to cut the woman's throat with it. Blood spilled down from the knife blade. A few members of the audience gasped, and one excitable girl gave a small scream, while her friends giggled.

The cardinal and the spangled woman took their final bow. The lights went down. We followed the flashlights down a brick-lined corridor.

The Second Room

The smell of damp was worse in here; it smelled like a cellar, musty and forgotten. I could hear somewhere the drip of rain. The ringmaster introduced the Creature—"Stitched together in the laboratories of the night, the Creature is capable of astonishing feats of strength." The Frankenstein's monster makeup was less than convincing, but the Creature lifted a stone block with fat Uncle Fester sitting on it, and he held back the dune buggy (driven by the vampire woman) at full throttle. For his pièce de résistance he blew up a hot-water bottle, then popped it.

"Roll on the sushi," I muttered to Jonathan.

Miss Finch pointed out, quietly, that in addition to the danger of parasites, it was also the case that bluefin tuna, swordfish, and Chilean sea bass were all being overfished and could soon be rendered extinct, since they were not reproducing fast enough to catch up.

The Third Room

went up for a long way into the darkness. The original ceiling had been removed at some time in the past, and the new ceiling was the roof of the empty warehouse far above us. The room buzzed at the corners of vision with the blue-purple of ultraviolet light. Teeth and shirts and flecks of lint began to glow in the darkness. A low, throbbing music began. We looked up to see, high above us, a skeleton, an alien, a werewolf, and an angel. Their costumes fluoresced in the UV, and they glowed like old dreams high above us, on trapezes. They swung back and forth, in time with the music, and then, as one, they let go and tumbled down toward us.

We gasped, but before they reached us they bounced on the air, and rose up again, like yo-yos, and clambered back on their trapezes. We realized that they were attached to the roof by rubber cords, invisible in the darkness, and they bounced and dove and swam through the air above us while we clapped and gasped and watched them in happy silence.

The Fourth Room

was little more than a corridor: the ceiling was low, and the ringmaster strutted into the audience and picked two people out of the crowd—the stocky woman and a tall black man wearing a sheepskin coat and tan gloves—pulling them up in front of us. He announced that he would be demonstrating his hypnotic powers. He made a couple of passes in the air and rejected the stocky woman. Then he asked the man to step up onto a box.

"It's a setup," muttered Jane. "He's a plant."

A guillotine was wheeled on. The ringmaster cut a watermelon in half, to demonstrate how sharp the blade was. Then he made the man put his hand under the guillotine, and dropped the blade.

The gloved hand dropped into the basket, and blood spurted from the open cuff.

Miss Finch squeaked.

Then the man picked his hand out of the basket and chased the Ringmaster around us, while the *Benny Hill Show* music played.

"Artificial hand," said Jonathan.

"I saw it coming," said Jane.

Miss Finch blew her nose into a tissue. "I think it's all in very questionable taste," she said. Then they led us to

The Fifth Room

and all the lights went on. There was a makeshift wooden table along one wall, with a young bald man selling beer and orange juice and bottles of water, and signs showed the way to the toilets in the room next door. Jane went to get the drinks, and Jonathan went to use the toilets, which left me to make awkward conversation with Miss Finch.

"So," I said, "I understand you've not been back in England long."

"I've been in Komodo," she told me. "Studying the dragons. Do you know why they grew so big?"

"Er . . ."

"They adapted to prey upon the pygmy elephants."

"There were pygmy elephants?" I was interested. This was much more fun than being lectured on sushi flukes.

"Oh yes. It's basic island biogeology—animals will naturally tend toward either gigantism or pygmyism. There are equations, you see . . ." As Miss Finch talked her face became more animated, and I found myself warming to her as she explained why and how some animals grew while others shrank.

Jane brought us our drinks; Jonathan came back from the toilet, cheered and bemused by having been asked to sign an autograph while he was pissing.

"Tell me," said Jane, "I've been reading a lot of cryptozoological journals for the next of the *Guides to the Unexplained* I'm doing. As a biologist—"

"Biogeologist," interjected Miss Finch.

"Yes. What do you think the chances are of prehistoric animals being alive today, in secret, unknown to science?"

"It's very unlikely," said Miss Finch, as if she were telling us off. "There is, at any rate, no 'Lost World' off on some island, filled with mammoths and Smilodons and aepyornis "

"Sounds a bit rude," said Jonathan. "A what?"

"Aepyornis. A giant flightless prehistoric bird," said Jane.

"I knew that really," he told her.

"Although of course, they're *not* prehistoric," said Miss Finch. "The last aepyornises were killed off by Portuguese sailors on Madagascar about three hundred years ago. And there are fairly reliable accounts of a pygmy mammoth being presented at the Russian court in the sixteenth century, and a band of something which from the descriptions we have were almost definitely some kind of saber-tooth—the Smilodon—brought in from North Africa by Vespasian to die in the circus. So these things aren't all prehistoric. Often, they're historic."

"I wonder what the point of the saber teeth would be," I said. "You'd think they'd get in the way."

"Nonsense," said Miss Finch. "Smilodon was a most efficient hunter. Must have been—the saber teeth are repeated a number of times in the fossil record. I wish with all my heart that there were some left today. But there aren't. We know the world too well."

"It's a big place," said Jane, doubtfully, and then the lights were flickered on and off, and a ghastly, disembodied voice told us to walk into the next room, that the latter half of the show was not for the faint of heart, and that later tonight, for one night only, the Theater of Night's Dreaming would be proud to present the Cabinet of Wishes Fulfill'd.

We threw away our plastic glasses, and we shuffled into

The Sixth Room

"Presenting," announced the ringmaster, "The Painmaker!"

The spotlight swung up to reveal an abnormally thin young man in bathing trunks, hanging from hooks through his nipples. Two of the punk girls helped him down to the ground, and handed him his props. He hammered a six-inch nail into his nose, lifted weights with a piercing through his tongue, put several ferrets into his bathing trunks, and, for his final trick, allowed the taller of the punk girls to use his stomach as a dartboard for accurately flung hypodermic needles.

"Wasn't he on the show, years ago?" asked Jane.

"Yeah," said Jonathan. "Really nice guy. He lit a firework held in his teeth."

"I thought you said there were no animals," said Miss Finch. "How do you think those poor ferrets feel about being stuffed into that young man's nether regions?"

"I suppose it depends mostly on whether they're boy ferrets or girl ferrets," said Jonathan, cheerfully.

The Seventh Room

contained a rock-and-roll comedy act, with some clumsy slapstick. A nun's breasts were revealed, and the hunchback lost his trousers.

The Eighth Room

was dark. We waited in the darkness for something to happen. I wanted to sit down. My legs ached, I was tired and cold, and I'd had enough.

Then someone started to shine a light at us. We blinked and squinted and covered our eyes.

"Tonight," an odd voice said, cracked and dusty. Not the ringmaster, I was sure of that. "Tonight, one of you shall get a wish. One of you will gain all that you desire, in the Cabinet of Wishes Fulfill'd. Who shall it be?"

"Ooh. At a guess, another plant in the audience," I whispered, remembering the one-handed man in the fourth room.

"Shush," said Jane.

"Who will it be? You, sir? You, madam?" A figure came out of the darkness and shambled toward us. It was hard to see him properly, for he held a portable spotlight. I wondered if he were wearing some kind of ape costume, for his outline seemed inhuman, and he moved as gorillas move. Perhaps it was the man who played the Creature. "Who shall it be, eh?" We squinted at him, edged out of his way.

And then he pounced. "Aha! I think we have our volunteer," he said, leaping over the rope barrier that separated the audience from the show area around us. Then he grabbed Miss Finch by the hand.

"I really don't think so," said Miss Finch, but she was being dragged away from us, too nervous, too polite, fundamentally too English to make a scene. She was pulled into the darkness, and she was gone to us.

Jonathan swore. "I don't think she's going to let us forget this in a hurry," he said.

The lights went on. A man dressed as a giant fish then proceeded to ride a motorbike around the room several times. Then he stood up on the seat as it went around. Then he sat down and drove the bike up and down the walls of the room, and then he hit a brick and skidded and fell over, and the bike landed on top of him.

The hunchback and the topless nun ran on and pulled the bike off the man in the fish-suit and hauled him away.

"I just broke my sodding leg," he was saying, in a dull, numb voice. "It's sodding broken. My sodding leg," as they carried him out.

"Do you think that was meant to happen?" asked a girl in the crowd near to us.

"No," said the man beside her.

Slightly shaken, Uncle Fester and the vampire woman ushered us forward, into

The Ninth Room

where Miss Finch awaited us.

It was a huge room. I knew that, even in the thick darkness. Perhaps the dark intensifies the other senses; perhaps it's simply that we are always processing more information than we imagine. Echoes of our shuffling and coughing came back to us from walls hundreds of feet away.

And then I became convinced, with a certainty bordering upon madness, that there were great beasts in the darkness, and that they were watching us with hunger.

Slowly the lights came on, and we saw Miss Finch. I wonder to this day where they got the costume.

Her black hair was down. The spectacles were gone. The costume, what little there was of it, fitted her perfectly. She held a spear, and she stared at us without emotion. Then the great cats padded into the light next to her. One of them threw its head back and roared.

Someone began to wail. I could smell the sharp animal stench of urine.

The animals were the size of tigers, but unstriped; they were the color of a sandy beach at evening. Their eyes were topaz, and their breath smelled of fresh meat and of blood.

I stared at their jaws: the saber teeth were indeed teeth, not tusks: huge, overgrown fangs, made for rending, for tearing, for ripping meat from the bone.

The great cats began to pad around us, circling slowly. We huddled together, closing ranks, each of us remembering in our guts what it was like in the old times, when we hid in our caves when the night came and the beasts went on the prowl; remembering when we were prey.

The Smilodons, if that was what they were, seemed uneasy, wary. Their tails switched whiplike from side to side impatiently. Miss Finch said nothing. She just stared at her animals.

Then the stocky woman raised her umbrella and waved it at one of the great cats. "Keep back, you ugly brute," she told it.

It growled at her and tensed back, like a cat about to spring.

The stocky woman went pale, but she kept her umbrella pointed out like a sword. She made no move to run in the torchlit darkness beneath the city.

And then it sprang, batting her to the ground with one huge velvet paw. It stood over her, triumphantly, and roared so deeply that I could feel it in the pit of my stomach. The stocky woman seemed to have passed out, which was, I felt, a mercy: with luck, she would not know when the bladelike fangs tore at her old flesh like twin daggers.

I looked around for some way out, but the other tiger was prowling around us, keeping us herded within the rope enclosure, like frightened sheep.

I could hear Jonathan muttering the same three dirty words, over and over and over.

"We're going to die, aren't we?" I heard myself say.

"I think so," said Jane.

Then Miss Finch pushed her way through the rope barrier, and she took the great cat by the scruff of its neck and pulled it back. It resisted, and she thwacked it on the nose with the end of her spear. Its tail went down between its legs, and it backed away from the fallen woman, cowed and obedient.

There was no blood, that I could see, and I hoped that she was only unconscious.

In the back of the cellar room light was slowly coming up. It seemed as if dawn were breaking. I could see a jungle mist wreathing about huge ferns and hostas; and I could hear, as if from a great way off, the chirp of crickets and the call of strange birds awaking to greet the new day.

And part of me—the writer part of me, the bit that has noted the particular way the light hit the broken glass in the puddle of blood even as I staggered out from a car crash, and has observed in exquisite detail the way that my heart was broken, or did not break, in moments of real, profound, personal tragedy—it was that part of me that thought, *You could get that effect with a smoke machine, some plants, and a tape track. You'd need a really good lighting guy, of course.*

Miss Finch scratched her left breast, unselfconsciously, then she turned her back on us and walked toward the dawn and the jungle underneath the world, flanked by two padding saber-toothed tigers.

A bird screeched and chattered.

Then the dawn light faded back into darkness, and the mists shifted, and the woman and the animals were gone.

The stocky woman's son helped her to her feet. She opened her eyes. She looked shocked but unhurt. And when we knew that she was not hurt, for she picked up her umbrella, and leaned on it, and glared at us all, why then we began to applaud.

No one came to get us. I could not see Uncle Fester or the vampire woman anywhere. So unescorted we all walked on into

The Tenth Room

It was all set up for what would obviously have been the grand finale. There were even plastic seats arranged, for us to watch the show. We sat down on the seats and we waited, but nobody from the circus came on, and, it became apparent to us all after some time, no one was going to come.

People began to shuffle into the next room. I heard a door open, and the noise of traffic and the rain.

I looked at Jane and Jonathan, and we got up and walked out. In the last room was an unmanned table upon which were laid out souvenirs of the circus: posters and CDs and badges, and an open cash box. Sodium-yellow light spilled in from the street outside, through an open door, and the wind gusted at the unsold posters, flapping the corners up and down impatiently.

"Should we wait for her?" one of us said, and I wish I could say that it was me. But the others shook their heads, and we walked out into the rain, which had by now subsided to a low and gusty drizzle.

After a short walk down narrow roads, in the rain and the wind, we found our way to the car. I stood on the pavement, waiting for the back door to be unlocked to let me in, and over the rain and the noise of the city I thought I heard a tiger, for, somewhere close by, there was a low roar that made the whole world shake. But perhaps it was only the passage of a train.

CHANGES

1998

I.

LATER, THEY WOULD POINT to his sister's death, the cancer that ate her twelve-year-old life, tumors the size of duck eggs in her brain, and him a boy of seven, snot-nosed and crew-cut, watching her die in the white hospital with his wide brown eyes, and they would say, "That was the start of it all," and perhaps it was.

In *Reboot* (dir. Robert Zemeckis, 2018), the biopic, they jumpcut to his teens, and he's watching his science teacher die of AIDS, following their argument over dissecting a large pale-stomached frog.

"Why should we take it apart?" says the young Rajit as the music swells. "Instead, should we not give it life?" His teacher, played by the late James Earl Jones, looks shamed and then inspired, and he lifts his hand from his hospital bed to the boy's bony shoulder. "Well, if anyone can do it, Rajit, you can," he says in a deep bass rumble.

The boy nods and stares at us with a dedication in his eyes that borders upon fanaticism.

This never happened.

II.

IT IS A GRAY November day, and Rajit is now a tall man in his forties with dark-rimmed spectacles, which he is not currently wearing. The lack of spectacles emphasizes his nudity. He is sitting in the bath as the water gets cold, practicing the conclusion to his speech. He stoops a little in everyday life, although he is not stooping now, and he considers his words before he speaks. He is not a good public speaker.

The apartment in Brooklyn, which he shares with another research scientist and a librarian, is empty today. His penis is shrunken and nutlike in the tepid water. "What this means," he says loudly and slowly, "is that the war against cancer has been won."

Then he pauses, takes a question from an imaginary reporter on the other side of the bathroom.

"Side effects?" he replies to himself in an echoing bathroom voice. "Yes, there are some side effects. But as far as we have been able to ascertain, nothing that will create any permanent changes."

He climbs out of the battered porcelain bathtub and walks, naked, to the toilet bowl, into which he throws up, violently, the stage fright pushing through him like a gutting knife. When there is nothing more to throw up and the dry heaves have subsided, Rajit rinses his mouth with Listerine, gets dressed, and takes the subway into central Manhattan.

III.

IT IS, AS *TIME* magazine will point out, a discovery that would "change the nature of medicine every bit as fundamentally and as importantly as the discovery of penicillin."

"What if," says Jeff Goldblum, playing the adult Rajit in the biopic, "just—what if—you could reset the body's genetic code? So many ills come because the body has forgotten what it should be doing. The code has become scrambled. The program has become corrupted. What if . . . what if you could fix it?"

"You're crazy," retorts his lovely blonde girlfriend, in the movie. In real life he has no girlfriend; in real life Rajit's sex life is a fitful series of commercial transactions between Rajit and the young men of the AAA-Ajax Escort Agency.

"Hey," says Jeff Goldblum, putting it better than Rajit ever did, "it's like a computer. Instead of trying to fix the glitches caused by a corrupted program one by one, symptom by symptom, you can just reinstall the program. All the information's there all along. We just have to tell our bodies to go and recheck the RNA and the DNA— reread the program if you will. And then reboot."

The blonde actress smiles, and stops his words with a kiss, amused and impressed and passionate.

IV.

THE WOMAN HAS CANCER of the spleen and of the lymph nodes and abdomen: non-Hodgkin's lymphoma. She also has pneumonia. She has agreed to Rajit's request to use an experimental treatment on her. She also knows that claiming to cure cancer is illegal in America. She was a fat woman until recently. The weight has fallen from her, and she reminds Rajit of a snowman in the sun: each day she melts, each day she is, he feels, less defined.

"It is not a drug as you understand it," he tells her. "It is a set of chemical instructions." She looks blank. He injects two ampules of a clear liquid into her veins.

Soon she sleeps.

When she awakes, she is free of cancer. The pneumonia kills her soon after that.

Rajit has spent the two days before her death wondering how he will explain the fact that, as the autopsy demonstrates beyond a doubt, the patient now has a penis and is, in every respect, functionally and chromosomally male.

V.

IT IS TWENTY YEARS later in a tiny apartment in New Orleans (although it might as well be in Moscow, or Manchester, or Paris, or Berlin). Tonight is going to be a big night, and Jo/e is going to stun.

The choice is between a Polonaise crinoline-style eighteenth-century French court dress (fiberglass bustle, underwired décolletage setting off lace-embroidered crimson bodice) and a reproduction of Sir Philip Sidney's court dress in black velvet and silver thread, complete with ruff and codpiece. Eventually, and after weighing all the options, Jo/e plumps for cleavage over cock. Twelve hours to go: Jo/e opens the bottle with the red pills, each little red pill marked with an X, and pops two of them. It's 10 A.M., and Jo/e goes to bed, begins to masturbate, penis semihard, but falls asleep before coming.

The room is very small. Clothes hang from every surface. An empty pizza box sits on the floor. Jo/e snores loudly, normally, but when freebooting Jo/e makes no sound at all, and might as well be in some kind of coma.

Jo/e wakes at 10 P.M., feeling tender and new. Back when Jo/e first started on the party scene, each change would prompt a severe self-examination, peering at moles and nipples, foreskin or clit, finding out which scars had vanished and which ones had remained. But Jo/e's now an old hand at this and puts on the bustle, the petticoat, the bodice and the gown, new breasts (high and conical) pushed together, petticoat trailing the floor, which means Jo/e can wear the forty-year-old pair of Dr. Martens boots underneath (you never know when you'll need to run, or to walk or to kick, and silk slippers do no one any favors).

High, powder-look wig completes the look. And a spray of cologne. Then Jo/e's hand fumbles at the petticoat, a finger pushes between the legs (Jo/e wears no knickers, claiming a desire for authenticity to which the Doc Martens give the lie) and then dabs it behind the ears, for luck, perhaps, or to help pull. The taxi rings the door at 11:05, and Jo/e goes downstairs. Jo/e goes to the ball.

Tomorrow night Jo/e will take another dose; Jo/e's job identity during the week is strictly male.

VI.

RAJIT NEVER VIEWED THE gender-rewriting action of Reboot as anything more than a side effect. The Nobel Prize was for anti-cancer work (rebooting worked for most cancers, it was discovered, but not all of them).

For a clever man, Rajit was remarkably shortsighted. There were a few things he failed to foresee. For example:

That there would be people who, dying of cancer, would rather die than experience a change in gender.

That the Catholic Church would come out against Rajit's chemical trigger, marketed by this point under the brand name Reboot, chiefly because the gender change caused a female body to reabsorb into itself the flesh of a fetus as it rebooted itself: males cannot be pregnant. A number of other religious sects would come out against Reboot, most of them citing Genesis 1:27, "Male and female created He them," as their reason.

Sects that came out against Reboot included; Islam; Christian Science; the Russian Orthodox Church; the Roman Catholic Church (with a number of dissenting voices); the Unification Church; Orthodox Trek Fandom; Orthodox Judaism; the Fundamentalist Alliance of the U.S.A.

Sects that came out in favor of Reboot use where deemed the appropriate treatment by a qualified medical doctor included: most Buddhists; the Church of Jesus Christ of Latter-Day Saints; the Greek Orthodox Church; the Church of Scientology; the Anglican Church (with a number of dissenting voices); New Trek Fandom; Liberal and Reform Judaism; the New Age Coalition of America.

Sects that initially came out in favor of using Reboot recreationally: None.

While Rajit realized that Reboot would make gender reassignment surgery obsolete, it never occurred to him that anyone might wish to take it for reasons of desire or curiosity or escape. Thus, he never foresaw the black market in Reboot and similar chemical triggers; nor that, within fifteen years of Reboot's commercial release and FDA approval, illegal sales of the designer Reboot knock-offs

(*bootlegs*, as they were soon known) would outsell heroin and co-
caine, gram for gram, more than ten times over.

VII.

IN SEVERAL OF THE New Communist States of Eastern Europe possession of bootlegs carried a mandatory death sentence.

In Thailand and Mongolia it was reported that boys were being
forcibly rebooted into girls to increase their worth as prostitutes.

In China newborn girls were rebooted to boys: families would
save all they had for a single dose. The old people died of cancer as
before. The subsequent birthrate crisis was not perceived as a problem until it was too late, the proposed drastic solutions proved difficult to implement and led, in their own way, to the final revolution.

Amnesty International reported that in several of the PanArabic
countries men who could not easily demonstrate that they had
been born male and were not, in fact, women escaping the veil
were being imprisoned and, in many cases, raped and killed. Most
Arab leaders denied that either phenomenon was occurring or had
ever occurred.

VIII.

RAJIT IS IN HIS sixties when he reads in *The New Yorker* that the word
change is gathering to itself connotations of deep indecency and
taboo.

Schoolchildren giggle embarrassedly when they encounter
phrases like "I needed a change" or "Time for change" or "The
Winds of Change" in their studies of pre-twenty-first-century literature. In an English class in Norwich horrified smutty sniggers greet
a fourteen-year-old's discovery of "A change is as good as a rest."

A representative of the King's English Society writes a letter to
The Times, deploring the loss of another perfectly good word to the
English language.

Several years later a youth in Streatham is successfully prosecuted for publicly wearing a T-shirt with the slogan I'M A CHANGED MAN! printed clearly upon it.

IX.

JACKIE WORKS IN BLOSSOMS, a nightclub in West Hollywood. There are dozens, if not hundreds, of Jackies in Los Angeles, thousands of them across the country, hundreds of thousands across the world.

Some of them work for the government, some for religious organizations, or for businesses. In New York, London, and Los Angeles, people like Jackie are on the door at the places that the in-crowds go.

This is what Jackie does. Jackie watches the crowd coming in and thinks, *Born M now F, born F now M, born M now M, born M now F, born F now F . . .*

On "Natural Nights" (crudely, *unchanged*) Jackie says, "I'm sorry, you can't come in tonight" a lot. People like Jackie have a 97 percent accuracy rate. An article in *Scientific American* suggests that birth gender recognition skills might be genetically inherited: an ability that always existed but had no strict survival values until now.

Jackie is ambushed in the small hours of the morning, after work, in the back of the Blossoms parking lot. And as each new boot crashes or thuds into Jackie's face and chest and head and groin, Jackie thinks, *Born M now F, born F now F, born F now M, born M now M . . .*

When Jackie gets out of the hospital, vision in one eye only, face and chest a single huge purple-green bruise, there is a message, sent with an enormous bunch of exotic flowers, to say that Jackie's job is still open.

However, Jackie takes the bullet train to Chicago, and from there takes a slow train to Kansas City, and stays there, working as a house-painter and electrician, professions for which Jackie had trained a long time before, and does not go back.

X.

RAJIT IS NOW IN his seventies. He lives in Rio de Janeiro. He is rich enough to satisfy any whim; he will, however, no longer have sex with anyone. He eyes them all distrustfully from his apartment's window, staring down at the bronzed bodies on the Copacabana, wondering.

The people on the beach think no more of him than a teenager with chlamydia gives thanks to Alexander Fleming. Most of them imagine that Rajit must be dead by now. None of them care either way.

It is suggested that certain cancers have evolved or mutated to survive rebooting. Many bacterial and viral diseases can survive rebooting. A handful even thrive upon rebooting, and one—a strain of gonorrhea—is hypothesized to use the process in its vectoring, initially remaining dormant in the host body and becoming infectious only when the genitalia have reorganized into that of the opposite gender.

Still, the average Western human life span is increasing.

Why some freebooters—recreational Reboot users—appear to age normally, while others give no indication of aging at all, is something that puzzles scientists. Some claim that the latter group is actually aging on a cellular level. Others maintain that it is too soon to tell and that no one knows anything for certain.

Rebooting does not reverse the aging process; however, there is evidence that, for some, it may arrest it. Many of the older generation, who have until now been resistant to rebooting for pleasure, begin to take it regularly—freebooting—whether they have a medical condition that warrants it or no.

XI.

LOOSE COINS BECOME KNOWN as *coinage* or, occasionally, *specie.*

The process of making different or altering is now usually known as *shifting.*

XII.

RAJIT IS DYING OF prostate cancer in his Rio apartment. He is in his early nineties. He has never taken Reboot; the idea now terrifies him. The cancer has spread to the bones of his pelvis and to his testes.

He rings the bell. There is a short wait for the nurse's daily soap opera to be turned off, the cup of coffee put down. Eventually his nurse comes in.

"Take me out into the air," he says to the nurse, his voice hoarse. At first the nurse affects not to understand him. He repeats it, in his rough Portuguese. A shake of the head from his nurse.

He pulls himself out of the bed—a shrunken figure, stooped so badly as to be almost hunchbacked, and so frail that it seems that a storm would blow him over—and begins to walk toward the door of the apartment.

His nurse tries, and fails, to dissuade him. And then the nurse walks with him to the apartment hall and holds his arm as they wait for the elevator. He has not left the apartment in two years; even before the cancer, Rajit did not leave the apartment. He is almost blind.

The nurse walks him out into the blazing sun, across the road, and down onto the sand of the Copacabana.

The people on the beach stare at the old man, bald and rotten, in his antique pajamas, gazing about him with colorless once-brown eyes through bottle-thick dark-rimmed spectacles.

He stares back at them.

They are golden and beautiful. Some of them are asleep on the sand. Most of them are naked, or they wear the kind of bathing attire that emphasizes and punctuates their nakedness.

Rajit knows them, then.

Later, much later, they made another biopic. In the final sequence the old man falls to his knees on the beach, as he did in real life, and blood trickles from the open flap of his pajama bottoms, soaking the faded cotton and puddling darkly onto the soft sand. He stares at them all, looking from one to another with awe upon his face, like a man who has finally learned how to stare at the sun.

He said one word only as he died, surrounded by the golden people, who were not men, who were not women.

He said, "Angels."

And the people watching the biopic, as golden, as beautiful, as *changed* as the people on the beach, knew that that was the end of it all.

And in any way that Rajit would have understood, it was.

EXCERPT FROM *STARDUST*

1998

THE STAR HAD been soaked to the skin when she arrived at the pass, sad and shivering. She was worried about the unicorn; they had found no food for it on the last day's journey, as the grasses and ferns of the forest had been replaced by gray rocks and stunted thorn bushes. The unicorn's unshod hooves were not meant for the rocky road, nor was its back meant to carry riders, and its pace became slower and slower. As they traveled, the star cursed the day she had fallen to this wet, unfriendly world. It had seemed so gentle and welcoming when seen from high in the sky. That was before. Now, she hated everything about it, except the unicorn; and, saddle sore and uncomfortable, she would have even happily spent time away from the unicorn.

After a day of pelting rain, the lights of the inn were the most welcoming sight she had seen in her time on the Earth. *"Watch your step, watch your step,"* pattered the raindrops on the stone. The unicorn stopped fifty yards from the inn and would approach no closer. The door to the inn was opened, flooding the gray world with warm yellow light.

"Hello there, dearie," called a welcoming voice from the open doorway.

The star stroked the unicorn's wet neck and spoke softly to the animal, but it made no move, stood there frozen in the light of the inn like a pale ghost.

"Will you be coming in, dearie? Or will you be stopping out there in the rain?" The woman's friendly voice warmed the star, soothed her: just the right mixture of practicality and concern. "We can get you food, if it's food you're after. There's a fire blazing in the hearth and enough hot water for a tub that'll melt the chill from your bones."

"I . . . I will need help coming in . . ." said the star. "My leg . . ."

"Ach, poor mite," said the woman. "I'll have my husband Billy carry you inside. There's hay and fresh water in the stables, for your beast."

The unicorn looked about wildly as the woman approached. "There, there, dearie. I won't be coming too close. After all, it's been many a long year since I was maiden enough to touch a unicorn, and many a long year since such a one was seen in these parts. ."

Nervously, the unicorn followed the woman into the stables, keeping its distance from her. It walked along the stable to the furthest stall, where it lay down in the dry straw, and the star scrambled off its back, dripping and miserable.

Billy turned out to be a white-bearded, gruff sort of fellow. He said little, but carried the star into the inn and put her down on a three-legged stool in front of a crackling log fire.

"Poor dear," said the innkeeper's wife, who had followed them inside. "Look at you, wet as a water-nixie, look at the puddle under you, and your lovely dress, oh the state of it, you must be soaked to the bone." And, sending her husband away, she helped the star remove her dripping wet dress, which she placed on a hook near the fire, where each drip hissed and fizzed when it fell to the hot bricks of the hearth.

There was a tin tub in front of the fire, and the innkeeper's wife put up a paper screen around it. "How d'you like your baths?" she asked, solicitously, "warm, hot, or boil-a-lobster?"

"I do not know," said the star, naked but for the topaz stone on the silver chain about her waist, her head all in a whirl at the strange turn that events had taken, "for I have never had a bath before."

"Never had one?" The innkeeper's wife looked astonished. "Why, you poor duck; well, we won't make it too hot, then. Call me if you need another copperful of water, I've got some going over the kitchen fire; and when you're done with the bath, I'll bring you some mulled wine, and some sweet-roasted turnips."

And, before the star could protest that she neither ate nor drank, the woman had bustled off, leaving the star sitting in the tin tub, her broken leg in its splints sticking out of the water and resting on the three-legged stool. Initially the water was indeed too hot, but as she became used to the heat she relaxed, and was, for the first time since she had tumbled from the sky, utterly happy.

"There's a love," said the innkeeper's wife, returning. "How are you feeling now?"

"Much, much better, thank you," said the star.

"And your heart? How does your heart feel?" asked the woman.

"My heart?" It was a strange question, but the woman seemed genuinely concerned. "It feels happier. More easy. Less troubled."

"Good. That's good. Let us get it burning high and hot within you, eh? Burning bright inside you."

"I am sure that under your care my heart shall blaze and burn with happiness," said the star.

The innkeeper's wife leaned over and chucked the star under the chin. "There's a pet, such a duck it is, the fine things it says." And the woman smiled indulgently and ran a hand through her gray-streaked hair. She hung a thick toweling robe on the edge of the screen. "This is for you to wear when you are done with your bath—oh no, not to hurry, ducks—it'll be nice and warm for you, and your pretty dress will still be damp for a while now. Just give us a shout when you want to hop out of the tub and I'll come and give you a hand." Then she leaned over, and touched the star's chest, between her breasts, with one cold finger. And she smiled. "A good strong heart," she said.

There *were* good people on this benighted world, the star decided, warmed and contented. Outside the rain and the wind pattered and howled through the mountain pass, but in the inn, at the Sign of the Chariot, all was warm and comfortable. Eventually the innkeeper's wife, assisted by her dull-faced daughter, helped the star out of her bath. The firelight glinted on the topaz set in silver which the star wore on a knotted silver chain about her waist, until the topaz, and the star's body, vanished beneath the thick toweling of her robe.

"Now, my sweet," said the innkeeper's wife, "you come over here and make yourself comfortable." She helped the star over to a long wooden table, at the head of which were laid a cleaver and a knife, both of them with hilts of bone and blades of dark glass. Leaning and limping, the star made it to the table and sat down at the bench beside it.

Outside there was a gust of wind, and the fire flared up green and blue and white. Then a deep voice boomed from outside the inn, over the howl of the elements. "Service! Food! Wine! Fire! Where is the stableboy?"

Billy the innkeeper and his daughter made no move, but only looked at the woman in the red dress as if for instructions. She pursed her lips. And then she said, "It can wait. For a little. After all, you are not going anywhere, my dearie?" This last to the star. "Not on that leg of yours, and not until the rain lets up, eh?"

"I appreciate your hospitality more than I can say," said the star, simply and with feeling.

"Of course you do," said the woman in the red dress, and her fidgeting fingers brushed the black knives impatiently, as if there were something she could not wait to be doing. "Plenty of time when these nuisances have gone, eh?"

THE LIGHT OF the inn was the happiest and best thing Tristran had seen on his journey through Faerie. While Primus bellowed for assistance, Tristran unhitched the exhausted horses, and led them one by one into the stables on the side of the inn. There was a white horse asleep in the furthest stall, but Tristran was too busy to pause to inspect it.

He knew—somewhere in the odd place inside him that knew directions and distances of things he had never seen and the places he had never been—that the star was close at hand, and this comforted him, and made him nervous. He knew that the horses were more exhausted and more hungry than he was. His dinner—and thus, he suspected, his confrontation with the star—could wait. "I'll groom the horses," he told Primus. "They'll catch a chill otherwise."

The tall man rested his huge hand on Tristran's shoulder.

"Good lad. I'll send a pot-boy out with some burnt ale for you."

Tristran thought about the star as he brushed down the horses and picked out their hooves. What would he say? What would *she* say? He was brushing the last of the horses when a blank-looking pot-girl came out to him with a tankard of steaming wine.

"Put it down over there," he told her. "I'll drink it with goodwill as soon as my hands are free." She put it down on the top of a tack box and went out, without saying anything.

It was then that the horse in the end stall got to its feet and began to kick against the door.

"Settle down, there," called Tristran, "settle down, fellow, and I'll see if I cannot find warm oats and bran for all of you."

There was a large stone in the stallion's front inside hoof, and Tristran removed it with care. *Madam,* he had decided he would say, *please accept my heartfelt and most humble apologies. Sir,* the star would say in her turn, *that I shall do with all my heart. Now, let us go to your village, where you shall present me to your true love, as a token of your devotion to her. . . .*

His ruminations were interrupted by an enormous clattering, as a huge white horse—but, he realized immediately, it was not a horse—kicked down the door of its stall and came charging, desperately, toward him, its horn lowered.

Tristran threw himself onto the straw on the stable floor, his arms about his head.

Moments passed. He raised his head. The unicorn had stopped in front of the tankard, was lowering its horn into the mulled wine.

Awkwardly, Tristran got to his feet. The wine was steaming and bubbling, and it came to Tristran then—the information surfacing from some long-forgotten fairy tale or piece of children's lore—that a unicorn's horn was proof against . . .

"Poison?" he whispered, and the unicorn raised its head, and stared into Tristran's eyes, and Tristran knew that it was the truth. His heart was pounding hard in his chest. Around the inn the wind was screaming like a witch in her madness.

Tristran ran to the stable door, then he stopped and thought. He fumbled in his tunic pocket, finding the lump of wax, which was all that remained of his candle, with a dried copper leaf sticking to it. He peeled the leaf away from the wax with care. Then he raised the leaf to his ear and listened to what it told him.

"WINE, MILORD?" ASKED the middle-aged woman in the long red dress, when Primus had entered the inn.

"I am afraid not," he said. "I have a personal superstition that, until the day I see my brother's corpse cold on the ground before me, I shall drink only my own wine, and eat only food I have obtained and prepared myself. This I shall do here, if you have no objection. I shall, of course, pay you as if it were your own wine I was drinking. If I might trouble you to put this bottle of mine near the fire to take the chill from it? Now, I have a companion on my journey, a young man who is attending to the horses; he has sworn no such oath, and I am sure that if you could send him a mug of burnt ale it would help take the chill from his bones . . . ?"

The pot-maid bobbed a curtsey, and she scuttled back to the kitchens.

"So, mine host," said Primus to the white-bearded innkeeper, "how are your beds here at the back of beyond? Have you straw mattresses? Are there fires in the bedrooms? And I note with increasing pleasure that there is a bathtub in front of your fireplace—if there's a fresh copper of steaming water, I shall have a bath later. But I shall pay you no more than a small silver coin for it, mind."

The innkeeper looked to his wife, who said, "Our beds are good, and I shall have the maid make up a fire in the bedroom for you and your companion."

Primus removed his dripping black robe and hung it by the fire, beside the star's still-damp blue dress. Then he turned and saw the young lady sitting at the table. "Another guest?" he said. "Well-met, milady, in this noxious weather." At that, there was a loud clattering from the stable next door. "Something must have disturbed the horses," said Primus, concerned.

"Perhaps the thunder," said the innkeeper's wife.

"Aye, perhaps," said Primus. Something else was occupying his attention. He walked over to the star and stared into her eyes for several heartbeats. "You. ." he hesitated. Then, with certainty, "You have my father's stone. You have the Power of Stormhold."

The girl glared up at him with eyes the blue of sky. "Well, then," she said. "Ask me for it, and I can have done with the stupid thing."

The innkeeper's wife hurried over and stood at the head of the table. "I'll not have you bothering the other guests now, my dearie-ducks," she told him, sternly.

Primus's eyes fell upon the knives upon the wood of the table-top. He recognized them: there were tattered scrolls in the vaults of Stormhold in which those knives were pictured, and their names were given. They were old things, from the First Age of the world.

The front door of the inn banged open.

"Primus!" called Tristran, running in. "They have tried to poison me!"

The Lord Primus reached for his short-sword, but even as he went for it the witch-queen took the longest of the knives and drew the blade of it, in one smooth, practical movement, across his throat . . .

For Tristran, it all happened too fast to follow. He entered, saw the star and Lord Primus, and the innkeeper and his strange family, and then the blood was spurting in a crimson fountain in the firelight.

"Get him!" called the woman in the scarlet dress. "Get the brat!"

Billy and the maid ran toward Tristran; and it was then that the unicorn entered the inn.

Tristran threw himself out of the way. The unicorn reared up on its hind legs, and a blow from one of its sharp hooves sent the pot-maid flying.

Billy lowered his head and ran, headlong, at the unicorn, as if he were about to butt it with his forehead. The unicorn lowered its head also, and Billy the Innkeeper met his unfortunate end.

"*Stupid!*" screamed the innkeeper's wife, furiously, and she advanced upon the unicorn, a knife in each hand, blood staining her right hand and forearm the same color as her dress.

Tristran had thrown himself onto his hands and knees and had crawled toward the fireplace. In his left hand he had hold of the lump of wax, all that remained of the candle that had brought him here. He had been squeezing it in his hand until it was soft and malleable.

"This had better ought to work," said Tristran to himself. He hoped that the tree had known what she was talking about.

Behind him, the unicorn screamed in pain.

Tristran ripped a lace from his jerkin and closed the wax around it.

"What is happening?" asked the star, who had crawled toward Tristran on her hands and knees.

"I don't really know," he admitted.

The witch-woman howled, then; the unicorn had speared her with its horn, through the shoulder. It lifted her off the ground, triumphantly, preparing to hurl her to the ground and then to dash her to death beneath its sharp hooves, when, impaled as she was, the witch-woman swung around and thrust the point of the longer of the rock-glass knives into the unicorn's eye and far into its skull.

The beast dropped to the wooden floor of the inn, blood dripping from its side and from its eye and from its open mouth. First it fell to its knees, and then it collapsed, utterly, as the life fled. Its tongue was piebald, and it protruded most pathetically from the unicorn's dead mouth.

The witch-queen pulled her body from the horn, and, one hand gripping her wounded shoulder, the other holding her cleaver, she staggered to her feet.

Her eyes scanned the room, alighting on Tristran and the star huddled by the fire. Slowly, agonizingly slowly, she lurched toward them, a cleaver in her hand and a smile upon her face.

"The burning golden heart of a star at peace is so much finer than the flickering heart of a little frightened star," she told them, her voice oddly calm and detached, coming, as it was, from that blood-bespattered face. "But even the heart of a star who is afraid and scared is better by far than no heart at all."

Tristran took the star's hand in his right hand. "Stand up," he told her.

"I cannot," she said, simply.

"Stand, or we die now," he told her, getting to his feet. The star nodded, and, awkwardly, resting her weight on him, she began to try to pull herself to her feet.

"*Stand, or you die now?*" echoed the witch-queen. "Oh, you die now, children, standing or sitting. It is all the same to me." She took another step toward them.

"Now," said Tristran, one hand gripping the star's arm, the other holding his makeshift candle, "now, *walk!*"

And he thrust his left hand into the fire.

There was pain, and burning, such that he could have screamed, and the witch-queen stared at him as if he were madness personified.

Then his improvised wick caught and burned with a steady blue flame, and the world began to shimmer around them. "Please walk," he begged the star. "Don't let go of me."

And she took an awkward step.

They left the inn behind them, the howls of the witch-queen ringing in their ears.

They were underground, and the candlelight flickered from the wet cave walls; and with their next halting step they were in a desert of white sand, in the moonlight; and with their third step they were high above the earth, looking down on the hills and trees and rivers far below them.

And it was then that the last of the wax ran molten over Tristran's hand, and the burning became impossible for him to bear, and the last of the flame burned out forever.

HARLEQUIN VALENTINE

1999

IT IS FEBRUARY the fourteenth, at that hour of the morning when all the children have been taken to school and all the husbands have driven themselves to work or been dropped, steambreathing and greatcoated, at the rail station at the edge of the town for the Great Commute, when I pin my heart to Missy's front door. The heart is a deep dark red that is almost a brown, the color of liver. Then I knock on the door, sharply, *rat-a-tat-tat!*, and I grasp my wand, my stick, my oh-so-thrustable and beribboned lance and I vanish like cooling steam into the chilly air. . . .

Missy opens the door. She looks tired.

"My Columbine," I breathe, but she hears not a word. She turns her head, so she takes in the view from one side of the street to the other, but nothing moves. A truck rumbles in the distance. She walks back into the kitchen, and I dance, silent as a breeze, as a mouse, as a dream, into the kitchen beside her.

Missy takes a plastic sandwich bag from a paper box in the kitchen drawer, and a bottle of cleaning spray from under the sink. She pulls off two sections of paper towel from the roll on the kitchen counter. Then she walks back to the front door. She pulls the pin from the painted wood—it was my hatpin, which I had stumbled across where? I turn the matter over in my head: in Gascony, perhaps? or Twickenham? or Prague?

The face on the end of the hatpin is that of a pale Pierrot.

She removes the pin from the heart, and puts the heart into the plastic sandwich bag. She wipes the blood from the door with a squirt of cleaning spray and a rub of paper towel, and she inserts the pin into her lapel, where the little white-faced August stares out at the cold world with his blind silver eyes and his grave silver lips. Naples. Now it comes back to me. I purchased the hatpin in Naples, from an old woman with one eye. She smoked a clay pipe. This was a long time ago.

Missy puts the cleaning utensils down on the kitchen table, then she thrusts her arms through the sleeves of her old blue coat, which was once her mother's, does up the buttons, one, two, three, then she places the sandwich bag with the heart in it determinedly into her pocket and sets off down the street.

Secret, secret, quiet as a mouse I follow her, sometimes creeping, sometimes dancing, and she never sees me, not for a moment, just pulls her blue coat more tightly around her, and she walks through the little Kentucky town, and down the old road that leads past the cemetery.

The wind tugs at my hat, and I regret, for a moment, the loss of my hatpin. But I am in love, and this is Valentine's Day. Sacrifices must be made.

Missy is remembering in her head the other times she has walked into the cemetery, through the tall iron cemetery gates: when her father died; and when they came here as kids at All Hallows', the whole school mob and caboodle of them, partying and scaring each other; and when a secret lover was killed in a three-car pileup on the interstate, and she waited until the end of the funeral, when the day was all over and done with, and she came in the evening, just before sunset, and laid a white lily on the fresh grave.

Oh Missy, shall I sing the body and the blood of you, the lips and the eyes? A thousand hearts I would give you, as your valentine.

Proudly I wave my staff in the air and dance, singing silently of the gloriousness of me, as we skip together down Cemetery Road.

A low gray building, and Missy pushes open the door. She says Hi and How's it going to the girl at the desk who makes no intelligible reply, fresh out of school and filling in a crossword from a periodical filled with nothing but crosswords, page after page of them, and the girl would be making private phone calls on company time if only she had somebody to call, which she doesn't, and, I see, plain as elephants, she never will. Her face is a mass of blotchy acne pustules and acne scars and she thinks it matters, and talks to nobody. I see her life spread out before me: she will die, unmarried and unmolested, of breast cancer in fifteen years' time, and will be planted under a stone with her name on it in the meadow by Cemetery Road, and the first hands to have touched her breasts will have been those of the pathologist as he cuts out the cauliflowerlike stinking growth and mutters "Jesus, look at the size of this thing, why didn't she *tell* anyone?" which rather misses the point.

Gently, I kiss her on her spotty cheek, and whisper to her that she is beautiful. Then I tap her once, twice, *thrice,* on the head with my staff and wrap her with a ribbon.

She stirs and smiles. Perhaps tonight she will get drunk and dance and offer up her virginity upon Hymen's altar, meet a young man who cares more for her breasts than for her face, and will one day, stroking those breasts and suckling and rubbing them say "Honey, you seen anybody about that lump?" and by then her spots will be long gone, rubbed and kissed and frottaged into oblivion. . . .

But now I have mislaid Missy, and I run and caper down a dun-carpeted corridor until I see that blue coat pushing into a room at the end of the hallway and I follow her into an unheated room tiled in bathroom green.

The stench is unbelievable, heavy and rancid and wretched on the air. The fat man in the stained lab coat wears disposable rubber gloves and has a thick layer of mentholatum on his upper lip and about his nostrils. A dead man is on the table in front of him. The man is a thin, old black man with callused fingertips. He has a thin mustache. The fat man has not noticed Missy yet. He has made an incision, and now he peels back the skin with a wet, sucking sound, and how dark the brown of it is on the outside, and how pink, pretty the pink of it is on the inside.

Classical music plays from a portable radio, very loudly. Missy turns the radio off, then she says, "Hello, Vernon."

The fat man says, "Hello Missy. You come for your old job back?"

This is the Doctor, I decide, for he is too big, too round, too magnificently well-fed to be Pierrot, too unselfconscious to be Pantaloon. His face creases with delight to see Missy, and she smiles to see him, and I am jealous: I feel a stab of pain shoot through my heart (currently in a plastic sandwich bag in Missy's coat pocket) sharper than I felt when I stabbed it with my hatpin and stuck it to her door.

And speaking of my heart, she has pulled it from her pocket, and is waving it at the pathologist, Vernon. "Do you know what this is?" she says.

"Heart," he says. "Kidneys don't have the ventricles, and brains are bigger and squishier. Where'd you get it?"

"I was hoping that you could tell me," she says. "Doesn't it come from here? Is it your idea of a Valentine's card, Vernon? A human heart stuck to my front door?"

He shakes his head. "Don't come from here," he says. "You want I should call the police?"

She shakes her head. "With my luck," she says, "they'll decide I'm a serial killer and send me to the chair."

The Doctor opens the sandwich bag and prods at the heart with stubby fingers in latex gloves. "Adult, in pretty good shape, took care of his heart," he said. "Cut out by an expert."

I smile proudly at this, and bend down to talk to the dead black man on the table, with his chest all open and his callused string-bass-picking fingers. "Go 'way Harlequin," he mutters, quietly, not to offend Missy and his doctor. "Don't you go causing trouble here."

"Hush yourself. I will cause trouble wherever I wish," I tell him. "It is my function." But, for a moment, I feel a void about me: I am wistful, almost Pierrotish, which is a poor thing for a harlequin to be.

Oh Missy, I saw you yesterday in the street, and followed you into Al's Super-Valu Foods and More, elation and joy rising within me. In you, I recognized someone who could transport me, take me from myself. In you I recognized my Valentine, my Columbine.

I did not sleep last night, and instead I turned the town topsy and turvy, befuddling the unfuddled. I caused three sober bankers to make fools of themselves with drag queens from Madame Zora's

Revue and Bar. I slid into the bedrooms of the sleeping, unseen and unimagined, slipping the evidence of mysterious and exotic trysts into pockets and under pillows and into crevices, able only to imagine the fun that would ignite the following day as soiled split-crotch fantasy panties would be found poorly hidden under sofa cushions and in the inner pockets of respectable suits. But my heart was not in it, and the only face I could see was Missy's.

Oh, Harlequin in love is a sorry creature.

I wonder what she will do with my gift. Some girls spurn my heart; others touch it, kiss it, caress it, punish it with all manner of endearments before they return it to my keeping. Some never even see it.

Missy takes the heart back, puts it in the sandwich bag again, pushes the snap-shut top of it closed.

"Shall I incinerate it?" she asks.

"Might as well. You know where the incinerator is," says the Doctor, returning to the dead musician on the table. "And I meant what I said about your old job. I need a good lab assistant."

I imagine my heart trickling up to the sky as ashes and smoke, covering the world. I do not know what I think of this, but, her jaw set, she shakes her head and she bids good-bye to Vernon the pathologist. She has thrust my heart into her pocket and she is walking out of the building and up Cemetery Road and back into town.

I caper ahead of her. Interaction would be a fine thing, I decide, and fitting word to deed I disguise myself as a bent old woman on her way to the market, covering the red spangles of my costume with a tattered cloak, hiding my masked face with a voluminous hood, and at the top of Cemetery Road I step out and block her way.

Marvelous, marvelous, marvelous me, and I say to her, in the voice of the oldest of women, "Spare a copper coin for a bent old woman dearie and I'll tell you a fortune will make your eyes spin with joy," and Missy stops. She opens her purse and takes out a dollar bill.

"Here," says Missy.

And I have it in my head to tell her all about the mysterious man she will meet, all dressed in red and yellow, with his domino mask, who will thrill her and love her and never, never leave her (for it is not a good thing to tell your Columbine the *entire* truth), but instead I find myself saying, in a cracked old voice, "Have you ever heard of Harlequin?"

Missy looks thoughtful. Then she nods. "Yes," she says. "Character in the commedia dell'arte. Costume covered in little diamond shapes. Wore a mask. I think he was a clown of some sort, wasn't he?"

I shake my head, beneath my hood. "No clown," I tell her. "He was . . ."

And I find that I am about to tell her the truth, so I choke back the words and pretend that I am having the kind of coughing attack to which elderly women are particularly susceptible. I wonder if this could be the power of love. I do not remember it troubling me with other women I thought I had loved, other Columbines I have encountered over centuries now long gone.

I squint through old-woman eyes at Missy: she is in her early twenties, and she has lips like a mermaid's, full and well-defined and certain, and gray eyes, and a certain intensity to her gaze.

"Are you all right?" she asks.

I cough and splutter and cough some more, and gasp, "Fine, my dearie-duck, I'm just fine, thank you kindly."

"So," she said, "I thought you were going to tell me my fortune."

"Harlequin has given you his heart," I hear myself saying. "You must discover its beat yourself."

She stares at me, puzzled. I cannot change or vanish while her eyes are upon me, and I feel frozen, angry at my trickster tongue for betraying me. "Look," I tell her, "a rabbit!" and she turns, follows my pointing finger and as she takes her eyes off me I disappear, *pop!*, like a rabbit down a hole, and when she looks back there's not a trace of the old fortune-teller lady, which is to say me.

Missy walks on, and I caper after her, but there is no longer the spring in my step there was earlier in the morning.

Midday, and Missy has walked to Al's Super-Valu Foods and More, where she buys a small block of cheese, a carton of unconcentrated orange juice, two avocados, and on to the County One Bank where she withdraws two hundred and seventy-nine dollars and twenty-two cents, which is the total amount of money in her savings account, and I creep after her sweet as sugar and quiet as the grave.

"Morning Missy," says the owner of the Salt Shaker Café, when Missy enters. He has a trim beard, more pepper than salt, and my heart would have skipped a beat if it were not in the sandwich bag in Missy's pocket, for this man obviously lusts after her and my confidence, which is legendary, droops and wilts. *I am Harlequin,* I tell myself, *in my diamond-covered garments, and the world is my harlequinade. I am Harlequin, who rose from the dead to play his pranks upon the living. I am Harlequin, in my mask, with my wand.* I whistle to myself, and my confidence rises, hard and full once more.

"Hey, Harve," says Missy. "Give me a plate of hash browns and a bottle of ketchup."

"That all?" he asks.

"Yes," she says. "That'll be perfect. And a glass of water."

I tell myself that the man Harve is Pantaloon, the foolish merchant that I must bamboozle, baffle, confusticate, and confuse. Perhaps there is a string of sausages in the kitchen. I resolve to bring delightful disarray to the world, and to bed luscious Missy before midnight: my Valentine's present to myself. I imagine myself kissing her lips.

There is a handful of other diners. I amuse myself by swapping their plates while they are not looking, but I have difficulty finding the fun in it. The waitress is thin, and her hair hangs in sad ringlets about her face. She ignores Missy, whom she obviously considers entirely Harve's preserve.

Missy sits at the table and pulls the sandwich bag from her pocket. She places it on the table in front of her.

Harve-the-Pantaloon struts over to Missy's table, gives her a glass of water, a plate of hash-browned potatoes, and a bottle of Heinz 57 Varieties Tomato Ketchup. "And a steak knife," she tells him.

I trip him up on the way back to the kitchen. He curses, and I feel better, more like the former me, and I goose the waitress as she passes the table of an old man who is reading *USA Today* while toying with his salad. She gives the old man a filthy look. I chuckle, and then I find I am feeling most peculiar. I sit down upon the floor, suddenly.

"What's that, honey?" the waitress asks Missy.

"Health food, Charlene," says Missy. "Builds up iron." I peep over the tabletop. She is cutting up small slices of liver-colored meat on her plate, liberally doused in tomato sauce, and piling her fork high with hash browns. Then she chews.

I watch my heart disappearing into her rosebud mouth. My Valentine's jest somehow seems less funny.

"You anemic?" asks the waitress, on her way past once more, with a pot of steaming coffee.

"Not anymore," says Missy, popping another scrap of raw gristle cut small into her mouth, and chewing it, hard, before swallowing.

And as she finishes eating my heart, Missy looks down and sees me sprawled upon the floor. She nods. "Outside," she says. "Now." Then she gets up and leaves ten dollars beside her plate.

She is sitting on a bench on the sidewalk waiting for me. It is cold, and the street is almost deserted. I sit down beside her. I would caper around her, but it feels so foolish now I know someone is watching.

"You ate my heart," I tell her. I can hear the petulance in my voice, and it irritates me.

"Yes," she says. "Is that why I can see you?"

I nod.

"Take off that domino mask," she says. "You look stupid."

I reach up and take off the mask. She looks slightly disappointed. "Not much improvement," she says. "Now, give me the hat. And the stick."

I shake my head. Missy reaches out and plucks my hat from my head, takes my stick from my hand. She toys with the hat, her long fingers brushing and bending it. Her nails are painted crimson. Then she stretches and smiles, expansively. The poetry has gone from my soul, and the cold February wind makes me shiver.

"It's cold," I tell her.

"No," she says, "it's perfect, magnificent, marvelous and magical. It's Valentine's Day, isn't it? Who could be cold upon Valentine's Day? What a fine and fabulous time of the year."

I look down. The diamonds are fading from my suit, which is turning ghost-white, Pierrot-white.

"What do I do now?" I ask her.

"I don't know," says Missy. "Fade away, perhaps. Or find another role . . . A lovelorn swain, perchance, mooning and pining under the pale moon. All you need is a Columbine."

"You," I tell her. "You are my Columbine."

"Not anymore," she tells me. "That's the joy of a harlequinade, after all, isn't it? We change our costumes. We change our roles."

She flashes me such a smile, now. Then she puts my hat, my own hat, my harlequin hat, up onto her head. She chucks me under the chin.

"And you?" I ask.

She tosses the wand into the air: it tumbles and twists in a high arc, red and yellow ribbons twisting and swirling about it, and then it lands neatly, almost silently, back into her hand. She pushes the tip down to the sidewalk, pushes herself up from the bench in one smooth movement.

"I have things to do," she tells me. "Tickets to take. People to dream." Her blue coat that was once her mother's is no longer blue, but is canary yellow, covered with red diamonds.

Then she leans over, and kisses me, full and hard upon the lips.

SOMEWHERE A CAR backfired. I turned, startled, and when I looked back I was alone on the street. I sat there for several moments, on my own.

Charlene opened the door to the Salt Shaker Café. "Hey. Pete. Have you finished out there?"

"Finished?"

"Yeah. C'mon. Harve says your ciggie break is over. And you'll freeze. Back into the kitchen."

I stared at her. She tossed her pretty ringlets and, momentarily, smiled at me. I got to my feet, adjusted my white clothes, the uniform of the kitchen help, and followed her inside.

It's Valentine's Day, I thought. *Tell her how you feel. Tell her what you think.*

But I said nothing. I dared not. I simply followed her inside, a creature of mute longing.

Back in the kitchen a pile of plates was waiting for me: I began to scrape the leftovers into the pig bin. There was a scrap of dark meat on one of the plates, beside some half-finished ketchup-covered hash browns. It looked almost raw, but I dipped it into the congealing ketchup and, when Harve's back was turned, I picked it off the plate and chewed it. It tasted metallic and gristly, but I swallowed it anyhow, and could not have told you why.

A blob of red ketchup dripped from the plate onto the sleeve of my white uniform, forming one perfect diamond.

"Hey, Charlene," I called, across the kitchen. "Happy Valentine's Day." And then I started to whistle.

EXCERPT FROM *AMERICAN GODS*

2001

COMING TO AMERICA

813 A.D.

THEY NAVIGATED THE GREEN sea by the stars and by the shore, and when the shore was only a memory and the night sky was overcast and dark they navigated by faith, and they called on the all-father to bring them safely to land once more.

A bad journey they had of it, their fingers numb and with a shiver in their bones that not even wine could burn off. They would wake in the morning to see that the rime had frosted their beards, and, until the sun warmed them, they looked like old men, white-bearded before their time.

Teeth were loosening and eyes were deep-sunken in their sockets when they made landfall on the green land to the West. The men said, "We are far, far from our homes and our hearths, far from the seas we know and the lands we love. Here on the edge of the world we will be forgotten by our gods."

Their leader clambered to the top of a great rock, and he mocked them for their lack of faith. "The all-father made the world," he shouted. "He built it with his hands from the shattered bones and the flesh of Ymir, his grandfather. He placed Ymir's brains in the sky as clouds, and his salt blood became the seas we crossed. If he made the world, do you not realize that he created this land as well? And if we die here as men, shall we not be received into his hall?"

And the men cheered and laughed. They set to, with a will, to build a hall out of split trees and mud, inside a small stockade of sharpened logs, although as far as they knew they were the only men in the new land.

On the day that the hall was finished there was a storm: the sky at midday became as dark as night, and the sky was rent with forks of white flame, and the thunder-crashes were so loud that the men were almost deafened by them, and the ship's cat they had brought with them for good fortune hid beneath their beached longboat. The storm was hard enough and vicious enough that the men laughed and clapped each other on the back, and they said, "The thunderer is here with us, in this distant land," and they gave thanks, and rejoiced, and they drank until they were reeling.

In the smoky darkness of their hall, that night, the bard sang them the old songs. He sang of Odin, the all-father, who was sacrificed to himself as bravely and as nobly as others were sacrificed to him. He sang of the nine days that the all-father hung from the world-tree, his side pierced and dripping from the spear-point (at this point his song became, for a moment, a scream), and he sang them all the things the all-father had learned in his agony: nine names, and nine runes, and twice-nine charms. When he told them of the spear piercing Odin's side, the bard shrieked in pain, as the all-father himself had called out in his agony, and all the men shivered, imagining his pain.

They found the scraeling the following day, which was the all-father's own day. He was a small man, his long hair black as a crow's wing, his skin the color of rich red clay. He spoke in words none of them could understand, not even their bard, who had been on a ship that had sailed through the pillars of Hercules, and who could speak the trader's pidgin men spoke all across the Mediterranean. The stranger was dressed in feathers and in furs, and there were small bones braided into his long hair.

They led him into their encampment, and they gave him roasted meat to eat, and strong drink to quench his thirst. They laughed riotously at the man as he stumbled and sang, at the way his head rolled and lolled, and this on less than a drinking-horn of mead. They gave him more drink, and soon enough he lay beneath the table with his head curled under his arm.

Then they picked him up, a man at each shoulder, a man at each leg, carried him at shoulder height, the four men making him an eight-legged horse, and they carried him at the head of a procession to an ash tree on the hill overlooking the bay, where they put a rope around his neck and hung him high in the wind, their tribute to the all-father, the gallows lord. The screaling's body swung in the wind, his face blackening, his tongue protruding, his eyes popping, his penis hard enough to hang a leather helmet on, while the men cheered and shouted and laughed, proud to be sending their sacrifice to the Heavens.

And, the next day, when two huge ravens landed upon the screaling's corpse, one on each shoulder, and commenced to peck at its cheeks and eyes, the men knew their sacrifice had been accepted.

It was a long winter, and they were hungry, but they were cheered by the thought that, when spring came, they would send the boat back to the northlands, and it would bring settlers, and bring women. As the weather became colder, and the days became shorter, some of the men took to searching for the screaling village, hoping to find food, and women. They found nothing, save for the places where fires had been, where small encampments had been abandoned.

One midwinter's day, when the sun was as distant and cold as a dull silver coin, they saw that the remains of the screaling's body had been removed from the ash tree. That afternoon it began to snow, in huge, slow flakes.

The men from the northlands closed the gates of their encampment, retreated behind their wooden wall.

The screaling war party fell upon them that night: five hundred men to thirty. They climbed the wall, and, over the following seven days, they killed each of the thirty men, in thirty different ways. And the sailors were forgotten, by history and their people.

The wall they tore down, and the village they burned. The long-boat, upside-down and pulled high on the shingle, they also burned, hoping that the pale strangers had but one boat, and that by burning it they were ensuring that no other Northmen would come to their shores.

It was more than a hundred years before Leif the Fortunate, son of Erik the Red, rediscovered that land, which he would call Vine-land. His gods were already waiting for him when he arrived: Tyr, one-handed, and gray Odin gallows-god, and Thor of the thunders.

They were there.

They were waiting.

DINNER WITH MARGUERITE OLSEN

IT WAS SATURDAY MORNING. Shadow answered the door.

Marguerite Olsen was there. She did not come in, just stood there in the sunlight, looking serious. "Mister Ainsel . . . ?"

"Mike, please," said Shadow.

"Mike, yes. Would you like to come over for dinner tonight? About six-ish? It won't be anything exciting, just spaghetti and meatballs."

"Not a problem. I like spaghetti and meatballs."

"Obviously, if you have any other plans . . ."

"I have no other plans."

"Six o'clock."

"Should I bring flowers?"

"If you must. But this is a social gesture. Not a romantic one." She closed the door behind her.

He showered. He went for a short walk, down to the bridge and back. The sun was up, a tarnished quarter in the sky, and he was sweating in his coat by the time he got home. It had to be above freezing. He drove the 4Runner down to Dave's Finest Foods and bought a bottle of wine. It was a twenty-dollar bottle, which seemed to Shadow like some kind of guarantee of quality. He didn't know wines, but he figured that for twenty bucks it ought to taste good. He bought a Californian Cabernet, because Shadow had once seen a bumper sticker, back when he was younger and people still had bumper stickers on their cars, which said LIFE IS A CABERNET and it had made him laugh.

He bought a plant in a pot as a gift. Green leaves, no flowers. Nothing remotely romantic about that.

He bought a carton of milk, which he would never drink, and a selection of fruit, which he would never eat.

Then he drove over to Mabel's and bought a single lunchtime pasty. Mabel's face lit up when she saw him. "Did Hinzelmann catch up with you?"

"I didn't know he was looking for me."

"Yup. Wants to take you ice-fishing. And Chad Mulligan wanted to know if I'd seen you around. His cousin's here from out of state. She's a widow. His second cousin, what we used to call kissing cousins. Such a sweetheart. You'll love her." And she dropped the pasty into a brown paper bag, twisted the top of the bag over to keep the pasty warm.

Shadow drove the long way home, eating one-handed, the steaming pasty's pastry-crumbs tumbling onto his jeans and onto the floor of the 4Runner. He passed the library on the south shore of the lake. It was a black and white town in the ice and the snow. Spring seemed unimaginably far away: the klunker would always sit on the ice, with the ice-fishing shelters and the pickup trucks and the snowmobile tracks.

He reached his apartment, parked, walked up the drive, up the wooden steps to his apartment. The goldfinches and nuthatches on the bird feeder hardly gave him a glance. He went inside. He watered the plant, wondered whether or not to put the wine into the refrigerator.

There was a lot of time to kill until six.

Shadow wished he could comfortably watch television once more. He wanted to be entertained, not to have to think, just to sit and let the sounds and the light wash over him. *Do you want to see Lucy's tits?* something with a Lucy voice whispered in his memory, and he shook his head, although there was no one there to see him.

He was nervous, he realized. This would be his first real social interaction with other people—normal people, not people in jail, not gods or culture heroes or dreams—since he was first arrested, over three years ago. He would have to make conversation, as Mike Ainsel.

He checked his watch. It was two thirty. Marguerite Olsen had told him to be there at six. Did she mean six *exactly*? Should he be there a little early? A little late? He decided, eventually, to walk next door at five past six.

Shadow's telephone rang.

"Yeah?" he said.

"That's no way to answer the phone," growled Wednesday.

"When I get my telephone connected I'll answer it politely," said Shadow. "Can I help you?"

"I don't know," said Wednesday. There was a pause. Then he said, "Organizing gods is like herding cats into straight lines. They don't take naturally to it." There was a deadness, and an exhaustion, in Wednesday's voice that Shadow had never heard before.

"What's wrong?"

"It's hard. It's too fucking hard. I don't know if this is going to work. We might as well cut our throats. Just cut our own throats."

"You mustn't talk like that."

"Yeah. Right."

"Well, if you do cut your throat," said Shadow, trying to jolly Wednesday out of his darkness, "maybe it wouldn't even hurt."

"It would hurt. Even for my kind, pain still hurts. If you move and act in the material world, then the material world acts on you. Pain hurts, just as greed intoxicates and lust burns. We may not die easy and we sure as hell don't die well, but we can die. If we're still loved and remembered, something else a whole lot like us comes along and takes our place and the whole damn thing starts all over again. And if we're forgotten, we're done."

Shadow did not know what to say. He said, "So where are you calling from?"

"None of your goddamn business."

"Are you drunk?"

"Not yet. I just keep thinking about Thor. You never knew him. Big guy, like you. Good hearted. Not bright, but he'd give you the goddamned shirt off his back if you asked him. And he killed himself. He put a gun in his mouth and blew his head off in Philadelphia in 1932. What kind of a way is that for a god to die?"

"I'm sorry."

"You don't give two fucking cents, son. He was a whole lot like you. Big and dumb." Wednesday stopped talking. He coughed.

"What's wrong?" said Shadow, for the second time.

"They got in touch."

"Who did?"

"The opposition."

"And?"

"They want to discuss a truce. Peace talks. Live and let fucking live."

"So what happens now?"

"Now I go and drink bad coffee with the modern assholes in a Kansas City Masonic hall."

"Okay. You going to pick me up, or shall I meet you somewhere?"

"You stay there and you keep your head down. Don't get into any trouble. You hear me?"

"But—"

There was a click, and the line went dead and stayed dead. There was no dial tone, but then, there never was.

Nothing but time to kill. The conversation with Wednesday had left Shadow with a sense of disquiet. He got up, intending to go for a walk, but already the light was fading, and he sat back down again.

Shadow picked up the *Minutes of the Lakeside City Council 1872–1884* and turned the pages, his eyes scanning the tiny print, not actually reading it, occasionally scanning something that caught his eye.

In July of 1874, Shadow learned, the city council was concerned about the number of itinerant foreign loggers arriving in the town. An opera house was to be built on the corner of Third Street and Broadway. It was to be expected that the nuisances attendant to the damming of Mill Creek would abate once the millpond had become a lake. The council authorized the payment of seventy dollars to Mr. Samuel Samuels, and of eighty-five dollars to Mr. Heikki Salminen, in compensation for their land and for the expenses incurred in moving their domiciles out of the area to be flooded.

It had never occurred to Shadow before that the lake was man-made. Why call a town Lakeside, when the lake had begun as a dammed millpond? He read on, to discover that a Mr. Hinzelmann, originally of Hüdemuhlen in Brunswick, was in charge of the lake-building project, and that the city council had granted him the sum of $370 toward the project, any shortfall to be made up by public subscription. Shadow tore off a strip of a paper towel and placed it into the book as a bookmark. He could imagine Hinzelmann's pleasure in seeing the reference to his grandfather. He wondered if the old man knew that his family had been instrumental in building the lake. Shadow flipped forward through the book, scanning for more references to the lake-building project.

They had dedicated the lake in a ceremony in the spring of 1876, as a precursor to the town's centennial celebrations. A vote of thanks to Mr. Hinzelmann was taken by the council.

Shadow checked his watch. It was five thirty. He went into the bathroom, shaved, combed his hair. He changed his clothes. Somehow the final fifteen minutes passed. He got the wine and the plant, and he walked next door.

The door opened as he knocked. Marguerite Olsen looked almost as nervous as he felt. She took the wine bottle and the potted plant, and said thank you. The television was on, *The Wizard of Oz* on video. It was still in sepia, and Dorothy was still in Kansas, sitting with her eyes closed in Professor Marvel's wagon as the old fraud pretended to read her mind, and the twister-wind that would tear her away from her life was approaching. Leon sat in front of the screen, playing with a toy fire truck. When he saw Shadow an expression of delight touched his face; he stood up and ran, tripping over his feet in his excitement, into a back bedroom, from which he emerged a moment later, triumphantly waving a quarter.

"Watch, Mike Ainsel!" he shouted. Then he closed both his hands and he pretended to take the coin into his right hand, which he opened wide. "I made it disappear, Mike Ainsel!"

"You did," agreed Shadow. "After we've eaten, if it's okay with your mom, I'll show you how to do it even smoother than that."

"Do it now if you want," said Marguerite. "We're still waiting for Samantha. I sent her out for sour cream. I don't know what's taking her so long."

And, as if that was her cue, footsteps sounded on the wooden deck, and somebody shouldered open the front door. Shadow did not recognize her at first, then she said, "I didn't know if you wanted the kind with calories or the kind that tastes like wallpaper paste so I went for the kind with calories," and he knew her then: the girl from the road to Cairo.

"That's fine," said Marguerite. "Sam, this is my neighbor, Mike Ainsel. Mike, this is Samantha Black Crow, my sister."

I don't know you, thought Shadow desperately. *You've never met me before. We're total strangers.* He tried to remember how he had thought *snow*, how easy and light that had been: this was desperate. He put out his hand and said, "Pleased to meetcha."

She blinked, looked up at his face. A moment of puzzlement, then recognition entered her eyes and curved the corners of her mouth into a grin. "Hello," she said.

"I'll see how the food is doing," said Marguerite, in the taut voice of someone who burns things in kitchens if they leave them alone and unwatched even for a moment.

Sam took off her puffy coat and her hat. "So you're the melancholy but mysterious neighbor," she said. "Who'da thunk it?" She kept her voice down.

"And you," he said, "are girl Sam. Can we talk about this later?"

"If you promise to tell me what's going on."

"Deal."

Leon tugged at the leg of Shadow's pants. "Will you show me now?" he asked, and held out his quarter.

"Okay," said Shadow. "But if I show you, you have to remember that a master magician never tells anyone how it's done."

OTHER PEOPLE

2001

"TIME IS FLUID here," said the demon.

He knew it was a demon the moment he saw it. He knew it, just as he knew the place was Hell. There was nothing else that either of them could have been.

The room was long, and the demon waited by a smoking brazier at the far end. A multitude of objects hung on the rock-gray walls, of the kind that it would not have been wise or reassuring to inspect too closely. The ceiling was low, the floor oddly insubstantial.

"Come close," said the demon, and he did.

The demon was rake thin and naked. It was deeply scarred, and it appeared to have been flayed at some time in the distant past. It had no ears, no sex. Its lips were thin and ascetic, and its eyes were a demon's eyes: they had seen too much and gone too far, and under their gaze he felt less important than a fly.

"What happens now?" he asked.

"Now," said the demon, in a voice that carried with it no sorrow, no relish, only a dreadful flat resignation, "you will be tortured."

"For how long?"

But the demon shook its head and made no reply. It walked slowly along the wall, eyeing first one of the devices that hung there, then another. At the far end of the wall, by the closed door, was a cat-o'-nine-tails made of frayed wire. The demon took it down with one three-fingered hand and walked back, carrying it reverently. It placed the wire tines onto the brazier, and stared at them as they began to heat up.

"That's inhuman."

"Yes."

The tips of the cat's tails were glowing a dead orange.

As the demon raised its arm to deliver the first blow, it said, "In time you will remember even this moment with fondness."

"You are a liar."

"No," said the demon. "The next part," it explained, in the moment before it brought down the cat, "is worse."

Then the tines of the cat landed on the man's back with a crack and a hiss, tearing through the expensive clothes, burning and rending and shredding as they struck, and, not for the last time in that place, he screamed.

There were two hundred and eleven implements on the walls of that room, and in time he was to experience each of them.

When, finally, the Lazarene's Daughter, which he had grown to know intimately, had been cleaned and replaced on the wall in the two hundred and eleventh position, then, through wrecked lips, he gasped, "Now what?"

"Now," said the demon, "the true pain begins."

It did.

Everything he had ever done that had been better left undone. Every lie he had told—told to himself, or told to others. Every little hurt, and all the great hurts. Each one was pulled out of him, detail by detail, inch by inch. The demon stripped away the cover of forgetfulness, stripped everything down to truth, and it hurt more than anything.

"Tell me what you thought as she walked out the door," said the demon.

"I thought my heart was broken."

"No," said the demon, without hate, "you didn't." It stared at him with expressionless eyes, and he was forced to look away.

"I thought, now she'll never know I've been sleeping with her sister."

The demon took apart his life, moment by moment, instant to awful instant. It lasted a hundred years, perhaps, or a thousand—

they had all the time there ever was, in that gray room—and toward the end he realized that the demon had been right. The physical torture had been kinder.

And it ended.

And once it had ended, it began again. There was a self-knowledge there he had not had the first time, which somehow made everything worse.

Now, as he spoke, he hated himself. There were no lies, no evasions, no room for anything except the pain and the anger.

He spoke. He no longer wept. And when he finished, a thousand years later, he prayed that now the demon would go to the wall, and bring down the skinning knife, or the choke-pear, or the screws.

"Again," said the demon.

He began to scream. He screamed for a long time.

"Again," said the demon, when he was done, as if nothing had been said.

It was like peeling an onion. This time through his life he learned about consequences. He learned the results of things he had done; things he had been blind to as he did them; the ways he had hurt the world; the damage he had done to people he had never known, or met, or encountered. It was the hardest lesson yet.

"Again," said the demon, a thousand years later.

He crouched on the floor, beside the brazier, rocking gently, his eyes closed, and he told the story of his life, re-experiencing it as he told it, from birth to death, changing nothing, leaving nothing out, facing everything. He opened his heart.

When he was done, he sat there, eyes closed, waiting for the voice to say, "Again," but nothing was said. He opened his eyes.

Slowly, he stood up. He was alone.

At the far end of the room, there was a door, and as he watched, it opened.

A man stepped through the door. There was terror in the man's face, and arrogance, and pride. The man, who wore expensive clothes, took several hesitant steps into the room, and then stopped.

When he saw the man, he understood.

"Time is fluid here," he told the new arrival.

STRANGE LITTLE GIRLS

2001

THE GIRLS

New Age

S HE SEEMS SO cool, so focused, so quiet, yet her eyes remain fixed upon the horizon.

You think you know all there is to know about her immediately upon meeting her, but everything you think you know is wrong. Passion flows through her like a river of blood.

She only looked away for a moment, and the mask slipped, and you fell. All your tomorrows start here.

Bonnie's Mother

You know how it is when you love someone?

And the hard part, the bad part, the *Jerry Springer Show* part is that you never stop loving someone. There's always a piece of them in your heart.

Now that she is dead, she tries to remember only the love. She imagines every blow a kiss, the makeup that inexpertly covers the bruises, the cigarette burn on her thigh—all these things, she decides, were gestures of love.

She wonders what her daughter will do.

She wonders what her daughter will be.

She is holding a cake, in her death. It is the cake she was always going to bake for her little one. Maybe they would have mixed it together.

They would have sat and eaten it and smiled, all three of them, and the apartment would have slowly filled with laughter and with love.

Strange

There are a hundred things she has tried to chase away the things she won't remember and that she can't even let herself think about because that's when the birds scream and the worms crawl and somewhere in her mind it's always raining a slow and endless drizzle.

You will hear that she has left the country, that there was a gift she wanted you to have, but it is lost before it reaches you. Late one night the telephone will sing, and a voice that might be hers will say something that you cannot interpret before the connection crackles and is broken.

Several years later, from a taxi, you will see someone in a doorway who looks like her, but she will be gone by the time you persuade the driver to stop. You will never see her again.

Whenever it rains you will think of her.

Silence

Thirty-five years a showgirl that she admits to, and her feet hurt, day in, day out, from the high heels, but she can walk down steps with a forty-pound headdress in high heels, she's walked across a stage with a lion in high heels, she could walk through goddamn Hell in high heels if it came to that.

These are the things that have helped, that kept her walking and her head high: her daughter; a man from Chicago who loved her, although not enough; the national news anchor who paid her rent for a decade and didn't come to Vegas more than once a month; two bags of silicone gel; and staying out of the desert sun.

She will be a grandmother soon, very soon.

Love

And then there was the time that one of them simply wouldn't return her calls to his office. So she called the number he did not know that she had, and she said to the woman who answered that this was so embarrassing but as he was no longer talking to her could he be told that she was still waiting for the return of her lacy black underthings, which he had taken because, he said, they smelled of her, of both of them. Oh, and that reminded her, she said, as the woman on the other end of the phone said nothing, could they be laundered first, and then simply posted back to her. He has her address. And then, her business joyfully concluded, she forgets him utterly and forever, and she turns her attention to the next.

One day she won't love you, too. It will break your heart.

Time

She is not waiting. Not quite. It is more that the years mean nothing to her anymore, that the dreams and the street cannot touch her.

She remains on the edges of time, implacable, unhurt, beyond, and one day you will open your eyes and see her; and after that, the dark.

It is not a reaping. Instead, she will pluck you, gently, like a feather, or a flower for her hair.

Rattlesnake

She doesn't know who owned the jacket originally. Nobody claimed it after a party, and she figured it looked good on her.

It says KISS, and she does not like to kiss. People, men and women,

have told her that she is beautiful, and she has no idea what they
mean. When she looks in the mirror she does not see beauty looking
back at her. Only her face.

She does not read, watch TV, or make love. She listens to music.
She goes places with her friends. She rides roller coasters but never
screams when they plummet or twist and plunge upside down.

If you told her the jacket was yours she'd just shrug and give it
back to you. It's not like she cares, not one way or the other.

Heart of Gold

—sentences.

Sisters, maybe twins, possibly cousins. We won't know unless we
see their birth certificates, the real ones, not the ones they use to
get ID.

This is what they do for a living. They walk in, take what they
need, walk out again.

It's not glamorous. It's just business. It may not always be strictly
legal. It's just business.

They are too smart for this, and too tired.

They share clothes, wigs, makeup, cigarettes. Restless and hunting, they move on. Two minds. One heart.

Sometimes they even finish each other's—

Monday's Child

Standing in the shower, letting the water run over her, washing it
away, washing everything away, she realizes that what made it hardest was that it had smelled just like her own high school.

She had walked through the corridors, heart beating raggedly in
her chest, smelling that school smell, and it all came back to her.

It was only, what, six years, maybe less, since it had been her running from locker to classroom, since she had watched her friends
crying and raging and brooding over the taunts and the names and
the thousand hurts that plague the powerless. None of them had ever
gone this far.

She found the first body in a stairwell.

That night, after the shower, which could not wash what she had had to do away, not really, she said to her husband, "I'm scared."

"Of what?"

"That this job is making me hard. That it's making me someone else. Someone I don't know anymore."

He pulled her close and held her, and they stayed touching, skin to skin, until dawn.

Happiness

She feels at home on the range; ear protectors in position, man-shaped paper target up and waiting for her.

She imagines, a little, she remembers, a little, and she sights and squeezes and as her time on the range begins she feels rather than sees the head and the heart obliterate. The smell of cordite always makes her think of the Fourth of July.

You use the gifts God gave you. That was what her mother had said, which makes their falling-out even harder, somehow.

Nobody will ever hurt her. She'll just smile her faint vague wonderful smile and walk away.

It's not about the money. It's never about the money.

Raining Blood

Here: an exercise in choice. Your choice. One of these tales is true.

She lived through the war. In 1959 she came to America. She now lives in a condo in Miami, a tiny Frenchwoman with white hair, with a daughter and a granddaughter. She keeps herself to herself and smiles rarely, as if the weight of memory keeps her from finding joy.

Or that's a lie. Actually the Gestapo picked her up during a border crossing in 1943, and they left her in a meadow. First she dug her own grave, then a single bullet to the back of the skull.

Her last thought, before that bullet, was that she was four months' pregnant, and that if we do not fight to create a future there will be no future for any of us.

There is an old woman in Miami who wakes, confused, from a dream of the wind blowing the wildflowers in a meadow.

There are bones untouched beneath the warm French earth which dream of a daughter's wedding. Good wine is drunk. The only tears shed are happy ones.

Real Men

Some of the girls were boys.

The view changes from where you are standing.

Words can wound, and wounds can heal.

All of these things are true.

OCTOBER IN THE CHAIR

2002

OCTOBER WAS IN the chair, so it was chilly that evening, and the leaves were red and orange and tumbled from the trees that circled the grove. The twelve of them sat around a campfire roasting huge sausages on sticks, which spat and crackled as the fat dripped onto the burning applewood, and drinking fresh apple cider, tangy and tart in their mouths.

April took a dainty bite from her sausage, which burst open as she bit into it, spilling hot juice down her chin. "Beshrew and suck ordure on it," she said.

Squat March, sitting next to her, laughed, low and dirty, and then pulled out a huge, filthy handkerchief. "Here you go," he said.

April wiped her chin. "Thanks," she said. "The cursed bag of innards burned me. I'll have a blister there tomorrow."

September yawned. "You are *such* a hypochondriac," he said, across the fire. "And such *language.*" He had a pencil-thin mustache and was balding in the front, which made his forehead seem high and wise.

"Lay off her," said May. Her dark hair was cropped short against her skull, and she wore sensible boots. She smoked a small brown cigarillo that smelled heavily of cloves. "She's sensitive."

"Oh puh*lease,*" said September. "Spare me."

October, conscious of his position in the chair, sipped his apple cider, cleared his throat, and said, "Okay. Who wants to begin?" The chair he sat in was carved from one large block of oakwood, inlaid with ash, with cedar, and with cherrywood. The other eleven sat on tree stumps equally spaced about the small bonfire. The tree stumps had been worn smooth and comfortable by years of use.

"What about the minutes?" asked January. "We always do minutes when I'm in the chair."

"But you aren't in the chair now, are you, dear?" said September, an elegant creature of mock solicitude.

"What about the minutes?" repeated January. "You can't ignore them."

"Let the little buggers take care of themselves," said April, one hand running through her long blonde hair. "And I think September should go first."

September preened and nodded. "Delighted," he said.

"Hey," said February. "Hey-hey-hey-hey-hey-hey-hey. I didn't hear the chairman ratify that. Nobody starts till October says who starts, and then nobody else talks. Can we have maybe the tiniest semblance of order here?" He peered at them, small, pale, dressed entirely in blues and grays.

"It's fine," said October. His beard was all colors, a grove of trees in autumn, deep brown and fire-orange and wine-red, an untrimmed tangle across the lower half of his face. His cheeks were apple-red. He looked like a friend; like someone you had known all your life. "September can go first. Let's just get it rolling."

September placed the end of his sausage into his mouth, chewed daintily, and drained his cider mug. Then he stood up and bowed to the company and began to speak.

"Laurent DeLisle was the finest chef in all of Seattle, at least, Laurent DeLisle thought so, and the Michelin stars on his door confirmed him in his opinion. He was a remarkable chef, it is true—his minced lamb brioche had won several awards; his smoked quail and white truffle ravioli had been described in the *Gastronome* as 'the tenth wonder of the world.' But it was his wine cellar . . . ah, his wine cellar . . . that was his source of pride and his passion.

"I understand that. The last of the white grapes are harvested in me, and the bulk of the reds: I appreciate fine wines, the aroma, the taste, the aftertaste as well.

"Laurent DeLisle bought his wines at auctions, from private wine lovers, from reputable dealers: he would insist on a pedigree for each wine, for wine frauds are, alas, too common, when the bottle is selling for perhaps five, ten, a hundred thousand dollars, or pounds, or euros.

"The treasure—the jewel—the rarest of the rare and the *ne plus ultra* of his temperature-controlled wine cellar was a bottle of 1902 Château Lafite. It was on the wine list at one hundred and twenty thousand dollars, although it was, in true terms, priceless, for it was the last bottle of its kind."

"Excuse me," said August, politely. He was the fattest of them all, his thin hair combed in golden wisps across his pink pate.

September glared down at his neighbor. "Yes?"

"Is this the one where some rich dude buys the wine to go with the dinner, and the chef decides that the dinner the rich dude ordered isn't good enough for the wine, so he sends out a different dinner, and the guy takes one mouthful, and he's got, like, some rare allergy and he just dies like that, and the wine never gets drunk after all?"

September said nothing. He looked a great deal.

"Because if it is, you told it before. Years ago. Dumb story then. Dumb story now." August smiled. His pink cheeks shone in the firelight.

September said, "Obviously pathos and culture are not to everyone's taste. Some people prefer their barbecues and beer, and some of us like—"

February said, "Well, I hate to say this, but he kind of does have a point. It has to be a new story."

September raised an eyebrow and pursed his lips. "I'm done," he said, abruptly. He sat down on his stump.

They looked at one another across the fire, the months of the year.

June, hesitant and clean, raised her hand and said, "I have one about a guard on the X-ray machines at LaGuardia Airport, who could read all about people from the outlines of their luggage on the screen, and one day she saw a luggage X-ray so beautiful that she fell in love with the person, and she had to figure out which person in the line it was, and she couldn't, and she pined for months and months. And when the person came through again she knew it this time, and it was the man, and he was a wizened old Indian man and she was pretty and black and, like, twenty-five, and she knew it would never work out and she let him go, because she could also see from the shapes of his bags on the screen that he was going to die soon."

October said, "Fair enough, young June. Tell that one."

June stared at him, like a spooked animal. "I just did," she said.

October nodded. "So you did," he said, before any of the others could say anything. And then he said, "Shall we proceed to my story, then?"

February sniffed. "Out of order there, big fella. The man in the chair only tells his story when the rest of us are through. Can't go straight to the main event."

May was placing a dozen chestnuts on the grate above the fire, deploying them into patterns with her tongs. "Let him tell his story if he wants to," she said. "God knows it can't be worse than the one about the wine. And I have things to be getting back to. Flowers don't bloom by themselves. All in favor?"

"You're taking this to a formal vote?" February said. "I cannot believe this. I cannot believe this is happening." He mopped his brow with a handful of tissues, which he pulled from his sleeve.

Seven hands were raised. Four people kept their hands down—February, September, January, and July. ("I don't have anything personal on this," said July, apologetically. "It's purely procedural. We shouldn't be setting precedents.")

"It's settled then," said October. "Is there anything anyone would like to say before I begin?"

"Um. Yes. Sometimes," said June, "sometimes I think somebody's watching us from the woods, and then I look and there isn't anybody there. But I still think it."

April said, "That's because you're crazy."

"Mm," said September to everybody. "That's our April. She's sensitive, but she's still the cruelest."

"Enough," said October. He stretched in his chair. He cracked a cobnut with his teeth, pulled out the kernel, and threw the fragments of shell into the fire, where they hissed and spat and popped, and he began.

THERE WAS A BOY, OCTOBER SAID, who was miserable at home, although they did not beat him. He did not fit well, not his family, his town, nor even his life. He had two older brothers, who were twins, older than he was, and who hurt him or ignored him, and were popular. They played football: some games one twin would score more and be the hero, and some games the other would. Their little brother did not play football. They had a name for their brother. They called him the Runt.

They had called him the Runt since he was a baby, and at first their mother and father had chided them for it.

The twins said, "But he *is* the runt of the litter. Look at *him*. Look at *us*." The boys were six when they said this. Their parents thought it was cute. A name like the Runt can be infectious, so pretty soon the only person who called him Donald was his grandmother, when she telephoned him on his birthday, and people who did not know him.

Now, perhaps because names have power, he was a runt: skinny and small and nervous. He had been born with a runny nose, and it had not stopped running in a decade. At mealtimes, if the twins liked the food, they would steal his; if they did not, they would contrive to place their food on his plate and he would find himself in trouble for leaving good food uneaten.

Their father never missed a football game, and would buy an ice cream afterward for the twin who had scored the most, and a consolation ice cream for the other twin, who hadn't. Their mother described herself as a newspaperwoman, although she mostly sold advertising space and subscriptions: she had gone back to work full-time once the twins were capable of taking care of themselves.

The other kids in the boy's class admired the twins. They had called him Donald for several weeks in first grade, until the word trickled down that his brothers called him the Runt. His teachers rarely called him anything at all, although among themselves they could sometimes be heard to say that it was a pity the youngest Covay boy didn't have the pluck or the imagination or the life of his brothers.

The Runt could not have told you when he first decided to run away, nor when his daydreams crossed the border and became plans. By the time that he admitted to himself he was leaving he had a large Tupperware container hidden beneath a plastic sheet behind the garage containing three Mars bars, two Milky Ways, a bag of nuts, a small bag of licorice, a flashlight, several comics, an unopened packet of beef jerky, and thirty-seven dollars, most of it in quarters. He did not like the taste of beef jerky, but he had read that explorers had survived for weeks on nothing else; and it was when he put the packet of beef jerky into the Tupperware box and pressed the lid down with a pop that he knew he was going to have to run away.

He had read books, newspapers, and magazines. He knew that if you ran away you sometimes met bad people who did bad things to you; but he had also read fairy tales, so he knew that there were kind people out there, side by side with the monsters.

The Runt was a thin ten-year-old, small, with a runny nose and a blank expression. If you were to try and pick him out of a group of boys, you'd be wrong. He'd be the other one. Over at the side. The one your eye slipped over.

All through September he put off leaving. It took a really bad Friday, during the course of which both of his brothers sat on him (and the one who sat on his face broke wind and laughed uproariously), for him to decide that whatever monsters were waiting out in the world would be bearable, perhaps even preferable.

Saturday, his brothers were meant to be looking after him, but soon they went into town to see a girl they liked. The Runt went around the back of the garage and took the Tupperware container out from beneath the plastic sheeting. He took it up to his bedroom. He emptied his schoolbag onto his bed, filled it with his candies and comics and quarters and the beef jerky. He filled an empty soda bottle with water.

The Runt walked into town and got on the bus. He rode west, ten-dollars-in-quarters' worth of west, to a place he didn't know, which he thought was a good start, then he got off the bus and walked.

There was no sidewalk now, so when cars came past he would edge over into the ditch, to safety.

The sun was high. He was hungry, so he rummaged in his bag and pulled out a Mars bar. After he ate it he found he was thirsty, and he drank almost half of the water from his soda bottle before he realized he was going to have to ration it. He had thought that once he got out of the town he would see springs of fresh water everywhere, but there were none to be found. There was a river, though, that ran beneath a wide bridge.

The Runt stopped halfway across the bridge to stare down at the brown water. He remembered something he had been told in school: that, in the end, all rivers flowed into the sea. He had never been to the seashore. He clambered down the bank and followed the river. There was a muddy path along the side of the riverbank, and an occasional beer can or plastic snack packet to show that people had been that way before, but he saw no one as he walked.

He finished his water.

He wondered if they were looking for him yet. He imagined police cars and helicopters and dogs, all trying to find him. He would evade them. He would make it to the sea.

The river ran over some rocks, and it splashed. He saw a blue heron, its wings wide, glide past him, and he saw solitary end-of-season dragonflies, and sometimes small clusters of midges, enjoying the Indian summer. The blue sky became dusk-gray, and a bat swung down to snatch insects from the air. The Runt wondered where he would sleep that night.

Soon the path divided, and he took the branch that led away from the river, hoping it would lead to a house or to a farm with an empty barn. He walked for some time, as the dusk deepened, until at the end of the path he found a farmhouse, half tumbled-down and unpleasant-looking. The Runt walked around it, becoming increasingly certain as he walked that nothing could make him go inside, and then he climbed over a broken fence to an abandoned pasture, and settled down to sleep in the long grass with his schoolbag for his pillow.

He lay on his back, fully dressed, staring up at the sky. He was not in the slightest bit sleepy.

"They'll be missing me by now," he told himself. "They'll be worried."

He imagined himself coming home in a few years' time. The delight on his family's faces as he walked up the path to home. Their welcome. Their love. . . .

He woke some hours later, with the bright moonlight in his face. He could see the whole world—as bright as day, like in the nursery rhyme, but pale and without colors. Above him, the moon was full, or almost, and he imagined a face looking down at him, not unkindly, in the shadows and shapes of the moon's surface.

A voice said, "Where do you come from?"

He sat up, not scared, not yet, and looked around him. Trees. Long grass. "Where are you? I don't see you."

Something he had taken for a shadow moved, beside a tree on the edge of the pasture, and he saw a boy of his own age.

"I'm running away from home," said the Runt.

"Whoa," said the boy. "That must have taken a whole lot of guts."

The Runt grinned with pride. He didn't know what to say.

"You want to walk a bit?" said the boy.

"Sure," said the Runt. He moved his schoolbag so it was next to the fence post, so he could always find it again.

They walked down the slope, giving a wide berth to the old farmhouse.

"Does anyone live there?" asked the Runt.

"Not really," said the other boy. He had fair, fine hair that was almost white in the moonlight. "Some people tried a long time back, but they didn't like it, and they left. Then other folk moved in. But nobody lives there now. What's your name?"

"Donald," said the Runt. And then, "But they call me the Runt. What do they call you?"

The boy hesitated. "Dearly," he said.

"That's a cool name."

Dearly said, "I used to have another name, but I can't read it anymore."

They squeezed through a huge iron gateway, rusted part open, part closed, and they were in the little meadow at the bottom of the slope.

"This place is cool," said the Runt.

There were dozens of stones of all sizes in the small meadow. Tall stones, bigger than either of the boys, and small ones, just the right size for sitting on. There were some broken stones. The Runt knew what sort of a place this was, but it did not scare him. It was a loved place.

"Who's buried here?" he asked.

"Mostly okay people," said Dearly. "There used to be a town over there. Past those trees. Then the railroad came and they built a stop in the next town over, and our town sort of dried up and fell in and blew away. There's bushes and trees now, where the town was. You can hide in the trees and go into the old houses and jump out."

The Runt said, "Are they like that farmhouse up there? The houses?" He didn't want to go in them, if they were.

"No," said Dearly. "Nobody goes in them, except for me. And some animals, sometimes. I'm the only kid around here."

"I figured," said the Runt.

"Maybe we can go down and play in them," said Dearly.

"That would be pretty cool," said the Runt.

It was a perfect early October night: almost as warm as summer, and the harvest moon dominated the sky. You could see everything.

"Which one of these is yours?" asked the Runt.

Dearly straightened up proudly and took the Runt by the hand. He pulled him to an overgrown corner of the field. The two boys pushed aside the long grass. The stone was set flat into the ground, and it had dates carved into it from a hundred years before. Much of it was worn away, but beneath the dates it was possible to make out the words

DEARLY DEPARTED
WILL NEVER BE FORG

"Forgotten, I'd wager," said Dearly.

"Yeah, that's what I'd say, too," said the Runt.

They went out of the gate, down a gully, and into what remained of the old town. Trees grew through houses, and buildings had fallen in on themselves, but it wasn't scary. They played hide and seek.

They explored. Dearly showed the Runt some pretty cool places, including a one-room cottage that he said was the oldest building in that whole part of the county. It was in pretty good shape, too, considering how old it was.

"I can see pretty good by moonlight," said the Runt. "Even inside. I didn't know that it was so easy."

"Yeah," said Dearly. "And after a while you get good at seeing even when there ain't any moonlight."

The Runt was envious.

"I got to go to the bathroom," said the Runt. "Is there somewhere around here?"

Dearly thought for a moment. "I don't know," he admitted. "I don't do that stuff anymore. There are a few outhouses still standing, but they may not be safe. Best just to do it in the woods."

"Like a bear," said the Runt.

He walked out the back, into the woods that pushed up against the wall of the cottage, and went behind a tree. He'd never done that before, in the open air. He felt like a wild animal. When he was done he wiped himself off with fallen leaves. Then he went back out the front. Dearly was sitting in a pool of moonlight, waiting for him.

"How did you die?" asked the Runt.

"I got sick," said Dearly. "My maw cried and carried on something fierce. Then I died."

"If I stayed here with you," said the Runt, "would I have to be dead, too?"

"Maybe," said Dearly. "Well, yeah. I guess."

"What's it like? Being dead?"

"I don't mind it," admitted Dearly. "Worst thing is not having anyone to play with."

"But there must be lots of people up in that meadow," said the Runt. "Don't they ever play with you?"

"Nope," said Dearly. "Mostly, they sleep. And even when they walk, they can't be bothered to just go and see stuff and do things. They can't be bothered with me. You see that tree?"

It was a beech tree, its smooth gray bark cracked with age. It sat in what must once have been the town square, ninety years before.

"Yeah," said the Runt. "You want to climb it?"

"It looks kind of high."

"It is. Real high. But it's easy to climb. I'll show you."

It was easy to climb. There were handholds in the bark, and the boys went up the big beech like a couple of monkeys or pirates or warriors. From the top of the tree one could see the whole world. The sky was starting to lighten, just a hair, in the east.

Everything waited. The night was ending. The world was holding its breath, preparing to begin again.

"This was the best day I ever had," said the Runt.

"Me too," said Dearly. "What you going to do now?"

"I don't know," said the Runt.

He imagined himself going on across the world, all the way to the sea. He imagined himself growing up and growing older, bringing himself up by his bootstraps. Somewhere in there he would become fabulously wealthy. And then he would go back to the house with the twins in it, and he would drive up to their door in his wonderful car, or perhaps he would turn up at a football game (in his imagination the twins had neither aged nor grown) and look down at them, in a kindly way. He would buy them all, the twins, his parents, a meal at the finest restaurant in the city, and they would tell him how badly they had misunderstood him and mistreated him. They apologized and wept, and through it all he said nothing. He let their apologies wash over him. And then he would give each of them a gift, and afterward he would leave their lives once more, this time for good.

It was a fine dream.

In reality, he knew, he would keep walking, and be found tomorrow or the day after that, and go home and be yelled at, and everything would be the same as it ever was, and day after day, hour after hour until the end of time he'd still be the Runt, only they'd be mad at him for having dared to walk away.

"I have to go to bed soon," said Dearly. He started to climb down the big beech tree.

Climbing down the tree was harder, the Runt found. You couldn't see where you were putting your feet and had to feel around for somewhere to put them. Several times he slipped and slid, but Dearly went down ahead of him and would say things like "A little to the right, now," and they both made it down just fine.

The sky continued to lighten, and the moon was fading, and it was harder to see. They clambered back through the gully. Sometimes the Runt wasn't sure that Dearly was there at all, but when he got to the top, he saw the boy waiting for him.

They didn't say much as they walked up to the meadow filled with stones. The Runt put his arm over Dearly's shoulder, and they walked in step up the hill.

"Well," said Dearly. "Thanks for coming over."

"I had a good time," said the Runt.

"Yeah," said Dearly. "Me too."

Down in the woods somewhere a bird began to sing.

"If I wanted to stay—?" said the Runt, all in a burst. Then he stopped. *I might never get another chance to change it,* thought the Runt. He'd never get to the sea. They'd never let him.

Dearly didn't say anything, not for a long time. The world was gray. More birds joined the first.

"I can't do it," said Dearly, eventually. "But they might."

"Who?"

"The ones in there." The fair boy pointed up the slope to the tumbledown farmhouse with the jagged, broken windows, silhouetted against the dawn. The gray light had not changed it.

The Runt shivered. "There's people in there?" he said. "I thought you said it was empty."

"It ain't empty," said Dearly. "I said nobody lives there. Different things." He looked up at the sky. "I got to go now," he added. He squeezed the Runt's hand. And then he just wasn't there any longer.

The Runt stood in the little graveyard all on his own, listening to the birdsong on the morning air. Then he made his way up the hill. It was harder by himself.

He picked up his schoolbag from the place he had left it. He ate his last Milky Way and stared at the tumbledown building. The empty windows of the farmhouse were like eyes, watching him.

It was darker inside there. Darker than anything.

He pushed his way through the weed-choked yard. The door to

the farmhouse was mostly crumbled away. He stopped at the door-way, hesitating, wondering if this was wise. He could smell damp, and rot, and something else underneath. He thought he heard some-thing move, deep in the house, in the cellar, maybe, or the attic. A shuffle, maybe. Or a hop. It was hard to tell.

Eventually, he went inside.

NOBODY SAID ANYTHING. October filled his wooden mug with ap-ple cider when he was done, and drained it, and filled it again.

"It was a story," said December. "I'll say that for it." He rubbed his pale blue eyes with a fist. The fire was almost out.

"What happened next?" asked June, nervously. "After he went into the house?"

May, sitting next to her, put her hand on June's arm. "Better not to think about it," she said.

"Anyone else want a turn?" asked August. There was silence. "Then I think we're done."

"That needs to be an official motion," pointed out February.

"All in favor?" said October. There was a chorus of "Aye"s. "All against?" Silence. "Then I declare this meeting adjourned."

They got up from the fireside, stretching and yawning, and walked away into the wood, in ones and twos and threes, until only October and his neighbor remained.

"Your turn in the chair next time," said October.

"I know," said November. He was pale and thin-lipped. He helped October out of the wooden chair. "I like your stories. Mine are always too dark."

"I don't think so," said October. "It's just that your nights are lon-ger. And you aren't as warm."

"Put it like that," said November, "and I feel better. I suppose we can't help who we are."

"That's the spirit," said his brother. And they touched hands as they walked away from the fire's orange embers, taking their stories with them back into the dark.

FOR RAY BRADBURY

CLOSING TIME

2002

THERE ARE STILL clubs in London. Old ones, and mock-old, with elderly sofas and crackling fireplaces, newspapers, and traditions of speech or of silence, and new clubs, the Groucho and its many knockoffs, where actors and journalists go to be seen, to drink, to enjoy their glowering solitude, or even to talk. I have friends in both kinds of club, but am not myself a member of any club in London, not anymore.

Years ago, half a lifetime, when I was a young journalist, I joined a club. It existed solely to take advantage of the licensing laws of the day, which forced all pubs to stop serving drinks at eleven P.M., closing time. This club, the Diogenes, was a one-room affair located above a record shop in a narrow alley just off the Tottenham Court Road. It was owned by a cheerful, chubby, alcohol-fueled woman called Nora, who would tell anyone who asked and even if they didn't that she'd called the club the Diogenes, darling, because she was still looking for an honest man. Up a narrow flight of steps, and, at Nora's whim, the door to the club would be open, or not. It kept irregular hours.

It was a place to go once the pubs closed, that was all it ever was, and despite Nora's doomed attempts to serve food or even to send out a cheery monthly newsletter to all her club's members reminding them that the club now served food, that was all it would ever be.

I was saddened several years ago when I heard that Nora had died; and I was struck, to my surprise, with a real sense of desolation last month when, on a visit to England, walking down that alley, I tried to figure out where the Diogenes Club had been, and looked first in the wrong place, then saw the faded green cloth awnings shading the windows of a tapas restaurant above a mobile phone shop, and, painted on them, a stylized man in a barrel. It seemed almost indecent, and it set me remembering.

There were no fireplaces in the Diogenes Club, and no armchairs either, but still, stories were told.

Most of the people drinking there were men, although women passed through from time to time, and Nora had recently acquired a glamorous permanent fixture in the shape of a deputy, a blonde Polish émigrée who called everybody "darlink" and who helped herself to drinks whenever she got behind the bar. When she was drunk, she would tell us that she was by rights a countess, back in Poland, and swear us all to secrecy.

There were actors and writers, of course. Film editors, broadcasters, police inspectors, and drunks. People who did not keep fixed hours. People who stayed out too late or who did not want to go home. Some nights there might be a dozen people there, or more. Other nights I'd wander in and I'd be the only person around—on those occasions I'd buy myself a single drink, drink it down, and then leave.

That night, it was raining, and there were four of us in the club after midnight.

Nora and her deputy were sitting up at the bar, working on their sitcom. It was about a chubby-but-cheerful woman who owned a drinking club, and her scatty deputy, an aristocratic foreign blonde who made amusing English mistakes. It would be like *Cheers*, Nora used to tell people. She named the comical Jewish landlord after me. Sometimes they would ask me to read a script.

There was an actor named Paul (commonly known as Paul-the-actor, to stop people confusing him with Paul-the-police-inspector or Paul-the-struck-off-plastic-surgeon, who were also regulars), a computer gaming magazine editor named Martyn, and me. We knew each other vaguely, and the three of us sat at a table by the window and watched the rain come down, misting and blurring the lights of the alley.

There was another man there, older by far than any of the three of us. He was cadaverous and gray-haired and painfully thin, and he sat alone in the corner and nursed a single whiskey. The elbows of his tweed jacket were patched with brown leather, I remember that quite vividly. He did not talk to us, or read, or do anything. He just sat, looking out at the rain and the alley beneath, and, sometimes, he sipped his whiskey without any visible pleasure.

It was almost midnight, and Paul and Martyn and I had started telling ghost stories. I had just finished telling them a sworn-true ghostly account from my school days: the tale of the Green Hand. It had been an article of faith at my prep school that there was a disembodied, luminous hand that was seen, from time to time, by unfortunate schoolboys. If you saw the Green Hand you would die soon after. Fortunately, none of us were ever unlucky enough to encounter it, but there were sad tales of boys from before our time, boys who saw the Green Hand and whose thirteen-year-old hair had turned white overnight. According to school legend they were taken to the sanatorium, where they would expire after a week or so without ever being able to utter another word.

"Hang on," said Paul-the-actor. "If they never uttered another word, how did anyone know they'd seen the Green Hand? I mean, they could have seen anything."

As a boy, being told the stories, I had not thought to ask this, and now it was pointed out to me it did seem somewhat problematic.

"Perhaps they wrote something down," I suggested, a bit lamely.

We batted it about for a while, and agreed that the Green Hand was a most unsatisfactory sort of ghost. Then Paul told us a true story about a friend of his who had picked up a hitchhiker, and dropped her off at a place she said was her house, and when he went back the next morning, it turned out to be a cemetery. I mentioned that exactly the same thing had happened to a friend of mine as well. Martyn said that it had not only happened to a friend of his, but, because the hitchhiking girl looked so cold, the friend had lent her

his coat, and the next morning, in the cemetery, he found his coat all
neatly folded on her grave.

Martyn went and got another round of drinks, and we wondered
why all these ghost women were zooming around the country all
night and hitchhiking home, and Martyn said that probably living
hitchhikers these days were the exception, not the rule.

And then one of us said, "I'll tell you a true story, if you like. It's
a story I've never told a living soul. It's true—it happened to me, not
to a friend of mine—but I don't know if it's a ghost story. It probably
isn't."

This was over twenty years ago. I have forgotten so many things,
but I have not forgotten that night, or how it ended.

This is the story that was told that night, in the Diogenes Club.

I WAS NINE years old, or thereabouts, in the late 1960s, and I was
attending a small private school not far from my home. I was only
at that school less than a year—long enough to take a dislike to the
school's owner, who had bought the school in order to close it and to
sell the prime land on which it stood to property developers, which,
shortly after I left, she did.

For a long time—a year or more—after the school closed the
building stood empty before it was finally demolished and replaced
by offices. Being a boy, I was also a burglar of sorts, and one day
before it was knocked down, curious, I went back there. I wriggled
through a half-open window and walked through empty classrooms
that still smelled of chalk dust. I took only one thing from my visit,
a painting I had done in Art of a little house with a red door knocker
like a devil or an imp. It had my name on it, and it was up on a wall.
I took it home.

When the school was still open I walked home each day, through
the town, then down a dark road cut through sandstone hills and
all grown over with trees, and past an abandoned gatehouse. Then
there would be light, and the road would go past fields, and finally I
would be home.

Back then there were so many old houses and estates, Victorian
relics that stood in an empty half-life awaiting the bulldozers that

would transform them and their ramshackle grounds into blandly identical landscapes of desirable modern residences, every house neatly arranged side by side around roads that went nowhere.

The other children I encountered on my way home were, in my memory, always boys. We did not know each other, but, like gueril- las in occupied territory, we would exchange information. We were scared of adults, not each other. We did not have to know each other to run in twos or threes or in packs.

The day that I'm thinking of, I was walking home from school, and I met three boys in the road where it was at its darkest. They were looking for something in the ditches and the hedges and the weed-choked place in front of the abandoned gatehouse. They were older than me.

"What are you looking for?"

The tallest of them, a beanpole of a boy, with dark hair and a sharp face, said, "Look!" He held up several ripped-in-half pages from what must have been a very, very old pornographic magazine. The girls were all in black-and-white, and their hairstyles looked like the ones my great-aunts had in old photographs. Fragments of it had blown all over the road and into the abandoned gatehouse front garden.

I joined in the paper chase. Together, the three of us retrieved almost a whole copy of *The Gentleman's Relish* from that dark place. Then we climbed over a wall, into a deserted apple orchard, and looked at what we had gathered. Naked women from a long time ago. There is a smell, of fresh apples and of rotten apples moldering down into cider, which even today brings back the idea of the forbid- den to me.

The smaller boys, who were still bigger than I was, were called Simon and Douglas, and the tall one, who might have been as old as fifteen, was called Jamie. I wondered if they were brothers. I did not ask.

When we had all looked at the magazine, they said, "We're going to hide this in our special place. Do you want to come along? You mustn't tell, if you do. You mustn't tell anyone."

They made me spit on my palm, and they spat on theirs, and we pressed our hands together.

Their special place was an abandoned metal water tower in a field by the entrance to the lane near to where I lived. We climbed a high ladder. The tower was painted a dull green on the outside, and inside it was orange with rust, which covered the floor and the walls. There was a wallet on the floor with no money in it, only some cigarette cards. Jamie showed them to me: each card held a painting of a cricketer from a long time ago. They put the pages of the magazine down on the floor of the water tower, and the wallet on top of it.

Then Douglas said, "I say we go back to the Swallows next."

My house was not far from the Swallows, a sprawling manor house set back from the road. It had been owned, my father had told me once, by the Earl of Tenterden, but when he had died his son, the new earl, had simply closed the place up. I had wandered to the edges of the grounds, but had not gone further in. It did not feel abandoned. The gardens were too well-cared-for, and where there were gardens there were gardeners. Somewhere there had to be an adult.

I told them this.

Jamie said, "Bet there's not. Probably just someone who comes in and cuts the grass once a month or something. You're not scared, are you? We've been there hundreds of times. Thousands."

Of course I was scared, and of course I said that I was not. We went up the main drive until we reached the main gates. They were closed, and we squeezed beneath the bars to get in.

Rhododendron bushes lined the drive. Before we got to the house there was what I took to be a groundskeeper's cottage, and beside it on the grass were some rusting metal cages, big enough to hold a hunting dog, or a boy. We walked past them, up to a horseshoe-shaped drive and right up to the front door of the Swallows. We peered inside, looking in the windows but seeing nothing. It was too dark inside.

We slipped around the house, through a rhododendron thicket and out again, into some kind of fairyland. It was a magical grotto, all rocks and delicate ferns and odd, exotic plants I'd never seen before: plants with purple leaves, and leaves like fronds, and small half-hidden flowers like jewels. A tiny stream wound through it, a rill of water running from rock to rock.

Douglas said, "I'm going to wee-wee in it." It was very matter-of-fact. He walked over to it, pulled down his shorts, and urinated in the stream, splashing on the rocks. The other boys did it, too, both of them pulling out their penises and standing beside him to piss into the stream.

I was shocked. I remember that. I suppose I was shocked by the joy they took in this, or just by the way they were doing something like that in such a special place, spoiling the clear water and the magic of the place; making it into a toilet. It seemed wrong.

When they were done, they did not put their penises away. They shook them. They pointed them at me. Jamie had hair growing at the base of his.

"We're cavaliers," said Jamie. "Do you know what that means?" I knew about the English Civil War, Cavaliers (wrong but romantic) versus Roundheads (right but repulsive), but I didn't think that was what he was talking about. I shook my head.

"It means our willies aren't circumcised," he explained. "Are you a cavalier or a roundhead?"

I knew what they meant now. I muttered, "I'm a roundhead."

"Show us. Go on. Get it out."

"No. It's none of your business."

For a moment, I thought things were going to get nasty, but then Jamie laughed, and put his penis away, and the others did the same. They told dirty jokes to each other then, jokes I really didn't understand, for all that I was a bright child, but I heard and remembered them, and several weeks later was almost expelled from school for telling one of them to a boy who went home and told it to his parents.

The joke had the word *fuck* in it. That was the first time I ever heard the word, in a dirty joke in a fairy grotto.

The principal called my parents into the school, after I'd got in trouble, and said that I'd said something so bad they could not repeat it, not even to tell my parents what I'd done.

My mother asked me, when they got home that night.

"Fuck," I said.

"You must never, ever say that word," said my mother. She said this very firmly, and quietly, and for my own good. "That is the worst word anyone can say." I promised her that I wouldn't.

But after, amazed at the power a single word could have, I would whisper it to myself, when I was alone.

In the grotto, that autumn afternoon after school, the three big boys told jokes and they laughed and they laughed, and I laughed, too, although I did not understand any of what they were laughing about.

We moved on from the grotto. Into the formal gardens and over a small bridge that spanned a pond; we crossed it nervously, because it was out in the open, but we could see huge goldfish in the blackness of the pond below, which made it worthwhile. Then Jamie led Douglas and Simon and me down a gravel path into some woodland.

Unlike the gardens, the woods were abandoned and unkempt. They felt like there was no one around. The path was grown over. It led between trees and then, after a while, into a clearing.

In the clearing was a little house.

It was a playhouse, built perhaps forty years earlier for a child, or for children. The windows were Tudor style, leaded and crisscrossed into diamonds. The roof was mock Tudor. A stone path led straight from where we were to the front door.

Together, we walked up the path to the door.

Hanging from the door was a metal knocker. It was painted crimson and had been cast in the shape of some kind of imp, some kind of grinning pixie or demon, cross-legged, hanging by its hands from a hinge. Let me see . . . how can I describe this best? It wasn't a *good* thing. The expression on its face, for starters. I found myself wondering what kind of a person would hang something like that on a playhouse door.

It frightened me, there in that clearing, with the dusk gathering under the trees. I walked away from the house, back to a safe distance, and the others followed me.

"I think I have to go home now," I said.

It was the wrong thing to say. The three of them turned and laughed and jeered at me, called me pathetic, called me a baby. *They* weren't scared of the house, they said.

"I dare you!" said Jamie. "I dare you to knock on the door."

I shook my head.

"If you don't knock on the door," said Douglas, "you're too much of a baby ever to play with us again."

I had no desire ever to play with them again. They seemed like occupants of a land I was not yet ready to enter. But still, I did not want them to think me a baby.

"Go on. *We're* not scared," said Simon.

I try to remember the tone of voice he used. Was he frightened, too, and covering it with bravado? Or was he amused? It's been so long. I wish I knew.

I walked slowly back up the flagstone path to the house. I reached up, grabbed the grinning imp in my right hand, and banged it hard against the door.

Or rather, I tried to bang it hard, just to show the other three that I was not afraid at all. That I was not afraid of anything. But something happened, something I had not expected, and the knocker hit the door with a muffled sort of a thump.

"Now you have to go inside!" shouted Jamie. He was excited. I could hear it. I found myself wondering if they had known about this place already, before we came. If I was the first person they had brought there.

But I did not move.

"*You* go in," I said. "I knocked on the door. I did it like you said. Now *you* have to go inside. I dare you. I dare *all* of you."

I wasn't going in. I was perfectly certain of that. Not then. Not ever. I'd felt something move, I'd felt the knocker *twist* under my hand as I'd banged that grinning imp down on the door. I was not so old that I would deny my own senses.

They said nothing. They did not move.

Then, slowly, the door fell open. Perhaps they thought that I, standing by the door, had pushed it open. Perhaps they thought that I'd jarred it when I knocked. But I hadn't. I was certain of it. It opened because it was ready.

I should have run then. My heart was pounding in my chest. But the devil was in me, and instead of running I looked at the three big boys at the bottom of the path, and I simply said, "Or are you scared?"

They walked up the path toward the little house.

"It's getting dark," said Douglas.

Then the three boys walked past me, and one by one, reluctantly perhaps, they entered the playhouse. A white face turned to look at me as they went into that room, to ask why I wasn't following them in, I'll bet. But as Simon, who was the last of them, walked in, the door banged shut behind them, and I swear to God I did not touch it.

The imp grinned down at me from the wooden door, a vivid splash of crimson in the gray gloaming.

I walked around to the side of the playhouse and peered through all the windows, one by one, into the dark and empty room. Nothing moved in there. I wondered if the other three were inside hiding from me, pressed against the wall, trying their damnedest to stifle their giggles. I wondered if it was a big-boy game.

I didn't know. I couldn't tell.

I stood there in the courtyard of the playhouse, while the sky got darker, just waiting. The moon rose after a while, a big autumn moon the color of honey.

And then, after a while, the door opened, and nothing came out.

Now I was alone in the glade, as alone as if there had never been anyone else there at all. An owl hooted, and I realized that I was free to go. I turned and walked away, following a different path out of the glade, always keeping my distance from the main house. I climbed a fence in the moonlight, ripping the seat of my school shorts, and I walked—not ran, I didn't need to run—across a field of barley stubble, and over a stile, and into a flinty lane that would take me, if I followed it far enough, all the way to my house.

And soon enough, I was home.

My parents had not been worried, although they were irritated by the orange rust dust on my clothes, by the rip in my shorts. "Where were you, anyway?" my mother asked.

"I went for a walk," I said. "I lost track of time."

And that was where we left it.

IT WAS ALMOST two in the morning. The Polish countess had already gone. Now Nora began, noisily, to collect up the glasses and ashtrays and to wipe down the bar. "*This* place is haunted," she said, cheerfully. "Not that it's ever bothered me. I like a bit of company, darlings. If I didn't, I wouldn't have opened the club. Now, don't you have homes to go to?"

We said our good nights to Nora, and she made each of us kiss her on her cheek, and she closed the door of the Diogenes Club behind us. We walked down the narrow steps past the record shop, down into the alley and back into civilization.

The underground had stopped running hours ago, but there were always night buses, and cabs still out there for those who could afford them. (I couldn't. Not in those days.)

The Diogenes Club itself closed several years later, finished off by Nora's cancer and, I suppose, by the easy availability of late-night alcohol once the English licensing laws were changed. But I rarely went back after that night.

"Was there ever," asked Paul-the-actor, as we hit the street, "any news of those three boys? Did you see them again? Or were they reported as missing?"

"Neither," said the storyteller. "I mean, I never saw them again. And there was no local manhunt for three missing boys. Or if there was, I never heard about it."

"Is the playhouse still there?" asked Martyn.

"I don't know," admitted the storyteller.

"Well," said Martyn, as we reached the Tottenham Court Road and headed for the night bus stop, "I for one do not believe a word of it."

There were four of us, not three, out on the street long after closing time. I should have mentioned that before. There was still one of us who had not spoken, the elderly man with the leather elbow patches, who had left the club with the three of us. And now he spoke for the first time.

"I believe it," he said mildly. His voice was frail, almost apologetic. "I cannot explain it, but I believe it. Jamie died, you know, not long after Father did. It was Douglas who wouldn't go back, who sold the old place. He wanted them to tear it all down. But they kept the house itself, the Swallows. They weren't going to knock *that* down. I imagine that everything else must be gone by now."

It was a cold night, and the rain still spat occasional drizzle. I shivered, but only because I was cold.

"Those cages you mentioned," he said. "By the driveway. I haven't thought of them in fifty years. When we were bad he'd lock us up in them. We must have been bad a great deal, eh? Very naughty, naughty boys."

He was looking up and down the Tottenham Court Road, as if he were looking for something. Then he said, "Douglas killed himself, of course. Ten years ago. When I was still in the bin. So my memory's not as good. Not as good as it was. But that was Jamie all right, to the life. He'd never let us forget that he was the oldest. And you know, we weren't ever allowed in the playhouse. Father didn't build it for us." His voice quavered, and for a moment I could imagine this pale old man as a boy again. "Father had his own games."

And then he waved his arm and called "Taxi!" and a taxi pulled over to the curb. "Brown's Hotel," said the man, and he got in. He did not say good night to any of us. He pulled shut the door of the cab.

And in the closing of the cab door I could hear too many other doors closing. Doors in the past, which are gone now, and cannot be reopened.

A STUDY IN EMERALD

2003

1. THE NEW FRIEND

Fresh from Their Stupendous European Tour, where they performed before several of the CROWNED HEADS OF EUROPE, garnering their *plaudits* and *praise* with *magnificent dramatic performances*, combining both COMEDY and TRAGEDY, the <u>*Strand Players*</u> wish to make it known that they shall be appearing at the *Royal Court Theatre*, *Drury Lane*, for a LIMITED ENGAGEMENT in April, at which they will present *My Look-Alike Brother Tom!*, *The Littlest Violet-Seller* and *The Great Old Ones Come* (this last an Historical Epic of Pageantry and Delight); each an *entire play* in one act! Tickets are available now from the Box Office.

I T IS THE immensity, I believe. The hugeness of things below. The darkness of dreams.

But I am woolgathering. Forgive me. I am not a literary man.

I had been in need of lodgings. That was how I met him. I wanted

someone to share the cost of rooms with me. We were introduced
by a mutual acquaintance, in the chemical laboratories of St. Bart's.
"You have been in Afghanistan, I perceive," that was what he said to
me, and my mouth fell open and my eyes opened very wide.

"Astonishing," I said.

"Not really," said the stranger in the white lab coat, who was to
become my friend. "From the way you hold your arm, I see you have
been wounded, and in a particular way. You have a deep tan. You
also have a military bearing, and there are few enough places in the
Empire that a military man can be both tanned and, given the nature of the injury to your shoulder and the traditions of the Afghan
cave-folk, tortured."

Put like that, of course, it was absurdly simple. But then, it always
was. I had been tanned nut-brown. And I had indeed, as he had observed, been tortured.

The gods and men of Afghanistan were savages, unwilling to be
ruled from Whitehall or from Berlin or even from Moscow, and unprepared to see reason. I had been sent into those hills, attached to
the ——th Regiment. As long as the fighting remained in the hills
and mountains, we fought on an equal footing. When the skirmishes
descended into the caves and the darkness then we found ourselves,
as it were, out of our depth and in over our heads.

I shall not forget the mirrored surface of the underground lake,
nor the thing that emerged from the lake, its eyes opening and
closing, and the singing whispers that accompanied it as it rose,
wreathing their way about it like the buzzing of flies bigger than
worlds.

That I survived was a miracle, but survive I did, and I returned
to England with my nerves in shreds and tatters. The place that
leech-like mouth had touched me was tattooed forever, frog-white,
into the skin of my now-withered shoulder. I had once been a crack
shot. Now I had nothing, save a fear of the world-beneath-the-world
akin to panic, which meant that I would gladly pay sixpence of my
army pension for a Hansom cab rather than a penny to travel underground.

Still, the fogs and darknesses of London comforted me, took me in. I had lost my first lodgings because I screamed in the night. I had been in Afghanistan; I was there no longer.

"I scream in the night," I told him.

"I have been told that I snore," he said. "Also I keep irregular hours, and I often use the mantelpiece for target practice. I will need the sitting room to meet clients. I am selfish, private, and easily bored. Will this be a problem?"

I smiled, and I shook my head, and extended my hand. We shook on it.

The rooms he had found for us, in Baker Street, were more than adequate for two bachelors. I bore in mind all my friend had said about his desire for privacy, and I forbore from asking what it was he did for a living. Still, there was much to pique my curiosity. Visitors would arrive at all hours, and when they did I would leave the sitting room and repair to my bedroom, pondering what they could have in common with my friend: the pale woman with one eye bone-white, the small man who looked like a commercial traveler, the portly dandy in his velvet jacket, and the rest. Some were frequent visitors, many others came only once, spoke to him, and left, looking troubled or looking satisfied.

He was a mystery to me.

We were partaking of one of our landlady's magnificent breakfasts one morning, when my friend rang the bell to summon that good lady. "There will be a gentleman joining us, in about four minutes," he said. "We will need another place at table."

"Very good," she said, "I'll put more sausages under the grill."

My friend returned to perusing his morning paper. I waited for an explanation with growing impatience. Finally, I could stand it no longer. "I don't understand. How could you know that in four minutes we would be receiving a visitor? There was no telegram, no message of any kind."

He smiled, thinly. "You did not hear the clatter of a brougham several minutes ago? It slowed as it passed us—obviously as the driver identified our door—then it sped up and went past, up into the Marylebone Road. There is a crush of carriages and taxicabs letting off passengers at the railway station and at the waxworks, and it is in that crush that anyone wishing to alight without being observed will go. The walk from there to here is but four minutes . . ."

He glanced at his pocket watch, and as he did so I heard a tread on the stairs outside.

"Come in, Lestrade," he called. "The door is ajar, and your sausages are just coming out from under the grill."

A man I took to be Lestrade opened the door, then closed it carefully behind him. "I should not," he said. "But truth to tell, I have not had a chance to break my fast this morning. And I could certainly do justice to a few of those sausages." He was the small man I had observed on several occasions previously, whose demeanor was that of a traveler in rubber novelties or patent nostrums.

My friend waited until our landlady had left the room before he said, "Obviously, I take it this is a matter of national importance."

"My stars," said Lestrade, and he paled. "Surely the word cannot be out already. Tell me it is not." He began to pile his plate high with sausages, kipper fillets, kedgeree, and toast, but his hands shook, a little.

"Of course not," said my friend. "I know the squeak of your brougham wheels, though, after all this time: an oscillating G sharp above high C. And if Inspector Lestrade of Scotland Yard cannot publicly be seen to come into the parlor of London's only consulting detective, yet comes anyway, and without having had his breakfast, then I know that this is not a routine case. Ergo, it involves those above us and is a matter of national importance."

Lestrade dabbed egg yolk from his chin with his napkin. I stared at him. He did not look like my idea of a police inspector, but then, my friend looked little enough like my idea of a consulting detective—whatever that might be.

"Perhaps we should discuss the matter privately," Lestrade said, glancing at me.

My friend began to smile, impishly, and his head moved on his shoulders as it did when he was enjoying a private joke. "Nonsense," he said. "Two heads are better than one. And what is said to one of us is said to us both."

"If I am intruding—" I said, gruffly, but he motioned me to silence.

Lestrade shrugged. "It's all the same to me," he said, after a moment. "If you solve the case then I have my job. If you don't, then I have no job. You use your methods, that's what I say. It can't make things any worse."

"If there's one thing that a study of history has taught us, it is that things can always get worse," said my friend. "When do we go to Shoreditch?"

Lestrade dropped his fork. "This is too bad!" he exclaimed. "Here you were, making sport of me, when you know all about the matter! You should be ashamed—"

"No one has told me anything of the matter. When a police inspector walks into my room with fresh splashes of mud of that peculiar mustard-yellow hue on his boots and trouser legs, I can surely be forgiven for presuming that he has recently walked past the diggings at Hobbs Lane, in Shoreditch, which is the only place in London that particular mustard-colored clay seems to be found."

Inspector Lestrade looked embarrassed. "Now you put it like that," he said, "it seems so obvious."

My friend pushed his plate away from him. "Of course it does," he said, slightly testily.

We rode to the East End in a cab. Inspector Lestrade had walked up to the Marylebone Road to find his brougham, and left us alone.

"So you are truly a consulting detective?" I said.

"The only one in London, or, perhaps, the world," said my friend. "I do not take cases. Instead, I consult. Others bring me their insoluble problems, they describe them, and, sometimes, I solve them."

"Then those people who come to you—"

"Are, in the main, police officers, or are detectives themselves, yes."

It was a fine morning, but we were now jolting about the edges of the rookery of St. Giles, that warren of thieves and cutthroats which sits on London like a cancer on the face of a pretty flower seller, and the only light to enter the cab was dim and faint.

"Are you sure that you wish me along with you?"

In reply my friend stared at me without blinking. "I have a feeling," he said. "I have a feeling that we were meant to be together. That we have fought the good fight, side by side, in the past or in the future, I do not know. I am a rational man, but I have learned the value of a good companion, and from the moment I clapped eyes on you, I knew I trusted you as well as I do myself. Yes. I want you with me."

I blushed, or said something meaningless. For the first time since Afghanistan, I felt that I had worth in the world.

2. THE ROOM

Victor's VITAE! An electrical fluid! Do your limbs and nether regions lack life? Do you look back on the days of your youth with envy? Are the pleasures of the flesh now buried and forgot? Victor's VITAE will bring life where life has long been lost: even the oldest warhorse can be a proud stallion once more! Bringing life to the dead: from an old family recipe and the best of modern science. To receive signed attestations of the efficacy of Victor's VITAE write to the V. Von F. Company, 1b Cheap Street, London.

It was a cheap rooming house in Shoreditch. There was a policeman at the front door. Lestrade greeted him by name and made to usher us in, and I was ready to enter, but my friend squatted on the doorstep, and pulled a magnifying glass from his coat pocket. He examined the mud on the wrought iron boot-scraper, prodding at it with his forefinger. Only when he was satisfied would he let us go inside.

We walked upstairs. The room in which the crime had been committed was obvious: it was flanked by two burly constables.

Lestrade nodded to the men, and they stood aside. We walked in. I am not, as I said, a writer by profession, and I hesitate to describe that place, knowing that my words cannot do it justice. Still, I have begun this narrative, and I fear I must continue. A murder had been committed in that little bedsit. The body, what was left of it, was still there, on the floor. I saw it, but, at first, somehow, I did not see it. What I saw instead was what had sprayed and gushed from the throat and chest of the victim: in color it ranged from bile-green to grass-green. It had soaked into the threadbare carpet and spattered the wallpaper. I imagined it for one moment the work of some hellish artist who had decided to create a study in emerald.

After what seemed like a hundred years I looked down at the body, opened like a rabbit on a butcher's slab, and tried to make sense of what I saw. I removed my hat, and my friend did the same.

He knelt and inspected the body, examining the cuts and gashes. Then he pulled out his magnifying glass, and walked over to the wall, examining the gouts of drying ichor.

"We've already done that," said Inspector Lestrade.

"Indeed?" said my friend. "What did you make of this, then? I do believe it is a word."

Lestrade walked to the place my friend was standing, and looked up. There was a word, written in capitals, in green blood, on the faded yellow wallpaper, some little way above Lestrade's head. "R-A-C-H-E . . . ?" said Lestrade, spelling it out. "Obviously he was going to write 'Rachel,' but he was interrupted. So—we must look for a woman."

My friend said nothing. He walked back to the corpse and picked up its hands, one after the other. The fingertips were clean of ichor. "I think we have established that the word was not written by His Royal Highness—"

"What the Devil makes you say—?"

"My dear Lestrade. Please give me some credit for having a brain. The corpse is obviously not that of a man—the color of his blood, the number of limbs, the eyes, the position of the face, all these things bespeak the blood royal. While I cannot say *which* royal line, I would hazard that he is an heir, perhaps no, second in line to the throne in one of the German principalities."

"That is amazing." Lestrade hesitated, then he said, "This is Prince Franz Drago of Bohemia. He was here in Albion as a guest of Her Majesty Victoria. Here for a holiday and a change of air . . ."

"For the theaters, the whores, and the gaming tables, you mean."

"If you say so." Lestrade looked put out. "Anyway, you've given us a fine lead with this Rachel woman. Although I don't doubt we would have found her on our own."

"Doubtless," said my friend.

He inspected the room further, commenting acidly several times that the police, with their boots, had obscured footprints and moved things that might have been of use to anyone attempting to reconstruct the events of the previous night.

Still, he seemed interested in a small patch of mud he found behind the door.

Beside the fireplace he found what appeared to be some ash or dirt.

"Did you see this?" he asked Lestrade.

"Her Majesty's police," replied Lestrade, "tend not to be excited by ash in a fireplace. It's where ash tends to be found." And he chuckled at that.

My friend took a pinch of the ash and rubbed it between his fingers, then sniffed the remains. Finally, he scooped up what was left of the material and tipped it into a glass vial, which he stoppered and placed in an inner pocket of his coat.

He stood up. "And the body?"

Lestrade said, "The palace will send their own people."

My friend nodded at me, and together we walked to the door. My friend sighed. "Inspector. Your quest for Miss Rachel may prove fruitless. Among other things, *Rache* is a German word. It means 'revenge.' Check your dictionary. There are other meanings."

We reached the bottom of the stair and walked out onto the street. "You have never seen royalty before this morning, have you?" he asked. I shook my head. "Well, the sight can be unnerving, if you're unprepared. Why, my good fellow—you are trembling!"

"Forgive me. I shall be fine in moments."

"Would it do you good to walk?" he asked, and I assented, certain that if I did not walk then I would begin to scream.

"West, then," said my friend, pointing to the dark tower of the palace. And we commenced to walk.

"So," said my friend, after some time. "You have never had any personal encounters with any of the crowned heads of Europe?"

"No," I said.

"I believe I can confidently state that you shall," he told me. "And not with a corpse this time. Very soon."

"My dear fellow, whatever makes you believe—?"

In reply he pointed to a carriage, black-painted, that had pulled up fifty yards ahead of us. A man in a black top hat and a greatcoat stood by the door, holding it open, waiting, silently. A coat of arms familiar to every child in Albion was painted in gold upon the carriage door.

"There are invitations one does not refuse," said my friend. He doffed his own hat to the footman, and I do believe that he was smiling as he climbed into the boxlike space and relaxed back into the soft, leathery cushions.

When I attempted to speak with him during the journey to the palace, he placed his finger over his lips. Then he closed his eyes and seemed sunk deep in thought. I, for my part, tried to remember what I knew of German royalty, but, apart from the Queen's consort, Prince Albert, being German, I knew little enough.

I put a hand in my pocket, pulled out a handful of coins—brown and silver, black and copper-green. I stared at the portrait stamped on each of them of our Queen, and felt both patriotic pride and stark dread. I told myself I had once been a military man and a stranger to fear, and I could remember when this had been the plain truth. For a moment I remembered a time when I had been a crack shot—even, I liked to think, something of a marksman—but my right hand shook as if it were palsied, and the coins jingled and chinked, and I felt only regret.

3. THE PALACE

AT LONG LAST DOCTOR HENRY JEKYLL IS PROUD TO AN-
NOUNCE THE GENERAL RELEASE OF THE WORLD-RENOWNED
"JEKYLL'S POWDERS" FOR POPULAR CONSUMPTION. NO LON-
GER THE PROVINCE OF THE PRIVILEGED FEW. RELEASE
THE INNER YOU! FOR INNER AND OUTER CLEANLI-
NESS! TOO MANY PEOPLE, BOTH MEN AND WOMEN,
SUFFER FROM CONSTIPATION OF THE SOUL! RELIEF IS IM-
MEDIATE AND CHEAP—WITH JEKYLL'S POWDERS! (AVAILABLE
IN VANILLA AND ORIGINAL MENTHOLATUM FORMULATIONS.)

The Queen's consort, Prince Albert, was a big man with an impressive handlebar mustache and a receding hairline, and he was undeniably and entirely human. He met us in the corridor, nodded to my friend and to me, did not ask us for our names or offer to shake hands.

"The Queen is most upset," he said. He had an accent. He pronounced his *S*s as *Z*s: *Mozt. Upzet*. "Franz was one of her favorites. She has so many nephews. But he made her laugh so. You will find the ones who did this to him."

"I will do my best," said my friend.

"I have read your monographs," said Prince Albert. "It was I who told them that you should be consulted. I hope I did right."

"As do I," said my friend.

And then the great door was opened, and we were ushered into the darkness and the presence of the Queen.

She was called Victoria, because she had beaten us in battle, seven hundred years before, and she was called Gloriana, because she was glorious, and she was called the Queen, because the human mouth was not shaped to say her true name. She was huge, huger than I had imagined possible, and she squatted in the shadows staring down at us, without moving.

Thizsz muzzst be zsolved. The words came from the shadows.

"Indeed, ma'am," said my friend.

A limb squirmed and pointed at me. *Zstepp forward.*

I wanted to walk. My legs would not move.

My friend came to my rescue then. He took me by the elbow and walked me toward Her Majesty.

Isz not to be afraid. Isz to be worthy. Isz to be a companion. That was what she said to me. Her voice was a very sweet contralto, with a distant buzz. Then the limb uncoiled and extended, and she touched my shoulder. There was a moment, but only a moment, of a pain deeper and more profound than anything I have ever experienced, and then it was replaced by a pervasive sense of well-being. I could feel the muscles in my shoulder relax, and, for the first time since Afghanistan, I was free from pain.

Then my friend walked forward. Victoria spoke to him, yet I could not hear her words; I wondered if they went, somehow, directly from her mind to his, if this was the Queen's Counsel I had read about in the histories. He replied aloud.

"Certainly, ma'am. I can tell you that there were two other men with your nephew in that room in Shoreditch, that night. The footprints were, although obscured, unmistakable." And then, "Yes. I understand. . . . I believe so. Yes."

He was quiet when we left the palace, and said nothing to me as we rode back to Baker Street.

It was dark already. I wondered how long we had spent in the palace.

Fingers of sooty fog twined across the road and the sky.

Upon our return to Baker Street, in the looking glass of my room, I observed that the frog-white skin across my shoulder had taken on a pinkish tinge. I hoped that I was not imagining it, that it was not merely the moonlight through the window.

4. THE PERFORMANCE

LIVER COMPLAINTS?! BILIOUS ATTACKS?! NEURASTHENIC DISTURBANCES?! QUINSY?! ARTHRITIS?! THESE ARE JUST A HANDFUL OF THE COMPLAINTS FOR WHICH A PROFESSIONAL <u>EXSANGUINATION</u> CAN BE THE REMEDY. IN OUR OFFICES WE HAVE SHEAVES OF TESTIMONIALS WHICH CAN BE INSPECTED BY THE PUBLIC AT ANY TIME. DO NOT PUT YOUR HEALTH IN THE HANDS OF AMATEURS!! WE HAVE BEEN DOING THIS FOR A VERY LONG TIME: V. TEPES—PROFESSIONAL EXSANGUINATOR. (REMEMBER! IT IS PRONOUNCED TZSEP-PESH!) ROMANIA, PARIS, LONDON, WHITBY. YOU'VE TRIED THE REST—NOW TRY THE BEST!!

That my friend was a master of disguise should have come as no surprise to me, yet surprise me it did. Over the next ten days a strange assortment of characters came in through our door in Baker Street—an elderly Chinese man, a young roué, a fat, red-haired woman of whose former profession there could be little doubt, and a venerable old buffer, his foot swollen and bandaged from gout. Each of them would walk into my friend's room, and, with a speed that would have done justice to a music-hall "quick-change artist," my friend would walk out.

He would not talk about what he had been doing on these occasions, preferring to relax, staring off into space, occasionally making notations on any scrap of paper to hand, notations I found, frankly, incomprehensible. He seemed entirely preoccupied, so much so that I found myself worrying about his well-being. And then, late one afternoon, he came home dressed in his own clothes, with an easy grin upon his face, and he asked if I was interested in the theater.

"As much as the next man," I told him.

"Then fetch your opera glasses," he told me. "We are off to Drury Lane."

I had expected a light opera, or something of the kind, but instead I found myself in what must have been the worst theater in Drury Lane, for all that it had named itself after the royal court—and to be honest, it was barely in Drury Lane at all, being situated at the Shaftesbury Avenue end of the road, where the avenue approaches the rookery of St. Giles. On my friend's advice I concealed my wallet, and, following his example, I carried a stout stick.

Once we were seated in the stalls (I had bought a threepenny orange from one of the lovely young women who sold them to the members of the audience, and I sucked it as we waited), my friend said, quietly, "You should only count yourself lucky that you did not need to accompany me to the gambling dens or the brothels. Or the madhouses—another place that Prince Franz delighted in visiting, as I have learned. But there was nowhere he went to more than once. Nowhere but—"

The orchestra struck up, and the curtain was raised. My friend was silent.

It was a fine enough show in its way: three one-act plays were performed. Comic songs were sung between the acts. The leading man was tall, languid, and had a fine singing voice; the leading lady was elegant, and her voice carried through all the theater; the comedian had a fine touch for patter songs.

The first play was a broad comedy of mistaken identities: the leading man played a pair of identical twins who had never met, but had managed, by a set of comical misadventures, each to find himself engaged to be married to the same young lady—who, amusingly, thought herself engaged to only one man. Doors swung open and closed as the actor changed from identity to identity.

The second play was a heartbreaking tale of an orphan girl who starved in the snow selling hothouse violets—her grandmother recognized her at the last, and swore that she was the babe stolen ten years back by bandits, but it was too late, and the frozen little angel breathed her last. I must confess I found myself wiping my eyes with my linen handkerchief more than once.

The performance finished with a rousing historical narrative: the entire company played the men and women of a village on the shore of the ocean, seven hundred years before our modern times. They saw shapes rising from the sea, in the distance. The hero joyously proclaimed to the villagers that these were the Old Ones whose coming was foretold, returning to us from R'lyeh, and from dim Carcosa, and from the plains of Leng, where they had slept, or waited, or passed out the time of their death. The comedian opined that the other villagers had all been eating too many pies and drinking too much ale, and they were imagining the shapes. A portly gentleman playing a priest of the Roman God told the villagers that the shapes in the sea were monsters and demons, and must be destroyed.

At the climax, the hero beat the priest to death with his own crucifer, and prepared to welcome Them as They came. The heroine sang a haunting aria, whilst, in an astonishing display of magic-lantern trickery, it seemed as if we saw Their shadows cross the sky at the back of the stage: the Queen of Albion herself, and the Black One of Egypt (in shape almost like a man), followed by the Ancient Goat, Parent to a Thousand, Emperor of all China, and the Czar Unanswerable, and He Who Presides over the New World, and the White Lady of the Antarctic Fastness, and the others. And as each shadow crossed the stage, or appeared to, from out of every throat in the gallery came, unbidden, a mighty "Huzzah!" until the air itself seemed to vibrate. The moon rose in the painted sky, and then, at its height, in one final moment of theatrical magic, it turned from a pallid yellow, as it was in the old tales, to the comforting crimson of the moon that shines down upon us all today.

The members of the cast took their bows and their curtain calls to cheers and laughter, and the curtain fell for the last time, and the show was done.

"There," said my friend. "What did you think?"

"Jolly, jolly good," I told him, my hands sore from applauding.

"Stout fellow," he said, with a smile. "Let us go backstage."

We walked outside and into an alley beside the theater, to the stage door, where a thin woman with a wen on her cheek knitted busily. My friend showed her a visiting card, and she directed us into the building and up some steps to a small communal dressing room.

Oil lamps and candles guttered in front of smeared looking glasses, and men and women were taking off their makeup and costumes with no regard to the proprieties of gender. I averted my eyes. My friend seemed unperturbed. "Might I talk to Mr. Vernet?" he asked, loudly.

A young woman who had played the heroine's best friend in the first play, and the saucy innkeeper's daughter in the last, pointed us to the end of the room. "Sherry! Sherry Vernet!" she called.

The young man who stood up in response was lean; less conventionally handsome than he had seemed from the other side of the footlights. He peered at us quizzically. "I do not believe I have had the pleasure . . . ?"

"My name is Henry Camberley," said my friend, drawling his speech somewhat. "You may have heard of me."

"I must confess that I have not had that privilege," said Vernet.

My friend presented the actor with an engraved card.

The man looked at the card with unfeigned interest. "A theatrical promoter? From the New World? My, my. And this is . . . ?" He smiled at me.

"This is a friend of mine, Mister Sebastian. He is not of the profession."

I muttered something about having enjoyed the performance enormously, and shook hands with the actor.

My friend said, "Have you ever visited the New World?"

"I have not yet had that honor," admitted Vernet, "although it has always been my dearest wish."

"Well, my good man," said my friend, with the easy informality of a New Worlder. "Maybe you'll get your wish. That last play. I've never seen anything like it. Did you write it?"

"Alas, no. The playwright is a good friend of mine. Although I devised the mechanism of the magic-lantern shadow show. You'll not see finer on the stage today."

"Would you give me the playwright's name? Perhaps I should speak to him directly, this friend of yours."

Vernet shook his head. "That will not be possible, I am afraid. He is a professional man, and does not wish his connection with the stage publicly to be known."

"I see." My friend pulled a pipe from his pocket and put it in his mouth. Then he patted his pockets. "I am sorry," he began. "I have forgotten to bring my tobacco pouch."

"I smoke a strong black shag," said the actor, "but if you have no objection—"

"None!" said my friend, heartily. "Why, I smoke a strong shag myself," and he filled his pipe with the actor's tobacco, and the two men puffed away, while my friend described a vision he had for a play that could tour the cities of the New World, from Manhattan Island all the way to the furthest tip of the continent in the distant south. The first act would be the last play we had seen. The rest of the play might perhaps tell of the dominion of the Old Ones over humanity and its gods, perhaps telling what might have happened if people had had no Royal Families to look up to—a world of barbarism and darkness—"But your mysterious professional man would be the play's author, and what occurs would be his alone to decide," interjected my friend. "Our drama would be his. But I can guarantee you audiences beyond your imaginings, and a significant share of the takings at the door. Let us say fifty percent!"

"This is most exciting," said Vernet. "I hope it will not turn out to have been a pipe dream!"

"No sir, it shall not!" said my friend, puffing on his own pipe, chuckling at the man's joke. "Come to my rooms in Baker Street tomorrow

morning, after breakfast-time, say at ten, in company with your author friend, and I shall have the contracts drawn up and waiting."

With that the actor clambered up onto his chair and clapped his
hands for silence. "Ladies and gentlemen of the company, I have an
announcement to make," he said, his resonant voice filling the room.
"This gentleman is Henry Camberley, the theatrical promoter, and
he is proposing to take us across the Atlantic Ocean, and on to fame
and fortune."

There were several cheers, and the comedian said, "Well, it'll
make a change from herrings and pickled cabbage," and the company laughed.

And it was to the smiles of all of them that we walked out of the
theater and onto the fog-wreathed streets.

"My dear fellow," I said. "Whatever was—"

"Not another word," said my friend. "There are many ears in the
city."

And not another word was spoken until we had hailed a cab, and
clambered inside, and were rattling up the Charing Cross Road.

And even then, before he said anything, my friend took his pipe
from his mouth, and emptied the half-smoked contents of the bowl
into a small tin. He pressed the lid onto the tin, and placed it in his
pocket.

"There," he said. "That's the Tall Man found, or I'm a Dutchman.
Now, we just have to hope that the cupidity and the curiosity of the
Limping Doctor proves enough to bring him to us tomorrow morn-
ing."

"The Limping Doctor?"

My friend snorted. "That is what I have been calling him. It was
obvious, from footprints and much else besides, when we saw the
prince's body, that two men had been in that room that night: a tall
man, who, unless I miss my guess, we have just encountered, and a
smaller man with a limp, who eviscerated the prince with a professional skill that betrays the medical man."

"A doctor?"

"Indeed. I hate to say this, but it is my experience that when a
doctor goes to the bad, he is a fouler and darker creature than the

worst cutthroat. There was Huston, the acid-bath man, and Campbell, who brought the procrustean bed to Ealing . . ." and he carried on in a similar vein for the rest of our journey.

The cab pulled up beside the curb. "That'll be one and tenpence," said the cabbie. My friend tossed him a florin, which he caught and tipped to his ragged tall hat. "Much obliged to you both," he called out, as the horse clopped into the fog.

We walked to our front door. As I unlocked it, my friend said, "Odd. Our cabbie just ignored that fellow on the corner."

"They do that at the end of a shift," I pointed out.

"Indeed they do," said my friend.

I dreamed of shadows that night, vast shadows that blotted out the sun, and I called out to them in my desperation, but they did not listen.

5. THE SKIN AND THE PIT

THIS YEAR, STEP INTO THE SPRING—WITH A SPRING IN YOUR STEP! JACK'S. BOOTS, SHOES AND BROGUES. SAVE YOUR SOLES! HEELS OUR SPECIALITY. JACK'S. AND DO NOT FORGET TO VISIT OUR NEW CLOTHES AND FITTINGS EMPORIUM IN THE EAST END—FEATURING EVENING WEAR OF ALL KINDS, HATS, NOVELTIES, CANES, SWORDSTICKS &C. JACK'S OF PICCADILLY. *IT'S ALL IN THE SPRING!*

Inspector Lestrade was the first to arrive.

"You have posted your men in the street?" asked my friend.

"I have," said Lestrade. "With strict orders to let anyone in who comes, but to arrest anyone trying to leave."

"And you have handcuffs with you?"

In reply, Lestrade put his hand in his pocket, and jangled two pairs of cuffs, grimly.

"Now sir," he said. "While we wait, why do you not tell me what we are waiting for?"

My friend pulled his pipe out of his pocket. He did not put it in his mouth, but placed it on the table in front of him. Then he took the tin from the night before, and a glass vial I recognized as the one he had had in the room in Shoreditch.

"There," he said. "The coffin-nail, as I trust it shall prove, for our Master Vernet." He paused. Then he took out his pocket watch, laid it carefully on the table. "We have several minutes before they arrive." He turned to me. "What do you know of the Restorationists?"

"Not a blessed thing," I told him.

Lestrade coughed. "If you're talking about what I think you're talking about," he said, "perhaps we should leave it there. Enough's enough."

"Too late for that," said my friend. "For there are those who do not believe that the coming of the Old Ones was the fine thing we all know it to be. Anarchists to a man, they would see the old ways restored—mankind in control of its own destiny, if you will."

"I will not hear this sedition spoken," said Lestrade. "I must warn you—"

"I must warn you not to be such a fathead," said my friend. "Because it was the Restorationists that killed Prince Franz Drago. They murder, they kill, in a vain effort to force our masters to leave us alone in the darkness. The Prince was killed by a *rache*—it's an old term for a hunting dog, Inspector, as you would know if you had looked in a dictionary. It also means 'revenge.' And the hunter left his signature on the wallpaper in the murder room, just as an artist might sign a canvas. But he was not the one who killed the Prince."

"The Limping Doctor!" I exclaimed.

"Very good. There was a tall man there that night—I could tell his height, for the word was written at eye level. He smoked a pipe—the ash and dottle sat unburnt in the fireplace, and he had tapped out his pipe with ease on the mantel, something a smaller man would not have done. The tobacco was an unusual blend of shag. The footprints in the room had, for the most part, been almost obliterated by your men, but there were several clear prints behind the door and by the window. Someone had waited there: a smaller man from his stride, who put his weight on his right leg. On the path outside I had several clear prints, and the different colors of clay on the bootscraper gave me more information: a tall man, who had accompanied the Prince into those rooms, and had, later, walked out. Waiting for them to arrive was the man who had sliced up the Prince so impressively . . ."

Lestrade made an uncomfortable noise that did not quite become a word.

"I have spent many days retracing the movements of His Highness. I went from gambling hell to brothel to dining den to madhouse looking for our pipe-smoking man and his friend. I made no progress until I thought to check the newspapers of Bohemia, searching for a clue to the Prince's recent activities there, and in them I learned that an English Theatrical Troupe had been in Prague last month, and had performed before Prince Franz Drago . . ."

"Good Lord," I said. "So that Sherry Vernet fellow—"

"Is a Restorationist. Exactly."

I was shaking my head in wonder at my friend's intelligence and skills of observation, when there was a knock on the door.

"This will be our quarry!" said my friend. "Careful now!"

Lestrade put his hand deep into his pocket, where I had no doubt he kept a pistol. He swallowed, nervously.

My friend called out, "Please, come in!"

The door opened.

It was not Vernet, nor was it a Limping Doctor. It was one of the young street Arabs who earn a crust running errands—"in the employ of Messrs. Street and Walker," as we used to say when I was young. "Please sirs," he said. "Is there a Mister Henry Camberley here? I was asked by a gentleman to deliver a note."

"I'm he," said my friend. "And for a sixpence, what can you tell me about the gentleman who gave you the note?"

The young lad, who volunteered that his name was Wiggins, bit the sixpence before making it vanish, then told us that the cheery cove who gave him the note was on the tall side, with dark hair, and, he added, he had been smoking a pipe.

I have the note here, and take the liberty of transcribing it.

My Dear Sir,

I do not address you as Henry Camberley, for it is a name to which you have no claim. I am surprised that you did not announce yourself under your own name, for it is a fine one, and one that does you credit. I have read a number of your papers, when I have been able to obtain them. Indeed, I corresponded with you quite profitably two years ago about certain theoretical anomalies in your paper on the Dynamics of an Asteroid.

I was amused to meet you, yesterday evening. A few tips which might save you bother in times to come, in the profession you currently follow. Firstly, a pipe-smoking man might possibly have a brand-new, unused pipe in his pocket, and no tobacco, but it is exceedingly unlikely—at least as unlikely as a theatrical promoter with no idea of the usual customs of recompense on a tour, who is accompanied by a taciturn ex-army officer (Afghanistan, unless I miss my guess). Incidentally, while you are correct that the streets of London have ears, it might also behoove you in future not to take the first cab that comes along. Cab drivers have ears too, if they choose to use them.

You are certainly correct in one of your suppositions: it was indeed I who lured the halfblood creature back to the room in Shoreditch.

If it is any comfort to you, having learned a little of his recreational predilections, I had told him I had procured for him a girl, abducted from a convent in Cornwall where she had never seen a man, and that it would only take his touch, and the sight of his face, to tip her over into a perfect madness.

Had she existed, he would have feasted on her madness while he took her, like a man sucking the flesh from a ripe peach leaving nothing behind but the skin and the pit. I have seen them do this. I have seen them do far worse. And it is not the price we pay for peace and prosperity. It is too great a price for that.

The good doctor—who believes as I do, and who did indeed write our little performance, for he has some crowd-pleasing skills—was waiting for us, with his knives.

I send this note, not as a catch-me-if-you-can taunt, for we are gone, the estimable doctor and I, and you shall not find us, but to tell you that it was good to feel that, if only for a moment, I had a worthy adversary. Worthier by far than inhuman creatures from beyond the Pit.

I fear the Strand Players will need to find themselves a new leading man.

I will not sign myself Vernet, and until the hunt is done and the world restored, I beg you to think of me simply as,

Rache.

Inspector Lestrade ran from the room, calling to his men. They made young Wiggins take them to the place where the man had given him the note, for all the world as if Vernet the actor would be waiting there for them, a-smoking of his pipe. From the window we watched them run, my friend and I, and we shook our heads.

"They will stop and search all the trains leaving London, all the ships leaving Albion for Europe or the New World," said my friend, "looking for a tall man, and his companion, a smaller, thickset medical man, with a slight limp. They will close the ports. Every way out of the country will be blocked."

"Do you think they will catch him, then?"

My friend shook his head. "I may be wrong," he said, "but I would wager that he and his friend are even now only a mile or so away, in the rookery of St. Giles, where the police will not go except by the dozen. And they will hide up there until the hue and cry have died away. And then they will be about their business."

"What makes you say that?"

"Because," said my friend, "if our positions were reversed, it is what I would do. You should burn the note, by the way."

I frowned. "But surely it's evidence," I said.

"It's seditionary nonsense," said my friend.

And I should have burned it. Indeed, I told Lestrade I *had* burned it, when he returned, and he congratulated me on my good sense. Lestrade kept his job, and Prince Albert wrote a note to my friend congratulating him on his deductions, while regretting that the perpetrator was still at large.

They have not yet caught Sherry Vernet, or whatever his name really is, nor was any trace found of his murderous accomplice, tentatively identified as a former military surgeon named John (or perhaps James) Watson. Curiously, it was revealed that he had also been in Afghanistan. I wonder if we ever met.

My shoulder, touched by the Queen, continues to improve, the flesh fills and it heals. Soon I shall be a dead shot once more.

One night when we were alone, several months ago, I asked my friend if he remembered the correspondence referred to in the letter from the man who signed himself Rache. My friend said that he remembered it well, and that "Sigerson" (for so the actor had called himself then, claiming to be an Icelander) had been inspired by an equation of my friend's to suggest some wild theories furthering the relationship between mass, energy, and the hypothetical speed of light. "Nonsense, of course," said my friend, without smiling. "But inspired and dangerous nonsense nonetheless."

The palace eventually sent word that the Queen was pleased with my friend's accomplishments in the case, and there the matter has rested.

I doubt my friend will leave it alone, though; it will not be over until one of them has killed the other.

I kept the note. I have said things in this retelling of events that are not to be said. If I were a sensible man I would burn all these pages, but then, as my friend taught me, even ashes can give up their secrets. Instead, I shall place these papers in a strongbox at my bank with instructions that the box may not be opened until long after anyone now living is dead. Although, in the light of the recent events in Russia, I fear that day may be closer than any of us would care to think.

S——M——Major (Ret'd)
Baker Street,
London, New Albion, 1881

BITTER GROUNDS

2003

1. "COME BACK EARLY OR NEVER COME"

IN EVERY WAY THAT counted, I was dead. Inside somewhere maybe I was screaming and weeping and howling like an animal, but that was another person deep inside, another person who had no access to the face and lips and mouth and head, so on the surface I just shrugged and smiled and kept moving. If I could have physically passed away, just let it all go, like that, without doing anything, stepped out of life as easily as walking through a door, I would have done. But I was going to sleep at night and waking in the morning, disappointed to be there and resigned to existence.

Sometimes I telephoned her. I let the phone ring once, maybe even twice, before I hung up.

The me who was screaming was so far inside nobody knew he was even there at all. Even I forgot that he was there, until one day I got into the car—I had to go to the store, I had decided, to bring back some apples—and I went past the store that sold apples and I kept driving, and driving. I was going south, and west, because if I went north or east I would run out of world too soon.

A couple of hours down the highway my cell phone started to

ring. I wound down the window and threw the cell phone out. I wondered who would find it, whether they would answer the phone and find themselves gifted with my life.

When I stopped for gas I took all the cash I could on every card I had. I did the same for the next couple of days, ATM by ATM, until the cards stopped working.

The first two nights I slept in the car.

I was halfway through Tennessee when I realized I needed a bath badly enough to pay for it. I checked into a motel, stretched out in the bath and slept in it until the water got cold and woke me. I shaved with a motel courtesy kit plastic razor and a sachet of foam. Then I stumbled to the bed, and I slept.

Awoke at 4:00 A.M., and knew it was time to get back on the road.

I went down to the lobby.

There was a man standing at the front desk when I got there: silver-gray hair although I guessed he was still in his thirties, if only just, thin lips, good suit rumpled, saying, "I *ordered* that cab an *hour* ago. One *hour* ago." He tapped the desk with his wallet as he spoke, the beats emphasizing his words.

The night manager shrugged. "I'll call again," he said. "But if they don't have the car, they can't send it." He dialed a phone number, said, "This is the Night's Out Inn front desk again. Yeah, I told him. Yeah, I told him."

"Hey," I said. "I'm not a cab, but I'm in no hurry. You need a ride somewhere?"

For a moment the man looked at me like I was crazy, and for a moment there was fear in his eyes. Then he looked at me like I'd been sent from Heaven. "You know, by God, I do," he said.

"You tell me where to go," I said. "I'll take you there. Like I said, I'm in no hurry."

"Give me that phone," said the silver-gray man to the night clerk. He took the handset and said, "You can *cancel* your cab, because God just sent me a Good Samaritan. People come into your life for a reason. That's right. And I want you to think about that."

He picked up his briefcase—like me he had no luggage—and together we went out to the parking lot.

We drove through the dark. He'd check a hand-drawn map on his lap, with a flashlight attached to his key ring, then he'd say, *left here,* or *this way.*

"It's good of you," he said.

"No problem. I have time."

"I appreciate it. You know, this has that pristine urban legend quality, driving down country roads with a mysterious Samaritan. A Phantom Hitchhiker story. After I get to my destination, I'll describe you to a friend, and they'll tell me you died ten years ago, and still go round giving people rides."

"Be a good way to meet people."

He chuckled. "What do you do?"

"Guess you could say I'm between jobs," I said. "You?"

"I'm an anthropology professor." Pause. "I guess I should have introduced myself. Teach at a Christian college. People don't believe we teach anthropology at Christian colleges, but we do. Some of us."

"I believe you."

Another pause. "My car broke down. I got a ride to the motel from the highway patrol, as they said there was no tow truck going to be there until morning. Got two hours of sleep. Then the highway patrol called my hotel room. Tow truck's on the way. I got to be there when they arrive. Can you believe that? I'm not there, they won't touch it. Just drive away. Called a cab. Never came. Hope we get there before the tow truck."

"I'll do my best."

"I guess I should have taken a plane. It's not that I'm scared of flying. But I cashed in the ticket. I'm on my way to New Orleans. Hour's flight, four hundred and forty dollars. Day's drive, thirty dollars. That's four hundred and ten dollars' spending money, and I don't have to account for it to anybody. Spent fifty dollars on the motel room, but that's just the way these things go. Academic conference. My first. Faculty doesn't believe in them. But things change. I'm looking forward to it. Anthropologists from all over the world." He named several, names that meant nothing to me. "I'm presenting a paper on the Haitian coffee girls."

"They grow it, or drink it?"

"Neither. They sold it, door-to-door in Port-au-Prince, early in the morning, in the early years of the last century."

It was starting to get light now.

"People thought they were zombies," he said. "You know. The walking dead. I think it's a right turn here."

"Were they? Zombies?"

He seemed very pleased to have been asked. "Well, anthropologically, there are several schools of thought about zombies. It's not as cut-and-dried as popularist works like *The Serpent and the Rainbow* would make it appear. First we have to define our terms: are we talking folk belief, or zombie dust, or the walking dead?"

"I don't know," I said. I was pretty sure *The Serpent and the Rainbow* was a horror movie.

"They were children, little girls, five to ten years old, who went door-to-door through Port-au-Prince selling the chicory coffee mixture. Just about this time of day, before the sun was up. They belonged to one old woman. Hang a left just before we go into the next turn. When she died, the girls vanished. That's what the books tell you."

"And what do you believe?" I asked.

"That's my car," he said, with relief in his voice. It was a red Honda Accord, on the side of the road. There was a tow truck beside it, lights flashing, a man beside the tow truck smoking a cigarette. We pulled up behind the tow truck.

The anthropologist had the door opened before I'd stopped; he grabbed his briefcase and was out of the car.

"Was giving you another five minutes, then I was going to take off," said the tow truck driver. He dropped his cigarette into a puddle on the tarmac. "Okay, I'll need your triple-A card and a credit card."

The man reached for his wallet. He looked puzzled. He put his hands in his pockets. He said, "My wallet." He came back to my car, opened the passenger-side door and leaned back inside. I turned on the light. He patted the empty seat. "My wallet," he said again. His voice was plaintive and hurt.

"You had it back in the motel," I reminded him. "You were holding it. It was in your hand."

He said, "God *damn it*. God fucking *damn* it to Hell."

"Everything okay there?" called the tow truck driver.

"Okay," said the anthropologist to me, urgently. "This is what we'll do. You drive back to the motel. I must have left the wallet on the desk. Bring it back here. I'll keep him happy until then. Five minutes, it'll take you five minutes." He must have seen the expression on my face. He said, "Remember. People come into your life for a reason."

I shrugged, irritated to have been sucked into someone else's story.

Then he shut the car door and gave me a thumbs-up.

I wished I could just have driven away and abandoned him, but it was too late, I was driving to the hotel. The night clerk gave me the wallet, which he had noticed on the counter, he told me, moments after we left.

I opened the wallet. The credit cards were all in the name of Jackson Anderton.

It took me half an hour to find my way back, as the sky grayed into full dawn. The tow truck was gone. The rear window of the red Honda Accord was broken, and the driver's-side door hung open. I wondered if it was a different car, if I had driven the wrong way to the wrong place; but there were the tow truck driver's cigarette stubs crushed on the road, and in the ditch nearby I found a gaping briefcase, empty, and beside it, a manila folder containing a fifteen-page typescript, a prepaid hotel reservation at a Marriott in New Orleans in the name of Jackson Anderton, and a packet of three condoms, ribbed for extra pleasure.

On the title page of the typescript was printed:

" *'This was the way Zombies are spoken of: They are the bodies without souls. The living dead. Once they were dead, and after that they were called back to life again.'* Hurston. *Tell My Horse*."

I took the manila folder but left the briefcase where it was. I drove south under a pearl-colored sky.

People come into your life for a reason. Right.

I could not find a radio station that would hold its signal. Eventually I pressed the scan button on the radio and just left it on, left it scanning from channel to channel in a relentless quest for signal, scurrying from gospel to oldies to Bible talk to sex talk to country, three seconds a station with plenty of white noise in between.

. . . Lazarus, who was dead, you make no mistake about that, he was dead, and Jesus brought him back to show us, I say to show us . . .

What I call a Chinese dragon, can I say this on the air? Just as you, y'know, get your rocks off, you whomp her round the backatha head, it all spurts outta her nose, I damn near laugh my ass off . . .

If you come home tonight I'll be waiting in the darkness for my woman with my bottle and my gun . . .

When Jesus says will you be there will you be there? No man knows the day or the hour so will you be there . . .

President unveiled an initiative today . . .

Fresh-brewed in the morning. For you, for me. For every day. Because every day is freshly ground . . .

Over and over. It washed over me, driving through the day, on the back roads. Just driving and driving.

They become more personable as you head south, the people. You sit in a diner and, along with your coffee and your food, they bring you comments, questions, smiles, and nods.

It was evening, and I was eating fried chicken and collard greens and hush puppies, and a waitress smiled at me. The food seemed tasteless, but I guessed that might have been my problem, not theirs.

I nodded at her, politely, which she took as an invitation to come over and refill my coffee cup. The coffee was bitter, which I liked. At least it tasted of something.

"Looking at you," she said, "I would guess that you are a professional man. May I inquire as to your profession?" That was what she said, word for word.

"Indeed you may," I said, feeling almost possessed by something, and affably pompous, like W. C. Fields or the Nutty Professor (the fat one, not the Jerry Lewis one, although I am actually within pounds of the optimum weight for my height), "I happen to be . . . an anthropologist, on my way to a conference in New Orleans, where I shall confer, consult, and otherwise hobnob with my fellow anthropologists."

"I knew it," she said. "Just looking at you. I had you figured for a professor. Or a dentist, maybe."

She smiled at me one more time. I thought about stopping forever in that little town, eating in that diner every morning and every night. Drinking their bitter coffee and having her smile at me until I ran out of coffee and money and days.

Then I left her a good tip, and went south and west.

2. "TONGUE BROUGHT ME HERE"

THERE WERE NO HOTEL rooms in New Orleans, or anywhere in the New Orleans sprawl. A Jazz Festival had eaten them, every one. It was too hot to sleep in my car, and, even if I'd cranked a window and been prepared to suffer the heat, I felt unsafe. New Orleans is a real place, which is more than I can say about most of the cities I've lived in, but it's not a safe place, not a friendly one.

I stank, and itched. I wanted to bathe, and to sleep, and for the world to stop moving past me.

I drove from fleabag motel to fleabag motel, and then, at the last, as I had always known I would, I drove into the parking lot of the downtown Marriott on Canal Street. At least I knew they had one free room. I had a voucher for it in the manila folder.

"I need a room," I said to one of the women behind the counter.

She barely looked at me. "All rooms are taken," she said. "We won't have anything until Tuesday."

I needed to shave, and to shower, and to rest. *What's the worst she can say?* I thought. *I'm sorry, you've already checked in?*

"I have a room, prepaid by my university. The name's Anderton."

She nodded, tapped a keyboard, said "Jackson?" then gave me a key to my room, and I initialed the room rate. She pointed me to the elevators.

A short man with a ponytail and a dark, hawkish face dusted with white stubble cleared his throat as we stood beside the elevators. "You're the Anderton from Hopewell," he said. "We were neighbors in the *Journal of Anthropological Heresies*." He wore a white T-shirt that said "Anthropologists Do It While Being Lied To."

"We were?"

"We were. I'm Campbell Lakh. University of Norwood and Streatham. Formerly North Croydon Polytechnic. England. I wrote the paper about Icelandic spirit-walkers and fetches."

"Good to meet you," I said, and shook his hand. "You don't have a London accent."

"I'm a Brummie," he said. "From Birmingham," he added. "Never seen you at one of these things before."

"It's my first conference," I told him.

"Then you stick with me," he said. "I'll see you're all right. I remember my first one of these conferences, I was scared shitless I'd do something stupid the entire time. We'll stop on the mezzanine, get our stuff, then get cleaned up. There must have been a hundred babies on my plane over, Isweartogod. They took it in shifts to scream, shit, and puke, though. Never less than ten of them screaming at a time."

We stopped on the mezzanine, collected our badges and programs. "Don't forget to sign up for the ghost walk," said the smiling woman behind the table. "Ghost walks of Old New Orleans each night, limited to fifteen people in each party, so sign up fast."

I bathed, and washed my clothes out in the basin, then hung them up in the bathroom to dry.

I sat naked on the bed and examined the former contents of Anderton's briefcase. I skimmed through the paper he had intended to present, without taking in the content.

On the clean back of page five he had written, in a tight, mostly legible, scrawl, "*In a perfect world you could fuck people without giving them a piece of your heart. And every glittering kiss and every touch of flesh is another shard of heart you'll never see again.*

"*Until walking (waking? calling?) on your own is unsupportable.*"

When my clothes were pretty much dry I put them back on and went down to the lobby bar. Campbell was already there. He was drinking a gin and tonic, with a gin and tonic on the side.

He had out a copy of the conference program and had circled each of the talks and papers he wanted to see. ("Rule one, if it's before midday, fuck it unless you're the one doing it," he explained.) He showed me my talk, circled in pencil.

"I've never done this before," I told him. "Presented a paper at a conference."

"It's a piece of piss, Jackson," he said. "Piece of piss. You know what I do?"

"No," I said.

"I just get up and read the paper. Then people ask questions, and I just bullshit," he said. "Actively bullshit, as opposed to passively. That's the best bit. Just bullshitting. Piece of utter piss."

"I'm not really good at, um, bullshitting," I said. "Too honest."

"Then nod, and tell them that that's a really perceptive question, and that it's addressed at length in the longer version of the paper, of which the one you are reading is an edited abstract. If you get some nut job giving you a really difficult time about something you got wrong, just get huffy and say that it's not about what's fashionable to believe, it's about the truth."

"Does that work?"

"Christ yes, I gave a paper a few years back about the origins of the Thuggee sects in Persian military troops—it's why you could get Hindus and Muslims equally becoming Thuggee, you see, the Kali worship was tacked on later. It would have begun as some sort of Manichaean secret society—"

"Still spouting that nonsense?" She was a tall, pale woman with a shock of white hair, wearing clothes that looked both aggressively, studiedly Bohemian, and far too warm for the climate. I could imagine her riding a bicycle, the kind with a wicker basket in the front.

"Spouting it? I'm writing a fucking book about it," said the Englishman. "So, what I want to know is, who's coming with me to the French Quarter to taste all that New Orleans can offer?"

"I'll pass," said the woman, unsmiling. "Who's your friend?"

"This is Jackson Anderton, from Hopewell College."

"The Zombie Coffee Girls paper?" She smiled. "I saw it in the program. Quite fascinating. Yet another thing we owe Zora, eh?"

"Along with *The Great Gatsby*," I said.

"Hurston knew F. Scott Fitzgerald?" said the bicycle woman. "I did not know that. We forget how small the New York literary world was back then, and how the color bar was often lifted for a Genius."

The Englishman snorted. "Lifted? Only under sufferance. The woman died in penury as a cleaner in Florida. Nobody knew she'd written any of the stuff she wrote, let alone that she'd worked with Fitzgerald on *The Great Gatsby*. It's pathetic, Margaret."

"Posterity has a way of taking these things into account," said the tall woman. She walked away.

Campbell stared after her. "When I grow up," he said, "I want to be her."

"Why?"

He looked at me. "Yeah, that's the attitude. You're right. Some of us write the bestsellers, some of us read them, some of us get the prizes, some of us don't. What's important is being human, isn't it? It's how good a person you are. Being alive."

He patted me on the arm.

"Come on. Interesting anthropological phenomenon I've read about on the Internet I shall point out to you tonight, of the kind you probably don't see back in Dead Rat, Kentucky. *Id est,* women who would, under normal circumstances, not show their tits for a hundred quid, who will be only too pleased to get 'em out for the crowd for some cheap plastic beads."

"Universal trading medium," I said. "Beads."

"Fuck," he said. "There's a paper in that. Come on. You ever had a Jell-O shot, Jackson?"

"No."

"Me neither. Bet they'll be disgusting. Let's go and see." We paid for our drinks. I had to remind him to tip.

"By the way," I said. "F. Scott Fitzgerald. What was his wife's name?"

"Zelda? What about her?"

"Nothing," I said.

Zelda. Zora. Whatever. We went out.

3. "NOTHING, LIKE SOMETHING, HAPPENS ANYWHERE"

MIDNIGHT, GIVE OR TAKE. We were in a bar on Bourbon Street, me and the English anthropology prof, and he started buying drinks—real drinks, this place didn't do Jell-O shots—for a couple of dark-haired women at the bar. They looked so similar they could have been sisters. One wore a red ribbon in her hair, the other wore a white ribbon. Gauguin could have painted them, only he would have painted them bare-breasted and without the silver mouse skull earrings. They laughed a lot.

We had seen a small party of academics walk past the bar at one point, being led by a guide with a black umbrella. I pointed them out to Campbell.

The woman with the red ribbon raised an eyebrow. "They go on the Haunted History tours, looking for ghosts, you want to say, dude, this is where the ghosts come, this is where the dead stay. Easier to go looking for the living."

"You saying the tourists are *alive?*" said the other, mock-concern on her face.

"When they *get* here," said the first, and they both laughed at that. They laughed a lot.

The one with the white ribbon laughed at everything Campbell said. She would tell him, "Say fuck again," and he would say it, and she would say "Fook! Fook!" trying to copy him, and he'd say, "It's not *fook*, it's *fuck*," and she couldn't hear the difference, and would laugh some more.

After two drinks, maybe three, he took her by the hand and walked her into the back of the bar, where music was playing, and it was dark, and there were a couple of people already, if not dancing, then moving against each other.

I stayed where I was, beside the woman with the red ribbon in her hair.

She said, "So you're in the record company, too?"

I nodded. It was what Campbell had told them we did. "I hate telling people I'm a fucking academic," he had said, reasonably, when they were in the ladies' room. Instead he had told them that he had discovered Oasis.

"How about you? What do you do in the world?"

She said, "I'm a priestess of Santeria. Me, I got it all in my blood, my papa was Brazilian, my momma was Irish-Cherokee. In Brazil, everybody makes love with everybody and they have the best little brown babies. Everybody got black slave blood, everybody got Indian blood, my poppa even got some Japanese blood. His brother, my uncle, he looks Japanese. My poppa, he just a good-looking man. People think it was my poppa I got the Santeria from, but no, it was my grandmomma, said she was Cherokee, but I had her figgered for mostly high yaller when I saw the old photographs. When I was three I was talking to dead folks, when I was five I watched a huge black dog, size of a Harley-Davidson, walking behind a man in the street, no one could see it but me, when I told my mom, she told my grandmomma, they said, she's got to know, she's got to learn. There's people to teach me, even as a little girl.

"I was never afraid of dead folk. You know that? They never hurt you. So many things in this town can hurt you, but the dead don't hurt you. Living people hurt you. They hurt you so bad."

I shrugged.

"This is a town where people sleep with each other, you know. We make love to each other. It's something we do to show we're still alive."

I wondered if this was a come-on. It did not seem to be.

She said, "You hungry?"

I said, a little.

She said, "I know a place near here they got the best bowl of gumbo in New Orleans. Come on."

I said, "I hear it's a town you're best off not walking on your own at night."

"That's right," she said. "But you'll have me with you. You're safe, with me with you."

Out on the street college girls were flashing their breasts to the crowds on the balconies. For every glimpse of nipple the onlookers would cheer and throw plastic beads. I had known the red-ribbon woman's name earlier in the evening, but now it had evaporated.

"Used to be they only did this shit at Mardi Gras," she said. "Now the tourists expect it, so it's just tourists doing it for the tourists. The locals don't care. When you need to piss," she added, "you tell me."

"Okay. Why?"

"Because most tourists who get rolled, get rolled when they go into the alleys to relieve themselves. Wake up an hour later in Pirate's Alley with a sore head and an empty wallet."

"I'll bear that in mind."

She pointed to an alley as we passed it, foggy and deserted. "Don't go there," she said.

The place we wound up in was a bar with tables. A TV on above the bar showed the *Tonight Show* with the sound off and subtitles on, although the subtitles kept scrambling into numbers and fractions. We ordered the gumbo, a bowl each.

I was expecting more from the best gumbo in New Orleans. It was almost tasteless. Still, I spooned it down, knowing that I needed food, that I had had nothing to eat that day.

Three men came into the bar. One sidled, one strutted, one shambled. The sidler was dressed like a Victorian undertaker, high top hat and all. His skin was fishbelly pale; his hair was long and stringy; his beard was long and threaded with silver beads. The strutter was dressed in a long black leather coat, dark clothes underneath. His skin was very black. The last one, the shambler, hung back, waiting by the door. I could not see much of his face, nor decode his race: what I could see of his skin was a dirty gray. His lank hair hung over his face. He made my skin crawl.

The first two men made straight to our table, and I was, momentarily, scared for my skin, but they paid no attention to me. They looked at the woman with the red ribbon, and both of the men kissed her on the cheek. They asked about friends they had not seen, about who did what to whom in which bar and why. They reminded me of the fox and the cat from *Pinocchio*.

"What happened to your pretty girlfriend?" the woman asked the black man.

He smiled, without humor. "She put a squirrel tail on my family tomb."

She pursed her lips. "Then you better off without her."

"That's what I say."

I glanced over at the one who gave me the creeps. He was a filthy thing, junkie-thin, gray-lipped. His eyes were downcast. He barely moved. I wondered what the three men were doing together: the fox and the cat and the ghost.

Then the white man took the woman's hand and pressed it to his lips, bowed to her, raised a hand to me, in a mock salute, and the three of them were gone.

"Friends of yours?"

"Bad people," she said. "Macumba. Not friends of anybody."

"What was up with the guy by the door? Is he sick?"

She hesitated, then she shook her head. "Not really. I'll tell you when you're ready."

"Tell me now."

On the TV, Jay Leno was talking to a thin, blonde woman. IT&S NOT .UST T½E MOVIE said the caption. SO H.VE SS YOU SE¾N THE AC ION F!GURE? He picked up a small toy from his desk, pretended to check under its skirt to make sure it was anatomically correct. [LAUGHTER], said the caption.

She finished her bowl of gumbo, licked the spoon with a red, red tongue, and put it down in the bowl. "A lot of kids they come to New Orleans. Some of them read Anne Rice books and figure they learn about being vampires here. Some of them have abusive parents, some are just bored. Like stray kittens living in drains, they come here. They found a whole new breed of cat living in a drain in New Orleans, you know that?"

"No."

SLAUGHTER S] said the caption, but Jay was still grinning, and the *Tonight Show* went to a car commercial.

"He was one of the street kids, only he had a place to crash at night. Good kid. Hitchhiked from L.A. to New Orleans. Wanted to be left alone to smoke a little weed, listen to his Doors cassettes, study up on Chaos magick and read the complete works of Aleister Crowley. Also get his dick sucked. He wasn't particular about who did it. Bright eyes and bushy tail."

"Hey," I said. "That was Campbell. Going past. Out there."

"Campbell?"

"My friend."

"The record producer?" She smiled as she said it, and I thought, *She knows. She knows he was lying. She knows what he is.*

I put down a twenty and a ten on the table, and we went out onto the street, to find him, but he was already gone.

"I thought he was with your sister," I told her.

"No sister," she said. "No sister. Only me. Only me."

We turned a corner and were engulfed by a crowd of noisy tourists, like a sudden breaker crashing onto the shore. Then, as fast as they had come, they were gone, leaving only a handful of people behind them. A teenaged girl was throwing up in a gutter, a young man nervously standing near her, holding her purse and a plastic cup half full of booze.

The woman with the red ribbon in her hair was gone. I wished I had made a note of her name, or the name of the bar in which I'd met her.

I had intended to leave that night, to take the interstate west to Houston and from there to Mexico, but I was tired and two-thirds drunk, and instead I went back to my room, and when the morning came I was still in the Marriott. Everything I had worn the night before smelled of perfume and rot.

I put on my T-shirt and pants, went down to the hotel gift shop, picked out a couple more T-shirts and a pair of shorts. The tall woman, the one without the bicycle, was in there, buying some Alka-Seltzer.

She said, "They've moved your presentation. It's now in the Audubon Room, in about twenty minutes. You might want to clean your teeth first. Your best friends won't tell you, but I hardly know you, Mister Anderton, so I don't mind telling you at all."

I added a traveling toothbrush and toothpaste to the stuff I was buying. Adding to my possessions, though, troubled me. I felt I should be shedding them. I needed to be transparent, to have nothing.

I went up to the room, cleaned my teeth, put on the Jazz Festival T-shirt. And then, because I had no choice in the matter, or because I was doomed to confer, consult, and otherwise hobnob, or because I was pretty certain Campbell would be in the audience and I wanted to say good-bye to him before I drove away, I picked up the type-script and went down to the Audubon Room, where fifteen people were waiting. Campbell was not one of them.

I was not scared. I said hello, and I looked at the top of page one.

It began with another quote from Zora Neale Hurston:

Big Zombies who come in the night to do malice are talked about. Also the little girl Zombies who are sent out by their owners in the dark dawn to sell little packets of roasted coffee. Before sun-up their cries of "Café grillé" can be heard from dark places in the streets and one can only see them if one calls out for the seller to come with the goods. Then the little dead one makes herself visible and mounts the steps.

Anderton continued on from there, with quotations from Hurston's contemporaries, several extracts from old interviews with older Haitians, the man's paper leaping, as far as I was able to tell, from conclusion to conclusion, spinning fancies into guesses and suppositions and weaving those into facts.

Halfway through, Margaret, the tall woman without the bicycle, came in and simply stared at me. I thought, *She knows I'm not him. She knows.* I kept reading though. What else could I do?

At the end, I asked for questions.

Somebody asked me about Zora Neale Hurston's research prac-tices. I said that was a very good question, which was addressed at greater length in the finished paper, of which what I had read was essentially an edited abstract.

Someone else, a short, plump woman, stood up and announced that the zombie girls could not have existed: Zombie drugs and pow-ders numbed you, induced deathlike trances, but still worked fun-damentally on belief—the belief that you were now one of the dead and had no will of your own. How, she asked, could a child of four or five be induced to believe such a thing? No. The coffee girls were, she said, one with the Indian Rope Trick, just another of the urban legends of the past.

Personally I agreed with her, but I nodded and said that her points were well made and well taken. And that, from my perspective— which was, I hoped, a genuinely anthropological perspective—what mattered was not what it was easy to believe, but, much more importantly, the truth.

They applauded, and afterward a man with a beard asked me whether he might be able to get a copy of the paper for a journal he edited. It occurred to me that it was a good thing I had come to New Orleans, that Anderton's career would not be harmed by his absence from the conference.

The plump woman, whose badge said her name was Shanelle Gravely-King, was waiting for me at the door. She said, "I really enjoyed that. I don't want you to think that I didn't."

Campbell didn't turn up for his presentation. Nobody ever saw him again.

Margaret introduced me to someone from New York, and mentioned that Zora Neale Hurston had worked on *The Great Gatsby*. The man said yes, that was pretty common knowledge these days. I wondered if she had called the police, but she seemed friendly enough. I was starting to stress, I realized. I wished I had not thrown away my cell phone.

Shanelle Gravely-King and I had an early dinner in the hotel, at the beginning of which I said, "Oh, let's not talk shop," and she agreed that only the very dull talked shop at the table, so we talked about rock bands we had seen live, fictional methods of slowing the decomposition of a human body, and about her partner, who was a woman older than she was and who owned a restaurant, and then we went up to my room. She smelled of baby powder and jasmine, and her naked skin was clammy against mine.

Over the next couple of hours I used two of the three condoms. She was sleeping by the time I returned from the bathroom, and I climbed into the bed next to her. I thought about the words Anderton had written, hand-scrawled on the back of the typescript page, and I wanted to check them, but I fell asleep, a soft-fleshed jasmine-scented woman pressing close to me.

After midnight, I woke from a dream, and a woman's voice was whispering in the darkness.

She said, "So he came into town, with his Doors cassettes and his Crowley books, and his handwritten list of the secret URLs for Chaos magick on the Web, and everything was good, he even got a few disciples, runaways like him, and he got his dick sucked whenever he wanted, and the world was good.

"And then he started to believe his own press. He thought he was the real thing. That he was the dude. He thought he was a big mean tiger cat, not a little kitten. So he dug up . . . something . . . someone else wanted.

"He thought the something he dug up would look after him. Silly boy. And that night, he's sitting in Jackson Square, talking to the tarot readers, telling them about Jim Morrison and the kabbalah, and someone taps him on the shoulder, and he turns, and someone blows powder into his face, and he breathes it in.

"Not all of it. And he is going to do something about it, when he realizes there's nothing to be done, because he's all paralyzed, there's fugu fish and toad skin and ground bone and everything else in that powder, and he's breathed it in.

"They take him down to emergency, where they don't do much for him, figuring him for a street rat with a drug problem, and by the next day he can move again, although it's two, three days until he can speak.

"Trouble is, he needs it. He wants it. He knows there's some big secret in the zombie powder, and he was almost there. Some people say they mixed heroin with it, some shit like that, but they didn't even need to do that. He wants it.

"And they told him they wouldn't sell it to him. But if he did jobs for them, they'd give him a little zombie powder, to smoke, to sniff, to rub on his gums, to swallow. Sometimes they'd give him nasty jobs to do no one else wanted. Sometimes they just humiliate him because they could—make him eat dog shit from the gutter, maybe.

Kill for them, maybe. Anything but die. All skin and bones. He do anything for his zombie powder.

"And he still thinks, in the little bit of his head that's still him, that he's not a zombie. That he's not dead, that there's a threshold he hasn't stepped over. But he crossed it long time ago."

I reached out a hand, and touched her. Her body was hard, and slim, and lithe, and her breasts felt like breasts that Gauguin might have painted. Her mouth, in the darkness, was soft and warm against mine.

People come into your life for a reason.

4. "THOSE PEOPLE OUGHT TO KNOW WHO WE ARE AND TELL THAT WE ARE HERE"

WHEN I WOKE, IT was still almost dark, and the room was silent. I turned on the light, looked on the pillow for a ribbon, white or red, or for a mouse-skull earring, but there was nothing to show that there had ever been anyone in the bed that night but me.

I got out of bed and pulled open the drapes, looked out of the window. The sky was graying in the east.

I thought about moving south, about continuing to run, continuing to pretend I was alive. But it was, I knew now, much too late for that. There are doors, after all, between the living and the dead, and they swing in both directions.

I had come as far as I could.

There was a faint tap-tapping on the hotel room door. I pulled on my pants and the T-shirt I had set out in and, barefoot, I pulled the door open.

The coffee girl was waiting for me.

Everything beyond the door was touched with light, an open, wonderful predawn light, and I heard the sound of birds calling on the morning air. The street was on a hill, and the houses facing me were little more than shanties. There was mist in the air, low to the ground, curling like something from an old black-and-white film, but it would be gone by noon.

The girl was thin and small; she did not appear to be more than six years old. Her eyes were cobwebbed with what might have been cataracts, her skin was as gray as it had once been brown. She was holding a white hotel cup out to me, holding it carefully, with one small hand on the handle, one hand beneath the saucer. It was half-filled with a steaming mud-colored liquid.

I bent to take it from her, and I sipped it. It was a very bitter drink, and it was hot, and it woke me the rest of the way.

I said, "Thank you."

Someone, somewhere, was calling my name.

The girl waited, patiently, while I finished the coffee. I put the cup down on the carpet, then I put out my hand and touched her shoulder. She reached up her hand, spread her small gray fingers, and took hold of my hand. She knew I was with her. Wherever we were headed now, we were going there together.

I remembered something somebody had once said to me. "It's okay. Every day is freshly ground," I told her.

The coffee girl's expression did not change, but she nodded, as if she had heard me, and gave my arm an impatient tug. She held my hand tight with her cold cold fingers, and we walked, finally, side by side into the misty dawn.

THE PROBLEM OF SUSAN

2004

*S*HE HAS THE *dream again that night.*

    In the dream, she is standing, with her brothers and her sister, on the edge of the battlefield. It is summer, and the grass is a peculiarly vivid shade of green: a wholesome green, like a cricket pitch or the welcoming slope of the South Downs as you make your way north from the coast. There are bodies on the grass. None of the bodies are human; she can see a centaur, its throat slit, on the grass near her. The horse half of it is a vivid chestnut. Its human skin is nut-brown from the sun. She finds herself staring at the horse's penis, wondering about centaurs mating, imagines being kissed by that bearded face. Her eyes flick to the cut throat, and the sticky red-black pool that surrounds it, and she shivers.

    Flies buzz about the corpses.

    The wildflowers tangle in the grass. They bloomed yesterday for the first time in . . . how long? A hundred years? A thousand? A hundred thousand? She does not know.

    All this was snow, she thinks, as she looks at the battlefield.

    Yesterday, all this was snow. Always winter, and never Christmas.

    Her sister tugs her hand, and points. On the brow of the green hill they stand, deep in conversation. The lion is golden, his arms folded behind his back. The witch is dressed all in white. Right now she is shouting at the lion, who is simply listening. The children cannot make out any of their words, not her cold anger, nor the lion's thrum-deep replies. The witch's hair is black and shiny, her lips are red.

In her dream she notices these things.

They will finish their conversation soon, the lion and the witch . . .

THERE ARE THINGS about herself that the professor despises. Her smell, for example. She smells like her grandmother smelled, like old women smell, and for this she cannot forgive herself, so on waking she bathes in scented water and, naked and towel-dried, dabs several drops of Chanel toilet water beneath her arms and on her neck. It is, she believes, her sole extravagance.

Today she dresses in her dark brown dress suit. She thinks of these as her interview clothes, as opposed to her lecture clothes or her knocking-about-the-house clothes. Now she is in retirement, she wears her knocking-about-the-house clothes more and more. She puts on lipstick.

After breakfast, she washes a milk bottle, places it at her back door. She discovers that the next-door's cat has deposited a mouse head and a paw, on the doormat. It looks as though the mouse is swimming through the coconut matting, as though most of it is submerged. She purses her lips, then she folds her copy of yesterday's *Daily Telegraph,* and she folds and flips the mouse head and the paw into the newspaper, never touching them with her hands.

Today's *Daily Telegraph* is waiting for her in the hall, along with several letters, which she inspects, without opening any of them, then places on the desk in her tiny study. Since her retirement she visits her study only to write. Now she walks into the kitchen and seats herself at the old oak table. Her reading glasses hang about her neck on a silver chain, and she perches them on her nose and begins with the obituaries.

She does not actually expect to encounter anyone she knows there, but the world is small, and she observes that, perhaps with cruel humor, the obituarists have run a photograph of Peter Burrell-Gunn as he was in the early 1950s, and not at all as he was the last time the professor had seen him, at a *Literary Monthly* Christmas party several years before, all gouty and beaky and trembling, and reminding her of nothing so much as a caricature of an owl. In the photograph, he is very beautiful. He looks wild, and noble.

She had spent an evening once kissing him in a summer house: she remembers that very clearly, although she cannot remember for the life of her in which garden the summer house had belonged.

It was, she decides, Charles and Nadia Reid's house in the country. Which meant that it was before Nadia ran away with that Scottish artist, and Charles took the professor with him to Spain, although she was certainly not a professor then. This was many years before people commonly went to Spain for their holidays; it was an exotic and dangerous place in those days. He asked her to marry him, too, and she is no longer certain why she said no, or even if she had entirely said no. He was a pleasant-enough young man, and he took what was left of her virginity on a blanket on a Spanish beach, on a warm spring night. She was twenty years old, and had thought herself so old . . .

The doorbell chimes, and she puts down the paper, and makes her way to the front door, and opens it.

Her first thought is how young the girl looks.

HER FIRST THOUGHT is how old the woman looks. "Professor Hastings?" she says. "I'm Greta Campion. I'm doing the profile on you. For the *Literary Chronicle*."

The older woman stares at her for a moment, vulnerable and ancient, then she smiles. It's a friendly smile, and Greta warms to her. "Come in, dear," says the professor. "We'll be in the sitting room."

"I brought you this," says Greta. "I baked it myself." She takes the cake tin from her bag, hoping its contents hadn't disintegrated en route. "It's a chocolate cake. I read online that you liked them."

The old woman nods and blinks. "I do," she says. "How kind. This way."

Greta follows her into a comfortable room, is shown to her armchair, and told, firmly, not to move. The professor bustles off and returns with a tray, on which are teacups and saucers, a teapot, a plate of chocolate biscuits, and Greta's chocolate cake.

Tea is poured, and Greta exclaims over the professor's brooch, and then she pulls out her notebook and pen, and a copy of the professor's last book, *A Quest for Meanings in Children's Fiction,* the copy bristling with Post-it notes and scraps of paper. They talk about the early chapters, in which the hypothesis is set forth that there was originally no distinct branch of fiction that was only intended for children, until the Victorian notions of the purity and sanctity of childhood demanded that fiction for children be made . . .

"Well, pure," says the professor.

"And sanctified?" asks Greta, with a smile.

"And sanctimonious," corrects the old woman. "It is difficult to read *The Water Babies* without wincing."

And then she talks about ways that artists used to draw children— as adults, only smaller, without considering the child's proportions— and how the Grimms' stories were collected for adults and, when the Grimms realized the books were being read in the nursery, were bowdlerized to make them more appropriate. She talks of Perrault's "Sleeping Beauty in the Wood," and of its original coda in which the Prince's cannibal ogre mother attempts to frame the Sleeping Beauty for having eaten her own children, and all the while Greta nods and takes notes, and nervously tries to contribute enough to the conversation that the professor will feel that it is a conversation or at least an interview, not a lecture.

"Where," asks Greta, "do you feel your interest in children's fiction came from?"

The professor shakes her head. "Where do any of our interests come from? Where does *your* interest in children's books come from?"

Greta says, "They always seemed the books that were most important to me. The ones that mattered. When I was a kid, and when I grew. I was like Dahl's Matilda. Were your family great readers?"

"Not really. . . . I say that it was a long time ago that they died. Were killed. I should say."

"All your family died at the same time? Was this in the war?"

"No, dear. We were evacuees, in the war. This was in a train crash, several years after. I was not there."

"Just like in Lewis's *Narnia* books," says Greta, and immediately feels like a fool, and an insensitive fool. "I'm sorry. That was a terrible thing to say, wasn't it?"

"Was it, dear?"

Greta can feel herself blushing, and she says, "It's just I remember that sequence so vividly. In *The Last Battle*. Where you learn there was a train crash on the way back to school, and everyone was killed. Except for Susan, of course."

The professor says, "More tea, dear?" and Greta knows that she should leave the subject, but she says, "You know, that used to make me so angry."

"What did, dear?"

"Susan. All the other kids go off to Paradise, and Susan can't go. She's no longer a friend of Narnia because she's too fond of lipsticks and nylons and invitations to parties. I even talked to my English teacher about it, about the problem of Susan, when I was twelve."

She'll leave the subject now, talk about the role of children's fiction in creating the belief systems we adopt as adults, but the professor says, "And tell me, dear, what did your teacher say?"

"She said that even though Susan had refused Paradise then, she still had time while she lived to repent."

"Repent *what?*"

"Not believing, I suppose. And the sin of Eve."

The professor cuts herself a slice of chocolate cake. She seems to be remembering. And then she says, "I doubt there was much opportunity for nylons and lipsticks after her family was killed. There certainly wasn't for me. A little money—less than one might imagine—from her parents' estate, to lodge and feed her. No luxuries . . ."

"There must have been something else wrong with Susan," says the young journalist, "something they didn't tell us. Otherwise she wouldn't have been damned like that—denied the Heaven of further up and further in. I mean, all the people she had ever cared for had gone on to their reward, in a world of magic and waterfalls and joy. And she was left behind."

"I don't know about the girl in the books," says the professor, "but remaining behind would also have meant that she was available to identify her brothers' and her little sister's bodies. There were a lot of people dead in that crash. I was taken to a nearby school—it was the first day of term, and they had taken the bodies there. My older brother looked okay. Like he was asleep. The other two were a bit messier."

"I suppose Susan would have seen their bodies, and thought, they're on holidays now. The perfect school holidays. Romping in meadows with talking animals, world without end."

"She might have done. I only remember thinking what a great deal of damage a train can do, when it hits another train, to the people who were traveling inside. I suppose you've never had to identify a body, dear?"

"No."

"That's a blessing. I remember looking at them and thinking, *What if I'm wrong, what if it's not him after all?* My younger brother was decapitated, you know. A god who would punish me for liking nylons and parties by making me walk through that school dining room, with the flies, to identify Ed, well . . . he's enjoying himself a bit too much, isn't he? Like a cat, getting the last ounce of enjoyment out of a mouse. Or a gram of enjoyment, I suppose it must be these days. I don't know, really."

She trails off. And then, after some time, she says, "I'm sorry dear. I don't think I can do any more of this today. Perhaps if your editor gives me a ring, we can set a time to finish our conversation."

Greta nods and says of course, and knows in her heart, with a peculiar finality, that they will talk no more.

THAT NIGHT, THE professor climbs the stairs of her house, slowly, painstakingly, floor by floor. She takes sheets and blankets from the airing cupboard, and makes up a bed in the spare bedroom, at the back. It is empty but for a wartime austerity dressing table, with a mirror and drawers, an oak bed, and a dusty applewood wardrobe, which contains only coat hangers and a cardboard box. She places a vase on the dressing table, containing purple rhododendron flowers, sticky and vulgar.

She takes from the box in the wardrobe a plastic shopping bag containing four old photographic albums. Then she climbs into the bed that was hers as a child, and lies there between the sheets, looking at the black-and-white photographs, and the sepia photographs, and the handful of unconvincing color photographs. She looks at her brothers, and her sister, and her parents, and she wonders how they could have been that young, how anybody could have been that young.

After a while she notices that there are several children's books beside the bed, which puzzles her slightly, because she does not believe she keeps books on the bedside table in that room. Nor, she decides, does she usually have a bedside table there. On the top of the pile is an old paperback book—it must be more than forty years old: the price on the cover is in shillings. It shows a lion, and two girls twining a daisy chain into its mane.

The professor's lips prickle with shock. And only then does she understand that she is dreaming, for she does not keep those books in the house. Beneath the paperback is a hardback, in its jacket, of a book that, in her dream, she has always wanted to read: *Mary Poppins Brings in the Dawn*, which P. L. Travers had never written while alive.

She picks it up and opens it to the middle, and reads the story waiting for her: Jane and Michael follow Mary Poppins on her day off, to Heaven, and they meet the boy Jesus, who is still slightly scared of Mary Poppins because she was once his nanny, and the Holy Ghost, who complains that he has not been able to get his sheet properly white since Mary Poppins left, and God the Father, who says, "There's no making her do anything. Not her. *She's* Mary Poppins."

"But you're God," said Jane. "You created everybody and everything. They have to do what you say."

"Not her," said God the Father once again, and he scratched his golden beard flecked with white. "I didn't create *her*. She's Mary Poppins."

And the professor stirs in her sleep, and afterward dreams that she is reading her own obituary. It has been a good life, she thinks, as she reads it, discovering her history laid out in black and white. Everyone is there. Even the people she had forgotten.

GRETA SLEEPS BESIDE her boyfriend, in a small flat in Camden, and she, too, is dreaming.

In the dream, the lion and the witch come down the hill together.

She is standing on the battlefield, holding her sister's hand. She looks up at the golden lion, and the burning amber of his eyes. "He's not a tame lion, is he?" she whispers to her sister, and they shiver.

The witch looks at them all, then she turns to the lion, and says, coldly, "I am satisfied with the terms of our agreement. You take the girls: for myself, I shall have the boys."

She understands what must have happened, and she runs, but the beast is upon her before she has covered a dozen paces.

The lion eats all of her except her head, in her dream. He leaves the head, and one of her hands, just as a housecat leaves the parts of a mouse it has no desire for, for later, or as a gift.

She wishes that he had eaten her head, then she would not have had to look. Dead eyelids cannot be closed, and she stares, unflinching, at the twisted thing her brothers have become. The great beast eats her little sister more slowly, and, it seems to her, with more relish and pleasure than it had eaten her; but then, her little sister had always been its favorite.

The witch removes her white robes, revealing a body no less white, with high, small breasts, and nipples so dark they are almost black. The witch lies back upon the grass, spreads her legs. Beneath her body, the grass becomes rimed with frost. "Now," she says.

The lion licks her white cleft with its pink tongue, until she can take no more of it, and she pulls its huge mouth to hers, and wraps her icy legs into its golden fur. . . .

Being dead, the eyes in the head on the grass cannot look away. Being dead, they miss nothing.

And when the two of them are done, sweaty and sticky and sated, only then does the lion amble over to the head on the grass and devour it in its huge mouth, crunching her skull in its powerful jaws, and it is then, only then, that she wakes.

Her heart is pounding. She tries to wake her boyfriend, but he snores and grunts and will not be roused.

It's true, Greta thinks, irrationally, in the darkness. *She grew up. She carried on. She didn't die.*

She imagines the professor, waking in the night and listening to the noises coming from the old applewood wardrobe in the corner:

to the rustlings of all these gliding ghosts, which might be mistaken for the scurries of mice or rats, to the padding of enormous velvet paws, and the distant, dangerous music of a hunting horn.

She knows she is being ridiculous, although she will not be surprised when she reads of the professor's demise. *Death comes in the night*, she thinks, before she returns to sleep. *Like a lion.*

THE WHITE WITCH *rides naked on the lion's golden back. Its muzzle is spotted with fresh, scarlet blood. Then the vast pinkness of its tongue wipes around its face, and once more it is perfectly clean.*

FORBIDDEN BRIDES OF THE FACELESS SLAVES IN THE SECRET HOUSE OF THE NIGHT OF DREAD DESIRE

2004

I.

SOMEWHERE IN THE NIGHT, someone was writing.

II.

HER FEET SCRUNCHED THE gravel as she ran, wildly, up the tree-lined drive. Her heart was pounding in her chest, her lungs felt as if they were bursting, heaving breath after breath of the cold night air. Her eyes fixed on the house ahead, the single light in the topmost room drawing her toward it like a moth to a candle flame. Above her, and away in the deep forest behind the house, night-things whooped and skrarked. From the road behind her, she heard something scream briefly—a small animal that had been the victim of some beast of prey, she hoped, but could not be certain.

She ran as if the legions of hell were close on her heels, and spared
not even a glance behind her until she reached the porch of the old
mansion. In the moon's pale light the white pillars seemed skeletal,
like the bones of a great beast. She clung to the wooden doorframe,
gulping air, staring back down the long driveway, as if she were waiting for something, and then she rapped on the door—timorously at
first, and then harder. The rapping echoed through the house. She
imagined, from the echo that came back to her, that, far away, someone was knocking on another door, muffled and dead.

"Please!" she called. "If there's someone here—anyone—please let
me in. I beseech you. I implore you." Her voice sounded strange to
her ears.

The flickering light in the topmost room faded and vanished, to
reappear in successive descending windows. One person, then, with
a candle. The light vanished into the depths of the house. She tried to
catch her breath. It seemed like an age passed before she heard footsteps on the other side of the door and spied a chink of candlelight
through a crack in the ill-fitting doorframe.

"Hello?" she said.

The voice, when it spoke, was dry as old bone—a desiccated voice,
redolent of crackling parchment and musty grave hangings. "Who
calls?" it said. "Who knocks? Who calls, on this night of all nights?"

The voice gave her no comfort. She looked out at the night that
enveloped the house, then pulled herself straight, tossed her raven
locks, and said in a voice that, she hoped, betrayed no fear, "'Tis I,
Amelia Earnshawe, recently orphaned and now on my way to take
up a position as a governess to the two small children—a boy and a
girl—of Lord Falconmere, whose cruel glances I found, during our
interview in his London residence, both repellent and fascinating,
but whose aquiline face haunts my dreams."

"And what do you do here, then, at this house, on this night of all
nights? Falconmere Castle lies a good twenty leagues on from here,
on the other side of the moors."

"The coachman—an ill-natured fellow, and a mute, or so he pretended to be, for he formed no words, but made his wishes known
only by grunts and gobblings—reined in his team a mile or so back

down the road, or so I judge, and then he shewed me by gestures that he would go no further, and that I was to alight. When I did refuse to do so, he pushed me roughly from the carriage to the cold earth, then, whipping the poor horses into a frenzy, he clattered off the way he had come, taking my several bags and my trunk with him. I called after him, but he did not return, and it seemed to me that a deeper darkness stirred in the forest gloom behind me. I saw the light in your window and I . . . I . . . ." She was able to keep up her pretense of bravery no longer, and she began to sob.

"Your father," came the voice from the other side of the door. "Would he have been the Honorable Hubert Earnshawe?"

Amelia choked back her tears. "Yes. Yes, he was."

"And you—you say you are an orphan?"

She thought of her father, of his tweed jacket, as the maelstrom seized him and whipped him onto the rocks and away from her forever.

"He died trying to save my mother's life. They both were drowned."

She heard the dull chunking of a key being turned in a lock, then twin booms as iron bolts were drawn back. "Welcome, then, Miss Amelia Earnshawe. Welcome to your inheritance, in this house without a name. Aye, welcome—on this night of all nights." The door opened.

The man held a black tallow candle; its flickering flame illuminated his face from below, giving it an unearthly and eldritch appearance. He could have been a jack-o'-lantern, she thought, or a particularly elderly axe-murderer.

He gestured for her to come in.

"Why do you keep saying that?" she asked.

"Why do I keep saying what?"

" 'On this night of all nights.' You've said it three times so far." He simply stared at her for a moment. Then he beckoned again, with one bone-colored finger. As she entered, he thrust the candle close to her face and stared at her with eyes that were not truly mad but were still far from sane. He seemed to be examining her, and eventually he grunted, and nodded. "This way," was all he said.

She followed him down a long corridor. The candle-flame threw fantastic shadows about the two of them, and in its light the grandfather clock and the spindly chairs and table danced and capered. The old man fumbled with his keychain and unlocked a door in the wall beneath the stairs. A smell came from the darkness beyond, of must and dust and abandonment.

"Where are we going?" she asked.

He nodded, as if he had not understood her. Then he said, "There are some as are what they are. And there are some as aren't what they seem to be. And there are some as only seem to be what they seem to be. Mark my words, and mark them well, Hubert Earnshawe's daughter. Do you understand me?"

She shook her head. He began to walk and did not look back.

She followed the old man down the stairs.

III.

FAR AWAY AND FAR along the young man slammed his quill down upon the manuscript, spattering sepia ink across the ream of paper and the polished table.

"It's no good," he said, despondently. He dabbed at a circle of ink he had just made on the table with a delicate forefinger, smearing the teak a darker brown, then, unthinking, he rubbed the finger against the bridge of his nose. It left a dark smudge.

"No, sir?" The butler had entered almost soundlessly.

"It's happening again, Toombes. Humor creeps in. Self-parody whispers at the edges of things. I find myself guying literary convention and sending up both myself and the whole scrivening profession."

The butler gazed unblinking at his young master. "I believe humor is very highly thought of in certain circles, sir."

The young man rested his head in his hands, rubbing his forehead pensively with his fingertips. "That's not the point, Toombes. I'm trying to create a slice of life here, an accurate representation of the world as it is, and of the human condition. Instead, I find myself indulging, as I write, in schoolboy parody of the foibles of my fellows. I make little jokes." He had smeared ink all over his face. "Very little."

From the forbidden room at the top of the house an eerie, ululating cry rang out, echoing through the house. The young man sighed. "You had better feed Aunt Agatha, Toombes."

"Very good, sir."

The young man picked up the quill pen and idly scratched his ear with the tip.

Behind him, in a bad light, hung the portrait of his great-great-grandfather. The painted eyes had been cut out most carefully, long ago, and now real eyes stared out of the canvas face, looking down at the writer. The eyes glinted a tawny gold. If the young man had turned around and remarked upon them, he might have thought them the golden eyes of some great cat or of some misshapen bird of prey, were such a thing possible. These were not eyes that belonged in any human head. But the young man did not turn. Instead, oblivious, he reached for a new sheet of paper, dipped his quill into the glass inkwell, and commenced to write:

IV.

"AYE . . ." said the old man, putting down the black tallow candle on the silent harmonium. "He is our master, and we are his slaves, though we pretend to ourselves that it is not so. But when the time is right, then he demands what he craves, and it is our duty and our compulsion to provide him with . . ." He shuddered, and drew a breath. Then he said only, "With what he needs."

The bat-wing curtains shook and fluttered in the glassless casement as the storm drew closer. Amelia clutched the lace handkerchief to her breast, her father's monogram upward. "And the gate?" she asked, in a whisper.

"It was locked in your ancestor's time, and he charged, before he vanished, that it should always remain so. But there are still tunnels, folk do say, that link the old crypt with the burial grounds."

"And Sir Frederick's first wife . . . ?"

He shook his head, sadly. "Hopelessly insane, and but a mediocre harpsichord player. He put it about that she was dead, and perhaps some believed him."

She repeated his last four words to herself. Then she looked up at him, a new resolve in her eyes. "And for myself? Now I have learned why I am here, what do you advise me to do?"

He peered around the empty hall. Then he said, urgently, "Fly from here, Miss Earnshawe. Fly while there is still time. Fly for your life, fly for your immortal aagh."

"My what?" she asked, but even as the words escaped her crimson lips, the old man crumpled to the floor. A silver crossbow quarrel protruded from the back of his head.

"He is dead," she said, in shocked wonderment.

"Aye," affirmed a cruel voice from the far end of the hall. "But he was dead before this day, girl. And I do think that he has been dead a monstrous long time."

Under her shocked gaze, the body began to putresce. The flesh dripped and rotted and liquified, the bones revealed crumbled and oozed, until there was nothing but a stinking mass of foetor where once there had been a man.

Amelia squatted beside it, then dipped her fingertip into the noxious stuff. She licked her finger, and she made a face. "You would appear to be right, sir, whoever you are," she said. "I would estimate that he has been dead for the better part of a hundred years."

V.

"I AM ENDEAVORING," SAID the young man to the chambermaid, "to write a novel that reflects life as it is, mirrors it down to the finest degree. Yet as I write it turns to dross and gross mockery. What should I do? Eh, Ethel? What should I do?"

"I'm sure I don't know, sir," said the chambermaid, who was pretty and young, and had come to the great house in mysterious circumstances several weeks earlier. She gave the bellows several more squeezes, making the heart of the fire glow an orange-white. "Will that be all?"

"Yes. No. Yes," he said. "You may go, Ethel."

The girl picked up the now-empty coal scuttle and walked at a steady pace across the drawing room.

The young man made no move to return to his writing-desk; instead he stood in thought by the fireplace, staring at the human skull on the mantel, at the twin crossed swords that hung above it upon the wall. The fire crackled and spat as a lump of coal broke in half.

Footsteps, close behind him. The young man turned. "You?"

The man facing him was almost his double—the white streak in the auburn hair proclaimed them of the same blood, if any proof were needed. The stranger's eyes were dark and wild, his mouth petulant yet oddly firm.

"Yes—I! I, your elder brother, whom you thought dead these many years. But I am not dead—or, perhaps, I am no longer dead— and I have come back—aye, come back from ways that are best left untraveled—to claim what is truly mine."

The young man's eyebrows raised. "I see. Well, obviously all this is yours—if you can prove that you are who you say you are."

"Proof? I need no proof. I claim birth-right, and blood-right—and death-right!" So saying, he pulled both the swords down from above the fireplace, and passed one, hilt first, to his younger brother. "Now guard you, my brother—and may the best man win."

Steel flashed in the firelight and kissed and clashed and kissed again in an intricate dance of thrust and parry. At times it seemed no more than a dainty minuet, or a courtly and deliberate ritual, while at other times it seemed pure savagery, a wildness that moved faster than the eye could easily follow. Around and around the room they went, and up the steps to the mezzanine, and down the steps to the main hall. They swung from drapes and from chandeliers. They leapt up on tables and down again.

The older brother obviously was more experienced, and, perhaps, was a better swordsman, but the younger man was fresher and he fought like a man possessed, forcing his opponent back and back and back to the roaring fire itself. The older brother reached out with his left hand and grasped the poker. He swung it wildly at the younger, who ducked, and, in one elegant motion, ran his brother through.

"I am done for. I am a dead man."

The younger brother nodded his ink-stained face.

"Perhaps it is better this way. Truly, I did not want the house, or the lands. All I wanted, I think, was peace." He lay there, bleeding crimson onto the gray flagstone. "Brother? Take my hand."

The young man knelt, and clasped a hand that already, it seemed to him, was becoming cold.

"Before I go into that night where none can follow, there are things I must tell you. Firstly, with my death, I truly believe the curse is lifted from our line. The second . . ." His breath now came in a bubbling wheeze, and he was having difficulty speaking. "The second . . . is . . . the . . . the thing in the abyss . . . beware the cellars . . . the rats . . . the—*it follows!*"

And with this his head lolled on the stone, and his eyes rolled back and saw nothing, ever again.

Outside the house, the raven cawed thrice. Inside, strange music had begun to skirl up from the crypt, signifying that, for some, the wake had already started.

The younger brother, once more, he hoped, the rightful possessor of his title, picked up a bell and rang for a servant. Toombes the butler was there in the doorway before the last ring had died away.

"Remove this," said the young man. "But treat it well. He died to redeem himself. Perhaps to redeem us both."

Toombes said nothing, merely nodded to show that he had understood.

The young man walked out of the drawing room. He entered the Hall of Mirrors—a hall from which all the mirrors had carefully been removed, leaving irregularly shaped patches on the paneled walls—and, believing himself alone, he began to muse aloud.

"This is precisely what I was talking about," he said. "Had such a thing happened in one of my tales—and such things happen all the time—I would have felt myself constrained to guy it unmercifully." He slammed a fist against a wall, where once a hexagonal mirror had hung. "What is wrong with me? Wherefore this flaw?"

Strange scuttling things gibbered and cheetled in the black drapes at the end of the room, and high in the gloomy oak beams, and behind the wainscoting, but they made no answer. He had expected none.

He walked up the grand staircase and along a darkened hall, to enter his study. Someone, he suspected, had been tampering with his papers. He suspected that he would find out who later that evening, after the Gathering.

He sat down at his desk, dipped his quill pen once more, and continued to write.

VI.

OUTSIDE THE ROOM THE ghoul-lords howled with frustration and hunger, and they threw themselves against the door in their ravenous fury, but the locks were stout, and Amelia had every hope that they would hold.

What had the woodcutter said to her? His words came back to her then, in her time of need, as if he were standing close to her, his manly frame mere inches from her feminine curves, the very scent of his honest laboring body surrounding her like the headiest perfume, and she heard his words as if he were, that moment, whispering them in her ear. "I was not always in the state you see me in now, lassie," he had told her. "Once I had another name, and a destiny unconnected to the hewing of cords of firewood from fallen trees. But know you this—in the escritoire there is a secret compartment, or so my great-uncle claimed, when he was in his cups. . . ."

The escritoire! Of course!

She rushed to the old writing desk. At first she could find no trace of a secret compartment. She pulled out the drawers, one after another, and then perceived that one of them was much shorter than the rest, which seeing she forced her white hand into the space where formerly the drawer had been, and found, at the back, a button. Frantically, she pressed it. Something opened, and she put her hand on a tightly rolled paper scroll.

Amelia withdrew her hand. The scroll was tied with a dusty black ribbon, and with fumbling fingers she untied the knot and opened the paper. Then she read, trying to make sense of the antiquated handwriting, of the ancient words. As she did so, a ghastly pallor suffused her handsome face, and even her violet eyes seemed clouded and distracted.

The knockings and the scratchings redoubled. In but a short time they would burst through, she had no doubt. No door could hold them forever. They would burst through, and she would be their prey. Unless, unless . . .

"Stop!" she called, her voice trembling. "I abjure you, every one of you, and thee most of all, O Prince of Carrion. In the name of the ancient compact between thy people and mine."

The sounds stopped. It seemed to the girl that there was shock in that silence. Finally, a cracked voice said, "The compact?" and a dozen voices, as ghastly again, whispered "The compact," in a susurrus of unearthly sound.

"Aye!" called Amelia Earnshawe, her voice no longer unsteady. "The compact."

For the scroll, the long-hidden scroll, had been the compact—the dread agreement between the Lords of the House and the denizens of the crypt in ages past. It had described and enumerated the nightmarish rituals that had chained them one to another over the centuries—rituals of blood, and of salt, and more.

"If you have read the compact," said a deep voice from beyond the door, "then you know what we need, Hubert Earnshawe's daughter."

"Brides," she said, simply.

"The brides!" came the whisper from beyond the door, and it redoubled and resounded until it seemed to her that the very house itself throbbed and echoed to the beat of those words—two syllables invested with longing, and with love, and with hunger.

Amelia bit her lip. "Aye. The brides. I will bring thee brides. I shall bring brides for all."

She spoke quietly, but they heard her, for there was only silence, a deep and velvet silence, on the other side of the door.

And then one ghoul voice hissed, "Yes, and do you think we could get her to throw in a side order of those little bread roll things?"

VII.

HOT TEARS STUNG THE young man's eyes. He pushed the papers from him and flung the quill pen across the room. It spattered its inky load over the bust of his great-great-great-grandfather, the brown ink soiling the patient white marble. The occupant of the bust, a large and mournful raven, startled, nearly fell off, and only kept its place by dint of flapping its wings several times. It turned, then, in an awkward step and hop, to stare with one black bead eye at the young man.

"Oh, this is intolerable!" exclaimed the young man. He was pale and trembling. "I cannot do it, and I shall never do it. I swear now, by . . ." and he hesitated, casting his mind around for a suitable curse from the extensive family archives.

The raven looked unimpressed. "Before you start cursing, and probably dragging peacefully dead and respectable ancestors back from their well-earned graves, just answer me one question." The voice of the bird was like stone striking against stone.

The young man said nothing, at first. It is not unknown for ravens to talk, but this one had not done so before, and he had not been expecting it to. "Certainly. Ask your question."

The raven tipped its head to one side. "Do you *like* writing that stuff?"

"Like?"

"That life-as-it-is stuff you do. I've looked over your shoulder sometimes. I've even read a little here and there. Do you enjoy writing it?"

The young man looked down at the bird. "It's literature," he explained, as if to a child. "Real literature. Real life. The real world. It's an artist's job to show people the world they live in. We hold up mirrors."

Outside the room lightning clove the sky. The young man glanced out of the window: a jagged streak of blinding fire created warped and ominous silhouettes from the bony trees and the ruined abbey on the hill.

The raven cleared its throat. "I said, do you enjoy it?"

The young man looked at the bird, then he looked away and, wordlessly, he shook his head.

"That's why you keep trying to pull it apart," said the bird. "It's not the satirist in you that makes you lampoon the commonplace and the humdrum. Merely boredom with the way things are. D'you see?" It paused to preen a stray wing-feather back into place with its beak. Then it looked up at him once more. "Have you ever thought of writing fantasy?" it asked.

The young man laughed. "Fantasy? Listen, I write literature. Fantasy isn't life. Esoteric dreams, written by a minority for a minority, it's—"

"What you'd be writing if you knew what was good for you."

"I'm a classicist," said the young man. He reached out his hand to a shelf of the classics—*Udolpho, The Castle of Otranto, The Saragossa Manuscript, The Monk*, and the rest of them. "It's literature."

"Nevermore," said the raven. It was the last word the young man ever heard it speak. It hopped from the bust, spread its wings, and glided out of the study door into the waiting darkness.

The young man shivered. He rolled the stock themes of fantasy over in his mind: cars and stockbrokers and commuters, housewives and police, agony columns and commercials for soap, income tax and cheap restaurants, magazines and credit cards and streetlights and computers . . .

"It is escapism, true," he said, aloud. "But is not the highest impulse in mankind the urge toward freedom, the drive to escape?" The young man returned to his desk, and he gathered together the pages of his unfinished novel and dropped them, unceremoniously, in the bottom drawer, amongst the yellowing maps and cryptic testaments and the documents signed in blood. The dust, disturbed, made him cough.

He took up a fresh quill; sliced at its tip with his pen-knife. In five deft strokes and cuts he had a pen. He dipped the tip of it into the glass inkwell. Once more he began to write:

VIII.

AMELIA EARNSHAWE PLACED THE slices of whole-wheat bread into the toaster and pushed it down. She set the timer to dark brown, just as George liked it. Amelia preferred her toast barely singed. She liked white bread as well, even if it didn't have the vitamins. She hadn't eaten white bread for a decade now.

At the breakfast table, George read his paper. He did not look up. He never looked up.

I hate him, she thought, and simply putting the emotion into words surprised her. She said it again in her head. *I hate him.* It was like a song. *I hate him for his toast, and for his bald head, and for the way he chases the office crumpet—girls barely out of school who laugh at him behind his back, and for the way he ignores me whenever he doesn't want to be bothered with me, and for the way he says "What, love?" when I ask him a simple question, as if he's long ago forgotten my name. As if he's forgotten that I even* have *a name.*

"Scrambled or boiled?" she said aloud.

"What, love?"

George Earnshawe regarded his wife with fond affection, and would have found her hatred of him astonishing. He thought of her in the same way, and with the same emotions, that he thought of anything which had been in the house for ten years and still worked well. The television, for example. Or the lawnmower. He thought it was love. "You know, we ought to go on one of those marches," he said, tapping the newspaper's editorial. "Show we're committed. Eh, love?"

The toaster made a noise to show that it was done. Only one dark brown slice had popped up. She took a knife and fished out the torn second slice with it. The toaster had been a wedding present from her uncle John. Soon she'd have to buy another, or start cooking toast under the grill, the way her mother had done.

"George? Do you want your eggs scrambled or boiled?" she asked, very quietly, and there was something in her voice that made him look up.

"Any way you like it, love," he said amiably, and could not for the life of him, as he told everyone in the office later that morning, understand why she simply stood there holding her slice of toast or why she started to cry.

IX.

THE QUILL PEN WENT *scritch scritch* across the paper, and the young man was engrossed in what he was doing. His face was strangely content, and a smile flickered between his eyes and his lips.

He was rapt.

Things scratched and scuttled in the wainscot but he hardly heard them.

High in her attic room Aunt Agatha howled and yowled and rattled her chains. A weird cachinnation came from the ruined abbey: it rent the night air, ascending into a peal of manic glee. In the dark woods beyond the great house, shapeless figures shuffled and loped, and raven-locked young women fled from them in fear.

"Swear!" said Toombes the butler, down in the butler's pantry, to the brave girl who was passing herself off as chambermaid. "Swear to me, Ethel, on your life, that you'll never reveal a word of what I tell you to a living soul . . ."

There were faces at the windows and words written in blood; deep in the crypt a lonely ghoul crunched on something that might once have been alive; forked lightnings slashed the ebony night; the faceless were walking; all was right with the world.

THE MONARCH OF THE GLEN

2004

*She herself is a haunted house. She does not possess
herself; her ancestors sometimes come and peer out of the
windows of her eyes and that is very frightening.*

ANGELA CARTER,
"THE LADY OF THE HOUSE OF LOVE"

I.

"IF YOU ASK ME," said the little man to Shadow, "you're something of
a monster. Am I right?"

They were the only two people, apart from the barmaid, in the
bar of a hotel in a town on the north coast of Scotland. Shadow
had been sitting there on his own, drinking a lager, when the man
came over and sat at his table. It was late summer, and it seemed
to Shadow that everything was cold and small and damp. He had a
small book of Pleasant Local Walks in front of him, and was studying the walk he planned to do tomorrow, along the coast, toward
Cape Wrath.

He closed the book.

"I'm American," said Shadow, "if that's what you mean."

The little man cocked his head to one side, and he winked, the-atrically. He had steel-gray hair, and a gray face, and a gray coat, and he looked like a small-town lawyer. "Well, perhaps that is what I mean, at that," he said. Shadow had had problems understanding Scottish accents in his short time in the country, all rich burrs and strange words and trills, but he had no trouble understanding this man. Everything the little man said was small and crisp, each word so perfectly enunciated that it made Shadow feel like he himself was talking with a mouthful of oatmeal.

The little man sipped his drink and said, "So you're American. Oversexed, overpaid, and over here. Eh? D'you work on the rigs?"

"Sorry?"

"An oilman? Out on the big metal platforms. We get oil people up here, from time to time."

"No. I'm not from the rigs."

The little man took out a pipe from his pocket, and a small penknife, and began to remove the dottle from the bowl. Then he tapped it out into the ashtray. "They have oil in Texas, you know," he said, after a while, as if he were confiding a great secret. "That's in America."

"Yes," said Shadow.

He thought about saying something about Texans believing that Texas was actually in Texas, but he suspected that he'd have to start explaining what he meant, so he said nothing.

Shadow had been away from America for the better part of two years. He had been away when the towers fell. He told himself sometimes that he did not care if he ever went back, and some-times he almost came close to believing himself. He had reached the Scottish mainland two days ago, landed in Thurso on the ferry from Orkney, and had traveled to the town he was staying in by bus.

The little man was talking. "So there's a Texas oilman, down in Aberdeen, he's talking to an old fellow he meets in a pub, much like you and me meeting actually, and they get talking, and the Texan, he says, Back in Texas I get up in the morning, I get into my car—I won't try to do the accent, if you don't mind—I'll turn the key in the ignition, and put my foot down on the accelerator, what you call the, the—"

"Gas pedal," said Shadow, helpfully.

"Right. Put my foot down on the gas pedal at breakfast, and by lunchtime I still won't have reached the edge of my property. And the canny old Scot, he just nods and says, Aye, well, I used to have a car like that myself."

The little man laughed raucously, to show that the joke was done. Shadow smiled and nodded to show that he knew it was a joke.

"What are you drinking? Lager? Same again over here, Jennie love. Mine's a Lagavulin." The little man tamped tobacco from a pouch into his pipe. "Did you know that Scotland's bigger than America?"

There had been no one in the hotel bar when Shadow came downstairs that evening, just the thin barmaid reading a newspaper and smoking her cigarette. He'd come down to sit by the open fire, as his bedroom was cold, and the metal radiators on the bedroom wall were colder than the room. He hadn't expected company.

"No," said Shadow, always willing to play straight man. "I didn't. How'd you reckon that?"

"It's all fractal," said the little man. "The smaller you look, the more things unpack. It could take you as long to drive across America as it would to drive across Scotland, if you did it the right way. It's like, you look on a map, and the coastlines are solid lines. But when you walk them, they're all over the place. I saw a whole program on it on the telly the other night. Great stuff."

"Okay," said Shadow.

The little man's pipe lighter flamed, and he sucked and puffed and sucked and puffed until he was satisfied that the pipe was burning well, then he put the lighter, the pouch, and the penknife back into his coat pocket.

"Anyway, anyway," said the little man. "I believe you're planning on staying here through the weekend."

"Yes," said Shadow. "Do you . . . are you with the hotel?"

"No, no. Truth to tell, I was standing in the hall when you arrived. I heard you talking to Gordon on the reception desk."

Shadow nodded. He had thought that he had been alone in the reception hall when he had registered, but it was possible that the little man had passed through. But still . . . there was a wrongness to this conversation. There was a wrongness to everything.

Jennie the barmaid put their drinks onto the bar. "Five pounds twenty," she said. She picked up her newspaper, and started to read once more. The little man went to the bar, paid, and brought back the drinks.

"So how long are you in Scotland?" asked the little man.

Shadow shrugged. "I wanted to see what it was like. Take some walks. See the sights. Maybe a week. Maybe a month."

Jennie put down her newspaper. "It's the arse-end of nowhere up here," she said, cheerfully. "You should go somewhere interesting."

"That's where you're wrong," said the little man. "It's only the arse-end of nowhere if you look at it wrong. See that map, laddie?" He pointed to a fly-specked map of Northern Scotland on the opposite wall of the bar. "You know what's wrong with it?"

"No."

"It's upside down!" the man said, triumphantly. "North's at the top. It's saying to the world that this is where things stop. Go no further. The world ends here. But you see, that's not how it was. This wasn't the north of Scotland. This was the southernmost tip of the Viking world. You know what the second most northern county in Scotland is called?"

Shadow glanced at the map, but it was too far away to read. He shook his head.

"Sutherland!" said the little man. He showed his teeth. "The South Land. Not to anyone else in the world it wasn't, but it was to the Vikings."

Jennie the barmaid walked over to them. "I won't be gone long," she said. "Call the front desk if you need anything before I get back." She put a log on the fire, then she went out into the hall.

"Are you a historian?" Shadow asked.

"Good one," said the little man. "You may be a monster, but you're funny. I'll give you that."

"I'm not a monster," said Shadow.

"Aye, that's what monsters always say," said the little man. "I was a specialist once. In St. Andrews. Now I'm in general practice. Well, I was. I'm semiretired. Go in to the surgery a couple of days a week, just to keep my hand in."

"Why do you say I'm a monster?" asked Shadow.

"Because," said the little man, lifting his whisky glass with the air of one making an irrefutable point, "I am something of a monster myself. Like calls to like. We are all monsters, are we not? Glorious monsters, shambling through the swamps of unreason. " He sipped his whisky, then said, "Tell me, a big man like you, have you ever been a bouncer? 'Sorry mate, I'm afraid you can't come in here to-night, private function going on, sling your hook and get on out of it,' all that?"

"No," said Shadow.

"But you must have done something like that?"

"Yes," said Shadow, who had been a bodyguard once, to an old god; but that was in another country.

"You, uh, you'll pardon me for asking, don't take this the wrong way, but do you need money?"

"Everyone needs money. But I'm okay." This was not entirely true; but it was a truth that, when Shadow needed money, the world seemed to go out of its way to provide it.

"Would you like to make a wee bit of spending money? Being a bouncer? It's a piece of piss. Money for old rope."

"At a disco?"

"Not exactly. A private party. They rent a big old house near here, come in from all over at the end of the summer. So last year, everybody's having a grand old time, champagne out of doors, all that, and there was some trouble. A bad lot. Out to ruin everybody's weekend."

"These were locals?"

"I don't think so."

"Was it political?" asked Shadow. He did not want to be drawn into local politics.

"Not a bit of it. Yobs and hairies and idiots. Anyway. They probably won't come back this year. Probably off in the wilds of nowhere demonstrating against international capitalism. But just to be on the safe side, the folk up at the house've asked me to look out for someone who could do a spot of intimidating. You're a big lad, and that's what they want."

"How much?" asked Shadow.

"Can you handle yourself in a fight, if it came down to it?" asked the man.

Shadow didn't say anything. The little man looked him up and down, and then he grinned again, showing tobacco-stained teeth. "Fifteen hundred pounds, for a long weekend's work. That's good money. And it's cash. Nothing you'd ever need to report to the tax man."

"This weekend coming?" said Shadow.

"Starting Friday morning. It's a big old house. Part of it used to be a castle. West of Cape Wrath."

"I don't know," said Shadow.

"If you do it," said the little gray man, "you'll get a fantastic weekend in a historical house, and I can guarantee you'll get to meet all kinds of interesting people. Perfect holiday job. I just wish I was younger. And, uh, a great deal taller, actually."

Shadow said, "Okay," and as soon as he said it, wondered if he would regret it.

"Good man. I'll get you more details as and when." The little gray man stood up, and gave Shadow's shoulder a gentle pat as he walked past. Then he went out, leaving Shadow in the bar on his own.

II.

SHADOW HAD BEEN ON the road for about eighteen months. He had backpacked across Europe and down into northern Africa. He had picked olives and fished for sardines and driven a truck and sold wine from the side of a road. Finally, several months ago, he had hitch-hiked his way back to Norway, to Oslo, where he had been born thirty-five years before.

He was not sure what he had been looking for. He only knew that he had not found it, although there were moments, in the high ground, in the crags and waterfalls, when he was certain that whatever he needed was just around the corner: behind a jut of granite, or in the nearest pine wood.

Still, it was a deeply unsatisfactory visit, and when, in Bergen, he was asked if he would be half of the crew of a motor yacht on its way to meet its owner in Cannes, he said yes.

They had sailed from Bergen to the Shetlands, and then to Orkney, where they spent the night in a bed-and-breakfast in Stromness. Next morning, leaving the harbor, the engines had failed, ultimately and irrevocably, and the boat had been towed back to port.

Bjorn, who was the captain and the other half of the crew, stayed with the boat, to talk to the insurers and field the angry calls from the boat's owner. Shadow saw no reason to stay: he took the ferry to Thurso, on the north coast of Scotland.

He was restless. At night he dreamed of freeways, of entering the neon edges of a city where the people spoke English. Sometimes it was in the Midwest, sometimes it was in Florida, sometimes on the East Coast, sometimes on the West.

When he got off the ferry he bought a book of scenic walks, and picked up a bus timetable, and he set off into the world.

Jennie the barmaid came back, and started to wipe all the surfaces with a cloth. Her hair was so blonde it was almost white, and it was tied up at the back in a bun.

"So what is it people do around here for fun?" asked Shadow.

"They drink. They wait to die," she said. "Or they go south. That pretty much exhausts your options."

"You sure?"

"Well, think about it. There's nothing up here but sheep and hills. We feed off the tourists, of course, but there's never really enough of you. Sad, isn't it?" Shadow shrugged.

"Are you from New York?" she asked.

"Chicago, originally. But I came here from Norway."

"You speak Norwegian?"

"A little."

"There's somebody you should meet," she said, suddenly. Then she looked at her watch. "Somebody who came here from Norway, a long time ago. Come on."

She put her cleaning cloth down, turned off the bar lights, and walked over to the door. "Come on," she said, again.

"Can you do that?" asked Shadow.

"I can do whatever I want," she said. "It's a free country, isn't it?"

"I guess."

She locked the bar with a brass key. They walked into the reception hall. "Wait here," she said. She went through a door marked PRIVATE, and reappeared several minutes later, wearing a long brown coat. "Okay. Follow me."

They walked out into the street. "So, is this a village or a small town?" asked Shadow.

"It's a fucking graveyard," she said. "Up this way. Come on."

They walked up a narrow road. The moon was huge and a yellowish brown. Shadow could hear the sea, although he could not yet see it. "You're Jennie?" he said.

"That's right. And you?"

"Shadow."

"Is that your real name?"

"It's what they call me."

"Come on, then, Shadow," she said.

At the top of the hill, they stopped. They were on the edge of the village, and there was a gray stone cottage. Jennie opened the gate and led Shadow up a path to the front door. He brushed a small bush at the side of the path, and the air filled with the scent of sweet lavender. There were no lights on in the cottage.

"Whose house is this?" asked Shadow. "It looks empty."

"Don't worry," said Jennie. "She'll be home in a second."

She pushed open the unlocked front door, and they went inside. She turned on the light switch by the door. Most of the inside of the cottage was taken up by a kitchen sitting room. There was a

tiny staircase leading up to what Shadow presumed was an attic bedroom. A CD player sat on the pine counter.

"This is your house," said Shadow.

"Home sweet home," she agreed. "You want coffee? Or something to drink?"

"Neither," said Shadow. He wondered what Jennie wanted. She
had barely looked at him, hadn't even smiled at him.

"Did I hear right? Was Doctor Gaskell asking you to help look
after a party on the weekend?"

"I guess."

"So what are you doing tomorrow and Friday?"

"Walking," said Shadow. "I've got a book. There are some beautiful walks."

"Some of them are beautiful. Some of them are treacherous," she
told him. "You can still find winter snow here, in the shadows, in the
summer. Things last a long time, in the shadows."

"I'll be careful," he told her.

"That was what the Vikings said," she said, and she smiled. She
took off her coat and dropped it on the bright purple sofa. "Maybe
I'll see you out there. I like to go for walks." She pulled at the bun at
the back of her head, and her pale hair fell free. It was longer than
Shadow had thought it would be.

"Do you live here alone?"

She took a cigarette from a packet on the counter, lit it with a
match. "What's it to you?" she asked. "You won't be staying the
night, will you?"

Shadow shook his head.

"The hotel's at the bottom of the hill," she told him. "You can't
miss it. Thanks for walking me home."

Shadow said good night, and walked back, through the lavender
night, out to the lane. He stood there for a little while, staring at the
moon on the sea, puzzled. Then he walked down the hill until he got
to the hotel. She was right: you couldn't miss it. He walked up the
stairs, unlocked his room with a key attached to a short stick, and
went inside. The room was colder than the corridor.

He took off his shoes, and stretched out on the bed in the dark.

III.

THE SHIP WAS MADE of the fingernails of dead men, and it lurched through the mist, bucking and rolling hugely and unsteadily on the choppy sea.

There were shadowy shapes on the deck, men as big as hills or houses, and as Shadow got closer he could see their faces: proud men and tall, each one of them. They seemed to ignore the ship's motion, each man waiting on the deck as if frozen in place.

One of them stepped forward, and he grasped Shadow's hand with his own huge hand. Shadow stepped onto the gray deck.

"Well come to this accursed place," said the man holding Shadow's hand, in a deep, gravel voice.

"Hail!" called the men on the deck. "Hail sun-bringer! Hail Baldur!" The name on Shadow's birth certificate was Balder Moon, but he shook his head. "I am not him," he told them. "I am not the one you are waiting for."

"We are dying here," said the gravel-voiced man, not letting go of Shadow's hand.

It was cold in the misty place between the worlds of waking and the grave. Salt spray crashed on the bows of the gray ship, and Shadow was drenched to the skin.

"Bring us back," said the man holding his hand. "Bring us back or let us go."

Shadow said, "I don't know how."

At that, the men on the deck began to wail and howl. Some of them crashed the hafts of their spears against the deck, others struck the flats of their short swords against the brass bowls at the center of their leather shields, setting up a rhythmic din accompanied by cries that moved from sorrow to a full-throated berserker ululation. . . .

A seagull was screaming in the early-morning air. The bedroom window had blown open in the night and was banging in the wind. Shadow was lying on the top of his bed in his narrow hotel room. His skin was damp, perhaps with sweat.

Another cold day at the end of the summer had begun.

The hotel packed him a Tupperware box containing several chicken sandwiches, a hard-boiled egg, a small packet of cheese-and-onion crisps, and an apple. Gordon on the reception desk, who handed him the box, asked when he'd be back, explaining that if he was more than a couple of hours late they'd call out the rescue services, and asking for the number of Shadow's mobile phone.

Shadow did not have a mobile phone.

He set off on the walk, heading toward the coast. It was beautiful, a desolate beauty that chimed and echoed with the empty places inside Shadow. He had imagined Scotland as being a soft place, all gentle heathery hills, but here on the North Coast everything seemed sharp and jutting, even the gray clouds that scudded across the pale blue sky. It was as if the bones of the world showed through. He followed the route in his book, across scrubby meadows and past splashing burns, up rocky hills and down.

Sometimes he imagined that he was standing still and the world was moving underneath him, that he was simply pushing it past with his legs.

The route was more tiring than he had expected. He had planned to eat at one o'clock, but by midday his legs were tired and he wanted a break. He followed his path to the side of a hill, where a boulder provided a convenient windbreak, and he crouched to eat his lunch. In the distance, ahead of him, he could see the Atlantic.

He had thought himself alone.

She said, "Will you give me your apple?"

It was Jennie, the barmaid from the hotel. Her too-fair hair gusted about her head.

"Hello, Jennie," said Shadow. He passed her his apple. She pulled a clasp knife from the pocket of her brown coat, and sat beside him. "Thanks," she said.

"So," said Shadow, "from your accent, you must have come from Norway when you were a kid. I mean, you sound like a local to me."

"Did I say that I came from Norway?"

"Well, didn't you?"

She speared an apple slice, and ate it, fastidiously, from the tip of the knife blade, only touching it with her teeth. She glanced at him. "It was a long time ago."

"Family?"

She moved her shoulders in a shrug, as if any answer she could give him was beneath her.

"So you like it here?"

She looked at him and shook her head. "I feel like a *hulder*."

He'd heard the word before, in Norway. "Aren't they a kind of troll?"

"No. They are mountain creatures, like the trolls, but they come from the woods, and they are very beautiful. Like me." She grinned as she said it, as if she knew that she was too pallid, too sulky, and too thin ever to be beautiful. "They fall in love with farmers."

"Why?"

"Damned if I know," she said. "But they do. Sometimes the farmer realizes that he is talking to a hulder woman, because she has a cow's tail hanging down behind, or worse, sometimes from behind there is nothing there, she is just hollow and empty, like a shell. Then the farmer says a prayer or runs away, flees back to his mother or his farm.

"But sometimes the farmers do not run. Sometimes they throw a knife over her shoulder, or just smile, and they marry the hulder woman. Then her tail falls off. But she is still stronger than any human woman could ever be. And she still pines for her home in the forests and the mountains. She will never be truly happy. She will never be human."

"What happens to her then?" asked Shadow. "Does she age and die with her farmer?"

She had sliced the apple down to the core. Now, with a flick of the wrist, she sent the apple core arcing off the side of the hill. "When her man dies . . . I think she goes back to the hills and the woods." She stared out at the hillside. "There's a story about one of them who was married to a farmer who didn't treat her well. He shouted at her, wouldn't help around the farm, he came home from the village drunk and angry. Sometimes he beat her.

"Now, one day she's in the farmhouse, making up the morning's fire, and he comes in and starts shouting at her, for his food is not ready, and he is angry, nothing she does is right, he doesn't know why he married her, and she listens to him for a while, and then, saying nothing, she reaches down to the fireplace, and she picks up the poker. A heavy black iron jobbie. She takes that poker and, without an effort, she bends it into a perfect circle, just like her wedding ring. She doesn't grunt or sweat, she just bends it, like you'd bend a reed. And her farmer sees this and he goes white as a sheet, and doesn't say anything else about his breakfast. He's seen what she did to the poker and he knows that at any time in the last five years she could have done the same to him. And until he died, he never laid another finger on her, never said one harsh word. Now, you tell me something, Mister everybody-calls-you-Shadow, if she could do that, why did she let him beat her in the first place? Why would she want to be with someone like that? You tell me."

"Maybe," said Shadow. "Maybe she was lonely."

She wiped the blade of the knife on her jeans.

"Doctor Gaskell kept saying you were a monster," she said. "Is it true?"

"I don't think so," said Shadow.

"Pity," she said. "You know where you are with monsters, don't you?"

"You do?"

"Absolutely. At the end of the day, you're going to be dinner. Talking about which, I'll show you something." She stood up, and led him to the top of the hill. "See. Over there? On the far side of that hill, where it drops into the glen, you can just see the house you'll be working at this weekend. Do you see it, over there?"

"No."

"Look. I'll point. Follow the line of my finger." She stood close to him, held out her hand and pointed to the side of a distant ridge. He could see the overhead sun glinting off something he supposed was a lake—or a loch, he corrected himself, he was in Scotland after all—and above that a gray outcropping on the side of a hill. He had taken it for rocks, but it was too regular to be anything but a building.

"That's the castle?"

"I'd not call it that. Just a big house in the glen."

"Have you been to one of the parties there?"

"They don't invite locals," she said. "And they wouldn't ask me. You shouldn't do it, anyway. You should say no."

"They're paying good money," he told her.

She touched him then, for the first time, placed her pale fingers on the back of his dark hand. "And what good is money to a monster?" she asked, and smiled, and Shadow was damned if he didn't think that maybe she *was* beautiful, at that.

And then she put down her hand and backed away. "Well?" she said. "Shouldn't you be off on your walk? You've not got much longer before you'll have to start heading back again. The light goes fast when it goes, this time of year."

And she stood and watched him as he hefted his rucksack, and began to walk down the hill. He turned around when he reached the bottom and looked up. She was still looking at him. He waved, and she waved back.

The next time he looked back she was gone.

He took the little ferry across the kyle to the cape, and walked up to the lighthouse. There was a minibus from the lighthouse back to the ferry, and he took it.

He got back to the hotel at eight that night, exhausted but feeling satisfied. It had rained once, in the late afternoon, but he had taken shelter in a tumbledown bothy, and read a five-year-old newspaper while the rain drummed against the roof. It had ended after half an hour, but Shadow had been glad that he had good boots, for the earth had turned to mud.

He was starving. He went into the hotel restaurant. It was empty. Shadow said, "Hello?"

An elderly woman came to the door between the restaurant and the kitchen and said, "Aye?"

"Are you still serving dinner?"

"Aye." She looked at him disapprovingly, from his muddy boots to his tousled hair. "Are you a guest?"

"Yes. I'm in room eleven."

"Well . . . you'll probably want to change before dinner," she said. "It's kinder to the other diners."

"So you *are* serving."

"Aye."

He went up to his room, dropped his rucksack on the bed, and took off his boots. He put on his sneakers, ran a comb through his hair, and went back downstairs.

The dining room was no longer empty. Two people were sitting at a table in the corner, two people who seemed different in every way that people could be different: a small woman who looked to be in her late fifties, hunched and birdlike at the table, and a young man, big and awkward and perfectly bald. Shadow decided that they were mother and son.

He sat down at a table in the center of the room.

The elderly waitress came in with a tray. She gave both of the other diners a bowl of soup. The man began to blow on his soup, to cool it; his mother tapped him, hard, on the back of his hand, with her spoon. "Stop that," she said. She began to spoon the soup into her mouth, slurping it noisily.

The bald man looked around the room, sadly. He caught Shadow's eye, and Shadow nodded at him. The man sighed, and returned to his steaming soup.

Shadow scanned the menu without enthusiasm. He was ready to order, but the waitress had vanished again.

A flash of gray; Dr. Gaskell peered in at the door of the restaurant. He walked into the room, came over to Shadow's table.

"Do you mind if I join you?"

"Not at all. Please. Sit down."

He sat down, opposite Shadow. "Have a good day?"

"Very good. I walked."

"Best way to work up an appetite. So. First thing tomorrow they're sending a car out here to pick you up. Bring your things. They'll take you out to the house. Show you the ropes."

"And the money?" asked Shadow.

"They'll sort that out. Half at the beginning, half at the end. Anything else you want to know?"

The waitress stood at the edge of the room, watching them, making no move to approach. "Yeah. What do I have to do to get some food around here?"

"What do you want? I recommend the lamb chops. The lamb's local."

"Sounds good."

Gaskell said loudly, "Excuse me, Maura. Sorry to trouble you, but could we both have the lamb chops?"

She pursed her lips, and went back to the kitchen.

"Thanks," said Shadow.

"Don't mention it. Anything else I can help you with?"

"Yeah. These folk coming in for the party. Why don't they hire their own security? Why hire me?"

"They'll be doing that too, I have no doubt," said Gaskell. "Bringing in their own people. But it's good to have local talent."

"Even if the local talent is a foreign tourist?"

"Just so."

Maura brought two bowls of soup, put them down in front of Shadow and the doctor. "They come with the meal," she said. The soup was too hot, and it tasted faintly of reconstituted tomatoes and vinegar. Shadow was hungry enough that he'd finished most of the bowl off before he realized that he did not like it.

"You said I was a monster," said Shadow to the steel-gray man.

"I did?"

"You did."

"Well, there's a lot of monsters in this part of the world." He tipped his head toward the couple in the corner. The little woman had picked up her napkin, dipped it into her water glass, and was dabbing vigorously with it at the spots of crimson soup on her son's mouth and chin. He looked embarrassed. "It's remote. We don't get into the news unless a hiker or a climber gets lost, or starves to death. Most people forget we're here."

The lamb chops arrived, on a plate with overboiled potatoes, underboiled carrots, and something brown and wet that Shadow thought might have started life as spinach. He started to cut at the chops with his knife. The doctor picked his up in his fingers, and began to chew.

"You've been inside," said the doctor.

"Inside?"

"Prison. You've been in prison." It wasn't a question.

"Yes."

"So you know how to fight. You could hurt someone, if you had to."

Shadow said, "If you need someone to hurt people, I'm probably not the guy you're looking for."

The little man grinned, with greasy gray lips. "I'm sure you are. I was just asking. You can't give a man a hard time for asking. Anyway. *He's* a monster," he said, gesturing across the room with a mostly chewed lamb chop. The bald man was eating some kind of white pudding with a spoon. "So's his mother."

"They don't look like monsters to me," said Shadow.

"I'm teasing you, I'm afraid. Local sense of humor. They should warn you about mine when you enter the village. Warning, loony old doctor at work. Talking about monsters. Forgive an old man. You mustn't listen to a word I say." A flash of tobacco-stained teeth. He wiped his hands and mouth on his napkin. "Maura, we'll be needing the bill over here. The young man's dinner is on me."

"Yes, Doctor Gaskell."

"Remember," said the doctor to Shadow. "Eight fifteen tomorrow morning, be in the lobby. No later. They're busy people. If you aren't there, they'll just move on, and you'll have missed out on fifteen hundred pounds, for a weekend's work. A bonus, if they're happy."

Shadow decided to have his after-dinner coffee in the bar. There was a log fire there, after all. He hoped it would take the chill from his bones.

Gordon from reception was working behind the bar. "Jennie's night off?" asked Shadow.

"What? No, she was just helping out. She'll do it if we're busy, sometimes."

"Mind if I put another log on the fire?"

"Help yourself."

If this is how the Scots treat their summers, thought Shadow, remembering something Oscar Wilde had once said, *they don't deserve to have any.*

The bald young man came in. He nodded a nervous greeting to

Shadow. Shadow nodded back. The man had no hair that Shadow could see: no eyebrows, no eyelashes. It made him look babyish, and unformed. Shadow wondered if it was a disease, or if it was perhaps a side effect of chemotherapy. He smelled of damp.

"I heard what he said," stammered the bald man. "He said I was a monster. He said my ma was a monster too. I've got good ears on me. I don't miss much."

He did have good ears on him. They were a translucent pink, and they stuck out from the sides of his head like the fins of some huge fish.

"You've got great ears," said Shadow.

"You taking the mickey?" The bald man's tone was aggrieved. He looked like he was ready to fight. He was only a little shorter than Shadow, and Shadow was a big man.

"If that means what I think it does, not at all."

The bald man nodded. "That's good," he said. He swallowed, and hesitated. Shadow wondered if he should say something conciliatory, but the bald man continued, "It's not my fault. Making all that noise. I mean, people come up here to get away from the noise. And the people. Too many damned people up here anyway. Why don't you just go back to where you came from and stop making all that bluidy noise?"

The man's mother appeared in the doorway. She smiled nervously at Shadow, then walked hurriedly over to her son. She pulled at his sleeve. "Now then," she said. "Don't you get yourself all worked up over nothing. Everything's all right." She looked up at Shadow, birdlike, placatory. "I'm sorry. I'm sure he didn't mean it." She had a length of toilet paper sticking to the bottom of her shoe, and she hadn't noticed yet.

"Everything's all right," said Shadow. "It's good to meet people."

She nodded. "That's all right then," she said. Her son looked relieved. *He's scared of her,* thought Shadow.

"Come on pet," said the woman to her son. She pulled at his sleeve, and he followed her to the door.

Then he stopped, obstinately, and turned. "You tell them," said the bald young man, "not to make so much noise."

"I'll tell them," said Shadow.

"It's just that I can hear everything."

"Don't worry about it," said Shadow.

"He really is a good boy," said the bald young man's mother, and she led her son by the sleeve, into the corridor and away, trailing a tag of toilet paper.

Shadow walked out into the hall. "Excuse me," he said. They turned, the man and his mother.

"You've got something on your shoe," said Shadow.

She looked down. Then she stepped on the strip of paper with her other shoe, and lifted her foot, freeing it. She nodded at Shadow, approvingly, and walked away.

Shadow went to the reception desk. "Gordon, have you got a good local map?"

"Like an Ordnance Survey? Absolutely. I'll bring it into the lounge for you."

Shadow went back into the bar and finished his coffee. Gordon brought in a map. Shadow was impressed by the detail: it seemed to show every goat-track. He inspected it closely, tracing his walk. He found the hill where he had stopped and eaten his lunch. He ran his finger southwest.

"There aren't any castles around here, are there?"

"I'm afraid not. There are some to the east. I've got a guide to the castles of Scotland I could let you look at—"

"No, no. That's fine. Are there any big houses in this area? The kind people would call castles? Or big estates?"

"Well, there's the Cape Wrath Hotel, just over here," and he pointed to it on the map. "But it's a fairly empty area. Technically, for human occupation, what do they call it, for population density, it's a desert up here. Not even any interesting ruins, I'm afraid. Not that you could walk to."

Shadow thanked him, then asked him for an early-morning alarm call. He wished he had been able to find the house he had seen from the hill on the map, but perhaps he had been looking in the wrong place. It wouldn't be the first time.

The couple in the room next door were fighting, or making love.

Shadow could not tell, but each time he began to drift off to sleep raised voices or cries would jerk him awake.

Later, he was never certain if it had really happened, if she had really come to him, or if it had been the first of that night's dreams: but in truth or in dreams, shortly before midnight by the bedside clock radio, there was a knock on his bedroom door. He got up. Called, "Who is it?"

"Jennie."

He opened the door, winced at the light in the hall.

She was wrapped in her brown coat, and she looked up at him hesitantly.

"Yes?" said Shadow.

"You'll be going to the house tomorrow," she said.

"Yes."

"I thought I should say good-bye," she said. "In case I don't get a chance to see you again. And if you don't come back to the hotel. And you just go on somewhere. And I never see you."

"Well, good-bye, then," said Shadow.

She looked him up and down, examining the T-shirt and the boxers he slept in, at his bare feet, then up at his face. She seemed worried. "You know where I live," she said, at last. "Call me if you need me."

She reached her index finger out and touched it gently to his lips. Her finger was very cold. Then she took a step back into the corridor and just stood there, facing him, making no move to go.

Shadow closed the hotel room door, and he heard her footsteps walking away down the corridor. He climbed back into bed.

He was sure that the next dream was a dream, though. It was his life, jumbled and twisted: one moment he was in prison, teaching himself coin tricks and telling himself that his love for his wife would get him through this. Then Laura was dead, and he was out of prison; he was working as a bodyguard to an old grifter who had told Shadow to call him Wednesday. And then his dream was filled with gods: old, forgotten gods, unloved and abandoned, and new gods, transient scared things, duped and confused. It was a tangle of improbabilities, a cat's cradle which became a web which became a net which became a skein as big as a world. . . .

In his dream he died on the tree.

In his dream he came back from the dead.

And after that there was darkness.

IV.

THE TELEPHONE BESIDE THE bed shrilled at seven. He showered, shaved, dressed, packed his world into his backpack. Then he went down to the restaurant for breakfast: salty porridge, limp bacon, and oily fried eggs. The coffee, though, was surprisingly good.

At ten past eight he was in the lobby, waiting.

At fourteen minutes past eight, a man came in, wearing a sheepskin coat. He was sucking on a hand-rolled cigarette. The man stuck out his hand, cheerfully. "You'll be Mister Moon," he said. "My name's Smith. I'm your lift out to the big house." The man's grip was firm. "You *are* a big feller, aren't you?"

Unspoken was, "But I could take you," although Shadow knew that it was there.

Shadow said, "So they tell me. You aren't Scottish."

"Not me, matey. Just up for the week to make sure that everything runs like it's s'posed to. I'm a London boy." A flash of teeth in a hatchet-blade face. Shadow guessed that the man was in his mid-forties. "Come on out to the car. I can bring you up to speed on the way. Is that your bag?"

Shadow carried his backpack out to the car, a muddy Land Rover, its engine still running. He dropped it in the back, climbed into the passenger seat. Smith pulled one final drag on his cigarette, now little more than a rolled stub of white paper, and threw it out of the open driver's-side window into the road.

They drove out of the village.

"So how do I pronounce your name?" asked Smith. "Bal-der or Borl-der, or something else? Like *Cholmondely* is actually pronounced *Chumley.*"

"Shadow," said Shadow. "People call me Shadow."

"Right."

Silence.

"So," said Smith. "Shadow. I don't know how much old Gaskell told you about the party this weekend."

"A little."

"Right, well, the most important thing to know is this. Anything that happens, you keep *shtum* about. Right? Whatever you see, people having a little bit of fun, you don't say nothing to anybody, even if you recognize them, if you take my meaning."

"I don't recognize people," said Shadow.

"That's the spirit. We're just here to make sure that everyone has a good time without being disturbed. They've come a long way for a nice weekend."

"Got it," said Shadow.

They reached the ferry to the cape. Smith parked the Land Rover beside the road, took their bags, and locked the car.

On the other side of the ferry crossing, an identical Land Rover waited. Smith unlocked it, threw their bags in the back, and started along the dirt track.

They turned off before they reached the lighthouse, drove for a while in silence down a dirt road that rapidly turned into a sheep track. Several times Shadow had to get out and open gates; he waited while the Land Rover drove through, closed the gates behind it.

There were ravens in the fields and on the low stone walls, huge black birds that stared at Shadow with implacable eyes.

"So you were in the nick?" said Smith, suddenly.

"Sorry?"

"Prison. Pokey. Porridge. Other words beginning with a P, indicating poor food, no nightlife, inadequate toilet facilities, and limited opportunities for travel."

"Yeah."

"You're not very chatty, are you?"

"I thought that was a virtue."

"Point taken. Just conversation. The silence was getting on my nerves. You like it up here?"

"I guess. I've only been here for a few days."

"Gives me the fucking willies. Too remote. I've been to parts of Siberia that felt more welcoming. You been to London yet? No? When you come down south I'll show you around. Great pubs. Real food. And there's all that tourist stuff you Americans like. Traffic's hell, though. At least up here, we can drive. No bloody traffic lights. There's this traffic light at the bottom of Regent Street, I swear, you sit there for five minutes on a red light, then you get about ten seconds on a green light. Two cars max. Sodding ridiculous. They say it's the price we pay for progress. Right?"

"Yeah," said Shadow. "I guess."

They were well off-road now, thumping and bumping along a scrubby valley between two high hills. "Your party guests," said Shadow. "Are they coming in by Land Rover?"

"Nah. We've got helicopters. They'll be in in time for dinner tonight. Choppers in, then choppers out on Monday morning."

"Like living on an island."

"I wish we were living on an island. Wouldn't get loony locals causing problems, would we? Nobody complains about the noise coming from the island next door."

"You make a lot of noise at your party?"

"It's not my party, chum. I'm just a facilitator. Making sure that everything runs smoothly. But yes. I understand that they can make a lot of noise when they put their minds to it."

The grassy valley became a sheep path, the sheep path became a driveway running almost straight up a hill. A bend in the road, a sudden turn, and they were driving toward a house that Shadow recognized. Jennie had pointed to it yesterday, at lunch.

The house was old. He could see that at a glance. Parts of it seemed older than others: there was a wall on one wing of the building built out of gray rocks and stones, heavy and hard. That wall jutted into another, built of brown bricks. The roof, which covered the whole building, both wings, was a dark gray slate. The house looked out onto a gravel drive and then down the hill onto the loch. Shadow climbed out of the Land Rover. He looked at the house and felt small. He felt as though he were coming home, and it was not a good feeling.

There were several other four-wheel-drive vehicles parked on the gravel. "The keys to the cars are hanging in the pantry, in case you need to take one out. I'll show you as we go past."

Through a large wooden door, and now they were in a central courtyard, partly paved. There was a small fountain in the middle of the courtyard, and a plot of grass, a ragged green viperous swath bounded by gray flagstones.

"This is where the Saturday-night action will be," said Smith. "I'll show you where you'll be staying."

Into the smaller wing through an unimposing door, past a room hung with keys on hooks, each key marked with a paper tag, and another room filled with empty shelves. Down a dingy hall, and up some stairs. There was no carpeting on the stairs, nothing but whitewash on the walls. ("Well, this is the servants' quarters, innit? They never spent any money on it.") It was cold, in a way that Shadow was starting to become familiar with: colder inside the building than out. He wondered how they did that, if it was a British building secret.

Smith led Shadow to the top of the house and showed him into a dark room containing an antique wardrobe, an iron-framed single bed that Shadow could see at a glance would be smaller than he was, an ancient washstand, and a small window which looked out onto the inner courtyard.

"There's a loo at the end of the hall," said Smith. "The servants' bathroom's on the next floor down. Two baths, one for men, one for women, no showers. The supplies of hot water on this wing of the house are distinctly limited, I'm afraid. Your monkey suit's hanging in the wardrobe. Try it on now, see if it all fits, then leave it off until this evening, when the guests come in. Limited dry-cleaning facilities. We might as well be on Mars. I'll be in the kitchen if you need me. It's not as cold down there, if the Aga's working. Bottom of the stairs and left, then right, then yell if you're lost. Don't go into the other wing unless you're told to."

He left Shadow alone.

Shadow tried on the black tuxedo jacket, the white dress shirt, the black tie. There were highly polished black shoes, as well. It all fitted, as if it had been tailored for him. He hung everything back in the wardrobe.

He walked down the stairs, found Smith on the landing, stabbing angrily at a small silver mobile phone. "No bloody reception. The thing rang, now I'm trying to call back it won't give me a signal. It's the bloody Stone Age up here. How was your suit? All right?"

"Perfect."

"That's my boy. Never use five words if you can get away with one, eh? I've known dead men talk more than you do."

"Really?"

"Nah. Figure of speech. Come on. Fancy some lunch?"

"Sure. Thank you."

"Right. Follow me. It's a bit of a warren, but you'll get the hang of it soon enough."

They ate in the huge, empty kitchen: Shadow and Smith piled enameled tin plates with slices of translucent orange smoked salmon on crusty white bread, and slices of sharp cheese, accompanied by mugs of strong, sweet tea. The Aga was, Shadow discovered, a big metal box, part oven, part water heater. Smith opened one of the many doors on its side and shoveled in several large scoops of coal.

"So where's the rest of the food? And the waiters, and the cooks?" asked Shadow. "It can't just be us."

"Well spotted. Everything's coming up from Edinburgh. It'll run like clockwork. Food and party workers will be here at three, and unpack. Guests get brought in at six. Buffet dinner is served at eight. Talk a lot, eat, have a bit of a laugh, nothing too strenuous. Tomorrow there's breakfast from seven to midday. Guests get to go for walks, scenic views, all that in the afternoon. Bonfires are built in the courtyard. Then in the evening the bonfires are lit, everybody has a wild Saturday night in the north, hopefully without being bothered by our neighbors. Sunday morning we tiptoe around, out of respect for everybody's hangover, Sunday afternoon the choppers land and we wave everybody on their way. You collect your pay packet, and I'll drive you back to the hotel, or you can ride south with me, if you fancy a change. Sounds good?"

"Sounds just dandy," said Shadow. "And the folks who may show up on the Saturday night?"

"Just killjoys. Locals out to ruin everybody's good time."

"What locals?" asked Shadow. "There's nothing but sheep for miles."

"Locals. They're all over the place," said Smith. "You just don't see them. Tuck themselves away like Sawney Bean and his family."

Shadow said, "I think I've heard of him. The name rings a bell . . ."

"He's *historical*," said Smith. He slurped his tea, and leaned back in his chair. "This was, what, six hundred years back—after the Vikings had buggered off back to Scandinavia, or intermarried and converted until they were just another bunch of Scots, but before Queen Elizabeth died and James came down from Scotland to rule both countries. Somewhere in there." He took a swig of his tea. "So. Travelers in Scotland kept vanishing. It wasn't that unusual. I mean, if you set out on a long journey back then, you didn't always get home. Sometimes it would be months before anyone knew you weren't coming home again, and they'd blame the wolves or the weather, and resolve to travel in groups, and only in the summer.

"One traveler, though, he was riding with a bunch of companions through a glen, and there came over the hill, dropped from the trees, up from the ground, a swarm, a flock, a pack of children, armed with daggers and knives and bone clubs and stout sticks, and they pulled the travelers off their horses, and fell on them, and finished them off. All but this one geezer, and he was riding a little behind the others, and he got away. He was the only one, but it only takes one, doesn't it? He made it to the nearest town, and raised the hue and cry, and they gather a troop of townsfolk and soldiers and they go back there, with dogs.

"It takes them days to find the hideout, they're ready to give up, when, at the mouth of a cave by the seashore, the dogs start to howl. And they go down.

"Turns out there's caves, under the ground, and in the biggest and deepest of the caves is old Sawney Bean and his brood, and carcasses, hanging from hooks, smoked and slow-roast. Legs, arms, thighs, hands, and feet of men, women, and children are hung up in rows, like dried pork. There are limbs pickled in brine, like salt beef. There's money in heaps, gold and silver, with watches, rings, swords, pistols, and clothes, riches beyond imagining, as they never spent a single penny of it. Just stayed in their caves, and ate, and bred, and hated.

"He'd been living there for years. King of his own little kingdom, was old Sawney, him and his wife, and their children and grand-children, and some of those grandchildren were also their children. An incestuous little bunch."

"Did this really happen?"

"So I'm told. There are court records. They took the family to Leith to be tried. The court decision was interesting—they decided that Sawney Beane, by virtue of his acts, had removed himself from the human race. So they sentenced him as an animal. They didn't hang him or behead him. They just got a big fire going and threw the Beanies onto it, to burn to death."

"All of his family?"

"I don't remember. They may have burned the little kids, or they may not. Probably did. They tend to deal very efficiently with mon-sters in this part of the world."

Smith washed their plates and mugs in the sink, left them in a rack to dry. The two men walked out into the courtyard. Smith rolled himself a cigarette expertly. He licked the paper, smoothed it with his fingers, lit the finished tube with a Zippo. "Let's see. What d'you need to know for tonight? Well, basics are easy: speak when you're spoken to—not that you're going to find that one a problem, eh?"

Shadow said nothing.

"Right. If one of the guests asks you for something, do your best to provide it, ask me if you're in any doubt, but do what the guests ask as long as it doesn't take you off what you're doing, or violate the prime directive."

"Which is?"

"Don't. Shag. The posh totty. There's sure to be some young la-dies who'll take it into their heads, after half a bottle of wine, that what they really need is a bit of rough. And if that happens, you do a *Sunday People*."

"I have no idea what you're talking about."

"*Our reporter made his excuses and left.* Yes? You can look, but you can't touch. Got it?"

"Got it."

"Smart boy."

Shadow found himself starting to like Smith. He told himself that liking this man was not a sensible thing to do. He had met people like Smith before, people without consciences, without scruples, without hearts, and they were uniformly as dangerous as they were likeable.

In the early afternoon the servants arrived, brought in by a helicopter that looked like a troop carrier: they unpacked boxes of wine and crates of food, hampers and containers with astonishing efficiency. There were boxes filled with napkins and with tablecloths. There were cooks and waiters, waitresses and chambermaids.

But, first off the helicopter, there were the security guards: big, solid men with earpieces and what Shadow had no doubt were gun-bulges beneath their jackets. They reported one by one to Smith, who set them to inspecting the house and the grounds. Shadow was helping out, carrying boxes filled with vegetables from the chopper to the kitchen. He could carry twice as much as anyone else. The next time he passed Smith he stopped and said, "So, if you've got all these security guys, what am I here for?"

Smith smiled affably. "Look, son. There's people coming to this do who're worth more than you or I will ever see in a lifetime. They need to be sure they'll be looked after. Kidnappings happen. People have enemies. Lots of things happen. Only with those lads around, they won't. But having them deal with grumpy locals, it's like setting a landmine to stop trespassers. Yeah?"

"Right," said Shadow. He went back to the chopper, picked up another box marked *baby aubergines* and filled with small, black egg-plants, put it on top of a crate of cabbages and carried them both to the kitchen, certain now that he was being lied to. Smith's reply was reasonable. It was even convincing. It simply wasn't true. There was no reason for him to be there, or if there was it wasn't the reason he'd been given.

He chewed it over, trying to figure out why he was in that house, and hoped that he was showing nothing on the surface. Shadow kept it all on the inside. It was safer there.

V.

MORE HELICOPTERS CAME DOWN in the early evening, as the sky was turning pink, and a score or more of smart people clambered out. Several of them were smiling and laughing. Most of them were in their thirties and forties. Shadow recognized none of them.

Smith moved casually but smoothly from person to person, greeting them confidently. "Right, now you go through there and turn left, and wait in the main hall. Lovely big log fire there. Someone'll come and take you up to your room. Your luggage should be waiting for you there. You call me if it's not, but it will be. 'Ullo your ladyship, you do look a treat—shall I 'ave someone carry your 'andbag? Looking forward to termorrer? Aren't we all."

Shadow watched, fascinated, as Smith dealt with each of the guests, his manner an expert mixture of familiarity and deference, of amiability and Cockney charm: aitches, consonants, and vowel sounds came and went and transformed according to who he was talking to.

A woman with short dark hair, very pretty, smiled at Shadow as he carried her bags inside. "Posh totty," muttered Smith, as he went past. "Hands off."

A portly man who Shadow estimated to be in his early sixties was the last person off the chopper. He walked over to Smith, leaned on a cheap wooden walking stick, said something in a low voice. Smith replied in the same fashion.

He's in charge, thought Shadow. It was there in the body language. Smith was no longer smiling, no longer cajoling. He was reporting, efficiently and quietly, telling the old man everything he should know.

Smith crooked a finger at Shadow, who walked quickly over to them.

"Shadow," said Smith. "This is Mister Alice."

Mr. Alice put out his hand, shook Shadow's big, dark hand with his pink, pudgy one. "Great pleasure to meet you," he said. "Heard good things about you."

"Good to meet you," said Shadow.

"Well," said Mr. Alice, "carry on."

Smith nodded at Shadow, a gesture of dismissal.

"If it's okay by you," said Shadow to Smith, "I'd like to take a look around while there's still some light. Get a sense of where the locals could come from."

"Don't go too far," said Smith. He picked up Mr. Alice's briefcase, and led the older man into the building.

Shadow walked the outside perimeter of the house. He had been set up. He did not know why, but he knew he was right. There was too much that didn't add up. Why hire a drifter to do security, while bringing in real security guards? It made no sense, no more than Smith introducing him to Mr. Alice, after two dozen other people had treated Shadow as no more human than a decorative ornament.

There was a low stone wall in front of the house. Behind the house, a hill that was almost a small mountain, in front of it a gentle slope down to the loch. Off to the side was the track by which he had arrived that morning. He walked to the far side of the house and found what seemed to be a kitchen garden, with a high stone wall and wilderness beyond. He took a step down into the kitchen garden, and walked over to inspect the wall.

"You doing a recce, then?" said one of the security guards, in his black tuxedo. Shadow had not seen him there, which meant, he supposed, that he was very good at his job. Like most of the servants, his accent was Scottish.

"Just having a look around."

"Get the lay of the land, very wise. Don't you worry about this side of the house. A hundred yards that way there's a river leads down to the loch, and beyond that just wet rocks for a hundred feet or so, straight down. Absolutely treacherous."

"Oh. So the locals, the ones who come and complain, where do they come from?"

"I wouldnae have a clue."

"I should head on over there and take a look at it," said Shadow. "See if I can figure out the ways in and out."

"I wouldnae do that," said the guard. "Not if I were you. It's really treacherous. You go poking around over there, one slip, you'll be crashing down the rocks into the loch. They'll never find your body, if you head out that way."

"I see," said Shadow, who did.

He kept walking around the house. He spotted five other security guards, now that he was looking for them. He was sure there were others that he had missed.

In the main wing of the house he could see, through the french windows, a huge, wood-paneled dining room, and the guests seated around a table, talking and laughing.

He walked back into the servants' wing. As each course was done with, the serving plates were put out on a sideboard, and the staff helped themselves, piling food high on paper plates. Smith was sitting at the wooden kitchen table, tucking into a plate of salad and rare beef.

"There's caviar over there," he said to Shadow. "It's golden osetra, top quality, very special. What the party officials used to keep for themselves in the old days. I've never been a fan of the stuff, but help yourself."

Shadow put a little of the caviar on the side of his plate, to be polite. He took some tiny boiled eggs, some pasta, and some chicken. He sat next to Smith and started to eat.

"I don't see where your locals are going to come from," he said. "Your men have the drive sealed off. Anyone who wants to come here would have to come over the loch."

"You had a good poke around, then?"

"Yes," said Shadow.

"You met some of my boys?"

"Yes."

"What did you think?"

"I wouldn't want to mess with them."

Smith smirked. "Big fellow like you? You could take care of yourself."

"They're killers," said Shadow, simply.

"Only when they need to be," said Smith. He was no longer smiling. "Why don't you stay up in your room? I'll give you a shout when I need you."

"Sure," said Shadow. "And if you don't need me, this is going to be a very easy weekend."

Smith stared at him. "You'll earn your money," he said.

Shadow went up the back stairs to the long corridor at the top of the house. He went into his room. He could hear party noises, and looked out of the small window. The french windows opposite were wide open, and the partygoers, now wearing coats and gloves, holding their glasses of wine, had spilled out into the inner court-yard. He could hear fragments of conversations that transformed and reshaped themselves; the noises were clear but the words and the sense were lost. An occasional phrase would break free of the susurrus. A man said, "I told him, judges like you, I don't own, I sell. . . ." Shadow heard a woman say, "It's a monster, darling. An absolute monster. Well, what can you do?" and another woman saying, "Well, if only I could say the same about my boyfriend's!" and a bray of laughter.

He had two alternatives. He could stay, or he could try to go.

"I'll stay," he said, aloud.

VI.

IT WAS A NIGHT of dangerous dreams.

In Shadow's first dream he was back in America, standing beneath a streetlight. He walked up some steps, pushed through a glass door, and stepped into a diner, the kind that had once been a dining car on a train. He could hear an old man singing, in a deep gravelly voice, to the tune of "My Bonnie Lies Over the Ocean,"

> *"My grandpa sells condoms to sailors*
> *He punctures the tips with a pin*
> *My grandma does back-street abortions*
> *My God how the money rolls in."*

Shadow walked along the length of the dining car. At a table at the end of the car, a grizzled man was sitting, holding a beer bottle, and singing, *"Rolls in, rolls in, my God how the money rolls in."* When he caught sight of Shadow his face split into a huge monkey grin, and he gestured with the beer bottle. "Sit down, sit down," he said.

Shadow sat down opposite the man he had known as Wednesday.

"So what's the trouble?" asked Wednesday, dead for almost two years, or as dead as his kind of creature was going to get. "I'd offer you a beer, but the service here stinks."

Shadow said that was okay. He didn't want a beer.

"Well?" asked Wednesday, scratching his beard.

"I'm in a big house in Scotland with a shitload of really rich folks, and they have an agenda. I'm in trouble, and I don't know what kind of trouble I'm in. But I think it's pretty bad trouble."

Wednesday took a swig of his beer. "The rich are different, m'boy," he said, after a while.

"What the hell does *that* mean?"

"Well," said Wednesday. "For a start, most of them are probably mortal. Not something *you* have to worry about."

"Don't give me that shit."

"But you *aren't* mortal," said Wednesday. "You died on the tree, Shadow. You died and you came back."

"So? I don't even remember how I did that. If they kill me this time, I'll still be dead."

Wednesday finished his beer. Then he waved his beer bottle around, as if he were conducting an invisible orchestra with it, and sang another verse:

"My brother's a missionary worker
He saves fallen women from sin
For five bucks he'll save you a redhead
My God how the money rolls in."

"You aren't helping," said Shadow. The diner was a train carriage now, rattling through a snowy night.

Wednesday put down his beer bottle, and he fixed Shadow with his real eye, the one that wasn't glass. "It's patterns," he said. "If they think you're a hero, they're wrong. After you die, you don't get to be

Beowulf or Perseus or Rama anymore. Whole different set of rules. Chess, not checkers. *Go*, not chess. You understand?"

"Not even a little," said Shadow, frustrated.

People, in the corridor of the big house, moving loudly and drunkenly, shushing each other as they stumbled and giggled their way down the hall.

Shadow wondered if they were servants, or if they were strays from the other wing, slumming. And the dreams took him once again. . . .

Now he was back in the bothy where he had sheltered from the rain, the day before. There was a body on the floor: a boy, no more than five years old. Naked, on his back, limbs spread. There was a flash of intense light, and someone pushed through Shadow as if he was not there and rearranged the position of the boy's arms. Another flash of light.

Shadow knew the man taking the photographs. It was Dr. Gaskell, the little steel-haired man from the hotel bar.

Gaskell took a white paper bag from his pocket, and fished about in it for something that he popped into his mouth.

"Dolly mixtures," he said to the child on the stone floor. "Yum yum. Your favorites."

He smiled and crouched down, and took another photograph of the dead boy.

Shadow pushed through the stone wall of the cottage, flowing through the cracks in the stones like the wind. He flowed down to the seashore. The waves crashed on the rocks and Shadow kept moving across the water, through gray seas, up the swells and down again, toward the ship made of dead men's nails.

The ship was far away, out at sea, and Shadow passed across the surface of the water like the shadow of a cloud.

The ship was huge. He had not understood before how huge it was. A hand reached down and grasped his arm, pulled him up from the sea onto the deck.

"Bring us back," said a voice as loud as the crashing of the sea, urgent and fierce. "Bring us back, or let us go." Only one eye burned in that bearded face.

"I'm not keeping you here."

They were giants, on that ship, huge men made of shadows and frozen sea-spray, creatures of dream and foam.

One of them, huger than all the rest, red-bearded, stepped forward. "We cannot land," he boomed. "We cannot leave."

"Go home," said Shadow.

"We came with our people to this southern country," said the one-eyed man. "But they left us. They sought other, tamer gods, and they renounced us in their hearts, and gave us over."

"Go home," repeated Shadow.

"Too much time has passed," said the red-bearded man. By the hammer at his side, Shadow knew him. "Too much blood has been spilled. You are of our blood, Baldur. Set us free."

And Shadow wanted to say that he was not theirs, was not anybody's, but the thin blanket had slipped from the bed, and his feet stuck out at the bottom, and thin moonlight filled the attic room.

There was silence, now, in that huge house. Something howled in the hills, and Shadow shivered.

He lay in a bed that was too small for him, and imagined time as something that pooled and puddled, wondered if there were places where time hung heavy, places where it was heaped and held—cities, he thought, must be filled with time: all the places where people congregated, where they came and brought time with them.

And if that were true, Shadow mused, then there could be other places, where the people were thin on the ground, and the land waited, bitter and granite, and a thousand years was an eyeblink to the hills—a scudding of clouds, a wavering of rushes and nothing more, in the places where time was as thin on the ground as the people . . .

"They are going to kill you," whispered Jennie, the barmaid.

Shadow sat beside her now, on the hill, in the moonlight. "Why would they want to do that?" he asked. "I don't matter."

"It's what they do to monsters," she said. "It's what they have to do. It's what they've always done."

He reached out to touch her, but she turned away from him. From behind, she was empty and hollow. She turned again, so she was facing him. "Come away," she whispered.

"You can come to me," he said.

"I can't," she said. "There are things in the way. The path there is hard, and it is guarded. But you can call. If you call me, I'll come."

Then dawn came, and with it a cloud of midges from the boggy land at the foot of the hill. Jennie flicked at them with her tail, but it was no use; they descended on Shadow like a cloud, until he was breathing midges, his nose and mouth filling with the tiny, crawling stinging things, and he was choking on the darkness. . . .

He wrenched himself back into his bed and his body and his life, into wakefulness, his heart pounding in his chest, gulping for breath.

VII.

BREAKFAST WAS KIPPERS, GRILLED tomatoes, scrambled eggs, toast, two stubby, thumblike sausages, and slices of something dark and round and flat that Shadow didn't recognize.

"What's this?" asked Shadow.

"Black pudden'," said the man sitting next to him. He was one of the security guards, and was reading a copy of yesterday's *Sun* as he ate. "Blood and herbs. They cook the blood until it congeals into a sort of a dark, herby scab." He forked some eggs onto his toast, ate it with his fingers. "I don't know. What is it they say, you should never see anyone making sausages or the law? Something like that."

Shadow ate the rest of the breakfast, but he left the black pudding alone.

There was a pot of real coffee now, and he drank a mug of it, hot and black, to wake him up and to clear his head.

Smith walked in. "Shadow-man. Can I borrow you for five minutes?"

"You're paying," said Shadow. They walked out into the corridor.

"It's Mr. Alice," said Smith. "He wants a quick word." They crossed from the dismal whitewashed servants' wing into the wood-paneled vastness of the old house. They walked up the huge wooden stair-case and into a vast library. No one was there.

"He'll just be a minute," said Smith. "I'll make sure he knows you're waiting."

The books in the library were protected from mice and dust and people by locked doors of glass and wire mesh. There was a painting of a stag on the wall, and Shadow walked over to look at it. The stag was haughty and superior: behind it, a valley filled with mist.

"*The Monarch of the Glen*," said Mr. Alice, walking in slowly, lean-ing on his stick. "The most reproduced picture of Victorian times. That's not the original, but it was done by Landseer in the late 1850s as a copy of his own painting. I love it, although I'm sure I shouldn't. He did the lions in Trafalgar Square, Landseer. Same bloke."

He walked over to the bay window, and Shadow walked with him. Below them in the courtyard, servants were putting out chairs and tables. By the pond in the center of the courtyard other people, party guests, were building bonfires out of logs and wood.

"Why don't they have the servants build the fires?" asked Shadow.

"Why should *they* have the fun?" said Mr. Alice. "It'd be like send-ing your man out into the rough some afternoon to shoot pheasants for you. There's something about building a bonfire, when you've hauled over the wood, and put it down in the perfect place, that's special. Or so they tell me. I've not done it myself." He turned away from the window. "Take a seat," he said. "I'll get a crick in my neck looking up at you."

Shadow sat down.

"I've heard a lot about you," said Mr. Alice. "Been wanting to meet you for a while. They said you were a smart young man who was going places. That's what they said."

"So you didn't just hire a tourist to keep the neighbors away from your party?"

"Well, yes and no. We had a few other candidates, obviously. It's just you were perfect for the job. And when I realized who you were. Well, a gift from the gods really, weren't you?"

"I don't know. Was I?"

"Absolutely. You see, this party goes back a very long way. Almost a thousand years, they've been having it. Never missed a single year. And every year there's a fight, between our man and their man. And our man wins. This year, our man is you."

"Who . . ." said Shadow. "Who are *they*? And who are *you*?"

"I am your host," said Mr. Alice. "I suppose. . . ." He stopped, for a moment, tapped his walking stick against the wooden floor. "*They* are the ones who lost, a long time ago. *We* won. We were the knights, and they were the dragons, we were the giant-killers, they were the ogres. We were the men and they were the monsters. And *we won*. They know their place now. And tonight is all about not letting them forget it. It's humanity you'll be fighting for, tonight. We can't let them get the upper hand. Not even a little. Us versus them."

"Doctor Gaskell said that I was a monster," said Shadow.

"Doctor Gaskell?" said Mr. Alice. "Friend of yours?"

"No," said Shadow. "He works for you. Or for the people who work for you. I think he kills children and takes pictures of them."

Mr. Alice dropped his walking stick. He bent down, awkwardly, to pick it up. Then he said, "Well, I don't think you're a monster, Shadow. I think you're a hero."

No, thought Shadow. *You think I'm a monster. But you think I'm your monster.*

"Now, you do well tonight," said Mr. Alice, "and I know you will—and you can name your price. You ever wondered why some people were film stars, or famous, or rich? Bet you think, *He's got no talent. What's he got that I haven't got?* Well, sometimes the answer is, he's got someone like me on his side."

"Are you a god?" asked Shadow.

Mr. Alice laughed then, a deep, full-throated chuckle. "Nice one, Mister Moon. Not at all. I'm just a boy from Streatham who's done well for himself."

"So who do I fight?" asked Shadow.

"You'll meet him tonight," said Mr. Alice. "Now, there's stuff needs to come down from the attic. Why don't you lend Smithie a hand? Big lad like you, it'll be a doddle."

The audience was over and, as if on cue, Smith walked in.

"I was just saying," said Mr. Alice, "that our boy here would help you bring the stuff down from the attic."

"Triffic," said Smith. "Come on, Shadow. Let's wend our way upwards."

They went up, through the house, up a dark wooden stairway, to a padlocked door, which Smith unlocked, into a dusty wooden attic, piled high with what looked like . . .

"Drums?" said Shadow.

"Drums," said Smith. They were made of wood and of animal skins. Each drum was a different size. "Right, let's take them down."

They carried the drums downstairs. Smith carried one at a time, holding it as if it was precious. Shadow carried two.

"So what really happens tonight?" asked Shadow, on their third trip, or perhaps their fourth.

"Well," said Smith. "Most of it, as I understand, you're best off figuring out on your own. As it happens."

"And you and Mr. Alice. What part do you play in this?"

Smith gave him a sharp look. They put the drums down at the foot of the stairs, in the great hall. There were several men there, talking in front of the fire.

When they were back up the stairs again, and out of earshot of the guests, Smith said, "Mr. Alice will be leaving us late this afternoon. I'll stick around."

"He's leaving? Isn't he part of this?"

Smith looked offended. "He's the host," he said. "But." He stopped. Shadow understood. Smith didn't talk about his employer. They carried more drums down the stairs. When they had brought down all the drums, they carried down heavy leather bags.

"What's in these?" asked Shadow.

"Drumsticks," said Smith.

Smith continued, "They're old families. That lot downstairs. Very old money. They know who's boss, but that doesn't make him one of them. See? They're the only ones who'll be at tonight's party. They'd not want Mr. Alice. See?"

And Shadow did see. He wished that Smith hadn't spoken to him about Mr. Alice. He didn't think Smith would have said anything to anyone he thought would live to talk about it.

But all he said was, "Heavy drumsticks."

VIII

A SMALL HELICOPTER TOOK Mr. Alice away late that afternoon. Land Rovers took away the staff. Smith drove the last one. Only Shadow was left behind, and the guests, with their smart clothes and their smiles.

They stared at Shadow as if he were a captive lion who had been brought for their amusement, but they did not talk to him.

The dark-haired woman, the one who had smiled at Shadow as she had arrived, brought him food to eat: a steak, almost rare. She brought it to him on a plate, without cutlery, as if she expected him to eat it with his fingers and his teeth, and he was hungry, and he did.

"I am not your hero," he told them, but they would not meet his gaze. Nobody spoke to him, not directly. He felt like an animal.

And then it was dusk. They led Shadow to the inner courtyard, by the rusty fountain, and they stripped him naked, at gunpoint, and the women smeared his body with some kind of thick yellow grease, rubbing it in.

They put a knife on the grass in front of him. A gesture with a gun, and Shadow picked the knife up. The hilt was black metal, rough and easy to hold. The blade looked sharp.

Then they threw open the great door, from the inner courtyard to the world outside, and two of the men lit the two high bonfires: they crackled and blazed.

They opened the leather bags, and each of the guests took out a single carved black stick, like a cudgel, knobbly and heavy. Shadow found himself thinking of Sawney Bean's children, swarming up from the darkness holding clubs made of human thighbones . . .

Then the guests arranged themselves around the edge of the courtyard, and they began to beat the drums with the sticks.

They started slow, and they started quietly, a deep, throbbing pounding, like a heartbeat. Then they began to crash and slam into strange rhythms, staccato beats that wove and wound, louder and louder, until they filled Shadow's mind and his world. It seemed to him that the firelight flickered to the rhythms of the drums.

And then, from outside the house, the howling began.

There was pain in the howling, and anguish, and it echoed across the hills above the drumbeats, a wail of pain and loss and hate.

The figure that stumbled through the doorway to the courtyard was clutching its head, covering its ears, as if to stop the pounding of the drumbeats.

The firelight caught it.

It was huge, now: bigger than Shadow, and naked. It was perfectly hairless, and dripping wet.

It lowered its hands from its ears, and it stared around, its face twisted into a mad grimace. "Stop it!" it screamed. "Stop making all that noise!"

And the people in their pretty clothes beat their drums harder, and faster, and the noise filled Shadow's head and chest.

The monster stepped into the center of the courtyard. It looked at Shadow. "You," it said. "I told you. I told you about the noise," and it howled, a deep throaty howl of hatred and challenge.

The creature edged closer to Shadow. It saw the knife, and stopped. "Fight me!" it shouted. "Fight me fair! Not with cold iron! Fight me!"

"I don't want to fight you," said Shadow. He dropped the knife on the grass, raised his hands to show them empty.

"Too late," said the bald thing that was not a man. "Too late for that."

And it launched itself at Shadow.

Later, when Shadow thought of that fight, he remembered only fragments: he remembered being slammed to the ground, and throwing himself out of the way. He remembered the pounding of the drums, and the expressions on the faces of the drummers as they stared, hungrily, between the bonfires, at the two men in the firelight.

They fought, wrestling and pounding each other.

Salt tears ran down the monster's face as it wrestled with Shadow.

They were equally matched, it seemed to Shadow.

The monster slammed its arm into Shadow's face, and Shadow could taste his own blood. He could feel his own anger beginning to rise, like a red wall of hate.

He swung a leg out, hooking the monster behind the knee, and as it stumbled back Shadow's fist crashed into its gut, making it cry out and roar with anger and pain.

A glance at the guests: Shadow saw the bloodlust on the faces of the drummers.

There was a cold wind, a sea wind, and it seemed to Shadow that there were huge shadows in the sky, vast figures that he had seen on a ship made of the fingernails of dead men, and that they were staring down at him, that this fight was what was keeping them frozen on their ship, unable to land, unable to leave.

This fight was old, Shadow thought, older than even Mr. Alice knew, and he was thinking that even as the creature's talons raked his chest. It was the fight of man against monster, and it was old as time: it was Theseus battling the Minotaur, it was Beowulf and Grendel, it was the fight of every hero who had ever stood between the firelight and the darkness and wiped the blood of something in- human from his sword.

The bonfires burned, and the drums pounded and throbbed and pulsed like the beating of a thousand hearts.

Shadow slipped on the damp grass, as the monster came at him, and he was down. The creature's fingers were around Shadow's neck, and it was squeezing; Shadow could feel everything starting to thin, to become distant.

He closed his hand around a patch of grass, and pulled at it, dug his fingers deep, grabbing a handful of grass and clammy earth, and he smashed the clod of dirt into the monster's face, momentarily blinding it.

He pushed up, and was on top of the creature, now. He rammed his knee hard into its groin, and it doubled into a fetal position, and howled, and sobbed.

Shadow realized that the drumming had stopped, and he looked up. The guests had put down their drums.

They were all approaching him, in a circle, men and women, still

holding their drumsticks, but holding them like cudgels. They were
not looking at Shadow, though: they were staring at the monster on
the ground, and they raised their black sticks and moved toward it in
the light of the twin fires.

Shadow said, "Stop!"

The first club blow came down on the creature's head. It wailed
and twisted, raising an arm to ward off the next blow.

Shadow threw himself in front of it, shielding it with his body.
The dark-haired woman who had smiled at him before now brought
down her club on his shoulder, dispassionately, and another club,
from a man this time, hit him a numbing blow in the leg, and a third
struck him on his side.

They'll kill us both, he thought. *Him first, then me. That's what they
do. That's what they always do.* And then, *She said she would come. If I
called her.*

Shadow whispered, "Jennie?"

There was no reply. Everything was happening so slowly. Another club was coming down, this one aimed at his head. Shadow
rolled out of the way awkwardly, watched the heavy wood smash
into the turf.

"Jennie," he said, picturing her too-fair hair in his mind, her thin
face, her smile. "I call you. Come now. *Please.*"

A gust of cold wind.

The dark-haired woman had raised her club high, and brought it
down now, fast, hard, aiming for Shadow's face.

The blow never landed. A small hand caught the heavy stick as if
it were a twig.

Fair hair blew about her head, in the cold wind. He could not have
told you what she was wearing.

She looked at him. Shadow thought that she looked disappointed.

One of the men aimed a cudgel blow at the back of her head. It
never connected. She turned . . .

A rending sound, as if something was tearing itself apart . . .

And then the bonfires exploded. That was how it seemed. There
was blazing wood all over the courtyard, even in the house. And the
people were screaming in the bitter wind.

Shadow staggered to his feet.

The monster lay on the ground, bloodied and twisted. Shadow did not know if it was alive or not. He picked it up, hauled it over his shoulder, and staggered out of the courtyard with it.

He stumbled out onto the gravel forecourt, as the massive wooden doors slammed closed behind them. Nobody else would be coming out. Shadow kept moving down the slope, one step at a time, down toward the loch.

When he reached the water's edge he stopped, and sank to his knees, and let the bald man down onto the grass as gently as he could.

He heard something crash, and looked back up the hill.

The house was burning.

"How is he?" said a woman's voice.

Shadow turned. She was knee-deep in the water, the creature's mother, wading toward the shore.

"I don't know," said Shadow. "He's hurt."

"You're both hurt," she said. "You're all bluid and bruises."

"Yes," said Shadow.

"Still," she said. "He's not dead. And that makes a nice change."

She had reached the shore now. She sat on the bank, with her son's head in her lap. She took a packet of tissues from her handbag, and spat on a tissue, and began fiercely to scrub at her son's face with it, rubbing away the blood.

The house on the hill was roaring now. Shadow had not imagined that a burning house would make so much noise.

The old woman looked up at the sky. She made a noise in the back of her throat, a clucking noise, and then she shook her head. "You know," she said, "you've let them in. They'd been bound for so long, and you've let them in."

"Is that a good thing?" asked Shadow.

"I don't know, love," said the little woman, and she shook her head again. She crooned to her son as if he were still her baby, and dabbed at his wounds with her spit.

Shadow was naked, at the edge of the loch, but the heat from the burning building kept him warm. He watched the reflected flames in the glassy water of the loch. A yellow moon was rising.

He was starting to hurt. Tomorrow, he knew, he would hurt much worse.

Footsteps on the grass behind him. He looked up.

"Hello, Smithie," said Shadow.

Smith looked down at the three of them.

"Shadow," he said, shaking his head. "Shadow, Shadow, Shadow, Shadow, Shadow. This was not how things were meant to turn out."

"Sorry," said Shadow.

"This will cause real embarrassment to Mr. Alice," said Smith. "Those people were his guests."

"They were animals," said Shadow.

"If they were," said Smith, "they were rich and important animals. There'll be widows and orphans and God knows what to take care of. Mr. Alice will not be pleased." He said it like a judge pronouncing a death sentence.

"Are you threatening him?" asked the old lady.

"I don't threaten," said Smith, flatly.

She smiled. "Ah," she said. "Well, I do. And if you or that fat bastard you work for hurt this young man, it'll be the worse for both of you." She smiled then, with sharp teeth, and Shadow felt the hairs on the back of his neck prickle. "There's worse things than dying," she said. "And I know most of them. I'm not young, and I'm not one for idle talk. So if I were you," she said, with a sniff, "I'd look after this lad."

She picked up her son with one arm, as if he were a child's doll, and she clutched her handbag close to her with the other.

Then she nodded to Shadow and walked away, into the glass-dark water, and soon she and her son were gone beneath the surface of the loch.

"Fuck," muttered Smith. Shadow didn't say anything.

Smith fumbled in his pocket. He pulled out the pouch of tobacco, and rolled himself a cigarette. Then he lit it. "Right," he said.

"Right?" said Shadow.

"We better get you cleaned up, and find you some clothes. You'll catch your death, otherwise. You heard what she said."

IX.

THEY HAD THE BEST room waiting for Shadow, that night, back at the hotel. And, less than an hour after Shadow returned, Gordon on the front desk brought up a new backpack, a box of new clothes, even new boots. He asked no questions.

There was a large envelope on top of the pile of clothes.

Shadow ripped it open. It contained his passport, slightly scorched, his wallet, and money: several bundles of new fifty-pound notes, wrapped in rubber bands.

My God, how the money rolls in, he thought, without pleasure, and tried, without success, to remember where he had heard that song before.

He took a long bath, to soak away the pain.

And then he slept.

In the morning he dressed, and walked up the lane next to the hotel, that led up the hill and out of the village. There had been a cottage at the top of the hill, he was sure of it, with lavender in the garden, a stripped pine countertop, and a purple sofa, but no matter where he looked there was no cottage on the hill, nor any evidence that there ever had been anything there but grass and a hawthorn tree.

He called her name, but there was no reply, only the wind coming in off the sea, bringing with it the first promises of winter.

Still, she was waiting for him, when he got back to the hotel room. She was sitting on the bed, wearing her old brown coat, inspecting her fingernails. She did not look up when he unlocked the door and walked in.

"Hello, Jennie," he said.

"Hello," she said. Her voice was very quiet.

"Thank you," he said. "You saved my life."

"You called," she said dully. "I came."

He said, "What's wrong?"

She looked at him, then. "I could have been yours," she said, and there were tears in her eyes. "I thought you would love me. Perhaps. One day."

"Well," he said, "maybe we could find out. We could take a walk tomorrow together, maybe. Not a long one, I'm afraid, I'm a bit of a mess physically."

She shook her head.

The strangest thing, Shadow thought, was that she did not look human any longer: she now looked like what she was, a wild thing, a forest thing. Her tail twitched on the bed, under her coat. She was very beautiful, and, he realized, he wanted her, very badly.

"The hardest thing about being a hulder," said Jennie, "even a hulder very far from home, is that, if you don't want to be lonely, you have to love a man."

"So love me. Stay with me," said Shadow. "Please."

"You," she said, sadly and finally, "are not a man."

She stood up.

"Still," she said, "everything's changing. Maybe I can go home again now. After a thousand years I don't even know if I remember any *Norsk*."

She took his hands in her small hands, that could bend iron bars, that could crush rocks to sand, and she squeezed his fingers very gently. And she was gone.

He stayed another day in that hotel, and then he caught the bus to Thurso, and the train from Thurso to Inverness.

He dozed on the train, although he did not dream.

When he woke, there was a man on the seat next to him. A hatchet-faced man, reading a paperback book. He closed the book when he saw that Shadow was awake. Shadow looked down at the cover: Jean Cocteau's *The Difficulty of Being*.

"Good book?" asked Shadow.

"Yeah, all right," said Smith. "It's all essays. They're meant to be personal, but you feel that every time he looks up innocently and says 'This is me,' it's some kind of double bluff. I liked *Belle et la Bête*, though. I felt closer to him watching that than through any of these essays."

"It's all on the cover," said Shadow.

"How d'you mean?"

"The difficulty of being Jean Cocteau."

Smith scratched his nose.

"Here," he said. He passed Shadow a copy of the *Scotsman*. "Page nine."

At the bottom of page nine was a small story: retired doctor kills himself. Gaskell's body had been found in his car, parked in a picnic spot on the coast road. He had swallowed quite a cocktail of painkillers, washed down with most of a bottle of Lagavulin.

"Mr. Alice hates being lied to," said Smith. "Especially by the hired help."

"Is there anything in there about the fire?" asked Shadow.

"What fire?"

"Oh. Right."

"It wouldn't surprise me if there wasn't a terrible run of luck for the great and the good over the next couple of months, though. Car crashes. Train crash. Maybe a plane'll go down. Grieving widows and orphans and boyfriends. Very sad."

Shadow nodded.

"You know," said Smith, "Mr. Alice is very concerned about your health. He worries. I worry, too."

"Yeah?" said Shadow.

"Absolutely. I mean, if something happens to you while you're in the country. Maybe you look the wrong way crossing the road. Flash a wad of cash in the wrong pub. I dunno. The point is, if you got hurt, then whatsername, Grendel's mum, might take it the wrong way."

"So?"

"So we think you should leave the U.K. Be safer for everyone, wouldn't it?"

Shadow said nothing for a while. The train began to slow.

"Okay," said Shadow.

"This is my stop," said Smith. "I'm getting out here. We'll arrange the ticket, first class of course, to anywhere you're heading. One-way ticket. You just have to tell me where you want to go."

Shadow rubbed the bruise on his cheek. There was something about the pain that was almost comforting.

The train came to a complete stop. It was a small station, seemingly in the middle of nowhere. There was a large black car parked by the station building, in the thin sunshine. The windows were tinted, and Shadow could not see inside.

Mr. Smith pushed down the train window, reached outside to open the carriage door, and he stepped out onto the platform. He looked back in at Shadow through the open window. "Well?"

"I think," said Shadow, "that I'll spend a couple of weeks looking around the U.K. And you'll just have to pray that I look the right way when I cross your roads."

"And then?"

Shadow knew it, then. Perhaps he had known it all along. "Chicago," he said to Smith, as the train gave a jerk, and began to move away from the station. He felt older, as he said it. But he could not put it off forever.

And then he said, so quietly that only he could have heard it, "I guess I'm going home."

Soon afterward it began to rain: huge, pelting drops that rattled against the windows and blurred the world into grays and greens. Deep rumbles of thunder accompanied Shadow on his journey south: the storm grumbled, the wind howled, and the lightning made huge shadows across the sky, and in their company Shadow slowly began to feel less alone.

THE RETURN OF THE
THIN WHITE DUKE

2004

H E WAS THE monarch of all he surveyed, even when he stood
out on the palace balcony at night listening to reports and he
glanced up into the sky at the bitter twinkling clusters and whorls
of stars. He ruled the worlds. He had tried for so long to rule wisely,
and well, and to be a good monarch, but it is hard to rule, and wisdom can be painful. And it is impossible, he had found, if you rule,
to do only good, for you cannot build anything without tearing
something down, and even he could not care about every life, every
dream, every population of every world.

Bit by bit, moment by moment, death by little death, he ceased to
care.

He would not die, for only inferior people died, and he was the
inferior of no one.

Time passed. One day, in the deep dungeons, a man with blood on
his face looked at the Duke and told him he had become a monster.
The next moment, the man was no more; a footnote in a history
book.

The Duke gave this conversation much thought over the next
several days, and eventually he nodded his head. "The traitor was
right," he said. "I have become a monster. Ah well. I wonder if any of
us set out to be monsters?"

Once, long ago, there had been lovers, but that had been in the dawn days of the Dukedom. Now, in the dusk of the world, with all pleasures available freely (but what we attain with no effort we cannot value), and with no need to deal with any issues of succession (for even the notion that another would one day succeed the Duke bordered upon blasphemy), there were no more lovers, just as there were no challenges. He felt as if he were asleep while his eyes were open and his lips spoke, but there was nothing to wake him.

The day after it had occurred to the Duke that he was now a monster was the Day of Strange Blossoms, celebrated by the wearing of flowers brought to the Ducal Palace from every world and every plane. It was a day that all in the Ducal Palace, which covered a continent, were traditionally merry, and in which they cast off their cares and darknesses, but the Duke was not happy.

"How can you be made happy?" asked the information beetle on his shoulder, there to relay his master's whims and desires to a hundred hundred worlds. "Give the word, Your Grace, and empires will rise and fall to make you smile. Stars will flame novae for your entertainment."

"Perhaps I need a heart," said the Duke.

"I shall have a hundred hundred hearts immediately plucked, ripped, torn, incised, sliced and otherwise removed from the chests of ten thousand perfect specimens of humanity," said the information beetle. "How do you wish them prepared? Shall I alert the chefs or the taxidermists, the surgeons or the sculptors?"

"I need to care about something," said the Duke. "I need to value life. I need to wake."

The beetle chittered and chirrupped on his shoulder; it could access the wisdom of ten thousand worlds, but it could not advise its master when he was in this mood, so it said nothing. It relayed its concern to its predecessors, the older information beetles and scarabs, now sleeping in ornate boxes on a hundred hundred worlds, and the scarabs consulted among themselves with regret, because, in the vastness of time, even this had happened before, and they were prepared to deal with it.

A long-forgotten subroutine from the morning of the worlds was set into motion. The Duke was performing the final ritual of the Day of Strange Blossoms with no expression on his thin face, a man seeing his world as it was and valuing it not at all, when a small winged creature fluttered out from the blossom in which she had been hiding.

"Your Grace," she whispered. "My mistress needs you. Please. You are her only hope."

"Your mistress?" asked the Duke.

"The creature comes from Beyond," clicked the beetle on his shoulder. "From one of the places that does not acknowledge the Ducal Overlordship, from the lands beyond life and death, between being and unbeing. It must have hidden itself inside an imported off-world orchid blossom. Its words are a trap, or a snare. I shall have it destroyed."

"No," said the Duke. "Let it be." He did something he had not done for many years, and stroked the beetle with a thin white finger. Its green eyes turned black and it chittered into perfect silence.

He cupped the tiny thing in his hands, and walked back to his quarters, while she told him of her wise and noble Queen, and of the giants, each more beautiful than the last, and each more huge and dangerous and more monstrous, who kept her Queen a captive.

And as she spoke, the Duke remembered the days when a lad from the stars had come to World to seek his fortune (for in those days there were fortunes everywhere, just waiting to be found); and in remembering he discovered that his youth was less distant than he had thought. His information beetle lay quiescent upon his shoulder.

"Why did she send you to me?" he asked the little creature. But, her task accomplished, she would speak no more, and in moments she vanished, as instantly and as permanently as a star that had been extinguished upon Ducal order.

He entered his private quarters, and placed the deactivated information beetle in its case beside his bed. In his study, he had his servants bring him a long black case. He opened it himself, and, with a touch, he activated his master advisor. It shook itself, then wriggled up and about his shoulders in viper form, its serpent tail forking into the neural plug at the base of his neck.

The Duke told the serpent what he intended to do.

"This is not wise," said the master advisor, the intelligence and advice of every Ducal advisor in memory available to it, after a moment's examination of precedent.

"I seek adventure, not wisdom," said the Duke. A ghost of a smile began to play at the edges of his lips; the first smile that his servants had seen in longer than they could remember.

"Then, if you will not be dissuaded, take a battle-steed," said the advisor. It was good advice. The Duke deactivated his master advisor and he sent for the key to the battle-steeds' stable. The key had not been played in a thousand years: its strings were dusty.

There had once been six battle-steeds, one for each of the Lords and Ladies of the Evening. They were brilliant, beautiful, unstoppable, and when the Duke had been forced, with regret, to terminate the career of each of the Rulers of the Evening, he had declined to destroy their battle-steeds, instead placing them where they could be of no danger to the worlds.

The Duke took the key and played an opening arpeggio. The gate opened, and an ink-black, jet-black, coal-black battle-steed strutted out with feline grace. It raised its head and stared at the world with proud eyes.

"Where do we go?" asked the battle-steed. "What do we fight?"

"We go Beyond," said the Duke. "And as to whom we shall fight . . . well, that remains to be seen."

"I can take you anywhere," said the battle-steed. "And I will kill those who try to hurt you."

The Duke clambered onto the battle-steed's back, the cold metal yielding as live flesh between his thighs, and he urged it forward.

A leap and it was racing through the froth and flux of Underspace: together they were tumbling through the madness between the worlds. The Duke laughed, then, where no man could hear him, as they traveled together through Underspace, traveling forever in the Undertime (that is not reckoned against the seconds of a person's life).

"This feels like a trap of some kind," said the battle-steed, as the space beneath galaxies evaporated about them.

"Yes," said the Duke. "I am sure that it is."

"I have heard of this Queen," said the battle-steed, "or of something like her. She lives between life and death, and calls warriors and heroes and poets and dreamers to their doom."

"That sounds right," said the Duke.

"And when we return to real-space, I would expect an ambush," said the battle-steed.

"That sounds more than probable," said the Duke, as they reached their destination, and erupted out of Underspace back into existence.

The guardians of the palace were as beautiful as the messenger had warned him, and as ferocious, and they were waiting.

"What are you doing?" they called, as they came in for the assault. "Do you know that strangers are forbidden here? Stay with us. Let us love you. We will devour you with our love."

"I have come to rescue your Queen," he told them.

"Rescue the Queen?" they laughed. "She will have your head on a plate before she looks at you. Many people have come to save her, over the years. Their heads sit on golden plates in her palace. Yours will simply be the freshest."

There were men who looked like fallen angels and women who looked like demons risen. There were people so beautiful that they would have been all that the Duke had ever desired, had they been human, and they pressed close to him, skin to carapace and flesh against armor, so they could feel the coldness of him, and he could feel the warmth of them.

"Stay with us. Let us love you," they whispered, and they reached out with sharp talons and teeth.

"I do not believe your love will prove to be good for me," said the Duke. One of the women, fair of hair, with eyes of a peculiar translucent blue, reminded him of someone long forgotten, of a lover who had passed out of his life a long time before. He found her name in his mind, and would have called it aloud, to see if she turned, to see if she knew him, but the battle-steed lashed out with sharp claws, and the pale blue eyes were closed forever.

The battle-steed moved fast, like a panther, and each of the guardians fell to the ground, and writhed and was still.

The Duke stood before the Queen's palace. He slipped from his battle-steed to the fresh earth.

"Here, I go on alone," he said. "Wait, and one day I shall return."

"I do not believe you will ever return," said the battle-steed. "I shall wait until time itself is done, if need be. But still, I fear for you."

The Duke touched his lips to the black steel of the steed's head, and bade it farewell. He walked on to rescue the Queen. He remembered a monster who had ruled worlds and who would never die, and he smiled, because he was no longer that man. For the first time since his first youth he had something to lose, and the discovery of that made him young again. His heart began to pound in his chest as he walked through the empty palace, and he laughed out loud.

She was waiting for him, in the place where flowers die. She was everything he had imagined that she would be. Her skirt was simple and white, her cheekbones were high and very dark, her hair was long and the infinitely dark color of a crow's wing.

"I am here to rescue you," he told her.

"You are here to rescue yourself," she corrected him. Her voice was almost a whisper, like the breeze that shook the dead blossoms.

He bowed his head, although she was as tall as he was.

"Three questions," she whispered. "Answer them correctly, and all you desire shall be yours. Fail, and your head will rest forever on a golden dish." Her skin was the brown of the dead rose petals. Her eyes were the dark gold of amber.

"Ask your three questions," he said, with a confidence he did not feel.

The Queen reached out a finger and she ran the tip of it gently along his cheek. The Duke could not remember the last time that anybody had touched him without his permission.

"What is bigger than the universe?" she asked.

"Underspace and Undertime," said the Duke. "For they both include the universe, and also all that is not the universe. But I suspect you seek a more poetic, less accurate answer. The mind, then, for it can hold a universe, but also imagine things that have never been, and are not."

The Queen said nothing.

"Is that right? Is that wrong?" asked the Duke. He wished, momentarily, for the snakelike whisper of his master advisor, unloading, through its neural plug, the accumulated wisdom of his advisors over the years, or even the chitter of his information beetle.

"The second question," said the Queen. "What is greater than a King?"

"Obviously, a Duke," said the Duke. "For all Kings, Popes, Chancellors, Empresses and such serve at and only at my will. But again, I suspect that you are looking for an answer that is less accurate and more imaginative. The mind, again, is greater than a King. Or a Duke. Because, although I am the inferior of nobody, there are those who could imagine a world in which there is something superior to me, and something else again superior to that, and so on. No! Wait! I have the answer. It is from the Great Tree: *Kether,* the Crown, the concept of monarchy, is greater than any King."

The Queen looked at the Duke with amber eyes, and she said, "The final question for you. What can you never take back?"

"My word," said the Duke. "Although, now I come to think of it, once I give my word, sometimes circumstances change and sometimes the worlds themselves change in unfortunate or unexpected ways. From time to time, if it comes to that, my word needs to be modified in accordance with realities. I would say Death, but, truly, if I find myself in need of someone I have previously disposed of, I simply have them reincorporated . . ."

The Queen looked impatient.

"A kiss," said the Duke.

She nodded.

"There is hope for you," said the Queen. "You believe you are my only hope, but, truthfully, I am yours. Your answers were all quite wrong. But the last was not as wrong as the rest of them."

The Duke contemplated losing his head to this woman, and found the prospect less disturbing than he would have expected.

A wind blew through the garden of dead flowers, and the Duke was put in mind of perfumed ghosts.

"Would you like to know the answer?" she asked.

"Answers," he said. "Surely."

"Only one answer, and it is this: the heart," said the Queen. "The heart is greater than the universe, for it can find pity in it for everything in the universe, and the universe itself can feel no pity. The heart is greater than a King, because a heart can know a King for what he is, and still love him. And once you give your heart, you cannot take it back."

"I *said* a kiss," said the Duke.

"It was not as wrong as the other answers," she told him. The wind gusted higher and wilder and for a heartbeat the air was filled with dead petals. Then the wind was gone as suddenly as it appeared, and the broken petals fell to the floor.

"So. I have failed, in the first task you set me. Yet I do not believe my head would look good upon a golden dish," said the Duke. "Or upon any kind of a dish. Give me a task, then, a quest, something I can achieve to show that I am worthy. Let me rescue you from this place."

"I am never the one who needs rescuing," said the Queen. "Your advisors and scarabs and programs are done with you. They sent you here, as they sent those who came before you, long ago, because it is better for you to vanish of your own volition, than for them to kill you in your sleep. And less dangerous." She took his hand in hers. "Come," she said. They walked away from the garden of dead flowers, past the fountains of light, spraying their lights into the void, and into the citadel of song, where perfect voices waited at each turn, sighing and chanting and humming and echoing, although nobody was there to sing.

Beyond the citadel was only mist.

"There," she told him. "We have reached the end of everything, where nothing exists but what we create, by act of will or by desperation. Here in this place I can speak freely. It is only us, now." She looked into his eyes. "You do not have to die. You can stay with me. You will be happy to have finally found happiness, a heart, and the value of existence. And I will love you."

The Duke looked at her with a flash of puzzled anger. "I asked to care. I asked for something to care about. I asked for a heart."

"And they have given you all you asked for. But you cannot be their monarch and have those things. So you cannot return."

"I . . . I asked them to make this happen," said the Duke. He no longer looked angry. The mists at the edge of that place were pale, and they hurt the Duke's eyes when he stared at them too deeply or too long.

The ground began to shake, as if beneath the footsteps of a giant.

"Is anything true here?" asked the Duke. "Is anything permanent?"

"Everything is true," said the Queen. "The giant comes. And it will kill you, unless you defeat it."

"How many times have you been through this?" asked the Duke. "How many heads have wound up on golden dishes?"

"Nobody's head has ever wound up on a golden platter," she said. "I am not programmed to kill them. They battle for me and they win me and they stay with me, until they close their eyes for the last time. They are content to stay, or I make them content. But you . . . you need your discontent, don't you?"

He hesitated. Then he nodded.

She put her arms around him and kissed him, slowly and gently. The kiss, once given, could not be taken back.

"So now, I will fight the giant and save you?"

"It is what happens."

He looked at her. He looked down at himself, at his engraved armor, at his weapons. "I am no coward. I have never walked away from a fight. I cannot return, but I will not be content to stay here with you. So I will wait here, and I will let the giant kill me."

She looked alarmed. "Stay with me. Stay."

The Duke looked behind him, into the blank whiteness. "What lies out there?" he asked. "What is beyond the mist?"

"You would run?" she asked. "You would leave me?"

"I will walk," he said. "And I will not walk away. But I will walk towards. I wanted a heart. What is on the other side of that mist?"

She shook her head. "Beyond the mist is *Malkuth:* the Kingdom. But it does not exist unless you make it so. It becomes as you create it. If you dare to walk into the mist, then you will build a world or you will cease to exist entirely. And you can do this thing. I do not know what will happen, except for this: if you walk away from me you can never return."

He heard a pounding still, but was no longer certain that it was the feet of a giant. It felt more like the beat, beat, beat of his own heart.

He turned towards the mist, before he could change his mind, and he walked into the nothingness, cold and clammy against his skin. With each step he felt himself becoming less. His neural plugs died, and gave him no new information, until even his name and his status were lost to him.

He was not certain if he was seeking a place or making one. But he remembered dark skin and her amber eyes. He remembered the stars—there would be stars where he was going, he decided. There must be stars.

He pressed on. He suspected he had once been wearing armor, but he felt the damp mist on his face, and on his neck, and he shivered in his thin coat against the cold night air.

He stumbled, his foot glancing against the curb.

Then he pulled himself upright, and peered at the blurred streetlights through the fog. A car drove close—too close—and vanished past him, the red rear lights staining the mist crimson.

My old manor, he thought, fondly, and that was followed by a moment of pure puzzlement, at the idea of Beckenham as his old anything. He'd only just moved there. It was somewhere to use as a base. Somewhere to escape from. Surely, that was the point?

But the idea, of a man running away (a lord or a duke, perhaps, he thought, and liked the way it felt in his head), hovered and hung in his mind, like the beginning of a song.

"I'd rather write a something song than rule the world," he said aloud, tasting the words in his mouth. He rested his guitar case against a wall, put his hand in the pocket of his duffel coat, found a pencil stub and a shilling notebook, and wrote them down. He'd find a good two-syllable word for the *something* soon enough, he hoped.

Then he pushed his way into the pub. The warm, beery atmosphere embraced him as he walked inside. The low fuss and grumble of pub conversation. Somebody called his name, and he waved a pale hand at them, pointed to his wristwatch and then to the stairs. Cigarette smoke gave the air a faint blue sheen. He coughed, once, deep in his chest, and craved a cigarette of his own.

Up the stairs with the threadbare red carpeting, holding his guitar case like a weapon, whatever had been in his mind before he turned the corner into the High Street evaporating with each step. He paused in the dark corridor before opening the door to the pub's upstairs room. From the buzz of small talk and the clink of glasses, he knew there were already a handful of people waiting and working. Someone was tuning a guitar.

Monster? thought the young man. *That's got two syllables.*

He turned the word around in his mind several times before he decided that he could find something better, something bigger, something more fitting for the world he intended to conquer, and, with only a momentary regret, he let it go forever, and walked inside.

EXCERPT FROM *ANANSI BOYS*

2005

HOW ANANSI TRICKED TIGER

NOW, PROBABLY YOU know some Anansi stories. Probably there's no one in the whole wide world doesn't know some Anansi stories.

Anansi was a spider, when the world was young, and all the stories were being told for the first time. He used to get himself into trouble, and he used to get himself out of trouble. The story of the Tar-Baby, the one they tell about Bre'r Rabbit? That was Anansi's story first. Some people think he was a rabbit. But that's their mistake. He wasn't a rabbit. He was a spider.

Anansi stories go back as long as people been telling each other stories. Back in Africa, where everything began, even before people were painting cave lions and bears on rock walls, even then they were telling stories, about monkeys and lions and buffalo: big dream stories. People always had those proclivities. That was how they made sense of their worlds. Everything that ran or crawled or swung or snaked got to walk through those stories, and different tribes of people would venerate different creatures.

Lion was the king of beasts, even then, and Gazelle was the fleetest of foot, and Monkey was the most foolish, and Tiger was the most terrible, but it wasn't stories about them people wanted to hear.

Anansi gave his name to stories. Every story is Anansi's. Once, before the stories were Anansi's, they all belonged to Tiger (which is the name the people of the islands call all the big cats), and the tales were dark and evil, and filled with pain, and none of them ended happily. But that was a long time ago. These days, the stories are Anansi's.

Seeing we were just at a funeral, let me tell you a story about Anansi, the time his grandmother died. (It's okay: she was a very old woman, and she went in her sleep. It happens.) She died a long way from home, so Anansi, he goes across the island with his handcart, and he gets his grandmother's body, and puts it on the handcart, and he wheels it home. He's going to bury her by the banyan tree out the back of his hut, you see.

Now, he's passing through the town, after pushing his grandmother's corpse in the cart all morning, and he thinks, *I need some whisky.* So he goes into the shop, for there is a shop in that village, a store that sells everything, where the shopkeeper is a very hasty-tempered man. Anansi, he goes in and he drinks some whisky. He drinks a little more whisky, and he thinks, *I shall play a trick on this fellow,* so he says to the shopkeeper, go take some whisky to my grandmother, sleeping in the cart outside. You may have to wake her, for she's a sound sleeper.

So the shopkeeper, he goes out to the cart with a bottle, and he says to the old lady in the cart, "Hey, here's your whisky," but the old lady she not say anything. And the shopkeeper, he's just getting angrier and angrier, for he was such a hasty-tempered man, saying get up, old woman, get up and drink your whisky, but the old woman she says nothing. Then she does something that the dead sometimes do in the heat of the day: she flatulates loudly. Well, the shopkeeper, he's so angry with this old woman for flatulating at him that he hits her, and then he hits her again, and now he hits her one more time and she tumbles down from the handcart onto the ground.

Anansi, he runs out and he starts a-crying and a-wailing and a-carrying on, and saying my grandmother, she's a dead woman, look what you did! Murderer! Evildoer! Now the shopkeeper, he says to Anansi, don't you tell anyone I done this, and he gives Anansi five whole bottles of whisky, and a bag of gold, and a sack of plantains and pineapples and mangos, to make him hush his carrying-on, and to go away.

(He thinks he killed Anansi's grandmother, you see.)

So Anansi, he wheels his handcart home, and he buries his grandmother underneath the banyan tree.

Now the next day, Tiger, he's passing by Anansi's house, and he smells cooking smells. So he invites himself over, and there's Anansi having a feast, and Anansi, having no other option, asks Tiger to sit and eat with them.

Tiger says, Brother Anansi, where did you get all that fine food from, and don't you lie to me? And where did you get these bottles of whisky from, and that big bag filled with gold pieces? If you lie to me, I'll tear out your throat.

So Anansi, he says, I cannot lie to you, Brother Tiger. I got them all for I take my dead grandmother to the village on a handcart. And the storekeeper gave me all these good things for bringing him my dead grandmother.

Now, Tiger, he didn't have a living grandmother, but his wife had a mother, so he goes home and he calls his wife's mother out to see him, saying, grandmother, you come out now, for you and I must have a talk. And she comes out and peers around, and says what is it? Well, Tiger, he kills her, even though his wife loves her, and he places her body on a handcart.

Then he wheels his handcart to the village, with his dead mother-in-law on it. Who want a dead body? he calls. Who want a dead grandmother? But all the people they just jeered at him, and they laughed at him, and they mocked him, and when they saw that he was serious and he wasn't going anywhere, they pelted him with rotten fruit until he ran away.

It wasn't the first time Tiger was made a fool of by Anansi, and it wouldn't be the last time. Tiger's wife never let him forget how he killed her mother. Some days it's better for Tiger if he's never been born.

That's an Anansi story.

'Course, all stories are Anansi stories. Even this one.

Olden days, all the animals wanted to have stories named after them, back in the days when the songs that sung the world were still being sung, back when they were still singing the sky and the rainbow and the ocean. It was in those days when animals were people as well as animals that Anansi the spider tricked all of them, especially Tiger, because he wanted all the stories named after him.

Stories are like spiders, with all they long legs, and stories are like spiderwebs, which man gets himself all tangled up in but which look so pretty when you see them under a leaf in the morning dew, and in the elegant way that they connect to one another, each to each.

What's that? You want to know if Anansi looked like a spider? Sure he did, except when he looked like a man.

No, he never changed his shape. It's just a matter of how you tell the story. That's all.

THE MORNING AFTER

FAT CHARLIE WAS THIRSTY.

Fat Charlie was thirsty and his head hurt.

Fat Charlie was thirsty and his head hurt and his mouth tasted evil and his eyes were too tight in his head and all his teeth twinged and his stomach burned and his back was aching in a way that started around his knees and went up to his forehead and his brains had been removed and replaced with cotton balls and needles and pins which was why it hurt to try and think, and his eyes were not just too tight in his head but they must have rolled out in the night and been reattached with roofing nails; and now he noticed that anything louder than the gentle Brownian motion of air molecules drifting softly past each other was above his pain threshold. Also, he wished he were dead.

Fat Charlie opened his eyes, which was a mistake, in that it let daylight in, which hurt. It also told him where he was (in his own bed, in his bedroom), and because he was staring at the clock on his bedside table, it told him that the time was 11:30.

That, he thought, one word at a time, was about as bad as things could get: he had the kind of hangover that an Old Testament God might have smitten the Midianites with, and the next time he saw Grahame Coats he would undoubtedly learn that he had been fired.

He wondered if he could sound convincingly sick over the phone, then realized that the challenge would be convincingly sounding anything else.

He could not remember getting home last night.

He would phone the office, the moment he was able to remember the telephone number. He would apologize—crippling twenty-four-hour flu, flat on his back, nothing that could be done. . . .

"You know," said someone in the bed next to him, "I think there's a bottle of water on your side. Could you pass it over here?"

Fat Charlie wanted to explain that there was no water on his side of the bed, and that there was, in fact, no water closer than the bath-room sink, if he disinfected the toothbrush mug first, but he realized he was staring at one of several bottles of water, sitting on the bed-side table. He reached his hand out, and closed fingers that felt like they belonged to someone else around one of them, then, with the sort of effort people usually reserve for hauling themselves up the final few feet of a sheer rock face, he rolled over in bed.

It was the vodka and orange.

Also, she was naked. At least, the bits of her he could see were.

She took the water, and pulled the sheet up to cover her chest. "Ta. He said to tell you," she said, "when you woke, not to worry about calling work and telling them you were ill. He said to tell you he's already taken care of it."

Fat Charlie's mind was not put at rest. His fears and worries were not allayed. Then again, in the condition he was in, he only had room in his head for a single thing to worry about at once, and right now he was worrying about whether or not he would make it to the bathroom in time.

"You'll need more liquids," said the girl. "You'll need to replenish your electrolytes."

Fat Charlie made it to the bathroom in time. Afterward, seeing he was there already, he stood under the shower until the room stopped undulating, and then he brushed his teeth without throwing up.

When he returned to the bedroom, the vodka and orange was no longer there, which was a relief to Fat Charlie, who had started to hope that she might have been an alcohol-induced delusion, like pink elephants or the nightmarish idea that he had taken to the stage to sing on the previous evening.

He could not find his dressing gown, so he pulled on a tracksuit, in order to feel dressed enough to visit the kitchen, at the far end of the hall.

His phone chimed, and he rummaged through his jacket, which was on the floor beside the bed, until he found it, and flipped it open. He grunted into it, as anonymously as he could, just in case it was someone from the Grahame Coats Agency trying to discern his whereabouts.

"It's me," said Spider's voice. "Everything's okay."

"You told them I was dead?"

"Better than that. I told them I was you."

"But." Fat Charlie tried to think clearly. "But you're not me."

"Hey. I know that. I told them I was."

"You don't even look like me."

"Brother of mine, you are harshing a potential mellow here. It's all taken care of. Oops. Gotta go. The big boss needs to talk to me."

"Grahame Coats? Look, Spider—"

But Spider had put down the phone, and the screen blanked.

Fat Charlie's dressing gown came through the door. There was a girl inside it. It looked significantly better on her than it ever had on him. She was carrying a tray, on which was a water glass with a fizzing Alka-Seltzer in it, along with something in a mug.

"Drink both of these," she told him. "The mug first. Just knock it back."

"What's in the mug?"

"Egg yolk, Worcestershire sauce, Tabasco, salt, dash of vodka, things like that," she said. "Kill or cure. Now," she told him, in tones that brooked no argument. "Drink."

Fat Charlie drank. "Oh my god," he said.

"Yeah," she agreed. "But you're still alive."

He wasn't sure about that. He drank the Alka-Seltzer anyway. Something occurred to him.

"Um," said Fat Charlie. "Um. Look. Last night. Did we. Um." She looked blank.

"Did we what?"

"Did we. You know. *Do* it?"

"You mean you don't remember?" Her face fell. "You said it was the best you'd ever had. That it was as if you'd never made love to a woman before. You were part god, part animal, and part unstoppable sex machine . . ."

Fat Charlie didn't know where to look. She giggled.

"I'm just winding you up," she said. "I'd helped your brother get you home, we cleaned you up, and, after that, you know."

"No," he said. "I don't know."

"Well," she said, "you were completely out cold, and it's a big bed. I'm not sure where your brother slept. He must have the constitution of an ox. He was up at the crack of dawn, all bright and smiling."

"He went into work," said Fat Charlie. "He told them he was me."

"Wouldn't they be able to tell the difference? I mean, you're not exactly twins."

"Apparently not." He shook his head. Then he looked at her. She stuck out a small, extremely pink tongue at him.

"What's your name?"

"You mean you've forgotten? I remember *your* name. You're Fat Charlie."

"Charles," he said. "Just Charles is fine."

"I'm Daisy," she said, and stuck out her hand. "Pleased to meet you."

They shook hands solemnly.

"I feel a bit better," said Fat Charlie.

"Like I said," she said. "Kill or cure."

SPIDER WAS HAVING a great day at the office. He almost never worked in offices. He almost never worked. Everything was new, everything was marvelous and strange, from the tiny lift that lurched him up to the fifth floor, to the warrenlike offices of the Grahame Coats Agency. He stared, fascinated, at the glass case in the lobby filled with dusty awards. He wandered through the offices, and when anyone asked him who he was, he would say "I'm Fat Charlie Nancy," and he'd say it in his god-voice, which would make whatever he said practically true.

He found the tea-room, and made himself several cups of tea. Then he carried them back to Fat Charlie's desk, and arranged them around it in an artistic fashion. He started to play with the computer network. It asked him for a password. "I'm Fat Charlie Nancy," he told the computer, but there were still places it didn't want him to go, so he said, "I'm Grahame Coats," and it opened to him like a flower.

He looked at things on the computer until he got bored.

He dealt with the contents of Fat Charlie's in basket. He dealt with Fat Charlie's pending basket.

It occurred to him that Fat Charlie would be waking up around now, so he called him at home, in order to reassure him; he just felt that he was making a little headway when Grahame Coats put his head around the door, ran his fingers across his stoatlike lips, and beckoned.

"Gotta go," Spider said to his brother. "The big boss needs to talk to me." He put down the phone.

"Making private phone calls on company time, Nancy," stated Grahame Coats.

"Abso-friggin'-lutely," agreed Spider.

"And was that myself you were referring to as 'the big boss'?" asked Grahame Coats. They walked to the end of the hallway and into his office.

"You're the biggest," said Spider. "And the bossest."

Grahame Coats looked puzzled; he suspected he was being made fun of, but he was not certain, and this disturbed him.

"Well, sit ye down, sit ye down," he said.

Spider sat him down.

It was Grahame Coats's custom to keep the turnover of staff at the Grahame Coats Agency fairly constant. Some people came and went. Others came and remained until just before their jobs would begin to carry some kind of employment protection. Fat Charlie had been there longer than anyone: one year and eleven months. One month to go before redundancy payments or industrial tribunals could become a part of his life.

There was a speech that Grahame Coats gave, before he fired someone. He was very proud of his speech.

"Into each life," he began, "a little rain must fall. There's no cloud without a silver lining."

"It's an ill wind," offered Spider, "that blows no one good."

"Ah. Yes. Yes indeed. Well. As we pass through this vale of tears, we must pause to reflect that—"

"The first cut," said Spider, "is the deepest."

"What? Oh." Grahame Coats scrabbled to remember what came next. "Happiness," he pronounced, "is like a butterfly."

"Or a bluebird," agreed Spider.

"Quite. If I may finish?"

"Of course. Be my guest," said Spider, cheerfully.

"And the happiness of every soul at the Grahame Coats Agency is as important to me as my own."

"I cannot tell you," said Spider, "how happy that makes me."

"Yes," said Grahame Coats.

"Well, I better get back to work," said Spider. "It's been a blast, though. Next time you want to share some more, just call me. You know where I am."

"Happiness," said Grahame Coats. His voice was taking on a faintly strangulated quality. "And what I wonder, Nancy, Charles, is this—are you happy here? And do you not agree that you might be rather happier elsewhere?"

"That's not what I wonder," said Spider. "You want to know what I wonder?"

Grahame Coats said nothing. It had never gone like this before. Normally, at this point, their faces fell, and they went into shock. Sometimes they cried. Grahame Coats had never minded when they cried.

"What I wonder," said Spider, "is what the accounts in the Cayman Islands are for. You know, because it almost sort of looks like money that should go to our client accounts sometimes just goes into the Cayman Island accounts instead. And it seems a funny sort of way to organize the finances, for the money coming in to rest in those accounts. I've never seen anything like it before. I was hoping you could explain it to me."

Grahame Coats had gone off-white—one of those colors that turn up in paint catalogs with names like "parchment" or "magnolia." He said, "How did you get access to those accounts?"

"Computers," said Spider. "Do they drive you as nuts as they drive me? What can you do?"

Grahame Coats thought for several long moments. He had always liked to imagine that his financial affairs were so deeply tangled that, even if the Fraud Squad were ever able to conclude that financial crimes had been committed, they would find it extremely difficult to explain to a jury exactly what kind of crimes they were.

"There's nothing illegal about having offshore accounts," he said, as carelessly as possible.

"Illegal?" said Spider. "I should hope not. I mean, if I saw anything illegal, I should have to report it to the appropriate authorities."

Grahame Coats picked up a pen from his desk, then he put it down again. "Ah," he said. "Well, delightful though it is to chat, converse, spend time, and otherwise hobnob with you, Charles, I suspect that both of us have work we should be getting on with. Time and tide, after all, wait for no man. Procrastination is the thief of time."

"Life is a rock," suggested Spider, "but the radio rolled me."

"Whatever."

SUNBIRD

2005

THEY WERE A rich and a rowdy bunch at the Epicurean Club in those days. They certainly knew how to party. There were five of them:

There was Augustus TwoFeathers McCoy, big enough for three men, who ate enough for four men and who drank enough for five. His great-grandfather had founded the Epicurean Club with the proceeds of a tontine, which he had taken great pains, in the traditional manner, to ensure that he had collected in full.

There was Professor Mandalay, small and twitchy and gray as a ghost (and perhaps he was a ghost; stranger things have happened), who drank nothing but water, and who ate doll-portions from plates the size of saucers. Still, you do not need the gusto for the gastronomy, and Mandalay always got to the heart of every dish placed in front of him.

There was Virginia Boote, the food and restaurant critic, who had once been a great beauty but was now a grand and magnificent ruin, and who delighted in her ruination.

There was Jackie Newhouse, the descendant (on the left-handed route) of the great lover, gourmand, violinist, and duelist Giacomo Casanova. Jackie Newhouse had, like his notorious ancestor, both broken his share of hearts and eaten his share of great dishes.

And there was Zebediah T. Crawcrustle, who was the only one

of the Epicureans who was flat-out broke: he shambled in unshaven from the street when they had their meetings, with half a bottle of rotgut in a brown paper bag, hatless and coatless and, too often, partly shirtless, but he ate with more of an appetite than any of them.

Augustus TwoFeathers McCoy was talking—

"We have eaten everything that can be eaten," said Augustus TwoFeathers McCoy, and there was regret and glancing sorrow in his voice. "We have eaten vulture, mole, and fruitbat."

Mandalay consulted his notebook. "Vulture tasted like rotten pheasant. Mole tasted like carrion slug. Fruitbat tasted remarkably like sweet guinea pig."

"We have eaten kakapo, aye-aye, and giant panda—"

"Oh, that broiled panda steak," sighed Virginia Boote, her mouth watering at the memory.

"We have eaten several long-extinct species," said Augustus Two-Feathers McCoy. "We have eaten flash-frozen mammoth and Patagonian giant sloth."

"If we had but gotten the mammoth a little faster," sighed Jackie Newhouse. "I could tell why the hairy elephants went so fast, though, once people got a taste of them. I am a man of elegant pleasures, but after only one bite, I found myself thinking only of Kansas City barbecue sauce, and what the ribs on those things would be like, if they were fresh."

"Nothing wrong with being on ice for a millennium or two," said Zebediah T. Crawcrustle. He grinned. His teeth may have been crooked, but they were sharp and strong. "Even so, for real taste you had to go for honest-to-goodness mastodon every time. Mammoth was always what people settled for, when they couldn't get mastodon."

"We've eaten squid, and giant squid, and humongous squid," said Augustus TwoFeathers McCoy. "We've eaten lemmings and Tasmanian tigers. We've eaten bower bird and ortolan and peacock. We've eaten the dolphin fish (which is not the mammal dolphin) and the giant sea turtle and the Sumatran rhino. We've eaten everything there is to eat."

"Nonsense. There are many hundreds of things we have not yet tasted," said Professor Mandalay. "Thousands, perhaps. Think of all the species of beetle there are, still untasted."

"Oh Mandy," sighed Virginia Boote. "When you've tasted one beetle, you've tasted them all. And we all tasted several hundred species. At least the dung-beetles had a real kick to them."

"No," said Jackie Newhouse, "that was the dung-beetle balls. The beetles themselves were singularly unexceptional. Still, I take your point. We have scaled the heights of gastronomy, we have plunged down into the depths of gustation. We have become cosmonauts exploring undreamed-of worlds of delectation and gourmanderie."

"True, true, true," said Augustus TwoFeathers McCoy. "There has been a meeting of the Epicureans every month for over a hundred and fifty years, in my father's time, and my grandfather's time, and my great-grandfather's time, and now I fear that I must hang it up for there is nothing left that we, or our predecessors in the club, have not eaten."

"I wish I had been here in the twenties," said Virginia Boote, "when they legally had Man on the menu."

"Only after it had been electrocuted," said Zebediah T. Crawcrustle. "Half-fried already it was, all char and crackling. It left none of us with a taste for long pig, save one who was already that way inclined, and he went out pretty soon after that anyway."

"Oh, Crusty, *why* must you pretend that you were there?" asked Virginia Boote, with a yawn. "Anyone can see you aren't that old. You can't be more than sixty, even allowing for the ravages of time and the gutter."

"Oh, they ravage pretty good," said Zebediah T. Crawcrustle. "But not as good as you'd imagine. Anyway there's a host of things we've not eaten yet."

"Name one," said Mandalay, his pencil poised precisely above his notebook.

"Well, there's Suntown Sunbird," said Zebediah T. Crawcrustle. And he grinned his crookedy grin at them, with his teeth ragged but sharp.

"I've never heard of it," said Jackie Newhouse. "You're making it up."

"I've heard of it," said Professor Mandalay, "but in another context. And besides, it is imaginary."

"Unicorns are imaginary," said Virginia Boote, "but gosh, that unicorn flank tartare was tasty. A little bit horsy, a little big goatish, and all the better for the capers and raw quail eggs."

"There's something about the Sunbird in one of the minutes of the Epicurean Club from bygone years," said Augustus TwoFeathers McCoy. "But what it was, I can no longer remember."

"Did they say how it tasted?" asked Virginia.

"I do not believe that they did," said Augustus, with a frown. "I would need to inspect the bound proceedings, of course."

"Nah," said Zebediah T. Crawcrustle. "That's only in the charred volumes. You'll never find out about it from there."

Augustus TwoFeathers McCoy scratched his head. He really did have two feathers, which went through the knot of black-hair-shot-with-silver at the back of his head, and the feathers had once been golden although by now they were looking kind of ordinary and yellow and ragged. He had been given them when he was a boy.

"Beetles," said Professor Mandalay. "I once calculated that, if a man such as myself were to eat six different species of beetle each day, it would take him more than twenty years to eat every beetle that has been identified. And over that twenty years enough new species of beetle might have been discovered to keep him eating for another five years. And in those five years enough beetles might have been discovered to keep him eating for another two and a half years, and so on, and so on. It is a paradox of inexhaustibility. I call it Mandalay's Beetle. You would have to enjoy eating beetles, though," he added, "or it would be a very bad thing indeed."

"Nothing wrong with eating beetles if they're the right kind of beetle," said Zebediah T. Crawcrustle. "Right now, I've got a hankering on me for lightning bugs. There's a kick from the glow of a lightning bug that might be just what I need."

"While the lightning bug or firefly (*Photinus pyralis*) is more of a beetle than it is a glowworm," said Mandalay, "it is by no stretch of the imagination edible."

"They may not be edible," said Crawcrustle. "But they'll get you into shape for the stuff that is. I think I'll roast me some. Fireflies and habañero peppers. Yum."

Virginia Boote was an eminently practical woman. She said, "Suppose we did want to eat Suntown Sunbird. Where should we start looking for it?"

Zebediah T. Crawcrustle scratched the bristling seventh-day beard that was sprouting on his chin (it never grew any longer than that; seventh-day beards never do). "If it was me," he told them, "I'd head down to Suntown of a noon in midsummer, and I'd find somewhere comfortable to sit—Mustapha Stroheim's coffeehouse, for example—and I'd wait for the Sunbird to come by. Then I'd catch him in the traditional manner, and cook him in the traditional manner as well."

"And what would the traditional manner of catching him be?" asked Jackie Newhouse.

"Why, the same way your famous ancestor poached quails and wood grouse," said Crawcrustle.

"There's nothing in Casanova's memoirs about poaching quail," said Jackie Newhouse.

"Your ancestor was a busy man," said Crawcrustle. "He couldn't be expected to write everything down. But he poached a good quail nonetheless."

"Dried corn and dried blueberries, soaked in whiskey," said Augustus TwoFeathers McCoy. "That's how my folk always did it."

"And that was how Casanova did it," said Crawcrustle, "although he used barley grains mixed with raisins, and he soaked the raisins in brandy. He taught me himself."

Jackie Newhouse ignored this statement. It was easy to ignore much that Zebediah T. Crawcrustle said. Instead, Jackie Newhouse asked, "And where is Mustapha Stroheim's coffeehouse in Suntown?"

"Why, where it always is, third lane after the old market in the Suntown district, just before you reach the old drainage ditch that was once an irrigation canal, and if you find yourself outside Oneeye Khayam's carpet shop you have gone too far," began Crawcrustle. "But I see by the expressions of irritation upon your faces that you were expecting a less succinct, less accurate description. Very well.

It is in Suntown, and Suntown is in Cairo, in Egypt, where it always is, or almost always."

"And who will pay for an expedition to Suntown?" asked Augustus TwoFeathers McCoy. "And who will be on this expedition? I ask the question although I already know the answer, and I do not like it."

"Why, you will pay for it, Augustus, and we will all come," said Zebediah T. Crawcrustle. "You can deduct it from our Epicurean membership dues. And I shall bring my chef's apron and my cooking utensils."

Augustus knew that Crawcrustle had not paid his Epicurean Club membership in much too long a time, but the Epicurean Club would cover him; Crawcrustle had been a member of the Epicureans in Augustus's father's day. He simply said, "And when shall we leave?"

Crawcrustle fixed him with a mad old eye and shook his head in disappointment. "Why, Augustus," he said. "We're going to Suntown, to catch the Sunbird. When else should we leave?"

"Sunday!" sang Virginia Boote. "Darlings, we'll leave on a Sunday!"

"There's hope for you yet, young lady," said Zebediah T. Crawcrustle. "We shall leave Sunday indeed. Three Sundays from now. And we shall travel to Egypt. We shall spend several days hunting and trapping the elusive Sunbird of Suntown, and, finally, we shall deal with it in the traditional way."

Professor Mandalay blinked a small gray blink. "But," he said, "I am teaching a class on Monday. On Mondays I teach mythology, on Tuesdays I teach tap dancing, and on Wednesdays, woodwork."

"Get a teaching assistant to take your course, Mandalay O Mandalay. On Monday you'll be hunting the Sunbird," said Zebediah T. Crawcrustle. "And how many other professors can say that?"

THEY WENT, ONE by one, to see Crawcrustle, in order to discuss the journey ahead of them, and to announce their misgivings.

Zebediah T. Crawcrustle was a man of no fixed abode. Still, there were places he could be found, if you were of a mind to find him. In the early mornings he slept in the bus terminal, where the benches were comfortable and the transport police were inclined to let him lie; in the heat of the afternoons he hung in the park by the statues of long-forgotten generals, with the dipsos and the winos and the hopheads, sharing their company and the contents of their bottles, and offering his opinion, which was, as that of an Epicurean, always considered and always respected, if not always welcomed.

Augustus TwoFeathers McCoy sought out Crawcrustle in the park; he had with him his daughter, Hollyberry NoFeathers McCoy. She was small, but she was sharp as a shark's tooth.

"You know," said Augustus, "there is something very familiar about this."

"About what?" asked Zebediah.

"All of this. The expedition to Egypt. The Sunbird. It seemed to me like I heard about it before."

Crawcrustle merely nodded. He was crunching something from a brown paper bag.

Augustus said, "I went to the bound annals of the Epicurean Club, and I looked it up. And there was what I took to be a reference to the Sunbird in the index for forty years ago, but I was unable to learn anything more."

"And why was that?" asked Zebediah T. Crawcrustle, swallowing noisily.

Augustus TwoFeathers McCoy sighed. "I found the relevant page in the annals," he said, "but it was burned away, and afterward there was some great confusion in the administration of the Epicurean Club."

"You're eating lightning bugs from a paper bag," said Hollyberry NoFeathers McCoy. "I seen you doing it."

"I am indeed, little lady," said Zebediah T. Crawcrustle.

"Do you remember the days of great confusion, Crawcrustle?" asked Augustus.

"I do indeed," said Crawcrustle. "And I remember you. You were only the age that young Hollyberry is now. But there is always confusion, Augustus, and then there is no confusion. It is like the rising and the setting of the sun."

Jackie Newhouse and Professor Mandalay found Crawcrustle that evening, behind the railroad tracks. He was roasting something in a tin can over a small charcoal fire.

"What are you roasting, Crawcrustle?" asked Jackie Newhouse. "More charcoal," said Crawcrustle. "Cleans the blood, purifies the spirit."

There was basswood and hickory, cut up into little chunks at the bottom of the can, all black and smoking.

"And will you actually eat this charcoal, Crawcrustle?" asked Professor Mandalay.

In response, Crawcrustle licked his fingers and picked out a lump of charcoal from the can. It hissed and fizzed in his grip.

"A fine trick," said Professor Mandalay. "That's how fire-eaters do it, I believe."

Crawcrustle popped the charcoal into his mouth and crunched it between his ragged old teeth. "It is indeed," he said. "It is indeed."

Jackie Newhouse cleared his throat. "The truth of the matter is," he said, "Professor Mandalay and I have deep misgivings about the journey that lies ahead."

Zebediah merely crunched his charcoal. "Not hot enough," he said. He took a stick from the fire and nibbled off the orange-hot tip of it. "That's good," he said.

"It's all an illusion," said Jackie Newhouse.

"Nothing of the sort," said Zebediah T. Crawcrustle, primly. "It's prickly elm."

"I have extreme misgivings about all this," said Jackie Newhouse. "My ancestors and I have a finely tuned sense of personal preservation, one that has often left us shivering on roofs and hiding in rivers—one step away from the law, or from gentlemen with guns and legitimate grievances—and that sense of self-preservation is telling me not to go to Suntown with you."

"I am an academic," said Professor Mandalay, "and thus have no finely developed senses that would be comprehensible to anyone who has not ever needed to grade papers without actually reading the blessed things. Still, I find the whole thing remarkably suspicious. If this Sunbird is so tasty, why have I not heard of it?"

"You have, Mandy old fruit. You have," said Zebediah T. Crawcrustle.

"And I am, in addition, an expert on geographical features from

Tulsa, Oklahoma, to Timbuktu," continued Professor Mandalay. "Yet I have never seen a mention in any book of a place called Suntown in Cairo."

"Seen it mentioned? Why, you've taught it," said Crawcrustle, and he doused a lump of smoking charcoal with hot pepper sauce before popping it in his mouth and chomping it down.

"I don't believe you're really eating that," said Jackie Newhouse. "But even being around the trick of it is making me uncomfortable. I think it is time that I was elsewhere."

And he left. Perhaps Professor Mandalay left with him: that man was so gray and so ghostie it was always a toss-up whether he was there or not.

Virginia Boote tripped over Zebediah T. Crawcrustle while he rested in her doorway, in the small hours of the morning. She was returning from a restaurant she had needed to review. She got out of a taxi, tripped over Crawcrustle, and went sprawling. She landed nearby. "Whee!" she said. "That was some trip, wasn't it?"

"Indeed it was, Virginia," said Zebediah T. Crawcrustle. "You would not happen to have such a thing as a box of matches on you, would you?"

"I have a book of matches on me somewhere," she said, and she began to rummage in her purse, which was very large and very brown. "Here you are."

Zebediah T. Crawcrustle was carrying a bottle of purple methylated spirits, which he proceeded to pour into a plastic cup.

"Meths?" said Virginia Boote. "Somehow you never struck me as a meths drinker, Zebby."

"Nor am I," said Crawcrustle. "Foul stuff. It rots the guts and spoils the taste buds. But I could not find any lighter fluid at this time of night."

He lit a match, then dipped it near the surface of the cup of spirits, which began to burn with a flickery light. He ate the match. Then he gargled with the flaming liquid, and blew a sheet of flame into the street, incinerating a sheet of newspaper as it blew by.

"Crusty," said Virginia Boote, "that's a good way to get yourself killed."

Zebediah T. Crawcrustle grinned through black teeth. "I don't actually drink it," he told her. "I just gargle and breathe it out."

"You're playing with fire," she warned him.

"That's how I know I'm alive," said Zebediah T. Crawcrustle.

Virginia said, "Oh, Zeb. I *am* excited. I am so excited. What do you think the Sunbird tastes like?"

"Richer than quail and moister than turkey, fatter than ostrich and lusher than duck," said Zebediah T. Crawcrustle. "Once eaten it's never forgotten."

"We're going to Egypt," she said. "I've never been to Egypt." Then she said, "Do you have anywhere to stay the night?"

He coughed, a small cough that rattled around in his old chest. "I'm getting too old to sleep in doorways and gutters," he said. "Still, I have my pride."

"Well," she said, looking at the man, "you could sleep on my sofa."

"It is not that I am not grateful for the offer," he said, "but there is a bench in the bus station that has my name on it."

And he pushed himself away from the wall and tottered majestically down the street.

There really *was* a bench in the bus station that had his name on it. He had donated the bench to the bus station back when he was flush, and his name was attached to the back of it, engraved upon a small brass plaque. Zebediah T. Crawcrustle was not always poor. Sometimes he was rich, but he had difficulty in holding on to his wealth, and whenever he had become wealthy he discovered that the world frowned on rich men eating in hobo jungles at the back of the railroad, or consorting with the winos in the park, so he would fritter his wealth away as best he could. There were always little bits of it here and there that he had forgotten about, and sometimes he would forget that he did not like being rich, and then he would set out again and seek his fortune, and find it.

He had needed a shave for a week, and the hairs of his seven-day beard were starting to come through snow white.

THEY LEFT FOR Egypt on a Sunday, the Epicureans. There were five of them there, and Hollyberry NoFeathers McCoy waved good-bye to them at the airport. It was a very small airport, which still permitted waves good-bye.

"Good-bye, Father!" called Hollyberry NoFeathers McCoy.

Augustus TwoFeathers McCoy waved back at her as they walked along the asphalt to the little prop plane, which would begin the first leg of their journey.

"It seems to me," said Augustus TwoFeathers McCoy, "that I remember, albeit dimly, a day like this long, long ago. I was a small boy, in that memory, waving good-bye. I believe it was the last time I saw my father, and I am struck once more with a sudden presentiment of doom." He waved one last time at the small child at the other end of the field, and she waved back at him.

"You waved just as enthusiastically back then," agreed Zebediah T. Crawcrustle, "but I think she waves with slightly more aplomb."

It was true. She did.

They took a small plane and then a larger plane, then a smaller plane, a blimp, a gondola, a train, a hot-air balloon, and a rented Jeep.

They rattled through Cairo in the Jeep. They passed the old market, and they turned off on the third lane they came to (if they had continued on they would have come to a drainage ditch that was once an irrigation canal). Mustapha Stroheim himself was sitting outside in the street, perched on an elderly wicker chair. All of the tables and chairs were on the side of the street, and it was not a particularly wide street.

"Welcome, my friends, to my *kahwa*," said Mustapha Stroheim. "*Kahwa* is Egyptian for café, or for coffeehouse. Would you like tea? Or a game of dominoes?"

"We would like to be shown to our rooms," said Jackie Newhouse.

"Not me," said Zebediah T. Crawcrustle. "I'll sleep in the street. It's warm enough, and that doorstep over there looks mighty comfortable."

"I'll have coffee, please," said Augustus TwoFeathers McCoy. "Of course."

"Do you have water?" asked Professor Mandalay.

"Who said that?" said Mustapha Stroheim. "Oh, it was you, little gray man. My mistake. When I first saw you I thought you were someone's shadow."

"I will have *ShaySokkar Bosta*," said Virginia Boote, which is a glass of hot tea with the sugar on the side. "And I will play backgammon with anyone who wishes to take me on. There's not a soul in Cairo I cannot beat at backgammon, if I can remember the rules."

AUGUSTUS TWOFEATHERS MCCOY was shown to his room. Professor Mandalay was shown to his room. Jackie Newhouse was shown to his room. This was not a lengthy procedure; they were all in the same room, after all. There was another room in the back where Virginia would sleep, and a third room for Mustapha Stroheim and his family.

"What's that you're writing?" asked Jackie Newhouse.

"It's the procedures, annals, and minutes of the Epicurean Club," said Professor Mandalay. He was writing in a large leather-bound book with a small black pen. "I have chronicled our journey here, and all the things that we have eaten on the way. I shall keep writing as we eat the Sunbird, to record for posterity all the tastes and textures, all the smells and the juices."

"Did Crawcrustle say how he was going to cook the Sunbird?" asked Jackie Newhouse.

"He did," said Augustus TwoFeathers McCoy. "He says that he will drain a beer can, so it is only a third full. And then he will add herbs and spices to the beer can. He will stand the bird up on the can, with the can in its inner cavity, and place it up on the barbecue to roast. He says it is the traditional way."

Jackie Newhouse sniffed. "It sounds suspiciously modern to me."

"Crawcrustle says it is the traditional method of cooking the Sunbird," repeated Augustus.

"Indeed I did," said Crawcrustle, coming up the stairs. It was a small building. The stairs weren't that far away, and the walls were not thick ones. "The oldest beer in the world is Egyptian beer, and they've been cooking the Sunbird with it for over five thousand years now."

"But the beer can is a relatively modern invention," said Professor Mandalay, as Zebediah T. Crawcrustle came through the door. Crawcrustle was holding a cup of Turkish coffee, black as tar, which steamed like a kettle and bubbled like a tarpit.

"That coffee looks pretty hot," said Augustus TwoFeathers McCoy.

Crawcrustle knocked back the cup, draining half the contents. "Nah," he said. "Not really. And the beer can isn't really that new an invention. We used to make them out of an amalgam of copper and tin in the old days, sometimes with a little silver in there, sometimes not. It depended on the smith, and what he had to hand. You needed something that would stand up to the heat. I see that you are all looking at me doubtfully. Gentlemen, consider: of course the Ancient Egyptians made beer cans; where else would they have kept their beer?"

From outside the window, at the tables in the street, came a wailing, in many voices. Virginia Boote had persuaded the locals to start playing backgammon for money, and she was cleaning them out. That woman was a backgammon shark.

OUT BACK OF Mustapha Stroheim's coffeehouse there was a courtyard containing a broken-down old barbecue, made of clay bricks and a half-melted metal grating, and an old wooden table. Crawcrustle spent the next day rebuilding the barbecue and cleaning it, oiling down the metal grille.

"That doesn't look like it's been used in forty years," said Virginia Boote. Nobody would play backgammon with her any longer, and her purse bulged with grubby piasters.

"Something like that," said Crawcrustle. "Maybe a little more. Here, Ginnie, make yourself useful. I've written a list of things I need from the market. It's mostly herbs and spices and wood chips. You can take one of the children of Mustapha Stroheim to translate for you."

"My pleasure, Crusty."

The other three members of the Epicurean Club were occupying themselves in their own way. Jackie Newhouse was making friends with many of the people of the area, who were attracted by his elegant suits and his skill at playing the violin. Augustus TwoFeathers

McCoy went for long walks. Professor Mandalay spent time translating the hieroglyphics he had noticed were incised upon the clay bricks in the barbecue. He said that a foolish man might believe that they proved the barbecue in Mustapha Stroheim's backyard was once sacred to the sun. "But I, who am an intelligent man," he said, "I see immediately that what has happened is that bricks that were once, long ago, part of a temple, have, over the millennia, been reused. I doubt that these people know the value of what they have here."

"Oh, they know all right," said Zebediah T. Crawcrustle. "And these bricks weren't part of any temple. They've been right here for five thousand years, since we built the barbecue. Before that we made do with stones."

Virginia Boote returned with a filled shopping basket. "Here," she said. "Red sandalwood and patchouli, vanilla beans, lavender twigs and sage and cinnamon leaves, whole nutmegs, garlic bulbs, cloves, and rosemary: everything you wanted and more."

Zebediah T. Crawcrustle grinned with delight. "The Sunbird will be so happy," he told her.

He spent the afternoon preparing a barbecue sauce. He said it was only respectful, and besides, the Sunbird's flesh was often slightly on the dry side.

The Epicureans spent that evening sitting at the wicker tables in the street out front, while Mustapha Stroheim and his family brought them tea and coffee and hot mint drinks. Zebediah T. Crawcrustle had told the Epicureans that they would be having the Sunbird of Suntown for Sunday lunch, and that they might wish to avoid food the night before, to ensure that they had an appetite.

"I have a presentiment of doom upon me," said Augustus Two-Feathers McCoy that night, in a bed that was far too small for him, before he slept. "And I fear it shall come to us with barbecue sauce."

THEY WERE ALL so hungry the following morning. Zebediah T. Crawcrustle had a comedic apron on, with the words KISS THE COOK written upon it in violently green letters. He had already sprinkled the brandy-soaked raisins and grain beneath the stunted avocado tree behind the house, and he was arranging the scented woods, the herbs, and the spices on the bed of charcoal. Mustapha Stroheim and his family had gone to visit relatives on the other side of Cairo.

"Does anybody have a match?" Crawcrustle asked.

Jackie Newhouse pulled out a Zippo lighter, and passed it to Crawcrustle, who lit the dried cinnamon leaves and dried laurel leaves beneath the charcoal. The smoke drifted up into the noon air. "The cinnamon and sandalwood smoke will bring the Sunbird," said Crawcrustle.

"Bring it from where?" asked Augustus TwoFeathers McCoy.

"From the sun," said Crawcrustle. "That's where he sleeps."

Professor Mandalay coughed discreetly. He said, "The Earth is, at its closest, 91 million miles from the sun. The fastest dive by a bird ever recorded is that of the peregrine falcon, at 273 miles per hour. Flying at that speed, from the sun, it would take a bird a little over thirty-eight years to reach us—if it could fly through the dark and cold and vacuum of space, of course."

"Of course," agreed Zebediah T. Crawcrustle. He shaded his eyes and squinted and looked upward. "Here it comes," he said.

It looked almost as if the bird was flying out of the sun; but that could not have been the case. You could not look directly at the noonday sun, after all.

First it was a silhouette, black against the sun and against the blue sky, then the sunlight caught its feathers, and the watchers on the ground caught their breath. You have never seen anything like sunlight on the Sunbird's feathers; seeing something like that would take your breath away.

The Sunbird flapped its wide wings once, then it began to glide in ever-decreasing circles in the air above Mustapha Stroheim's coffeehouse.

The bird landed in the avocado tree. Its feathers were golden, and purple, and silver. It was smaller than a turkey, larger than a rooster, and had the long legs and high head of a heron, though its head was more like the head of an eagle.

"It is very beautiful," said Virginia Boote. "Look at the two tall feathers on its head. Aren't they lovely?"

"It is indeed quite lovely," said Professor Mandalay.

"There is something familiar about that bird's headfeathers," said Augustus TwoFeathers McCoy.

"We pluck the headfeathers before we roast the bird," said Zebediah T. Crawcrustle. "It's the way it's always done."

The Sunbird perched on a branch of the avocado tree, in a patch of sun. It seemed almost as if it were glowing, gently, in the sunlight, as if its feathers were made of sunlight, iridescent with purples and greens and golds. It preened itself, extending one wing in the sunlight. It nibbled and stroked at the wing with its beak until all the feathers were in their correct position, and oiled. Then it extended the other wing, and repeated the process. Finally, the bird emitted a contented chirrup, and flew the short distance from the branch to the ground.

It strutted across the dried mud, peering from side to side short-sightedly.

"Look!" said Jackie Newhouse. "It's found the grain."

"It seemed almost that it was looking for it," said Augustus Two-Feathers McCoy. "That it was expecting the grain to be there."

"That's where I always leave it," said Zebediah T. Crawcrustle.

"It's so lovely," said Virginia Boote. "But now I see it closer, I can see that it's much older than I thought. Its eyes are cloudy and its legs are shaking. But it's still lovely."

"The Bennu bird is the loveliest of birds," said Zebediah T. Crawcrustle.

Virginia Boote spoke good restaurant Egyptian, but beyond that she was all at sea. "What's a Bennu bird?" she asked. "Is that Egyptian for Sunbird?"

"The Bennu bird," said Professor Mandalay, "roosts in the Persea tree. It has two feathers on its head. It is sometimes represented as being like a heron, and sometimes like an eagle. There is more, but it is too unlikely to bear repeating."

"It's eaten the grain and the raisins!" exclaimed Jackie Newhouse. "Now it's stumbling drunkenly from side to side—such majesty, even in its drunkenness!"

Zebediah T. Crawcrustle walked over to the Sunbird, which, with a great effort of will, was staggering back and forth on the mud beneath the avocado tree, not tripping over its long legs. He stood directly in front of the bird, and then, very slowly, he bowed to it. He bent like a very old man, slowly and creakily, but still he bowed. And the Sunbird bowed back to him, then it toppled to the mud. Zebediah T. Crawcrustle picked it up reverently, and placed it in his arms, carrying it as one would carry a child, and he took it back to the plot of land behind Mustapha Stroheim's coffeehouse, and the others followed him.

First he plucked the two majestic headfeathers, and set them aside.

And then, without plucking the bird, he gutted it, and placed the guts on the smoking twigs. He put the half-filled beer can inside the body cavity, and placed the bird upon the barbecue.

"Sunbird cooks fast," warned Crawcrustle. "Get your plates ready."

The beers of the ancient Egyptians were flavored with cardamom and coriander, for the Egyptians had no hops; their beers were rich and flavorsome and thirst-quenching. You could build pyramids after drinking that beer, and sometimes people did. On the barbecue the beer steamed the inside of the Sunbird, keeping it moist. As the heat of the charcoal reached them, the feathers of the bird burned off, igniting with a flash like a magnesium flare, so bright that the Epicureans were forced to avert their eyes.

The smell of roast fowl filled the air, richer than peacock, lusher than duck. The mouths of the assembled Epicureans began to water. It seemed like it had been cooking for no time at all, but Zebediah lifted the Sunbird from the charcoal bed and put it on the table. Then, with a carving knife, he sliced it up and placed the steaming meat on the plates. He poured a little barbecue sauce over each piece of meat. He placed the carcass directly onto the flames.

Each member of the Epicurean Club sat in the back of Mustapha Stroheim's coffeehouse, sat around an elderly wooden table, and they ate with their fingers.

"Zebby, this is amazing!" said Virginia Boote, talking as she ate. "It melts in your mouth. It tastes like heaven."

"It tastes like the sun," said Augustus TwoFeathers McCoy, putting his food away as only a big man can. He had a leg in one hand, and some breast in the other. "It is the finest thing I have ever eaten, and I do not regret eating it, but I do believe that I shall miss my daughter."

"It is perfect," said Jackie Newhouse. "It tastes like love and fine music. It tastes like truth."

Professor Mandalay was scribbling in the bound annals of the Epicurean Club. He was recording his reaction to the meat of the bird, and recording the reactions of the other Epicureans, and trying not to drip on the page while he wrote, for with the hand that was not writing he was holding a wing, and, fastidiously, he was nibbling the meat off it.

"It is strange," said Jackie Newhouse, "for as I eat it, it gets hotter and hotter in my mouth and in my stomach."

"Yup. It'll do that. It's best to prepare for it ahead of time," said Zebediah T. Crawcrustle. "Eat coals and flames and lightning bugs to get used to it. Otherwise it can be a trifle hard on the system."

Zebediah T. Crawcrustle was eating the head of the bird, crunching its bones and beak in his mouth. As he ate, the bones sparked small lightnings against his teeth. He just grinned and chewed the more.

The bones of the Sunbird's carcass burned orange on the barbecue, and then they began to burn white. There was a thick heat-haze in the courtyard at the back of Mustapha Stroheim's coffeehouse, and in it everything shimmered, as if the people around the table were seeing the world through water or a dream.

"It is so good!" said Virginia Boote as she ate. "It is the best thing I have ever eaten. It tastes like my youth. It tastes like forever." She licked her fingers, then picked up the last slice of meat from her plate. "The Sunbird of Suntown," she said. "Does it have another name?"

"It is the Phoenix of Heliopolis," said Zebediah T. Crawcrustle. "It is the bird that dies in ashes and flame, and is reborn, generation after generation. It is the Bennu bird, which flew across the waters when all was dark. When its time is come it is burned on the fire of rare woods and spices and herbs, and in the ashes it is reborn, time after time, world without end."

"Fire!" exclaimed Professor Mandalay. "It feels as if my insides are burning up!" He sipped his water, but seemed no happier.

"My fingers," said Virginia Boote. "Look at my fingers." She held them up. They were glowing inside, as if lit with inner flames.

Now the air was so hot you could have baked an egg in it.

There was a spark and a sputter. The two yellow feathers in Augustus TwoFeathers McCoy's hair went up like sparklers. "Crawcrustle," said Jackie Newhouse, aflame, "answer me truly. How long have you been eating the Phoenix?"

"A little over ten thousand years," said Zebediah. "Give or take a few thousand. It's not hard, once you master the trick of it; it's just mastering the trick of it that's hard. But this is the best Phoenix I've ever prepared. Or do I mean, 'this is the best I've ever cooked this Phoenix'?"

"The years!" said Virginia Boote. "They are burning off you!"

"They do that," admitted Zebediah. "You've got to get used to the heat, though, before you eat it. Otherwise you can just burn away."

"Why did I not remember this?" said Augustus TwoFeathers McCoy, through the bright flames that surrounded him. "Why did I not remember that this was how my father went, and his father before him, that each of them went to Heliopolis to eat the Phoenix? And why do I only remember it now?"

"Because the years are burning off you," said Professor Mandalay. He had closed the leather book as soon as the page he had been writing on caught fire. The edges of the book were charred, but the rest of the book would be fine. "When the years burn, the memories of those years come back." He looked more solid now, through the wavering burning air, and he was smiling. None of them had ever seen Professor Mandalay smile before.

"Shall we burn away to nothing?" asked Virginia, now incandescent. "Or shall we burn back to childhood and burn back to ghosts and angels and then come forward again? It does not matter. Oh Crusty, this is all such *fun!*"

"Perhaps," said Jackie Newhouse, through the fire, "there might have been a little more vinegar in the sauce. I feel a meat like this could have dealt with something more robust." And then he was gone, leaving only an afterimage.

"*Chacun à son goût,*" said Zebediah T. Crawcrustle, which is French for "each to his own taste," and he licked his fingers and he shook his head. "Best it's ever been," he said, with enormous satisfaction.

"Good-bye, Crusty," said Virginia. She put her flame-white hand out, and held his dark hand tightly, for one moment, or perhaps for two.

And then there was nothing in the courtyard back of Mustapha Stroheim's *kahwa* (or coffeehouse) in Heliopolis (which was once the city of the sun, and is now a suburb of Cairo) but white ash, which blew up in the momentary breeze, and settled like powdered sugar or like snow; and nobody there but a young man with dark, dark hair and even, ivory-colored teeth, wearing an apron that said KISS THE COOK.

A tiny golden-purple bird stirred in the thick bed of ashes on top of the clay bricks, as if it were waking for the first time. It made a high-pitched "peep!" and it looked directly into the sun, as an infant looks at a parent. It stretched its wings as if to dry them, and, eventually, when it was quite ready, it flew upward, toward the sun, and nobody watched it leave but the young man in the courtyard.

There were two long golden feathers at the young man's feet, beneath the ash that had once been a wooden table, and he gathered them up, and brushed the white ash from them and placed them, reverently, inside his jacket. Then he removed his apron, and he went upon his way.

HOLLYBERRY TWOFEATHERS MCCOY is a grown woman, with children of her own. There are silver hairs on her head, in there with the black, beneath the golden feathers in the bun at the back. You can see that once the feathers must have looked pretty special, but that would have been a long time ago. She is the president of the Epicurean Club—a rich and rowdy bunch—having inherited the position, many long years ago, from her father.

I hear that the Epicureans are beginning to grumble once again. They are saying that they have eaten everything.

(FOR HMG—A BELATED BIRTHDAY PRESENT)

HOW TO TALK TO
GIRLS AT PARTIES

2006

COME ON," SAID Vic. "It'll be great."

"No, it won't," I said, although I'd lost this fight hours ago, and I knew it.

"It'll be brilliant," said Vic, for the hundredth time. "Girls! Girls! Girls!" He grinned with white teeth.

We both attended an all-boys' school in south London. While it would be a lie to say that we had no experience with girls—Vic seemed to have had many girlfriends, while I had kissed three of my sister's friends—it would, I think, be perfectly true to say that we both chiefly spoke to, interacted with, and only truly understood, other boys. Well, I did, anyway. It's hard to speak for someone else, and I've not seen Vic for thirty years. I'm not sure that I would know what to say to him now if I did.

We were walking the back streets that used to twine in a grimy maze behind East Croydon station—a friend had told Vic about a party, and Vic was determined to go whether I liked it or not, and I didn't. But my parents were away that week at a conference, and I was Vic's guest at his house, so I was trailing along beside him.

"It'll be the same as it always is," I said. "After an hour you'll be off somewhere snogging the prettiest girl at the party, and I'll be in the kitchen listening to somebody's mum going on about politics or poetry or something."

"You just have to *talk* to them," he said. "I think it's probably that road at the end here." He gestured cheerfully, swinging the bag with the bottle in it.

"Don't you know?"

"Alison gave me directions and I wrote them on a bit of paper, but I left it on the hall table. S'okay. I can find it."

"How?" Hope welled slowly up inside me.

"We walk down the road," he said, as if speaking to an idiot child. "And we look for the party. Easy."

I looked, but saw no party: just narrow houses with rusting cars or bikes in their concreted front gardens; and the dusty glass fronts of newsagents, which smelled of alien spices and sold everything from birthday cards and secondhand comics to the kind of magazines that were so pornographic that they were sold already sealed in plastic bags. I had been there when Vic had slipped one of those magazines beneath his sweater, but the owner caught him on the pavement outside and made him give it back.

We reached the end of the road and turned into a narrow street of terraced houses. Everything looked very still and empty in the summer's evening. "It's all right for you," I said. "They fancy you. You don't actually *have* to talk to them." It was true: one urchin grin from Vic and he could have his pick of the room.

"Nah. S'not like that. You've just got to talk."

The times I had kissed my sister's friends I had not spoken to them. They had been around while my sister was off doing something elsewhere, and they had drifted into my orbit, and so I had kissed them. I do not remember any talking. I did not know what to say to girls, and I told him so.

"They're just girls," said Vic. "They don't come from another planet."

As we followed the curve of the road around, my hopes that the party would prove unfindable began to fade: a low pulsing noise, music muffled by walls and doors, could be heard from a house up ahead. It was eight in the evening, not that early if you aren't yet six-teen, and we weren't. Not quite.

I had parents who liked to know where I was, but I don't think Vic's parents cared that much. He was the youngest of five boys. That in itself seemed magical to me: I merely had two sisters, both younger than I was, and I felt both unique and lonely. I had wanted a brother as far back as I could remember. When I turned thirteen, I stopped wishing on falling stars or first stars, but back when I did, a brother was what I had wished for.

We went up the garden path, crazy paving leading us past a hedge and a solitary rosebush to a pebble-dashed facade. We rang the door-bell, and the door was opened by a girl. I could not have told you how old she was, which was one of the things about girls I had be-gun to hate: when you start out as kids you're just boys and girls, going through time at the same speed, and you're all five, or seven, or eleven, together. And then one day there's a lurch and the girls just sort of sprint off into the future ahead of you, and they know all about everything, and they have periods and breasts and makeup and God-only-knew-what-else—for I certainly didn't. The diagrams in biology textbooks were no substitute for being, in a very real sense, young adults. And the girls of our age were.

Vic and I weren't young adults, and I was beginning to suspect that even when I started needing to shave every day, instead of once every couple of weeks, I would still be way behind.

The girl said, "Hello?"

Vic said, "We're friends of Alison's." We had met Alison, all freck-les and orange hair and a wicked smile, in Hamburg, on a German exchange. The exchange organizers had sent some girls with us, from a local girls' school, to balance the sexes. The girls, our age, more or less, were raucous and funny, and had more or less adult boyfriends with cars and jobs and motorbikes and—in the case of one girl with crooked teeth and a raccoon coat, who spoke to me about it sadly at the end of a party in Hamburg, in, of course, the kitchen—a wife and kids.

"She isn't here," said the girl at the door. "No Alison."

"Not to worry," said Vic, with an easy grin. "I'm Vic. This is Enn." A beat, and then the girl smiled back at him. Vic had a bottle of white wine in a plastic bag, removed from his parents' kitchen cabinet. "Where should I put this, then?"

She stood out of the way, letting us enter. "There's a kitchen in the back," she said. "Put it on the table there, with the other bottles." She had golden, wavy hair, and she was very beautiful. The hall was dim in the twilight, but I could see that she was beautiful.

"What's your name, then?" said Vic.

She told him it was Stella, and he grinned his crooked white grin and told her that that had to be the prettiest name he had ever heard. Smooth bastard. And what was worse was that he said it like he meant it.

Vic headed back to drop off the wine in the kitchen, and I looked into the front room, where the music was coming from. There were people dancing in there. Stella walked in, and she started to dance, swaying to the music all alone, and I watched her.

This was during the early days of punk. On our own record players we would play the Adverts and the Jam, the Stranglers and the Clash and the Sex Pistols. At other people's parties you'd hear ELO or 10cc or even Roxy Music. Maybe some Bowie, if you were lucky. During the German exchange, the only LP that we had all been able to agree on was Neil Young's *Harvest,* and his song "Heart of Gold" had threaded through the trip like a refrain: *I crossed the ocean for a heart of gold. . . .*

The music playing in that front room wasn't anything I recognized.

It sounded a bit like a German electronic pop group called Kraftwerk, and a bit like an LP I'd been given for my last birthday, of strange sounds made by the BBC Radiophonic Workshop. The music had a beat, though, and the half-dozen girls in that room were moving gently to it, although I only looked at Stella. She shone.

Vic pushed past me, into the room. He was holding a can of lager. "There's booze back in the kitchen," he told me. He wandered over to Stella and he began to talk to her. I couldn't hear what they were saying over the music, but I knew that there was no room for me in that conversation.

I didn't like beer, not back then. I went off to see if there was something I wanted to drink. On the kitchen table stood a large bottle of Coca-Cola, and I poured myself a plastic tumblerful, and I didn't dare say anything to the pair of girls who were talking in the under-lit kitchen. They were animated and utterly lovely. Each of them had very black skin and glossy hair and movie star clothes, and their accents were foreign, and each of them was out of my league.

I wandered, Coke in hand.

The house was deeper than it looked, larger and more complex than the two-up two-down model I had imagined. The rooms were underlit—I doubt there was a bulb of more than 40 watts in the building—and each room I went into was inhabited: in my memory, inhabited only by girls. I did not go upstairs.

A girl was the only occupant of the conservatory. Her hair was so fair it was white, and long, and straight, and she sat at the glass-topped table, her hands clasped together, staring at the garden outside, and the gathering dusk. She seemed wistful.

"Do you mind if I sit here?" I asked, gesturing with my cup. She shook her head, and then followed it up with a shrug, to indicate that it was all the same to her. I sat down.

Vic walked past the conservatory door. He was talking to Stella, but he looked in at me, sitting at the table, wrapped in shyness and awkwardness, and he opened and closed his hand in a parody of a speaking mouth. *Talk*. Right.

"Are you from around here?" I asked the girl.

She shook her head. She wore a low-cut silvery top, and I tried not to stare at the swell of her breasts.

I said, "What's your name? I'm Enn."

"Wain's Wain," she said, or something that sounded like it. "I'm a second."

"That's uh. That's a different name."

She fixed me with huge, liquid eyes. "It indicates that my progenitor was also Wain, and that I am obliged to report back to her. I may not breed."

"Ah. Well. Bit early for that anyway, isn't it?"

She unclasped her hands, raised them above the table, spread her fingers. "You see?" The little finger on her left hand was crooked, and it bifurcated at the top, splitting into two smaller fingertips. A minor deformity. "When I was finished a decision was needed. Would I be retained, or eliminated? I was fortunate that the decision was with me. Now, I travel, while my more perfect sisters remain at home in stasis. They were firsts. I am a second.

"Soon I must return to Wain, and tell her all I have seen. All my impressions of this place of yours."

"I don't actually live in Croydon," I said. "I don't come from here." I wondered if she was American. I had no idea what she was talking about.

"As you say," she agreed, "neither of us comes from here." She folded her six-fingered left hand beneath her right, as if tucking it out of sight. "I had expected it to be bigger, and cleaner, and more colorful. But still, it is a jewel."

She yawned, covered her mouth with her right hand, only for a moment, before it was back on the table again. "I grow weary of the journeying, and I wish sometimes that it would end. On a street in Río, at Carnival, I saw them on a bridge, golden and tall and insect-eyed and winged, and elated I almost ran to greet them, before I saw that they were only people in costumes. I said to Hola Colt, 'Why do they try so hard to look like us?' and Hola Colt replied, 'Because they hate themselves, all shades of pink and brown, and so small.' It is what I experience, even me, and I am not grown. It is like a world of children, or of elves." Then she smiled, and said, "It was a good thing they could not any of them see Hola Colt."

"Um," I said, "do you want to dance?"

She shook her head immediately. "It is not permitted," she said. "I can do nothing that might cause damage to property. I am Wain's."

"Would you like something to drink, then?"

"Water," she said.

I went back to the kitchen and poured myself another Coke, and filled a cup with water from the tap. From the kitchen back to the hall, and from there into the conservatory, but now it was quite empty.

I wondered if the girl had gone to the toilet, and if she might change her mind about dancing later. I walked back to the front room and stared in. The place was filling up. There were more girls dancing, and several lads I didn't know, who looked a few years older than me and Vic. The lads and the girls all kept their distance, but Vic was holding Stella's hand as they danced, and when the song ended he put an arm around her, casually, almost proprietorially, to make sure that nobody else cut in.

I wondered if the girl I had been talking to in the conservatory was now upstairs, as she did not appear to be on the ground floor.

I walked into the living room, which was across the hall from the room where the people were dancing, and I sat down on the sofa. There was a girl sitting there already. She had dark hair, cut short and spiky, and a nervous manner.

Talk, I thought. "Um, this mug of water's going spare," I told her, "if you want it?"

She nodded, and reached out her hand and took the mug, extremely carefully, as if she were unused to taking things, as if she could trust neither her vision nor her hands.

"I love being a tourist," she said, and smiled hesitantly. She had a gap between her two front teeth, and she sipped the tap water as if she were an adult sipping a fine wine. "The last tour, we went to sun, and we swam in sunfire pools with the whales. We heard their histories and we shivered in the chill of the outer places, then we swam deepward where the heat churned and comforted us.

"I wanted to go back. This time, I wanted it. There was so much I had not seen. Instead we came to world. Do you like it?"

"Like what?"

She gestured vaguely to the room—the sofa, the armchairs, the curtains, the unused gas fire.

"It's all right, I suppose."

"I told them I did not wish to visit world," she said. "My parent-teacher was unimpressed. 'You will have much to learn,' it told me. I said, 'I could learn more in sun, again. Or in the deeps. Jessa spun webs between galaxies. I want to do that.'

"But there was no reasoning with it, and I came to world. Parent-teacher engulfed me, and I was here, embodied in a decaying lump of meat hanging on a frame of calcium. As I incarnated I felt things deep inside me, fluttering and pumping and squishing. It was my first experience with pushing air through the mouth, vibrating the vocal cords on the way, and I used it to tell parent-teacher that I wished that I would die, which it acknowledged was the inevitable exit strategy from world."

There were black worry beads wrapped around her wrist, and she fiddled with them as she spoke. "But knowledge is there, in the meat," she said, "and I am resolved to learn from it."

We were sitting close at the center of the sofa now. I decided I should put an arm around her, but casually. I would extend my arm along the back of the sofa and eventually sort of creep it down, almost imperceptibly, until it was touching her. She said, "The thing with the liquid in the eyes, when the world blurs. Nobody told me, and I still do not understand. I have touched the folds of the Whisper and pulsed and flown with the tachyon swans, and I still do not understand."

She wasn't the prettiest girl there, but she seemed nice enough, and she was a girl, anyway. I let my arm slide down a little, tentatively, so that it made contact with her back, and she did not tell me to take it away.

Vic called to me then, from the doorway. He was standing with his arm around Stella, protectively, waving at me. I tried to let him know, by shaking my head, that I was onto something, but he called my name and, reluctantly, I got up from the sofa and walked over to the door. "What?"

"Er. Look. The party," said Vic, apologetically. "It's not the one I thought it was. I've been talking to Stella and I figured it out. Well, she sort of explained it to me. We're at a different party."

"Christ. Are we in trouble? Do we have to go?"

Stella shook her head. He leaned down and kissed her, gently, on the lips. "You're just happy to have me here, aren't you darlin'?"

"You know I am," she told him.

He looked from her back to me, and he smiled his white smile: roguish, lovable, a little bit Artful Dodger, a little bit wide-boy Prince Charming. "Don't worry. They're all tourists here anyway. It's a foreign exchange thing, innit? Like when we all went to Germany."

"It is?"

"Enn. You got to *talk* to them. And that means you got to listen to them, too. You understand?"

"I *did*. I already talked to a couple of them."

"You getting anywhere?"

"I was till you called me over."

"Sorry about that. Look, I just wanted to fill you in. Right?"

And he patted my arm and he walked away with Stella. Then, together, the two of them went up the stairs.

Understand me, all the girls at that party, in the twilight, were lovely; they all had perfect faces but, more important than that, they had whatever strangeness of proportion, of oddness or humanity, it is that makes a beauty something more than a shop window dummy. Stella was the most lovely of any of them, but she, of course, was Vic's, and they were going upstairs together, and that was just how things would always be.

There were several people now sitting on the sofa, talking to the gap-toothed girl. Someone told a joke, and they all laughed. I would have had to push my way in there to sit next to her again, and it didn't look like she was expecting me back, or cared that I had gone, so I wandered out into the hall. I glanced in at the dancers, and found myself wondering where the music was coming from. I couldn't see a record player or speakers.

From the hall I walked back to the kitchen.

Kitchens are good at parties. You never need an excuse to be there, and, on the good side, at this party I couldn't see any signs of some-one's mum. I inspected the various bottles and cans on the kitchen table, then I poured a half an inch of Pernod into the bottom of my plastic cup, which I filled to the top with Coke. I dropped in a couple of ice cubes and took a sip, relishing the sweet-shop tang of the drink.

"What's that you're drinking?" A girl's voice.

"It's Pernod," I told her. "It tastes like aniseed balls, only it's alco-holic." I didn't say that I only tried it because I'd heard someone in the crowd ask for a Pernod on a live Velvet Underground LP.

"Can I have one?" I poured another Pernod, topped it off with Coke, passed it to her. Her hair was a coppery auburn, and it tumbled around her head in ringlets. It's not a hairstyle you see much now, but you saw it a lot back then.

"What's your name?" I asked.

"Triolet," she said.

"Pretty name," I told her, although I wasn't sure that it was. She was pretty, though.

"It's a verse form," she said, proudly. "Like me."

"You're a poem?"

She smiled, and looked down and away, perhaps bashfully. Her profile was almost flat—a perfect Grecian nose that came down from her forehead in a straight line. We did *Antigone* in the school theater the previous year. I was the messenger who brings Creon the news of Antigone's death. We wore half-masks that made us look like that. I thought of that play, looking at her face, in the kitchen, and I thought of Barry Smith's drawings of women in the *Conan* comics: five years later I would have thought of the Pre-Raphaelites, of Jane Morris and Lizzie Siddall. But I was only fifteen then.

"You're a poem?" I repeated.

She chewed her lower lip. "If you want. I am a poem, or I am a pattern, or a race of people whose world was swallowed by the sea."

"Isn't it hard to be three things at the same time?"

"What's your name?"

"Enn."

"So you are Enn," she said. "And you are a male. And you are a biped. Is it hard to be three things at the same time?"

"But they aren't different things. I mean, they aren't contradictory." It was a word I had read many times but never said aloud before that night, and I put the stresses in the wrong places. *Contradictory.*

She wore a thin dress made of a white, silky fabric. Her eyes were a pale green, a color that would now make me think of tinted contact lenses; but this was thirty years ago; things were different then. I remember wondering about Vic and Stella, upstairs. By now, I was sure that they were in one of the bedrooms, and I envied Vic so much it almost hurt.

Still, I was talking to this girl, even if we were talking nonsense, even if her name wasn't really Triolet (my generation had not been

given hippie names: all the Rainbows and the Sunshines and the Moons, they were only six, seven, eight years old back then). She said, "We knew that it would soon be over, and so we put it all into a poem, to tell the universe who we were, and why we were here, and what we said and did and thought and dreamed and yearned for. We wrapped our dreams in words and patterned the words so that they would live forever, unforgettable. Then we sent the poem as a pattern of flux, to wait in the heart of a star, beaming out its message in pulses and bursts and fuzzes across the electromagnetic spectrum, until the time when, on worlds a thousand sun systems distant, the pattern would be decoded and read, and it would become a poem once again."

"And then what happened?"

She looked at me with her green eyes, and it was as if she stared out at me from her own Antigone half-mask; but as if her pale green eyes were just a different, deeper, part of the mask. "You cannot hear a poem without it changing you," she told me. "They heard it, and it colonized them. It inherited them and it inhabited them, its rhythms becoming part of the way that they thought; its images permanently transmuting their metaphors; its verses, its outlook, its aspirations becoming their lives. Within a generation their children would be born already knowing the poem, and, sooner rather than later, as these things go, there were no more children born. There was no need for them, not any longer. There was only a poem, which took flesh and walked and spread itself across the vastness of the known."

I edged closer to her, so I could feel my leg pressing against hers. She seemed to welcome it: she put her hand on my arm, affectionately, and I felt a smile spreading across my face.

"There are places that we are welcomed," said Triolet, "and places where we are regarded as a noxious weed, or as a disease, something immediately to be quarantined and eliminated. But where does contagion end and art begin?"

"I don't know," I said, still smiling. I could hear the unfamiliar music as it pulsed and scattered and boomed in the front room.

She leaned into me then and—I suppose it was a kiss . . . I sup-

pose. She pressed her lips to my lips, anyway, and then, satisfied, she pulled back, as if she had now marked me as her own.

"Would you like to hear it?" she asked, and I nodded, unsure what she was offering me, but certain that I needed anything she was willing to give me.

She began to whisper something in my ear. It's the strangest thing about poetry—you can tell it's poetry, even if you don't speak the language. You can hear Homer's Greek without understanding a word, and you still know it's poetry. I've heard Polish poetry, and Inuit poetry, and I knew what it was without knowing. Her whisper was like that. I didn't know the language, but her words washed through me, perfect, and in my mind's eye I saw towers of glass and diamond; and people with eyes of the palest green; and, unstoppable, beneath every syllable, I could feel the relentless advance of the ocean.

Perhaps I kissed her properly. I don't remember. I know I wanted to.

And then Vic was shaking me violently. "Come on!" he was shouting. "Quickly. Come on!"

In my head I began to come back from a thousand miles away. "Idiot. Come on. Just get a move on," he said, and he swore at me. There was fury in his voice.

For the first time that evening I recognized one of the songs being played in the front room. A sad saxophone wail followed by a cascade of liquid chords, a man's voice singing cut-up lyrics about the sons of the silent age. I wanted to stay and hear the song.

She said, "I am not finished. There is yet more of me."

"Sorry love," said Vic, but he wasn't smiling any longer. "There'll be another time," and he grabbed me by the elbow and he twisted and pulled, forcing me from the room. I did not resist. I knew from experience that Vic could beat the stuffing out me if he got it into his head to do so. He wouldn't do it unless he was upset or angry, but he was angry now.

Out into the front hall. As Vic pulled open the door, I looked back one last time, over my shoulder, hoping to see Triolet in the doorway to the kitchen, but she was not there. I saw Stella, though, at the top of the stairs. She was staring down at Vic, and I saw her face.

This all happened thirty years ago. I have forgotten much, and

I will forget more, and in the end I will forget everything; yet, if I have any certainty of life beyond death, it is all wrapped up not in psalms or hymns, but in this one thing alone: I cannot believe that I will ever forget that moment, or forget the expression on Stella's face as she watched Vic hurrying away from her. Even in death I shall remember that.

Her clothes were in disarray, and there was makeup smudged across her face, and her eyes—

You wouldn't want to make a universe angry. I bet an angry universe would look at you with eyes like that.

We ran then, me and Vic, away from the party and the tourists and the twilight, ran as if a lightning storm was on our heels, a mad helter-skelter dash down the confusion of streets, threading through the maze, and we did not look back, and we did not stop until we could not breathe; and then we stopped and panted, unable to run any longer. We were in pain. I held on to a wall, and Vic threw up, hard and long, into the gutter.

He wiped his mouth.

"She wasn't a—" He stopped.

He shook his head.

Then he said, "You know . . . I think there's a thing. When you've gone as far as you dare. And if you go any further, you wouldn't be *you* anymore? You'd be the person who'd done *that*? The places you just can't go . . . I think that happened to me tonight."

I thought I knew what he was saying. "Screw her, you mean?" I said.

He rammed a knuckle hard against my temple, and twisted it violently. I wondered if I was going to have to fight him—and lose—but after a moment he lowered his hand and moved away from me, making a low, gulping noise.

I looked at him curiously, and I realized that he was crying: his face was scarlet; snot and tears ran down his cheeks. Vic was sobbing in the street, as unselfconsciously and heartbreakingly as a little boy. He walked away from me then, shoulders heaving, and he hurried down the road so he was in front of me and I could no longer see his face. I wondered what had occurred in that upstairs room to make him behave like that, to scare him so, and I could not even begin to guess.

The streetlights came on, one by one; Vic stumbled on ahead, while I trudged down the street behind him in the dusk, my feet treading out the measure of a poem that, try as I might, I could not properly remember and would never be able to repeat.

FEMININE ENDINGS

2007

MY DARLING,

Let us begin this letter, this prelude to an encounter, formally, as a declaration, in the old-fashioned way: I love you. You do not know me (although you have seen me, smiled at me, placed coins in the palm of my hand). I know you (although not so well as I would like. I want to be there when your eyes flutter open in the morning, and you see me, and you smile. Surely this would be paradise enough?). So I do declare myself to you now, with pen set to paper. I declare it again: I love you.

I write this in English, your language, a language I also speak. My English is good. I was some years ago in England and in Scotland. I spent a whole summer standing in Covent Garden, except for the month of Edinburgh Festival, when I am in Edinburgh. People who put money in my box in Edinburgh included Mr. Kevin Spacey the actor, and Mr. Jerry Springer the American television star, who was in Edinburgh for an opera about his life.

I have put off writing this for so long, although I have wanted to, although I have composed it many times in my head. Shall I write about you? About me?

First you.

I love your hair, long and red. The first time I saw you I believed you to be a dancer, and I still believe that you have a dancer's body.

The legs, and the posture, head up and back. It was your smile that told me you were a foreigner, before ever I heard you speak. In my country we smile in bursts, like the sun coming out and illuminating the fields and then retreating again behind a cloud too soon. Smiles are valuable here, and rare. But you smiled all the time, as if everything you saw delighted you. You smiled the first time you saw me, even wider than before. You smiled and I was lost, like a small child in a great forest never to find its way home again.

I learned when young that the eyes give too much away. Some in my profession adopt dark spectacles, or even (and these I scorn with bitter laughter as amateurs) masks that cover the whole face. What good is a mask? My solution is that of full-sclera theatrical contact lenses, purchased from an American website for a little under five hundred euro, which cover the whole eye. They are dark gray, of course, and look like stone. They have made me more than five hundred euro, paid for themselves over and over. You may think, given my profession, that I must be poor, but you would be wrong. Indeed, I fancy that you must be surprised by how much I have collected. My needs have been small and my earnings always very good.

Except when it rains.

Sometimes even when it rains. The others as perhaps you have observed, my love, retreat when it rains, put up the umbrellas, run away. I remain where I am. Always. I simply wait, unmoving. It all adds to the conviction of the performance.

And it is a performance, as much as when I was a theatrical actor, a magician's assistant, even when I myself was a dancer. (That is how I am so familiar with the bodies of dancers.) Always, I was aware of the audience as individuals. I have found this with all actors and all dancers, except the shortsighted ones for whom the audience is a blur. My eyesight is good, even through the contact lenses.

"Did you see the man with the moustache in the third row?" we would say. "He is staring at Minou with lustful glances."

And Minou would reply, "Ah yes. But the woman on the aisle, who looks like the German chancellor, she is now fighting to stay awake." If one person falls asleep, you can lose the whole audience, so we would play the rest of the evening to a middle-aged woman who wished only to succumb to drowsiness.

The second time you stood near me you were so close I could smell your shampoo. It smelled like flowers and fruit. I imagine America as being a whole continent full of women who smell of flowers and fruit. You were talking to a young man from the university. You were complaining about the difficulties of our language for an American. "I understand what gives a man or a woman gender," you were saying. "But what makes a chair masculine or a pigeon feminine? Why should a statue have a feminine ending?"

The young man, he laughed and pointed straight at me then. But truly, if you are walking through the square, you can tell nothing about me. The robes look like old marble, water-stained and time-worn and lichened. The skin could be granite. Until I move I am stone and old bronze, and I do not move if I do not want to. I simply stand. Some people wait in the square for much too long, even in the rain, to see what I will do. They are uncomfortable not knowing, only happy once they have assured themselves that I am a natural, not an artificial. It is the uncertainty that traps people, like a mouse in a glue trap.

I am writing about myself perhaps too much. I know that this is a letter of introduction as much as it is a love letter. I should write about you. Your smile. Your eyes so green. (You do not know the true color of my eyes. I will tell you. They are brown.) You like classical music, but you have also ABBA and Kid Loco on your iPod Nano. You wear no perfume. Your underwear is, for the most part, faded and comfortable, although you have a single set of red-lace brassiere and panties which you wear for special occasions.

People watch me in the square, but the eye is only attracted by motion. I have perfected the tiny movement, so tiny that the passer can scarcely tell if it is something he saw or not. Yes? Too often people will not see what does not move. The eyes see it but do not see it, they discount it. I am human-shaped, but I am not human. So in order to make them see me, to make them look at me, to stop their eyes from sliding off me and paying me no attention, I am forced to make the tiniest motions, to draw their eyes to me. Then, and only then, do they see me. But they do not always know what they have seen.

I think of you as a code to be broken, or as a puzzle to be cracked. Or a jigsaw puzzle, to be put together. I walk through your life, and I stand motionless at the edge of my own. My gestures—statuesque, precise—are too often misinterpreted. I want you. I do not doubt this.

You have a younger sister. She has a MySpace account, and a Facebook account. We talk sometimes on messenger. All too often people assume that a medieval statue exists only in the fifteenth century. This is not so true: I have a room, I have a laptop. My computer is passworded. I practice safe computing. Your password is your first name. That is not safe. Anyone could read your email, look at your photographs, reconstruct your interests from your web history. Someone who was interested and who cared could spend endless hours building up a complex schematic of your life, matching the people in the photographs to the names in the emails, for example. It would not be hard reconstructing a life from a computer, or from cell phone messages. It would be like filling a crossword puzzle.

I remember when I actually admitted to myself that you had taken to watching me, and only me, on your way across the square. You paused. You admired me. You saw me move once, for a child, and you told a woman with you, loud enough to be heard, that I might be a real statue. I take it as the highest compliment. I have many different styles of movement, of course—I can move like clockwork, in a set of tiny jerks and stutters, I can move like a robot or an automaton. I can move like a statue coming to life after hundreds of years of being stone.

Within my hearing you have spoken many times of the beauty of this small city. How, for you, to be standing inside the stained-glass confection of the old church was like being imprisoned inside a kaleidoscope of jewels. It was like being in the heart of the sun. Also, you are concerned about your mother's illness.

When you were an undergraduate you worked as a cook, and your fingertips are covered with the scar-marks of a thousand tiny knife-cuts.

I love you, and it is my love for you that drives me to know all about you. The more I know the closer I am to you. You were to come to my country with a young man, but he broke your heart, and still you came here to spite him, and still you smiled. I close my eyes and I can see you smiling. I close my eyes and I see you striding across the town square in a clatter of pigeons. The women of this country do not stride. They move diffidently, unless they are dancers. And when you sleep your eyelashes flutter. The way your cheek touches the pillow. The way you dream.

I dream of dragons. When I was a small child, at the home, they told me that there was a dragon beneath the old city. I pictured the dragon wreathing like black smoke beneath the buildings, inhabiting the cracks between the cellars, insubstantial and yet always present. That is how I think of the dragon, and how I think of the past, now. A black dragon made of smoke. When I perform I have been eaten by the dragon and have become part of the past. I am, truly, seven hundred years old. Kings come and kings go. Armies arrive and are absorbed or return home again, leaving only damaged buildings, widows and bastard children behind them, but the statues remain, and the dragon of smoke, and the past.

I say this, although the statue that I emulate is not from this town at all. It stands in front of a church in southern Italy, where it is believed to represent either the sister of John the Baptist, or a local lord who endowed the church to celebrate that he had not died of the plague, or the angel of death.

I had imagined you perfectly pure, my love, pure as I am, yet one time I found that the red lace panties were pushed to the bottom of your laundry hamper, and upon close examination I was able to assure myself that you had, unquestionably, been unchaste the previous evening. Only you know who with, for you did not talk of the incident in your letters home, or allude to it in your online journal.

A small girl looked up at me once, and turned to her mother, and said, "Why is she so unhappy?" (I translate into English for you, obviously. The girl was referring to me as a statue and thus she used the feminine ending.)

"Why do you believe her to be unhappy?"

"Why else would people make themselves into statues?"

Her mother smiled. "Perhaps she is unhappy in love," she said.

I was not unhappy in love. I was prepared to wait until everything was right, something very different.

There is time. There is always time. It is the gift I took from being a statue—one of the gifts, I should say.

You have walked past me and looked at me and smiled, and you have walked past me and other times you barely noticed me as anything other than an object. Truly, it is remarkable how little regard you, or any human, gives to something that remains completely motionless. You have woken in the night, got up, walked to the little toilet, micturated, walked back to your bed, slept once more, peacefully. You would not notice something perfectly still, would you? Something in the shadows?

If I could I would have made the paper for this letter for you out of my body. I thought about mixing in with the ink my blood or spittle, but no. There is such a thing as overstatement, yet great loves demand grand gestures, yes? I am unused to grand gestures. I am more practiced in the tiny gestures. I made a small boy scream once, simply by smiling at him when he had convinced himself that I was made of marble. It is the smallest of gestures that will never be forgotten.

I love you, I want you, I need you. I am yours just as you are mine. There. I have declared my love for you.

Soon, I hope, you will know this for yourself. And then we will never part. It will be time, in a moment, to turn around, put down the letter. I am with you, even now, in these old apartments with the Iranian carpets on the walls.

You have walked past me too many times.

No more.

I am here with you. I am here now.

When you put down this letter. When you turn and look across this old room, your eyes sweeping it with relief or with joy or even with terror . . .

Then I will move. Move, just a fraction. And, finally, you will see me.

ORANGE

2008

(Third Subject's Responses to Investigator's Written Questionnaire.)

EYES ONLY.

1. Jemima Glorfindel Petula Ramsey.

2. Seventeen on June the ninth.

3. The last five years. Before that we lived in Glasgow (Scotland). Before that, Cardiff (Wales).

4. I don't know. I think he's in magazine publishing now. He doesn't talk to us anymore. The divorce was pretty bad and Mum wound up paying him a lot of money. Which seems sort of wrong to me. But maybe it was worth it just to get shot of him.

5. An inventor and entrepreneur. She invented the Stuffed Muffin™, and started the Stuffed Muffin chain. I used to like them when I was a kid, but you can get kind of sick of stuffed muffins for every meal, especially because Mum used us as guinea pigs. The Complete Turkey Dinner Christmas Stuffed Muffin was the worst. But she sold out her interest in the Stuffed Muffin chain about five years

ago, to start work on My Mum's Colored Bubbles (not actually ™ yet).

6. Two. My sister, Nerys, who was just fifteen, and my brother, Pryderi, twelve.

7. Several times a day.

8. No.

9. Through the Internet. Probably on eBay.

10. She's been buying colors and dyes from all over the world ever since she decided that the world was crying out for brightly colored Day-Glo bubbles. The kind you can blow, with bubble mixture.

11. It's not really a laboratory. I mean, she calls it that, but really it's just the garage. Only she took some of the Stuffed Muffins™ money and converted it, so it has sinks and bathtubs and Bunsen burners and things, and tiles on the walls and the floor to make it easier to clean.

12. I don't know. Nerys used to be pretty normal. When she turned thirteen she started reading these magazines and putting pictures of these strange bimbo women up on her wall like Britney Spears and so on. Sorry if anyone reading this is a Britney fan ;) but I just don't get it. The whole orange thing didn't start until last year.

13. Artificial tanning creams. You couldn't go near her for hours after she put it on. And she'd never give it time to dry after she smeared it on her skin, so it would come off on her sheets and on the fridge door and in the shower, leaving smears of orange everywhere. Her friends would wear it too, but they never put it on like she did. I mean, she'd slather on the cream, with no attempt to look even human-colored, and she thought she looked great. She did the tanning salon thing once, but I don't think she liked it, because she never went back.

14. Tangerine Girl. The Oompa-Loompa. Carrot-top. GoMango. Orangina.

15. Not very well. But she didn't seem to care, really. I mean, this is a girl who said that she couldn't see the point of science or maths because she was going to be a pole dancer as soon as she left school. I

said, nobody's going to pay to see you in the altogether, and she said how do you know? and I told her that I saw the little QuickTime films she'd made of herself dancing nuddy and left in the camera and she screamed and said give me that, and I told her I'd wiped them. But honestly, I don't think she was ever going to be the next Bettie Page or whoever. She's a sort of squarish shape, for a start.

16. German measles, mumps, and I think Pryderi had chicken pox when he was staying in Melbourne with the grandparents.

17. In a small pot. It looked a bit like a jam jar, I suppose.

18. I don't think so. Nothing that looked like a warning label anyway. But there was a return address. It came from abroad, and the return address was in some kind of foreign lettering.

19. You have to understand that Mum had been buying colors and dyes from all over the world for five years. The thing with the Day-Glo bubbles is not that someone can blow glowing colored bubbles, it's that they don't pop and leave splashes of dye all over everything. Mum says that would be a lawsuit waiting to happen. So, no.

20. There was some kind of shouting match between Nerys and Mum to begin with, because Mum had come back from the shops and not bought anything from Nerys's shopping list except the shampoo. Mum said she couldn't find the tanning cream at the supermarket but I think she just forgot. So Nerys stormed off and slammed the door and went into her bedroom and played something that was probably Britney Spears really loudly. I was out the back, feeding the three cats, the chinchilla, and a guinea pig named Roland who looks like a hairy cushion, and I missed it all.

21. On the kitchen table.

22. When I found the empty jam jar in the back garden the next morning. It was underneath Nerys's window. It didn't take Sherlock Holmes to figure it out.

23. Honestly, I couldn't be bothered. I figured it would just be more yelling, you know? And Mum would work it out soon enough.

24. Yes, it was stupid. But it wasn't uniquely stupid, if you see what I mean. Which is to say, it was par-for-the-course-for-Nerys stupid.

25. That she was glowing.

26. A sort of pulsating orange.

27. When she started telling us that she was going to be worshipped like a god, as she was in the dawn times.

28. Pryderi said she was floating about an inch above the ground. But I didn't actually see this. I thought he was just playing along with her newfound weirdness.

29. She didn't answer to "Nerys" anymore. She described herself mostly as either My Immanence, or the Vehicle. ("It is time to feed the Vehicle.")

30. Dark chocolate. Which was weird because in the old days I was the only one in the house who even sort of liked it. But Pryderi had to go out and buy her bars and bars of it.

31. No. Mum and me just thought it was more Nerys. Just a bit more imaginatively weirdo Nerys than usual.

32. That night, when it started to get dark. You could see the orange pulsing under the door. Like a glowworm or something. Or a light show. The weirdest thing was that I could still see it with my eyes closed.

33. The next morning. All of us.

34. It was pretty obvious by this point. She didn't really even look like Nerys any longer. She looked sort of *smudged*. Like an afterimage. I thought about it, and it's . . . Okay. Suppose you were staring at something really bright, that was a blue color. Then you closed your eyes, and you'd see this glowing yellowy-orange afterimage in your eyes? That was what she looked like.

35. They didn't work either.

36. She let Pryderi leave to get her more chocolate. Mum and I weren't allowed to leave the house anymore.

37. Mostly I just sat in the back garden and read a book. There wasn't very much else I really could do. I started wearing dark glasses, so did Mum, because the orange light hurt our eyes. Other than that, nothing.

38. Only when we tried to leave or call anybody. There was food in the house, though. And Stuffed Muffins™ in the freezer.

39. "If you'd just stopped her wearing that stupid tanning cream a year ago we wouldn't be in this mess!" But it was unfair, and I apologized afterwards.

40. When Pryderi came back with the dark chocolate bars. He said he'd gone up to a traffic warden and told him that his sister had turned into a giant orange glow and was controlling our minds. He said the man was extremely rude to him.

41. I don't have a boyfriend. I did, but we broke up after he went to a Rolling Stones concert with the evil bottle-blonde former friend whose name I do not mention. Also, I mean, the Rolling Stones? These little old goatmen hopping around the stage pretending to be all rock-and-roll? Please. So, no.

42. I'd quite like to be a vet. But then I think about having to put animals down, and I don't know. I want to travel for a bit before I make any decisions.

43. The garden hose. We turned it on full, while she was eating her chocolate bars, and distracted, and we sprayed it at her.

44. Just orange steam, really. Mum said that she had solvents and things in the laboratory, if we could get in there, but by now Her Immanence was hissing mad (literally) and she sort of fixed us to the floor. I can't explain it. I mean, I wasn't stuck, but I couldn't leave or move my legs. I was just where she left me.

45. About half a meter above the carpet. She'd sink down a bit to go through doors, so she didn't bump her head. And after the hose incident she didn't go back to her room, just stayed in the main room and floated about grumpily, the color of a luminous carrot.

46. Complete world domination.

47. I wrote it down on a piece of paper and gave it to Pryderi.

48. He had to carry it back. I don't think Her Immanence really understood money.

49. I don't know. It was Mum's idea more than mine. I think she hoped

that the solvent might remove the orange. And at that point, it couldn't hurt. Nothing could have made things worse.

50. It didn't even upset her, like the hose-water did. I'm pretty sure she liked it. I think I saw her dipping her chocolate bars into it, before she ate them, although I had to sort of squint up my eyes to see anything where she was. It was all a sort of a great orange glow.

51. That we were all going to die. Mum told Pryderi that if the Great Oompa-Loompa let him out to buy chocolate again, he just shouldn't bother coming back. And I was getting really upset about the animals—I hadn't fed the chinchilla or Roland the guinea pig for two days, because I couldn't go into the back garden. I couldn't go anywhere. Except the loo, and then I had to ask.

52. I suppose because they thought the house was on fire. All the orange light. I mean, it was a natural mistake.

53. We were glad she hadn't done that to us. Mum said it proved that Nerys was still in there somewhere, because if she had the power to turn us into goo, like she did the firefighters, she would have done. I said that maybe she just wasn't powerful enough to turn us into goo at the beginning and now she couldn't be bothered.

54. You couldn't even see a person in there anymore. It was a bright orange pulsing light, and sometimes it talked straight into your head.

55. When the spaceship landed.

56. I don't know. I mean, it was bigger than the whole block, but it didn't crush anything. It sort of materialized around us, so that our whole house was inside it. And the whole street was inside it too.

57. No. But what else could it have been?

58. A sort of pale blue. They didn't pulse, either. They twinkled.

59. More than six, less than twenty. It's not that easy to tell if this is the same intelligent blue light you were just speaking to five minutes ago.

60. Three things. First of all, a promise that Nerys wouldn't be hurt or harmed. Second, that if they were ever able to return her to the way she was, they'd let us know, and bring her back. Thirdly, a recipe for fluorescent bubble mixture. (I can only assume they were read-

ing Mum's mind, because she didn't say anything. It's possible that Her Immanence told them, though. She definitely had access to some of "the Vehicle's" memories.) Also, they gave Pryderi a thing like a glass skateboard.

61. A sort of a liquid sound. Then everything became transparent. I was crying, and so was Mum. And Pryderi said, "Cool beans," and I started to giggle while crying, and then it was just our house again.

62. We went out into the back garden and looked up. There was something blinking blue and orange, very high, getting smaller and smaller, and we watched it until it was out of sight.

63. Because I didn't want to.

64. I fed the remaining animals. Roland was in a state. The cats just seemed happy that someone was feeding them again. I don't know how the chinchilla got out.

65. Sometimes. I mean, you have to bear in mind that she was the single most irritating person on the planet, even before the whole Her Immanence thing. But yes, I guess so. If I'm honest.

66. Sitting outside at night, staring up at the sky, wondering what she's doing now.

67. He wants his glass skateboard back. He says that it's his, and the government has no right to keep it. (You are the government, aren't you?) Mum seems happy to share the patent for the Colored Bubbles recipe with the government though. The man said that it might be the basis of a whole new branch of molecular something or other. Nobody gave me anything, so I don't have to worry.

68. Once, in the back garden, looking up at the night sky. I think it was only an orangeyish star, actually. It could have been Mars, I know they call it the red planet. Although once in a while I think that maybe she's back to herself again, and dancing, up there, wherever she is, and all the aliens love her pole dancing because they just don't know any better, and they think it's a whole new art form, and they don't even mind that she's sort of square.

69. I don't know. Sitting in the back garden talking to the cats, maybe. Or blowing silly-colored bubbles.

70. Until the day that I die.

I ATTEST THAT this is a true statement of events.
Jemima Glorfindel Petula Ramsey

MYTHICAL CREATURES

2008

GIANTS

IF IT WERE NOT for the giants, Britain would look very different.

In the dawn days they feefifofummed across the land, picking up rocks and throwing them at other giants in friendly rivalry, or alone they would break mountains, crush rocks into causeways, leave henges and stone seats to mark their passing.

The giants were big, but not bright. They were outsmarted by clever boys named Jack and fell from beanstalks or were tricked to death. They died but not all of them are dead.

The remaining giants sleep, lost in deep slow dreams, covered in earth and trees and wild grass. Some have clouds on their shoulders or long men carved in their sides. We see them from the windows of cars and tell each other that from some angles they look almost like people.

Even giants can only sleep for so long. Do not make too much noise the next time you walk in the hills.

PIXIES

THEY'LL HELP YOU, FOLK say, unless you thank them: if you leave them gifts or payment they'll be off into the night, never again to sweep your floor or sew your shoes or stack your CDs into alphabetical order.

But there are some that wouldn't take a thank-you. Those are the bad hats that sour the milk, vinegar the wine, crash the computer, freeze every mobile phone.

One family had enough. They loaded up their SUV in the middle of the night with all the possessions they could not bear to part with, and drove away with their headlights off. When they reached the village they stopped for petrol.

"Going somewhere?" asked the attendant.

From the back of the car, from the cardboard boxes of the last good wine, the ancestral china wrapped in rolled-up duvets, a pixie voice called out, "That's right, George. We're flitting."

The family turned around and went home again. When a pixie has your number, they said, there's nothing else you can do.

DRAGONS

THE NATIVE DRAGONS OF the British Isles, called wyrms, had poisonous breath and coiled snakelike around hills. They could not fly or breathe fire. They demanded oxen or maidens. They grew slowly, ate rarely and slept much.

Local species can be fragile: the new dragons, the firedrakes, came south with the Norsemen, crossed the stormy seas with the Saxons, accompanied the Crusaders back from the hot lands in the center of the world. Nature can be cruel, and soon the wyrms were gone, their bones turned to stone.

The new ones spread, alien and invasive, until the time came for them to lay their eggs. Dragons nest on golden treasure, and British gold was hard to find, and soon they slipped away, another species that came and flourished and dwindled once again. A handful of dragons hung on, half-starved in the Welsh wilderness, until time and the wet winters extinguished their fires.

They went, like the wolf or the beaver; and they exit from the pages of history, pursued by a cave bear.

MERMAIDS

SHE KEEPS THE SOULS of the drowned in lobster pots that she finds on the seabed. They sing, the captive souls, and they light her way home beneath the gray Atlantic.

She had sisters once, but long ago they shed their tails and scales and stepped gingerly ashore to live with fishermen in their dry-land cottages. Now she's lonely, and not even the souls of the dead are company.

Walk the sea's edge in winter and you may see her, too far away, waving to you. Wave back and she will take you down to her world, deep below the waves, and show you cold wonders, and teach you the songs of the merfolk and the lonely ways beneath the sea.

UNICORNS

NOBODY REMEMBERS WHO SENT the first King of Scotland a unicorn. They are long-lived creatures, after all. The Kings of Scotland were proud of owning a unicorn, and left it to run, tangle-maned and alone, across the stark highlands, an ivory flash against the heather.

And then James VI got the news from the south and he sent a maiden into the hills. She sat and waited until it came and placed its head in her lap, then she bridled it with a silver bridle and walked it, skittish and straining, to the King.

The royal procession was made all the more exciting by the presence of the fabulous beast at the head. And then they were in London, and the Tower rose before them.

The unicorn was led into its stall. It scented the animal, caged across the way, and heard it roar before it saw the golden mane, the tawny eyes. The only lion in England was caged in the Tower, beside the only unicorn. The artists placed them on each side of the crown.

Two hundred years later, the unicorn's horn in the Tower was valued at 20,000 guineas; but now even that is lost to us.

FAIRIES

IT'S NOT THAT THEY'RE small, the fair folk. Especially not the queen of them all, Mab of the flashing eyes and the slow smile with lips that can conjure your heart under the hills for a hundred years.

It's not that they're small. It's that we're so far away.

"THE TRUTH IS A CAVE IN THE
BLACK MOUNTAINS . . ."

2010

YOU ASK ME if I can forgive myself? I can forgive myself for many things. For where I left him. For what I did. But I will not forgive myself for the year that I hated my daughter, when I believed her to have run away, perhaps to the city. During that year I forbade her name to be mentioned, and if her name entered my prayers when I prayed, it was to ask that she would one day learn the meaning of what she had done, of the dishonor that she had brought to our family, of the red that ringed her mother's eyes.

I hate myself for that, and nothing will ease the hatred, not even what happened that final night, on the side of the mountain.

I had searched for nearly ten years, although the trail was cold. I would say that I found him by accident, but I do not believe in accidents. If you walk the path, eventually you must arrive at the cave.

But that was later. First, there was the valley on the mainland, the whitewashed house in the gentle meadow with the burn splashing through it, a house that sat like a square of white sky against the green of the grass and the heather just beginning to purple.

And there was a boy outside the house, picking wool from off a thornbush. He did not see me approaching, and he did not look up until I said, "I used to do that. Gather the wool from the thorn-bushes and twigs. My mother would wash it, then she would make me things with it. A ball, and a doll."

He turned. He looked shocked, as if I had appeared out of nowhere. And I had not. I had walked many a mile, and had many more miles to go. I said, "I walk quietly. Is this the house of Calum MacInnes?"

The boy nodded, drew himself up to his full height, which was perhaps two fingers bigger than mine, and he said, "I am Calum MacInnes."

"Is there another of that name? For the Calum MacInnes that I seek is a grown man."

The boy said nothing, just unknotted a thick clump of sheep's wool from the clutching fingers of the thornbush. I said, "Your father, perhaps? Would he be Calum MacInnes as well?"

The boy was peering at me. "What are you?" he asked.

"I am a small man," I told him. "But I am a man, nonetheless, and I am here to see Calum MacInnes."

"Why?" The boy hesitated. Then, "And why are you so small?"

I said, "Because I have something to ask your father. Man's business." And I saw a smile start at the tips of his lips. "It's not a bad thing to be small, young Calum. There was a night when the Campbells came knocking on my door, a whole troop of them, twelve men with knives and sticks, and they demanded of my wife, Morag, that she produce me, as they were there to kill me, in revenge for some imagined slight. And she said, 'Young Johnnie, run down to the far meadow, and tell your father to come back to the house, that I sent for him.' And the Campbells watched as the boy ran out the door. They knew that I was a most dangerous person. But nobody had told them that I was a wee man, or if that had been told them, it had not been believed."

"Did the boy call you?" said the lad.

"It was no boy," I told him, "but me myself, it was. And they'd had me, and still I walked out the door and through their fingers."

The boy laughed. Then he said, "Why were the Campbells after you?"

"It was a disagreement about the ownership of cattle. They thought the cows were theirs. I maintained the Campbells' ownership of them had ended the first night the cows had come with me over the hills."

"Wait here," said young Calum MacInnes.

I sat by the burn and looked up at the house. It was a good-sized house: I would have taken it for the house of a doctor or a man of law, not of a border reaver. There were pebbles on the ground and I made a pile of them, and I tossed the pebbles, one by one, into the burn. I have a good eye, and I enjoyed rattling the pebbles over the meadow and into the water. I had thrown a hundred stones when the boy returned, accompanied by a tall, loping man. His hair was streaked with gray, his face was long and wolfish. There are no wolves in those hills, not any longer, and the bears have gone too.

"Good day to you," I said.

He said nothing in return, only stared. I am used to stares. I said, "I am seeking Calum MacInnes. If you are he, say so, I will greet you. If you are not he, tell me now, and I will be on my way."

"What business would you have with Calum MacInnes?"

"I wish to hire him, as a guide."

"And where is it you would wish to be taken?"

I stared at him. "That is hard to say," I told him. "For there are some who say it does not exist. There is a certain cave on the Misty Isle."

He said nothing. Then he said, "Calum, go back to the house."

"But, Da—"

"Tell your mother I said she was to give you some tablet. You like that. Go on."

Expressions crossed the boy's face—puzzlement, hunger, happiness—and then he turned and ran back to the white house.

Calum MacInnes said, "Who sent you here?"

I pointed to the burn as it splashed its way between us on its journey down the hill. "What's that?" I asked.

"Water," he replied.

"And they say there is a king across it," I told him.

I did not know him then at all, and never knew him well, but his eyes became guarded, and his head cocked to one side. "How do I know you are who you say you are?"

"I have claimed nothing," I said. "Just that there are those who have heard there is a cave on the Misty Isle, and that you might know the way."

He said, "I will not tell you where the cave is."

"I am not here asking for directions. I seek a guide. And two travel more safely than one."

He looked me up and down, and I waited for the joke about my size, but he did not make it, and for that I was grateful. He just said, "When we reach the cave, I will not go inside. You must bring out the gold yourself."

I said, "It is all one to me."

He said, "You can only take what you carry. I will not touch it. But yes, I will take you."

I said, "You will be paid well for your trouble." I reached into my jerkin, handed him the pouch I had in there. "This for taking me. Another, twice the size, when we return."

He poured the coins from the pouch into his huge hand, and he nodded. "Silver," he said. "Good." Then, "I will say good-bye to my wife and son."

"Is there nothing you need to bring?"

He said, "I was a reaver in my youth, and reavers travel light. I'll bring a rope, for the mountains." He patted his dirk, which hung from his belt, and went back into the whitewashed house. I never saw his wife, not then, nor at any other time. I do not know what color her hair was.

I threw another fifty stones into the burn as I waited, until he returned, with a coil of rope thrown over one shoulder, and then we walked together away from a house too grand for any reaver, and we headed west.

THE MOUNTAINS BETWEEN the rest of the world and the coast are gradual hills, visible from a distance as gentle, purple, hazy things, like clouds. They seem inviting. They are slow mountains, the kind you can walk up easily, like walking up a hill, but they are hills that take a full day and more to climb. We walked up the hill, and by the end of the first day we were cold.

I saw snow on the peaks above us, although it was high summer.

We said nothing to each other that first day. There was nothing to be said. We knew where we were going.

We made a fire, from dried sheep dung and a dead thornbush: we boiled water and made our porridge, each of us throwing a handful of oats and a fingerpinch of salt into the little pan I carried. His handful was huge, and my handful was small, like my hands, which made him smile and say, "I hope you will not be eating half of the porridge."

I said I would not and indeed, I did not, for my appetite is smaller than that of a full-grown man. But this is a good thing, I believe, for I can keep going in the wild on nuts and berries that would not keep a bigger person from starving.

A path of sorts ran across the high hills, and we followed it and encountered almost nobody: a tinker and his donkey, piled high with old pots, and a girl leading the donkey, who smiled at me when she thought me to be a child, and then scowled when she perceived me to be what I am, and would have thrown a stone at me had the tinker not slapped her hand with the switch he had been using to encourage the donkey; and, later, we overtook an old woman and a man she said was her grandson, on their way back across the hills. We ate with her, and she told us that she had attended the birth of her first greatgrandchild, that it was a good birth. She said she would tell our fortunes from the lines in our palms, if we had coins to cross her palm. I gave the old biddy a clipped lowland groat, and she looked at the palm of my right hand.

She said, "I see death in your past and death in your future."

"Death waits in all our futures," I said.

She paused, there in the highest of the highlands, where the summer winds have winter on their breath, where they howl and whip and slash the air like knives. She said, "There was a woman in a tree. There will be a man in a tree."

I said, "Will this mean anything to me?"

"One day. Perhaps." She said, "Beware of gold. Silver is your friend." And then she was done with me.

To Calum MacInnes she said, "Your palm has been burned." He

said that was true. She said, "Give me your other hand, your left hand." He did so. She gazed at it, intently. Then, "You return to where you began. You will be higher than most other men. And there is no grave waiting for you, where you are going."

He said, "You tell me that I will not die?"

"It is a left-handed fortune. I know what I have told you, and no more."

She knew more. I saw it in her face.

That was the only thing of any importance that occurred to us on the second day.

We slept in the open that night. The night was clear and cold, and the sky was hung with stars that seemed so bright and close I felt as if I could have reached out my arm and gathered them, like berries.

We lay side by side beneath the stars, and Calum MacInnes said, "Death awaits you, she said. But death does not wait for me. I think mine was the better fortune."

"Perhaps."

"Ah," he said. "It is all a nonsense. Old-woman talk. It is not truth." I woke in the dawn mist to see a stag, watching us, curiously.

The third day we crested those mountains, and we began to walk downhill.

My companion said, "When I was a boy, my father's dirk fell into the cooking fire. I pulled it out, but the metal hilt was as hot as the flames. I did not expect this, but I would not let the dirk go. I carried it away from the fire, and plunged the sword into the water. It made steam. I remember that. My palm was burned, and my hand curled, as if it was meant to carry a sword until the end of time."

I said, "You, with your hand. Me, only a little man. It's fine heroes we are, who seek our fortunes on the Misty Isle."

He barked a laugh, short and without humor. "Fine heroes," was all he said.

The rain began to fall then, and did not stop falling. That night we passed a small croft house. There was a trickle of smoke from its chimney, and we called out for the owner, but there was no response.

I pushed open the door and called again. The place was dark, but I could smell tallow, as if a candle had been burning and had recently been snuffed.

"No one at home," said Calum, but I shook my head and walked forward, then leaned down into the darkness beneath the bed.

"Would you care to come out?" I asked. "For we are travelers, seeking warmth and shelter and hospitality. We would share with you our oats and our salt and our whisky. And we will not harm you."

At first the woman hidden beneath the bed said nothing, and then she said, "My husband is away in the hills. He told me to hide myself away if the strangers come, for fear of what they might do to me."

I said, "I am but a little man, good lady, no bigger than a child, you could send me flying with a blow. My companion is a full-sized man, but I do swear that he shall do nothing to you, save partake of your hospitality, and we would dry ourselves. Please do come out."

All covered with dust and spiderwebs she was when she emerged, but even with her face all begrimed, she was beautiful, and even with her hair all webbed and grayed with dust it was still long and thick, and golden-red. For a heartbeat she put me in the mind of my daughter, but that my daughter would look a man in the eye, while this one glanced only at the ground fearfully, like something expecting to be beaten.

I gave her some of our oats, and Calum produced strips of dried meat from his pocket, and she went out to the field and returned with a pair of scrawny turnips, and she prepared food for the three of us.

I ate my fill. She had no appetite. I believe that Calum was still hungry when his meal was done. He poured whisky for the three of us: she took but a little, and that with water. The rain rattled on the roof of the house, and dripped in the corner, and, unwelcoming though it was, I was glad that I was inside.

It was then that a man came through the door. He said nothing, only stared at us, untrusting, angry. He pulled off his cape of sheepskin, and his hat, and he dropped them on the earth floor. They dripped and puddled. The silence was oppressive.

Calum MacInnes said, "Your wife gave us hospitality, when we found her. Hard enough she was in the finding."

"We asked for hospitality," I said. "As we ask it of you."

The man said nothing, only grunted.

In the highlands, people spend words as if they were golden coins. But the custom is strong there: strangers who ask for hospitality must be granted it, though you have blood-feud against them and their clan or kin.

The woman—little more than a girl she was, while her husband's beard was gray and white, so I wondered if she was his daughter for a moment, but no: there was but one bed, scarcely big enough for two—went outside, into the sheep-pen that adjoined the house, and returned with oatcakes and a dried ham she must have hidden there, which she sliced thin, and placed on a wooden trencher before the man.

Calum poured the man whisky, and said, "We seek the Misty Isle. Do you know if it is there?"

The man looked at us. The winds are bitter in the highlands, and they would whip the words from a man's lips. He pursed his mouth, then he said, "Aye. I saw it from the peak this morning. It's there. I cannot say if it will be there tomorrow."

We slept on the hard-earth floor of that cottage. The fire went out, and there was no warmth from the hearth. The man and his woman slept in their bed, behind the curtain. He had his way with her, beneath the sheepskin that covered that bed, and before he did that, he beat her for feeding us and for letting us in. I heard them, and could not stop hearing them, and sleep was hard in the finding that night.

I have slept in the homes of the poor, and I have slept in palaces, and I have slept beneath the stars, and would have told you before that night that all places were one to me. But I woke before first light, convinced we had to be gone from that place, but not knowing why, and I woke Calum by putting a finger to his lips, and silently we left that croft on the mountainside without saying our farewells, and I have never been more pleased to be gone from anywhere.

We were a mile from that place when I said, "The island. You asked if it would be there. Surely, an island is there, or it is not there."

Calum hesitated. He seemed to be weighing his words, and then he said, "The Misty Isle is not as other places. And the mist that surrounds it is not like other mists."

We walked down a path worn by hundreds of years of sheep and deer and few enough men.

He said, "They also call it the Winged Isle. Some say it is because the island, if seen from above, would look like butterfly wings. And I do not know the truth of it." Then, *"And what is truth? said jesting Pilate."*

It is harder coming down than it is going up.

I thought about it. "Sometimes I think that truth is a place. In my mind, it is like a city: there can be a hundred roads, a thousand paths, that will all take you, eventually, to the same place. It does not matter where you come from. If you walk toward the truth, you will reach it, whatever path you take."

Calum MacInnes looked down at me and said nothing. Then, "You are wrong. The truth is a cave in the black mountains. There is one way there, and one only, and that way is treacherous and hard, and if you choose the wrong path you will die alone, on the mountainside."

We crested the ridge, and we looked down to the coast. I could see villages below, beside the water. And I could see high black mountains before me, on the other side of the sea, coming out of the mist.

Calum said, "There's your cave. In those mountains."

The bones of the earth, I thought, seeing them. And then I became uncomfortable, thinking of bones, and to distract myself, I said, "And how many times is it you have been there?"

"Only once." He hesitated. "I searched for it all my sixteenth year, for I had heard the legends, and I believed if I sought I should find. I was seventeen when I reached it, and brought back all the gold coins I could carry."

"And were you not frightened of the curse?"

"When I was young, I was afraid of nothing."

"What did you do with your gold?"

"A portion I buried and I alone know where. The rest I used as bride-price for the woman I loved, and to build a fine house."

He stopped as if he had already said too much.

There was no ferryman at the jetty. Only a small boat on the shore, hardly big enough for three full-sized men, tied to a tree trunk all twisted and half-dead, and a bell beside it.

I sounded the bell, and soon enough a fat man came down the shore.

He said to Calum, "It will cost you a shilling for the ferry, and your boy, three pennies."

I stood tall. I am not as big as other men are, but I have as much pride as any of them. "I am also a man," I said, "I'll pay your shilling." The ferryman looked me up and down, then he scratched his beard. "I beg your pardon. My eyes are not what they once were. I shall take you to the island."

I handed him a shilling. He weighed it in his hand. "That's nine-pence you did not cheat me out of. Nine pennies are a lot of money in this dark age." The water was the color of slate, although the sky was blue, and whitecaps chased one another across the water's surface. He untied the boat and hauled it, rattling, down the shingle to the water. We waded out into the cold channel, and clambered inside.

The splash of oars on seawater, and the boat was propelled forward in easy movements. I sat closest to the ferryman. I said, "Nine-pence. It is good wages. But I have heard of a cave in the mountains on the Misty Isle, filled with gold coins, the treasure of the ancients."

He shook his head dismissively.

Calum was staring at me, lips pressed together so hard they were white. I ignored him and asked the man again, "A cave filled with golden coins, a gift from the Norsemen or the Southerners or from those who they say were here long before any of us: those who fled into the West as the people came."

"Heard of it," said the ferryman. "Heard also of the curse of it. I reckon that the one can take care of the other." He spat into the sea. Then he said, "You're an honest man, dwarf. I see it in your face. Do not seek this cave. No good can come of it."

"I am sure you are right," I told him, without guile.

"I am certain I am," he said. "For not every day it is that I take a reaver and a little dwarfy man to the Misty Isle." Then he said, "In this part of the world, it is not considered lucky to talk about those who went to the West."

We rode the rest of the boat journey in silence, though the sea became choppier, and the waves splashed into the side of the boat, such that I held on with both hands for fear of being swept away.

And after what seemed like half a lifetime the boat was tied to a long jetty of black stones. We walked the jetty, as the waves crashed around us, the salt spray kissing our faces. There was a humpbacked man at the landing selling oatcakes and plums dried until they were almost stones. I gave him a penny and filled my jerkin pockets with them.

We walked on into the Misty Isle.

I am old now, or at least, I am no longer young, and everything I see reminds me of something else I've seen, such that I see nothing for the first time. A bonny girl, her hair fiery red, reminds me only of another hundred such lasses, and their mothers, and what they were as they grew, and what they looked like when they died. It is the curse of age, that all things are reflections of other things.

I say that, but my time on the Misty Isle that is also called, by the wise, the Winged Isle, reminds me of nothing but itself.

It is a day from that jetty until you reach the black mountains. Calum MacInnes looked at me, half his size or less, and he set off at a loping stride, as if challenging me to keep up. His legs propelled him across the ground, which was wet, and all ferns and heather.

Above us, low clouds were scudding, gray and white and black, hiding each other and revealing and hiding again.

I let him get ahead of me, let him press on into the rain, until he was swallowed by the wet, gray haze. Then, and only then, I ran.

This is one of the secret things of me, the things I have not revealed to any person, save to Morag, my wife, and Johnnie and James, my sons, and Flora, my daughter (may the Shadows rest her poor soul): I can run, and I can run well, and, if I need to, I can run faster and longer and more sure-footedly than any full-sized man; and it was like this that I ran then, through the mist and the rain, taking to the high ground and the black-rock ridges, yet keeping below the skyline. He was ahead of me, but I spied him soon, and I ran on and I ran past him, on the high ground, with the brow of the hill between us.

Below us was a stream. I can run for days without stopping. That is the first of my secrets, but there is one secret I have revealed to no man.

We had discussed already where we would camp that first night on the Misty Isle, and Calum had told me that we would spend the night beneath the rock that is called Man and Dog, for it is said that it looks like an old man with his dog by his side, and I reached it late in the afternoon. There was a shelter beneath the rock, which was protected and dry, and some of those who had been before us had left firewood behind, sticks and twigs and branches. I made a fire and dried myself in front of it and took the chill from my bones. The wood smoke blew out across the heather.

It was dark when Calum loped into the shelter and looked at me as if he had not expected to see me that side of midnight. I said, "What took you so long, Calum MacInnes?"

He said nothing, only stared at me. I said, "There is trout, boiled in mountain water, and a fire to warm your bones."

He nodded. We ate the trout, drank whisky to warm ourselves. There was a mound of heather and of ferns, dried and brown, piled high in the rear of the shelter, and we slept upon that, wrapped tight in our damp cloaks.

I woke in the night. There was cold steel against my throat—the flat of the blade, not the edge. I said, "And why would you ever kill me in the night, Calum MacInnes? For our way is long, and our journey is not yet over."

He said, "I do not trust you, dwarf."

"It is not me you must trust," I told him, "but those that I serve. And if you left with me but return without me, there are those who will know the name of Calum MacInnes, and cause it to be spoken in the shadows."

The cold blade remained at my throat. He said, "How did you get ahead of me?"

"And here was I, repaying ill with good, for I made you food and a fire. I am a hard man to lose, Calum MacInnes, and it ill-becomes a guide to do as you did today. Now, take your dirk from my throat and let me sleep."

He said nothing, but after a few moments, the blade was removed. I forced myself neither to sigh nor to breathe, hoping he could not hear my heart pounding in my chest; and I slept no more that night.

For breakfast, I made porridge, and threw in some dried plums to soften them.

The mountains were black and gray against the white of the sky. We saw eagles, huge and ragged of wing, circling above us. Calum set a sober pace and I walked beside him, taking two steps for every one of his.

"How long?" I asked him.

"A day. Perhaps two. It depends upon the weather. If the clouds come down then two days, or even three . . ."

The clouds came down at noon and the world was blanketed by a mist that was worse than rain: droplets of water hung in the air, soaked our clothes and our skin; the rocks we walked upon became treacherous and Calum and I slowed in our ascent, stepped carefully. We were walking up the mountain, not climbing, up goat paths and craggy sharp ways. The rocks were black and slippery: we walked, and climbed and clambered and clung, we slipped and slid and stumbled and staggered, yet even in the mist, Calum knew where he was going, and I followed him.

He paused at a waterfall that splashed across our path, thick as the trunk of an oak. He took the thin rope from his shoulders, wrapped it about a rock.

"This waterfall was not here before," he told me. "I'll go first." He tied the other end of the rope about his waist and edged out along the path, into the waterfall, pressing his body against the wet rockface, edging slowly, intently through the sheet of water.

I was scared for him, scared for both of us: holding my breath as he passed through, only breathing when he was on the other side of the waterfall. He tested the rope, pulled on it, motioned me to follow him, when a stone gave way beneath his foot and he slipped on the wet rock, and fell into the abyss.

The rope held, and the rock beside me held. Calum MacInnes dangled from the end of the rope. He looked up at me, and I sighed, anchored myself by a slab of crag, and I wound and pulled him up and up. I hauled him back onto the path, dripping and cursing.

He said, "You're stronger than you look," and I cursed myself for a fool. He must have seen it on my face for, after he shook himself (like a dog, sending droplets flying), he said, "My boy Calum told me the tale you told him about the Campbells coming for you, and you being sent into the fields by your wife, with them thinking she was your ma, and you a boy."

"It was just a tale," I said. "Something to pass the time."

"Indeed?" he said. "For I heard tell of a raiding party of Campbells sent out a few years ago, seeking revenge on someone who had taken their cattle. They went, and they never came back. If a small fellow like you can kill a dozen Campbells . . . well, you must be strong, and you must be fast."

I must be *stupid*, I thought ruefully, telling that child that tale.

I had picked them off one by one, like rabbits, as they came out to piss or to see what had happened to their friends: I had killed seven of them before my wife killed her first. We buried them in the glen, built a small cairn of stacking stones above them, to weigh them down so their ghosts would not walk, and we were sad: that Campbells had come so far to kill me, that we had been forced to kill them in return. I take no joy in killing: no man should, and no woman. Sometimes death is necessary, but it is always an evil thing. That is something I am in no doubt of, even after the events I speak of here.

I took the rope from Calum MacInnes, and I clambered up and up, over the rocks, to where the waterfall came out of the side of the hill, and it was narrow enough for me to cross. It was slippery there, but I made it over without incident, tied the rope in place, came down it, threw the end of it to my companion, walked him across.

He did not thank me, neither for rescuing him, nor for getting us across: and I did not expect thanks. I also did not expect what he actually said, though, which was: "You are not a whole man, and you are ugly. Your wife: is she also small and ugly, like yourself?"

I decided to take no offense, whether offense had been intended or no. I simply said, "She is not. She is a tall woman, almost as tall

as you, and when she was young—when we were both younger—
she was reckoned by some to be the most beautiful girl in the lowlands. The bards wrote songs praising her green eyes and her long
red-golden hair."

I thought I saw him flinch at this, but it is possible that I imagined
it, or more likely, wished to imagine I had seen it.

"How did you win her, then?"

I spoke the truth: "I wanted her, and I get what I want. I did not
give up. She said I was wise and I was kind, and I would always provide for her. And I have."

The clouds began to lower, once more, and the world blurred at
the edges, became softer.

"She said I would be a good father. And I have done my best to raise
my children. Who are also, if you are wondering, normal-sized."

"I beat sense into young Calum," said older Calum. "He is not a
bad child."

"You can only do that as long as they are there with you," I said.
And then I stopped talking, and I remembered that long year, and
also I remembered Flora when she was small, sitting on the floor
with jam on her face, looking up at me as if I were the wisest man in
the world.

"Ran away, eh? I ran away when I was a lad. I was twelve. I went as
far as the court of the king over the water. The father of the current
king."

"That's not something you hear spoken aloud."

"I am not afraid," he said. "Not here. Who's to hear us? Eagles? I
saw him. He was a fat man, who spoke the language of the foreign-
ers well, and our own tongue only with difficulty. But he was still
our king." He paused. "And if he is to come to us again, he will need
gold, for vessels and weapons and to feed the troops that he raises."

I said, "So I believe. That is why we go in search of the cave."

He said, "This is bad gold. It does not come free. It has its cost."

"Everything has its cost."

I was remembering every landmark: climb at the sheep skull,
cross the first three streams, then walk along the fourth until the
five heaped stones and find where the rock looks like a seagull and

walk on between two sharply jutting walls of black rock, and let the slope bring you with it . . .

I could remember it, I knew. Well enough to find my way down again. But the mists confused me, and I could not be certain.

We reached a small loch, high in the mountains, and drank fresh water, caught huge white creatures that were not shrimps or lobsters or crayfish, and ate them raw like sausages, for we could not find any dry wood to make our fire, that high.

We slept on a wide ledge beside the icy water and woke into clouds before sunrise, when the world was gray and blue.

"You were sobbing in your sleep," said Calum.

"I had a dream," I told him.

"I do not have bad dreams," Calum said.

"It was a good dream," I said. It was true. I had dreamed that Flora still lived. She was grumbling about the village boys, and telling me of her time in the hills with the cattle, and of things of no consequence, smiling her great smile and tossing her hair the while, red-golden like her mother's, although her mother's hair is now streaked with white.

"Good dreams should not make a man cry out like that," said Calum. A pause, then, "I have no dreams, not good, not bad."

"No?"

"Not since I was a young man."

We rose. A thought struck me: "Did you stop dreaming after you came to the cave?"

He said nothing. We walked along the mountainside, into the mist, as the sun came up.

The mist seemed to thicken and fill with light, in the sunshine, but did not fade away and I realized that it must be a cloud. The world glowed. And then it seemed to me that I was staring at a man of my size, a small, humpty man, his face a shadow, standing in the air in front of me, like a ghost or an angel, and it moved as I moved. It was haloed by the light, and shimmered, and I could not have told you how near it was or how far away. I have seen miracles and I have seen evil things, but never have I seen anything like that.

"Is it magic?" I asked, although I smelled no magic on the air.

Calum said, "It is nothing. A property of the light. A shadow. A reflection. No more. I see a man beside me, as well. He moves as I move." I glanced back, but I saw nobody beside him.

And then the little glowing man in the air faded, and the cloud, and it was day, and we were alone.

We climbed all that morning, ascending. Calum's ankle had twisted the day before, when he had slipped at the waterfall. Now it swelled in front of me, swelled and went red, but his pace did not ever slow, and if he was in discomfort or in pain it did not show upon his face.

I said, "How long?" as the dusk began to blur the edges of the world.

"An hour, less, perhaps. We will reach the cave, and then we will sleep for the night. In the morning you will go inside. You can bring out as much gold as you can carry, and we will make our way back off the island."

I looked at him, then: gray-streaked hair, gray eyes, so huge and wolfish a man, and I said, "You would sleep outside the cave?"

"I would. There are no monsters in the cave. Nothing that will come out and take you in the night. Nothing that will eat us. But you should not go in until daylight."

And then we rounded a rockfall, all black rocks and gray half-blocking our path, and we saw the cave mouth. I said, "Is that all?"

"You expected marble pillars? Or a giant's cave from a gossip's fireside tales?"

"Perhaps. It looks like nothing. A hole in the rock-face. A shadow. And there are no guards?"

"No guards. Only the place, and what it is."

"A cave filled with treasure. And you are the only one who can find it?"

Calum laughed then, like a fox's bark. "The islanders know how to find it. But they are too wise to come here, to take its gold. They say that the cave makes you evil: that each time you visit it, each time you enter to take gold, it eats the good in your soul, so they do not enter."

"And is that true? Does it make you evil?"

". . . No. The cave feeds on something else. Not good and evil. Not really. You can take your gold, but afterwards, things are"—

he paused—"things are *flat*. There is less beauty in a rainbow, less meaning in a sermon, less joy in a kiss . . ." He looked at the cave mouth and I thought I saw fear in his eyes. "Less."

I said, "There are many for whom the lure of gold outweighs the beauty of a rainbow."

"Me, when young, for one. You, now, for another."

"So we go in at dawn."

"You will go in. I will wait for you out here. Do not be afraid. No monster guards the cave. No spells to make the gold vanish, if you do not know some cantrip or rhyme."

We made our camp, then: or rather we sat in the darkness, against the cold rock wall. There would be no sleep there.

I said, "You took the gold from here, as I will do tomorrow. You bought a house with it, a bride, a good name."

His voice came from the darkness. "Aye. And they meant nothing to me, once I had them, or less than nothing. And if your gold pays for the king over the water to come back to us and rule us and bring about a land of joy and prosperity and warmth, it will still mean nothing to you. It will be as something you heard of that happened to a man in a tale."

"I have lived my life to bring the king back," I told him.

He said, "You take the gold back to him. Your king will want more gold, because kings want more. It is what they do. Each time you come back, it will mean less. The rainbow means nothing. Killing a man means nothing."

Silence then, in the darkness. I heard no birds: only the wind that called and gusted about the peaks like a mother seeking her babe.

I said, "We have both killed men. Have you ever killed a woman, Calum MacInnes?"

"I have not. I have killed no women, no girls."

I ran my hands over my dirk in the darkness, seeking the wood and silver of the hilt, the steel of the blade. It was there in my hands. I had not intended ever to tell him, only to strike when we were out of the mountains, strike once, strike deep, but now I felt the words being pulled from me, would I or never-so. "They say there was a girl," I told him. "And a thornbush."

Silence. The whistling of the wind. "Who told you?" he asked. Then, "Never mind. I would not kill a woman. No man of honor would kill a woman"

If I said a word, I knew, he would be silent on the subject, and never talk about it again. So I said nothing. Only waited.

Calum MacInnes began to speak, choosing his words with care, talking as if he was remembering a tale he had heard as a child and had almost forgotten. "They told me the kine of the lowlands were fat and bonny, and that a man could gain honor and glory by adventuring off to the south and returning with the fine red cattle. So I went south, and never a cow was good enough, until on a hillside in the lowlands I saw the finest, reddest, fattest cows that ever a man has seen. So I began to lead them away, back the way I had come.

"She came after me with a stick. The cattle were her father's, she said, and I was a rogue and a knave and all manner of rough things. But she was beautiful, even when angry, and had I not already a young wife I might have dealt more kindly with her. Instead I pulled a knife, and touched it to her throat, and bade her to stop speaking. And she did stop.

"I would not kill her—I would not kill a woman, and that is the truth—so I tied her, by her hair, to a thorn tree, and I took her knife from her waistband, to slow her as she tried to free herself, and pushed the blade of it deep into the sod. I tied her to the thorn tree by her long hair, and I thought no more of her as I made off with her cattle.

"It was another year before I was back that way. I was not after cows that day, but I walked up the side of that bank—it was a lonely spot, and if you had not been looking, you might not have seen it. Perhaps nobody searched for her."

"I heard they searched," I told him. "Although some believed her taken by reavers, and others believed her run away with a tinker, or gone to the city. But still, they searched."

"Aye. I saw what I did see—perhaps you'd have to have stood where I was standing, to see what I did see. It was an evil thing I did, perhaps."

"Perhaps?"

He said, "I have taken gold from the cave of the mists. I cannot tell any longer if there is good or there is evil. I sent a message, by a child, at an inn, telling them where she was, and where they could find her."

I closed my eyes but the world became no darker.

"There is evil," I told him.

I saw it in my mind's eye: her skeleton picked clean of clothes, picked clean of flesh, as naked and white as anyone would ever be, hanging like a child's puppet against the thornbush, tied to a branch above it by its red-golden hair.

"At dawn," said Calum MacInnes, as if we had been talking of provisions or the weather, "you will leave your dirk behind, for such is the custom, and you will enter the cave, and bring out as much gold as you can carry. And you will bring it back with you, to the mainland. There's not a soul in these parts, knowing what you carry or where it's from, would take it from you. Then send it to the king over the water, and he will pay his men with it, and feed them, and buy their weapons. One day, he will return. Tell me on that day, that there is evil, little man."

WHEN THE SUN was up, I entered the cave. It was damp in there. I could hear water running down one wall, and I felt a wind on my face, which was strange, because there was no wind inside the mountain.

In my mind, the cave would be filled with gold. Bars of gold would be stacked like firewood, and bags of golden coins would sit between them. There would be golden chains and golden rings, and golden plates, heaped high like the china plates in a rich man's house.

I had imagined riches, but there was nothing like that here. Only shadows. Only rock.

Something was here, though. Something that waited.

I have secrets, but there is a secret that lies beneath all my other secrets, and not even my children know it, although I believe my wife suspects, and it is this: my mother was a mortal woman, the daughter of a miller, but my father came to her from out of the West, and to the West he returned, when he had had his sport with her. I cannot be sentimental about my parentage: I am sure he does not think of her, and doubt that he ever knew of me. But he left me a body that is small, and fast, and strong; and perhaps I take after him in other ways—I do not know. I am ugly, and my father was beautiful, or so my mother told me once, but I think that she might have been deceived.

I wondered what I would have seen in that cave if my father had been an innkeeper from the lowlands.

You would be seeing gold, said a whisper that was not a whisper, from deep in the heart of the mountain. It was a lonely voice, and distracted, and bored.

"I would see gold," I said aloud. "Would it be real, or would it be an illusion?"

The whisper was amused. *You are thinking like a mortal man, making things always to be one thing or another. It is gold they would see, and touch. Gold they would carry back with them, feeling the weight of it the while, gold they would trade with other mortals for what they needed. What does it matter if it is there or no, if they can see it, touch it, steal it, murder for it? Gold they need and gold I give them.*

"And what do you take, for the gold you give them?"

Little enough, for my needs are few, and I am old; too old to follow my sisters into the West. I taste their pleasure and their joy. I feed, a little, feed on what they do not need and do not value. A taste of heart, a lick and a nibble of their fine consciences, a sliver of soul. And in return a fragment of me leaves this cave with them and gazes out at the world through their eyes, sees what they see until their lives are done and I take back what is mine.

"Will you show yourself to me?"

I could see, in the darkness, better than any man born of man and woman could see. I saw something move in the shadows, and then the shadows congealed and shifted, revealing formless things at the edge of my perception, where it meets imagination. Troubled, I said the thing it is proper to say at times such as this: "Appear before me in a form that neither harms nor is offensive to me."

Is that what you wish?

The drip of distant water. "Yes," I said.

From out of the shadows it came, and it stared down at me with empty sockets, smiled at me with wind-weathered ivory teeth. It was all bone, save its hair, and its hair was red and gold, and wrapped about the branch of a thornbush.

"That offends my eyes."

I took it from your mind, said a whisper that surrounded the skeleton. Its jawbone did not move. *I chose something you loved. This was your daughter, Flora, as she was the last time you saw her.*

I closed my eyes, but the figure remained.

It said, *The reaver waits for you at the mouth of the cave. He waits for you to come out, weaponless and weighed down with gold. He will kill you, and take the gold from your dead hands.*

"But I'll not be coming out with gold, will I?"

I thought of Calum MacInnes, the wolf-gray in his hair, the gray of his eyes, the line of his dirk. He was bigger than I am, but all men are bigger than I am. Perhaps I was stronger, and faster, but he was also fast, and he was strong.

He killed my daughter, I thought, then wondered if the thought was mine or if it had crept out of the shadows into my head. Aloud, I said, "Is there another way out of this cave?"

You leave the way you entered, through the mouth of my home.

I stood there and did not move, but in my mind I was like an animal in a trap, questing and darting from idea to idea, finding no purchase and no solace and no solution.

I said, "I am weaponless. He told me that I could not enter this place with a weapon. That it was not the custom."

It is the custom now, to bring no weapon into my place. It was not always the custom. Follow me, said the skeleton of my daughter.

I followed her, for I could see her, even when it was so dark that I could see nothing else.

In the shadows it said, *It is beneath your hand.*

I crouched and felt it. The haft felt like bone—perhaps an antler. I touched the blade cautiously in the darkness, discovered that I was holding something that felt more like an awl than a knife. It was thin, sharp at the tip. It would be better than nothing.

"Is there a price?"

There is always a price.

"Then I will pay it. And I ask one other thing. You say that you can see the world through his eyes."

There were no eyes in that hollow skull, but it nodded. "Then tell me when he sleeps."

It said nothing. It melded with the darkness, and I felt alone in that place.

Time passed. I followed the sound of the dripping water, found a rock-pool, and drank. I soaked the last of the oats and I ate them, chewing them until they dissolved in my mouth. I slept and woke and slept again, and dreamed of my wife, Morag, waiting for me as the seasons changed, waiting for me just as we had waited for our daughter, waiting for me forever.

Something, a finger I thought, touched my hand: it was not bony and hard. It was soft, and human-like, but too cold. *He sleeps.*

I left the cave in the blue light, before dawn. He slept across the cave, cat-like, I knew, such that the slightest touch would have woken him. I held my weapon in front of me, a bone handle and a needle-like blade of blackened silver, and I reached out and took what I was after, without waking him.

Then I stepped closer, and his hand grasped for my ankle and his eyes opened.

"Where is the gold?" asked Calum MacInnes.

"I have none." The wind blew cold on the mountainside. I had danced back, out of his reach, when he had grabbed at me. He stayed on the ground, pushed himself up onto one elbow.

Then he said, "Where is my dirk?"

"I took it," I told him. "While you slept."

He looked at me, sleepily. "And why ever would you do that? If I was going to kill you I would have done it on the way here. I could have killed you a dozen times."

"But I did not have gold, then, did I?"

He said nothing.

I said, "If you think you could have got me to bring the gold from the cave, and that not bringing it out yourself would have saved your miserable soul, then you are a fool."

He no longer looked sleepy. "A fool, am I?"

He was ready to fight. It is good to make people who are ready to fight angry.

I said, "Not a fool. No. For I have met fools and idiots, and they are happy in their idiocy, even with straw in their hair. You are too wise for foolishness. You seek only misery and you bring misery with you and you call down misery on all you touch."

He rose then, holding a rock in his hand like an axe, and he came at me. I am small, and he could not strike me as he would have struck a man of his own size. He leaned over to strike. It was a mistake.

I held the bone haft tightly, and stabbed upward, striking fast with the point of the awl, like a snake. I knew the place I was aiming for, and I knew what it would do.

He dropped his rock, clutched at his right shoulder. "My arm," he said. "I cannot feel my arm."

He swore then, fouling the air with curses and threats. The dawn-light on the mountaintop made everything so beautiful and blue. In that light, even the blood that had begun to soak his garments was purple. He took a step back, so he was between me and the cave. I felt exposed, the rising sun at my back.

"Why do you not have gold?" he asked me. His arm hung limply at his side.

"There was no gold there for such as I," I said.

He threw himself forward, then, ran at me and kicked at me. My awl-blade went flying from my hand. I threw my arms around his leg, and I held on to him as together we hurtled off the mountainside.

His head was above me, and I saw triumph in it, and then I saw sky, and then the valley floor was above me and I was rising to meet it and then it was below me and I was falling to my death.

A jar and a bump, and now we were turning over and over on the side of the mountain, the world a dizzying whirligig of rock and pain and sky, and I knew I was a dead man, but still I clung to the leg of Calum MacInnes.

I saw a golden eagle in flight, but below me or above me I could no longer say. It was there, in the dawn sky, in the shattered fragments of time and perception, there in the pain. I was not afraid: there was no time and no space to be afraid in: no space in my mind and no space in my heart. I was falling through the sky, holding tightly to the leg of a man who was trying to kill me; we were crashing into rocks, scraping and bruising and then . . .

. . . we stopped.

Stopped with force enough that I felt myself jarred, and I was almost thrown off Calum MacInnes and to my death beneath. The side of the mountain had crumbled, there, long ago, sheared off, leaving a sheet of blank rock, as smooth and as featureless as glass. But that was below us. Where we were, there was a ledge, and on the ledge there was a miracle: stunted and twisted, high above the tree line, where no trees have any right to grow, was a twisted hawthorn tree, not much larger than a bush, although it was old. Its roots grew into the side of the mountain, and it was this hawthorn that had caught us in its gray arms.

I let go of the leg, clambered off Calum MacInnes's body and onto the side of the mountain. I stood on the narrow ledge and looked down at the sheer drop. There was no way down from here. No way down at all.

I looked up. It might be possible, I thought, climbing slowly, with fortune on my side, to make it up that mountain. If it did not rain. If the wind was not too hungry. And what choice did I have? The only alternative was death.

A voice: "So. Will you leave me here to die, dwarf?"

I said nothing. I had nothing to say.

His eyes were open. He said, "I cannot move my right arm, since you stabbed it. I think I broke a leg in the fall. I cannot climb with you."

I said, "I may succeed, or I may fail."

"You'll make it. I've seen you climb. After you rescued me, crossing that waterfall. You went up those rocks like a squirrel going up a tree."

I did not have his confidence in my climbing abilities.

He said, "Swear to me by all you hold holy. Swear by your king, who waits over the sea as he has since we drove his subjects from this land. Swear by the things you creatures hold dear—swear by shadows and eagle-feathers and by silence. Swear that you will come back for me."

"You know what I am?" I said.

"I know nothing," he said. "Only that I want to live."

I thought. "I swear by these things," I told him. "By shadows and by eagle-feathers and by silence. I swear by green hills and standing stones. I will come back."

"I would have killed you," said the man in the hawthorn bush, and he said it with humor, as if it was the biggest joke that ever one man had told another. "I had planned to kill you, and take the gold back as my own."

"I know."

His hair framed his face like a wolf-gray halo. There was red blood on his cheek where he had scraped it in the fall. "You could come back with ropes," he said. "My rope is still up there, by the cave mouth. But you'd need more than that."

"Yes," I said. "I will come back with ropes." I looked up at the rock above us, examined it as best I could. Sometimes good eyes mean the difference between life and death, if you are a climber. I saw where I would need to be as I went, the shape of my journey up the face of the mountain. I thought I could see the ledge outside the cave, from which we had fallen as we fought. I would head for there. Yes.

I blew on my hands, to dry the sweat before I began to climb. "I will come back for you," I said. "With ropes. I have sworn."

"When?" he asked, and he closed his eyes.

"In a year," I told him. "I will come here in a year."

I began to climb. The man's cries followed me as I stepped and crawled and squeezed and hauled myself up the side of that mountain, mingling with the cries of the great raptors; and they followed me back from the Misty Isle, with nothing to show for my pains and my time, and I will hear him screaming, at the edge of my mind, as I fall asleep or in the moments before I wake, until I die.

It did not rain, and the wind gusted and plucked at me, but did not throw me down. I climbed, and I climbed in safety.

When I reached the ledge the cave entrance seemed like a darker shadow in the noonday sun. I turned from it, turned my back on the mountain, and from the shadows that were already gathering in the cracks and the crevices and deep inside my skull, and I began my slow journey away from the Misty Isle. There were a hundred roads and a thousand paths that would take me back to my home in the lowlands, where my wife would be waiting.

THE THING ABOUT CASSANDRA

2010

SO THERE'S SCALLIE and me wearing Starsky-and-Hutch wigs, complete with sideburns, at five o'clock in the morning by the side of a canal in Amsterdam. There had been ten of us that night, including Rob, the groom, last seen handcuffed to a bed in the red-light district with shaving foam covering his nether regions and his future brother-in-law giggling and patting the hooker holding the straight razor on the arse, which was the point I looked at Scallie and he looked at me, and he said, "Maximum deniability?" and I nodded, because there are some questions you don't want to be able to answer when a bride starts asking pointed questions about the stag weekend, so we slipped off for a drink, leaving eight men in Starsky-and-Hutch wigs (one of whom was mostly naked, attached to a bed by fluffy pink handcuffs, and seemed to be starting to think that this adventure wasn't such a good idea after all) behind us, in a room that smelled of disinfectant and cheap incense, and we went and sat by a canal and drank cans of Danish lager and talked about the old days.

Scallie—whose real name is Jeremy Porter, and these days people call him Jeremy, but he had been Scallie when we were eleven—and the groom-to-be, Rob Cunningham, had been at school with me. We had drifted out of touch, more or less, had found each other the lazy way you do these days, through Friends Reunited and Facebook and such, and now Scallie and I were together for the first time since we were nineteen. The Starsky-and-Hutch wigs, which had been Scallie's idea, made us look like we were playing brothers in some made-for-TV movie—Scallie the short, stocky brother with the thick moustache, me, the tall one. Given that I've made a significant part of my income since leaving school modeling, I'd add the tall good-looking one, but nobody looks good in a Starsky-and-Hutch wig complete with sideburns.

Also, the wig itched.

We sat by the canal, and when the lager had all gone we kept talking and we watched the sun come up.

Last time I saw Scallie he was nineteen and filled with big plans. He had just joined the RAF as a cadet. He was going to fly planes, and do double duty using the flights to smuggle drugs, and so get incredibly rich while helping his country. It was the kind of mad idea he used to have all the way through school. Usually the whole thing would fall apart. Sometimes he'd get the rest of us into trouble on the way.

Now, twelve years later, his six months in the RAF ended early because of an unspecified problem with his ankle, he was a senior executive in a firm that manufactured double-glazed windows, he told me, with, since the divorce, a smaller house than he felt that he deserved and only a golden retriever for company.

He was sleeping with a woman in the double-glazing firm, but had no expectations of her leaving her boyfriend for him, seemed to find it easier that way. "Of course, I wake up crying sometimes, since the divorce. Well, you do," he said at one point. I could not imagine him crying, and anyway he said it with a huge, Scallie grin.

I told him about me: still modeling, helping out in a friend's antique shop to keep busy, more and more painting. I was lucky; people bought my paintings. Every year I would have a small gallery show at the Little Gallery in Chelsea, and while initially the only people to buy anything had been people I knew—photographers, old girlfriends and the like—these days I have actual collectors. We talked about the days that only Scallie seemed to remember, when he and Rob and I had been a team of three, inviolable, unbreakable. We talked about teenage heartbreak, about Caroline Minton (who was now Caroline Keen, and married to a vicar), about the first time we brazened our way into an 18 film, although neither of us could remember what the film actually was.

Then Scallie said, "I heard from Cassandra the other day."

"Cassandra?"

"Your old girlfriend. Cassandra. Remember?"

"No."

"The one from Reigate. You had her name written on all your books." I must have looked particularly dense or drunk or sleepy, because he said, "You met her on a skiing holiday. Oh, for heaven's sake. *Your first shag.* Cassandra."

"Oh," I said, remembering, remembering everything. "Cassandra." And I did remember.

"Yeah," said Scallie. "She dropped me a line on Facebook. She's running a community theater in East London. You should talk to her."

"Really?"

"I think, well, I mean, reading between the lines of her message, she may still have a thing for you. She asked after you."

I wondered how drunk he was, how drunk I was, staring at the canal in the early light. I said something, I forget what, then I asked whether Scallie remembered where our hotel was, because I had forgotten, and he said he had forgotten too, and that Rob had all the hotel details and really we should go and find him and rescue him from the clutches of the nice hooker with the handcuffs and the shaving kit, which, we realized, would be easier if we knew how to get back to where we'd left him, and looking for some clue to where we had left Rob I found a card with the hotel's address on it in my back pocket, so we headed back there and the last thing I did before I walked away from the canal and that whole strange evening was to pull the itchy Starsky-and-Hutch wig off my head and throw it into the canal.

It floated.

Scallie said, "There was a deposit on that, you know. If you didn't want to wear it, I'd've carried it." Then he said, "You should drop Cassandra a line."

I shook my head. I wondered who he had been talking to online, who he had confused for her, knowing it definitely wasn't Cassandra.

The thing about Cassandra is this: I'd made her up.

I WAS FIFTEEN, almost sixteen. I was awkward. I had just experienced my teenage growth spurt and was suddenly taller than most of my friends, self-conscious about my height. My mother owned and ran a small riding stables, and I helped out there, but the girls—competent, horsey, sensible types—intimidated me. At home I wrote bad poetry and painted watercolors, mostly of ponies in fields; at school—there were only boys at my school—I played cricket competently, acted a little, hung around with my friends playing records (the CD was newly around, but CD players were expensive and rare, and we had all inherited record players and hi-fis from parents or older siblings). When we didn't talk about music, or sports, we talked about girls.

Scallie was older than me. So was Rob. They liked having me as part of their gang, but they liked teasing me, too. They acted like I was a kid, and I wasn't. They had both done it with girls. Actually, that's not entirely true; they had both done it with the same girl, Caroline Minton, famously free with her favors and always up for it once, as long as the person she was with had a moped.

I did not have a moped. I was not old enough to get one, my mother could not afford one (my father had died when I was small, of an accidental overdose of anesthetic, when he was in hospital to have a minor operation on an infected toe. To this day, I avoid hospitals). I had seen Caroline Minton at parties, but she terrified me and even had I owned a moped, I would not have wanted my first sexual experience to be with her.

Scallie and Rob also had girlfriends. Scallie's girlfriend was taller than he was, had huge breasts and was interested in football, which meant Scallie had to feign an interest in football, mostly Crystal Palace, while Rob's girlfriend thought that Rob and she should have things in common, which meant that Rob stopped listening to the mideighties electropop the rest of us liked and started listening to hippy bands from before we were born, which was bad, and that Rob got to raid her dad's amazing collection of old TV on video, which was good.

I had no girlfriend.

Even my mother began to comment on it.

There must have been a place where it came from, the name, the idea: I don't remember though. I just remember writing "Cassandra" on my exercise books. Then, carefully, not saying anything.

"Who's Cassandra?" asked Scallie, on the bus to school.

"Nobody," I said.

"She must be somebody. You wrote her name on your maths exercise book."

"She's just a girl I met on the skiing holiday." My mother and I had gone skiing, with my aunt and cousins, the month before, in Austria.

"Are we going to meet her?"

"She's from Reigate. I expect so. Eventually."

"Well, I hope so. And you *like* her?"

I paused, for what I hoped was the right amount of time, and said, "She's a really good kisser," then Scallie laughed and Rob wanted to know if this was French kissing, with tongues and everything, and I said, "What do *you* think," and by the end of the day, they both believed in her.

My mum was pleased to hear I'd met someone. Her questions—what Cassandra's parents did, for example—I simply shrugged away. I went on three "dates" with Cassandra. On each of our dates, I took the train up to London, and took myself to the cinema. It was exciting, in its own way.

I returned from the first trip with more stories of kissing, and of breast-feeling.

Our second date (in reality, spent watching *Weird Science* on my own in Leicester Square) was, as told to my mum, merely spent holding hands together at what she still called "the pictures," but as reluctantly revealed to Rob and Scallie (and, over that week, to several other school friends who had heard rumors from sworn-to-secrecy Rob and Scallie, and now needed to find out if any of it was true) it was actually The Day I Lost My Virginity, in Cassandra's aunt's flat in London: the aunt was away, Cassandra had a key. I had (for proof) a packet of three condoms missing the one I had thrown away and a strip of four black-and-white photographs I had found on my first trip to London, abandoned in the basket of a photo booth in Victoria Station. The photo strip showed a girl about my age with long straight hair (I could not be certain of the color. Dark blond? Red? Light brown?) and a friendly, freckly, not unpretty, face. I pocketed it. In art class I did a pencil sketch of the third of the pictures, the one I liked the best, her head half-turned as if calling out to an unseen friend beyond the tiny curtain. She looked sweet, and charming. I would have liked her to be my girlfriend.

I put the drawing up on my bedroom wall, where I could see it from my bed.

After our third date (it was to see *Who Framed Roger Rabbit?*) I came back to school with bad news: Cassandra's family was going to Canada (a place that sounded more convincing to my ears than America), something to do with her father's job, and I would not see her for a long time. We hadn't really broken up, but we were being practical: those were the days when transatlantic phone calls were too expensive for teenagers. It was over.

I was sad. Everyone noticed how sad I was. They said they would have loved to have met her, and maybe when she comes back at Christmas? I was confident that by Christmas, she would be forgotten.

She was. By Christmas I was going out with Nikki Blevins and the only evidence that Cassandra had ever been a part of my life was her name, written on a couple of my exercise books, and the pencil drawing of her on my bedroom wall, with "Cassandra, February 19th, 1985" written underneath it.

When my mother sold the riding stable, the drawing was lost in the move. I was at art college at the time, considered my old pencil drawings as embarrassing as the fact that I had once invented a girlfriend, and did not care.

I do not believe I had thought of Cassandra for twenty years.

MY MOTHER SOLD the stables, the attached house and the meadows to a property developer, who built a housing estate where we had once lived, and, as part of the deal, gave her a small, detached house at the end of Seton Close. I visit her at least once a fortnight, arriving on Friday night, leaving Sunday morning, a routine as regular as the grandmother clock in the hall.

Mother is concerned that I am happy in life. She has started to mention that various of her friends have eligible daughters. This trip we had an extremely embarrassing conversation that began with her asking if I would like her to introduce me to the organist at her church, a very nice young man of about my age.

"Mother. I'm not gay."

"There's nothing wrong with it, dear. All sorts of people do it. They even get married. Well, not proper marriage, but it's the same thing."

"I'm still not gay."

"I just thought, still not married, and the painting and the modeling."

"I've had girlfriends, Mummy. You've even met some of them."

"Nothing that ever stuck, dear. I just thought there might be something you wanted to tell me."

"I'm not gay, Mother. I would tell you if I was." And then I said, "I snogged Tim Carter at a party when I was at art college but we were drunk and it never went beyond that."

She pursed her lips. "That's quite enough of that, young man." And then, changing the subject, as if to get rid of an unpleasant taste in her mouth, she said, "You'll never guess who I bumped into in Tesco's last week."

"No, I won't. Who?"

"Your old girlfriend. Your first girlfriend, I should say."

"Nikki Blevins? Hang on, she's married, isn't she? Nikki Woodbridge?"

"The one before her, dear. Cassandra. I was behind her, in the line. I would have been ahead of her, but I forgot that I needed cream for the berries today, so I went back to get it, and she was in front of me, and I knew her face was familiar. At first, I thought she was Joanie Simmond's youngest, the one with the speech disorder, what we used to call a stammer but apparently you can't say that anymore, but then I thought, *I* know where I know that face from, it was over your bed for five years, of course I said, 'It's not Cassandra, is it?' and she said, 'It is,' and I said, 'You'll laugh when I say this, but I'm Stuart Innes's mum.' She says, 'Stuart Innes?' and her face lit up. Well, she hung around while I was putting my groceries in my shopping bag, and she said she'd already been in touch with your friend Jeremy Porter on Bookface, and they'd been talking about you—"

"You mean Facebook? She was talking to Scallie on Facebook?"

"Yes, dear."

I drank my tea and wondered who my mother had actually been talking to. I said, "You're quite sure this was the Cassandra from over my bed?"

"Oh yes, dear. She told me about how you took her to Leicester Square, and how sad she was when they had to move to Canada. They went to Vancouver. I asked her if she ever met my cousin Leslie, he went to Vancouver after the war, but she said she didn't believe so, and it turns out it's actually a big sort of a place. I told her about the pencil drawing you did, and she seemed very up-to-date on your activities. She was thrilled when I told her that you were having a gallery opening this week."

"You *told* her that?"

"Yes, dear. I thought she'd like to know." Then my mother said, almost wistfully, "She's very pretty, dear. I think she's doing something in community theater." Then the conversation went over to the retirement of Dr. Dunnings, who had been our GP since before I was born, and how he was the only non-Indian doctor left in his practice and how my mother felt about this.

I lay in bed that night in my small bedroom at my mother's house and turned over the conversation in my head. I am no longer on Facebook and thought about rejoining to see who Scallie's friends were, and if this pseudo-Cassandra was one of them, but there were too many people I was happy not to see again, and I let it be, certain that when there was an explanation, it would prove to be a simple one, and I slept.

I HAVE BEEN showing in the Little Gallery in Chelsea for over a decade now. In the old days, I had a quarter of a wall and nothing priced at more than three hundred pounds. Now I get my own show every October, for a month, and it would be fair to say that I only have to sell a dozen paintings to know that my needs, rent and life are covered for another year. The unsold paintings remain on the gallery walls until they are gone and they are always gone by Christmas.

The couple who own the gallery, Paul and Barry, still call me "the beautiful boy" as they did twelve years ago, when I first exhibited with them, when it might actually have been true. Back then, they wore flowery, open-necked shirts and gold chains: now, in middle age, they wear expensive suits and talk too much for my liking about the stock exchange. Still, I enjoy their company. I see them three times a year: in September when they come to my studio to see what I've been working on, and select the paintings for the show; at the gallery, hanging and opening in October; and in February, when we settle up.

Barry runs the gallery. Paul co-owns it, comes out for the parties, but also works in the wardrobe department of the Royal Opera House. The preview party for this year's show was on a Friday evening. I had spent a nervous couple of days hanging the paintings. Now, my part was done, and there was nothing to do but wait, and hope people liked my art, and not to make a fool of myself. I did as I had done for the previous twelve years, on Barry's instructions: "Nurse the champagne. Fill up on water. There's nothing worse for the collector than encountering a drunken artist, unless he's famous for being drunk, and you are not, dear. Be amiable but enigmatic, and when people ask for the story behind the painting, say, 'My lips are sealed.' But for god's sake, imply there *is* one. It's the story they're buying."

I rarely invite people to the preview any longer: some artists do, regarding it as a social event. I do not. While I take my art seriously, as art, and am proud of my work (the latest exhibition was called "People in Landscapes," which pretty much says it all about my work anyway), I understand that the party exists solely as a commercial event, a come-on for eventual buyers and those who might say the right thing to other eventual buyers. I tell you this so you will not be surprised that Barry and Paul manage the guest list to the preview, not I.

The preview always begins at six thirty P.M. I had spent the afternoon hanging paintings, making sure everything looked as good as it could, as I have done every other year. The only thing that was different about the day of this particular event was how excited Paul looked, like a small boy struggling with the urge to tell you what he had bought you for a birthday present. That, and Barry, who said, while we were hanging, "I think tonight's show will put you on the map."

I said, "I think there's a typo on the Lake District one." An over-sized painting of Windermere at sunset, with two children staring lostly at the viewer from the banks. "It should say three thousand pounds. It says three hundred thousand."

"Does it?" said Barry, blandly. "My, my." But he did nothing to change it.

It was perplexing, but the first guests had arrived, a little early, and the mystery could wait. A young man invited me to eat a mushroom puff from a silver tray. I took my glass of nurse-this-slowly champagne from the table in the corner, and I prepared to mingle.

All the prices were high, and I doubted that the Little Gallery would be able to sell the paintings at those prices, and I worried about the year ahead.

Barry and Paul always take responsibility for moving me around the room, saying, "This is the artist, the beautiful boy who makes all these beautiful things, Stuart Innes," and I shake hands, and smile. By the end of the evening I will have met everyone, and Paul and Barry are very good about saying, "Stuart, you remember David, he writes about art for the *Telegraph* . . . ," and I for my part am good about saying, "Of course, how are you? So glad you could come."

The room was at its most crowded when a striking red-haired woman to whom I had not yet been introduced began shouting, "Representational bullshit!"

I was in conversation with the *Daily Telegraph* art critic and we turned. He said, "Friend of yours?"

I said, "I don't think so."

She was still shouting, although the sounds of the party had now quieted. She shouted, "Nobody's interested in this shit! Nobody!" Then she reached her hand into her coat pocket and pulled out a bottle of ink, shouted, "Try selling this now!" and threw ink at *Windermere Sunset*. It was blue-black ink.

Paul was by her side then, pulling the ink bottle away from her, saying, "That was a three-hundred-thousand-pound painting, young lady." Barry took her arm, said, "I think the police will want a word with you," and walked her back into his office. She shouted at us as she went, "I'm not afraid! I'm proud! Artists like him, just feeding off you gullible art buyers. You're all sheep! Representational crap!"

And then she was gone, and the party people were buzzing, and inspecting the ink-fouled painting and looking at me, and the *Telegraph* man was asking if I would like to comment and how I felt about seeing a three-hundred-thousand-pound painting destroyed, and I mumbled about how I was proud to be a painter, and said something about the transient nature of art, and he said that he supposed that tonight's event was an artistic happening in its own right, and we agreed that, artistic happening or not, the woman was not quite right in the head.

Barry reappeared, moving from group to group, explaining that Paul was dealing with the young lady, and that her eventual disposition would be up to me. The guests were still buzzing excitedly as he ushered them out of the door. Barry apologized as he did so, agreed that we lived in exciting times, explained that he would be open at the regular time tomorrow.

"That went well," he said, when we were alone in the gallery.

"*Well?* That was a disaster."

"Mm. 'Stuart Innes, the one who had the three-hundred-thousand-pound painting destroyed.' I think you need to be forgiving, don't you? She was a fellow artist, even one with different goals. Sometimes you need a little something to kick you up to the next level."

We went into the back room.

I said, "Whose idea was this?"

"Ours," said Paul. He was drinking white wine in the back room with the red-haired woman. "Well, Barry's mostly. But it needed a good little actress to pull it off, and I found her." She grinned, modestly: managed to look both abashed and pleased with herself.

"If this doesn't get you the attention you deserve, beautiful boy," said Barry, smiling at me, "nothing will. *Now* you're important enough to be attacked."

"The Windermere painting's ruined," I pointed out.

Barry glanced at Paul, and they giggled. "It's already sold, ink-splatters and all, for seventy-five thousand pounds," Barry said. "It's like I always say, people think they are buying the art, but really, they're buying the story."

Paul filled our glasses: "And we owe it all to you," he said to the woman. "Stuart, Barry, I'd like to propose a toast. *To Cassandra.*"

"Cassandra," we repeated, and we drank. This time I did not nurse my drink. I needed it.

Then, as the name was still sinking in, Paul said, "Cassandra, this ridiculously attractive and talented young man is, as I am sure you know, Stuart Innes."

"I know," she said. "Actually, we're very old friends."

"Do tell," said Barry.

"Well," said Cassandra, "twenty years ago, Stuart wrote my name on his maths exercise notebook."

She looked like the girl in my drawing, yes. Or like the girl in the photographs, all grown-up. Sharp-faced. Intelligent. Assured.

I had never seen her before in my life.

"Hello, Cassandra," I said. I couldn't think of anything else to say.

WE WERE IN the wine bar beneath my flat. They serve food there, too. It's more than just a wine bar.

I found myself talking to her as if she was someone I had known since childhood. And, I reminded myself, she wasn't. I had only met her that evening. She still had ink stains on her hands.

We had glanced at the menu, ordered the same thing—the vegetarian meze—and when it had arrived, both started with the dolmades, then moved on to the hummus.

"I made you up," I told her.

It was not the first thing I had said: first we had talked about her community theater, how she had become friends with Paul, his offer to her—a thousand pounds for this evening's show—and how she had needed the money but mostly said yes to him because it sounded like a fun adventure. Anyway, she said, she couldn't say no when she heard my name mentioned. She thought it was fate.

That was when I said it. I was scared she would think I was mad, but I said it. "I made you up."

"No," she said. "You didn't. I mean, obviously you didn't. I'm really here." Then she said, "Would you like to touch me?"

I looked at her. At her face, and her posture, at her eyes. She was everything I had ever dreamed of in a woman. Everything I had been missing in other women. "Yes," I said. "Very much."

"Let's eat our dinner first," she said. Then she said, "How long has it been since you were with a woman?"

"I'm not gay," I protested. "I have girlfriends."

"I know," she said. "When was the last one?"

I tried to remember. Was it Brigitte? Or the stylist the ad agency had sent me to Iceland with? I was not certain. "Two years," I said. "Perhaps three. I just haven't met the right person yet."

"You did once," she said. She opened her handbag then, a big floppy purple thing, pulled out a cardboard folder, opened it, removed a piece of paper, tape-browned at the corners. "See?"

I remembered it. How could I not? It had hung above my bed for years. She was looking around, as if talking to someone beyond the curtain. *Cassandra*, it said, *February 19th, 1985.* And it was signed, *Stuart Innes.* There is something at the same time both embarrassing and heartwarming about seeing your handwriting from when you were fifteen.

"I came back from Canada in '89," she said. "My parents' marriage fell apart out there, and Mum wanted to come home. I wondered about you, what you were doing, so I went to your old address. The house was empty. Windows were broken. It was obvious nobody lived there anymore. They'd knocked down the riding stables already—that made me so sad, I'd loved horses as a girl, obviously, but I walked through the house until I found your bedroom. It was obviously your bedroom, although all the furniture was gone. It still smelled like you. And this was still pinned to the wall. I didn't think anyone would miss it."

She smiled.

"Who *are* you?"

"Cassandra Carlisle. Aged thirty-four. Former actress. Failed playwright. Now running a community theater in Norwood. Drama therapy. Hall for rent. Four plays a year, plus workshops, and a local panto. Who are *you*, Stuart?"

"You know who I am." Then, "You know I've never met you before, don't you?"

She nodded. She said, "Poor Stuart. You live just above here, don't you?"

"Yes. It's a bit loud sometimes. But it's handy for the tube. And the rent isn't painful."

"Let's pay the bill, and go upstairs."

I reached out to touch the back of her hand. "Not yet," she said, moving her hand away before I could touch her. "We should talk first."

So we went upstairs.

"I like your flat," she said. "It looks exactly like the kind of place I imagine you being."

"It's probably time to start thinking about getting something a bit bigger," I told her. "But it does me fine. There's good light out the back for my studio—you can't get the effect now, at night. But it's great for painting."

It's strange, bringing someone home. It makes you see the place you live as if you've not been there before. There are two oil paintings of me in the lounge, from my short-lived career as an artists' model (I did not have the patience to stand and pose for very long, a failing I know), blown-up advertising photos of me in the little kitchen and the loo, book covers with me on—romance covers, mostly—over the stairs.

I showed her the studio, and then the bedroom. She examined the Edwardian barbers' chair I had rescued from an ancient place that closed down in Shoreditch. She sat down on the chair, pulled off her shoes.

"Who was the first grown-up you liked?" she asked.

"Odd question. My mother, I suspect. Don't know. Why?"

"I was three, perhaps four. He was a postman called Mister Postie. He'd come in his little post van and bring me lovely things. Not every day. Just sometimes. Brown paper packages with my name on, and inside would be toys or sweets or something. He had a funny, friendly face with a knobby nose."

"And he was real? He sounds like somebody a kid would make up."

"He drove a post van inside the house. It wasn't very big."

She began to unbutton her blouse. It was cream-colored, still flecked with splatters of ink. "What's the first thing you actually remember? Not something you were told you did. That you really remember."

"Going to the seaside when I was three, with my mum and my dad."

"Do you remember it? Or do you remember being told about it?"

"I don't see what the point of this is . . ."

She stood up, wiggled, stepped out of her skirt. She wore a white bra, dark green panties, frayed. Very human: not something you would wear to impress a new lover. I wondered what her breasts would look like, when the bra came off. I wanted to stroke them, to touch them to my lips.

She walked from the chair to the bed, where I was sitting.

"Lie down, now. On that side of the bed. I'll be next to you. Don't touch me."

I lay down, my hands at my sides. She looked down at me. She said, "You're so beautiful. I'm not honestly sure whether you're my type. You would have been when I was fifteen, though. Nice and sweet and unthreatening. Artistic. Ponies. A riding stable. And I bet you never make a move on a girl unless you're sure she's ready, do you?"

"No," I said. "I don't suppose that I do."

She lay down beside me.

"You can touch me now," said Cassandra.

I HAD STARTED thinking about Stuart again late last year. Stress, I think. Work was going well, up to a point, but I'd broken up with Pavel, who may or may not have been an actual bad hat although he certainly had his finger in many dodgy East European pies, and I was thinking about Internet dating. I had spent a stupid week joining the kind of websites that link you to old friends, and from there it was no distance to Jeremy "Scallie" Porter, and to Stuart Innes.

I don't think I could do it anymore. I lack the singlemindedness, the attention to detail. Something else you lose when you get older.

Mister Postie used to come in his van when my parents had no time for me. He would smile his big gnomey smile, wink an eye at me, hand me a brown-paper parcel with *Cassandra* written on it in big block letters, and inside would be a chocolate, or a doll, or a book. His final present was a pink plastic microphone, and I would walk around the house singing into it or pretending to be on TV. It was the best present I had ever been given.

My parents did not ask about the gifts. I did not wonder who was actually sending them. They came with Mister Postie, who drove his little van down the hall and up to my bedroom door, and who always knocked three times. I was a demonstrative girl, and the next time I saw him, after the plastic microphone, I ran to him and threw my arms around his legs.

It's hard to describe what happened then. He fell like snow, or like ash. For a moment I had been holding someone, then there was just powdery white stuff, and nothing.

I used to wish that Mister Postie would come back, after that, but he never did. He was over. After a while, he became embarrassing to remember: I had fallen for *that*.

So strange, this room.

I wonder why I could ever have thought that somebody who made me happy when I was fifteen would make me happy now. But Stuart was perfect: the riding stables (with ponies), and the painting (which showed me he was sensitive), and the inexperience with girls (so I could be his first) and how very, very tall, dark and handsome he would be. I liked the name, too: it was vaguely Scottish and (to my mind) sounded like the hero of a novel.

I wrote Stuart's name on my exercise books.

I did not tell my friends the most important thing about Stuart: that I had made him up.

And now I'm getting up off the bed and looking down at the out-line of a man, a silhouette in flour or ash or dust on the black satin bedspread, and I am getting into my clothes.

The photographs on the wall are fading, too. I didn't expect that. I wonder what will be left of his world in a few hours, wonder if I should have left well enough alone, a masturbatory fantasy, some-thing reassuring and comforting. He would have gone through his life without ever really touching anyone, just a picture and a painting and a half-memory for a handful of people who barely ever thought of him anymore.

I leave the flat. There are still people at the wine bar downstairs. They are sitting at the table, in the corner, where Stuart and I had been sitting earlier. The candle has burned way down but I imagine that it could almost be us. A man and a woman, in conversation. And soon enough, they will get up from their table and walk away, and the candle will be snuffed and the lights turned off and that will be that for another night.

I hail a taxi. Climb in. For a moment—for, I hope, the last time—I find myself missing Stuart Innes.

Then I sit back in the seat of the taxi, and I let him go. I hope I can afford the taxi fare and find myself wondering whether there will be a check in my bag in the morning, or just another blank sheet of paper. Then, more satisfied than not, I close my eyes, and I wait to be home.

THE CASE OF DEATH AND HONEY

2011

It was a mystery in those parts for years what had happened to the old white ghost man, the barbarian with his huge shoulder-bag. There were some who supposed him to have been murdered, and, later, they dug up the floor of Old Gao's little shack high on the hillside, looking for treasure, but they found nothing but ash and fire-blackened tin trays.

This was after Old Gao himself had vanished, you understand, and before his son came back from Lijiang to take over the beehives on the hill.

This is the problem, *wrote Holmes in 1899:* Ennui. And lack of interest. Or rather, it all becomes too easy. When the joy of solving crimes is the challenge, the possibility that you cannot, why then the crimes have something to hold your attention. But when each crime is soluble, and so easily soluble at that, why then there is no point in solving them.

Look: this man has been murdered. Well then, someone murdered him. He was murdered for one or more of a tiny handful of reasons: he inconvenienced someone, or he had something that someone wanted, or he had angered someone. Where is the challenge in that?

I would read in the dailies an account of a crime that had the police baffled, and I would find that I had solved it, in broad strokes if not in detail, before I had finished the article. Crime is too soluble. It dissolves. Why call the police and tell them the answers to their mysteries? I leave it, over and over again, as a challenge for them, as it is no challenge for me.

I am only alive when I perceive a challenge.

The bees of the misty hills, hills so high that they were sometimes called a mountain, were humming in the pale summer sun as they moved from spring flower to spring flower on the slope. Old Gao listened to them without pleasure. His cousin, in the village across the valley, had many dozens of hives, all of them already filling with honey, even this early in the year; also, the honey was as white as snow-jade. Old Gao did not believe that the white honey tasted any better than the yellow or light-brown honey that his own bees produced, although his bees produced it in meager quantities, but his cousin could sell his white honey for twice what Old Gao could get for the best honey he had.

On his cousin's side of the hill, the bees were earnest, hardworking, golden-brown workers, who brought pollen and nectar back to the hives in enormous quantities. Old Gao's bees were ill-tempered and black, shiny as bullets, who produced as much honey as they needed to get through the winter and only a little more: enough for Old Gao to sell from door to door, to his fellow villagers, one small lump of honeycomb at a time. He would charge more for the brood-comb, filled with bee-larvae, sweet-tasting morsels of protein, when he had brood-comb to sell, which was rarely, for the bees were angry and sullen and everything they did, they did as little as possible, including make more bees, and Old Gao was always aware that each piece of brood-comb he sold were bees he would not have to make honey for him to sell later in the year.

Old Gao was as sullen and as sharp as his bees. He had had a wife once, but she had died in childbirth. The son who had killed her lived for a week, then died himself. There would be nobody to say the funeral rites for Old Gao, no one to clean his grave for festivals or to put offerings upon it. He would die unremembered, as unremarkable and as unremarked as his bees.

The old white stranger came over the mountains in late spring of that year, as soon as the roads were passable, with a huge brown bag strapped to his shoulders. Old Gao heard about him before he met him.

"There is a barbarian who is looking at bees," said his cousin.

Old Gao said nothing. He had gone to his cousin to buy a pail-ful of second-rate comb, damaged or uncapped and liable soon to spoil. He bought it cheaply to feed to his own bees, and if he sold some of it in his own village, no one was any the wiser. The two men were drinking tea in Gao's cousin's hut on the hillside. From late spring, when the first honey started to flow, until first frost, Gao's cousin left his house in the village and went to live in the hut on the hillside, to live and to sleep beside his beehives, for fear of thieves. His wife and his children would take the honeycomb and the bottles of snow-white honey down the hill to sell.

Old Gao was not afraid of thieves. The shiny black bees of Old Gao's hives would have no mercy on anyone who disturbed them. He slept in his village, unless it was time to collect the honey.

"I will send him to you," said Gao's cousin. "Answer his questions, show him your bees and he will pay you."

"He speaks our tongue?"

"His dialect is atrocious. He said he learned to speak from sailors, and they were mostly Cantonese. But he learns fast, although he is old."

Old Gao grunted, uninterested in sailors. It was late in the morning, and there was still four hours' walking across the valley to his village, in the heat of the day. He finished his tea. His cousin drank finer tea than Old Gao had ever been able to afford.

He reached his hives while it was still light, put the majority of the uncapped honey into his weakest hives. He had eleven hives. His cousin had over a hundred. Old Gao was stung twice doing this, on the back of the hand and the back of the neck. He had been stung over a thousand times in his life. He could not have told you how many times. He barely noticed the stings of other bees, but the stings of his own black bees always hurt, even if they no longer swelled or burned.

The next day a boy came to Old Gao's house in the village, to tell him that there was someone—and that the someone was a giant foreigner—who was asking for him. Old Gao simply grunted. He walked across the village with the boy at his steady pace, while the boy ran ahead, and soon was lost to sight.

Old Gao found the stranger sitting drinking tea on the porch of the Widow Zhang's house. Old Gao had known the Widow Zhang's mother, fifty years ago. She had been a friend of his wife. Now she was long dead. He did not believe anyone who had known his wife still lived. The Widow Zhang fetched Old Gao tea, introduced him to the elderly barbarian, who had removed his bag and sat beside the small table.

They sipped their tea. The barbarian said, "I wish to see your bees."

Mycroft's death was the end of Empire, and no one knew it but the two of us. He lay in that pale room, his only covering a thin white sheet, as if he were already becoming a ghost from the popular imagination, and needed only eyeholes in the sheet to finish the impression.

I had imagined that his illness might have wasted him away, but he seemed huger than ever, his fingers swollen into white suet sausages.

I said, "Good evening, Mycroft. Doctor Hopkins tells me you have two weeks to live, and stated that I was under no circumstances to inform you of this."

"The man's a dunderhead," said Mycroft, his breath coming in huge wheezes between the words. "I will not make it to Friday."

"Saturday at least," I said.

"You always were an optimist. No, Thursday evening and then I shall be nothing more than an exercise in practical geometry for Hopkins and the funeral directors at Snigsby and Malterson, who will have the challenge, given the narrowness of the doors and corridors, of getting my carcass out of this room and out of the building."

"I had wondered," I said. "Particularly given the staircase. But they will take out the window-frame and lower you to the street like a grand piano."

Mycroft snorted at that. Then, "I am fifty-four years old, Sherlock. In my head is the British government. Not the ballot and hustings nonsense, but the business of the thing. There is no one else knows what the troop movements in the hills of Afghanistan have to do with the desolate shores of North Wales, no one else who sees the whole picture. Can you imagine the mess that this lot and their children will make of Indian Independence?"

I had not previously given any thought to the matter. "*Will* it become independent?"

"Inevitably. In thirty years, at the outside. I have written several recent memoranda on the topic. As I have on so many other subjects. There are memoranda on the Russian Revolution—that'll be along within the decade I'll wager—and on the German problem and . . . oh, so many others. Not that I expect them to be read or understood." Another wheeze. My brother's lungs rattled like the windows in an empty house. "You know, if I were to live, the British Empire might last another thousand years, bringing peace and improvement to the world."

In the past, especially when I was a boy, whenever I heard Mycroft make a grandiose pronouncement like that I would say something to bait him. But not now, not on his deathbed. And also I was certain that he was not speaking of the Empire as it was, a flawed and fallible construct of flawed and fallible people, but of a British Empire that existed only in his head, a glorious force for civilization and universal prosperity.

I do not, and did not, believe in empires. But I believed in Mycroft.

Mycroft Holmes. Four-and-fifty years of age. He had seen in the new century but the Queen would still outlive him by several months. She was more than thirty years older than he was, and in every way a tough old bird. I wondered to myself whether this unfortunate end might have been avoided.

Mycroft said, "You are right of course, Sherlock. Had I forced myself to exercise. Had I lived on birdseed and cabbages instead of porterhouse steak. Had I taken up country dancing along with a wife and a puppy and in all other ways behaved contrary to my nature, I might have bought myself another dozen or so years. But what is that in the scheme of things? Little enough. And sooner or later, I would enter my dotage. No. I am of the opinion that it would take two hundred years to train a functioning civil service, let alone a secret service . . ."

I had said nothing.

The pale room had no decorations on the wall of any kind. None of Mycroft's citations. No illustrations, photographs or paintings. I compared his austere digs to my own cluttered rooms in Baker Street and I wondered, not for the first time, at Mycroft's mind. He needed nothing on the outside, for it was all on the inside—everything he had seen, everything he had experienced, everything he had read. He could close his eyes and walk through the National Gallery, or browse the British Museum Reading Room—or, more likely, compare intelligence reports from the edge of the Empire with the price of wool in Wigan and the unemployment statistics in Hove, and then, from this and only this, order a man promoted or a traitor's quiet death.

Mycroft wheezed enormously, and then he said, "It is a crime, Sherlock."

"I beg your pardon?"

"A crime. It is a crime, my brother, as heinous and as monstrous as any of the penny-dreadful massacres you have investigated. A crime against the world, against nature, against order."

"I must confess, my dear fellow, that I do not entirely follow you. What is a crime?"

"My death," said Mycroft, "in the specific. And Death in general." He looked into my eyes. "I mean it," he said. "Now isn't *that* a crime worth investigating, Sherlock, old fellow? One that might keep your attention for longer than it will take you to establish that the poor fellow who used to conduct the brass band in Hyde Park was murdered by the third cornet using a preparation of strychnine."

"Arsenic," I corrected him, almost automatically.

"I think you will find," wheezed Mycroft, "that the arsenic, while present, had in fact fallen in flakes from the green-painted bandstand itself onto his supper. Symptoms of arsenical poison a complete red herring. No, it was strychnine that did for the poor fellow."

Mycroft said no more to me that day or ever. He breathed his last the following Thursday, late in the afternoon, and on the Friday the worthies of Snigsby and Malterson removed the casing from the window of the pale room, and lowered my brother's remains into the street, like a grand piano.

His funeral service was attended by me, by my friend Watson, by our cousin Harriet and, in accordance with Mycroft's express wishes—by no one else. The Civil Service, the Foreign Office, even the Diogenes Club—these institutions and their representatives were absent. Mycroft had been reclusive in life; he was to be equally as reclusive in death. So it was the three of us, and the parson, who had not known my brother, and had no conception that it was the more omniscient arm of the British government itself that he was consigning to the grave.

Four burly men held fast to the ropes and lowered my brother's remains to their final resting place, and did, I daresay, their utmost not to curse at the weight of the thing. I tipped each of them half a crown.

Mycroft was dead at fifty-four, and, as they lowered him into his grave, in my imagination I could still hear his clipped, gray wheeze as he seemed to be saying, "Now *there* is a crime worth investigating."

The stranger's accent was not too bad, although his vocabulary was limited, but he seemed to be talking in the local dialect, or something near to it. He was a fast learner. Old Gao hawked and spat into the dust of the street. He said nothing. He did not wish to take the stranger up the hillside; he did not wish to disturb his bees. In Old Gao's experience, the less he bothered his bees, the better they did. And if they stung the barbarian, what then?

The stranger's hair was silver-white, and sparse; his nose, the first barbarian nose that Old Gao had seen, was huge and curved and put Old Gao in mind of the beak of an eagle; his skin was tanned the same color as Old Gao's own, and was lined deeply. Old Gao was not certain that he could read a barbarian's face as he could read the face of a person, but he thought the man seemed most serious and, perhaps, unhappy.

"Why?"

"I study bees. Your brother tells me you have big black bees here. Unusual bees."

Old Gao shrugged. He did not correct the man on the relationship with his cousin.

The stranger asked Old Gao if he had eaten, and when Gao said that he had not the stranger asked the Widow Zhang to bring them soup and rice and whatever was good that she had in her kitchen, which turned out to be a stew of black tree-fungus and vegetables and tiny transparent river-fish, little bigger than tadpoles. The two men ate in silence. When they had finished eating, the stranger said, "I would be honored if you would show me your bees."

Old Gao said nothing, but the stranger paid Widow Zhang well and he put his bag on his back. Then he waited, and, when Old Gao began to walk, the stranger followed him. He carried his bag as if it weighed nothing to him. He was strong for an old man, thought Old Gao, and wondered whether all such barbarians were so strong.

"Where are you from?"

"England," said the stranger.

Old Gao remembered his father telling him about a war with the English, over trade and over opium, but that was long ago.

They walked up the hillside, that was, perhaps, a mountainside. It was steep, and the hillside was too rocky to be cut into fields. Old Gao tested the stranger's pace, walking faster than usual, and the stranger kept up with him, with his pack on his back.

The stranger stopped several times, however. He stopped to examine flowers—the small white flowers that bloomed in early spring elsewhere in the valley, but in late spring here on the side of the hill. There was a bee on one of the flowers, and the stranger knelt and observed it. Then he reached into his pocket, produced a large magnifying glass and examined the bee through it, and made notes in a small pocket notebook, in an incomprehensible writing.

Old Gao had never seen a magnifying glass before, and he leaned in to look at the bee, so black and so strong and so very different from the bees elsewhere in that valley.

"One of your bees?"

"Yes," said Old Gao. "Or one like it."

"Then we shall let her find her own way home," said the stranger, and he did not disturb the bee, and he put away the magnifying glass.

The Croft
East Dene, Sussex
August 11th, 1922

My dear Watson,

I have taken our discussion of this afternoon to heart, considered it carefully, and am prepared to modify my previous opinions.

I am amenable to your publishing your account of the incidents of 1903, specifically of the final case before my retirement, under the following condition.

In addition to the usual changes that you would make to disguise actual people and places, I would suggest that you replace the entire scenario we encountered (I speak of Professor Presbury's garden. I shall not write of it further here) with monkey glands, or some such extract from the testes of an ape or lemur, sent by some foreign mystery-man. Perhaps the monkey-extract could have the effect of making Professor Presbury move like an ape—he could be some kind of "creeping man," perhaps?—or possibly make him able to clamber up the sides of buildings and up trees. Perhaps he could grow a tail, but this might be too fanciful even for you, Watson, although no more fanciful than many of the rococo additions you have made in your histories to otherwise humdrum events in my life and work.

In addition, I have written the following speech, to be delivered by myself, at the end of your narrative. Please make certain that something much like this is there, in which I inveigh against living too long, and the foolish urges that push foolish people to do foolish things to prolong their foolish lives.

> *There is a very real danger to humanity. If one could live forever, if youth were simply there for the taking, that the material, the sensual, the worldly would all prolong their*

worthless lives. The spiritual would not avoid the call to
something higher. It would be the survival of the least fit.
What sort of cesspool may not our poor world become?
Something along those lines, I fancy, would set my mind at rest.
Let me see the finished article, please, before you submit it to be
published.

I remain, old friend, your most obedient servant,

Sherlock Holmes

They reached Old Gao's bees late in the afternoon. The beehives were gray wooden boxes piled behind a structure so simple it could barely be called a shack. Four posts, a roof, and hangings of oiled cloth that served to keep out the worst of the spring rains and the summer storms. A small charcoal brazier served for warmth, if you placed a blanket over it and yourself, and to cook upon; a wooden pallet in the center of the structure, with an ancient ceramic pillow, served as a bed on the occasions that Old Gao slept up on the mountainside with the bees, particularly in the autumn, when he harvested most of the honey. There was little enough of it compared to the output of his cousin's hives, but it was enough that he would sometimes spend two or three days waiting for the comb that he had crushed and stirred into a slurry to drain through the cloth into the buckets and pots that he had carried up the mountainside. He would melt the remainder, the sticky wax and bits of pollen and dirt and bee slurry, in a pot, to extract the beeswax, and he would give the sweet water back to the bees. Then he would carry the honey and the wax blocks down the hill to the village to sell.

He showed the barbarian stranger the eleven hives, watched impassively as the stranger put on a veil and opened a hive, examining first the bees, then the contents of a brood box, and finally the queen, through his magnifying glass. He showed no fear, no discomfort: in everything he did the stranger's movements were gentle and slow, and he was not stung, nor did he crush or hurt a single bee. This impressed Old Gao. He had assumed that barbarians were inscrutable, unreadable, mysterious creatures, but this man seemed overjoyed to have encountered Gao's bees. His eyes were shining.

Old Gao fired up the brazier, to boil some water. Long before the charcoal was hot, however, the stranger had removed from his bag a contraption of glass and metal. He had filled the upper half of it with water from the stream, lit a flame, and soon a kettleful of water was steaming and bubbling. Then the stranger took two tin mugs from his bag, and some green tea leaves wrapped in paper, and dropped the leaves into the mug, and poured on the water.

It was the finest tea that Old Gao had ever drunk: better by far than his cousin's tea. They drank it cross-legged on the floor. "I would like to stay here for the summer, in this house," said the stranger.

"Here? This is not even a house," said Old Gao. "Stay down in the village. Widow Zhang has a room."

"I will stay here," said the stranger. "Also I would like to rent one of your beehives."

Old Gao had not laughed in years. There were those in the village who would have thought such a thing impossible. But still, he laughed then, a guffaw of surprise and amusement that seemed to have been jerked out of him.

"I am serious," said the stranger. He placed four silver coins on the ground between them. Old Gao had not seen where he got them from: three silver Mexican pesos, a coin that had become popular in China years before, and a large silver yuan. It was as much money as Old Gao might see in a year of selling honey. "For this money," said the stranger, "I would like someone to bring me food: every three days should suffice."

Old Gao said nothing. He finished his tea and stood up. He pushed through the oiled cloth to the clearing high on the hillside. He walked over to the eleven hives: each consisted of two brood boxes with one, two, three or, in one case, even four boxes above that. He took the stranger to the hive with four boxes above it, each box filled with frames of comb.

"This hive is yours," he said.

They were plant extracts. That was obvious. They worked, in their way, for a limited time, but they were also extremely poisonous. But watching poor Professor Presbury during those final days—his skin, his eyes, his gait—had convinced me that he had not been on entirely the wrong path.

I took his case of seeds, of pods, of roots, and of dried extracts and I thought. I pondered. I cogitated. I reflected. It was an intellectual problem, and could be solved, as my old maths tutor had always sought to demonstrate to me, by intellect.

They were plant extracts, and they were lethal.

Methods I used to render them nonlethal rendered them quite ineffective.

It was not a three-pipe problem. I suspect it was something approaching a three-hundred-pipe problem before I hit upon an initial idea—a notion perhaps—of a way of processing the plants that might allow them to be ingested by human beings.

It was not a line of investigation that could easily be followed in Baker Street. So it was, in the autumn of 1903, that I moved to Sussex, and spent the winter reading every book and pamphlet and monograph so far published, I fancy, upon the care and keeping of bees. And so it was that in early April of 1904, armed only with theoretical knowledge, I took delivery from a local farmer of my first package of bees.

I wonder, sometimes, that Watson did not suspect anything. Then again, Watson's glorious obtuseness has never ceased to surprise me, and sometimes, indeed, I had relied upon it. Still, he knew what I was like when I had no work to occupy my mind, no case to solve. He knew my lassitude, my black moods when I had no case to occupy me.

So how could he believe that I had truly retired? He knew my methods.

Indeed, Watson was there when I took receipt of my first bees. He watched, from a safe distance, as I poured the bees from the package into the empty, waiting hive, like slow, gently humming treacle.

He saw my excitement, and he saw nothing.

And the years passed, and we watched the Empire crumble, we

watched the government unable to govern, we watched those poor heroic boys sent to the trenches of Flanders to die, all these things confirmed me in my opinions. I was not doing the right thing. I was doing the only thing.

As my face grew unfamiliar, and my finger joints swelled and ached (not so much as they might have done, though, which I attributed to the many bee stings I had received in my first few years as an investigative apiarist), and as Watson, dear, brave, obtuse Watson, faded with time and paled and shrank, his skin becoming grayer, his moustache becoming the same shade of gray as his skin, my resolve to conclude my researches did not diminish. If anything, it increased.

So: my initial hypotheses were tested upon the South Downs, in an apiary of my own devising, each hive modeled upon Langstroth's. I do believe that I made every mistake that ever a novice beekeeper could or has ever made, and in addition, due to my investigations, an entire hiveful of mistakes that no beekeeper has ever made before, or shall, I trust, ever make again. *The Case of the Poisoned Beehive,* Watson might have called many of them, although *The Mystery of the Transfixed Women's Institute* would have drawn more attention to my researches, had anyone been interested enough to investigate. (As it was, I chided Mrs. Telford for simply taking a jar of honey from the shelves here without consulting me, and I ensured that, in the future, she was given several jars for her cooking from the more regular hives, and that honey from the experimental hives was locked away once it had been collected. I do not believe that this ever drew comment.)

I experimented with Dutch bees, with German bees and with Italians, with Carniolans and Caucasians. I regretted the loss of our British bees to blight and, even where they had survived, to interbreeding, although I found and worked with a small hive I purchased and grew up from a frame of brood and a queen cell, from an old abbey in St. Albans, which seemed to me to be original British breeding stock.

I experimented for the best part of two decades, before I concluded that the bees that I sought, if they existed, were not to be found in England, and would not survive the distances they would need to travel to reach me by international parcel post. I needed to examine bees in India. I needed to travel perhaps further afield than that.

I have a smattering of languages.

I had my flower-seeds, and my extracts and tinctures in syrup. I needed nothing more.

I packed them up, arranged for the cottage on the Downs to be cleaned and aired once a week, and for Master Wilkins—to whom I am afraid I had developed the habit of referring, to his obvious distress, as "Young Villikins"—to inspect the beehives, and to harvest and sell surplus honey in Eastbourne market, and to prepare the hives for winter.

I told them I did not know when I should be back.

I am an old man. Perhaps they did not expect me to return. And, if this was indeed the case, they would, strictly speaking, have been right.

Old Gao was impressed, despite himself. He had lived his life among bees. Still, watching the stranger shake the bees from the boxes, with a practiced flick of his wrist, so cleanly and so sharply that the black bees seemed more surprised than angered, and simply flew or crawled back into their hive, was remarkable. The stranger then stacked the boxes filled with comb on top of one of the weaker hives, so Old Gao would still have the honey from the hive the stranger was renting.

So it was that Old Gao gained a lodger.

Old Gao gave the Widow Zhang's granddaughter a few coins to take the stranger food three times a week—mostly rice and vegetables, along with an earthenware pot filled, when she left at least, with boiling soup.

Every ten days Old Gao would walk up the hill himself. He went initially to check on the hives, but soon discovered that under the stranger's care all eleven hives were thriving as they had never thrived before. And indeed, there was now a twelfth hive, from a captured swarm of the black bees the stranger had encountered while on a walk along the hill.

Old Gao brought wood, the next time he came up to the shack, and he and the stranger spent several afternoons wordlessly working together, making extra boxes to go on the hives, building frames to fill the boxes.

One evening the stranger told Old Gao that the frames they were making had been invented by an American, only seventy years before. This seemed like nonsense to Old Gao, who made frames as his father had, and as they did across the valley, and as, he was certain, his grandfather and his grandfather's grandfather had, but he said nothing.

He enjoyed the stranger's company. They made hives together, and Old Gao wished that the stranger was a younger man. Then he would stay there for a long time, and Old Gao would have someone to leave his beehives to, when he died. But they were two old men, nailing boxes together, with thin frosty hair and old faces, and neither of them would see another dozen winters.

Old Gao noticed that the stranger had planted a small, neat garden beside the hive that he had claimed as his own, which he had moved away from the rest of the hives. He had covered it with a net. He had also created a "back door" to the hive, so that the only bees that could reach the plants came from the hive that he was renting. Old Gao also observed that, beneath the netting, there were several trays filled with what appeared to be sugar solution of some kind, one colored bright red, one green, one a startling blue, one yellow. He pointed to them, but all the stranger did was nod and smile.

The bees were lapping up the syrups, though, clustering and crowding on the sides of the tin dishes with their tongues down, eating until they could eat no more, and then returning to the hive.

The stranger had made sketches of Old Gao's bees. He showed the sketches to Old Gao, tried to explain the ways that Old Gao's bees differed from other honeybees, talked of ancient bees preserved in stone for millions of years, but here the stranger's Chinese failed him, and, truthfully, Old Gao was not interested. They were his bees, until he died, and after that, they were the bees of the mountainside. He had brought other bees here, but they had sickened and died, or been killed in raids by the black bees, who took their honey and left them to starve.

The last of these visits was in late summer. Old Gao went down the mountainside. He did not see the stranger again.

It is done.

It works. Already I feel a strange combination of triumph and of disappointment, as if of defeat, or of distant storm clouds teasing at my senses.

It is strange to look at my hands and to see, not my hands as I know them, but the hands I remember from my younger days: knuckles unswollen, dark hairs, not snow-white, on the backs.

It was a quest that had defeated so many, a problem with no apparent solution. The first emperor of China died and nearly destroyed his empire in pursuit of it, three thousand years ago, and all it took me was, what, twenty years?

I do not know if I did the right thing or not (although any "retirement" without such an occupation would have been, literally, maddening). I took the commission from Mycroft. I investigated the problem. I arrived, inevitably, at the solution.

Will I tell the world? I will not.

And yet, I have half a pot of dark brown honey remaining in my bag; a half a pot of honey that is worth more than nations. (I was tempted to write, *worth more than all the tea in China,* perhaps because of my current situation, but fear that even Watson would deride it as cliché.)

And speaking of Watson . . .

There is one thing left to do. My only remaining goal, and it is small enough. I shall make my way to Shanghai, and from there I shall take ship to Southampton, a half a world away.

And once I am there, I shall seek out Watson, if he still lives— and I fancy he does. It is irrational, I acknowledge, and yet I am certain that I would know, somehow, had Watson passed beyond the veil.

I shall buy theatrical makeup, disguise myself as an old man, so as not to startle him, and I shall invite my old friend over for tea.

There will be honey on buttered toast served with the tea that afternoon, I fancy.

There were tales of a barbarian who passed through the village on his way east, but the people who told Old Gao this did not believe that it could have been the same man who had lived in Gao's shack. This one was young and proud, and his hair was dark. It was not the old man who had walked through those parts in the spring, although, one person told Gao, the bag was similar.

Old Gao walked up the mountainside to investigate, although he suspected what he would find before he got there.

The stranger was gone, and the stranger's bag.

There had been much burning, though. That was clear. Papers had been burnt—Old Gao recognized the edge of a drawing the stranger had made of one of his bees, but the rest of the papers were ash, or blackened beyond recognition, even had Old Gao been able to read barbarian writing. The papers were not the only things to have been burnt; parts of the hive that stranger had rented were now only twisted ash; there were blackened, twisted strips of tin that might once have contained brightly colored syrups.

The color was added to the syrups, the stranger had told him once, so that he could tell them apart, although for what purpose Old Gao had never inquired.

He examined the shack like a detective, searching for a clue as to the stranger's nature or his whereabouts. On the ceramic pillow four silver coins had been left for him to find—two yuan coins and two silver pesos—and he put them away.

Behind the shack he found a heap of used slurry, with the last bees of the day still crawling upon it, tasting whatever sweetness was still on the surface of the still-sticky wax.

Old Gao thought long and hard before he gathered up the slurry, wrapped it loosely in cloth, and put it in a pot, which he filled with water. He heated the water on the brazier, but did not let it boil. Soon enough the wax floated to the surface, leaving the dead bees and the dirt and the pollen and the propolis inside the cloth.

He let it cool.

Then he walked outside, and he stared up at the moon. It was almost full.

He wondered how many villagers knew that his son had died as a baby. He remembered his wife, but her face was distant, and he had no portraits or photographs of her. He thought that there was nothing he was so suited for on the face of the earth as to keep the black, bullet-like bees on the side of this high, high hill. There was no other man who knew their temperament as he did.

The water had cooled. He lifted the now solid block of bees-wax out of the water, placed it on the boards of the bed to finish cooling. Then he took the cloth filled with dirt and impurities out of the pot. And then, because he too was, in his way, a detective, and once you have eliminated the impossible whatever remains, however unlikely, must be the truth, he drank the sweet water in the pot. There is a lot of honey in slurry, after all, even after the majority of it has dripped through a cloth and been purified. The water tasted of honey, but not a honey that Gao had ever tasted before. It tasted of smoke, and metal, and strange flowers, and odd perfumes. It tasted, Gao thought, a little like sex.

He drank it all down, and then he slept, with his head on the ceramic pillow.

When he woke, he thought, he would decide how to deal with his cousin, who would expect to inherit the twelve hives on the hill when Old Gao went missing.

He would be an illegitimate son, perhaps, the young man who would return in the days to come. Or perhaps a son. Young Gao. Who would remember, now? It did not matter.

He would go to the city and then he would return, and he would keep the black bees on the side of the mountain for as long as days and circumstances would allow.

THE MAN WHO FORGOT
RAY BRADBURY

2012

I AM FORGETTING THINGS, which scares me.

I am losing words, although I am not losing concepts. I hope that I am not losing concepts. If I am losing concepts, I am not aware of it. If I am losing concepts, how would I know?

Which is funny, because my memory was always so good. Everything was in there. Sometimes my memory was so good that I even thought that I could remember things I didn't know yet. Remembering forward . . .

I don't think there's a word for that, is there? Remembering things that haven't happened yet. I don't have that feeling I get when I go looking in my head for a word that isn't there, as if someone must have come and taken it in the night.

When I was a young man I lived in a big, shared house. I was a student, then. We had our own shelves in the kitchen, neatly marked with our names, and our own shelves in the fridge, upon which we kept our own eggs, cheese, yogurt, milk. I was always punctilious about using only my own provisions. Others were not so . . . there. I lost a word. One that would mean, "careful to obey the rules." The other people in the house were . . . not so. I would go to the fridge, but my eggs would have vanished.

I am thinking of a sky filled with spaceships, so many of them that they seem like a plague of locusts, silver against the luminous mauve of the night.

Things would go missing from my room back then as well. Boots. I remember my boots going. Or "being gone," I should say, as I did not ever actually catch them in the act of leaving. Boots do not just "go." Somebody "went" them. Just like my big dictionary. Same house, same time period. I went to the small bookshelf beside my bed (everything was by my bed: it was my room, but it was not much larger than a cupboard with a bed in it). I went to the shelf and the dictionary was gone, just a dictionary-sized hole in my shelf to show where my dictionary wasn't.

All the words and the book they came in were gone. Over the next month they also took my radio, a can of shaving foam, a pad of note-paper and a box of pencils. And my yogurt. And, I discovered during a power cut, my candles.

Now I am thinking of a boy with new tennis shoes, who believes he can run forever. No, that is not giving it to me. A dry town in which it rained forever. A road through the desert, on which good people see a mirage. A dinosaur that is a movie producer. The mirage was the pleasure dome of Kublai Khan. No . . .

Sometimes when the words go away I can find them by creeping up on them from another direction. Say I go and look for a word—I am discussing the inhabitants of the planet Mars, say, and I realize that the word for them has gone. I might also realize that the missing word occurs in a sentence or a title. The _____ Chronicles. My Favorite _____. If that does not give it to me I circle the idea. Little green men, I think, or tall, dark-skinned, gentle: Dark they were and golden-eyed . . . and suddenly the word Martians is waiting for me, like a friend or a lover at the end of a long day.

I left that house when my radio went. It was too wearing, the slow disappearance of the things I had thought so safely mine, item by item, thing by thing, object by object, word by word.

When I was twelve I was told a story by an old man that I have never forgotten.

A poor man found himself in a forest as night fell, and he had no prayer book to say his evening prayers. So he said, "God who knows all things, I have no prayer book and I do not know any prayers by heart. But you know all the prayers. You are God. So this is what I am going to do. I am going to say the alphabet, and I will let you put the words together."

There are things missing from my mind, and it scares me.

Icarus! It's not as if I have forgotten all names. I remember Icarus. He flew too close to the sun. In the stories, though, it's worth it. Always worth it to have tried, even if you fail, even if you fall like a meteor forever. Better to have flamed in the darkness, to have inspired others, to have *lived,* than to have sat in the darkness, cursing the people who borrowed, but did not return, your candle.

I have lost people, though.

It's strange when it happens. I don't actually *lose* them. Not in the way one loses one's parents, either as a small child, when you think you are holding your mother's hand in a crowd and then you look up, and it's not your mother, or later. When you have to find the words to describe them at a funeral service or a memorial, or when you are scattering ashes on a garden of flowers or into the sea.

I sometimes imagine I would like my ashes to be scattered in a library. But then the librarians would just have to come in early the next morning to sweep them up again, before the people got there.

I would like my ashes scattered in a library or, possibly, a funfair. A 1930s funfair, where you ride the black . . . the black . . . the . . . I have lost the word. Carousel? Roller coaster? The thing you ride, and you become young again. The Ferris wheel. Yes. There is another carnival that comes to town as well, bringing evil. "By the pricking of my thumbs . . ."

Shakespeare.

I remember Shakespeare, and I remember his name, and who he was and what he wrote. He's safe for now. Perhaps there are people who forget Shakespeare. They would have to talk about "the man who wrote to be or not to be"—not the film, starring Jack Benny, whose real name was Benjamin Kubelsky, who was raised in Waukegan, Illinois, an hour or so outside Chicago. Waukegan, Illinois, was later immortalized as Green Town, Illinois, in a series of stories and books by an American author who left Waukegan and went to live in

Los Angeles. I mean, of course, the man I am thinking of. I can see him in my head when I close my eyes.

I used to look at his photographs on the back of his books. He looked mild and he looked wise, and he looked kind.

He wrote a story about Poe, to stop Poe being forgotten, about a future where they burn books and they forget them, and in the story we are on Mars although we might as well be in Waukegan or Los Angeles, as critics, as those who would repress or forget books, as those who would take the words, all the words, dictionaries and radios full of words, as those people are walked through a house and murdered, one by one, by orangutan, by pit and pendulum, for the love of God, Montressor . . .

Poe. I know Poe. And Montressor. And Benjamin Kubelsky and his wife, Sadie Marks, who was no relation to the Marx Brothers and who performed as Mary Livingstone. All these names in my head.

I was twelve.

I had read the books, I had seen the film, and the burning point of paper was the moment where I knew that I would have to remember this. Because people would have to remember books, if other people burn them or forget them. We will commit them to memory. We will become them. We become authors. We become their books.

I am sorry. I lost something there. Like a path I was walking that dead-ended, and now I am alone and lost in the forest, and I am here and I do not know where here is anymore.

You must learn a Shakespeare play: I will think of you as *Titus Andronicus*. Or *you*, whoever you are, you could learn an Agatha Christie novel: you will be *Murder on the Orient Express*. Someone else can learn the poems of John Wilmot, Earl of Rochester, and you, whoever you are reading this, can learn a Dickens book and when I want to know what happened to Barnaby Rudge I will come to you. You can tell me.

And the people who would burn the words, the people who would take the books from the shelves, the firemen and the ignorant, the ones afraid of tales and words and dreams and Hallowe'en and people who have tattooed themselves with stories and Boys! You Can Grow Mushrooms in Your Cellar! and as long as your words which are people which are days which are my life, as long as your words survive, then you lived and you mattered and you changed the world and I cannot remember your name.

I learned your books. Burned them into my mind. In case the firemen come to town.

But who you are is gone. I wait for it to return to me. Just as I waited for my dictionary or for my radio, or for my boots, and with as meager a result.

All I have left is the space in my mind where you used to be. And I am not so certain about even that.

I was talking to a friend. And I said, "Are these stories familiar to you?" I told him all the words I knew, the ones about the monsters coming home to the house with the human child in it, the ones about the lightning salesman and the wicked carnival that followed him, and the Martians and their fallen glass cities and their perfect canals. I told him all the words, and he said he hadn't heard of them. That they didn't exist.

And I worry.

I worry I was keeping them alive. Like the people in the snow at the end of the story, walking backwards and forwards, remembering, repeating the words of the stories, making them real.

I think it's God's fault.

I mean, he can't be expected to remember everything, God can't. Busy chap. So perhaps he delegates things, sometimes, just goes, "You! I want you to remember the dates of the Hundred Years' War. And you, you remember okapi. You, remember Jack Benny who was Benjamin Kubelsky from Waukegan, Illinois." And then, when you forget the things that God has charged you with remembering, bam. No more okapi. Just an okapi-shaped hole in the world, which is halfway between an antelope and a giraffe. No more Jack Benny. No more Waukegan. Just a hole in your mind where a person or a concept used to be.

I don't know.

I don't know where to look. Have I lost an author, just as once I lost a dictionary? Or worse: did God give me this one small task, and now I have failed him, and because I have forgotten him he has gone from the shelves, gone from the reference works, and now he only exists in our dreams . . .

My dreams. I do not know your dreams. Perhaps you do not dream of a veldt that is only wallpaper but that eats two children. Perhaps you do not know that Mars is heaven, where our beloved dead go to wait for us, then consume us in the night. You do not dream of a man arrested for the crime of being a pedestrian.

I dream these things.

If he existed, then I have lost him. Lost his name. Lost his book titles, one by one by one. Lost the stories.

And I fear that I am going mad, for I cannot just be growing old.

If I have failed in this one task, oh God, then only let me do this thing, that you may give the stories back to the world.

Because, perhaps, if this works, they will remember him. All of them will remember him. His name will once more become synonymous with small American towns at Hallowe'en, when the leaves skitter across the sidewalk like frightened birds, or with Mars, or with love. And my name will be forgotten.

I am willing to pay that price, if the empty space in the bookshelf of my mind can be filled again, before I go.

Dear God, hear my prayer.

A . . . B . . . C . . . D . . . E . . . F . . . G . . .

EXCERPT FROM *THE OCEAN*
AT THE END OF THE LANE

2013

I T WAS THE first day of the spring holidays: three weeks of no
school. I woke early, thrilled by the prospect of endless days to fill
however I wished. I would read. I would explore.

I pulled on my shorts, my T-shirt, my sandals. I went downstairs
to the kitchen. My father was cooking, while my mother slept in. He
was wearing his dressing gown over his pajamas. He often cooked
breakfast on Saturdays. I said, "Dad! Where's my comic?" He always
bought me a copy of *SMASH!* before he drove home from work on
Fridays, and I would read it on Saturday mornings.

"In the back of the car. Do you want toast?"

"Yes," I said. "But not burnt."

My father did not like toasters. He toasted bread under the grill,
and, usually, he burnt it.

I went outside into the drive. I looked around. I went back into the
house, pushed the kitchen door, went in. I liked the kitchen door. It
swung both ways, in and out, so servants sixty years ago would be
able to walk in or out with their arms laden with dishes empty or full.

"Dad? Where's the car?"

"In the drive."

"No, it isn't."

"*What?*"

The telephone rang, and my father went out into the hall, where the phone was, to answer it. I heard him talking to someone.

The toast began to smoke under the grill. I got up on a chair and turned the grill off.

"That was the police," my father said. "Someone's reported seeing our car abandoned at the bottom of the lane. I said I hadn't even reported it stolen yet. Right. We can head down now, meet them there. *Toast!*"

He pulled the pan out from beneath the grill. The toast was smoking and blackened on one side.

"Is my comic there? Or did they steal it?"

"I don't know. The police didn't mention your comic."

My father put peanut butter on the burnt side of each piece of toast, replaced his dressing gown with a coat worn over his pajamas, put on a pair of shoes, and we walked down the lane together. He munched his toast as we walked. I held my toast, and did not eat it. We had walked for perhaps five minutes down the narrow lane which ran through fields on each side, when a police car came up behind us. It slowed, and the driver greeted my father by name.

I hid my piece of burnt toast behind my back while my father talked to the policeman. I wished my family would buy normal sliced white bread, the kind that went into toasters, like every other family I knew. My father had found a local baker's shop where they made thick loaves of heavy brown bread, and he insisted on buying them. He said they tasted better, which was, to my mind, nonsense. Proper bread was white, and pre-sliced, and tasted like almost nothing: that was the point.

The driver of the police car got out, opened the passenger door, told me to get in. My father rode up front beside the driver.

The police car went slowly down the lane. The whole lane was unpaved back then, just wide enough for one car at a time, a puddly, precipitous, bumpy way, with flints sticking up from it, the whole thing rutted by farm equipment and rain and time.

"These kids," said the policeman. "They think it's funny. Steal a car, drive it around, abandon it. They'll be locals."

"I'm just glad it was found so fast," said my father.

Past Caraway Farm, where a small girl with hair so blonde it was almost white, and red, red cheeks, stared at us as we went past. I held my piece of burnt toast on my lap.

"Funny them leaving it down here, though," said the policeman, "because it's a long walk back to anywhere from here."

We passed a bend in the lane and saw the white Mini over on the side, in front of a gate leading into a field, tires sunk deep in the brown mud. We drove past it, parked on the grass verge. The policeman let me out, and the three of us walked over to the Mini, while the policeman told my dad about crime in this area, and why it was obviously the local kids had done it, then my dad was opening the passenger side door with his spare key.

He said, "Someone left something on the back seat." My father reached back and pulled the blue blanket away, that covered the thing in the back seat, even as the policeman was telling him that he shouldn't do that, and I was staring at the back seat because that was where my comic was, so I saw it.

It was an *it*, the thing I was looking at, not a *him*.

Although I was an imaginative child, prone to nightmares, I had persuaded my parents to take me to Madame Tussauds waxworks in London, when I was six, because I had wanted to visit the Chamber of Horrors, expecting the movie-monster Chambers of Horrors I'd read about in my comics. I had wanted to thrill to waxworks of Dracula and Frankenstein's Monster and the Wolf-man. Instead I was walked through a seemingly endless sequence of dioramas of unremarkable, glum-looking men and women who had murdered people—usually lodgers, and members of their own families—and who were then murdered in their turn: by hanging, by the electric chair, in gas chambers. Most of them were depicted with their victims in awkward, social situations—seated around a dinner table, perhaps, as their poisoned family members expired. The plaques that explained who they were also told me that the majority of them had murdered their families and sold the bodies to anatomy. It was then that the word *anatomy* garnered its own edge of horror for me. I did not know what anatomy was. I knew only that *anatomy* made people kill their children.

The only thing that had kept me from running screaming from the Chamber of Horrors as I was led around it was that none of the waxworks had looked fully convincing. They could not truly look dead, because they did not ever look alive.

The thing in the back seat that had been covered by the blue blanket (I *knew* that blanket. It was the one that had been in my old bedroom, on the shelf, for when it got cold) was not convincing either. It looked a little like the opal miner, but it was dressed in a black suit, with a white, ruffled shirt and a black bow tie. Its hair was slicked back and artificially shiny. Its eyes were staring. Its lips were bluish, but its skin was very red. It looked like a parody of health. There was no gold chain around its neck.

I could see, underneath it, crumpled and bent, my copy of *SMASH!* with Batman, looking just as he did on the television, on the cover.

I don't remember who said what then, just that they made me stand away from the Mini. I crossed the road, and I stood there on my own while the policeman talked to my father and wrote things down in a notebook.

I stared at the Mini. A length of green garden hose ran from the exhaust pipe up to the driver's window. There was thick brown mud all over the exhaust, holding the hosepipe in place.

Nobody was watching me. I took a bite of my toast. It was burnt and cold.

At home, my father ate all the most burnt pieces of toast. "Yum!" he'd say, and "Charcoal! Good for you!" and "Burnt toast! My favorite!" and he'd eat it all up. When I was much older he confessed to me that he had not ever liked burnt toast, had only eaten it to prevent it from going to waste, and, for a fraction of a moment, my entire childhood felt like a lie: it was as if one of the pillars of belief that my world had been built upon had crumbled into dry sand.

The policeman spoke into a radio in the front of his car.

Then he crossed the road and came over to me. "Sorry about this, sonny," he said. "There's going to be a few more cars coming down this road in a minute. We should find you somewhere to wait that you won't be in the way. Would you like to sit in the back of my car again?"

I shook my head. I didn't want to sit there again.

Somebody, a girl, said, "He can come back with me to the farm-house. It's no trouble."

She was much older than me, at least eleven. Her red-brown hair was worn relatively short, for a girl, and her nose was snub. She was freckled. She wore a red skirt—girls didn't wear jeans much back then, not in those parts. She had a soft Sussex accent and sharp gray-blue eyes.

The girl went, with the policeman, over to my father, and she got permission to take me away, and then I was walking down the lane with her.

I said, "There is a dead man in our car."

"That's why he came down here," she told me. "The end of the road. Nobody's going to find him and stop him around here, three o'clock in the morning. And the mud there is wet and easy to mold."

"Do you think he killed himself?"

"Yes. Do you like milk? Gran's milking Bessie now."

I said, "You mean, real milk from a cow?" and then felt foolish, but she nodded, reassuringly.

I thought about this. I'd never had milk that didn't come from a bottle. "I think I'd like that."

We stopped at a small barn where an old woman, much older than my parents, with long gray hair, like cobwebs, and a thin face, was standing beside a cow. Long black tubes were attached to each of the cow's teats. "We used to milk them by hand," she told me. "But this is easier."

She showed me how the milk went from the cow down the black tubes and into the machine, through a cooler and into huge metal churns. The churns were left on a heavy wooden platform outside the barn, where they would be collected each day by a lorry.

The old lady gave me a cup of creamy milk from Bessie the cow, the fresh milk before it had gone through the cooler. Nothing I had drunk had ever tasted like that before: rich and warm and perfectly happy in my mouth. I remembered that milk after I had forgotten everything else.

"There's more of them up the lane," said the old woman, suddenly. "All sorts coming down with lights flashing and all. Such a palaver. You should get the boy into the kitchen. He's hungry, and a cup of milk won't do a growing boy."

The girl said, "Have you eaten?"

"Just a piece of toast. It was burned."

She said, "My name's Lettie. Lettie Hempstock. This is Hempstock Farm. Come on." She took me in through the front door, and into their enormous kitchen, sat me down at a huge wooden table, so stained and patterned that it looked as if faces were staring up at me from the old wood.

"We have breakfast here early," she said. "Milking starts at first light. But there's porridge in the saucepan, and jam to put in it."

She gave me a china bowl filled with warm porridge from the stovetop, with a lump of homemade blackberry jam, my favorite, in the middle of the porridge, then she poured cream on it. I swished it around with my spoon before I ate it, swirling it into a purple mess, and was as happy as I have ever been about anything. It tasted perfect.

A stocky woman came in. Her red-brown hair was streaked with gray, and cut short. She had apple cheeks, a dark green skirt that went to her knees, and Wellington boots. She said, "This must be the boy from the top of the lane. Such a business going on with that car. There'll be five of them needing tea soon."

Lettie filled a huge copper kettle from the tap. She lit a gas hob with a match and put the kettle onto the flame. Then she took down five chipped mugs from a cupboard, and hesitated, looking at the woman. The woman said, "You're right. Six. The doctor will be here too."

Then the woman pursed her lips and made a *tchutch!* noise. "They've missed the note," she said. "He wrote it so carefully too, folded it and put it in his breast pocket, and they haven't looked there yet."

"What does it say?" asked Lettie.

"Read it yourself," said the woman. I thought she was Lettie's mother. She seemed like she was somebody's mother. Then she said, "It says that he took all the money that his friends had given him to smuggle out of South Africa and bank for them in England, along with all the money he'd made over the years mining for opals, and he went to the casino in Brighton, to gamble, but he only meant to gamble with his own money. And then he only meant to dip into the money his friends had given him until he had made back the money he had lost.

"And then he didn't have anything," said the woman, "and all was dark."

"That's not what he wrote, though," said Lettie, squinting her eyes. "What he wrote was,

"To all my friends,

"Am so sorry it was not like I meant to and hope you can find it in your hearts to forgive me for I cannot forgive myself."

"Same thing," said the older woman. She turned to me. "I'm Lettie's ma," she said. "You'll have met my mother already, in the milking shed. I'm Mrs. Hempstock, but she was Mrs. Hempstock before me, so she's Old Mrs. Hempstock. This is Hempstock Farm. It's the oldest farm hereabouts. It's in the Domesday Book."

I wondered why they were all called Hempstock, those women, but I did not ask, any more than I dared to ask how they knew about the suicide note or what the opal miner had thought as he died. They were perfectly matter-of-fact about it.

Lettie said, "I nudged him to look in the breast pocket. He'll think he thought of it himself."

"There's a good girl," said Mrs. Hempstock. "They'll be in here when the kettle boils to ask if I've seen anything unusual and to have their tea. Why don't you take the boy down to the pond?"

"It's not a pond," said Lettie. "It's my ocean." She turned to me and said, "Come on." She led me out of the house the way we had come.

The day was still gray.

We walked around the house, down the cow path.

"Is it a real ocean?" I asked.

"Oh yes," she said.

We came on it suddenly: a wooden shed, an old bench, and between them, a duck pond, dark water spotted with duckweed and lily pads. There was a dead fish, silver as a coin, floating on its side on the surface.

"That's not good," said Lettie.

"I thought you said it was an ocean," I told her. "It's just a pond, really."

"It *is* an ocean," she said. "We came across it when I was just a baby, from the old country."

Lettie went into the shed and came out with a long bamboo pole, with what looked like a shrimping net on the end. She leaned over, carefully pushed the net beneath the dead fish. She pulled it out.

"But Hempstock Farm is in the Domesday Book," I said. "Your mum said so. And that was William the Conqueror."

"Yes," said Lettie Hempstock.

She took the dead fish out of the net and examined it. It was still soft, not stiff, and it flopped in her hand. I had never seen so many colors: it was silver, yes, but beneath the silver was blue and green and purple and each scale was tipped with black.

"What kind of fish is it?" I asked.

"This is very odd," she said. "I mean, mostly fish in this ocean don't die anyway." She produced a horn-handled pocketknife, although I could not have told you from where, and she pushed it into the stomach of the fish, and sliced along, toward the tail.

"This is what killed her," said Lettie.

She took something from inside the fish. Then she put it, still greasy from the fish-guts, into my hand. I bent down, dipped it into the water, rubbed my fingers across it to clean it off. I stared at it. Queen Victoria's face stared back at me.

"Sixpence?" I said. "The fish ate a sixpence?"

"It's not good, is it?" said Lettie Hempstock. There was a little sunshine now: it showed the freckles that clustered across her cheeks and nose, and, where the sunlight touched her hair, it was a coppery red. And then she said, "Your father's wondering where you are. Time to be getting back."

I tried to give her the little silver sixpence, but she shook her head. "You keep it," she said. "You can buy chocolates, or sherbet lemons."

"I don't think I can," I said. "It's too small. I don't know if shops will take sixpences like these nowadays."

"Then put it in your piggy bank," she said. "It might bring you luck." She said this doubtfully, as if she were uncertain what kind of luck it would bring.

The policemen and my father and two men in brown suits and ties were standing in the farmhouse kitchen. One of the men told me he was a policeman, but he wasn't wearing a uniform, which I thought was disappointing: if I were a policeman, I was certain, I would wear my uniform whenever I could. The other man with a suit and tie I recognized as Doctor Smithson, our family doctor. They were finishing their tea.

My father thanked Mrs. Hempstock and Lettie for taking care of me, and they said I was no trouble at all, and that I could come again. The policeman who had driven us down to the Mini now drove us back to our house, and dropped us off at the end of the drive.

"Probably best if you don't talk about this to your sister," said my father.

I didn't want to talk about it to anybody. I had found a special place, and made a new friend, and lost my comic, and I was holding an old-fashioned silver sixpence tightly in my hand.

I said, "What makes the ocean different to the sea?"

"Bigger," said my father. "An ocean is much bigger than the sea. Why?"

"Just thinking," I said. "Could you have an ocean that was as small as a pond?"

"No," said my father. "Ponds are pond-sized, lakes are lake-sized. Seas are seas and oceans are oceans. Atlantic, Pacific, Indian, Arctic. I think that's all of the oceans there are."

My father went up to his bedroom, to talk to my mum and to be on the phone up there. I dropped the silver sixpence into my piggy bank. It was the kind of china piggy bank from which nothing could be removed. One day, when it could hold no more coins, I would be allowed to break it, but it was far from full.

CLICK-CLACK THE RATTLEBAG

2013

B EFORE YOU TAKE me up to bed, will you tell me a story?"
"Do you actually need me to take you up to bed?" I asked
the boy.

He thought for a moment. Then, with intense seriousness, "Yes,
actually I think I do. It's because of, I've finished my homework, and
so it's my bedtime, and I am a bit scared. Not very scared. Just a bit.
But it is a very big house, and lots of times the lights don't work and
it's sort of dark."

I reached over and tousled his hair.

"I can understand that," I said. "It is a very big old house." He
nodded. We were in the kitchen, where it was light and warm. I put
down my magazine on the kitchen table. "What kind of story would
you like me to tell you?"

"Well," he said, thoughtfully. "I don't think it should be *too* scary,
because then when I go up to bed, I will just be thinking about monsters the whole time. But if it isn't just a *little* bit scary then I won't
be interested. And you make up scary stories, don't you? I know she
says that's what you do."

"She exaggerates. I write stories, yes. Nothing that's really been
published, yet, though. And I write lots of different kinds of stories."

"But you *do* write scary stories?"

"Yes."

The boy looked up at me from the shadows by the door, where he was waiting. "Do you know any stories about Click-Clack the Rattle-bag?"

"I don't think so."

"Those are the best sorts of stories."

"Do they tell them at your school?"

He shrugged. "Sometimes."

"What's a Click-Clack the Rattlebag story?"

He was a precocious child, and was unimpressed by his sister's boyfriend's ignorance. You could see it on his face. "Everybody knows them."

"I don't," I said, trying not to smile.

He looked at me as if he was trying to decide whether or not I was pulling his leg. He said, "I think maybe you should take me up to my bedroom, and then you can tell me a story before I go to sleep, but probably it should be a not-scary story because I'll be up in my bedroom then, and it's actually a bit dark up there, too."

I said, "Shall I leave a note for your sister, telling her where we are?"

"You can. But you'll hear when they get back. The front door is very slammy."

We walked out of the warm and cozy kitchen into the hallway of the big house, where it was chilly and drafty and dark. I flicked the light switch, but the hall remained dark.

"The bulb's gone," the boy said. "That always happens."

Our eyes adjusted to the shadows. The moon was almost full, and blue-white moonlight shone in through the high windows on the staircase, down into the hall. "We'll be all right," I said.

"Yes," said the boy, soberly. "I am very glad you're here." He seemed less precocious now. His hand found mine, and he held on to my fingers comfortably, trustingly, as if he'd known me all his life. I felt responsible and adult. I did not know if the feeling I had for his sister, who was my girlfriend, was love, not yet, but I liked that the child treated me as one of the family. I felt like his big brother, and I stood taller, and if there was something unsettling about the empty house I would not have admitted it for worlds.

The stairs creaked beneath the threadbare stair-carpet. "Click-Clacks," said the boy, "are the best monsters ever."

"Are they from television?"

"I don't think so. I don't think any people know where they come from. Mostly they come from the dark."

"Good place for a monster to come."

"Yes."

We walked along the upper corridor in the shadows, moving from patch of moonlight to patch of moonlight. It really was a big house. I wished I had a flashlight.

"They come from the dark," said the boy, holding on to my hand. "I think probably they're made of dark. And they come in when you don't pay attention. That's when they come in. And then they take you back to their . . . not nests. What's a word that's like *nests,* but not?"

"*House?*"

"No. It's not a house."

"*Lair?*"

He was silent. Then, "I think that's the word, yes. *Lair.*" He squeezed my hand. He stopped talking.

"Right. So they take the people who don't pay attention back to their lair. And what do they do then, your monsters? Do they suck all the blood out of you, like vampires?"

He snorted. "Vampires don't suck all the blood out of you. They only drink a little bit. Just to keep them going, and, you know, flying around. Click-Clacks are much scarier than vampires."

"I'm not scared of vampires," I told him.

"Me neither. I'm not scared of vampires either. Do you want to know what Click-Clacks do? They *drink* you," said the boy.

"Like a Coke?"

"Coke is very bad for you," said the boy. "If you put a tooth in Coke, in the morning, it will be dissolved into nothing. That's how bad Coke is for you and why you must always clean your teeth, every night."

I'd heard the Coke story as a boy, and had been told, as an adult, that it wasn't true, but was certain that a lie which promoted dental hygiene was a good lie, and I let it pass.

"Click-Clacks drink you," said the boy. "First they bite you, and then you go all *ishy* inside, and all your meat and all your brains and everything except your bones and your skin turns into a wet, milkshakey stuff and then the Click-Clack sucks it out through the holes where your eyes used to be."

"That's disgusting," I told him. "Did you make it up?"

We'd reached the last flight of stairs, all the way into the big house. "No."

"I can't believe you kids make up stuff like that."

"You didn't ask me about the rattlebag," he said. "Right. What's the rattlebag?"

"Well," he said, sagely, soberly, a small voice from the darkness beside me, "once you're just bones and skin, they hang you up on a hook, and you rattle in the wind."

"So what do these Click-Clacks look like?" Even as I asked him, I wished I could take the question back, and leave it unasked. I thought: *Huge spidery creatures. Like the one in the shower this morning.* I'm afraid of spiders.

I was relieved when the boy said, "They look like what you aren't expecting. What you aren't paying attention to."

We were climbing wooden steps now. I held on to the railing on my left, held his hand with my right, as he walked beside me. It smelled like dust and old wood, that high in the house. The boy's tread was certain, though, even though the moonlight was scarce.

"Do you know what story you're going to tell me, to put me to bed?" he asked. "Like I said. It doesn't actually have to be scary."

"Not really."

"Maybe you could tell me about this evening. Tell me what you did?"

"That won't make much of a story for you. My girlfriend just moved into a new place on the edge of town. She inherited it from an aunt or someone. It's very big and very old. I'm going to spend my first night with her, tonight, so I've been waiting for an hour or so for her and her housemates to come back with the wine and an Indian takeaway."

"See?" said the boy. There was that precocious amusement again;

but all kids can be insufferable sometimes, when they think they know something you don't. It's probably good for them. "You know all that. But you don't think. You just let your brain fill in the gaps."

He pushed open the door to the attic room. It was perfectly dark, now, but the opening door disturbed the air, and I heard things rattle gently, like dry bones in thin bags, in the slight wind. Click. Clack. Click. Clack. Like that.

I would have pulled away then, if I could; but small, firm fingers pulled me forward, unrelentingly, into the dark.

THE SLEEPER AND THE SPINDLE

2013

I T WAS THE closest kingdom to the queen's, as the crow flies, but not even the crows flew it. The high mountain range that served as the border between the two kingdoms discouraged crows as much as it discouraged people, and it was considered unpassable.

More than one enterprising merchant, on each side of the mountains, had commissioned folk to hunt for the mountain pass that would, if it were there, have made a rich man or woman of anyone who controlled it. The silks of Dorimar could have been in Kanselaire in weeks, in months, not years. But there was no such pass to be found and so, although the two kingdoms shared a common border, nobody crossed from one kingdom to the next.

Even the dwarfs, who were tough, and hardy, and composed of magic as much as of flesh and blood, could not go over the mountain range.

This was not a problem for the dwarfs. They did not go over the mountain range. They went under it.

THREE DWARFS, TRAVELING as swiftly as one through the dark paths beneath the mountains:

"Hurry! Hurry!" said the dwarf in the rear. "We have to buy her the finest silken cloth in Dorimar. If we do not hurry, perhaps it will be sold, and we will be forced to buy her the second-finest cloth."

"We know! We know!" said the dwarf in the front. "And we shall buy her a case to carry the cloth back in, so it will remain perfectly clean and untouched by dust."

The dwarf in the middle said nothing. He was holding his stone tightly, not dropping it or losing it, and was concentrating on nothing else but this. The stone was a ruby, rough-hewn from the rock and the size of a hen's egg. It would be worth a kingdom when cut and set, and would be easily exchanged for the finest silks of Dorimar.

It would not have occurred to the dwarfs to give the young queen anything they had dug themselves from beneath the earth. That would have been too easy, too routine. It's the distance that makes a gift magical, so the dwarfs believed.

THE QUEEN WOKE early that morning.

"A week from today," she said aloud. "A week from today, I shall be married."

It seemed both unlikely and extremely final. She wondered how she would feel to be a married woman. It would be the end of her life, she decided, if life was a time of choices. In a week from now she would have no choices. She would reign over her people. She would have children. Perhaps she would die in childbirth, perhaps she would die as an old woman, or in battle. But the path to her death, heartbeat by heartbeat, would be inevitable.

She could hear the carpenters in the meadows beneath the castle, building the seats that would allow her people to watch her marry. Each hammer blow sounded like the dull pounding of a huge heart.

THE THREE DWARFS scrambled out of a hole in the side of the river-bank, and clambered up into the meadow, one, two, three. They climbed to the top of a granite outcrop, stretched, kicked, jumped and stretched themselves once more. Then they sprinted north, toward the cluster of low buildings that made the village of Giff, and in particular to the village inn.

The innkeeper was their friend: they had brought him a bottle of Kanselaire wine—deep red, sweet and rich, and nothing like the sharp, pale wines of those parts—as they always did. He would feed them, and send them on their way, and advise them.

The innkeeper, chest as huge as his barrels, beard as bushy and as orange as a fox's brush, was in the taproom. It was early in the morning, and on the dwarfs' previous visits at that time of day the room had been empty, but now there must have been thirty people in that place, and not a one of them looked happy.

The dwarfs, who had expected to sidle into an empty taproom, found all eyes upon them.

"Goodmaster Foxen," said the tallest dwarf to the innkeeper.

"Lads," said the innkeeper, who thought that the dwarfs were boys, for all that they were four, perhaps five times his age, "I know you travel the mountain passes. We need to get out of here."

"What's happening?" said the smallest of the dwarfs.

"Sleep!" said the sot by the window.

"Plague!" said a finely dressed woman.

"Doom!" exclaimed a tinker, his saucepans rattling as he spoke. "Doom is coming!"

"We travel to the capital," said the tallest dwarf, who was no bigger than a child, and had no beard. "Is there plague in the capital?"

"It is not plague," said the sot by the window, whose beard was long and gray, and stained yellow with beer and wine. "It is sleep, I tell you."

"How can sleep be a plague?" asked the smallest dwarf, who was also beardless.

"A witch!" said the sot.

"A bad fairy," corrected a fat-faced man.

"She was an enchantress, as I heard it," interposed the pot girl.

"Whatever she was," said the sot, "she was not invited to a birthing celebration."

"That's all tosh," said the tinker. "She would have cursed the princess whether she'd been invited to the naming-day party or not. She was one of those forest witches, driven to the margins a thousand years ago, and a bad lot. She cursed the babe at birth, such that when the girl was eighteen she would prick her finger and sleep forever."

The fat-faced man wiped his forehead. He was sweating, although it was not warm. "As I heard it, she was going to die, but another fairy, a good one this time, commuted her magical death sentence to one of sleep. Magical sleep," he added.

"So," said the sot. "She pricked her finger on something-or-other. And she fell asleep. And the other people in the castle—the lord and the lady, the butcher, baker, milkmaid, lady-in-waiting—all of them slept, as she slept. None of them have aged a day since they closed their eyes."

"There were roses," said the pot girl. "Roses that grew up around the castle. And the forest grew thicker, until it became impassable. This was, what, a hundred years ago?"

"Sixty. Perhaps eighty," said a woman who had not spoken until now. "I know, because my aunt Letitia remembered it happening, when she was a girl, and she was no more than seventy when she died of the bloody flux, and that was only five years ago come Summer's End."

". . . and brave men," continued the pot girl. "Aye, and brave women too, they say, have attempted to travel to the Forest of Acaire, to the castle at its heart, to wake the princess, and, in waking her, to wake all the sleepers, but each and every one of those heroes ended their lives lost in the forest, murdered by bandits, or impaled upon the thorns of the rosebushes that encircle the castle—"

"Wake her how?" asked the middle-sized dwarf, hand still clutching his rock, for he thought in essentials.

"The usual method," said the pot girl, and she blushed. "Or so the tales have it."

"Right," said the tallest dwarf. "So, bowl of cold water poured on the face and a cry of 'Wakey! Wakey!'?"

"A kiss," said the sot. "But nobody has ever got that close. They've been trying for sixty years or more. They say the witch—"

"Fairy," said the fat man.

"Enchantress," corrected the pot girl.

"Whatever she is," said the sot. "She's still there. That's what they say. If you get that close. If you make it through the roses, she'll be waiting for you. She's old as the hills, evil as a snake, all malevolence and magic and death."

The smallest dwarf tipped his head on one side. "So, there's a sleeping woman in a castle, and perhaps a witch or fairy there with her. Why is there also a plague?"

"Over the last year," said the fat-faced man. "It started in the north, beyond the capital. I heard about it first from travelers coming from Stede, which is near the Forest of Acaire."

"People fell asleep in the towns," said the pot girl.

"Lots of people fall asleep," said the tallest dwarf. Dwarfs sleep rarely: twice a year at most, for several weeks at a time, but he had slept enough in his long lifetime that he did not regard sleep as anything special or unusual.

"They fall asleep whatever they are doing, and they do not wake up," said the sot. "Look at us. We fled the towns to come here. We have brothers and sisters, wives and children, sleeping now in their houses or cowsheds, at their workbenches. All of us."

"It is moving faster and faster," said the thin, red-haired woman who had not spoken previously. "Now it covers a mile, perhaps two miles, each day."

"It will be here tomorrow," said the sot, and he drained his flagon, gestured to the innkeeper to fill it once more. "There is nowhere for us to go to escape it. Tomorrow, everything here will be asleep. Some of us have resolved to escape into drunkenness before the sleep takes us."

"What is there to be afraid of in sleep?" asked the smallest dwarf. "It's just sleep. We all do it."

"Go and look," said the sot. He threw back his head, and drank as much as he could from his flagon. Then he looked back at them, with eyes unfocused, as if he were surprised to still see them there. "Well, go on. Go and look for yourselves." He swallowed the remaining drink, then he lay his head upon the table.

They went and looked.

"ASLEEP?" ASKED THE queen. "Explain yourselves. How so, asleep?"

The dwarf stood upon the table so he could look her in the eye. "Asleep," he repeated. "Sometimes crumpled upon the ground. Sometimes standing. They sleep in their smithies, at their awls, on milking stools. The animals sleep in the fields. Birds, too, slept, and we saw them in trees or dead and broken in fields where they had fallen from the sky."

The queen wore a wedding gown, whiter than the snow. Around her, attendants, maids of honor, dressmakers and milliners clustered and fussed.

"And why did you three also not fall asleep?"

The dwarf shrugged. He had a russet-brown beard that had always made the queen think of an angry hedgehog attached to the lower portion of his face. "Dwarfs are magical things. This sleep is a magical thing also. I felt sleepy, mind."

"And then?"

She was the queen, and she was questioning him as if they were alone. Her attendants began removing her gown, taking it away, folding and wrapping it, so the final laces and ribbons could be attached to it, so it would be perfect.

Tomorrow was the queen's wedding day. Everything needed to be perfect.

"By the time we returned to Foxen's Inn they were all asleep, every man jack-and-jill of them. It is expanding, the zone of the spell, a few miles every day."

The mountains that separated the two lands were impossibly high, but not wide. The queen could count the miles. She pushed one pale hand through her raven-black hair, and she looked most serious. "What do you think, then?" she asked the dwarf. "If I went there. Would I sleep, as they did?"

He scratched his arse, unselfconsciously. "You slept for a year," he said. "And then you woke again, none the worse for it. If any of the bigguns can stay awake there, it's you."

Outside, the townsfolk were hanging bunting in the streets and decorating their doors and windows with white flowers. Silverware had been polished and protesting children had been forced into tubs of lukewarm water (the oldest child always got the first dunk and the hottest, cleanest water) and then scrubbed with rough flannels until their faces were raw and red. They were then ducked under the water, and the backs of their ears were washed as well.

"I am afraid," said the queen, "that there will be no wedding tomorrow."

She called for a map of the kingdom, identified the villages closest to the mountains, sent messengers to tell the inhabitants to evacuate to the coast or risk royal displeasure.

She called for her first minister and informed him that he would be responsible for the kingdom in her absence, and that he should do his best neither to lose it nor to break it.

She called for her fiancé and told him not to take on so, and that they would still be married, even if he was but a prince and she already a queen, and she chucked him beneath his pretty chin and kissed him until he smiled.

She called for her mail shirt.

She called for her sword.

She called for provisions, and for her horse, and then she rode out of the palace, toward the east.

IT WAS A full day's ride before she saw, ghostly and distant, like clouds against the sky, the shape of the mountains that bordered the edge of her kingdom.

The dwarfs were waiting for her, at the last inn in the foothills of the mountains, and they led her down deep into the tunnels, the way that the dwarfs travel. She had lived with them, when she was little more than a child, and she was not afraid.

The dwarfs did not speak to her as they walked the deep paths, except, on more than one occasion, to say, "Mind your head."

"HAVE YOU NOTICED," asked the shortest of the dwarfs, "something unusual?" They had names, the dwarfs, but human beings were not permitted to know what they were, such things being sacred.

The queen had a name, but nowadays people only ever called her Your Majesty. Names are in short supply in this telling.

"I have noticed many unusual things," said the tallest of the dwarfs.

They were in Goodmaster Foxen's inn.

"Have you noticed, that even amongst all the sleepers, there is something that does not sleep?"

"I have not," said the second tallest, scratching his beard. "For each of them is just as we left him or her. Head down, drowsing, scarcely breathing enough to disturb the cobwebs that now festoon them . . ."

"The cobweb spinners do not sleep," said the tallest dwarf.

It was the truth. Industrious spiders had threaded their webs from finger to face, from beard to table. There was a modest web in the deep cleavage of the pot girl's breasts. There was a thick cobweb that stained the sot's beard gray. The webs shook and swayed in the draft of air from the open door.

"I wonder," said one of the dwarfs, "whether they will starve and die, or whether there is some magical source of energy that gives them the ability to sleep for a long time."

"I would presume the latter," said the queen. "If, as you say, the original spell was cast by a witch, seventy years ago, and those who were there sleep even now, like Red-beard beneath his hill, then obviously they have not starved or aged or died."

The dwarfs nodded. "You are very wise," said a dwarf. "You always were wise."

The queen made a sound of horror and of surprise.

"That man," she said, pointing. "He looked at me."

It was the fat-faced man. He had moved slowly, tearing the webbing, moved his face so that he was facing her. He had looked at her, yes, but he had not opened his eyes.

"People move in their sleep," said the smallest dwarf.

"Yes," said the queen. "They do. But not like that. That was too slow, too stretched, too *meant*."

"Or perhaps you imagined it," said a dwarf.

The rest of the sleeping heads in that place moved slowly, in a stretched way, as if they meant to move. Now each of the sleeping faces was facing the queen.

"You did not imagine it," said the same dwarf. He was the one with the red-brown beard. "But they are only looking at you with their eyes closed. That is not a bad thing."

The lips of the sleepers moved in unison. No voice, only the whisper of breath through sleeping lips.

"Did they just say what I thought they said?" asked the shortest dwarf.

"They said, 'Mama. It is my birthday,' " said the queen, and she shivered.

THEY RODE NO horses. The horses they passed all slept, standing in fields, and could not be woken.

The queen walked fast. The dwarfs walked twice as fast as she did, in order to keep up.

The queen found herself yawning.

"Bend over, towards me," said the tallest dwarf. She did so. The dwarf slapped her around the face. "Best to stay awake," he said, cheerfully.

"I only yawned," said the queen.

"How long, do you think, to the castle?" asked the smallest dwarf.

"If I remember my tales and my maps correctly," said the queen, "the Forest of Acaire is about seventy miles from here. Three days' march." And then she said, "I will need to sleep tonight. I cannot walk for another three days."

"Sleep, then," said the dwarfs. "We will wake you at sunrise."

She went to sleep that night in a hayrick, in a meadow, with the dwarfs around her, wondering if she would ever wake to see another morning.

THE CASTLE IN the Forest of Acaire was a gray, blocky thing, all grown over with climbing roses. They tumbled down into the moat and grew almost as high as the tallest tower. Each year the roses grew out further: close to the stone of the castle there were only dead, brown stems and creepers, with old thorns sharp as knives. Fifteen feet away the plants were green and the blossoming roses grew thickly. The climbing roses, living and dead, were a brown skeleton, splashed with color, that rendered the gray fastness less precise.

The trees in the Forest of Acaire were pressed thickly together, and the forest floor was dark. A century before, it had been a forest only in name: it had been hunting lands, a royal park, home to deer and wild boar and birds beyond counting. Now the forest was a dense tangle, and the old paths through the forest were overgrown and forgotten.

THE FAIR-HAIRED GIRL in the high tower slept.

All the people in the castle slept. Each of them was fast asleep, excepting only one.

The old woman's hair was gray, streaked with white, and was so sparse her scalp showed. She hobbled, angrily, through the castle, leaning on her stick, as if she were driven only by hatred, slamming doors, talking to herself as she walked. "Up the blooming stairs and past the blooming cook and what are you cooking now, eh, great lardarse, nothing in your pots and pans but dust and more dust, and all you ever ruddy do is snore."

Into the kitchen garden, neatly tended. The old woman picked rampion and rocket, and she pulled a large turnip from the ground.

Eighty years before, the palace had held five hundred chickens; the pigeon coop had been home to hundreds of fat white doves; rabbits had run, white-tailed, across the greenery of the grass square inside the castle walls; and fish had swum in the moat and the pond: carp and trout and perch. There remained now only three chickens. All the sleeping fish had been netted and carried out of the water. There were no more rabbits, no more doves.

She had killed her first horse sixty years back, and eaten as much of it as she could before the flesh went rainbow-colored and the carcass began to stink and crawl with blue flies and maggots. Now she only butchered the larger mammals in midwinter, when nothing rotted and she could hack and sear frozen chunks of the animal's corpse until the spring thaw.

The old woman passed a mother, asleep, with a baby dozing at her breast. She dusted them, absently, as she passed, made certain that the baby's sleepy mouth remained on the nipple.

She ate her meal of turnips and greens in silence.

IT WAS THE first great grand city they had come to. The city gates were high and impregnably thick, but they were open wide.

The three dwarfs were all for going around it, for they were not comfortable in cities, distrusted houses and streets as unnatural things, but they followed their queen.

Once in the city, the sheer numbers of people made them uncomfortable. There were sleeping riders on sleeping horses; sleeping cabmen up on still carriages that held sleeping passengers; sleeping children clutching their balls and hoops and the whips for their spinning tops;

sleeping flower women at their stalls of brown, rotten, dried flowers; even sleeping fishmongers beside their marble slabs. The slabs were covered with the remains of stinking fish, and they were crawling with maggots. The rustle and movement of the maggots was the only movement and noise the queen and the dwarfs encountered.

"We should not be here," grumbled the dwarf with the angry brown beard.

"This road is more direct than any other road we could follow," said the queen. "Also it leads to the bridge. The other roads would force us to ford the river."

The queen's temper was equable. She went to sleep at night, and she woke in the morning, and the sleeping sickness had not touched her.

The maggots' rustlings, and, from time to time, the gentle snores and shifts of the sleepers, were all that they heard as they made their way through the city. And then a small child, asleep on a step, said, loudly and clearly, "Are you spinning? Can I see?"

"Did you hear that?" asked the queen.

The tallest dwarf said only, "Look! The sleepers are waking!"

He was wrong. They were not waking.

The sleepers were standing, however. They were pushing themselves slowly to their feet, and taking hesitant, awkward, sleeping steps. They were sleepwalkers, trailing gauze cobwebs behind them. Always, there were cobwebs being spun.

"How many people, human people I mean, live in a city?" asked the smallest dwarf.

"It varies," said the queen. "In our kingdom, no more than twenty, perhaps thirty thousand people. This seems bigger than our cities. I would think fifty thousand people. Or more. Why?"

"Because," said the dwarf, "they appear to all be coming after us."

Sleeping people are not fast. They stumble, they stagger, they move like children wading through rivers of treacle, like old people whose feet are weighed down by thick, wet mud.

The sleepers moved towards the dwarfs and the queen. They were easy for the dwarfs to outrun, easy for the queen to outwalk. And yet, and yet, there were so many of them. Each street they came to was filled with sleepers, cobweb-shrouded, eyes tight closed or eyes open and rolled back in their heads showing only the whites, all of them shuffling sleepily forward.

The queen turned and ran down an alleyway and the dwarfs ran with her.

"This is not honorable," said a dwarf. "We should stay and fight."

"There is no honor," gasped the queen, "in fighting an opponent who has no idea that you are even there. No honor in fighting someone who is dreaming of fishing or of gardens or of long-dead lovers."

"What would they do if they caught us?" asked the dwarf beside her.

"Do you wish to find out?" asked the queen.

"No," admitted the dwarf.

They ran, and they ran, and they did not stop from running until they had left the city by the far gates, and had crossed the bridge that spanned the river.

THE OLD WOMAN had not climbed the tallest tower in a dozen years. It was a laborious climb, and each step took its toll on her knees and on her hips. She walked up the curving stone stairwell, each small shuffling step she took an agony. There were no railings there, nothing to make the steep steps easier. She leaned on her stick, sometimes, to catch her breath, and then she kept climbing.

She used the stick on the webs, too: thick cobwebs hung and covered the stairs, and the old woman shook her stick at them, pulling the webs apart, leaving spiders scurrying for the walls.

The climb was long, and arduous, but eventually she reached the tower room.

There was nothing in the room but a spindle and a stool, beside one slitted window, and a bed in the center of the round room. The bed was opulent: crimson and gold cloth was visible beneath the dusty netting that covered it and protected its sleeping occupant from the world.

The spindle sat on the ground, beside the stool, where it had fallen almost eighty years before.

The old woman pushed at the netting with her stick, and dust filled the air. She stared at the sleeper on the bed.

The girl's hair was the golden-yellow of meadow flowers. Her lips were the pink of the roses that climbed the palace walls. She had not seen daylight in a long time, but her skin was creamy, neither pallid nor unhealthy.

Her chest rose and fell, almost imperceptibly, in the semidarkness.

The old woman reached down, and picked up the spindle. She said, aloud, "If I drove this spindle through your heart, then you'd not be so pretty-pretty, would you? Eh? Would you?"

She walked towards the sleeping girl in the dusty white dress. Then she lowered her hand. "No. I can't. I wish to all the gods I could."

All of her senses were fading with age, but she thought she heard voices from the forest. Long ago she had seen them come, the princes and the heroes, watched them perish, impaled upon the thorns of the roses, but it had been a long time since anyone, hero or otherwise, had reached as far as the castle.

"Eh," she said aloud, as she said so much aloud, for who was to hear her? "Even if they come, they'll die screaming on the blinking thorns. There's nothing they can do—that anyone can do. Nothing at all."

A WOODCUTTER, ASLEEP by the bole of a tree half-felled half a century before, and now grown into an arch, opened his mouth as the queen and the dwarfs passed and said, "My! What an unusual naming-day present that must have been!"

Three bandits, asleep in the middle of what remained of the trail, their limbs crooked as if they had fallen asleep while hiding in a tree above and had tumbled, without waking, to the ground below, said, in unison, without waking, "Will you bring me roses?"

One of them, a huge man, fat as a bear in autumn, seized the queen's ankle as she came close to him. The smallest dwarf did not even hesitate: he lopped the hand off with his hand-axe, and the queen pulled the man's fingers away, one by one, until the hand fell on the leaf mold.

"Bring me roses," said the three bandits as they slept, with one voice, while the blood oozed indolently onto the ground from the stump of the fat man's arm. "I would be so happy if only you would bring me roses."

THEY FELT THE castle long before they saw it: felt it as a wave of sleep that pushed them away. If they walked towards it their heads fogged, their minds frayed, their spirits fell, their thoughts clouded. The moment they turned away they woke up into the world, felt brighter, saner, wiser.

The queen and the dwarfs pushed deeper into the mental fog.

Sometimes a dwarf would yawn and stumble. Each time the other dwarfs would take him by the arms and march him forward, struggling and muttering, until his mind returned.

The queen stayed awake, although the forest was filled with people she knew could not be there. They walked beside her on the path. Sometimes they spoke to her.

"Let us now discuss how diplomacy is affected by matters of natural philosophy," said her father.

"My sisters ruled the world," said her stepmother, dragging her iron shoes along the forest path. They glowed a dull orange, yet none of the dry leaves burned where the shoes touched them. "The mortal folk rose up against us, they cast us down. And so we waited, in crevices, in places they do not see us. And now, they adore me. Even you, my stepdaughter. Even you adore me."

"You are so beautiful," said her mother, who had died so very long ago. "Like a crimson rose fallen in the snow."

Sometimes wolves ran beside them, pounding dust and leaves up from the forest floor, although the passage of the wolves did not disturb the huge cobwebs that hung like veils across the path. Also, sometimes the wolves ran through the trunks of trees and off into the darkness.

The queen liked the wolves, and was sad when one of the dwarfs began shouting, saying that the spiders were bigger than pigs, and the wolves vanished from her head and from the world. (It was not so. They were only spiders of a regular size, used to spinning their webs undisturbed by time and by travelers.)

THE DRAWBRIDGE ACROSS the moat was down, and they crossed it, although everything seemed to be pushing them away. They could not enter the castle, however: thick thorns filled the gateway, and fresh growth covered with roses.

The queen saw the remains of men in the thorns: skeletons in armor and skeletons unarmored. Some of the skeletons were high on the sides of the castle, and the queen wondered if they had climbed up, seeking an entry, and died there, or if they had died on the ground, and been carried upwards as the roses grew.

She came to no conclusions. Either way was possible.

And then her world was warm and comfortable, and she became certain that closing her eyes for only a handful of moments would not be harmful. Who would mind?

"Help me," croaked the queen.

The dwarf with the brown beard pulled a thorn from the rosebush nearest to him, and jabbed it hard into the queen's thumb, and pulled it out again. A drop of dark blood dripped onto the flagstones of the gateway.

"Ow!" said the queen. And then, "Thank you!"

They stared at the thick barrier of thorns, the dwarfs and the queen. She reached out and picked a rose from the thorn-creeper nearest her, and bound it into her hair.

"We could tunnel our way in," said the dwarfs. "Go under the moat and into the foundations and up. Only take us a couple of days."

The queen pondered. Her thumb hurt, and she was pleased her thumb hurt. She said, "This began here eighty or so years ago. It began slowly. It only spread recently. It is spreading faster and faster. We do not know if the sleepers can ever wake. We do not know anything, save that we may not actually have another two days."

She eyed the dense tangle of thorns, living and dead, decades of dried, dead plants, their thorns as sharp in death as ever they were when alive. She walked along the wall until she reached a skeleton, and she pulled the rotted cloth from its shoulders, and felt it as she did so. It was dry, yes. It would make good kindling.

"Who has the tinder box?" she asked.

THE OLD THORNS burned so hot and so fast. In fifteen minutes orange flames snaked upwards: they seemed, for a moment, to engulf the building, and then they were gone, leaving just blackened stone.

The remaining thorns, those strong enough to have withstood

the heat, were easily cut through by the queen's sword, and were hauled away and tossed into the moat.

The four travelers went into the castle.

The old woman peered out of the slitted window at the flames below her. Smoke drifted in through the window, but neither the flames nor the roses reached the highest tower. She knew that the castle was being attacked, and she would have hidden in the tower room, had there been anywhere to hide, had the sleeper not been on the bed.

She swore, and began, laboriously, to walk down the steps, one at a time. She intended to make it down as far as the castle's battlements, where she could head over to the far side of the building, to the cellars. She could hide there. She knew the building better than anybody. She was slow, but she was cunning, and she could wait. Oh, she could wait.

She heard their calls rising up the stairwell.

"This way!"

"Up here!"

"It feels worse this way. Come on! Quickly!"

She turned around, then, did her best to hurry upward, but her legs moved no faster than they had when she was climbing earlier that day. They caught her just as she reached the top of the steps, three men, no higher than her hips, closely followed by a young woman in travel-stained clothes, with the blackest hair the old woman had ever seen.

The young woman said, "Seize her," in a tone of casual command. The little men took her stick.

"She's stronger than she looks," said one of them, his head still ringing from the blow she had got in with the stick, before he had taken it. They walked her back into the round tower room.

"The fire?" said the old woman, who had not talked to anyone who could answer her for decades. "Was anyone killed in the fire? Did you see the king or the queen?"

The young woman shrugged. "I don't think so. The sleepers we passed were all inside, and the walls are thick. Who are you?"

Names. Names. The old woman squinted, then she shook her head. She was herself, and the name she had been born with had been eaten by time and lack of use.

"Where is the princess?"

The old woman just stared at her.

"And why are you awake?"

She said nothing. They spoke urgently to one another then, the little men and the queen. "Is she a witch? There's a magic about her, but I do not think it's of her making."

"Guard her," said the queen. "If she is a witch, that stick might be important. Keep it from her."

"It's my stick," said the old woman. "I think it was my father's. But he had no more use for it."

The queen ignored her. She walked to the bed, pulled down the silk netting. The sleeper's face stared blindly up at them.

"So this is where it began," said one of the little men.

"On her birthday," said another.

"Well," said the third. "Somebody's got to do the honors."

"I shall," said the queen, gently. She lowered her face to the sleeping woman's. She touched the pink lips to her own carmine lips and she kissed the sleeping girl long and hard.

"DID IT WORK?" asked a dwarf.

"I do not know," said the queen. "But I feel for her, poor thing. Sleeping her life away."

"You slept for a year in the same witch-sleep," said the dwarf. "You did not starve. You did not rot."

The figure on the bed stirred, as if she were having a bad dream from which she was fighting to wake herself.

The queen ignored her. She had noticed something on the floor beside the bed. She reached down and picked it up. "Now this," she said. "This smells of magic."

"There's magic all through this," said the smallest dwarf.

"No, *this*," said the queen. She showed him the wooden spindle, the base half wound around with yarn. "*This* smells of magic."

"It was here, in this room," said the old woman, suddenly. "And I was little more than a girl. I had never gone so far before, but I climbed all the steps, and I went up and up and round and round until I came to the topmost room. I saw that bed, the one you see, although there was nobody in it. There was only an old woman, sitting on the stool, spinning wool into yarn with her spindle. I had never seen a spindle before. She asked if I would like a go. She took the wool in her hand and gave me the spindle to hold. And then, she held my thumb and pressed it against the point of the spindle until blood flowed, and she touched the blooming blood to the thread. And then she said—"

A voice interrupted her. A young voice it was, a girl's voice, but still sleep-thickened. "I said, now I take your sleep from you, girl, just as I take from you your ability to harm me in my sleep, for someone needs to be awake while I sleep. Your family, your friends, your world will sleep too. And then I lay down on the bed, and I slept, and they slept, and as each of them slept I stole a little of their life, a little of their dreams, and as I slept I took back my youth and my beauty and my power. I slept and I grew strong. I undid the ravages of time and I built myself a world of sleeping slaves."

She was sitting up in the bed. She looked so beautiful, and so very young.

The queen looked at the girl, and saw what she was searching for: the same look that she had seen in her stepmother's eyes, and she knew what manner of creature this girl was.

"We had been led to believe," said the tallest dwarf, "that when you woke, the rest of the world would wake with you."

"Why ever would you think that?" asked the golden-haired girl, all childlike and innocent (ah, but her eyes! Her eyes were so old). "I like them asleep. They are more *biddable*." She stopped for a moment. Then she smiled. "Even now they come for you. I have called them here."

"It's a high tower," said the queen. "And sleeping people do not move fast. We still have a little time to talk, Your Darkness."

"Who are you? Why would we talk? Why do you know to address me that way?" The girl climbed off the bed and stretched deliciously, pushing each finger out before running her fingertips through her golden hair. She smiled, and it was as if the sun shone into that dim room. "The little people will stop where they are, now. I do not like them. And you, girl. You will sleep too."

"No," said the queen.

She hefted the spindle. The yarn wrapped around it was black with age and with time.

The dwarfs stopped where they stood, and they swayed, and closed their eyes.

The queen said, "It's always the same with your kind. You need youth and you need beauty. You used your own up so long ago, and now you find ever-more-complex ways of obtaining them. And you always want power."

They were almost nose to nose, now, and the fair-haired girl seemed so much younger than the queen.

"Why don't you just go to sleep?" asked the girl, and she smiled guilelessly, just as the queen's stepmother had smiled when she wanted something. There was a noise on the stairs, far below them.

"I slept for a year in a glass coffin," said the queen. "And the woman who put me there was much more powerful and dangerous than you will ever be."

"More powerful than I am?" The girl seemed amused. "I have a million sleepers under my control. With every moment that I slept I grew in power, and the circle of dreams grows faster and faster with every passing day. I have my youth—so much youth! I have my beauty. No weapon can harm me. Nobody alive is more powerful than I am."

She stopped and stared at the queen.

"You are not of our blood," she said. "But you have some of the skill." She smiled, the smile of an innocent girl who has woken on a spring morning. "Ruling the world will not be easy. Nor will maintaining order among those of the Sisterhood who have survived into this degenerate age. I will need someone to be my eyes and ears, to administer justice, to attend to things when I am otherwise engaged. I will stay at the center of the web. You will not rule with me, but beneath me, but you will still rule, and rule continents, not just a tiny kingdom." She reached out a hand and stroked the queen's pale skin, which, in the dim light of that room, seemed almost as white as snow.

The queen said nothing.

"Love me," said the girl. "All will love me, and you, who woke me, you must love me most of all."

The queen felt something stirring in her heart. She remembered her stepmother then. Her stepmother had liked to be adored. Learning how to be strong, to feel her own emotions and not another's, had been hard; but once you learned the trick of it, you did not forget. And she did not wish to rule continents.

The girl smiled at her with eyes the color of the morning sky.

The queen did not smile. She reached out her hand. "Here," she said. "This is not mine."

She passed the spindle to the old woman beside her. The old woman hefted it, thoughtfully. She began to unwrap the yarn from the spindle with arthritic fingers. "This was my life," she said. "This thread was my life . . ."

"It *was* your life. You gave it to me," said the sleeper, irritably. "And it has gone on much too long."

The tip of the spindle was still sharp after so many decades.

The old woman, who had once been a princess, held the yarn tightly in her hand, and she thrust the point of the spindle at the golden-haired girl's breast.

The girl looked down as a trickle of red blood ran down her breast and stained her white dress crimson.

"No weapon can harm me," she said, and her girlish voice was petulant. "Not anymore. Look. It's only a scratch."

"It's not a weapon," said the queen, who understood what had happened. "It's your own magic. And a scratch is all that was needed."

The girl's blood soaked into the thread that had once been wrapped about the spindle, the thread that ran from the spindle to the raw wool in the old woman's hand.

The girl looked down at the blood staining her dress, and at the blood on the thread, and she said only, "It was just a prick of the skin, nothing more." She seemed confused.

The noise on the stairs was getting louder. A slow, irregular shuffling, as if a hundred sleepwalkers were coming up a stone spiral staircase with their eyes closed.

The room was small, and there was nowhere to hide, and the room's window was a narrow slit in the stones.

The old woman, who had not slept in so many decades, she who had once been a princess, said, "You took my dreams. You took my sleep. Now, that's enough of all that." She was a very old woman: her fingers were gnarled, like the roots of a hawthorn bush. Her nose was long, and her eyelids drooped, but there was a look in her eyes in that moment that was the look of someone young.

She swayed, and then she staggered, and she would have fallen to the floor if the queen had not caught her first.

The queen carried the old woman to the bed, marveling at how little she weighed, and placed her on the crimson counterpane. The old woman's chest rose and fell.

The noise on the stairs was louder now. Then a silence, followed, suddenly, by a hubbub, as if a hundred people were talking at once, all surprised and angry and confused.

The beautiful girl said, "But—" and now there was nothing girlish or beautiful about her. Her face fell, and became less shapely. She reached down to the smallest dwarf, pulled his hand-axe from his belt. She fumbled with the axe, held it up threateningly, with hands all wrinkled and worn.

The queen drew her sword (the blade-edge was notched and damaged from the thorns) but instead of striking, she took a step backwards.

"Listen! They are waking up," she said. "They are all waking up. Tell me again about the youth you stole from them. Tell me again about your beauty and your power. Tell me again how clever you were, Your Darkness."

When the people reached the tower room, they saw an old woman asleep on a bed, and they saw the queen, standing tall, and beside her, the dwarfs, who were shaking their heads, or scratching them.

They saw something else on the floor also: a tumble of bones, a hank of hair as fine and as white as fresh-spun cobwebs, a tracery of gray rags across it, and over all of it, an oily dust.

"Take care of her," said the queen, pointing with the dark wooden spindle at the old woman on the bed. "She saved your lives."

She left, then, with the dwarfs. None of the people in that room or on the steps dared to stop them or would ever understand what had happened.

A MILE OR SO from the castle, in a clearing in the Forest of Acaire, the queen and the dwarfs lit a fire of dry twigs, and in it they burned the thread and the fiber. The smallest dwarf chopped the spindle into fragments of black wood with his axe, and they burned them too. The wood chips gave off a noxious smoke as they burned, which made the queen cough, and the smell of old magic was heavy in the air.

Afterwards, they buried the charred wooden fragments beneath a rowan tree.

By evening they were on the outskirts of the forest, and had reached a cleared track. They could see a village across the hill, and smoke rising from the village chimneys.

"So," said the dwarf with the beard. "If we head due west, we can be at the mountains by the end of the week, and we'll have you back in your palace in Kanselaire within ten days."

"Yes," said the queen.

"And your wedding will be late, but it will happen soon after your return, and the people will celebrate, and there will be joy unbounded through the kingdom."

"Yes," said the queen. She said nothing, but sat on the moss beneath an oak tree and tasted the stillness, heartbeat by heartbeat.

There are choices, she thought, when she had sat long enough. *There are always choices.*

She made her choice.

The queen began to walk, and the dwarfs followed her.

"You *do* know we're heading east, don't you?" said one of the dwarfs.

"Oh yes," said the queen.

"Well, *that's* all right then," said the dwarf.

They walked to the east, all four of them, away from the sunset and the lands they knew, and into the night.

A CALENDAR OF TALES

2013

JANUARY TALE

WHAP!

"Is it always like this?" The kid seemed disoriented. He was glancing around the room, unfocused. That would get him killed, if he wasn't careful.

Twelve tapped him on the arm. "Nope. Not always. If there's any trouble, it'll come from up there."

He pointed to an attic door, in the ceiling above them. The door was askew, and the darkness waited behind it like an eye.

The kid nodded. Then he said, "How long have we got?"

"Together? Maybe another ten minutes."

"One thing I kept asking them at Base, they wouldn't answer. They said I'd see for myself. Who *are* they?"

Twelve didn't answer. Something had changed, ever so slightly, in the darkness of the attic above them. He touched his finger to his lips, then raised his weapon, and indicated for the kid to do likewise.

They came tumbling down from the attic-hole: brick-gray and mold-green, sharp-toothed and fast, so fast. The kid was still fumbling at the trigger when Twelve started shooting, and he took them out, all five of them, before the kid could fire a shot.

He glanced to his left. The kid was shaking.

"There you go," he said.

"I guess I mean, *what* are they?"

"What or who. Same thing. They're the enemy. Slipping in at the edges of time. Right now, at handover, they're going to be coming out in force."

They walked down the stairs together. They were in a small, suburban house. A woman and a man sat in the kitchen, at a table with a bottle of champagne upon it. They did not appear to notice the two men in uniform who walked through the room. The woman was pouring the champagne.

The kid's uniform was crisp and dark blue and looked unworn. His yearglass hung on his belt, full of pale sand. Twelve's uniform was frayed and faded to a bluish gray, patched up where it had been sliced into, or ripped, or burned. They reached the kitchen door and—

Whap!

They were outside, in a forest, somewhere very cold indeed.

"DOWN!" called Twelve.

The sharp thing went over their heads and crashed into a tree behind them.

The kid said, "I thought you said it wasn't always like this."

Twelve shrugged.

"Where are they coming from?"

"Time," said Twelve. "They're hiding behind the seconds, trying to get in."

In the forest close to them something went *whumpf,* and a tall fir tree began to burn with a flickering copper-green flame.

"Where are they?"

"Above us, again. They're normally above you or beneath you." They came down like sparks from a sparkler, beautiful and white and possibly slightly dangerous.

The kid was getting the hang of it. This time the two of them fired together.

"Did they brief you?" asked Twelve. As they landed, the sparks looked less beautiful and much more dangerous.

"Not really. They just told me that it was only for a year."

Twelve barely paused to reload. He was grizzled and scarred. The kid looked barely old enough to pick up a weapon. "Did they tell you that a year would be a lifetime?"

The kid shook his head. Twelve remembered when he was a kid like this, his uniform clean and unburned. Had he ever been so fresh-faced? So innocent?

He dealt with five of the spark-demons. The kid took care of the remaining three.

"So it's a year of fighting," said the kid.

"Second by second," said Twelve.

Whap!

The waves crashed on the beach. It was hot here, a Southern Hemisphere January. It was still night, though. Above them fireworks hung in the sky, unmoving. Twelve checked his yearglass: there were only a couple of grains left. He was almost done.

He scanned the beach, the waves, the rocks.

"I don't see it," he said.

"I do," said the kid.

It rose from the sea as he pointed, something huge beyond the mind's holding, all bulk and malevolent vastness, all tentacles and claws, and it roared as it rose.

Twelve had the rocket launcher off his back and over his shoulder. He fired it, and watched as flame blossomed on the creature's body.

"Biggest I've seen yet," he said. "Maybe they save the best for last."

"Hey," said the kid, "I'm only at the beginning."

It came for them then, crab-claws flailing and snapping, tentacles lashing, maw opening and vainly closing. They sprinted up the sandy ridge.

The kid was faster than Twelve: he was young, but sometimes that's an advantage. Twelve's hip ached, and he stumbled. His final grain of sand was falling through the yearglass when something—a tentacle, he figured—wrapped itself around his leg, and he fell.

He looked up.

The kid was standing on the ridge, feet planted like they teach you in boot camp, holding a rocket launcher of unfamiliar design—something after Twelve's time, he assumed. He began mentally to say his good-byes as he was hauled down the beach, sand scraping his face, and then a dull bang and the tentacle was whipped from his leg as the creature was blown backwards, into the sea.

He was tumbling through the air as the final grain fell and Midnight took him.

Twelve opened his eyes in the place the old years go. Fourteen helped him down from the dais.

"How'd it go?" asked Nineteen Fourteen. She wore a floor-length white skirt and long, white gloves.

"They're getting more dangerous every year," said Twenty Twelve. "The seconds, and the things behind them. But I like the new kid. I think he's going to do fine."

FEBRUARY TALE

GRAY FEBRUARY SKIES, MISTY white sands, black rocks, and the sea seemed black too, like a monochrome photograph, with only the girl in the yellow raincoat adding any color to the world.

Twenty years ago the old woman had walked the beach in all weathers, bowed over, staring at the sand, occasionally bending, laboriously, to lift a rock and look beneath it. When she had stopped coming down to the sands, a middle-aged woman, her daughter I assumed, came, and walked the beach with less enthusiasm than her mother. Now that woman had stopped coming, and in her place there was the girl.

She came towards me. I was the only other person on the beach in that mist. I don't look much older than her.

"What are you looking for?" I called.

She made a face. "What makes you think I'm looking for anything?"

"You come down here every day. Before you it was the lady, before her the very old lady, with the umbrella."

"That was my grandmother," said the girl in the yellow raincoat. "What did she lose?"

"A pendant."

"It must be very valuable."

"Not really. It has sentimental value."

"Must be worth more than that, if your family has been looking for it for umpteen years."

"Yes." She hesitated. Then she said, "Grandma said it would take her home again. She said she only came here to look around. She was curious. And then she got worried about having the pendant on her, so she hid it under a rock, so she'd be able to find it again, when she got back. And then, when she got back, she wasn't sure which rock it was, not anymore. That was fifty years ago."

"Where was her home?"

"She never told us."

The way the girl was talking made me ask the question that scared me. "Is she still alive? Your grandmother?"

"Yes. Sort of. But she doesn't talk to us these days. She just stares out at the sea. It must be horrible to be so old."

I shook my head. It isn't. Then I put my hand into my coat pocket and held it out to her. "Was it anything like this? I found it on this beach a year ago. Under a rock."

The pendant was untarnished by sand or by salt water.

The girl looked amazed, then she hugged me, and thanked me, and she took the pendant, and ran up the misty beach, in the direction of the little town.

I watched her go: a splash of gold in a black-and-white world, carrying her grandmother's pendant in her hand. It was a twin to the one I wore around my own neck.

I wondered about her grandmother, my little sister, whether she would ever go home; whether she would forgive me for the joke I had played on her if she did. Perhaps she would elect to stay on the earth, and would send the girl home in her place. That might be fun.

Only when my great-niece was gone and I was alone did I swim upward, letting the pendant pull me home, up into the vastness above us, where we wander with the lonely sky-whales and the skies and seas are one.

MARCH TALE

. . . only this we know, that she was not executed.

—CHARLES JOHNSON,
*A General History of the Robberies and
Murders of the Most Notorious Pirates*

IT WAS TOO WARM in the great house, and so the two of them went out onto the porch. A spring storm was brewing far to the west. Already the flicker of lightning, and the unpredictable chilly gusts blew about them and cooled them. They sat decorously on the porch swing, the mother and the daughter, and they talked of when the woman's husband would be home, for he had taken ship with a tobacco crop to faraway England.

Mary, who was thirteen, so pretty, so easily startled, said, "I do declare. I am glad that all the pirates have gone to the gallows, and Father will come back to us safely."

Her mother's smile was gentle, and it did not fade as she said, "I do not care to talk about pirates, Mary."

SHE WAS DRESSED as a boy when she was a girl, to cover up her father's scandal. She did not wear a woman's dress until she was on the ship with her father, and with her mother, his serving-girl mistress whom he would call wife in the New World, and they were on their way from Cork to the Carolinas.

She fell in love for the first time, on that journey, enveloped in unfamiliar cloth, clumsy in her strange skirts. She was eleven, and it was no sailor who took her heart but the ship itself: Anne would sit in the bows, watching the gray Atlantic roll beneath them, listening to the gulls scream, and feeling Ireland recede with each moment, taking with it all the old lies.

She left her love when they landed, with regret, and even as her father prospered in the new land she dreamed of the creak and slap of the sails.

Her father was a good man. He had been pleased when she had returned, and did not speak of her time away: the young man whom she had married, how he had taken her to Providence. She had returned to her family three years after, with a baby at her breast. Her husband had died, she said, and although tales and rumors abounded, even the sharpest of the gossiping tongues did not think to suggest that Annie Riley was the pirate-girl Anne Bonny, Red Rackham's first mate.

"If you had fought like a man, you would not have died like a dog." Those had been Anne Bonny's last words to the man who put the baby in her belly, or so they said.

MRS. RILEY WATCHED the lightning play, and heard the first rumble of distant thunder. Her hair was graying now, and her skin just as fair as that of any local woman of property.

"It sounds like cannon fire," said Mary (Anne had named her for her own mother, and for her best friend in the years she was away from the great house).

"Why would you say such things?" asked her mother, primly. "In this house, we do not speak of cannon fire."

The first of the March rain fell, then, and Mrs. Riley surprised her daughter by getting up from the porch swing and leaning into the rain, so it splashed her face like sea spray. It was quite out of character for a woman of such respectability.

As the rain splashed her face she thought herself there: the captain of her own ship, the cannonade around them, the stench of the gunpowder smoke blowing on the salt breeze. Her ship's deck would be painted red, to mask the blood in battle. The wind would fill her billowing canvas with a snap as loud as cannon's roar, as they prepared to board the merchant ship, and take whatever they wished, jewels or coin—and burning kisses with her first mate when the madness was done . . .

"Mother?" said Mary. "I do believe you must be thinking of a great secret. You have such a strange smile on your face."

"Silly girl, *acushla*," said her mother. And then she said, "I was thinking of your father." She spoke the truth, and the March winds blew madness about them.

APRIL TALE

YOU KNOW YOU'VE BEEN pushing the ducks too hard when they stop trusting you, and my father had been taking the ducks for everything he could since the previous summer.

He'd walk down to the pond. "Hey, ducks," he'd say to the ducks.

By January they'd just swim away. One particularly irate drake—we called him Donald, but only behind his back, ducks are sensitive to that kind of thing—would hang around and berate my father. "We ain't interested," he'd say. "We don't want to buy nothing you're selling: not life insurance, not encyclopedias, not aluminum siding, not safety matches, and especially not damp-proofing."

" 'Double or nothing'!" quacked a particularly indignant mallard. "Sure, you'll toss us for it. With a double-sided quarter . . . !"

The ducks, who had got to examine the quarter in question when my father had dropped it into the pond, all honked in agreement, and drifted elegantly and grumpily to the other side of the pond.

My father took it personally. "Those ducks," he said. "They were always there. Like a cow you could milk. They were suckers—the best kind. The kind you could go back to again and again. And I queered the pitch."

"You need to make them trust you again," I told him. "Or better still, you could just start being honest. Turn over a new leaf. You have a real job now."

He worked at the village inn, opposite the duck pond.

My father did not turn over a new leaf. He barely even turned over the old leaf. He stole fresh bread from the inn kitchens, he took unfinished bottles of red wine, and he went down to the duck pond to win the ducks' trust.

All of March he entertained them, he fed them, he told them jokes, he did whatever he could to soften them up. It was not until

April, when the world was all puddles, and the trees were new and green and the world had shaken off winter, that he brought out a pack of cards.

"How about a friendly game?" asked my father. "Not for money?"

The ducks eyed each other nervously. "I don't know . . . ," some of them muttered, warily.

Then one elderly mallard I did not recognize extended a wing graciously. "After so much fresh bread, after so much good wine, we would be churlish to refuse your offer. Perhaps, gin rummy? Or happy families?"

"How about poker?" said my father, with his poker face on, and the ducks said yes.

My father was so happy. He didn't even have to suggest that they start playing for money, just to make the game more interesting— the elderly mallard did that.

I'd learned a little over the years about dealing off the bottom: I'd watch my father sitting in our room at night, practicing, over and over, but that old mallard could have taught my father a thing or two. He dealt from the bottom. He dealt from the middle. He knew where every card in that deck was, and it just took a flick of the wing to put them exactly where he wanted them.

The ducks took my father for everything: his wallet, his watch, his shoes, his snuffbox, and the clothes he stood up in. If the ducks had accepted a boy as a bet, he would have lost me as well, and per- haps, in a lot of ways, he did.

He walked back to the inn in just his underwear and socks. Ducks don't like socks, they said. It's a duck thing.

"At least you kept your socks," I told him.

That was the April that my father learned not to trust ducks.

MAY TALE

IN MAY I RECEIVED an anonymous Mother's Day card. This puzzled me. I would have noticed if I had ever had children, surely?

In June I found a notice saying, "Normal Service Will Be Resumed as Soon as Possible," taped to my bathroom mirror, along with several small tarnished copper coins of uncertain denomination and origin.

In July I received three postcards, at weekly intervals, all postmarked from the Emerald City of Oz, telling me the person who sent them was having a wonderful time, and asking me to remind Doreen about changing the locks on the back door and to make certain that she had canceled the milk. I do not know anyone named Doreen.

In August someone left a box of chocolates on my doorstep. It had a sticker attached saying it was evidence in an important legal case, and under no circumstances were the chocolates inside to be eaten before they had been dusted for fingerprints. The chocolates had melted in the August heat into a squidgy brown mass, and I threw the whole box away.

In September I received a package containing *Action Comics* #1, a first folio of Shakespeare's plays, and a privately published copy of a novel by Jane Austen I was unfamiliar with, called *Wit and Wilderness*. I have little interest in comics, Shakespeare, or Jane Austen, and I left the books in the back bedroom. They were gone a week later, when I needed something to read in the bath, and went looking.

In October I found a notice saying, "Normal Service Will Be Resumed as Soon as Possible. Honest," taped to the side of the goldfish tank. Two of the goldfish appeared to have been taken and replaced by identical substitutes.

In November I received a ransom note telling me exactly what to do if ever I wished to see my Uncle Theobald alive again. I do not have an Uncle Theobald, but I wore a pink carnation in my buttonhole and ate nothing but salads for the entire month anyway.

In December I received a Christmas card postmarked THE NORTH POLE, letting me know that, this year, due to a clerical error, I was on neither the Naughty nor the Nice list. It was signed with a name that began with an S. It might have been Santa but it seemed more like Steve.

In January I woke to find someone had painted SECURE YOUR OWN MASK BEFORE HELPING OTHERS on the ceiling of my tiny kitchen, in vermilion paint. Some of the paint had dripped onto the floor.

In February a man came over to me at the bus stop and showed me the black statue of a falcon in his shopping bag. He asked for my help keeping it safe from the Fat Man, and then he saw someone behind me and he ran away.

In March I received three pieces of junk mail, the first telling me I might have already won a million dollars, the second telling me that I might already have been elected to the Académie Française, and the last telling me I might already have been installed as the titular head of the Holy Roman Empire.

In April I found a note on my bedside table apologizing for the problems in service, and assuring me that henceforward all faults in the universe had now been remedied forever. WE APOLOGIZE OF THE INCONVENIENTS, it concluded.

In May I received another Mother's Day card. Not anonymous, this time. It was signed, but I could not read the signature. It started with an S but it almost definitely wasn't Steve.

JUNE TALE

MY PARENTS DISAGREE. IT'S what they do. They do more than disagree. They argue. About everything. I'm still not sure that I understand how they ever stopped arguing about things long enough to get married, let alone to have me and my sister.

My mum believes in the redistribution of wealth, and thinks that the big problem with Communism is it doesn't go far enough. My dad has a framed photograph of the Queen on his side of the bed, and he votes as Conservative as he can. My mum wanted to name me Susan. My dad wanted to name me Henrietta, after his aunt. Neither of them would budge an inch. I am the only Susietta in my school or, probably, anywhere. My sister's name is Alismima, for similar reasons.

There is nothing that they agree on, not even the temperature. My dad is always too hot, my mum always too cold. They turn the radiators on and off, open and close windows, whenever the other one goes out of the room. My sister and I get colds all year, and we think that's probably why.

They couldn't even agree on what month we'd go on holiday. Dad said definitely August, Mum said unquestionably July. Which meant we wound up having to take our summer holiday in June, inconveniencing everybody.

Then they couldn't decide where to go. Dad was set on pony trekking in Iceland, while Mum was only willing to compromise as far as a camelback caravan across the Sahara, and both of them simply looked at us as if we were being a bit silly when we suggested that we'd quite like to sit on a beach in the South of France or somewhere. They stopped arguing long enough to tell us that that wasn't going to happen, and neither was a trip to Disneyland, and then they went back to disagreeing with each other.

They finished the Where Are We Going for Our Holidays in June Disagreement by slamming a lot of doors and shouting a lot of things like "Right then!" at each other through them.

When the inconvenient holiday rolled around, my sister and I were only certain of one thing: we weren't going anywhere. We took a huge pile of books out of the library, as many as we could between us, and prepared to listen to lots of arguing for the next ten days.

Then the men came in vans and brought things into the house and started to install them.

Mum had them put a sauna in the cellar. They poured masses of sand onto the floor. They hung a sunlamp from the ceiling. She put a towel on the sand beneath the sunlamp, and she'd lie down on it. She had pictures of sand dunes and camels taped to the cellar walls until they peeled off in the extreme heat.

Dad had the men put the fridge—the biggest fridge he could find, so big you could walk into it—in the garage. It filled the garage so completely that he had to start parking the car in the driveway. He'd get up in the morning, dress warmly in a thick Icelandic wool sweater, he'd get a book and thermos-flask filled with hot cocoa, and some Marmite and cucumber sandwiches, and he'd head in there in the morning with a huge smile on his face, and not come out until dinner.

I wonder if anybody else has a family as weird as mine. My parents never agree on anything at all.

"Did you know Mum's been putting her coat on and sneaking

into the garage in the afternoons?" said my sister suddenly, while we were sitting in the garden, reading our library books.

I didn't, but I'd seen Dad wearing just his bathing trunks and dressing gown heading down into the cellar that morning to be with Mum, with a big, goofy smile on his face.

I don't understand parents. Honestly, I don't think anybody ever does.

JULY TALE

THE DAY THAT MY wife walked out on me, saying she needed to be alone and to have some time to think things over, on the first of July, when the sun beat down on the lake in the center of the town, when the corn in the meadows that surrounded my house was knee-high, when the first few rockets and firecrackers were let off by overenthusiastic children to startle us and to speckle the summer sky, I built an igloo out of books in my backyard.

I used paperbacks to build it, scared of the weight of falling hardbacks or encyclopedias if I didn't build it soundly.

But it held. It was twelve feet high, and had a tunnel, through which I could crawl to enter, to keep out the bitter arctic winds.

I took more books into the igloo I had made out of books, and I read in there. I marveled at how warm and comfortable I was inside. As I read the books, I would put them down, make a floor out of them, and then I got more books, and I sat on them, eliminating the last of the green July grass from my world.

My friends came by the next day. They crawled on their hands and knees into my igloo. They told me I was acting crazy. I told them that the only thing that stood between me and the winter's cold was my father's collection of 1950s paperbacks, many of them with racy titles and lurid covers and disappointingly staid stories.

My friends left.

I sat in my igloo imagining the arctic night outside, wondering whether the Northern Lights would be filling the sky above me. I looked out, but saw only a night filled with pinprick stars.

I slept in my igloo made of books. I was getting hungry. I made a hole in the floor, lowered a fishing line and waited until something bit. I pulled it up: a fish made of books—green-covered vintage Penguin detective stories. I ate it raw, fearing a fire in my igloo.

When I went outside I observed that someone had covered the whole world with books: pale-covered books, all shades of white and blue and purple. I wandered the ice floes of books.

I saw someone who looked like my wife out there on the ice. She was making a glacier of autobiographies.

"I thought you left me," I said to her. "I thought you left me alone."

She said nothing, and I realized she was only a shadow of a shadow.

It was July, when the sun never sets in the Arctic, but I was getting tired, and I started back towards the igloo.

I saw the shadows of the bears before I saw the bears themselves: huge they were, and pale, made of the pages of fierce books: poems ancient and modern prowled the ice floes in bear-shape, filled with words that could wound with their beauty. I could see the paper, and the words winding across them, and I was frightened that the bears could see me.

I crept back to my igloo, avoiding the bears. I may have slept in the darkness. And then I crawled out, and I lay on my back on the ice and stared up at the unexpected colors of the shimmering Northern Lights, and listened to the cracks and snaps of the distant ice as an iceberg of fairy tales calved from a glacier of books on mythology.

I do not know when I became aware that there was someone else lying on the ground near to me. I could hear her breathing.

"They are very beautiful, aren't they?" she said.

"It is aurora borealis, the Northern Lights," I told her.

"It's the town's Fourth of July fireworks, baby," said my wife.

She held my hand and we watched the fireworks together.

When the last of the fireworks had vanished in a cloud of golden stars, she said, "I came home."

I didn't say anything. But I held her hand very tightly, and I left my igloo made of books, and I went with her back into the house we lived in, basking like a cat in the July heat.

I heard distant thunder, and in the night, while we slept, it began to rain, tumbling my igloo of books, washing away the words from the world.

AUGUST TALE

THE FOREST FIRES STARTED early that August. All the storms that might have dampened the world went south of us, and they took their rain with them. Each day we would see the helicopters going over above us, with their cargoes of lake water ready to drop on the distant flames.

Peter, who is Australian, and owns the house in which I live, cooking for him, and tending the place, said, "In Australia, the eucalypts use fire to survive. Some eucalyptus seeds won't germinate unless a forest fire has gone through and cleared out all the undergrowth. They need the intense heat."

"Weird thought," I said. "Something hatching out of the flames."

"Not really," said Peter. "Very normal. Probably a lot more normal when the Earth was hotter."

"Hard to imagine a world any hotter than this."

He snorted. "This is nothing," he said, and then talked about intense heat he had experienced in Australia when he was younger.

The next morning the TV news said that people in our area were advised to evacuate their property: we were in a high-risk area for fire.

"Load of old tosh," said Peter, crossly. "It'll never cause a problem for us. We're on high ground, and we've got the creek all around us."

When the water was high, the creek could be four, even five feet deep. Now it was no more than a foot, or two at the most.

By late afternoon, the smell of woodsmoke was heavy on the air, and the TV and the radio were both telling us to get out, now, if we could. We smiled at each other, and drank our beers, and congratulated each other on our understanding of a difficult situation, on not panicking, on not running away.

"We're complacent, humanity," I said. "All of us. People. We see the leaves cooking on the trees on a hot August day, and we still don't believe anything's really going to change. Our empires will go on forever."

"Nothing lasts forever," said Peter, and he poured himself another beer and told me about a friend of his back in Australia who had stopped a bushfire burning down the family farm by pouring beer on the little fires whenever they sprang up.

The fire came down the valley towards us like the end of the world, and we realized how little protection the creek would be. The air itself was burning.

We fled then, at last, pushing ourselves, coughing in the choking smoke, ran down the hill until we reached the creek, and we lay down in it, with only our heads above the water.

From the inferno we saw them hatch from the flames, and rise, and fly. They reminded me of birds, pecking at the flaming ruins of the house on the hill. I saw one of them lift its head, and call out triumphantly. I could hear it over the crackling of the burning leaves, over the roar of the flames. I heard the call of the phoenix, and I understood that nothing lasts forever.

A hundred birds of fire ascended into the skies as the creek water began to boil.

SEPTEMBER TALE

MY MOTHER HAD A ring in the shape of a lion's head. She used it to do small magics—find parking spaces, make the queue she was in at the supermarket move a bit faster, make the squabbling couple at the next table stop squabbling and fall in love again, that sort of thing. She left it to me when she died.

The first time I lost it I was in a café. I think I had been fiddling with it nervously, pulling it off my finger, putting it on again. Only when I got home did I realize that I was no longer wearing it.

I returned to the café, but there was no sign of it.

Several days later, it was returned to me by a taxi driver, who had found it on the pavement outside the café. He told me my mother had appeared to him in a dream and given him my address and her recipe for old-fashioned cheesecake.

The second time I lost the ring I was leaning over a bridge, idly tossing pinecones into the river below. I didn't think it was loose, but the ring left my hand with a pinecone. I watched its arc as it fell. It landed in the wet dark mud at the edge of the river with a loud *pollup* noise, and was gone.

A week later, I bought a salmon from a man I met in the pub: I collected it from a cooler in the back of his ancient green van. It was for a birthday dinner. When I cut the salmon open, my mother's lion ring tumbled out.

The third time I lost it, I was reading and sunbathing in the back garden. It was August. The ring was on the towel beside me, along with my dark glasses and some suntan lotion, when a large bird (I suspect it was a magpie or a jackdaw, but I may be wrong. It was definitely a corvid of some kind) flew down, and flapped away with my mother's ring in its beak.

The ring was returned the following night by a scarecrow, awkwardly animated. He gave me quite a start as he stood there, unmoving under the back door light, and then he lurched off into the darkness once again as soon as I had taken the ring from his straw-stuffed glove hand.

"Some things aren't meant to be kept," I told myself.

The next morning, I put the ring into the glove compartment of my old car. I drove the car to a wrecker, and I watched, satisfied, as the car was crushed into a cube of metal the size of an old television set, and then put in a container to be shipped to Romania, where it would be processed into useful things.

In early September I cleared out my bank account. I moved to Brazil, where I took a job as a web designer under an assumed name.

So far there's been no sign of Mother's ring. But sometimes I wake from a deep sleep with my heart pounding, soaked in sweat, wondering how she's going to give it back to me next time.

OCTOBER TALE

"THAT FEELS GOOD," I said, and I stretched my neck to get out the last of the cramp.

It didn't just feel good, it felt great, actually. I'd been squashed up inside that lamp for so long. You start to think that nobody's ever going to rub it again.

"You're a genie," said the young lady with the polishing cloth in her hand.

"I am. You're a smart girl, toots. What gave me away?"

"The appearing in a puff of smoke," she said. "And you look like a genie. You've got the turban and the pointy shoes."

I folded my arms and blinked. Now I was wearing blue jeans, gray sneakers, and a faded gray sweater: the male uniform of this time and this place. I raised a hand to my forehead, and I bowed deeply.

"I am the genie of the lamp," I told her. "Rejoice, O fortunate one. I have it in my power to grant you three wishes. And don't try the 'I wish for more wishes' thing—I won't play and you'll lose a wish. Right. Go for it."

I folded my arms again.

"No," she said. "I mean thanks and all that, but it's fine. I'm good."

"Honey," I said. "Toots. Sweetie. Perhaps you misheard me. I'm a genie. And the three wishes? We're talking anything you want. You ever dreamed of flying? I can give you wings. You want to be wealthy, richer than Croesus? You want power? Just say it. Three wishes. Whatever you want."

"Like I said," she said, "thanks. I'm fine. Would you like something to drink? You must be parched after spending so much time in that lamp. Wine? Water? Tea?"

"Uh . . ." Actually, now she came to mention it, I was thirsty. "Do you have any mint tea?"

She made me some mint tea in a teapot that was almost a twin to the lamp in which I'd spent the greater part of the last thousand years.

"Thank you for the tea."

"No problem."

"But I don't get it. Everyone I've ever met, they start asking for things. A fancy house. A harem of gorgeous women—not that you'd want that, of course . . ."

"I might," she said. "You can't just make assumptions about people. Oh, and don't call me toots, or sweetie, or any of those things. My name's Hazel."

"Ah!" I understood. "You want a beautiful woman then? My apologies. You have but to wish." I folded my arms.

"No," she said. "I'm good. No wishes. How's the tea?"

I told her that the mint tea was the finest I had ever tasted.

She asked me when I had started feeling a need to grant people's wishes, and whether I felt a desperate need to please. She asked about my mother, and I told her that she could not judge me as she would judge mortals, for I was a djinn, powerful and wise, magical and mysterious.

She asked me if I liked hummus, and when I said that I did, she toasted a pita bread, and sliced it up, for me to dip into the hummus. I dipped my bread slices into the hummus, and ate it with delight. The hummus gave me an idea.

"Just make a wish," I said, helpfully, "and I could have a meal fit for a sultan brought in to you. Each dish would be finer than the one before, and all served upon golden plates. And you could keep the plates afterwards."

"It's good," she said, with a smile. "Would you like to go for a walk?"

We walked together through the town. It felt good to stretch my legs after so many years in the lamp. We wound up in a public park, sitting on a bench by a lake. It was warm, but gusty, and the autumn leaves fell in flurries each time the wind blew.

I told Hazel about my youth as a djinn, of how we used to eavesdrop on the angels and how they would throw comets at us if they spied us listening. I told her of the bad days of the djinn-wars, and how King Suleiman had imprisoned us inside hollow objects: bottles, lamps, clay pots, that kind of thing.

She told me of her parents, who were both killed in the same plane crash, and who had left her the house. She told me of her job, illustrating children's books, a job she had backed into, accidentally, at the point she realized she would never be a really competent medical illustrator, and of how happy she became whenever she was sent a new book to illustrate. She told me she taught life drawing to adults at the local community college one evening a week.

I saw no obvious flaw in her life, no hole that she could fill by wishing, save one.

"Your life is good," I told her. "But you have no one to share it with. Wish, and I will bring you the perfect man. Or woman. A film star. A rich . . . person . . ."

"No need. I'm good," she said.

We walked back to her house, past houses dressed for Hallowe'en.

"This is not right," I told her. "People always want things."

"Not me. I've got everything I need."

"Then what do I do?"

She thought for a moment. Then she pointed at her front yard. "Can you rake the leaves?"

"Is that your wish?"

"Nope. Just something you could do while I'm getting our dinner ready."

I raked the leaves into a heap by the hedge, to stop the wind from blowing it apart. After dinner, I washed up the dishes. I spent the night in Hazel's spare bedroom.

It wasn't that she didn't want help. She let me help. I ran errands for her, picked up art supplies and groceries. On days she had been painting for a long time, she let me rub her neck and shoulders. I have good, firm hands.

Shortly before Thanksgiving I moved out of the spare bedroom, across the hall, into the main bedroom, and Hazel's bed.

I watched her face this morning as she slept. I stared at the shapes her lips make when she sleeps. The creeping sunlight touched her face, and she opened her eyes and stared at me, and she smiled.

"You know what I never asked," she said, "is what about you? What would you wish for if I asked what your three wishes were?"

I thought for a moment. I put my arm around her, and she snuggled her head into my shoulder.

"It's okay," I told her. "I'm good."

NOVEMBER TALE

THE BRAZIER WAS SMALL and square and made of an aged and fire-blackened metal that might have been copper or brass. It had caught Eloise's eye at the garage sale because it was twined with animals that might have been dragons and might have been sea-snakes. One of them was missing its head.

It was only a dollar, and Eloise bought it, along with a red hat with a feather on the side. She began to regret buying the hat even before she got home, and thought perhaps she would give it to someone as a gift. But the letter from the hospital had been waiting for her when she got home, and she put the brazier in the back garden and the hat in the closet as you went into the house, and had not thought of either of them again.

The months had passed, and so had the desire to leave the house. Every day made her weaker, and each day took more from her. She moved her bed to the room downstairs, because it hurt to walk, because she was too exhausted to climb the stairs, because it was simpler.

November came, and with it the knowledge that she would never see Christmas.

There are things you cannot throw away, things you cannot leave for your loved ones to find when you are gone. Things you have to burn.

She took a black cardboard folder filled with papers and letters and old photographs out into the garden. She filled the brazier with fallen twigs and brown paper shopping bags, and she lit it with a barbecue lighter. Only when it was burning did she open the folder.

She started with the letters, particularly the ones she would not want other people to see. When she had been at university there had been a professor and a relationship, if you could call it that, which had gone very dark and very wrong very fast. She had all his letters paperclipped together, and she dropped them, one by one, into the flames. There was a photograph of the two of them together, and she dropped it into the brazier last of all, and watched it curl and blacken.

She was reaching for the next thing in the cardboard folder when she realized that she could not remember the professor's name, or what he taught, or why the relationship had hurt her as it did, left her almost suicidal for the following year.

The next thing was a photograph of her old dog, Lassie, on her back beside the oak tree in the backyard. Lassie was dead these seven years, but the tree was still there, leafless now in the November chill. She tossed the photograph into the brazier. She had loved that dog.

She glanced over to the tree, remembering . . .

There was no tree in the backyard.

There wasn't even a tree stump; only a faded November lawn, strewn with fallen leaves from the trees next door.

Eloise saw it, and she did not worry that she had gone mad. She got up stiffly and walked into the house. Her reflection in the mirror shocked her, as it always did these days. Her hair so thin, so sparse, her face so gaunt.

She picked up the papers from the table beside her makeshift bed: a letter from her oncologist was on the top, beneath it a dozen pages of numbers and words. There were more papers beneath it, all with the hospital logo on the top of the first page. She picked them up and, for good measure, she picked up the hospital bills as well. Insurance covered so much of it, but not all.

She walked back outside, pausing in the kitchen to catch her breath.

The brazier waited, and she threw her medical information into the flames. She watched them brown and blacken and turn to ash on the November wind.

Eloise got up, when the last of the medical records had burned away, and she walked inside. The mirror in the hall showed her an Eloise both familiar and new: she had thick brown hair, and she smiled at herself from the looking glass as if she loved life and trailed comfort in her wake.

Eloise went to the hall closet. There was a red hat on the shelf she could barely remember, but she put it on, worried that the red might make her face look washed out and sallow. She looked in the mirror. She appeared just fine. She tipped the hat at a jauntier angle.

Outside the last of the smoke from the black snake-wound brazier drifted on the chilly November air.

DECEMBER TALE

SUMMER ON THE STREETS is hard, but you can sleep in a park in the summer without dying from the cold. Winter is different. Winter can be lethal. And even if it isn't, the cold still takes you as its special homeless friend, and it insinuates itself into every part of your life.

Donna had learned from the old hands. The trick, they told her, is to sleep wherever you can during the day—the Circle line is good, buy a ticket and ride all day, snoozing in the carriage, and so are the kinds of cheap cafés where they don't mind an eighteen-year-old girl spending fifty pence on a cup of tea and then dozing off in a corner for an hour or three, as long as she looks more or less respectable—but to keep moving at night, when the temperatures plummet, and the warm places close their doors, and lock them, and turn off the lights.

It was nine at night and Donna was walking. She kept to well-lit areas, and she wasn't ashamed to ask for money. Not anymore. People could always say no, and mostly they did.

There was nothing familiar about the woman on the street corner. If there had been, Donna wouldn't have approached her. It was her nightmare, someone from Biddenden seeing her like this: the shame, and the fear that they'd tell her mum (who never said much, who only said "good riddance" when she heard Gran had died) and then her mum would tell her dad, and he might just come down here and look for her, and try to bring her home. And that would break her. She didn't ever want to see him again.

The woman on the corner had stopped, puzzled, and was looking around as if she was lost. Lost people were sometimes good for change, if you could tell them the way to where they wanted to go.

Donna stepped closer, and said, "Spare any change?"

The woman looked down at her. And then the expression on her face changed and she looked like . . . Donna understood the cliché then, understood why people would say *She looked like she had seen a ghost*. She did. The woman said, *"You?"*

"Me?" said Donna. If she had recognized the woman she might have backed away, she might even have run off, but she didn't know her. The woman looked a little like Donna's mum, but kinder, softer, plump where Donna's mum was pinched. It was hard to see what she really looked like because she was wearing thick black winter clothes, and a thick woolen bobble cap, but her hair beneath the cap was as orange as Donna's own.

The woman said, "Donna." Donna would have run then, but she didn't, she stayed where she was because it was just too crazy, too unlikely, too ridiculous for words.

The woman said, "Oh god. Donna. You are you, aren't you? I remember." Then she stopped. She seemed to be blinking back tears.

Donna looked at the woman, as an unlikely, ridiculous idea filled her head, and she said, "Are you who I think you are?"

The woman nodded. "I'm you," she said. "Or I will be. One day. I was walking this way remembering what it was like back when I . . . when you . . ." Again she stopped. "Listen. It won't be like this for you forever. Or even for very long. Just don't do anything stupid. And don't do anything permanent. I promise it will be all right. Like the YouTube videos, you know? *It Gets Better*."

"What's a you tube?" asked Donna.

"Oh, lovey," said the woman. And she put her arms around Donna and pulled her close and held her tight.

"Will you take me home with you?" asked Donna.

"I can't," said the woman. "Home isn't there for you yet. You haven't met any of the people who are going to help you get off the street, or help you get a job. You haven't met the person who's going to turn out to be your partner. And you'll both make a place that's safe, for each other and for your children. Somewhere warm."

Donna felt the anger rising inside her. "Why are you telling me this?" she asked.

"So you know it gets better. To give you hope."

Donna stepped back. "I don't want hope," she said. "I want some-where warm. I want a home. I want it now. Not in twenty years."

A hurt expression on the placid face. "It's sooner than twen—"

"I don't *care*! It's not tonight. I don't have anywhere to go. And I'm *cold*. Have you got any change?"

The woman nodded. "Here," she said. She opened her purse and took out a twenty-pound note. Donna took it, but the money didn't look like any currency she was familiar with. She looked back at the woman to ask her something, but she was gone, and when Donna looked back at her hand, so was the money.

She stood there shivering. The money was gone, if it had ever been there. But she had kept one thing: she knew it would all work out someday. In the end. And she knew that she didn't need to do anything stupid. She didn't have to buy one last Underground ticket just to be able to jump down onto the tracks when she saw a train coming, too close to stop.

The winter wind was bitter, and it bit her and it cut her to the bone, but still, she spotted something blown up against a shop door-way, and she reached down and picked it up: a five-pound note. Per-haps tomorrow would be easier. She didn't have to do any of the things she had imagined herself doing.

December could be lethal, when you were out on the streets. But not this year. Not tonight.

NOTHING O'CLOCK

2013

I.

THE TIME LORDS BUILT a prison. They built it in a time and place that are equally as unimaginable to any entity who has never left the solar system in which it was spawned, or who has only experienced the journey into the future one second at a time, and that going forward. It was built solely for the Kin. It was impregnable: a complex of small, nicely appointed rooms (for they were not monsters, the Time Lords. They could be merciful, when it suited them), out of temporal phase with the rest of the Universe.

There were, in that place, only those rooms: the gulf between microseconds was one that could not be crossed. In effect, those rooms became a Universe in themselves, one that borrowed light and heat and gravity from the rest of creation, always a fraction of a moment away.

The Kin prowled its rooms, patient and deathless, and always waiting.

It was waiting for a question. It could wait until the end of time. (But even then, when Time Ended, the Kin would never perceive it, imprisoned in the micro-moment away from time.)

The Time Lords maintained the prison with huge engines they built in the hearts of black holes, unreachable: no one would be able to get to the engines, save the Time Lords themselves. The multiple engines were a fail-safe. Nothing could ever go wrong.

As long as the Time Lords existed, the Kin would be in their prison, and the rest of the Universe would be safe. That was how it was, and how it always would be.

And if anything went wrong, then the Time Lords would know. Even if, unthinkably, any of the engines failed, then emergency signals would sound on Gallifrey long before the prison of the Kin returned to our time and our Universe. The Time Lords had planned for everything.

They had planned for everything except the possibility that one day there would be no Time Lords, and no Gallifrey. No Time Lords in the Universe, except for one.

So when the prison shook and crashed, as if in an earthquake, throwing the Kin down, and when the Kin looked up from its prison to see the light of galaxies and suns above it, unmediated and unfiltered, and it knew that it had returned to the Universe, it knew it would only be a matter of time until the question would be asked once more.

And, because the Kin was careful, it took stock of the Universe they found themselves in. It did not think of revenge: that was not in its nature. It wanted what it had always wanted. And besides . . .

There was still a Time Lord in the Universe.

The Kin needed to do something about that.

II.

ON WEDNESDAY, ELEVEN-YEAR-OLD POLLY Browning put her head around her father's office door. "Dad. There's a man at the front door in a rabbit mask who says he wants to buy the house."

"Don't be silly, Polly." Mr. Browning was sitting in the corner of the room he liked to call his office, and which the estate agent had optimistically listed as a third bedroom, although it was scarcely big enough for a filing cabinet and a card table, upon which rested a brand-new Amstrad computer. Mr. Browning was carefully entering the numbers from a pile of receipts onto the computer, and wincing. Every half an hour he would save the work he'd done so far, and the computer would make a grinding noise for a few minutes as it saved everything onto a floppy disk.

"I'm not being silly. He says he'll give you seven hundred and fifty thousand pounds for it."

"Now you're really being silly. It's on sale for a hundred and fifty thousand." *And we'd be lucky to get that in today's market,* he thought, but did not say. It was the summer of 1984, and Mr. Browning despaired of finding a buyer for the little house at the end of Claversham Row.

Polly nodded thoughtfully. "I think you should go and talk to him."

Mr. Browning shrugged. He needed to save the work he'd done so far anyway. As the computer made its grumbling sound, Mr. Browning went downstairs. Polly, who had planned to go up to her bedroom to write in her diary, decided to sit on the stairs and find out what was going to happen next.

Standing in the front garden was a tall man in a rabbit mask. It was not a particularly convincing mask. It covered his entire face, and two long ears rose above his head. He held a large, leather, brown bag, which reminded Mr. Browning of the doctors' bags of his childhood.

"Now, see here," began Mr. Browning, but the man in the rabbit mask put a gloved finger to his painted bunny lips, and Mr. Browning fell silent.

"Ask me what time it is," said a quiet voice that came from behind the unmoving muzzle of the rabbit mask.

Mr. Browning said, "I understand you're interested in the house." The FOR SALE sign by the front gate was grimy and streaked by the rain.

"Perhaps. You can call me Mister Rabbit. Ask me what time it is."

Mr. Browning knew that he ought to call the police. Ought to do something to make the man go away. What kind of crazy person wears a rabbit mask anyway?

"Why are you wearing a rabbit mask?"

"That was not the correct question. But I am wearing the rabbit mask because I am representing an extremely famous and important person who values his or her privacy. Ask me what time it is."

Mr. Browning sighed. "What time is it, Mister Rabbit?" he asked. The man in the rabbit mask stood up straighter. His body language was one of joy and delight. "Time for you to be the richest man on Claversham Row," he said. "I'm buying your house, for cash, and for more than ten times what it's worth, because it's just perfect for me now." He opened the brown leather bag, and produced blocks of money, each block containing five hundred—"count them, go on, count them"—crisp fifty-pound notes, and two plastic supermarket shopping bags, into which he placed the blocks of currency.

Mr. Browning inspected the money. It appeared to be real.

"I . . ." He hesitated. What did he need to do? "I'll need a few days. To bank it. Make sure it's real. And we'll need to draw up contracts, obviously."

"Contract's already drawn up," said the man in the rabbit mask. "Sign here. If the bank says there's anything funny about the money, you can keep it and the house. I'll be back on Saturday to take vacant possession. You can get everything out by then, can't you?"

"I don't know," said Mr. Browning. Then: "I'm sure I can. I mean, *of course.*"

"I'll be here on Saturday," said the man in the rabbit mask.

"This is a very unusual way of doing business," said Mr. Browning. He was standing at his front door holding two shopping bags, containing £750,000.

"Yes," agreed the man in the rabbit mask. "It is. See you on Saturday, then."

He walked away. Mr. Browning was relieved to see him go. He had been seized by the irrational conviction that, were he to remove the rabbit mask, there would be nothing underneath.

Polly went upstairs to tell her diary everything she had seen and heard.

ON THURSDAY, A tall young man with a tweed jacket and a bow tie knocked on the door. There was nobody at home, and nobody answered, and, after walking around the house, he went away.

ON SATURDAY, MR. Browning stood in his empty kitchen. He had banked the money successfully, which had wiped out all his debts. The furniture that they had wanted to keep had been put into a moving van and sent to Mr. Browning's uncle, who had an enormous garage he wasn't using.

"What if it's all a joke?" asked Mrs. Browning.

"Not sure what's funny about giving someone seven hundred and fifty thousand pounds," said Mr. Browning. "The bank says it's real. Not reported stolen. Just a rich and eccentric person who wants to buy our house for a lot more than it's worth."

They had booked two rooms in a local hotel, although hotel rooms had proved harder to find than Mr. Browning had expected. Also, he had had to convince Mrs. Browning, who was a nurse, that they could now afford to stay in a hotel.

"What happens if he never comes back?" asked Polly. She was sitting on the stairs, reading a book.

Mr. Browning said, "Now you're being silly."

"Don't call your daughter silly," said Mrs. Browning. "She's got a point. You don't have a name or a phone number or anything."

This was unfair. The contract was made out, and the buyer's name was clearly written on it: N. M. de Plume. There was an address, too, for a firm of London solicitors, and Mr. Browning had phoned them and been told that, yes, this was absolutely legitimate.

"He's eccentric," said Mr. Browning. "An eccentric millionaire."

"I bet it's him behind that rabbit mask," said Polly. "The eccentric millionaire."

The doorbell rang. Mr. Browning went to the front door, his wife and daughter beside him, each of them hoping to meet the new owner of their house.

"Hello," said the lady in the cat mask. It was not a very realistic mask. Polly saw her eyes glinting behind it, though.

"Are you the new owner?" asked Mrs. Browning.

"Either that, or I'm the owner's representative."

"Where's . . . your friend? In the rabbit mask?"

Despite the cat mask, the young lady (was she young? Her voice sounded young, anyway) seemed efficient and almost brusque. "You have removed all your possessions? I'm afraid anything left behind will become the property of the new owner."

"We've got everything that matters."

"Good."

Polly said, "Can I come and play in the garden? There isn't a garden at the hotel." There was a swing on the oak tree in the back garden, and Polly loved to sit on it and read.

"Don't be silly, love," said Mr. Browning. "We'll have a new house, and then you'll have a garden with swings. I'll put up new swings for you."

The lady in the cat mask crouched down. "I'm Mrs. Cat. Ask me what time it is, Polly."

Polly nodded. "What's the time, Mrs. Cat?"

"Time for you and your family to leave this place and never look back," said Mrs. Cat, but she said it kindly.

Polly waved good-bye to the lady in the cat mask when she got to the end of the garden path.

III.

THEY WERE IN THE TARDIS control room, going home.

"I still don't understand," Amy was saying. "Why were the Skeleton People so angry with you in the first place? I thought they *wanted* to get free from the rule of the Toad-King."

"They weren't angry with me about *that*," said the young man in the tweed jacket and the bow tie. He pushed a hand through his hair. "I think they were quite pleased to be free, actually." He ran his hands across the TARDIS control panel, patting levers, stroking dials. "They were just a bit upset with me because I'd walked off with their squiggly whatsit."

"Squiggly whatsit?"

"It's on the . . ." He gestured vaguely with arms that seemed to be mostly elbows and joints. "The tabley thing over there. I confiscated it."

Amy looked irritated. She wasn't irritated, but she sometimes liked to give him the impression she was, just to show him who was boss. "Why don't you ever call things by their proper names? *The tabley thing over there*? It's called 'a table.' "

She walked over to the table. The squiggly whatsit was glittery and elegant: it was the size and general shape of a bracelet, but it twisted in ways that made it hard for the eye to follow.

"Really? Oh good." He seemed pleased. "I'll remember that."

Amy picked up the squiggly whatsit. It was cold and much heavier than it looked. "Why did you confiscate it? And why are you saying *confiscate* anyway? That's like what teachers do, when you bring something you shouldn't to school. My friend Mels set a record at school for the number of things she'd got confiscated. One night she got me and Rory to make a disturbance while she broke into the teacher's supply cupboard, which was where her stuff was. She had to go over the roof and through the teachers' loo window . . ."

But the Doctor was not interested in Amy's old school friend's exploits. He never was. He said, "Confiscated. For their own safety. Technology they shouldn't have had. Probably stolen. Time looper and booster. Could have made a nasty mess of things." He pulled a lever. "And we're here. All change."

There was a rhythmic grinding sound, as if the engines of the Universe itself were protesting, a rush of displaced air, and a large blue police box materialized in the back garden of Amy Pond's house. It was the beginning of the second decade of the twenty-first century.

The Doctor opened the TARDIS door. Then he said, "That's odd."

He stood in the doorway, made no attempt to walk outside. Amy came over to him. He put out an arm to prevent her from leaving the TARDIS. It was a perfectly sunny day, almost cloudless.

"What's wrong?"

"Everything," he said. "Can't you feel it?" Amy looked at her garden. It was overgrown and neglected, but then it always had been, as long as she remembered.

"No," said Amy. And then she said, "It's quiet. No cars. No birds. Nothing."

"No radio waves," said the Doctor. "Not even Radio Four."

"You can hear radio waves?"

"Of course not. Nobody can hear radio waves," he said, uncon-vincingly.

And that was when the voice said, ATTENTION VISITORS. YOU ARE NOW ENTERING KIN SPACE. THIS WORLD IS THE PROP-ERTY OF THE KIN. YOU ARE TRESPASSING.

It was a strange voice, whispery and, mostly, Amy suspected, in her head.

"This is Earth," called Amy. "It doesn't belong to you." And then she said, "What have you done with the people?"

WE BOUGHT IT FROM THEM. THEY DIED OUT NATU-RALLY SHORTLY AFTERWARDS. IT WAS A PITY.

"I don't believe you," shouted Amy.

NO GALACTIC LAWS WERE VIOLATED. THE PLANET WAS PURCHASED LEGALLY AND LEGITIMATELY. A THOROUGH INVESTIGATION BY THE SHADOW PROCLAMATION VINDI-CATED OUR OWNERSHIP IN FULL.

"It's not yours! Where's Rory?"

"Amy? Who are you talking to?" asked the Doctor.

"The voice. The one in my head. Can't you hear it?"

TO WHOM ARE YOU TALKING? asked the Voice.

Amy closed the TARDIS door.

"Why did you do that?" asked the Doctor.

"Weird, whispery voice in my head. Said they'd bought the planet. And the, the Shadow Proclamation said it was all okay. It told me all the people died out naturally. You couldn't hear it. It didn't know you were here. Element of surprise. Closed the door." Amy Pond could be astonishingly efficient, when she was under stress. Right now, she was under stress, but you wouldn't have known it, if it wasn't for the squiggly whatsit, which she was holding between her hands and was bending and twisting into shapes that defied the imagination and seemed to be wandering off into peculiar dimensions.

"Did they say who they were?"

She thought for a moment. " 'You are now entering Kin space. This world is the property of the Kin.' "

He said, "Could be anyone. The Kin. I mean . . . it's like calling yourselves the People. It's what pretty much every race-name means. Except for *Dalek*. That means *Metal-Cased Hatey Death Machines* in Skaronian." And then he was running to the control panel. "Something like this. It can't occur overnight. People don't just die off. And this is 2010. Which means . . ."

"It means they've done something to Rory."

"It means they've done something to everyone." He pressed several keys on an ancient typewriter keyboard, and patterns flowed across the screen that hung above the TARDIS console. "I couldn't hear them . . . they couldn't hear me. You could hear both of us. *Aha!* Summer of 1984! That's the divergence point . . ." His hands began turning, twiddling and pushing levers, pumps, switches, and something small that went *ding*.

"Where's Rory? I want him, right now," demanded Amy as the TARDIS lurched away into space and time. The Doctor had only briefly met her fiancé, Rory Williams, once before. She did not think the Doctor understood what she saw in Rory. Some days, *she* was not entirely sure what she saw in Rory. But she was certain of this: nobody took her fiancé away from her.

"Good question. Where's Rory? Also, where's seven billion other people?" he asked.

"I want my Rory."

"Well, wherever the rest of them are, he's there too. And you ought to have been with them. At a guess, neither of you were ever born."

Amy looked down at herself, checking her feet, her legs, her elbows, her hands (the squiggly whatsit glittered like an Escher nightmare on her wrist. She dropped it onto the control panel). She reached up and grasped a handful of auburn hair. "If I wasn't born, what am I doing here?"

"You're an independent temporal nexus, chronosynclastically established as an inverse." He saw her expression, and stopped.

"You're telling me it's timey-wimey, aren't you?"

"Yes," he said, seriously. "I suppose I am. Right. We're here."

He adjusted his bow tie with precise fingers, tipping it to one side rakishly.

"But, Doctor. The human race didn't die out in 1984."

"New timeline. It's a paradox."

"And you're the paradoctor?"

"Just the Doctor." He adjusted his bow tie to its earlier alignment, stood up a little straighter. "There's something familiar about all this."

"What?"

"Don't know. Hmm. Kin. Kin. *Kin*. I keep thinking of masks. Who wears masks?"

"Bank robbers?"

"No."

"Really ugly people?"

"No."

"Hallowe'en? People wear masks at Hallowe'en."

"*Yes!* They *do!*"

"So that's important?"

"Not even a little bit. But it's true. Right. Big divergence in time stream. And it's not actually possible to take over a Level 5 planet in a way that would satisfy the Shadow Proclamation unless . . ."

"Unless what?"

The Doctor stopped moving. He bit his lower lip. Then: "Oh. They wouldn't."

"Wouldn't what?"

"They couldn't. I mean, that would be completely . . ."

Amy tossed her hair, and did her best to keep her temper. Shouting at the Doctor never worked, unless it did. "Completely what?"

"Completely impossible. You can't take over a Level 5 planet. Unless you do it legitimately." On the TARDIS control panel something whirled and something else went *ding*. "We're here. It's the nexus. Come on! Let's explore 1984."

"You're enjoying this," said Amy. "My whole world has been taken over by a mysterious voice. All the people are extinct. Rory's gone. And you're enjoying this."

"No, I'm not," said the Doctor, trying hard not to show how much he was enjoying it.

THE BROWNINGS STAYED in the hotel while Mr. Browning looked for a new house. The hotel was completely full. Coincidentally, the

Brownings learned, in conversation with other hotel guests over breakfast, they had also sold their houses and flats. None of them seemed particularly forthcoming about who had bought their previous residences.

"It's ridiculous," he said, after ten days. "There's nothing for sale in town. Or anywhere around here. They've all been snapped up."

"There must be something," said Mrs. Browning.

"Not in this part of the country," said Mr. Browning. "What does the estate agent say?"

"Not answering the phone," said Mr. Browning.

"Well, let's go and talk to her," said Mrs. Browning. "You coming with, Polly?"

Polly shook her head. "I'm reading my book," she said.

Mr. and Mrs. Browning walked into town, and they met the estate agent outside the door of the shop, putting up a notice saying "Under New Management." There were no properties for sale in the window, only a lot of houses and flats with SOLD on them.

"Shutting up shop?" asked Mr. Browning.

"Someone made me an offer I couldn't refuse," said the estate agent. She was carrying a heavy-looking plastic shopping bag. The Brownings could guess what was in it.

"Someone in a rabbit mask?" asked Mrs. Browning.

When they got back to the hotel, the manager was waiting in the lobby for them, to tell them they wouldn't be living in the hotel much longer.

"It's the new owners," she explained. "They are closing the hotel for refurbishing."

"New owners?"

"They just bought it. Paid a lot of money for it, I was told."

Somehow, this did not surprise the Brownings one little bit. They were not surprised until they got up to their hotel room, and Polly was nowhere to be seen.

IV.

"NINETEEN EIGHTY-FOUR," mused Amy Pond. "I thought somehow it would feel more, I don't know. Historical. It doesn't feel like a long time ago. But my parents hadn't even met yet." She hesitated, as if she were about to say something about her parents, but her attention drifted. They crossed the road.

"What were they like?" asked the Doctor. "Your parents?"

Amy shrugged. "The usual," she said, without thinking. "A mum and a dad."

"Sounds likely," agreed the Doctor much too readily. "So, I need you to keep your eyes open."

"What are we looking for?"

It was a little English town, and it looked like a little English town as far as Amy was concerned. Just like the one she'd left, only without the coffee shops, or the mobile phone shops.

"Easy. We're looking for something that shouldn't be here. Or we're looking for something that should be here but isn't."

"What kind of thing?"

"Not sure," said the Doctor. He rubbed his chin. "Gazpacho, maybe."

"What's gazpacho?"

"Cold soup. But it's meant to be cold. So if we looked all over 1984 and couldn't find any gazpacho, that would be a clue."

"Were you always like this?"

"Like what?"

"A madman. With a time machine."

"Oh, no. It took ages until I got the time machine."

They walked through the center of the little town, looking for something unusual, and finding nothing, not even gazpacho.

POLLY STOPPED AT the garden gate in Claversham Row, looking up at the house that had been her house since they had moved here, when she was seven. She walked up to the front door, rang the doorbell and waited, and was relieved when nobody answered it. She glanced down the street, then walked hurriedly around the house, past the rubbish bins, into the back garden.

The French window that opened onto the little back garden had a catch that didn't fasten properly. Polly thought it extremely unlikely that the house's new owners had fixed it. If they had, she'd come back when they were here, and she'd have to ask, and it would be awkward and embarrassing.

That was the trouble with hiding things. Sometimes, if you were in a hurry, you left them behind. Even important things. And there was nothing more important than her diary.

Polly had been keeping it since they had arrived in the town. It had been her best friend: she had confided in it, told it about the girls who had bullied her, the ones who befriended her, about the first boy she had ever liked. It was, sometimes, her best friend: she would turn to it in times of trouble, or turmoil and pain. It was the place she poured out her thoughts.

And it was hidden underneath a loose floorboard in the big cupboard in her bedroom.

Polly tapped the left French door hard with the palm of her hand, rapping it next to the casement, and the door wobbled, and then swung open.

She walked inside. She was surprised to see that they hadn't replaced any of the furniture her family had taken away. It still smelled like her house. It was silent: nobody home. Good. She hurried up the stairs, worried she might still be at home when Mr. Rabbit or Mrs. Cat returned.

She went up the stairs. On the landing something brushed her face—touched it gently, like a thread, or a cobweb. She looked up. That was odd. The ceiling seemed furry: hair-like threads, or thread-like hairs, came down from it. She hesitated then, thought about running—but she could see her bedroom door. The Duran Duran poster was still on it. Why hadn't they taken it down?

Trying not to look up at the hairy ceiling, she pushed open her bedroom door.

The room was different. There was no furniture, and where her bed had been were sheets of paper. She glanced down: photographs from newspapers, blown up to life-size. The eyeholes had been cut out already. She recognized Ronald Reagan, Margaret Thatcher, Pope John Paul, the Queen . . .

Perhaps they were going to have a party. The masks didn't look very convincing.

She went to the built-in cupboard at the end of the room. Her *Smash Hits* diary was sitting in the darkness, beneath the floorboard, in there. She opened the cupboard door.

"Hello, Polly," said the man in the cupboard. He wore a mask, like the others had. An animal mask: this was some kind of big gray dog.

"Hello," said Polly. She didn't know what else to say. "I . . . I left my diary behind."

"I know. I was reading it." He raised the diary. He was not the same as the man in the rabbit mask, the woman in the cat mask, but everything Polly had felt about them, about the wrongness, was intensified here. "Do you want it back?"

"Yes please," Polly said to the dog-masked man. She felt hurt and violated: this man had been reading her diary. But she wanted it back.

"You know what you need to do, to get it?"

She shook her head.

"Ask me what the time is."

She opened her mouth. It was dry. She licked her lips, and muttered, "What time is it?"

"And my name," he said. "Say my name. I'm Mister Wolf."

"What's the time, Mister Wolf?" asked Polly. A playground game rose unbidden to her mind.

Mister Wolf smiled (but how can a mask smile?) and he opened his mouth so wide to show row upon row of sharp, sharp teeth.

"Dinnertime," he told her.

Polly started to scream then, as he came towards her, but she didn't get to scream for very long.

V.

THE TARDIS WAS SITTING in a small grassy area, too small to be a park, too irregular to be a square, in the middle of the town, and the Doctor was sitting outside it, in a deck chair, walking through his memories.

The Doctor had a remarkable memory. The problem was, there was so much of it. He had lived eleven lives (or more: there was another life, was there not, that he tried his best never to think about) and he had a different way of remembering things in each life.

The worst part of being however old he was (and he had long since abandoned trying to keep track of it in any way that mattered to anybody but him) was that sometimes things didn't arrive in his head quite when they were meant to.

Masks. That was part of it. And Kin. That was part of it too.

And Time.

It was all about Time. Yes, that was it . . .

An old story. Before his time—he was sure of that. It was something he had heard as a boy. He tried to remember the stories he had been told as a small boy on Gallifrey, before he had been taken to the Time Lord Academy and his life had changed forever.

Amy was coming back from a sortie through the town.

"Maximelos and the three Ogrons!" he shouted at her.

"What about them?"

"One was too vicious, one was too stupid, one was just right."

"And this is relevant how?"

He tugged at his hair absently. "Er, probably not relevant at all. Just trying to remember a story from my childhood."

"Why?"

"No idea. Can't remember."

"You," said Amy Pond, "are very frustrating."

"Yes," said the Doctor, happily. "I probably am."

He had hung a sign on the front of the TARDIS. It said:

SOMETHING MYSTERIOUSLY WRONG?
JUST KNOCK! NO PROBLEM TOO SMALL.

"If it won't come to us, I'll go to it. No, scrap that. Other way round. And I've redecorated inside, so as not to startle people. What did you find?"

"Two things," she said. "First one was Prince Charles. I saw him in the newsagent's."

"Are you sure it was him?"

Amy thought. "Well, he looked like Prince Charles. Just much younger. And the newsagent asked him if he'd picked out a name for the next Royal Baby. I suggested Rory."

"Prince Charles in the newsagent's. Right. Next thing?"

"There aren't any houses for sale. I've walked every street in the town. No FOR SALE signs. There are people camping in tents on the edge of town. Lots of people leaving to find places to live, because there's nothing around here. It's just weird."

"Yes."

He almost had it, now. Amy opened the TARDIS door. She looked inside. "Doctor . . . it's the same size on the inside."

He beamed, and took her on an extensive tour of his new office, which consisted of standing inside the doorway and making a waving gesture with his right arm. Most of the space was taken up with a desk, with an old-fashioned telephone, and a typewriter on it. There was a back wall. Amy experimentally pushed her hands through the wall (it was hard to do with her eyes open, easy when she closed them), then she closed her eyes and pushed her head through the wall. Now she could see the TARDIS control room, all copper and glass. She took a step backwards, into the tiny office.

"Is it a hologram?"

"Sort of."

There was a hesitant rap at the door of the TARDIS. The Doctor opened it.

"Excuse me. The sign on the door." The man appeared harassed. His hair was thinning. He looked at the tiny room, mostly filled by a desk, and he made no move to come inside.

"Yes! Hello! Come in!" said the Doctor. "No problem too small!"

"Um. My name's Reg Browning. It's my daughter. Polly. She was meant to be waiting for us, back in the hotel room. She's not there."

"I'm the Doctor. This is Amy. Have you spoken to the police?"

"Aren't you police? I thought perhaps you were."

"Why?" asked Amy.

"This is a police call box. I didn't even know they were bringing them back."

"For some of us," said the tall young man with the bow tie, "they never went away. What happened when you spoke to the police?"

"They said they'd keep an eye out for her. But honestly, they seemed a bit preoccupied. The desk sergeant said the lease had run out on the police station, rather unexpectedly, and they're looking for somewhere to go. The desk sergeant said the whole lease thing came as a bit of a blow to them."

"What's Polly like?" asked Amy. "Could she be staying with friends?"

"I've checked with her friends. Nobody's seen her. We're living in the Rose Hotel, on Wednesbury Street, right now."

"Are you visiting?"

Mr. Browning told them about the man in the rabbit mask who had come to the door last week to buy their house for so much more than it was worth, and paid cash. He told them about the woman in the cat mask who had taken possession of the house . . .

"Oh. Right. Well, that makes sense of everything," said the Doctor, as if it actually did.

"It does?" said Mr. Browning. "Do you know where Polly is?"

The Doctor shook his head. "Mister Browning. Reg. Is there any chance she might have gone back to your house?"

The man shrugged. "Might have done. Do you think—?"

But the tall young man and the red-haired Scottish girl pushed past him, slammed the door of their police box, and sprinted away across the green.

VI.

AMY KEPT PACE WITH the Doctor, and panted out questions as they ran. "You think she's in the house?"

"I'm afraid she is. Yes. I've got a sort of an idea. Look, Amy, don't let anyone persuade you to ask *them* the time. And if they do, don't answer them. Safer that way."

"You mean it?"

"I'm afraid so. And watch out for masks."

"Right. So these are dangerous aliens we're dealing with? They wear masks and ask you what time it is?"

"It sounds like them. Yes. But my people dealt with them, so long ago. It's almost inconceivable . . ."

They stopped running as they reached Claversham Row.

"And if it is who I think it is, what I think it—they—it—are . . . there is only one sensible thing we should be doing."

"What's that?"

"Running away," said the Doctor, as he rang the doorbell.

A moment's silence, then the door opened and a girl looked up at them. She could not have been more than eleven, and her hair was in pigtails. "Hello," she said. "My name is Polly Browning. What's your names?"

"Polly!" said Amy. "Your parents are worried sick about you."

"I just came to get my diary back," said the girl. "It was under a loose floorboard in my old bedroom."

"Your parents have been looking for you all day!" said Amy. She wondered why the Doctor didn't say anything.

The little girl—Polly—looked at her wristwatch. "That's weird. It says I've only been here for five minutes. I got here at ten this morning."

Amy knew it was somewhere late in the afternoon. She said, "What time is it now?"

Polly looked up, delighted. This time Amy thought there was something strange about the girl's face. Something flat. Something almost mask-like . . .

"Time for you to come into my house," said the girl.

Amy blinked. It seemed to her that, without having moved, she and the Doctor were now standing in the entry hall. The girl was standing on the stairs facing them. Her face was level with theirs.

"What are you?" asked Amy.

"We are the Kin," said the girl, who was not a girl. Her voice was deeper, darker, and more guttural. She seemed to Amy like something crouching, something huge that wore a paper mask with the face of a girl crudely scrawled on it. Amy could not understand how she could ever have been fooled into thinking it was a real face.

"I've heard of you," said the Doctor. "My people thought you were—"

"An abomination," said the crouching thing with the paper mask. "And a violation of all the laws of time. They sectioned us off from the rest of Creation. But I escaped, and thus we escaped. And we are ready to begin again. Already we have started to purchase this world."

"You're recycling money through time," said the Doctor. "Buying up this world with it, starting with this house, the town—"

"Doctor? What's going on?" asked Amy. "Can you explain any of this?"

"All of it," said the Doctor. "Sort of wish I couldn't. They've come here to take over the Earth. They're going to become the population of the planet."

"Oh, no, Doctor," said the huge crouching creature in the paper mask. "You don't understand. That's not why we take over the planet. We will take over the world and let humanity become extinct simply in order to get you here, now."

The Doctor grabbed Amy's hand and shouted, "Run!" He headed for the front door—

—and found himself at the top of the stairs. He called, "Amy!" but there was no reply. Something brushed his face: something that felt almost like fur. He swatted it away.

There was one door open, and he walked towards it.

"Hello," said the person in the room, in a breathy, female voice. "*So* glad you could come, Doctor."

It was Margaret Thatcher, the prime minister of Great Britain.

"You *do* know who we are, dear?" she asked. "It would be such a *shame* if you didn't."

"The Kin," said the Doctor. "A population that only consists of one creature, but able to move through time as easily and instinctively as a human can cross the road. There was only one of you. But you'd populate a place by moving backwards and forwards in time until there were hundreds of you, then thousands and millions, all interacting with yourselves at different moments in your own timeline. And this would go on until the local structure of time would collapse, like rotten wood. You need other entities, at least in the beginning, to ask you the time, and create the quantum super-positioning that allows you to anchor to a place-time location."

"Very *good*," said Mrs. Thatcher. "Do you *know* what the Time Lords said, when they engulfed our world? They said that as *each* of us was the Kin at a different moment in time, to kill any one of us was to commit an act of genocide against our whole species. You cannot kill *me*, because to kill me is to kill *all* of us."

"You know I'm the last Time Lord?"

"Oh *yes*, dear."

"Let's see. You pick up the money from the mint as it's being printed, buy things with it, return it moments later. Recycle it through time. And the masks . . . I suppose they amplify the conviction field. People are going to be much more willing to sell things when they believe that the leader of their country is asking for them, personally . . . and eventually you've sold the whole place to yourselves. Will you kill the humans?"

"*No* need, dear. We'll even make reservations for them: Greenland, Siberia, Antarctica . . . but they *will* die out, nonetheless. Several billion people living in places that can barely support a few thousand. Well, dear . . . it *won't* be pretty." Mrs. Thatcher moved. The Doctor concentrated on seeing her as she was. He closed his eyes. Opened them to see a bulky figure wearing a crude black and white face mask, with a photograph of Margaret Thatcher on it.

The Doctor reached out his hand and pulled off the mask from the Kin.

The Doctor could see beauty where humans could not. He took joy in all creatures. But the face of the Kin was hard to appreciate.

"You . . . you revolt yourself," said the Doctor. "Blimey. It's why you wear masks. You don't like your face, do you?"

The Kin said nothing. Its face, if that was its face, writhed and squirmed.

"Where's Amy?" asked the Doctor.

"Surplus to requirements," said another, similar voice, from behind him. A thin man, in a rabbit mask. "We let her go. We only needed you, Doctor. Our Time Lord prison was a torment, because we were trapped in it and reduced to one of us. You are also only one of you. And you will stay here in this house forever."

The Doctor walked from room to room, examining his surroundings with care. The walls of the house were soft and covered with a light layer of fur. And they moved, gently, in and out, as if they were . . . "Breathing. It's a living room. Literally."

He said, "Give me Amy back. Leave this place. I'll find you somewhere you can go. You can't just keep looping and re-looping through time, over and over, though. It messes everything up."

"And when it does, we begin again, somewhere else," said the woman in the cat mask, on the stairs. "You will be imprisoned until your life is done. Age here, regenerate here, die here, over and over. Our prison will not end until the last Time Lord is no more."

"Do you really think you can hold me that easily?" the Doctor asked. It was always good to seem in control, no matter how much he was worried that he was going to be stuck here for good.

"Quickly! Doctor! Down here!" It was Amy's voice. He took the steps three at a time, heading towards the place her voice had come from: the front door.

"Doctor!"

"I'm here." He rattled the door. It was locked. He pulled out his screwdriver, and soniced the door handle.

There was a clunk and the door flew open: the sudden daylight was blinding. The Doctor saw, with delight, his friend, and a familiar big blue police box. He was not certain which to hug first.

"Why didn't you go inside?" he asked Amy, as he opened the TARDIS door.

"Can't find the key. Must have dropped it while they were chasing me. Where are we going now?"

"Somewhere safe. Well, safer." He closed the door. "Got any suggestions?"

Amy stopped at the bottom of the control room stairs and looked around at the gleaming coppery world, at the glass pillar that ran through the TARDIS controls, at the doors.

"Amazing, isn't she?" said the Doctor. "I never get tired of looking at the old girl."

"Yes, the old girl," said Amy. "I think we should go to the very dawn of time, Doctor. As early as we can go. They won't be able to find us there, and we can work out what to do next." She was looking over the Doctor's shoulder at the console, watching his hands move, as if she was determined not to forget anything he did. The TARDIS was no longer in 1984.

"The dawn of time? Very clever, Amy Pond. That's somewhere we've never gone before. Somewhere we shouldn't be able to go. It's a good thing I've got this." He held up the squiggly whatsit, then attached it to the TARDIS console, using alligator clips and what looked like a piece of string.

"There," he said proudly. "Look at that."

"Yes," said Amy. "We've escaped the Kin's trap."

The TARDIS engines began to groan, and the whole room began to judder and shake.

"What's that noise?"

"We're heading for somewhere the TARDIS isn't designed to go. Somewhere I wouldn't dare go without the squiggly whatsit giving us a boost and a time bubble. The noise is the engines complaining. It's like going up a steep hill in an old car. It may take us a few more minutes to get there. Still, you'll like it when we arrive: the dawn of time. Excellent suggestion."

"I'm sure I will like it," said Amy, with a smile. "It must have felt so good to escape the Kin's prison, Doctor."

"That's the funny thing," said the Doctor. "You ask me about escaping the Kin's prison. That house. And I mean, I did escape, just by sonicing a doorknob, which was a bit convenient. But what if the trap wasn't the house? What if the Kin didn't want a Time Lord to torture and kill? What if they wanted something much more important. What if they wanted a TARDIS?"

"Why would the Kin want a TARDIS?" asked Amy.

The Doctor looked at Amy. He looked at her with clear eyes, unclouded by hate or by illusion. "The Kin can't travel very far through time. Not easily. And doing what they do is slow, and it takes an effort. The Kin would have to travel back and forward in time fifteen million times just to populate London.

"What if the Kin had all of Time and Space to move through? What if it went back to the very beginning of the Universe, and began its existence there? It would be able to populate everything. There would be no intelligent beings in the whole of the SpaceTime Continuum that wasn't the Kin. One entity would fill the Universe, leaving no room for anything else. Can you imagine it?"

Amy licked her lips. "Yes," she said. "Yes I can."

"All you'd need would be to get into a TARDIS, and have a Time Lord at the controls, and the Universe would be your playground."

"Oh yes," said Amy, and she was smiling broadly, now. "It will be."

"We're almost there," said the Doctor. "The dawn of time. Please. Tell me that Amy's safe, wherever she is."

"Why ever would I tell you that?" asked the Kin in the Amy Pond mask. "It's not true."

VII.

AMY COULD HEAR THE Doctor running down the stairs. She heard a voice that sounded strangely familiar calling to him, and then she heard a sound that filled her chest with despair: the diminishing *vworp vworp* of a TARDIS as it leaves.

The door opened, at that moment, and she walked out into the downstairs hall.

"He's run out on you," said a deep voice. "How does it feel to be abandoned?"

"The Doctor doesn't abandon his friends," said Amy to the thing in the shadows.

"He does. He obviously did in this case. You can wait as long as you want to, he'll never come back," said the thing, as it stepped out of the darkness, and into the half-light.

It was huge. Its shape was humanoid, but also somehow animal (*Lupine*, thought Amy Pond, as she took a step backwards, away from the thing). It had a mask on, an unconvincing wooden mask, that seemed like it was meant to represent an angry dog, or perhaps a wolf.

"He's taking someone he believes to be you for a ride in the TARDIS. And in a few moments, reality is going to rewrite. The Time Lords reduced the Kin to one lonely entity cut off from the rest of Creation. So it is fitting that a Time Lord restores us to our rightful place in the order of things: all other things will serve me, or will be me, or will be food for me. Ask me what time it is, Amy Pond."

"Why?"

There were more of them, now, shadowy figures. A cat-faced woman on the stairs. A small girl in the corner. The rabbit-headed man standing behind her said, "Because it will be a clean way to die. An easy way to go. In a few moments you will never have existed anyway."

"Ask me," said the wolf-masked figure in front of her. "Say, 'What's the time, Mister Wolf?' "

In reply, Amy Pond reached up and pulled the wolf mask from the face of the huge thing, and she saw the Kin.

Human eyes were not meant to look at the Kin. The crawling, squirming, wriggling mess that was the face of the Kin was a frightful thing: the masks had been as much for its own protection as for everyone else's.

Amy Pond stared at the face of the Kin. She said, "Kill me if you're going to kill me. But I don't believe that the Doctor has abandoned me. And I'm not going to ask you what time it is."

"Pity," said the Kin, through a face that was a nightmare. And it moved toward her.

THE TARDIS ENGINES groaned once, loudly, and then were silent.

"We are here," said the Kin. Its Amy Pond mask was now just a flat, scrawled drawing of a girl's face.

"We're here at the beginning of it all," said the Doctor, "because that's where you want to be. But I'm prepared to do this another way. I could find a solution for you. For all of you."

"Open the door," grunted the Kin.

The Doctor opened the door. The winds that swirled about the TARDIS pushed the Doctor backwards.

The Kin stood at the door of the TARDIS. "It's so dark."

"We're at the very start of it all. Before light."

"I will walk into the Void," said the Kin. "And you will ask me, 'What time is it?' And I will tell myself, tell you, tell all Creation, *Time for the Kin to rule, to occupy, to invade. Time for the Universe to become only me and mine and whatever I keep to devour. Time for the first and final reign of the Kin, world without end, through all of time.*"

"I wouldn't do it," said the Doctor. "If I were you. You can still change your mind."

The Kin dropped the Amy Pond mask onto the TARDIS floor. It pushed itself out of the TARDIS door, into the Void.

"Doctor," it called. Its face was a writhing mass of maggots. "Ask me what time it is."

"I can do better than that," said the Doctor. "I can *tell* you exactly what time it is. It's no time. It's Nothing O'Clock. It's a microsecond before the Big Bang. We're not at the Dawn of Time. We're before the Dawn.

"The Time Lords really didn't like genocide. I'm not too keen on it myself. It's the potential you're killing off. What if one day there was a good Dalek? What if . . ." He paused. "Space is big. Time is bigger. I would have helped you to find a place your people could have lived. But there was a girl called Polly, and she left her diary behind. And you killed her. That was a mistake."

"You never even knew her," called the Kin from the Void.

"She was a kid," said the Doctor. "Pure potential, like every kid everywhere. I know all I need." The squiggly whatsit attached to the TARDIS console was beginning to smoke and spark. "You're out of time, literally. Because Time doesn't start until the Big Bang. And if any part of a creature that inhabits time gets removed from time . . . well, you're removing yourself from the whole picture."

The Kin understood. It understood that, at that moment, all of Time and Space was one tiny particle, smaller than an atom, and that until a microsecond passed, and the particle exploded, nothing would happen. Nothing could happen. And the Kin was on the wrong side of the microsecond.

Cut off from Time, all the other parts of the Kin were ceasing to be. The It that was They felt the wash of nonexistence sweeping over them.

In the beginning—before the beginning—was the word. And the word was "Doctor!"

But the door had been closed and the TARDIS vanished, implacably. The Kin was left alone, in the Void before Creation.

Alone, forever, in that moment, waiting for Time to begin.

VIII.

THE YOUNG MAN IN the tweed jacket walked around the house at the end of Claversham Row. He knocked at the door, but no one answered. He went back into the blue box, and fiddled with the tiniest of controls: it was always easier to travel a thousand years than it was to travel twenty-four hours.

He tried again.

He could feel the threads of time raveling and reraveling. Time is complex: not everything that has happened has happened, after all. Only the Time Lords understood it, and even they found it impossible to describe.

The house in Claversham Row had a grimy FOR SALE sign in the garden.

He knocked at the door.

"Hello," he said. "You must be Polly. I'm looking for Amy Pond." The girl's hair was in pigtails. She looked up at the Doctor suspiciously. "How do you know my name?" she asked.

"I'm very clever," said the Doctor, seriously.

Polly shrugged. She went back into the house, and the Doctor followed. There was, he was relieved to notice, no fur on the walls.

Amy was in the kitchen, drinking tea with Mrs. Browning. Radio Four was playing in the background. Mrs. Browning was telling Amy about her job as a nurse, and the hours she had to work, and Amy was saying that her fiancé was a nurse, and she knew all about it.

She looked up, sharply, when the Doctor came in: a look as if to say "You've got a lot of explaining to do."

"I thought you'd be here," said the Doctor. "If I just kept looking."

THEY LEFT THE house on Claversham Row: the blue police box was parked at the end of the road, beneath some chestnut trees.

"One moment," said Amy, "I was about to be eaten by that creature. The next I was sitting in the kitchen, talking to Mrs. Browning, and listening to *The Archers*. How did you do that?"

"I'm very clever," said the Doctor. It was a good line, and he was determined to use it as much as possible.

"Let's go home," said Amy. "Will Rory be there this time?"

"Everybody in the world will be there," said the Doctor. "Even Rory."

They went into the TARDIS. He had already removed the blackened remains of the squiggly whatsit from the console: the TARDIS would not again be able to reach the moment before time began, but then, all things considered, that had to be a good thing.

He was determined to take Amy straight home—with just a small side trip to Andalusia, during the age of chivalry, where, in a small inn on the road to Seville, he had once been served the finest gazpacho he had ever tasted.

The Doctor was almost completely sure he could find it again . . .

"We'll go straight home," he said. "After lunch. And over lunch, I'll tell you the story of Maximelos and the three Ogrons."

A LUNAR LABYRINTH

2013

WE WERE WALKING up a gentle hill on a summer's evening. It was gone eight thirty, but it still felt like midafternoon. The sky was blue. The sun was low on the horizon, and it splashed the clouds with gold and salmon and purple-gray.

"So how did it end?" I asked my guide.

"It never ends," he said.

"But you said it's gone," I said. "The maze."

I had found the lunar labyrinth mentioned online, a small footnote on a website that told you what was interesting and noteworthy wherever you were in the world. Unusual local attractions: the tackier and more manmade the better. I do not know why I am drawn to them: stoneless henges made of cars or of yellow school buses, polystyrene models of enormous blocks of cheese, unconvincing dinosaurs made of flaking powdery concrete and all the rest.

I need them, and they give me an excuse to stop driving, wherever I am, and actually to talk to people. I have been invited into people's houses and into their lives because I wholeheartedly appreciated the zoos they made from engine parts, the houses they had built from tin cans, stone blocks and then covered with aluminum foil, the historical pageants made from shop-window dummies, the paint on their faces flaking off. And those people, the ones who made the roadside attractions, they would accept me for what I am.

"WE BURNED IT down," said my guide. He was elderly, and he walked with a stick. I had met him sitting on a bench in front of the town's hardware store, and he had agreed to show me the site that the lunar labyrinth had once been built upon. Our progress across the meadow was not fast. "The end of the lunar labyrinth. It was easy. The rosemary hedges caught fire and they crackled and flared. The smoke was thick and drifted down the hill and made us all think of roast lamb."

"Why was it called a lunar labyrinth?" I asked. "Was it just the alliteration?"

He thought about this. "I wouldn't rightly know," he said. "Not one way or the other. We called it a labyrinth, but I guess it's just a maze . . ."

"Just amazed," I repeated.

"There were traditions," he said. "We would start to walk it the day *after* the full moon. Begin at the entrance. Make your way to the center, then turn around and trace your way back. Like I say, we'd only start walking the day the moon began to wane. It would still be bright enough to walk. We'd walk it any night the moon was bright enough to see by. Come out here. Walk. Mostly in couples. We'd walk until the dark of the moon."

"Nobody walked it in the dark?"

"Oh, some of them did. But they weren't like us. They were kids, and they brought flashlights, when the moon went dark. They walked it, the bad kids, the bad seeds, the ones who wanted to scare each other. For those kids it was Hallowe'en every month. They loved to be scared. Some of them said they saw a torturer."

"What kind of a torturer?" The word had surprised me. You did not hear it often, not in conversation.

"Just someone who tortured people, I guess. I never saw him."

A breeze came down toward us from the hilltop. I sniffed the air but smelled no burning herbs, no ash, nothing that seemed unusual on a summer evening. Somewhere there were gardenias.

"It was only kids when the moon was dark. When the crescent moon appeared, then the children got younger, and parents would come up to the hill and walk with them. Parents and children.

They'd walk the maze together to its center and the adults would point up to the new moon, how it looks like a smile in the sky, a huge yellow smile, and little Romulus and Remus, or whatever the kids were called, they'd smile and laugh, and wave their hands as if they were trying to pull the moon out of the sky and put it on their little faces.

"Then, as the moon waxed, the couples would come. Young couples would come up here, courting, and elderly couples, comfortable in each other's company, the ones whose courting days were long forgotten." He leaned heavily on his stick. "Not forgotten," he said. "You never forget. It must be somewhere inside you. Even if the brain has forgotten, perhaps the teeth remember. Or the fingers."

"Did they have flashlights?"

"Some nights they did. Some nights they didn't. The popular nights were always the nights where no clouds covered the moon, and you could just walk the labyrinth. And sooner or later, everybody did. As the moonlight increased, day by day—night by night, I should say. That world was so beautiful.

"They parked their cars down there, back where you parked yours, at the edge of the property, and they'd come up the hill on foot. Always on foot, except for the ones in wheelchairs, or the ones whose parents carried them. Then, at the top of the hill some of them'd stop to canoodle. They'd walk the labyrinth too. There were benches, places to stop as you walked it. And they'd stop and canoodle some more. You'd think it was just the young ones, canoodling, but the older folk did it, too. Flesh to flesh. You would hear them sometimes, on the other side of the hedge, making noises like animals, and that always was your cue to slow down, or maybe explore another branch of the path for a while. Doesn't come by too often, but when it does I think I appreciate it more now than I did then. Lips touching skin. Under the moonlight."

"How many years exactly was the lunar labyrinth here before it was burned down? Did it come before or after the house was built?"

My guide made a dismissive noise. "After, before . . . these things all go back. They talk about the labyrinth of Minos, but that was nothing by comparison to this. Just some tunnels with a horn-headed fellow wandering lonely and scared and hungry. He wasn't really a bull-head. You know that?"

"How do you know?"

"Teeth. Bulls and cows are ruminants. They don't eat flesh. The minotaur did."

"I hadn't thought of that."

"People don't." The hill was getting steeper now.

I thought, *There are no torturers, not any longer.* And I was no torturer. But all I said was, "How high were the bushes that made up the maze? Were they real hedges?"

"They were real. They were high as they needed to be."

"I don't know how high rosemary grows in these parts." I didn't. I was far from home.

"We have gentle winters. Rosemary flourishes here."

"So why exactly did the people burn it all down?"

He paused. "You'll get a better idea of how things lie when we get to the top of the hill."

"How do they lie?"

"At the top of the hill."

The hill was getting steeper and steeper. My left knee had been injured the previous winter, in a fall on the ice, which meant I could no longer run fast, and these days I found hills and steps extremely taxing. With each step my knee would twinge, reminding me, angrily, of its existence.

Many people, on learning that the local oddity they wished to visit had burned down some years before, would simply have gotten back into their cars and driven on toward their final destination. I am not so easily deterred. The finest things I have seen are dead places: a shuttered amusement park I entered by bribing a night watchman with the price of a drink; an abandoned barn in which, the farmer said, half a dozen bigfoots had been living the summer before. He said they howled at night, and that they stank, but that they had moved on almost a year ago. There was a rank animal smell that lingered in that place, but it might have been coyotes.

"When the moon waned, they walked the lunar labyrinth with love," said my guide. "As it waxed, they walked with desire, not with love. Do I have to explain the difference to you? The sheep and the goats?"

"I don't think so."

"The sick came, too, sometimes. The damaged and the disabled came, and some of them needed to be wheeled through the labyrinth, or carried. But even they had to choose the path they traveled, not the people carrying them or wheeling them. Nobody chose their paths but them. When I was a boy people called them cripples. I'm glad we don't call them cripples any longer. The lovelorn came, too. The alone. The lunatics—they were brought here, sometimes. Got their name from the moon, it was only fair the moon had a chance to fix things."

We were approaching the top of the hill. It was dusk. The sky was the color of wine, now, and the clouds in the west glowed with the light of the setting sun, although from where we were standing it had already dropped below the horizon.

"You'll see, when we get up there. It's perfectly flat, the top of the hill."

I wanted to contribute something, so I said, "Where I come from, five hundred years ago the local lord was visiting the king. And the king showed off his enormous table, his candles, his beautiful painted ceiling, and as each one was displayed, instead of praising it, the lord simply said, 'I have a finer, and bigger, and better one.' The king wanted to call his bluff, so he told him that the following month he would come and eat at this table, bigger and finer than the king's, lit by candles in candleholders bigger and finer than the king's, under a ceiling painting bigger and better than the king's."

My guide said, "Did he lay out a tablecloth on the flatness of the hill, and have twenty brave men holding candles, and did they dine beneath God's own stars? They tell a story like that in these parts, too."

"That's the story," I admitted, slightly miffed that my contribution had been so casually dismissed. "And the king acknowledged that the lord was right."

"Didn't the boss have him imprisoned, and tortured?" asked my guide. "That's what happened in the version of the story they tell hereabouts. They say that the man never even made it as far as the Cordon Bleu dessert his chef had whipped up. They found him on the following day with his hands cut off, his severed tongue placed neatly in his breast pocket and a final bullet-hole in his forehead."

"Here? In the house back there?"

"Good lord, no. They left his body in his nightclub. Over in the city."

I was surprised how quickly dusk had ended. There was still a glow in the west, but the rest of the sky had become night, plum-purple in its majesty.

"The days before the full of the moon, in the labyrinth," he said. "They were set aside for the infirm, and those in need. My sister had a women's condition. They told her it would be fatal if she didn't have her insides all scraped out, and then it might be fatal anyway. Her stomach had swollen up as if she was carrying a baby, not a tumor, although she must have been pushing fifty. She came up here when the moon was a day from full and she walked the labyrinth. Walked it from the outside in, in the moon's light, and she walked it from the center back to the outside, with no false steps or mistakes."

"What happened to her?"

"She lived," he said, shortly.

We crested the hill, but I could not see what I was looking at. It was too dark.

"They delivered her of the thing inside her. It lived as well, for a while." He paused. Then he tapped my arm. "Look over there."

I turned and looked. The size of the moon astonished me. I know it's an optical illusion, that the moon grows no smaller as it rises, but this moon seemed to take up so much of the horizon as it rose that I found myself thinking of the old Frank Frazetta paperback covers, where men with their swords raised would be silhouetted in front of huge moons, and I remembered paintings of wolves howling on hilltops, black cutouts against the circle of snow-white moon that framed them. The enormous moon that was rising was the creamy yellow of freshly churned butter.

"Is the moon full?" I asked.

"That's a full moon, all right." He sounded satisfied. "And there's the labyrinth."

We walked towards it. I had expected to see ash on the ground, or nothing. Instead, in the buttery moonlight, I saw a maze, complex and elegant, made of circles and whorls inside a huge square. I could not judge distances properly in that light, but I thought that each side of the square must be two hundred feet or more.

The plants that outlined the maze were low to the ground, though. None of them was more than a foot tall. I bent down, picked a needlelike leaf, black in the moonlight, and crushed it between finger and thumb. I inhaled, and thought of raw lamb, carefully dismembered and prepared, and placed in an oven on a bed of branches and needles that smelled just like this.

"I thought you people burned all this to the ground," I said.

"We did. They aren't hedges, not any longer. But things grow again, in their season. There's no killing some things. Rosemary's tough."

"Where's the entrance?"

"You're standing in it," he said. He was an old man, who walked with a stick and talked to strangers. Nobody would ever miss him.

"So what happened up here when the moon was full?"

"Locals didn't walk the labyrinth then. That was the one night that paid for all."

I took a step into the maze. There was nothing difficult about it, not with the bushes that marked it no higher than my shins, no higher than a kitchen garden. If I got lost, I could simply step over the bushes, walk back out. But for now I followed the path into the labyrinth. It was easy to make out in the light of the full moon. I could hear my guide, as he continued to talk.

"Some folk thought even that price was too high. That was why we came up here, why we burned the lunar labyrinth. We came up that hill when the moon was dark, and we carried burning torches, like in the old black-and-white movies. We all did. Even me. But you can't kill everything. It don't work like that."

"Why rosemary?" I asked.

"Rosemary's for remembering," he told me.

The butter-yellow moon was rising faster than I imagined or expected. Now it was a pale ghost-face in the sky, calm and compassionate, and its color was white, bone-white.

The man said, "There's always a chance that you could get out safely. Even on the night of the full moon. First you have to get to the center of the labyrinth. There's a fountain there. You'll see. You can't mistake it. Then you have to make it back from the center. No missteps, no dead ends, no mistakes on the way in or on the way out. It's probably easier now than it was when the bushes were high. It's a chance. Otherwise, the labyrinth gets to cure you of all that ails you. Of course, you'll have to run."

I looked back. I could not see my guide. Not any longer. There was something in front of me, beyond the bush-path pattern, a black shadow padding silently along the perimeter of the square. It was the size of a large dog, but it did not move like a dog.

It threw back its head and howled to the moon with amusement and with merriment. The huge flat table at the top of the hill echoed with joyous howls, and, my left knee aching from the long hill-climb, I stumbled forward.

The maze had a pattern; I could trace it. Above me the moon shone, bright as day. She had always accepted my gifts in the past. She would not play me false at the end.

"Run," said a voice that was almost a growl.

I ran like a lamb to his laughter.

DOWN TO A SUNLESS SEA

2013

THE THAMES IS a filthy beast: it winds through London like a blindworm, or a sea serpent. All the rivers flow into it, the Fleet and the Tyburn and the Neckinger, carrying all the filth and scum and waste, the bodies of cats and dogs and the bones of sheep and pigs down into the brown water of the Thames, which carries them east into the estuary and from there into the North Sea and oblivion.

It is raining in London. The rain washes the dirt into the gutters, and it swells streams into rivers, rivers into powerful things. The rain is a noisy thing, splashing and pattering and rattling the rooftops. If it is clean water as it falls from the skies it only needs to touch London to become dirt, to stir dust and make it mud.

Nobody drinks it, neither the rainwater nor the river water. They make jokes about Thames water killing you instantly, and it is not true. There are mudlarks who will dive deep for thrown pennies, then come up again, spout the river water, shiver and hold up their coins. They do not die, of course, or not of that, although there are no mudlarks over fifteen years of age.

The woman does not appear to care about the rain.

She walks the Rotherhithe docks, as she has done for years, for decades: nobody knows how many years, because nobody cares. She walks the docks, or she stares out to sea. She examines the ships, as they bob at anchor. She must do something, to keep body and soul from dissolving their partnership, but none of the folk of the dock have the foggiest idea what this could be.

You take refuge from the deluge beneath a canvas awning put up by a sailmaker. You believe yourself to be alone under there, at first, for she is statue-still and staring out across the water, even though there is nothing to be seen through the curtain of rain. The far side of the Thames has vanished.

And then she sees you. She sees you and she begins to talk, not to you, oh no, but to the gray water that falls from the gray sky into the gray river. She says, "My son wanted to be a sailor," and you do not know what to reply, or how to reply. You would have to shout to make yourself heard over the roar of the rain, but she talks, and you listen. You discover yourself craning and straining to catch her words.

"My son wanted to be a sailor.

"I told him not to go to sea. I'm your mother, I said. The sea won't love you like I love you, she's cruel. But he said, Oh Mother, I need to see the world. I need to see the sun rise in the tropics, and watch the Northern Lights dance in the arctic sky, and most of all I need to make my fortune and then, when it's made I will come back to you, and build you a house, and you will have servants, and we will dance, Mother, oh how we will dance . . .

"And what would I do in a fancy house? I told him. You're a fool with your fine talk. I told him of his father, who never came back from the sea—some said he was dead and lost overboard, while some swore blind they'd seen him running a whorehouse in Amsterdam.

"It's all the same. The sea took him.

"When he was twelve years old, my boy ran away, down to the docks, and he shipped on the first ship he found, to Flores in the Azores, they told me.

"There's ships of ill omen. Bad ships. They give them a lick of paint after each disaster, and a new name, to fool the unwary.

"Sailors are superstitious. The word gets around. This ship was run aground by its captain, on orders of the owners, to defraud the insurers; and then, all mended and as good as new, it gets taken by pirates; and then it takes a shipment of blankets and becomes a plague ship crewed by the dead, and only three men bring it into port in Harwich . . .

"My son had shipped on a stormcrow ship. It was on the homeward leg of the journey, with him bringing me his wages—for he was too young to have spent them on women and on grog, like his father—that the storm hit.

"He was the smallest one in the lifeboat.

"They said they drew lots fairly, but I do not believe it. He was smaller than them. After eight days adrift in the boat, they were so hungry. And if they did draw lots, they cheated.

"They gnawed his bones clean, one by one, and they gave them to his new mother, the sea. She shed no tears and took them without a word. She's cruel.

"Some nights I wish he had not told me the truth. He could have lied.

"They gave my boy's bones to the sea, but the ship's mate—who had known my husband, and known me too, better than my husband thought he did, if truth were told—he kept a bone, as a keepsake.

"When they got back to land, all of them swearing my boy was lost in the storm that sank the ship, he came in the night, and he told me the truth of it, and he gave me the bone, for the love there had once been between us.

"I said, you've done a bad thing, Jack. That was your son that you've eaten.

"The sea took him too, that night. He walked into her, with his pockets filled with stones, and he kept walking. He'd never learned to swim.

"And I put the bone on a chain to remember them both by, late at night, when the wind crashes the ocean waves and tumbles them onto the sand, when the wind howls around the houses like a baby crying."

The rain is easing, and you think she is done, but now, for the first time, she looks at you, and appears to be about to say something. She has pulled something from around her neck, and now she is reaching it out to you.

"Here," she says. Her eyes, when they meet yours, are as brown as the Thames. "Would you like to touch it?"

You want to pull it from her neck, to toss it into the river for the mudlarks to find or to lose. But instead you stumble out from under the canvas awning, and the water of the rain runs down your face like someone else's tears.

HOW THE MARQUIS GOT
HIS COAT BACK

2014

IT WAS BEAUTIFUL. It was remarkable. It was unique. It was the reason that the Marquis de Carabas was chained to a pole in the middle of a circular room, far, far underground, while the water level rose slowly higher and higher. It had thirty pockets, seven of which were obvious, nineteen of which were hidden, and four of which were more or less impossible to find—even, on occasion, for the Marquis himself.

He had (we shall return to the pole, and the room, and the rising water, in due course) once been given—although *given* might be considered an unfortunate, if justified, exaggeration—a magnifying glass, by Victoria herself. It was a marvelous piece of work: ornate, gilt, with a chain and tiny cherubs and gargoyles, and the lens had the unusual property of rendering transparent anything you looked at through it. The Marquis did not know where Victoria had originally obtained the magnifying glass, before he pilfered it from her, to make up for a payment he felt was not entirely what had been agreed—after all, there was only one Elephant, and obtaining the Elephant's diary had not been easy, nor had escaping the Elephant and Castle once it had been obtained. The Marquis had slipped Victoria's magnifying glass into one of the four pockets that practically weren't there at all, and had never been able to find it again.

In addition to its unusual pockets, it had magnificent sleeves, an imposing collar, and a slit up the back. It was made of some kind of leather, it was the color of a wet street at midnight, and, more important than any of these things, it had style.

There are people who will tell you that clothes make the man, and mostly they are wrong. However, it would be true to say that when the boy who would become the Marquis put that coat on for the very first time, and stared at himself in the looking glass, he stood up straighter, and his posture changed, because he knew, seeing his reflection, that the sort of person who wore a coat like that was no mere youth, no simple sneak-thief and favor-trader. The boy wearing the coat, which was, back then, too large for him, had smiled, looking at his reflection, and remembered an illustration from a book he had seen, of a miller's cat standing on its two hind legs. A jaunty cat wearing a fine coat and big, proud boots. And he named himself.

A coat like that, he knew, was the kind of coat that could only be worn by the Marquis de Carabas. He was never sure, not then and not later, how you pronounced *Marquis de Carabas*. Some days he said it one way, some days the other.

The water level had reached his knees, and he thought, *This would never have happened if I still had my coat.*

IT WAS THE market day after the worst week of the Marquis de Carabas's life and things did not seem to be getting any better. Still, he was no longer dead, and his cut throat was healing rapidly. There was even a rasp in his throat he found quite attractive. Those were definite upsides.

There were just as definite downsides to being dead, or at least, to having been recently dead, and missing his coat was the worst of them.

The Sewer Folk were not helpful.

"You sold my corpse," said the Marquis. "These things happen. You also sold my possessions. I want them back. I'll pay."

Dunnikin of the Sewer Folk shrugged. "Sold them," he said. "Just like we sold you. Can't go getting things back that you sold. Not good business."

"We are talking," said the Marquis de Carabas, "about my coat. And I fully intend to have it back."

Dunnikin shrugged.

"To whom did you sell it?" asked the Marquis.

The sewer dweller said nothing at all. He acted as if he had not even heard the question.

"I can get you perfumes," said the Marquis, masking his irritability with all the blandness he could muster. "Glorious, magnificent, odiferous perfumes. You know you want them."

Dunnikin stared, stony-faced, at the Marquis. Then he drew his finger across his throat. As gestures went, the Marquis reflected, it was in appalling taste. Still, it had the desired effect. He stopped asking questions; there would be no answers from this direction.

The Marquis walked over to the food court. That night, the Floating Market was being held in the Tate Gallery. The food court was in the Pre-Raphaelite room, and had already been mostly packed away. There were almost no stalls left: just a sad-looking little man selling some kind of sausage, and, in the corner, beneath a Burne-Jones painting of ladies in diaphanous robes walking downstairs, there were some Mushroom People, with some stools, tables and a grill. The Marquis had once eaten one of the sad-looking man's sausages, and he had a firm policy of never intentionally making the same mistake twice, so he walked to the Mushroom People's stall.

There were three of the Mushroom People looking after the stall, two young men and a young woman. They smelled damp. They wore old duffel coats and army-surplus jackets, and they peered out from beneath their shaggy hair as if the light hurt their eyes.

"What are you selling?" he asked.

"The Mushroom. The Mushroom on toast. Raw the Mushroom."

"I'll have some of the Mushroom on toast," he said, and one of the Mushroom People—a thin, pale young woman with the complexion of day-old porridge—cut a slice off a puffball fungus the size of a tree stump. "And I want it cooked properly all the way through," he told her.

"Be brave. Eat it raw," said the woman. "Join us."

"I have already had dealings with the Mushroom," said the Marquis. "We came to an understanding."

The woman put the slice of white puffball under the portable grill.

One of the young men, tall, with hunched shoulders, in a duffel coat that smelled like old cellars, edged over to the Marquis, and poured him a glass of mushroom tea. He leaned forward, and the Marquis could see the tiny crop of pale mushrooms splashed like pimples over his cheek.

The Mushroom person said, "You're de Carabas? The fixer?" The Marquis did not think of himself as a fixer.

He said, "I am."

"I hear you're looking for your coat. I was there when the Sewer Folk sold it. Start of the last Market it was. On Belfast. I saw who bought it."

The hair on the back of the Marquis's neck pricked up. "And what would you want for the information?"

The Mushroom's young man licked his lips with a lichenous tongue. "There's a girl I like as won't give me the time of day."

"A Mushroom girl?"

"Would I were so lucky. If we were as one both in love and in the body of the Mushroom, I wouldn't have nothing to worry about. No. She's one of the Raven's Court. But she eats here sometimes. And we talk. Just like you and I are talking now."

The Marquis did not smile in pity and he did not wince. He barely raised an eyebrow. "And yet she does not return your ardor. How strange. What do you want me to do about it?"

The young man reached one gray hand into the pocket of his long duffel coat. He pulled out an envelope, inside a clear plastic sandwich bag.

"I wrote her a letter. More of a poem, you might say, although I'm not much of a poet. To tell her how I feels about her. But I don't know that she'd read it, if I gived it to her. Then I saw you, and I thought, if it was you as was to give it to her, with all your fine words and your fancy flourishes . . ." He trailed off.

"You thought she would read it and then be more inclined to listen to your suit."

The young man looked down at his duffel coat with a puzzled expression. "I've not got a suit," he said. "Only what I've got on."

The Marquis tried not to sigh. The Mushroom woman put a cracked plastic plate down in front of him, with a steaming slice of grilled the Mushroom on it, soaking into a brown slice of crusty toast.

He poked at the Mushroom experimentally, making sure that it was cooked all the way through, and there were no active spores. You could never be too careful, and the Marquis considered himself much too selfish for symbiosis.

It was good. He chewed, and swallowed, though the food hurt his throat.

"So all you want is for me to make sure she reads your missive of yearning?"

"You mean my letter? My poem?"

"I do."

"Well, yes. And I want you to be there with her, to make sure she doesn't put it away unread, and I want you to bring her answer back to me." The Marquis looked at the young man. It was true that he had tiny mushrooms sprouting from his neck and cheeks, and his hair was heavy and unwashed, and there was a general smell about him of abandoned places, but it was also true that through his thick fringe his eyes were pale blue and intense, and that he was tall, and not unattractive. The Marquis imagined him washed and cleaned up and somewhat less fungal, and approved. "I put the letter in the sandwich bag," said the young man, "So it doesn't get wet on the way."

"Very wise. Now, tell me: who bought my coat?"

"Not yet, Mister Jumps-the-gun. You haven't asked about my true love. Her name is Drusilla. You'll know her because she is the most beautiful woman in all of the Raven's Court."

"Beauty is traditionally in the eye of the beholder. Give me more to go on."

"I told you. Her name's Drusilla. There's only one. And she has a big red birthmark on the back of her hand that looks like a star."

"It seems an unlikely love pairing. One of the Mushroom's folk, in love with a lady of the Raven's Court. What makes you think she'll give up her life for your damp cellars and fungoid joys?"

The Mushroom youth shrugged. "She'll love me," he said. "Once she's read my poem." He twisted the stem of a tiny parasol mushroom growing on his right cheek, and when it fell to the table, he picked it up and continued to twist it between his fingers. "We're on?"

"We're on."

"The cove as bought your coat," said the Mushroom youth, "carried a stick."

"Lots of people carry sticks," said de Carabas.

"This one had a crook on the end," said the Mushroom youth. "Looked a bit like a frog, he did. Short one. Bit fat. Hair the color of gravel. Needed a coat and took a shine to yours." He popped the parasol mushroom into his mouth.

"Useful information. I shall certainly pass your ardor and felicitations on to the fair Drusilla," said the Marquis de Carabas, with a cheer that he most definitely did not feel.

De Carabas reached across the table, and took the sandwich bag with the envelope in it from the young man's fingers. He slipped it into one of the pockets sewn inside his shirt.

And then he walked away, thinking about a man holding a crook.

THE MARQUIS DE Carabas wore a blanket as a substitute for his coat. He wore it swathed about him like hell's own poncho. It did not make him happy. He wished he had his coat. *Fine feathers do not make fine birds,* whispered a voice at the back of his mind, something someone had said to him when he was a boy; he suspected that it was his brother's voice, and he did his best to forget it had ever spoken.

A crook: the man who had taken his coat from the sewer people had been carrying a crook.

He pondered.

The Marquis de Carabas liked being who he was, and when he took risks he liked them to be calculated risks, and he was someone who double- and triple-checked his calculations.

He checked his calculations for the fourth time.

The Marquis de Carabas did not trust people. It was bad for business and it could set an unfortunate precedent. He did not trust his friends or his occasional lovers, and he certainly never trusted his employers. He reserved the entirety of his trust for the Marquis de Carabas, an imposing figure in an imposing coat, able to outtalk, outthink and outplan anybody.

There were only two sorts of people who carried crooks: bishops and shepherds.

In Bishopsgate, the crooks were decorative, nonfunctional, purely symbolic. And the bishops had no need of coats. They had robes, after all, nice, white, bishoppy robes.

The Marquis was not scared of the bishops. He knew the Sewer Folk were not scared of the bishops. The inhabitants of Shepherd's Bush were another matter entirely. Even in his coat, and at the best of times, at the peak of health and with a small army at his beck and call, the Marquis would not have wanted to encounter the shepherds.

He toyed with the idea of visiting Bishopsgate, of spending a pleasant handful of days establishing that his coat was not there.

And then he sighed, dramatically, and went to the Guide's Pen, and looked for a bonded guide who might be persuaded take him to Shepherd's Bush.

HIS GUIDE WAS quite remarkably short, with fair hair cut close. The Marquis had first thought she was in her teens, until, after traveling with her for half a day, he had decided she was in her twenties. He had talked to half a dozen guides before he found her. Her name was Knibbs, and she had seemed confident, and he needed confidence. He told her the two places he was going, as they walked out of the Guide's Pen.

"So where do you want to go first, then?" she asked. "Shepherd's Bush, or Raven's Court?"

"The visit to Raven's Court is a formality; it is merely to deliver a letter. To someone named Drusilla."

"A love letter?"

"I believe so. Why do you ask?"

"I have heard that the fair Drusilla is most wickedly beautiful, and she has the unfortunate habit of reshaping those who displease her into birds of prey. You must love her very much, to be writing letters to her."

"I am afraid I have never encountered the young lady," said the Marquis. "The letter is not from me. And it doesn't matter which we visit first."

"You know," said Knibbs, thoughtfully, "just in case something dreadfully unfortunate happens to you when you get to the shepherds, we should probably do Raven's Court first. So the fair Drusilla gets her letter. I'm not saying that something horrible will happen to you, mind. Just that it's better to be safe than, y'know, dead."

The Marquis de Carabas looked down at his blanketed shape. He was uncertain. Had he been wearing his coat, he knew, he would not have been uncertain; he would have known exactly what to do. He looked at the girl and he mustered the most convincing grin he could. "Raven's Court it is, then," he said.

Knibbs had nodded, and set off on the path, and the Marquis had followed her.

The paths of London Below are not the paths of London Above: they rely to no little extent on things like belief and opinion and tradition as much as they rely upon the realities of maps.

De Carabas and Knibbs were two tiny figures walking through a high, vaulted tunnel carved from old, white stone. Their footsteps echoed.

"You're de Carabas, aren't you?" said Knibbs. "You're famous. You know how to get places. What exactly do you need a guide for?"

"Two heads are better than one," he told her. "So are two sets of eyes."

"You used to have a posh coat, didn't you?" she said.

"I did. Yes."

"What happened to it?"

He said nothing. Then he said, "I've changed my mind. We're going to Shepherd's Bush first."

"Fair enough," said his guide. "Easy to take you one place as another. I'll wait for you outside the shepherds' trading post, mind."

"Very wise, girl."

"My name's Knibbs," she said. "Not girl. Do you want to know why I become a guide? It's an interesting story."

"Not particularly," said the Marquis de Carabas. He was not feeling particularly talkative, and the guide was being well recompensed for her trouble. "Why don't we try to move in silence?"

Knibbs nodded, and said nothing as they reached the end of the tunnel, nothing as they clambered down some metal rungs set in the side of a wall. It was not until they had reached the banks of the Mortlake, the vast underground Lake of the Dead, and she was lighting a candle on the shore to summon the boatman, that she spoke again.

Knibbs said, "The thing about being a proper guide is that you're bonded. So people know you won't steer them wrong."

The Marquis only grunted. He was wondering what to tell the shepherds at the trading post, trying out alternate routes through possibility and through probability. He had nothing that the shepherds would want, that was the trouble.

"You lead them wrong, you'll never work as a guide again," said Knibbs, cheerfully. "That's why we're bonded."

"I know," said the Marquis. She was a most irritating guide, he thought. Two heads were only better than one if the other head kept its mouth shut and did not start telling him things he already knew.

"I got bonded," she said, "in Bond Street." She tapped the little chain around her wrist.

"I don't see the ferryman," said the Marquis.

"He'll be here soon enough. You keep an eye out for him in that direction, and halloo when you sees him. I'll keep looking over here. One way or another, we'll spot him."

They stared out over the dark water of the lake. Knibbs began to talk again. "Before I was a guide, when I was just little, my people trained me up for this. They said it was the only way that honor could ever be satisfied."

The Marquis turned to face her. She held the candle in front of her, at eye level. *Everything is off, here*, thought the Marquis, and he realized he should have been listening to her from the beginning.

Everything is wrong. He said, "Who are your people, Knibbs? Where do you come from?"

"Somewhere you ain't welcome anymore," said the girl. "I was born and bred to give my fealty and loyalty to the Elephant and the Castle."

Something hard struck him on the back of the head then, hit him like a hammer blow, and lightning pulsed in the darkness of his mind as he crumpled to the floor.

THE MARQUIS DE Carabas could not move his arms. They were, he realized, tied behind him. He was lying on his side.

He had been unconscious. If the people who did this to him thought him unconscious then he would do nothing to disabuse them of the idea, he decided. He let his eyes slit open the merest crack, to sneak a glance at the world.

A deep, grinding voice said, "Oh, don't be silly, de Carabas. I don't believe you're still out. I've got big ears. I can hear your heartbeat. Open your eyes properly, you weasel. Face me like a man."

The Marquis recognized the voice, and hoped he was mistaken. He opened his eyes. He was staring at legs, human legs with bare feet. The toes were squat and pushed together. The legs and feet were the color of teak. He knew those legs. He had not been mistaken.

His mind bifurcated: A small part of it berated him for his inattention and his foolishness. Knibbs had *told* him, by the Temple and the Arch; he just had not listened to her. But even as he raged at his own foolishness, the rest of his mind took over, forced a smile, and said, "Why, this is indeed an honor. You really didn't have to arrange to meet me like this. Why, the merest inkling that your prominence might have had even the teeniest desire to see me would have—"

"Sent you scurrying off in the other direction as fast as your spindly little legs could carry you," said the person with the teak-colored legs. He reached over with his trunk, which was long and flexible, and a greenish-blue color, and which hung to his ankles, and he pushed the Marquis onto his back.

The Marquis began rubbing his bound wrists slowly against the concrete beneath them, while he said, "Not at all. Quite the opposite. Words cannot actually describe how much pleasure I take in your pachydermic presence. Might I suggest that you untie me, and allow me to greet you, man to—man to elephant?"

"I don't think so, given all the trouble I've been through to make this happen," said the other. He had the head of a greenish-gray elephant. His tusks were sharp and stained reddish brown at the tips. "You know, I swore when I found out what you had done that I would make you scream and beg for mercy. And I swore I'd say no, to giving you mercy, when you begged for it."

"You could say yes, instead," said the Marquis.

"I couldn't say yes. Hospitality abused," said the Elephant. "I never forget."

The Marquis had been commissioned to bring Victoria the Elephant's diary, when he and the world had been much younger. The Elephant ran his fiefdom arrogantly, sometimes viciously and with no tenderness or humor, and the Marquis had thought that the Elephant was stupid. He had even believed that there was no way that the Elephant would correctly identify his role in the disappearance of the diary. It had been a long time ago, though, when the Marquis was young and foolish.

"This whole spending years training up a guide to betray me just on the off chance I'd come along and hire her," said the Marquis. "Isn't that a bit of an overreaction?"

"Not if you know me," said the Elephant. "If you know me, it's pretty mild. I did lots of other things to find you too."

The Marquis tried to sit up. The Elephant pushed him back to the floor, with one bare foot. "Beg for mercy," said the Elephant.

That one was easy. "Mercy!" said the Marquis. "I beg! I plead! Show me mercy—the finest of all gifts. It befits you, mighty Elephant, as lord of your own demesne, to be merciful to one who is not even fit to wipe the dust from your excellent toes . . ."

"Did you know," said the Elephant, "that everything you say sounds sarcastic?"

"I didn't. I apologize. I meant every single word of it."

"Scream," said the Elephant.

The Marquis de Carabas screamed very loudly and very long. It is hard to scream when your throat has been recently cut, but he screamed as hard and piteously as he could.

"You even scream sarcastically," said the Elephant.

There was a large black cast-iron pipe jutting out from the wall. A wheel in the side of the pipe allowed whatever came out of the pipe to be turned on and turned off. The Elephant hauled on it with powerful arms, and a trickle of dark sludge came out, followed by a spurt of water.

"Drainage overflow," said the Elephant. "Now. Thing is, I do my homework. You keep your life well hidden, de Carabas. You have done all these years, since you and I first crossed paths. No point in even trying anything as long as you had your life elsewhere. I've had people all over London Below—people you've eaten with, people you've slept with or laughed with or wound up naked in the clock tower of Big Ben with—but there was never any point in taking it further, not as long as your life was still carefully tucked out of harm's way. Until last week, when the word under the street was that your life was out of its box. And that was when I put the word out, that I'd give the freedom of the Castle to the first person to let me see—"

"See me scream for mercy," said de Carabas. "You said."

"You interrupted me," said the Elephant, mildly. "I was going to say, I was going to give the freedom of the Castle to the first person to let me see your dead body."

He pulled the wheel the rest of the way and the spurt of water became a gush.

"I ought to warn you. There is," said de Carabas, "a curse on the hand of anyone who kills me."

"I'll take the curse," said the Elephant. "Although you're probably making it up. You'll like the next bit. The room fills with water, and then you drown. Then I let the water out, and I come in, and I laugh a lot." He made a trumpeting noise that might, de Carabas reflected, have been a laugh, if you were an elephant.

The Elephant stepped out of de Carabas's line of sight.

The Marquis heard a door bang. He was lying in a puddle. He writhed and wriggled, then got to his feet. He looked down: there was a metal cuff around his ankle, which was chained to a metal pole in the center of the room.

He wished he were wearing his coat: there were blades in his coat; there were picklocks; there were buttons that were nowhere nearly as innocent and buttonlike as they appeared to be. He rubbed the rope that bound his wrists against the metal pole, hoping to make it fray, feeling the skin of his wrists and palms rubbing off even as the rope absorbed the water and tightened about him. The water level continued to rise; already it was up to his waist.

De Carabas looked about the circular chamber. All he had to do was free himself from the bonds that tied his wrists—obviously by loosening the pole to which he was bound—and then he would open the cuff around his ankle, turn off the water, get out of the room, avoid a revenge-driven Elephant and any of his assorted thugs, and get away.

He tugged on the pole. It didn't move. He tugged on it harder. It didn't move some more.

He slumped against the pole, and he thought about death, a true, final death, and he thought about his coat.

A voice whispered in his ear. It said, "Quiet!"

Something tugged at his wrists, and his bonds fell away. It was only as life came back into his wrists that he realized how tightly he had been bound. He turned around.

He said, "What?"

The face that met his was as familiar as his own. The smile was devastating, the eyes were guileless and adventuresome.

"Ankle," said the man, with a new smile that was even more devastating than the previous one.

The Marquis de Carabas was not devastated. He raised his leg, and the man reached down, did something with a piece of wire, and removed the leg cuff.

"I heard you were having a spot of bother," said the man. His skin was as dark as the Marquis's own. He was less than an inch taller than de Carabas, but he held himself as if he were easily taller than anyone he was ever likely to meet.

"No. No bother. I'm fine," said the Marquis. "You aren't. I just rescued you."

De Carabas ignored this. "Where's the Elephant?"

"On the other side of that door, with a number of the people working for him. The doors lock automatically when the hall is filled with water. He needed to be certain that he wouldn't be trapped in here with you. It was what I was counting on."

"Counting on?"

"Of course. I'd been following them for several hours. Ever since I heard that you'd gone off with one of the Elephant's plants. I thought, *Bad move,* I thought. *He'll be needing a hand with that.*"

"You *heard . . . ?*"

"Look," said the man, who looked a little like the Marquis de Carabas, only he was taller, and perhaps some people—not the Marquis, obviously—might have thought him just a hair more attractive, "you don't think I was going to let anything happen to my little brother, did you?"

They were up to their waists in water. "I was fine," said de Carabas. "I had it all under control."

The man walked over to the far end of the room. He knelt down, fumbled in the water, then, from his backpack, he produced something that looked like a short crowbar. He pushed one end of it beneath the surface of the water. "Get ready," he said. "I think this should be our quickest way out of here."

The Marquis was still flexing his pins-and-needles cramping fingers, trying to rub life back into them. "What is it?" he said, trying to sound unimpressed.

The man said, "There we go," and pulled up a large square of metal. "It's the drain." De Carabas did not have a chance to protest, as his brother picked him up and dropped him down a hole in the floor.

Probably, thought de Carabas, *there are rides like this at funfairs.* He could imagine them. Upworlders might pay good money to take this ride, if they were certain they would survive it.

He crashed through pipes, swept along by the flow of water, always heading down and deeper. He was not certain he was going to survive the ride, and he was not having fun.

The Marquis's body was bruised and battered as he rode the water down the pipe. He tumbled out, facedown, onto a large metal grate, which seemed scarcely able to hold his weight. He crawled off the grate onto the rock floor beside it, and he shivered.

There was an unlikely sort of a noise, and it was immediately followed by his brother, who shot out of the pipe and landed on his feet, as if he'd been practicing. He smiled. "Fun, eh?"

"Not really," said the Marquis de Carabas. And then he had to ask. "Were you just going '*Whee!*'?"

"Of course! Weren't you?" asked his brother.

De Carabas got to his feet, unsteadily. He said only, "What are you calling yourself these days?"

"Still the same. I don't change."

"It's not your real name, Peregrine," said de Carabas.

"It'll do. It marks my territory and my intentions. You're still calling yourself a Marquis, then?" said Peregrine.

"I am, because I say I am," said the Marquis. He looked, he was sure, like a drowned thing, and sounded, he was certain, unconvincing. He felt small and foolish.

"Your choice. Anyway, I'm off. You don't need me anymore. Stay out of trouble. You don't actually have to thank me." His brother meant it, of course. That was what stung the hardest.

The Marquis de Carabas hated himself. He hadn't wanted to say it, but now it had to be said. "Thank you, Peregrine."

"Oh!" said Peregrine. "Your coat. Word on the street is, it wound up in Shepherd's Bush. That's all I know. So. Advice. Mean this most sincerely. I know you don't like advice. But, the coat? Let it go. Forget about it. Just get a new coat. Honest."

"Well then," said the Marquis.

"Well," said Peregrine, and he grinned, and shook himself like a dog, spraying water everywhere, before he slipped into the shadows and was gone.

The Marquis de Carabas stood and dripped balefully.

He had a little time before the Elephant discovered the lack of water in the room, and the lack of a body, and came looking for him.

He checked his shirt pocket: the sandwich bag was there, and the envelope appeared safe and dry inside it.

He wondered, for a moment, about something that had bothered him since the Market. Why would the Mushroom lad use him, de Carabas, to send a letter to the fair Drusilla? And what kind of letter could persuade a member of the Raven's Court, and one with a star on her hand at that, to give up her life at the court, and love one of the Mushroom folk?

A suspicion occurred to him. It was not a comfortable idea, nor a charitable one, but it was swept aside by more immediate problems.

He could hide: lie low, for a while. All this would pass. But there was the coat to think about. He had been rescued—rescued!—by his brother, something that would never have happened under normal circumstances. He could get a new coat. Of course he could. But it would not be his coat.

A shepherd had his coat.

The Marquis de Carabas always had a plan, and he always had a fallback plan; and beneath these plans he always had a real plan, one that he would not even let himself know about, for when the original plan and the fallback plan had both gone south.

Now, it pained him to admit to himself, he had no plan. He did not even have a normal, boring, obvious plan that he could abandon as soon as things got tricky. He just had a want, and it drove him as their need for food or love or safety drove those the Marquis considered lesser men.

He was planless. He just wanted his coat back.

The Marquis de Carabas began walking. He had an envelope containing a love poem in his pocket, he was wrapped in a damp blanket, and he hated his brother for rescuing him.

When you create yourself from scratch you need a model of some kind, something to aim towards or head away from—all the things you want to be, or intentionally want not to be.

The Marquis had known whom he had wanted not to be, when he was a boy. He had definitely not wanted to be like Peregrine. He had not wanted to be like anyone at all. He had, instead, wanted to be elegant, elusive, brilliant, and, above all things, he had wanted to be unique.

Just like Peregrine.

THE THING WAS, he had been told, by a former shepherd, on the run, whom he had helped across the Tyburn River, to freedom, and to a short but happy life as a camp entertainer for the Roman Legion who waited there, beside the river, for orders that would never come, that the shepherds never made you do anything. They just took your natural impulses and desires and they pushed them, reinforced them, so you acted quite naturally, only you acted in the ways that they wanted.

He remembered that, and then he forgot it, because he was scared of being alone.

The Marquis had not known until just this moment quite how scared he was of being alone, and was surprised by how happy he was to see several other people walking in the same direction as he was.

"I'm glad you're here," one of them called.

"I'm glad you're here," called another.

"I'm glad I'm here too," said de Carabas. Where was he going? Where were they going? So good that they were all traveling the same way together. There was safety in numbers.

"It's good to be together," said a thin white woman, with a happy sort of a sigh. And it was.

"It's good to be together," said the Marquis.

"Indeed it is. It's good to be together," said his neighbor on the other side. There was something familiar about this person. He had huge ears, like fans, and a nose like a thick, gray-green snake. The Marquis began to wonder if he had ever met this person before, and was trying to remember exactly where, when he was tapped gently on the shoulder by a man holding a large stick with a curved end.

"We never want to fall out of step, do we?" said the man, reasonably, and the Marquis thought, *Of course we don't,* and he sped up a little, so he was back in step once more.

"That's good. Out of step is out of mind," said the man with the stick, and he moved on.

"Out of step is out of mind," said the Marquis, aloud, wondering how he could have missed knowing something so obvious, so basic.

There was a tiny part of him, somewhere distant, that wondered what that actually meant.

They reached the place they were going, and it was good to be among friends.

Time passed strangely in that place, but soon enough the Marquis and his friend with the gray-green face and the long nose were given a job to do, a real job, and it was this: they disposed of those members of the flock who could no longer move or serve, once anything that might be of use had been removed and reused. They removed the last of what was left, hair and tallow fat and all, then they dragged them to the pit, and dropped the remnants in. The shifts were long and tiring, and the work was messy, but the two of them did it together and they stayed in step.

They had been working proudly together for several days when the Marquis noticed an irritant. Someone appeared to be trying to attract his attention. "I followed you," whispered the stranger. "I know you didn't want me to. But, well, needs must."

The Marquis did not know what the stranger was talking about.

"I've got an escape plan, as soon as I can wake you up," said the stranger. "Please wake up."

The Marquis was awake. Again, he found he did not know what the stranger was talking about. Why did the man think he was asleep? The Marquis would have said something, but he had to work. He pondered this, while dismembering the next former member of the flock, until he decided there was something he could say, to explain why the stranger was irritating him. He said it aloud. "It's good to work," said the Marquis.

His friend, with the long, flexible nose, and the huge ears, nodded his head at this.

They worked. After a while his friend hauled what was left of some former members of the flock over to the pit, and pushed them in. The pit went down a long way.

The Marquis tried to ignore the stranger, who was now standing behind him. He was quite put out when he felt something slapped over his mouth, and his hands being bound together behind his back. He was not certain what he was meant to do. It made him feel quite out of step with the flock, and he would have complained, would have called out to his friend, but his lips were now stuck together and he was unable to do more than make ineffectual noises.

"It's me," whispered the voice from behind him, urgently. "Peregrine. Your brother. You've been captured by the shepherds. We have to get you out of here." And then, "Uh-oh."

A noise in the air, like something barking. It came closer: a high yip-yipping that turned suddenly into a triumphant howl, and was answered by matching howls from around them.

A voice barked, "Where's your flockmate?"

A low, elephantine voice rumbled, "He went over there. With the other one."

"Other one?"

The Marquis hoped they would come and find him and sort this all out. There was obviously some sort of mistake going on. He wanted to be in step with the flock, and now he was out of step, an unwilling victim. He wanted to work.

"Lud's gate!" muttered Peregrine. And then they were surrounded by the shapes of people who were not exactly people: they were sharp of face, and dressed in furs. They spoke excitedly to each other.

The people untied the Marquis's hands, although they left the tape on his face. He did not mind. He had nothing to say.

The Marquis was relieved it was all over and looked forward to getting back to work, but, to his slight puzzlement, he, his kidnapper, and his friend with the huge long flexible nose were walked away from the pit, along a causeway, and, eventually, into a honeycomb of little rooms, each room filled with people toiling away in step.

Up some narrow stairs. One of their escorts, dressed in rough furs, scratched at a door. A voice called, "Enter!" and the Marquis felt a thrill that was almost sexual. That voice. That was the voice of someone the Marquis had spent his whole life wanting to please. (His whole life went back, what? A week? Two weeks?)

"A stray lamb," said one of the escorts. "And his predator. Also his flockmate."

The room was large, and hung with oil paintings: landscapes, mostly, stained with age and smoke and dust. "Why?" said the man, sitting at a desk in the back of the room. He did not turn around. "Why do you bother me with this nonsense?"

"Because," said a voice, and the Marquis recognized it as that of his would-be kidnapper, "you gave orders that if ever I were to be apprehended within the bounds of the Shepherd's Bush, I was to be brought to you to dispose of personally."

The man pushed his chair back and got up. He walked towards them, stepping into the light. There was a wooden crook propped against the wall, and he picked it up as he passed. For several long moments he looked at them.

"Peregrine?" he said, at last, and the Marquis thrilled at his voice. "I had heard that you had gone into retirement. Become a monk or something. I never dreamed you'd dare to come back."

(Something very big was filling the Marquis's head. Something was filling his heart and his mind. It was something enormous, something he could almost touch.)

The shepherd reached out a hand and ripped the tape from the Marquis's mouth. The Marquis knew he should have been overjoyed by this, should have been thrilled to get attention from this man.

"And now I see . . . who would have thought it?" The shepherd's voice was deep and resonant. "He is here already. And already one of ours? The Marquis de Carabas. You know, Peregrine, I had been looking forward to ripping out your tongue, to grinding your fingers away while you watched, but think how much more delightful it would be if the last thing you ever saw was your own brother, one of our flock, as the instrument of your doom."

(An enormous thing filled the Marquis's head.)

The shepherd was plump, well-fed, and was excellently dressed. He had sandy-gray-colored hair and a harassed expression. He wore a remarkable coat, even if it was somewhat tight on him. The coat was the color of a wet street at midnight.

The enormous thing filling his head, the Marquis realized, was rage. It was rage, and it burned through the Marquis like a forest fire, devouring everything in its path with a red flame.

The coat. It was elegant. It was beautiful. It was so close that he could have reached out and touched it.

And it was unquestionably *his*.

The Marquis de Carabas did nothing to indicate that he had woken up. That would have been a mistake. He thought, and he thought fast, and what he thought had nothing to do with the room he was in. The Marquis had only one advantage over the shepherd and his dogs: he knew he was awake and in control of his thoughts, and they did not.

He hypothesized. He tested his hypothesis in his head. And then, he acted. "Excuse me," he said, blandly. "But I'm afraid I do need to be getting along. Can we hurry this up? I'm late for something that's frightfully important."

The shepherd leaned on his crook. He did not appear to be concerned by this. He said only, "You've left the flock, de Carabas."

"It would appear so," said the Marquis. "Hello, Peregrine. Wonderful to see you looking so sprightly. And the Elephant. How delightful. The gang's all here." He turned his attention back to the shepherd. "Wonderful meeting you, delightful to spend a modicum of time as one of your little band of serious thinkers. But I really must be tootling off now. Important diplomatic mission. Letter to deliver. You know how it is."

Peregrine said, "My brother, I'm not sure that you understand the gravity of the situation here . . ."

The Marquis, who understood the gravity of the situation perfectly, said, "I'm sure these nice people"—he gestured to the shepherd and to the three fur-clad, sharp-faced sheepdog people who were standing about them—"will let me head out of here, leaving you behind. It's you they want, not me. And I have something extremely important to deliver."

Peregrine said, "I can handle this."

"You have to be quiet now," said the shepherd. He took the strip of tape he had removed from the Marquis's mouth and pressed it down over Peregrine's.

The shepherd was shorter than the Marquis, and fatter, and the magnificent coat looked faintly ridiculous on him. "Something important to deliver?" asked the shepherd, brushing dust from his fingers. "What exactly are we talking about here?"

"I am afraid I cannot possibly tell you that," said the Marquis. "You are, after all, not the intended recipient of this particular diplomatic communiqué."

"Why not? What's it say? Who's it for?"

The Marquis shrugged. His coat was so close that he could have reached out and stroked it. "Only the threat of death could force me even to show it to you," he said reluctantly.

"Well, that's easy. I threaten you with death. That's in addition to the death sentence you're already under as an apostate member of the flock. And as for laughing boy here"—the shepherd gestured with his crook towards Peregrine, who was not laughing—"he's tried to steal a member of the flock. That's a death sentence too, in addition to everything else we're planning to do to him."

The shepherd looked at the Elephant. "And, I know I should have asked before, but what in the Auld Witch's name is *this*?"

"I am a loyal member of the flock," said the Elephant, humbly, in his deep voice, and the Marquis wondered if he had himself sounded so soulless and flat when he had been part of the flock. "I have remained loyal and in step even when this one did not."

"And the flock is grateful for all your hard work," said the shepherd. He reached out a hand and touched the sharp tip of one Elephantine tusk, experimentally. "I've never seen anything like you before, and if I never see another one again it'll be too soon. Probably best if you die too."

The Elephant's ears twitched. "But I am of the flock . . ."

The shepherd looked up into the Elephant's huge face. "Better safe than sorry," he said. Then, to the Marquis: "Well? Where is this important letter?"

The Marquis de Carabas said, "It is inside my shirt. I must repeat that it is the most significant document that I have ever been charged to deliver. I must ask you not to look at it. For your own safety."

The shepherd tugged at the front of the Marquis's shirt. The buttons flew, and rattled off the walls onto the floor. The letter, in its sandwich bag, was in the pocket inside the shirt.

"This is most unfortunate. I trust you will read it aloud to us before we die," said the Marquis. "But whether or not you read it to us, I can promise that Peregrine and I will be holding our breath. Won't we, Peregrine?"

The shepherd opened the sandwich bag, then he looked at the envelope. He ripped it open and pulled a sheet of discolored paper from inside it. Dust came from the envelope as the paper came out. The dust hung in the still air in that dim room.

" 'My darling beautiful Drusilla,' " read the shepherd, aloud. " 'While I know that you do not presently feel about me as I feel about you . . . ' What is this nonsense?"

The Marquis said nothing. He did not even smile. He was, as he had stated, holding his breath; he was hoping that Peregrine had listened to him; and he was counting, because at that moment counting seemed like the best possible thing that he could do to distract himself from needing to breathe. He would soon need to breathe.

Thirty-five . . . thirty-six . . . thirty-seven . . .

He wondered how long mushroom spores remained in the air.

Forty-three . . . forty-four . . . forty-five . . . forty-six . . .

The shepherd had stopped speaking.

The Marquis took a step backward, fearing a knife in his ribs or teeth in his throat from the rough-furred guard-dog men, but there was nothing. He walked backward, away from the dog-men, and the Elephant.

He saw that Peregrine was also walking backward.

His lungs hurt. His heart was pounding in his temples, pounding almost loudly enough to drown out the thin ringing noise in his ears.

Only when the Marquis's back was against a bookcase on the wall and he was as far as he could possibly get from the envelope did he allow himself to take a deep breath. He heard Peregrine breathe in too.

There was a stretching noise. Peregrine opened his mouth wide, and the tape dropped to the ground. "What," asked Peregrine, "was all that about?"

"Our way out of this room, and our way out of Shepherd's Bush, if I am not mistaken," said de Carabas. "As I so rarely am. Would you mind unbinding my wrists?"

He felt Peregrine's hands on his bound hands, and then the bindings fell away. There was a low rumbling. "I'm going to kill somebody," said the Elephant. "As soon as I figure out who."

"Whoa, dear heart," said the Marquis, rubbing his hands together. "You mean *whom.*" The shepherd and the sheepdogs were taking awkward, experimental steps towards the door. "And I can assure you that you aren't going to kill anybody, not as long as you want to get home to the Castle safely."

The Elephant's trunk swished irritably. "I'm definitely going to kill *you.*"

The Marquis grinned. "You are going to force me to say *pshaw,*" he said. "Or *fiddlesticks.* Until this moment I have never had the slightest yearning to say *fiddlesticks.* But I can feel it right now welling up inside me—"

"What, by the Temple and the Arch, has got into you?" asked the Elephant.

"Wrong question. But I shall ask the right question on your behalf. The question is actually, what *hasn't* got into the three of us? It hasn't got into Peregrine and me because we were holding our breath. It hasn't got into you because, I don't know, probably because you're an elephant, with nice thick skin, more likely because you were breathing through your trunk, which is down at ground level—and what did get into our captors? And the answer is, what hasn't got into us are the selfsame spores that have got into our portly shepherd and his pseudocanine companions."

"Spores of the Mushroom?" asked Peregrine. "The Mushroom People's the Mushroom?"

"Indeed. That selfsame Mushroom," agreed the Marquis.

"Blimming heck," said the Elephant.

"Which is why," de Carabas told the Elephant, "if you attempt to kill me, or to kill Peregrine, you will not only fail but you will doom us all. Whereas if you shut up and we all do our best to look as if we are still part of the flock, then we have a chance. The spores will be threading their way into their brains now. And any moment now the Mushroom will begin calling them home."

A SHEPHERD WALKED, implacably. He held a wooden crook. Three men followed him. One of those men had the head of an elephant; one was tall and ridiculously handsome; and the last of the flock wore a most magnificent coat. It fit him perfectly, and it was the color of a wet street at night.

The flock were followed by guard dogs, who moved as if they were ready to walk through fire to get wherever they believed that they were going.

It was not unusual in Shepherd's Bush to see a shepherd and part of his flock moving from place to place, accompanied by several of the fiercest sheepdogs (who were human, or had been, once). So when they saw a shepherd and three sheepdogs apparently leading three members of the flock away from Shepherd's Bush, none of the greater flock paid them any mind. The members of the flock who saw them simply did the same things they had always done, as members of the flock, and if they were aware that the influence of the shepherds had waned a little, then they patiently waited for another shepherd to come and to take care of them and to keep them safe from predators and from the world. It was a scary thing to be alone, after all.

Nobody noticed as they crossed the bounds of Shepherd's Bush, and still they kept on walking.

The seven of them reached the banks of the Kilburn, where they stopped, and the former shepherd and the three shaggy dog-men strode out into the water.

There was, the Marquis knew, nothing in the four men's heads at that moment but a need to get to the Mushroom, to taste its flesh once more, to let it live inside them, to serve it, and to serve it well. In exchange, the Mushroom would fix all the things about themselves that they hated: it would make their interior lives much happier and more interesting.

"Should've let me kill 'em," said the Elephant as the former shepherd and sheepdogs waded away.

"No point," said the Marquis. "Not even for revenge. The people who captured us don't exist any longer."

The Elephant flapped his ears hard, then scratched them vigorously. "Talking about revenge, who the hell did you steal my diary for anyway?" he asked.

"Victoria," admitted de Carabas.

"Not actually on my list of potential thieves. She's a deep one," said the Elephant, after a moment.

"I'll not argue with that," said the Marquis. "Also, she failed to pay me the entire amount agreed. I wound up obtaining my own lagniappe to make up the deficit."

He reached a dark hand into the inside of his coat. His fingers found the obvious pockets, and the less obvious, and then, to his surprise, the least obvious of all. He reached inside it, and pulled out a magnifying glass on a chain. "It was Victoria's," he said. "I believe you can use it to see through solid things. Perhaps this could be considered a small payment against my debt to you . . . ?"

The Elephant took something out of its own pocket—the Marquis could not see what it was—and squinted at it through the magnifying glass. Then the Elephant made a noise halfway between a delighted snort and a trumpet of satisfaction. "Oh fine, very fine," it said. It pocketed both of the objects. Then it said, "I suppose that saving my life outranks stealing my diary. And while I wouldn't have needed saving if I hadn't followed you down the drain, further recriminations are pointless. Consider your life your own once more."

"I look forward to visiting you in the Castle someday," said the Marquis.

"Don't push your luck, mate," said the Elephant, with an irritable swish of his trunk.

"I won't," said the Marquis, resisting the urge to point out that pushing his luck was the only way he had made it this far. He looked around and realized that Peregrine had slipped mysteriously and irritatingly away into the shadows, once more, without so much as a good-bye.

The Marquis hated it when people did that.

He made a small, courtly bow to the Elephant, and the Marquis's coat, his glorious coat, caught the bow, amplified it, made it perfect, and made it the kind of bow that only the Marquis de Carabas could ever possibly make. Whoever he was.

THE NEXT FLOATING Market was being held in Derry and Tom's Roof Garden. There had been no Derry and Tom's since 1973, but time and space and London Below had their own uncomfortable agreement, and the roof garden was younger and more innocent than it is today. The folk from London Above (they were young, and in an intense discussion, and they had stacked heels and paisley tops and bell-bottom flares, the men and the women) ignored the folk from London Below entirely.

The Marquis de Carabas strode through the roof garden as if he owned the place, walking swiftly until he reached the food court. He passed a tiny woman selling curling cheese sandwiches from a wheelbarrow piled high with the things, a curry stall, a short man with a huge glass bowl of pale white blind fish and a toasting fork, until, finally, he reached the stall that was selling the Mushroom.

"Slice of the Mushroom, well grilled, please," said the Marquis de Carabas.

The man who took his order was shorter than he was, and still somewhat stouter. He had sandy, receding hair and a harried expression.

"Coming right up," said the man. "Anything else?"

"No, that's all." And then, curiously, the Marquis asked, "Do you remember me?"

"I am afraid not," said the Mushroom man. "But I must say, that is a most beautiful coat."

"Thank you," said the Marquis de Carabas. He looked around. "Where is the young fellow who used to work here?"

"Ah. That is a most curious story, sir," said the man. He did not yet smell of damp, although there was a small encrustation of mushrooms on the side of his neck. "I am informed that somebody told the fair Drusilla, of the Court of the Raven, that our Vince had designs upon her, and had—you may not credit it, but I am assured that it is so—apparently sent her a letter filled with spores with the intention of making her his bride in the Mushroom."

The Marquis raised an eyebrow quizzically, although he found none of this surprising. He had, after all, told Drusilla himself, and had even shown her the original letter. "Did she take well to the news?"

"I do not believe that she did, sir. I do not believe that she did. She and several of her sisters were waiting for Vince, and they all caught up with us on our way to the Market. She told him they had matters to discuss, of an intimate nature. He seemed delighted by this news, and went off with her, to find out what these matters were. I have been waiting for him to arrive at the Market and come and work all evening, but I no longer believe he will be coming." Then the man said, a little wistfully, "That is a very fine coat. It seems to me that I might have had one like it, in a former life."

"I do not doubt it," said the Marquis de Carabas, satisfied with what he had heard, cutting into his grilled slice of the Mushroom, "but this particular coat is most definitely mine."

As he made his way out of the Market, he passed a clump of people descending the stairs and he paused and nodded at a young woman of uncommon grace. She had the long orange hair and the flattened profile of a Pre-Raphaelite beauty, and there was a birthmark in the shape of a five-pointed star on the back of one hand. Her other hand was stroking the head of a large, rumpled owl, which glared uncomfortably out at the world with eyes that were, unusually for such a bird, of an intense, pale blue.

The Marquis nodded at her, and she glanced awkwardly at him, then she looked away in the manner of someone who had just begun to realize that she owed the Marquis a favor.

He nodded at her, amiably, and continued to descend.

Drusilla hurried after him. She looked as if she had something she wanted to say. The Marquis de Carabas reached the foot of the stairs ahead of her. He stopped for a moment, and he thought about people, and about things, and about how hard it is to do anything for the first time. And then, clad in his fine coat, he slipped mysteriously, even irritatingly, into the shadows, without so much as a good-bye, and he was gone.

BLACK DOG

2015

There were ten tongues within one head
And one went out to fetch some bread,
To feed the living and the dead.

—OLD RIDDLE

I. THE BAR GUEST

OUTSIDE THE PUB IT was raining cats and dogs.

Shadow was still not entirely convinced that he was in a pub. True, there was a tiny bar at the back of the room, with bottles behind it and a couple of the huge taps you pulled, and there were several high tables and people were drinking at the tables, but it all felt like a room in somebody's house. The dogs helped reinforce that impression. It seemed to Shadow that everybody in the pub had a dog except for him.

"What kind of dogs are they?" Shadow asked, curious. The dogs reminded him of greyhounds, but they were smaller and seemed saner, more placid and less high-strung than the greyhounds he had encountered over the years.

"Lurchers," said the pub's landlord, coming out from behind the bar. He was carrying a pint of beer that he had poured for himself. "Best dogs. Poacher's dogs. Fast, smart, lethal." He bent down, scratched a chestnut-and-white brindled dog behind the ears. The dog stretched and luxuriated in the ear-scratching. It did not look particularly lethal, and Shadow said so.

The landlord, his hair a mop of gray and orange, scratched at his beard reflectively. "That's where you'd be wrong," he said. "I walked with his brother last week, down Cumpsy Lane. There's a fox, a big red reynard, pokes his head out of a hedge, no more than twenty meters down the road, then, plain as day, saunters out onto the track. Well, Needles sees it, and he's off after it like the clappers. Next thing you know, Needles has his teeth in reynard's neck, and one bite, one hard shake, and it's all over."

Shadow inspected Needles, a gray dog sleeping by the little fireplace. He looked harmless too. "So what sort of a breed is a lurcher? It's an English breed, yes?"

"It's not actually a breed," said a white-haired woman without a dog who had been leaning on a nearby table. "They're crossbred for speed, stamina. Sighthound, greyhound, collie."

The man next to her held up a finger. "You must understand," he said, cheerfully, "that there used to be laws about who could own purebred dogs. The local folk couldn't, but they could own mongrels. And lurchers are better and faster than pedigree dogs." He pushed his spectacles up his nose with the tip of his forefinger. He had a muttonchop beard, brown flecked with white.

"Ask me, all mongrels are better than pedigree anything," said the woman. "It's why America is such an interesting country. Filled with mongrels." Shadow was not certain how old she was. Her hair was white, but she seemed younger than her hair.

"Actually, darling," said the man with the muttonchops, in his gentle voice, "I think you'll find that the Americans are keener on pedigree dogs than the British. I met a woman from the American Kennel Club, and honestly, she scared me. I was scared."

"I wasn't talking about dogs, Ollie," said the woman. "I was talking about . . . Oh, never mind."

"What are you drinking?" asked the landlord.

There was a handwritten piece of paper taped to the wall by the bar telling customers not to order a lager "as a punch in the face often offends."

"What's good and local?" asked Shadow, who had learned that this was mostly the wisest thing to say.

The landlord and the woman had various suggestions as to which of the various local beers and ciders were good. The little mutton-chopped man interrupted them to point out that in his opinion *good* was not the avoidance of evil, but something more positive than that: it was making the world a better place. Then he chuckled, to show that he was only joking and that he knew that the conversation was really only about what to drink.

The beer the landlord poured for Shadow was dark and very bitter. He was not certain that he liked it. "What is it?"

"It's called Black Dog," said the woman. "I've heard people say it was named after the way you feel after you've had one too many."

"Like Churchill's moods," said the little man.

"Actually, the beer is named after a local dog," said a younger woman. She was wearing an olive-green sweater, and standing against the wall. "But not a real one. Semi-imaginary."

Shadow looked down at Needles, then hesitated. "Is it safe to scratch his head?" he asked, remembering the fate of the fox.

"Course it is," said the white-haired woman. "He loves it. Don't you?"

"Well. He practically had that tosser from Glossop's finger off," said the landlord. There was admiration mixed with warning in his voice.

"I think he was something in local government," said the woman. "And I've always thought that there's nothing wrong with dogs biting *them*. Or VAT inspectors."

The woman in the green sweater moved over to Shadow. She was not holding a drink. She had dark, short hair, and a crop of freckles that spattered her nose and cheeks. She looked at Shadow. "You aren't in local government, are you?"

Shadow shook his head. He said, "I'm kind of a tourist." It was not actually untrue. He was traveling, anyway.

"You're Canadian?" said the muttonchop man.

"American," said Shadow. "But I've been on the road for a while now."

"Then," said the white-haired woman, "you aren't actually a tourist. Tourists turn up, see the sights and leave."

Shadow shrugged, smiled, and leaned down. He scratched the landlord's lurcher on the back of its head.

"You're not a dog person, are you?" asked the dark-haired woman.
"I'm not a dog person," said Shadow.

Had he been someone else, someone who talked about what was happening inside his head, Shadow might have told her that his wife had owned dogs when she was younger, and sometimes called Shadow *puppy* because she wanted a dog she could not have. But Shadow kept things on the inside. It was one of the things he liked about the British: even when they wanted to know what was happening on the inside, they did not ask. The world on the inside remained the world on the inside. His wife had been dead for three years now.

"If you ask me," said the man with the muttonchops, "people are either dog people or cat people. So would you then consider yourself a cat person?"

Shadow reflected. "I don't know. We never had pets when I was a kid, we were always on the move. But—"

"I mention this," the man continued, "because our host also has a cat, which you might wish to see."

"Used to be out here, but we moved it to the back room," said the landlord, from behind the bar.

Shadow wondered how the man could follow the conversation so easily while also taking people's meal orders and serving their drinks. "Did the cat upset the dogs?" he asked.

Outside, the rain redoubled. The wind moaned, and whistled, and then howled. The log fire burning in the little fireplace coughed and spat.

"Not in the way you're thinking," said the landlord. "We found it when we knocked through into the room next door, when we needed to extend the bar." The man grinned. "Come and look."

Shadow followed the man into the room next door. The mutton-chop man and the white-haired woman came with them, walking a little behind Shadow.

Shadow glanced back into the bar. The dark-haired woman was watching him, and she smiled warmly when he caught her eye.

The room next door was better lit, larger, and it felt a little less like somebody's front room. People were sitting at tables, eating. The food looked good and smelled better. The landlord led Shadow to the back of the room, to a dusty glass case.

"There she is," said the landlord, proudly.

The cat was brown, and it looked, at first glance, as if it had been constructed out of tendons and agony. The holes that were its eyes were filled with anger and with pain; the mouth was wide open, as if the creature had been yowling when she was turned to leather.

"The practice of placing animals in the walls of buildings is similar to the practice of walling up children alive in the foundations of a house you want to stay up," explained the muttonchop man, from behind him. "Although mummified cats always make me think of the mummified cats they found around the temple of Bast in Bubastis in Egypt. So many tons of mummified cats that they sent them to England to be ground up as cheap fertilizer and dumped on the fields. The Victorians also made paint out of mummies. A sort of brown, I believe."

"It looks miserable," said Shadow. "How old is it?"

The landlord scratched his cheek. "We reckon that the wall she was in went up somewhere between 1300 and 1600. That's from parish records. There's nothing here in 1300, and there's a house in 1600. The stuff in the middle was lost."

The dead cat in the glass case, furless and leathery, seemed to be watching them, from its empty black-hole eyes.

I got eyes wherever my folk walk, breathed a voice in the back of Shadow's mind. He thought, momentarily, about the fields fertilized with the ground mummies of cats, and what strange crops they must have grown.

"*They put him into an old house side,*" said the man called Ollie. "*And there he lived and there he died. And nobody either laughed or cried.*

All sorts of things were walled up, to make sure that things were guarded and safe. Children, sometimes. Animals. They did it in churches as a matter of course."

The rain beat an arrhythmic rattle on the windowpane. Shadow thanked the landlord for showing him the cat. They went back into the taproom. The dark-haired woman had gone, which gave Shadow a moment of regret. She had looked so friendly. Shadow bought a round of drinks for the muttonchop man, the white-haired woman, and one for the landlord.

The landlord ducked behind the bar. "They call me Shadow," Shadow told them. "Shadow Moon."

The muttonchop man pressed his hands together in delight. "Oh! How wonderful. I had an Alsatian named Shadow, when I was a boy. Is it your real name?"

"It's what they call me," said Shadow.

"I'm Moira Callanish," said the white-haired woman. "This is my partner, Oliver Bierce. He knows a lot, and he will, during the course of our acquaintance, undoubtedly tell you everything he knows."

They shook hands. When the landlord returned with their drinks, Shadow asked if the pub had a room to rent. He had intended to walk further that night, but the rain sounded like it had no intention of giving up. He had stout walking shoes, and weather-resistant outer clothes, but he did not want to walk in the rain.

"I used to, but then my son moved back in. I'll encourage people to sleep it off in the barn, on occasion, but that's as far as I'll go these days."

"Anywhere in the village I could get a room?"

The landlord shook his head. "It's a foul night. But Porsett is only a few miles down the road, and they've got a proper hotel there. I can call Sandra, tell her that you're coming. What's your name?"

"Shadow," said Shadow again. "Shadow Moon."

Moira looked at Oliver, and said something that sounded like "waifs and strays?" and Oliver chewed his lip for a moment, and then he nodded enthusiastically. "Would you fancy spending the night with us? The spare room's a bit of a box room, but it does have a bed in it. And it's warm there. And it's dry."

"I'd like that very much," said Shadow. "I can pay."

"Don't be silly," said Moira. "It will be nice to have a guest."

II. THE GIBBET

OLIVER AND MOIRA BOTH had umbrellas. Oliver insisted that Shadow carry his umbrella, pointing out that Shadow towered over him, and thus was ideally suited to keep the rain off both of them.

The couple also carried little flashlights, which they called torches. The word put Shadow in mind of villagers in a horror movie storming the castle on the hill, and the lightning and thunder added to the vision. *Tonight, my creature,* he thought, *I will give you life!* It should have been hokey but instead it was disturbing. The dead cat had put him into a strange set of mind.

The narrow roads between fields were running with rainwater. "On a nice night," said Moira, raising her voice to be heard over the rain, "we would just walk over the fields. But they'll be all soggy and boggy, so we're going down by Shuck's Lane. Now, that tree was a gibbet tree, once upon a time." She pointed to a massive-trunked sycamore at the crossroads. It had only a few branches left, sticking up into the night like afterthoughts.

"Moira's lived here since she was in her twenties," said Oliver. "I came up from London, about eight years ago. From Turnham Green. I'd come up here on holiday originally when I was fourteen and I never forgot it. You don't."

"The land gets into your blood," said Moira. "Sort of."

"And the blood gets into the land," said Oliver. "One way or another. You take that gibbet tree, for example. They would leave people in the gibbet until there was nothing left. Hair gone to make bird's nests, flesh all eaten by ravens, bones picked clean. Or until they had another corpse to display anyway."

Shadow was fairly sure he knew what a gibbet was, but he asked anyway. There was never any harm in asking, and Oliver was definitely the kind of person who took pleasure in knowing peculiar things and in passing his knowledge on.

"Like a huge iron birdcage. They used them to display the bodies of executed criminals, after justice had been served. The gibbets were locked, so the family and friends couldn't steal the body back and give it a good Christian burial. Keeping passersby on the straight and the narrow, although I doubt it actually deterred anyone from anything."

"Who were they executing?"

"Anyone who got unlucky. Three hundred years ago, there were over two hundred crimes punishable by death. Including traveling with Gypsies for more than a month, stealing sheep—and, for that matter, anything over twelve pence in value—and writing a threatening letter."

He might have been about to begin a lengthy list, but Moira broke in. "Oliver's right about the death sentence, but they only gibbeted murderers, up these parts. And they'd leave corpses in the gibbet for twenty years, sometimes. We didn't get a lot of murders." And then, as if trying to change the subject to something lighter, she said, "We are now walking down Shuck's Lane. The locals say that on a clear night, which tonight certainly is not, you can find yourself being followed by Black Shuck. He's a sort of a fairy dog."

"We've never seen him, not even on clear nights," said Oliver.

"Which is a very good thing," said Moira. "Because if you see him—you die."

"Except Sandra Wilberforce said she saw him, and she's healthy as a horse."

Shadow smiled. "What does Black Shuck do?"

"He doesn't do anything," said Oliver.

"He does. He follows you home," corrected Moira. "And then, a bit later, you die."

"Doesn't sound very scary," said Shadow. "Except for the dying bit."

They reached the bottom of the road. Rainwater was running like a stream over Shadow's thick hiking boots.

Shadow said, "So how did you two meet?" It was normally a safe question, when you were with couples.

Oliver said, "In the pub. I was up here on holiday, really."

Moira said, "I was with someone when I met Oliver. We had a very brief, torrid affair, then we ran off together. Most unlike both of us."

They did not seem like the kind of people who ran off together, thought Shadow. But then, all people were strange. He knew he should say something.

"I was married. My wife was killed in a car crash."

"I'm so sorry," said Moira.

"It happened," said Shadow.

"When we get home," said Moira, "I'm making us all whisky macs. That's whisky and ginger wine and hot water. And I'm having a hot bath. Otherwise I'll catch my death."

Shadow imagined reaching out his hand and catching death in it, like a baseball, and he shivered.

The rain redoubled, and a sudden flash of lightning burned the world into existence all around them: every gray rock in the drystone wall, every blade of grass, every puddle and every tree was perfectly illuminated, and then swallowed by a deeper darkness, leaving afterimages on Shadow's night-blinded eyes.

"Did you see that?" asked Oliver. "Damnedest thing." The thunder rolled and rumbled, and Shadow waited until it was done before he tried to speak.

"I didn't see anything," said Shadow. Another flash, less bright, and Shadow thought he saw something moving away from them in a distant field. "That?" he asked.

"It's a donkey," said Moira. "Only a donkey."

Oliver stopped. He said, "This was the wrong way to come home. We should have got a taxi. This was a mistake."

"Ollie," said Moira. "It's not far now. And it's just a spot of rain. You aren't made of sugar, darling."

Another flash of lightning, so bright as to be almost blinding. There was nothing to be seen in the fields.

Darkness. Shadow turned back to Oliver, but the little man was no longer standing beside him. Oliver's flashlight was on the ground. Shadow blinked his eyes, hoping to force his night vision to return. The man had collapsed, crumpled onto the wet grass on the side of the lane.

"Ollie?" Moira crouched beside him, her umbrella by her side. She shone her flashlight onto his face. Then she looked at Shadow. "He can't just sit here," she said, sounding confused and concerned. "It's pouring."

Shadow pocketed Oliver's flashlight, handed his umbrella to Moira, then picked Oliver up. The man did not seem to weigh much, and Shadow was a big man.

"Is it far?"

"Not far," she said. "Not really. We're almost home."

They walked in silence, across a churchyard on the edge of a village green, and into a village. Shadow could see lights on in the gray stone houses that edged the one street. Moira turned off, into a house set back from the road, and Shadow followed her. She held the back door open for him.

The kitchen was large and warm, and there was a sofa, half-covered with magazines, against one wall. There were low beams in the kitchen, and Shadow needed to duck his head. Shadow removed Oliver's raincoat and dropped it. It puddled on the wooden floor. Then he put the man down on the sofa.

Moira filled the kettle.

"Do we call an ambulance?"

She shook her head.

"This is just something that happens? He falls down and passes out?"

Moira busied herself getting mugs from a shelf. "It's happened before. Just not for a long time. He's narcoleptic, and if something surprises or scares him he can just go down like that. He'll come round soon. He'll want tea. No whisky mac tonight, not for him. Sometimes he's a bit dazed and doesn't know where he is, sometimes he's been following everything that happened while he was out. And he hates it if you make a fuss. Put your backpack down by the Aga."

The kettle boiled. Moira poured the steaming water into a teapot. "He'll have a cup of real tea. I'll have chamomile, I think, or I won't sleep tonight. Calm my nerves. You?"

"I'll drink tea, sure," said Shadow. He had walked more than twenty miles that day, and sleep would be easy in the finding. He wondered at Moira. She appeared perfectly self-possessed in the face of her partner's incapacity, and he wondered how much of it was not wanting to show weakness in front of a stranger. He admired her, although he found it peculiar. The English were strange. But he understood hating "making a fuss." Yes.

Oliver stirred on the couch. Moira was at his side with a cup of tea, helped him into a sitting position. He sipped the tea, in a slightly dazed fashion.

"It followed me home," he said, conversationally.

"What followed you, Ollie, darling?" Her voice was steady, but there was concern in it.

"The dog," said the man on the sofa, and he took another sip of his tea. "The black dog."

III. THE CUTS

THESE WERE THE THINGS Shadow learned that night, sitting around the kitchen table with Moira and Oliver:

He learned that Oliver had not been happy or fulfilled in his London advertising agency job. He had moved up to the village and taken an extremely early medical retirement. Now, initially for recreation and increasingly for money, he repaired and rebuilt drystone walls. There was, he explained, an art and a skill to wall building, it was excellent exercise, and, when done correctly, a meditative practice.

"There used to be hundreds of drystone-wall people around here. Now there's barely a dozen who know what they're doing. You see walls repaired with concrete, or with breeze blocks. It's a dying art. I'd love to show you how I do it. Useful skill to have. Picking the rock, sometimes, you have to let the rock tell you where it goes. And then it's immovable. You couldn't knock it down with a tank. Remarkable."

He learned that Oliver had been very depressed several years earlier, shortly after Moira and he got together, but that for the last few years he had been doing very well. Or, he amended, relatively well.

He learned that Moira was independently wealthy, that her family trust fund had meant that she and her sisters had not needed to work, but that, in her late twenties, she had gone for teacher training. That she no longer taught, but that she was extremely active in local affairs, and had campaigned successfully to keep the local bus routes in service.

Shadow learned, from what Oliver didn't say, that Oliver was scared of something, very scared, and that when Oliver was asked what had frightened him so badly, and what he had meant by saying that the black dog had followed him home, his response was to stammer and to sway. He learned not to ask Oliver any more questions.

This is what Oliver and Moira had learned about Shadow sitting around that kitchen table:

Nothing much.

Shadow liked them. He was not a stupid man; he had trusted people in the past who had betrayed him, but he liked this couple, and he liked the way their home smelled—like bread-making and jam and walnut wood-polish—and he went to sleep that night in his box-room bedroom worrying about the little man with the muttonchop beard. What if the thing Shadow had glimpsed in the field had *not* been a donkey? What if it *had* been an enormous dog? What then?

The rain had stopped when Shadow woke. He made himself toast in the empty kitchen. Moira came in from the garden, letting a gust of chilly air in through the kitchen door. "Sleep well?" she asked.

"Yes. Very well." He had dreamed of being at the zoo. He had been surrounded by animals he could not see, which snuffled and snorted in their pens. He was a child, walking with his mother, and he was safe and he was loved. He had stopped in front of a lion's cage, but what had been in the cage was a sphinx, half lion and half woman, her tail swishing. She had smiled at him, and her smile had been his mother's smile. He heard her voice, accented and warm and feline.

It said, *Know thyself.*

I know who I am, said Shadow in his dream, holding the bars of the cage. Behind the bars was the desert. He could see pyramids. He could see shadows on the sand.

Then who are you, Shadow? What are you running from? Where are you running to?

Who are you?

And he had woken, wondering why he was asking himself that question, and missing his mother, who had died twenty years before, when he was a teenager. He still felt oddly comforted, remembering the feel of his hand in his mother's hand.

"I'm afraid Ollie's a bit under the weather this morning."

"Sorry to hear that."

"Yes. Well, can't be helped."

"I'm really grateful for the room. I guess I'll be on my way."

Moira said, "Will you look at something for me?"

Shadow nodded, then followed her outside, and round the side of the house. She pointed to the rose bed. "What does that look like to you?"

Shadow bent down. *"The footprint of an enormous hound,"* he said. "To quote Dr. Watson."

"Yes," she said. "It really does."

"If there's a spectral ghost-hound out there," said Shadow, "it shouldn't leave footprints. Should it?"

"I'm not actually an authority on these matters," said Moira. "I had a friend once who could have told us all about it. But she . . ." She trailed off. Then, more brightly, "You know, Mrs. Camberley two doors down has a Doberman pinscher. Ridiculous thing." Shadow was not certain whether the ridiculous thing was Mrs. Camberley or her dog.

He found the events of the previous night less troubling and odd, more explicable. What did it matter if a strange dog had followed them home? Oliver had been frightened or startled, and had collapsed, from narcolepsy, from shock.

"Well, I'll pack you some lunch before you go," said Moira. "Boiled eggs. That sort of thing. You'll be glad of them on the way."

They went into the house. Moira went to put something away, and returned looking shaken.

"Oliver's locked himself in the bathroom," she said.

Shadow was not certain what to say.

"You know what I wish?" she continued.

"I don't."

"I wish you would talk to him. I wish he would open the door. I wish he'd talk to me. I can hear him in there. I can hear him."

And then, "I hope he isn't cutting himself again."

Shadow walked back into the hall, stood by the bathroom door, called Oliver's name. "Can you hear me? Are you okay?"

Nothing. No sound from inside.

Shadow looked at the door. It was solid wood. The house was old, and they built them strong and well back then. When Shadow had used the bathroom that morning he'd learned the lock was a hook and eye. He leaned on the handle of the door, pushing it down, then rammed his shoulder against the door. It opened with a noise of splintering wood.

He had watched a man die in prison, stabbed in a pointless argument. He remembered the way that the blood had puddled about the man's body, lying in the back corner of the exercise yard. The sight had troubled Shadow, but he had forced himself to look, and to keep looking. To look away would somehow have felt disrespectful.

Oliver was naked on the floor of the bathroom. His body was pale, and his chest and groin were covered with thick, dark hair. He held the blade from an ancient safety razor in his hands. He had sliced his arms with it, his chest above the nipples, his inner thighs and his penis. Blood was smeared on his body, on the black and white linoleum floor, on the white enamel of the bathtub. Oliver's eyes were round and wide, like the eyes of a bird. He was looking directly at Shadow, but Shadow was not certain that he was being seen.

"Ollie?" said Moira's voice, from the hall. Shadow realized that he was blocking the doorway and he hesitated, unsure whether to let her see what was on the floor or not.

Shadow took a pink towel from the towel rail and wrapped it around Oliver. That got the little man's attention. He blinked, as if seeing Shadow for the first time, and said, "The dog. It's for the dog. It must be fed, you see. We're making friends."

Moira said, "Oh my dear sweet god."

"I'll call the emergency services."

"Please don't," she said. "He'll be fine at home with me. I don't know what I'll . . . please?"

Shadow picked up Oliver, swaddled in the towel, carried him into the bedroom as if he were a child, and then placed him on the bed. Moira followed. She picked up an iPad by the bed, touched the screen, and music began to play. "Breathe, Ollie," she said. "Remember. Breathe. It's going to be fine. You're going to be fine."

"I can't really breathe," said Oliver, in a small voice. "Not really. I can feel my heart, though. I can feel my heart beating."

Moira squeezed his hand and sat down on the bed, and Shadow left them alone.

When Moira entered the kitchen, her sleeves rolled up, and her hands smelling of antiseptic cream, Shadow was sitting on the sofa, reading a guide to local walks.

"How's he doing?"

She shrugged.

"You have to get him help."

"Yes." She stood in the middle of the kitchen and looked about her, as if unable to decide which way to turn. "Do you . . . I mean, do you have to leave today? Are you on a schedule?"

"Nobody's waiting for me. Anywhere."

She looked at him with a face that had grown haggard in an hour. "When this happened before, it took a few days, but then he was right as rain. The depression doesn't stay long. So, just wondering, would you just, well, stick around? I phoned my sister but she's in the middle of moving. And I can't cope on my own. I really can't. Not again. But I can't ask you to stay, not if anyone is waiting for you."

"Nobody's waiting," repeated Shadow. "And I'll stick around. But I think Oliver needs specialist help."

"Yes," agreed Moira. "He does."

Dr. Scathelocke came over late that afternoon. He was a friend of Oliver and Moira's. Shadow was not entirely certain whether rural British doctors still made house calls, or whether this was a socially justified visit. The doctor went into the bedroom, and came out twenty minutes later.

He sat at the kitchen table with Moira, and he said, "It's all very shallow. Cry-for-help stuff. Honestly, there's not a lot we can do for him in hospital that you can't do for him here, what with the cuts. We used to have a dozen nurses in that wing. Now they are trying to close it down completely. Get it all back to the community."

Dr. Scathelocke had sandy hair, was as tall as Shadow but lankier. He reminded Shadow of the landlord in the pub, and he wondered idly if the two men were related. The doctor scribbled several prescriptions, and Moira handed them to Shadow, along with the keys to an old white Range Rover.

Shadow drove to the next village, found the little chemists' and waited for the prescriptions to be filled. He stood awkwardly in the overlit aisle, staring at a display of suntan lotions and creams, sadly redundant in this cold wet summer.

"You're Mr. American," said a woman's voice from behind him. He turned. She had short dark hair and was wearing the same olive-green sweater she had been wearing in the pub.

"I guess I am," he said.

"Local gossip says that you are helping out while Ollie's under the weather."

"That was fast."

"Local gossip travels faster than light. I'm Cassie Burglass."

"Shadow Moon."

"Good name," she said. "Gives me chills." She smiled. "If you're still rambling while you're here, I suggest you check out the hill just past the village. Follow the track up until it forks, and then go left. It takes you up Wod's Hill. Spectacular views. Public right of way. Just keep going left and up, you can't miss it."

She smiled at him. Perhaps she was just being friendly to a stranger.

"I'm not surprised you're still here though," Cassie continued. "It's hard to leave this place once it gets its claws into you." She smiled again, a warm smile, and she looked directly into his eyes, as if trying to make up her mind. "I think Mrs. Patel has your prescriptions ready. Nice talking to you, Mr. American."

IV. THE KISS

SHADOW HELPED MOIRA. HE walked down to the village shop and bought the items on her shopping list while she stayed in the house, writing at the kitchen table or hovering in the hallway outside the bedroom door. Moira barely talked. He ran errands in the white Range Rover, and saw Oliver mostly in the hall, shuffling to the bathroom and back. The man did not speak to him.

Everything was quiet in the house: Shadow imagined the black dog squatting on the roof, cutting out all sunlight, all emotion, all feeling and truth. Something had turned down the volume in that house, pushed all the colors into black and white. He wished he was some-where else, but could not run out on them. He sat on his bed, and stared out of the window at the rain puddling its way down the windowpane, and felt the seconds of his life counting off, never to come back.

It had been wet and cold, but on the third day the sun came out. The world did not warm up, but Shadow tried to pull himself out of the gray haze, and decided to see some of the local sights. He walked to the next village, through fields, up paths and along the side of a long drystone wall. There was a bridge over a narrow stream that was little more than a plank, and Shadow jumped the water in one easy bound. Up the hill: there were trees, oak and hawthorn, syc-amore and beech at the bottom of the hill, and then the trees be-came sparser. He followed the winding trail, sometimes obvious, sometimes not, until he reached a natural resting place, like a tiny meadow, high on the hill, and there he turned away from the hill and saw the valleys and the peaks arranged all about him in greens and grays like illustrations from a children's book.

He was not alone up there. A woman with short dark hair was sit-ting and sketching on the hill's side, perched comfortably on a gray boulder. There was a tree behind her, which acted as a windbreak. She wore a green sweater and blue jeans, and he recognized Cassie Burglass before he saw her face.

As he got close, she turned. "What do you think?" she asked, holding her sketchbook up for his inspection. It was an assured pen-cil drawing of the hillside.

"You're very good. Are you a professional artist?"

"I dabble," she said.

Shadow had spent enough time talking to the English to know that this meant either that she dabbled, or that her work was regu-larly hung in the National Gallery or the Tate Modern.

"You must be cold," he said. "You're only wearing a sweater."

"I'm cold," she said. "But, up here, I'm used to it. It doesn't really bother me. How's Ollie doing?"

"He's still under the weather," Shadow told her.

"Poor old sod," she said, looking from her paper to the hillside and back. "It's hard for me to feel properly sorry for him, though."

"Why's that? Did he bore you to death with interesting facts?"

She laughed, a small huff of air at the back of her throat. "You really ought to listen to more village gossip. When Ollie and Moira met, they were both with other people."

"I know that. They told me that." Shadow thought a moment. "So he was with you first?"

"No. *She* was. We'd been together since college." There was a pause. She shaded something, her pencil scraping the paper. "Are you going to try and kiss me?" she asked.

"I, uh. I, um," he said. Then, honestly, "It hadn't occurred to me."

"Well," she said, turning to smile at him, "it bloody well should. I mean, I asked you up here, and you came, up to Wod's Hill, just to see me." She went back to the paper and the drawing of the hill. "They say there's dark doings been done on this hill. Dirty dark doings. And I was thinking of doing something dirty myself. To Moira's lodger."

"Is this some kind of revenge plot?"

"It's not an anything plot. I just like you. And there's no one around here who wants me any longer. Not as a woman."

The last woman that Shadow had kissed had been in Scotland. He thought of her, and what she had become, in the end. "You *are* real, aren't you?" he asked. "I mean . . . you're a real person. I mean . . ."

She put the pad of paper down on the boulder and she stood up. "Kiss me and find out," she said.

He hesitated. She sighed, and she kissed him.

It was cold on that hillside, and Cassie's lips were cold. Her mouth was very soft. As her tongue touched his, Shadow pulled back.

"I don't actually know you," Shadow said.

She leaned away from him, looked up into his face. "You know," she said, "all I dream of these days is somebody who will look my way and see the real me. I had given up until you came along, Mr. American, with your funny name. But you looked at me, and I knew you saw me. And that's all that matters."

Shadow's hands held her, feeling the softness of her sweater. "How much longer are you going to be here? In the district?" she asked.

"A few more days. Until Oliver's feeling better."

"Pity. Can't you stay forever?"

"I'm sorry?"

"You have nothing to be sorry for, sweet man. You see that opening over there?"

He glanced over to the hillside, but could not see what she was pointing at. The hillside was a tangle of weeds and low trees and half-tumbled drystone walls. She pointed to her drawing, where she had drawn a dark shape, like an archway, in the middle of a clump of gorse bushes on the side of the hill. "There. Look." He stared, and this time he saw it immediately.

"What is it?" Shadow asked.

"The Gateway to Hell," she told him, impressively.

"Uh-huh."

She grinned. "That's what they call it round here. It was originally a Roman temple, I think, or something even older. But that's all that remains. You should check it out, if you like that sort of thing. Although it's a bit disappointing: just a little passageway going back into the hill. I keep expecting some archaeologists will come out this way, dig it up, catalog what they find, but they never do."

Shadow examined her drawing. "So what do you know about big black dogs?" he asked.

"The one in Shuck's Lane?" she said. He nodded. "They say the barghest used to wander all around here. But now it's just in Shuck's Lane. Dr. Scathelocke once told me it was folk memory. The Wish Hounds are all that are left of the wild hunt, which was based around the idea of Odin's hunting wolves, Freki and Geri. I think it's even older than that. Cave memory. Druids. The thing that prowls in the darkness beyond the fire circle, waiting to tear you apart if you edge too far out alone."

"Have you ever seen it, then?"

She shook her head. "No. I researched it, but never saw it. My semi-imaginary local beast. Have you?"

"I don't think so. Maybe."

"Perhaps you woke it up when you came here. You woke me up, after all."

She reached up, pulled his head down towards her and kissed him again. She took his left hand, so much bigger than hers, and placed it beneath her sweater.

"Cassie, my hands are cold," he warned her.

"Well, my everything is cold. There's nothing *but* cold up here. Just smile and look like you know what you're doing," she told him. She pushed Shadow's left hand higher, until it was cupping the lace of her bra, and he could feel, beneath the lace, the hardness of her nipple and the soft swell of her breast.

He began to surrender to the moment, his hesitation a mixture of awkwardness and uncertainty. He was not sure how he felt about this woman: she had history with his benefactors, after all. Shadow never liked feeling that he was being used; it had happened too many times before. But his left hand was touching her breast and his right hand was cradling the nape of her neck, and he was leaning down and now her mouth was on his, and she was clinging to him as tightly as if, he thought, she wanted to occupy the very same space that he was in. Her mouth tasted like mint and stone and grass and the chilly afternoon breeze. He closed his eyes, and let himself enjoy the kiss and the way their bodies moved together.

Cassie froze. Somewhere close to them, a cat mewed. Shadow opened his eyes.

"Jesus," he said.

They were surrounded by cats. White cats and tabbies, brown and ginger and black cats, long-haired and short. Well-fed cats with collars and disreputable ragged-eared cats that looked as if they had been living in barns and on the edges of the wild. They stared at Shadow and Cassie with green eyes and blue eyes and golden eyes, and they did not move. Only the occasional swish of a tail or the blinking of a pair of feline eyes told Shadow that they were alive.

"This is weird," said Shadow.

Cassie took a step back. He was no longer touching her now. "Are they with you?" she asked.

"I don't think they're with anyone. They're cats."

"I think they're jealous," said Cassie. "Look at them. They don't like me."

"That's . . ." Shadow was going to say "nonsense," but no, it was sense, of a kind. There had been a woman who was a goddess, a continent away and years in his past, who had cared about him, in her own way. He remembered the needle-sharpness of her nails and the catlike roughness of her tongue.

Cassie looked at Shadow dispassionately. "I don't know who you are, Mr. American," she told him. "Not really. I don't know why you can look at me and see the real me, or why I can talk to you when I find it so hard to talk to other people. But I can. And you know, you seem all normal and quiet on the surface, but you are so much weirder than I am. And I'm extremely fucking weird."

Shadow said, "Don't go."

"Tell Ollie and Moira you saw me," she said. "Tell them I'll be waiting where we last spoke, if they have anything they want to say to me." She picked up her sketchpad and pencils, and she walked off briskly, stepping carefully through the cats, who did not even glance at her, just kept their gazes fixed on Shadow, as she moved away through the swaying grasses and the blowing twigs.

Shadow wanted to call after her, but instead he crouched down and looked back at the cats. "What's going on?" he asked. "Bast? Are you doing this? You're a long way from home. And why would you still care who I kiss?"

The spell was broken when he spoke. The cats began to move, to look away, to stand, to wash themselves intently.

A tortoiseshell cat pushed her head against his hand, insistently, needing attention. Shadow stroked her absently, rubbing his knuckles against her forehead.

She swiped blinding-fast with claws like tiny scimitars, and drew blood from his forearm. Then she purred, and turned, and within moments the whole kit and caboodle of them had vanished into the

hillside, slipping behind rocks and into the undergrowth, and were
gone.

V. THE LIVING AND THE DEAD

OLIVER WAS OUT OF his room when Shadow got back to the house,
sitting in the warm kitchen, a mug of tea by his side, reading a book
on Roman architecture. He was dressed, and he had shaved his chin
and trimmed his beard. He was wearing pajamas, with a plaid bathrobe over them.

"I'm feeling a bit better," he said, when he saw Shadow. Then,
"Have you ever had this? Been depressed?"

"Looking back on it, I guess I did. When my wife died," said Shadow.
"Everything went flat. Nothing meant anything for a long time."

Oliver nodded. "It's hard. Sometimes I think the black dog is a real
thing. I lie in bed thinking about the painting of Fuseli's nightmare
on a sleeper's chest. Like Anubis. Or do I mean Set? Big black thing.
What was Set anyway? Some kind of donkey?"

"I never ran into Set," said Shadow. "He was before my time."

Oliver laughed. "Very dry. And they say you Americans don't do
irony." He paused. "Anyway. All done now. Back on my feet. Ready
to face the world." He sipped his tea. "Feeling a bit embarrassed. All
that Hound of the Baskervilles nonsense behind me now."

"You really have nothing to be embarrassed about," said Shadow,
reflecting that the English found embarrassment wherever they
looked for it.

"Well. All a bit silly, one way or another. And I really am feeling
much perkier."

Shadow nodded. "If you're feeling better, I guess I should start
heading south."

"No hurry," said Oliver. "It's always nice to have company. Moira
and I don't really get out as much as we'd like. It's mostly just a walk
up to the pub. Not much excitement here, I'm afraid."

Moira came in from the garden. "Anyone seen the secateurs? I
know I had them. Forget my own head next."

Shadow shook his head, uncertain what secateurs were. He thought of telling the couple about the cats on the hill, and how they had behaved, but could not think of a way to describe it that would explain how odd it was. So, instead, without thinking, he said, "I ran into Cassie Burglass on Wod's Hill. She pointed out the Gateway to Hell."

They were staring at him. The kitchen had become awkwardly quiet. He said, "She was drawing it."

Oliver looked at him and said, "I don't understand."

"I've run into her a couple of times since I got here," said Shadow.

"What?" Moira's face was flushed. "What are you saying?" And then, "Who the, who the *fuck* are you to come in here and say things like that?"

"I'm, I'm nobody," said Shadow. "She just started talking to me. She said that you and she used to be together."

Moira looked as if she were going to hit him. Then she just said, "She moved away after we broke up. It wasn't a good breakup. She was very hurt. She behaved appallingly. Then she just up and left the village in the night. Never came back."

"I don't want to talk about that woman," said Oliver, quietly. "Not now. Not ever."

"Look. She was in the pub with us," pointed out Shadow. "That first night. You guys didn't seem to have a problem with her then."

Moira just stared at him and did not respond, as if he had said something in a tongue she did not speak. Oliver rubbed his forehead with his hand. "I didn't see her," was all he said.

"Well, she said to say hi when I saw her today," said Shadow. "She said she'd be waiting, if either of you had anything you wanted to say to her."

"We have nothing to say to her. Nothing at all." Moira's eyes were wet, but she was not crying. "I can't believe that, that *fucking* woman has come back into our lives, after all she put us through." Moira swore like someone who was not very good at it.

Oliver put down his book. "I'm sorry," he said. "I don't feel very well." He walked out, back to the bedroom, and closed the door behind him.

Moira picked up Oliver's mug, almost automatically, and took it over to the sink, emptied it out and began to wash it.

"I hope you're pleased with yourself," she said, rubbing the mug with a white plastic scrubbing brush as if she were trying to scrub the picture of Beatrix Potter's cottage from the china. "He was coming back to himself again."

"I didn't know it would upset him like that," said Shadow. He felt guilty as he said it. He had known there was history between Cassie and his hosts. He could have said nothing, after all. Silence was always safer.

Moira dried the mug with a green and white tea towel. The white patches of the towel were comical sheep, the green were grass. She bit her lower lip, and the tears that had been brimming in her eyes now ran down her cheeks. Then, "Did she say anything about me?"

"Just that you two used to be an item."

Moira nodded, and wiped the tears from her young-old face with the comical tea towel. "She couldn't bear it when Ollie and I got together. After I moved out, she just hung up her paintbrushes and locked the flat and went to London." She blew her nose vigorously. "Still. Mustn't grumble. We make our own beds. And Ollie's a *good* man. There's just a black dog in his mind. My mother had depression. It's hard."

Shadow said, "I've made everything worse. I should go."

"Don't leave until tomorrow. I'm not throwing you out, dear. It's not your fault you ran into that woman, is it?" Her shoulders were slumped. "There they are. On top of the fridge." She picked up something that looked like a very small pair of garden shears. "Secateurs," she explained. "For the rosebushes, mostly."

"Are you going to talk to him?"

"No," she said. "Conversations with Ollie about Cassie never end well. And in this state, it could plunge him even further back into a bad place. I'll just let him get over it."

Shadow ate alone in the pub that night, while the cat in the glass case glowered at him. He saw no one he knew. He had a brief conversation with the landlord about how he was enjoying his time in the village. He walked back to Moira's house after the pub, past the old sycamore, the gibbet tree, down Shuck's Lane. He saw nothing moving in the fields in the moonlight: no dog, no donkey.

All the lights in the house were out. He went to his bedroom as quietly as he could, packed the last of his possessions into his backpack before he went to sleep. He would leave early, he knew.

He lay in bed, watching the moonlight in the box room. He remembered standing in the pub and Cassie Burglass standing beside him. He thought about his conversation with the landlord, and the conversation that first night, and the cat in the glass box, and, as he pondered, any desire to sleep evaporated. He was perfectly wide awake in the small bed.

Shadow could move quietly when he needed to. He slipped out of bed, pulled on his clothes and then, carrying his boots, he opened the window, reached over the sill and let himself tumble silently into the soil of the flower bed beneath. He got to his feet and put on the boots, lacing them up in the half dark. The moon was several days from full, bright enough to cast shadows.

Shadow stepped into a patch of darkness beside a wall, and he waited there.

He wondered how sane his actions were. It seemed very probable that he was wrong, that his memory had played tricks on him, or other people's had. It was all so very unlikely, but then, he had experienced the unlikely before, and if he was wrong he would be out, what? A few hours' sleep?

He watched a fox hurry across the lawn, watched a proud white cat stalk and kill a small rodent, and saw several other cats pad their way along the top of the garden wall. He watched a weasel slink from shadow to shadow in the flower bed. The constellations moved in slow procession across the sky.

The front door opened, and a figure came out. Shadow had half expected to see Moira, but it was Oliver, wearing his pajamas and, over them, a thick tartan dressing gown. He had Wellington boots on his feet, and he looked faintly ridiculous, like an invalid from a black and white movie, or someone in a play. There was no color in the moonlit world.

Oliver pulled the front door closed until it clicked, then he walked towards the street, but walking on the grass, instead of crunching down the gravel path. He did not glance back, or even look around. He set off up the lane, and Shadow waited until Oliver was almost out of sight before he began to follow. He knew where Oliver was going, had to be going.

Shadow did not question himself, not any longer. He knew where they were both headed, with the certainty of a person in a dream. He was not even surprised when, halfway up Wod's Hill, he found Oliver sitting on a tree stump, waiting for him. The sky was lightening, just a little, in the east.

"The Gateway to Hell," said the little man. "As far as I can tell, they've always called it that. Goes back years and years."

The two men walked up the winding path together. There was something gloriously comical about Oliver in his robe, in his striped pajamas and his oversized black rubber boots. Shadow's heart pumped in his chest.

"How did you bring her up here?" asked Shadow.

"Cassie? I didn't. It was her idea to meet up here on the hill. She loved coming up here to paint. You can see so far. And it's holy, this hill, and she always loved that. Not holy to Christians, of course. Quite the obverse. The old religion."

"Druids?" asked Shadow. He was uncertain what other old religions there were, in England.

"Could be. Definitely could be. But I think it predates the druids. Doesn't have much of a name. It's just what people in these parts practice, beneath whatever else they believe. Druids, Norse, Catholics, Protestants, doesn't matter. That's what people pay lip service to. The old religion is what gets the crops up and keeps your cock hard and makes sure that nobody builds a bloody great motorway through an area of outstanding natural beauty. The Gateway stands, and the hill stands, and the place stands. It's well, well over two thousand years old. You don't go mucking about with anything that powerful."

Shadow said, "Moira doesn't know, does she? She thinks Cassie moved away." The sky was continuing to lighten in the east, but it was still night, spangled with a glitter of stars, in the purple-black sky to the west.

"That was what she *needed* to think. I mean, what else was she going to think? It might have been different if the police had been interested . . . but it wasn't like . . . Well. It protects itself. The hill. The gate."

They were coming up to the little meadow on the side of the hill. They passed the boulder where Shadow had seen Cassie drawing. They walked toward the hill.

"The black dog in Shuck's Lane," said Oliver. "I don't actually think it is a dog. But it's been there so long." He pulled out a small LED flashlight from the pocket of his bathrobe. "You really talked to Cassie?"

"We talked, I even kissed her."

"Strange."

"I first saw her in the pub, the night I met you and Moira. That was what made me start to figure it out. Earlier tonight, Moira was talking as if she hadn't seen Cassie in years. She was baffled when I asked. But Cassie was standing just behind me that first night, and she spoke to us. Tonight, I asked at the pub if Cassie had been in, and nobody knew who I was talking about. You people all know each other. It was the only thing that made sense of it all. It made sense of what she said. Everything."

Oliver was almost at the place Cassie had called the Gateway to Hell. "I thought that it would be so simple. I would give her to the hill, and she would leave us both alone. Leave Moira alone. How could she have kissed you?"

Shadow said nothing.

"This is it," said Oliver. It was a hollow in the side of the hill, like a short hallway that went back. Perhaps, once, long ago, there had been a structure, but the hill had weathered, and the stones had returned to the hill from which they had been taken.

"There are those who think it's devil worship," said Oliver. "And I think they are wrong. But then, one man's god is another's devil. Eh?"

He walked into the passageway, and Shadow followed him.

"Such bullshit," said a woman's voice. "But you always were a bullshitter, Ollie, you pusillanimous little cock-stain."

Oliver did not move or react. He said, "She's here. In the wall.

That's where I left her." He shone the flashlight at the wall, in the short passageway into the side of the hill. He inspected the drystone wall carefully, as if he were looking for a place he recognized, then he made a little grunting noise of recognition. Oliver took out a compact metal tool from his pocket, reached as high as he could and levered out one little rock with it. Then he began to pull rocks out from the wall, in a set sequence, each rock opening a space to allow another to be removed, alternating large rocks and small.

"Give me a hand. Come on."

Shadow knew what he was going to see behind the wall, but he pulled out the rocks, placed them down on the ground, one by one.

There was a smell, which intensified as the hole grew bigger, a stink of old rot and mold. It smelled like meat sandwiches gone bad. Shadow saw her face first, and he barely knew it as a face: the cheeks were sunken, the eyes gone, the skin now dark and leathery, and if there were freckles they were impossible to make out; but the hair was Cassie Burglass's hair, short and black, and in the LED light, he could see that the dead thing wore an olive-green sweater, and the blue jeans were her blue jeans.

"It's funny. I knew she was still here," said Oliver. "But I still had to see her. With all your talk. I had to see it. To prove she was still here."

"Kill him," said the woman's voice. "Hit him with a rock, Shadow. He killed me. Now he's going to kill you."

"Are you going to kill me?" Shadow asked.

"Well, yes, obviously," said the little man, in his sensible voice. "I mean, you know about Cassie. And once you're gone, I can just finally forget about the whole thing, once and for all."

"Forget?"

"Forgive *and* forget. But it's hard. It's not easy to forgive myself, but I'm sure I can forget. There. I think there's enough room for you to get in there now, if you squeeze."

Shadow looked down at the little man. "Out of interest," he said, curious, "how are you going to make me get in there? You don't have a gun on you. And, Ollie, I'm twice your size. You know, I could just break your neck."

"I'm not a stupid man," said Oliver. "I'm not a bad man, either. I'm not a terribly well man, but that's neither here nor there, really. I mean, I did what I did because I was jealous, not because I was ill. But I wouldn't have come up here alone. You see, this is the temple of the Black Dog. These places were the first temples. Before the stone henges and the standing stones, they were waiting and they were worshipped, and sacrificed to, and feared, and placated. The black shucks and the barghests, the padfoots and the wish hounds. They were here and they remain on guard."

"Hit him with a rock," said Cassie's voice. "Hit him now, Shadow, *please.*"

The passage they stood in went a little way into the hillside, a man-made cave with drystone walls. It did not look like an ancient temple. It did not look like a gateway to hell. The predawn sky framed Oliver. In his gentle, unfailingly polite voice, he said, "He is in me. And I am in him."

The black dog filled the doorway, blocking the way to the world outside, and, Shadow knew, whatever it was, it was no true dog. Its eyes actually glowed, with a luminescence that reminded Shadow of rotting sea-creatures. It was to a wolf, in scale and in menace, what a tiger is to a lynx: pure carnivore, a creature made of danger and threat. It stood taller than Oliver and it stared at Shadow, and it growled, a rumbling deep in its chest. Then it sprang.

Shadow raised his arm to protect his throat, and the creature sank its teeth into his flesh, just below the elbow. The pain was excruciating. He knew he should fight back, but he was falling to his knees, and he was screaming, unable to think clearly, unable to focus on anything except his fear that the creature was going to use him for food, fear it was crushing the bone of his forearm.

On some deep level he suspected that the fear was being created by the dog: that he, Shadow, was not cripplingly afraid like that. Not really. But it did not matter. When the creature released Shadow's arm, he was weeping and his whole body was shaking.

Oliver said, "Get in there, Shadow. Through the gap in the wall. Quickly, now. Or I'll have him chew off your face."

Shadow's arm was bleeding, but he got up and squeezed through the gap into the darkness without arguing. If he stayed out there, with the beast, he would die soon, and die in pain. He knew that with as much certainty as he knew that the sun would rise tomorrow.

"Well, yes," said Cassie's voice in his head. "It's going to rise. But unless you get your shit together you are never going to see it."

There was barely space for him and Cassie's body in the cavity behind the wall. He had seen the expression of pain and fury on her face, like the face of the cat in the glass box, and then he knew she, too, had been entombed here while alive.

Oliver picked up a rock from the ground, and placed it onto the wall, in the gap. "My own theory," he said, hefting a second rock and putting it into position, "is that it is the prehistoric dire wolf. But it is bigger than ever the dire wolf was. Perhaps it is the monster of our dreams, when we huddled in caves. Perhaps it was simply a wolf, but we were smaller, little hominids who could never run fast enough to get away."

Shadow leaned against the rock face behind him. He squeezed his left arm with his right hand to try to stop the bleeding. "This is Wod's Hill," said Shadow. "And that's Wod's dog. I wouldn't put it past him."

"It doesn't matter." More stones were placed on stones.

"Ollie," said Shadow. "The beast is going to kill you. It's already inside you. It's not a good thing."

"Old Shuck's not going to hurt me. Old Shuck loves me. Cassie's in the wall," said Oliver, and he dropped a rock on top of the others with a crash. "Now you are in the wall with her. Nobody's waiting for you. Nobody's going to come looking for you. Nobody is going to cry for you. Nobody's going to miss you."

There were, Shadow knew, although he could never have told a soul how he knew, three of them, not two, in that tiny space. There was Cassie Burglass, there in body (rotted and dried and still stinking of decay) and there in soul, and there was also something else, something that twined about his legs, and then butted gently at his injured hand. A voice spoke to him, from somewhere close. He knew that voice, although the accent was unfamiliar.

It was the voice that a cat would speak in, if a cat were a woman:

expressive, dark, musical. The voice said, *You should not be here, Shadow. You have to stop, and you must take action. You are letting the rest of the world make your decisions for you.*

Shadow said aloud, "That's not entirely fair, Bast."

"You have to be quiet," said Oliver, gently. "I mean it." The stones of the wall were being replaced rapidly and efficiently. Already they were up to Shadow's chest.

Mrr. No? Sweet thing, you really have no idea. No idea who you are or what you are or what that means. If he walls you up in here to die in this hill, this temple will stand forever—and whatever hodgepodge of belief these locals have will work for them and will make magic. But the sun will still go down on them, and all the skies will be gray. All things will mourn, and they will not know what they are mourning for. The world will be worse—for people, for cats, for the remembered, for the forgotten. You have died and you have returned. You matter, Shadow, and you must not meet your death here, a sad sacrifice hidden in a hillside.

"So what are you suggesting I do?" he whispered.

Fight. The Beast is a thing of mind. It's taking its power from you, Shadow. You are near, and so it's become more real. Real enough to own Oliver. Real enough to hurt you.

"Me?"

"You think ghosts can talk to everyone?" asked Cassie Burglass's voice in the darkness, urgently. "We are moths. And you are the flame."

"What should I do?" asked Shadow. "It hurt my arm. It damn near ripped out my throat."

Oh, sweet man. It's just a shadow-thing. It's a night-dog. It's just an overgrown jackal.

"It's real," Shadow said. The last of the stones was being banged into place.

"Are you truly scared of your father's dog?" said a woman's voice.

Goddess or ghost, Shadow did not know.

But he knew the answer. Yes. Yes, he was scared.

His left arm was only pain, and unusable, and his right hand was slick and sticky with his blood. He was entombed in a cavity between a wall and rock. But he was, for now, alive.

"Get your shit together," said Cassie. "I've done everything I can. Do it."

He braced himself against the rocks behind the wall, and he raised his feet. Then he kicked both his booted feet out together, as hard as he could. He had walked so many miles in the last few months. He was a big man, and he was stronger than most. He put everything he had behind that kick.

The wall exploded.

The Beast was on him, the black dog of despair, but this time Shadow was prepared for it. This time he was the aggressor. He grabbed at it.

I will not be my father's dog.

With his right hand he held the beast's jaw closed. He stared into its green eyes. He did not believe the beast was a dog at all, not really. *It's daylight,* said Shadow to the dog, with his mind, not with his voice. *Run away. Whatever you are, run away. Run back to your gibbet, run back to your grave, little wish hound. All you can do is depress us, fill the world with shadows and illusions. The age when you ran with the wild hunt, or hunted terrified humans, it's over. I don't know if you're my father's dog or not. But you know what? I don't care.*

With that, Shadow took a deep breath and let go of the dog's muzzle.

It did not attack. It made a noise, a baffled whine deep in its throat that was almost a whimper.

"Go home," said Shadow, aloud.

The dog hesitated. Shadow thought for a moment then that he had won, that he was safe, that the dog would simply go away. But then the creature lowered its head, raised the ruff around its neck, and bared its teeth. It would not leave, Shadow knew, until he was dead.

The corridor in the hillside was filling with light: the rising sun shone directly into it. Shadow wondered if the people who had built it, so long ago, had aligned their temple to the sunrise. He took a step to the side, stumbled on something, and fell awkwardly to the ground.

Beside Shadow on the grass was Oliver, sprawled and unconscious. Shadow had tripped over his leg. The man's eyes were closed; he made a growling sound in the back of his throat, and Shadow heard the same sound, magnified and triumphant, from the dark beast that filled the mouth of the temple.

Shadow was down, and hurt, and was, he knew, a dead man.

Something soft touched his face, gently.

Something else brushed his hand. Shadow glanced to his side, and he understood. He understood why Bast had been with him in this place, and he understood who had brought her.

They had been ground up and sprinkled on these fields more than a hundred years before, stolen from the earth around the temple of Bastet and Beni Hasan. Tons upon tons of them, mummified cats in their thousands, each cat a tiny representation of the deity, each cat an act of worship preserved for an eternity.

They were there, in that space, beside him: brown and sand-colored and shadowy gray, cats with leopard spots and cats with tiger stripes, wild, lithe and ancient. These were not the local cats Bast had sent to watch him the previous day. These were the ancestors of those cats, of all our modern cats, from Egypt, from the Nile Delta, from thousands of years ago, brought here to make things grow.

They trilled and chirruped, they did not meow.

The black dog growled louder but now it made no move to attack. Shadow forced himself into a sitting position. "I thought I told you to go home, Shuck," he said.

The dog did not move. Shadow opened his right hand, and gestured. It was a gesture of dismissal, of impatience. *Finish this.*

The cats sprang, with ease, as if choreographed. They landed on the beast, each of them a coiled spring of fangs and claws, both as sharp as they had ever been in life. Pin-sharp claws sank into the black flanks of the huge beast, tore at its eyes. It snapped at them, angrily, and pushed itself against the wall, toppling more rocks, in an attempt to shake them off, but without success. Angry teeth sank into its ears, its muzzle, its tail, its paws.

The beast yelped and growled, and then it made a noise which, Shadow thought, would, had it come from any human throat, have been a scream.

Shadow was never certain what happened then. He watched the black dog put its muzzle down to Oliver's mouth, and push, hard. He could have sworn that the creature stepped *into* Oliver, like a bear stepping into a river.

Oliver shook, violently, on the sand.

The scream faded, and the beast was gone, and sunlight filled the space on the hill.

Shadow felt himself shivering. He felt like he had just woken up from a waking sleep; emotions flooded through him, like sunlight: fear and revulsion and grief and hurt, deep hurt.

There was anger in there, too. Oliver had tried to kill him, he knew, and he was thinking clearly for the first time in days.

A man's voice shouted, "Hold up! Everyone all right over there?"

A high bark, and a lurcher ran in, sniffed at Shadow, his back against the wall, sniffed at Oliver Bierce, unconscious on the ground, and at the remains of Cassie Burglass.

A man's silhouette filled the opening to the outside world, a gray paper cutout against the rising sun.

"Needles! Leave it!" he said. The dog returned to the man's side. The man said, "I heard someone screaming. Leastways, I wouldn't swear to it being a someone. But I heard it. Was that you?"

And then he saw the body, and he stopped. "Holy fucking mother of all fucking bastards," he said.

"Her name was Cassie Burglass," said Shadow.

"Moira's old girlfriend?" said the man. Shadow knew him as the landlord of the pub, could not remember whether he had ever known the man's name. "Bloody Nora. I thought she went to London."

Shadow felt sick.

The landlord was kneeling beside Oliver. "His heart's still beating," he said. "What happened to him?"

"I'm not sure," said Shadow. "He screamed when he saw the body—you must have heard him. Then he just went down. And your dog came in."

The man looked at Shadow, worried. "And you? Look at you! What happened to you, man?"

"Oliver asked me to come up here with him. Said he had something awful he had to get off his chest." Shadow looked at the wall on each side of the corridor. There were other bricked-in nooks there. Shadow had a good idea of what would be found behind them if any of them were opened. "He asked me to help him open the wall. I did. He knocked me over as he went down. Took me by surprise."

"Did he tell you why he had done it?"

"Jealousy," said Shadow. "Just jealous of Moira and Cassie, even after Moira had left Cassie for him."

The man exhaled, shook his head. "Bloody hell," he said. "Last bugger I'd expect to do anything like this. Needles! Leave it!" He pulled a cell phone from his pocket, and called the police. Then he excused himself. "I've got a bag of game to put aside until the police have cleared out," he explained.

Shadow got to his feet, and inspected his arms. His sweater and coat were both ripped in the left arm, as if by huge teeth, but his skin was unbroken beneath it. There was no blood on his clothes, no blood on his hands.

He wondered what his corpse would have looked like, if the black dog had killed him.

Cassie's ghost stood beside him, and looked down at her body, half-fallen from the hole in the wall. The corpse's fingertips and the fingernails were wrecked, Shadow observed, as if she had tried, in the hours or the days before she died, to dislodge the rocks of the wall.

"Look at that," she said, staring at herself. "Poor thing. Like a cat in a glass box." Then she turned to Shadow. "I didn't actually fancy you," she said. "Not even a little bit. I'm not sorry. I just needed to get your attention."

"I know," said Shadow. "I just wish I'd met you when you were alive. We could have been friends."

"I bet we would have been. It was hard in there. It's good to be done with all of this. And I'm sorry, Mr. American. Try not to hate me."

Shadow's eyes were watering. He wiped his eyes on his shirt. When he looked again, he was alone in the passageway.

"I don't hate you," he told her.

He felt a hand squeeze his hand. He walked outside, into the

morning sunlight, and he breathed and shivered, and listened to the
distant sirens.

Two men arrived and carried Oliver off on a stretcher, down the
hill to the road where an ambulance took him away, siren screaming
to alert any sheep on the lanes that they should shuffle back to the
grass verge.

A female police officer turned up as the ambulance disappeared,
accompanied by a younger male officer. They knew the landlord,
whom Shadow was not surprised to learn was also a Scathelocke,
and were both impressed by Cassie's remains, to the point that the
young male officer left the passageway and vomited into the ferns.

If it occurred to either of them to inspect the other bricked-in cav-
ities in the corridor, for evidence of centuries-old crimes, they managed to suppress the idea, and Shadow was not going to suggest it.

He gave them a brief statement, then rode with them to the local
police station, where he gave a fuller statement to a large police officer with a serious beard. The officer appeared mostly concerned that
Shadow was provided with a mug of instant coffee, and that Shadow,
as an American tourist, would not form a mistaken impression of
rural England. "It's not like this up here normally. It's really quiet.
Lovely place. I wouldn't want you to think we were all like this."

Shadow assured him that he didn't think that at all.

VI. THE RIDDLE

MOIRA WAS WAITING FOR him when he came out of the police station. She was standing with a woman in her early sixties, who looked
comfortable and reassuring, the sort of person you would want at
your side in a crisis.

"Shadow, this is Doreen. My sister."

Doreen shook hands, explaining she was sorry she hadn't been
able to be there during the last week, but she had been moving house.

"Doreen's a county court judge," explained Moira.

Shadow could not easily imagine this woman as a judge.

"They are waiting for Ollie to come around," said Moira. "Then they are going to charge him with murder." She said it thoughtfully, but in the same way she would have asked Shadow where he thought she ought to plant some snapdragons.

"And what are you going to do?"

She scratched her nose. "I'm in shock. I have no idea what I'm doing anymore. I keep thinking about the last few years. Poor, poor Cassie. She never thought there was any malice in him."

"I never liked him," said Doreen, and she sniffed. "Too full of facts for my liking, and he never knew when to stop talking. Just kept wittering on. Like he was trying to cover something up."

"Your backpack and your laundry are in Doreen's car," said Moira. "I thought we could give you a lift somewhere, if you needed one. Or if you want to get back to rambling, you can walk."

"Thank you," said Shadow. He knew he would never be welcome in Moira's little house, not anymore.

Moira said, urgently, angrily, as if it was all she wanted to know, "You said you saw Cassie. You *told* us, yesterday. That was what sent Ollie off the deep end. It hurt me so much. Why did you say you'd seen her, if she was dead? You *couldn't* have seen her."

Shadow had been wondering about that, while he had been giving his police statement. "Beats me," he said. "I don't believe in ghosts. Probably a local, playing some kind of game with the Yankee tourist."

Moira looked at him with fierce hazel eyes, as if she was trying to believe him but was unable to make the final leap of faith. Her sister reached down and held her hand. "More things in heaven and earth, Horatio. I think we should just leave it at that."

Moira looked at Shadow, unbelieving, angered, for a long time, before she took a deep breath and said, "Yes. Yes, I suppose we should."

There was silence in the car. Shadow wanted to apologize to Moira, to say something that would make things better.

They drove past the gibbet tree.

"*There were ten tongues within one head,*" recited Doreen, in a voice slightly higher and more formal than the one in which she had previously spoken. "*And one went out to fetch some bread, to feed the living and the dead.* That was a riddle written about this corner, and that tree."

"What does it mean?"

"A wren made a nest inside the skull of a gibbeted corpse, flying in and out of the jaw to feed its young. In the midst of death, as it were, life just keeps on happening."

Shadow thought about the matter for a little while, and told her that he guessed that it probably did.

October 2014
Florida/New York/Paris

MONKEY AND THE LADY

2018

MONKEY WAS IN the plum tree. He had only made the universe that morning, and he had been admiring it, particularly the moon, which was visible in the daytime sky, from the top of the tree. He had made the winds and the stars, the ocean waves and the towering cliffs. He had made fruit to eat, and he had been enthusiastically picking and eating fruit all day, and trees to climb and from which he could observe the world he had made. Now he was covered in sticky red juice. He laughed with delight, because it was a good world, and the plums were sweet and tart and sunwarmed, and it was good to be Monkey.

Something was walking, beneath the tree, something he did not remember having created. It was walking in a stately fashion, looking at the flowers and the plants.

Monkey dropped a half-eaten plum onto it, to see what it would do. It picked the plum from its shoulder and flicked the fruit uneaten into the bushes.

Monkey dropped to the ground. "Hello," said Monkey.

"You must be Monkey," said the person. She wore a high-collared blouse, and her gray skirts were full, and went almost to the ground. She even wore a hat, with a rose of a dusty orange color tucked into the hatband.

"Yes," said Monkey, and he scratched himself with his left foot. "I made all this."

"I am the Lady," said the woman. "I believe we are going to have to learn to live together."

"I don't remember making you," said Monkey, puzzled. "I made fruit and trees and ponds and sticks and—"

"You certainly didn't make me," said the woman.

Monkey scratched himself thoughtfully, this time with his right foot. Then he picked up a plum from the ground, and devoured it with relish, throwing the plum-stone down when he was done. He picked at the mushy remains of plum from the fur on the back of his arm, and sucked at the fruit he retrieved.

"Is that?" asked the Lady, "really acceptable behavior?"

"I'm Monkey," said Monkey. "I do whatever I want to."

"I am sure you do," said the Lady. "But not if you wish to be with me."

Monkey pondered.

"*Do* I wish to be with you?" he asked.

The Lady looked at Monkey gravely, then she smiled. It was the smile that did it. Somewhere between the beginning of the smile and the end of it, Monkey decided that spending time in this person's company would be a fine thing.

Monkey nodded.

"In which case," she said, "you will need clothes. And you will need manners. And you will need not to do that."

"What?"

"The thing you are doing with your hands."

Monkey looked at his hands, guiltily. He was not quite certain what they had been doing. Monkey's hands were part of him, he knew, but when he was not actually thinking about them they did whatever hands did when you were not watching them. They scratched and they investigated and they poked and they touched. They picked insects from crevices and pulled nuts from bushes.

Behave yourselves, Monkey thought at his hands. In reply one of the hands began to pick at the fingernails of the other.

This would not be easy, he decided. Not even a little. Making stars and trees and volcanoes and thunderclouds was easier. But it would be worth it.

He was almost certain it would be worth it.

Monkey had created everything, so he intuited immediately what clothes were: cloth coverings that people would wear. In order for clothes to exist, he needed to make people to wear them, to exchange them and to sell them.

He created a nearby village, in which there would be clothes, and he filled it with people. He created a little street market, and people who would sell things in the market. He created food stalls, where people made food that sizzled and smelled enticing, and stalls that sold strings of shells and beads.

Monkey saw some clothes on a market stall. They were colorful and strange, and Monkey liked the look of them immediately. He waited until the stallholder's back was turned, then he swung down and seized the clothes, and ran through the market while people shouted at him in anger or in amusement.

He put the clothes on, just as the humans wore them, and then, awkwardly, he went and found the Lady. She was in a small cafe, near the market.

"It's me," said Monkey.

The Lady examined him without approaching. Then she sighed. "It is you," she said. "And you are wearing clothes. They are very gaudy. But they are clothes."

"Shall we live together now?" asked Monkey.

In response, the Lady passed Monkey a plate with a cucumber sandwich on it. Monkey took a bite of the sandwich, broke the plate experimentally on a rock, cut himself on a section of broken plate, then peeled apart the sandwich, picked the cucumber from it with bloody fingers and threw the remaining bread onto the cafe floor.

"You will need to do a better impersonation of a person than that," said the Lady, and she walked away in her gray-leather shoes with buttons up the side.

I created all the people, thought Monkey. *I created them as gray dull land-bound things, to make Monkey seem wiser and funnier and freer and more alive. Why should I now pretend to be one?*

But he said nothing. He spent the next day, and the day after that, watching people and following them on the earth, almost never climbing walls or trees or flinging himself upwards or across spaces only to catch himself before he fell.

He pretended that he was not Monkey. He decided not to answer to "Monkey" anymore, when anything spoke to him. From now on, he told them, he was "Man."

He moved awkwardly on the earth. He only managed to conquer the urge to climb everything once he stole shoes and forced them onto his feet, which were not made for shoes. He hid his tail inside his trousers, and now he could only touch the world and move it or change it with his hands or his teeth. Monkey's hands were better behaved too—more responsible, now that his tail and his feet were hidden, less likely to poke or pry, to rip or to rub.

The Lady was drinking tea in a small cafe near the market, and he sat beside her.

"Sit on the chair," said the Lady. "Not the table."

Monkey was not sure he would always be able to tell the difference, but he did as she requested.

"Well?" said Monkey.

"You're getting there," said the Lady. "Now you just need a job."

Monkey frowned and chittered. "A job?" He knew what a job was, of course, because Monkey had created jobs when he had created everything else, rainbows and nebulae and plums and all the things in the oceans, but he had barely paid attention to them even as he created them. They were a joke, something for Monkey and his friends to laugh at.

"A job," repeated Monkey. "You want me to stop eating whatever I wish, and living where I wish, and sleeping where I wish, and instead to go to work in the mornings and come home tired in the evening, earning money enough to buy food to eat, and a place to live and to sleep . . . ? "

"A job," said the Lady. "Now you are getting the idea."

Monkey went into the village he had made, but there were no jobs there to be had, and the people laughed at him when he asked them to employ him.

He went into a town nearby, and found himself a job, sitting at a desk and writing lists of names into a huge ledger, bigger than he was. He did not enjoy sitting at the desk, and writing names made his hands hurt, and whenever he sucked absentmindedly on his pen and thought of the forests the blue ink tasted foul and it left ink stains on his face and his fingers.

On the last day of the week, Monkey took his pay and walked from the town back to the village where he had last seen the Lady. His shoes were dusty and they hurt his feet.

He put one foot in front of the other on the path.

Monkey went to the cafe, but it was empty. He asked if anyone there had seen the Lady. The owner shrugged her shoulders, but said that, on reflection, she thought she had seen the Lady in the rose gardens on the edge of the village the previous day, and perhaps Monkey should look there . . .

"Man," corrected Monkey. "Not Monkey."

But his heart was not in it. Monkey went to the rose gardens, but he did not see the Lady.

He was slouching along the path that would have taken him back to the cafe when he noticed something on the dry earth. It was a gray hat with a dusty orange rose in the hatband.

Monkey walked towards the hat, and picked it up, and examined it to see if, perhaps, the Lady was underneath it. She was not. But Monkey noticed something else, a minute's walk away. He hurried over to it. It was a gray shoe, with buttons up the side.

He walked on in the same direction and there, on the ground, was a second shoe, almost the twin of the first.

Monkey kept going, now. Soon, crumpled on the side of the road, he found a woman's jacket, and then he found a blouse. He found a skirt, abandoned on the edge of the village.

Outside the village he found more gray clothes, thin and unlikely, like the shed skins of some scanty reptile, hanging now from branches. The sun would soon be setting, and the moon was already high in the eastern sky.

Something about the branches the clothes were hanging on felt familiar. He walked further into the grove of trees.

Something hit Monkey on the shoulder: it was a half-eaten plum. Monkey looked up.

She was far above him, naked and hairy-arsed, her face and her breasts stained and sticky with red juice, sitting and laughing in the plum tree.

"Come and look at the moon, my love," she said, with delight. "Come and look at the moon."

HONORS LIST

This volume contains selections that have received or were nominated for various literary prizes, as follows.

"TROLL BRIDGE" (1993)
Nominee for the World Fantasy Award

"SNOW, GLASS, APPLES" (1994)
Winner of the Bram Stoker Award   *Nominee for the Seiun Award (Japan)*

NEVERWHERE (1996)
Nominee for the Mythopoeic Fantasy Award

STARDUST (1999)
Winner of the Mythopoeic Fantasy Award   *Winner of the Geffen Award (Israel)*
                                                  Finalist for the Locus Award
Winner of the ALA (American Library Association) Alex Award   *Nominee for the Deutsche Phantastik Preis (Germany)*

AMERICAN GODS (2001)
Winner of the Hugo Award   *Nominee for the British Science Fiction Association Award*
Winner of the Locus Award
Winner of the Bram Stoker Award   *Nominee for the International Horror Guild Award*
Winner of the Geffen Award (Israel)
                                                  Nominee for the Grand Prix de l'Imaginaire (France)
Nominee for the World Fantasy Award
Nominee for the Mythopoeic Fantasy Award   *Nominee for the Deutsche Phantastik Preis (Germany)*
Nominee for the British Fantasy Society/August Derleth Award   *Nominee for the Italia Award (Italy)*

"OCTOBER IN THE CHAIR" (2002)
Winner of the Locus Award   *Nominee for the World Fantasy Award*

"CLOSING TIME" (2002)
Winner of the Locus Award

"A STUDY IN EMERALD" (2003)
Winner of the Hugo Award   *Winner of the Seiun Award (Japan)*
Winner of the Locus Award

"BITTER GROUNDS" (2003)
Finalist for the Locus Award   *Nominee for the SLF Fountain Award*

"THE PROBLEM OF SUSAN" (2004)
*Nominee for the British Fantasy
  Award*

"FORBIDDEN BRIDES OF THE FACELESS SLAVES IN THE SECRET HOUSE
  OF THE NIGHT OF DREAD DESIRE" (2004)
Winner of the Locus Award

"THE MONARCH OF THE GLEN" (2004)
Finalist for the Locus Award

ANANSI BOYS (2005)
Winner of the Locus Award   *Winner of the Geffen Award (Israel)*
*Winner of the Mythopoeic Fantasy
  Award*   *Nominee for the ALA (American
     Library Association) Alex Award*
*Winner of the British Fantasy
  Society/August Derleth Award*

"SUNBIRD" (2005)
Winner of the Locus Award

"HOW TO TALK TO GIRLS AT PARTIES" (2006)
Winner of the Locus Award   *Nominee for the Hugo Award*

"THE TRUTH IS A CAVE IN THE BLACK MOUNTAINS" (2010)
Winner of the Locus Award   *Winner of the Shirley Jackson Award*

"THE THING ABOUT CASSANDRA" (2010)
Winner of the Locus Award

"THE CASE OF DEATH AND HONEY" (2011)

Winner of the Locus Award

Nominee for an Edgar Award

THE OCEAN AT THE END OF THE LANE (2013 NOVEL)

Winner of the Locus Award

Winner of the British National Book Award for Book of the Year

Winner of the Deutsche Phantastik Preis (Germany)

Winner of the Geffen Award (Israel)

Nominee for the World Fantasy Award

Nominee for the Nebula Award

Nominee for the Mythopoeic Fantasy Award

Nominee for the British Fantasy Award

"THE SLEEPER AND THE SPINDLE" (2013)

Winner of the Locus Award

"BLACK DOG" (2015)

Winner of the Locus Award

Most of the stories in this volume come from three previously published collections: *Smoke and Mirrors, Fragile Things,* and *Trigger Warning.* Those collections received or were nominated for various literary prizes, as follows.

SMOKE AND MIRRORS: SHORT FICTIONS AND ILLUSIONS (1998)

Winner of the Geffen Award (Israel) Finalist for the Locus Award

Nominee for the Bram Stoker Award

Nominee for the Grand Prix de l'Imaginaire (France)

FRAGILE THINGS: SHORT FICTIONS AND WONDERS (2006)

Winner of the Locus Award

Winner of the British Fantasy Award

Winner of the Grand Prix de l'Imaginaire (France)

TRIGGER WARNING: SHORT FICTIONS AND DISTURBANCES (2015)

Winner of the Locus Award

Winner of the Goodreads Choice Award for Best Fantasy

CREDITS